Charming Academy

Jessica L. Elliott

Copyright © 2011 Jessica L. Elliott
All rights reserved.
ISBN-10: 1463657218
ISBN-13: 978-1463657215

Dedication

To John for inspiring me to retell my favorite stories in a way that wasn't "girly".

To Mom for giving me constant encouragement along the way.

To Jonathan for being the real Prince Charming in my life. Thank you for sweeping me off my feet into a true-life happily ever after story.

Contents

Prologue		1
Year 1	Chapter 1	3
	Chapter 2	11
	Chapter 3	18
	Chapter 4	30
	Chapter 5	42
	Chapter 6	54
	Chapter 7	67
	Chapter 8	81
	Chapter 9	91
Year 2	Chapter 1	96
	Chapter 2	107
	Chapter 3	117
	Chapter 4	127
Year 3	Chapter 1	137
	Chapter 2	152
	Chapter 3	163
	Chapter 4	177
	Chapter 5	191
	Chapter 6	202
Year 4	Chapter 1	216
	Chapter 2	228
	Chapter 3	241
	Chapter 4	259
	Chapter 5	270
	Chapter 6	283
	Chapter 7	295
Year 5	Chapter 1	306
	Chapter 2	316
	Chapter 3	330
	Chapter 4	339
	Chapter 5	349
	Chapter 6	359
Year 6	Chapter 1	376
	Chapter 2	388
	Chapter 3	397
	Chapter 4	408
Epilogue		418

Prologue

"I won't go to bed," the child screeched. "I won't, I won't, I won't!"

"You will and you'll do so right now," the babysitter replied firmly, picking up the kicking boy and dropping him rather unceremoniously on his bed. She had long, red hair, tied back in a ponytail; though there was always a wisp or two that escaped. Her bright blue eyes took in everything around her and right now all she saw was the same screaming brat she'd been dealing with since six that evening. She was tall, which was emphasized by the way she presented herself; her mother always complimented her perfect posture. Dressed plainly in a pair of old blue jeans and a grey tee shirt, she sighed as the small boy strained against her freckled arms which were held resolutely across his belly to keep him in bed. "If you'll quiet down, I'll tell you a story."

"What kind of story?" the boy asked. He stopped squirming and eyed her suspiciously.

"A fairy tale," she replied in a mystic voice.

The boy scoffed, "I don't want to listen to a fairy tale. They're all about some guy named Prince Charming who goes around saving and marrying princesses. Seriously, who would name their kid Charming?"

"No one. It's a title," the babysitter explained. "Not every prince was a Prince Charming and he certainly wasn't just one person. There were many and they had to go to a special school to become one."

"What about the princesses? They have weird names too," the boy argued.

"Those were used to protect the people and their families. Don't you realize that if everyone knew Sleeping Beauty's family, they would never get any peace? They'd be bothered all the time by fans and the press," she said.

"Oh come on, those stories aren't real," he retorted.

"Actually, they are real," she replied. "They happened thousands of years ago. So long ago that they've become legends, changed and gilded through the years as people passed them down through the generations. Of course, it isn't helped by the fact that the fairies left Sanalbereth. That's why we don't have Charming Academy now. But if you promise to try to go to sleep, I'll tell you the honest to goodness, true story of the fairy tale."

Year 1

Chapter 1

Our story begins, as all fairy tales do, once upon a time in a land far away. More specifically, it begins in the province Maltisten, a small country within the fairy-ruled empire of Sanalbereth. In this province, lived a king and queen and their two children, Lucian and Allegra. Like all good parents, King Lysander and Queen Alexandra wanted the best for their children. So, they decided to request their placements in the two most sought-after schools in Sanalbereth; Charming Academy for Boys and Fair Damsels Academy for Young Ladies. The only problem with their plan was that each child secretly hoped that they would be rejected. Lucian, like most thirteen-year-old boys, firmly believed that females were to be avoided at all cost. Living with a little sister had proven that to him. Allegra, at twelve, firmly believed that she already knew everything and most vehemently disliked the idea of spending time with boys. They were far too boisterous and dirty for her tastes.

But unfortunately for both of them, life is what happens when you're making other plans. And life has a wicked way of doing precisely what you don't want it to do.

The day Lucian's life took its merry twist had already been shaping up to be a terrible day. It started before he woke up when his father left him at home; instead of taking him on the elk hunt like he was supposed to. It didn't matter that it was Lucian's own fault for oversleeping. That simply made it worse. Then at breakfast he'd gotten in trouble for sticking his tongue out at Allegra. Nobody would listen when he said Allegra had started it. Instead, Allegra grinned triumphantly and gave one last parting shot with her tongue while no one was watching. He scowled at her and walked up the stairs to his room. He had wanted to fight the wooden dragon in the corner, but his sword was missing. Thinking that perhaps Millie, the maid, had put it in the toy chest, Lucian began pulling out the contents and scattering them across the floor. But he soon stopped when he heard his mother screech, "Lucian, what are you doing?"

"I was trying to find my sword. I was just looking in the toy chest," Lucian replied.

"You don't have to make such a mess. Now you clean this up right now. No wonder Millie sighs so when she gets to your room," Alexandra said.

Lucian tried to argue, "But Mom…"

"No buts, Lucian. Clean this mess right now," Alexandra commanded. She turned and left leaving a scowling Lucian behind as well as revealing a very pleased Allegra.

"Looking for something?" Allegra asked, holding Lucian's sword above her head with a nasty smile.

"You give that back," Lucian hissed, jumping at her.

"You didn't say please," Allegra said in a singsong voice, sidestepping so that Lucian missed her.

"Please," Lucian snarled.

"Please what?" Allegra asked with an annoying smirk on her face.

Lucian scowled at her. "Please give me my sword."

Allegra held the sword in front of her, but as Lucian reached for it she jumped backwards. "Gotta catch me first," she called as she sprinted down the hall.

"Allegra, give that back," Lucian shouted as he ran after her. He thundered down the stairs and after skipping the bottom three entirely, tackled her to the ground. He had almost wrestled it away from her when his mother's voice pierced the air.

"Lucian Alexander, what on earth are you doing to your sister?" Alexandra cried.

"Mother, she stole my sword," Lucian replied angrily.

Using that whiny voice and horrible pout that their mother always fell for, Allegra lied, "Did not. I was trying to give it back and he attacked me."

"Lucian, you should be ashamed of yourself. You know better than to attack a lady," Alexandra scolded.

"But, Mom, she's lying," Lucian argued.

"That is not important. A young man never attacks a lady, whether or not she is behaving as one. Now you apologize and go finish your room," Alexandra said.

"But, Mom," Lucian began.

"No buts," Alexandra interrupted. "Apologize and clean your room."

Lucian scowled at Allegra who was smiling wickedly before saying through clenched teeth, "Sorry." He then ran back up the stairs to his room. It simply wasn't fair. Allegra got away with everything! He shoved his toys back in his toy chest. "Well today can't get any worse," he said bitterly. He should have known better than to tempt fate, but he was only thirteen. A knock at the door made him pause. "Who is it?"

Allegra walked into the room. "Here's your sword back. I'm sorry I got you in trouble."

"No you're not," Lucian said angrily. "You wanted to get me in trouble."

"Well, yeah, but I still feel bad," Allegra countered. "So I thought I'd say sorry. I shouldn't have done it."

Lucian softened. "What are siblings for?" he asked with a smile. "You want to play a game with me?" Allegra didn't have a chance to answer because just then they heard the doorbell. "I wonder who that is," Lucian said and the two of them raced down the stairs. A fairy with gold wings and long blonde hair was standing in the doorway handing Alexandra two large envelopes. "Just the mail." He and Allegra turned to go back up the stairs.

They had just reached the top when Alexandra began screaming at the top of her lungs. Immediately the two turned around and barreled down the stairs. Lysander, who had recently returned from his hunt, collided with Lucian as he reached the landing. Allegra laughed as Lucian, sprawled on the ground, tried to regain his breath.

"What's the matter, Alexandra?" Lysander asked as he pulled Lucian to his feet.

The queen seemed to have lost the ability to speak and was dancing from side to side waving a piece of paper in the king's face. He snatched at it a few times before finally getting it away from her. As the king read aloud, Lucian's heart sank farther into his shoes. He read:

> To Their Royal Highnesses King Lysander and Queen Alexandra,
> On behalf of the entire staff at Charming Academy, I thank you for your interest in sending your son to our school. After reviewing your request we have chosen to accept him into our program. Please arrive with Prince Lucian and his possessions on August 31 at 9:00 $_{AM}$ for a tour and orientation provided by myself. Congratulations to you and your son.
> Sincerely,
> Calista Periwinkle
> Headmistress of Charming Academy for Boys.

Lucian felt as though he'd been kicked in the stomach as he watched his parents dance about the rotunda. Allegra was laughing herself silly. In fact she was laughing so hard that she was clutching the banister for support. "Don't laugh," Lucian snapped.

"Your day is coming."

"You don't know that," Allegra gasped between giggles.

At the moment, she was right. But the fact was that lying on the ground forgotten was the second envelope, unopened. Lucian felt that this was the just the chance to prove to Allegra that in fact he did know that her day was coming by promptly picking the letter off the ground. "Mother, you dropped this," he said, holding it out for Alexandra to take.

"How clumsy of me," she said as she stopped dancing and took it from him. She read aloud, giving Lucian the opportunity to laugh. She read:

> *To Their Royal Highnesses King Lysander and Queen Alexandra,*
>
> *It is my pleasure and honor to inform you that we have received your request for Princess Allegra's placement in Fair Damsels Academy for Young Ladies. After reviewing the information sent, I am pleased to say that she has been accepted. However, our program does not start until age thirteen. Please see enclosed a schedule of important dates on which she will need to attend as well as the date on which you are to bring her for a tour and orientation next year.*
>
> *Congratulations to you all!*
>
> *Sincerely,*
> *Melantha Honeycomb*
> *Headmistress of Fair Damsels Academy for Young Ladies*

"Oh how wonderful!" Alexandra squealed and soon she and the king had once again begun a spirited polka around the rotunda.

Lucian dodged his parents to go stand by Allegra. "It could be worse."

"Not really," Allegra said.

"Hey, at least you have a year before you have to start going," Lucian pointed out. "I have to start right away."

Allegra patted Lucian's back. "I'm sorry," she said sympathetically.

"Sorry for what?" Lysander asked. He and the queen stopped dancing to look at the two children.

"I, um, I stepped on Lucian's foot," Allegra lied. They both knew how important it was to their parents that they go to the academies.

"Yeah," Lucian said, feigning a sore toe. "It's okay."

"Oh, alright," Lysander said, looking at the two suspiciously.

"We're going to have to go to town tomorrow to get all of Lucian's school supplies," Alexandra said. "This is quite an unusual list."

"May I see it?" Lucian asked. His mother handed him the paper and he looked over it as Allegra read over his shoulder.

School Supplies

Uniform:
Tailored jacket, cerulean, brass buttons, and single gold braid on sleeve. No other ornamentation allowed including ribbons and/or medals previously won or inherited.
Three pairs tan trousers with cerulean suspenders
Three white doublets and two cream doublets
Hunting apparel
Shield, no crest
Armor, lightweight
Supplies:
Beginner's epée

Bow and quiver of arrows
Horse, white or grey; no black
Hunting hound, medium size
Three writing pads
Pen and inkwell with ink, black or blue
One set charcoals
One set oil-color paints
Simple recorder

Please note that books and other necessities will be provided by the instructors.

"I guess you'll have to say goodbye to Marvello," Allegra said, speaking of Lucian's large pony. Marvello was sweet by nature and as black as a horse can possibly be.

"I guess so," Lucian admitted sadly.

"Don't worry about him," Allegra said kindly. "I'll take care of him while you're gone."

"Thanks," Lucian replied. He handed the list back to his mother before climbing up the stairs. What rotten luck! Nothing had been going well all day. All he needed now was a summer thunderstorm to complete his misery. As though hearing his silent thought, thunder rumbled in the distance. He walked to the window and looked out as the heavy, grey clouds that had been hovering in the sky throughout the day finally released their burden. Lightning flashed and he watched the rain pummel his window.

He didn't hear the knock on the door, nor did he hear his father come in. In fact, he didn't notice his father's presence until he was right next to him saying, "Dismal weather isn't it?"

"Yeah," Lucian said. He took a deep breath before continuing, "Dad, can I talk to you about something?"

"Of course, Lucian," Lysander replied. "You can talk to me about anything."

"Well," Lucian began, "it's about Charming Academy."

"What about it, son?" Lysander asked.

Lucian hesitated, "I'm, well, I'm just not sure that I…"

"You're afraid you're not good enough," Lysander said.

"No, Dad, it's just," Lucian tried to say, but his father didn't hear him.

"Son," Lysander interrupted, "you've got everything you need to go to that school. You're smart and brave. At your age, I dreamed about going to Charming Academy and becoming a Prince Charming. But your grandparents were too late in sending the request. We soon got a letter stating that all the available slots were taken. So I missed my opportunity. Your mother went to Fair Damsels Academy. The only reason I was able to marry her was her prince failed his mission."

"What if I fail, Dad?" Lucian asked.

"My son? Fail? Nonsense, Lucian," Lysander said confidently. "Why, I was able to save your mother and I didn't have any of the special training that her prince got. She would never say it, of course, but I sometimes think she regretted her prince giving up on her. She only got second best in me. That's why I'm so proud of you, son. Your princess will never have any regrets. She'll get the Prince Charming she deserves. So what are you concerned about?"

"Nothing," Lucian lied. He couldn't tell his father that his real concern was simply that he didn't want to go. It would break his heart. Instead he forced a smile on his face and said, "I wish you could come with me."

Lysander put his arm around Lucian and said with a smile, "I do too, son. But this is something that you need to do on your own. Don't worry, you'll do fine."

"I won't let you down, Dad," Lucian said.

The next morning the whole family rode into town to buy Lucian's school supplies. Alexandra and Allegra went to get the paper supplies while Lysander and Lucian went to the tailor for the uniforms. They walked into the tailor's small shop as a very tall, wiry, old man said, "Good morning, Your Highnesses. And what can I do for you? Lower a hem?"

"No, Lucian has been accepted at Charming Academy," Lysander replied. "We need his uniforms made."

"Oh, that is a high honor indeed, my young prince!" the tailor exclaimed. "Have no fears! Old Tom'll set you up right. Now what are the specifics?"

While the king and Tom went over the list's instructions, a young girl no older than Allegra was taking Lucian's measurements. She had long, blond hair pulled back with a turquoise ribbon. Her eyes were a light caramel brown and there was a depth to them that belied her smiling, cheerful countenance. "That'll about do it," she said before scampering over to Tom and disappearing into a back room.

"Well, now, Your Majesty, I'll have these ready for you by tomorrow afternoon. Bring him in then for a fitting," Tom said with a smile and low bow.

"Thank you, Tom. We'll be in around four," Lysander replied before he and Lucian walked back out to the street. "Now I suppose we should get your sword."

"Yeah," Lucian said. This was the only part he was looking forward to, but he was curious. "Dad, who was that girl in the tailor's?"

"Girl? What girl?" Lysander asked.

"The girl who took my measurements," Lucian specified.

"Oh, that's Tom's granddaughter, Gabriella. She's going to Fair Damsels Academy to work as a maid in the fall. Poor Tom isn't as young as he once was and they need the extra income," Lysander said.

"Why doesn't she live with her parents?" Lucian asked.

"They died when she was a baby. Carriage accident if I remember right," Lysander replied. "Very hard on Tom to lose his only son."

Their conversation ended as they entered a shop labeled *Bill Smith: Sword Master*. "King Lysander, what a pleasure!" Bill cried as the pair walked through his door. "Will you be needing a new rapier? I've got some beauties over here you might be interested in."

"Not today, Bill," Lysander replied. "I need a beginner's sword for Lucian. He's going to Charming Academy this fall."

"Well, you've come to the right place, Your Highness. I'll make sure he's got the very best epée in that whole school. Now," Bill said, turning his attention to Lucian, "which is your sword hand, young prince?"

"I'm left-handed," Lucian said.

"Ah, a leftie is it? Excellent! Let me see your arm," Bill requested. Lucian held his arm out and Bill started poking and prodding. "Lean, but strong. Not too long, nor too short. Hands, small, very small, but all in all very satisfactory. Very good, come by tomorrow morning and you'll have your first real sword young man."

"Thank you, Bill," Lysander said.

"Sure you won't have a look at the rapiers?" Bill asked.

"Perhaps in the morning, Bill," Lysander replied. "I'm under strict orders from the queen."

Bill laughed heartily. "Very well, Your Majesty. Tomorrow we'll play." He bowed and waved them from his shop.

"Well," Lysander said as they mounted their horses, "I think the last place to go is Phillip's to get your horse. Allegra and your mother are getting everything else. Come on." They rode to the edge of town to Phillip's Stables. When they arrived, Lysander led Lucian and Marvello into the stables after tying his own horse to the outside post.

"Why are you bringing Marvello in, Dad?" Lucian asked, afraid that he was in for a nasty surprise.

"We're getting you a horse, son. You don't need a pony anymore. Besides, he was getting too short for you anyway," Lysander said.

"But Marvello is my friend. What about Allegra?" Lucian asked desperately.

"Allegra already has a horse, Lucian. Not to mention she couldn't ride Marvello even if she wanted to with her height, especially those legs. She'd look ridiculous. You needn't make such a fuss," Lysander chided. "I'm sure you'll like your new horse just as much."

A teenage girl met them before Lucian could respond. She curtsied and said, "Good afternoon, Your Highnesses. How may I assist you?"

"We're looking for Phillip. We're here to buy and sell," Lysander replied.

"My father is out in the ring," the girl said, pushing a red curl behind her ear. "Follow me." She bobbed in curtsy before turning and leading them out of the stables past dozens of horses. Lucian didn't see a single one he liked. He doubted there would be any as good as Marvello.

Once outside, they saw a tall, red-headed man riding a fiery chestnut around the ring. On seeing his customers, he reined his horse in and dismounted. "Good afternoon, Your Majesties. What can I do for you?"

"They're here to buy and sell, Papa," the girl said.

"Thank you, Mariah," Phillip said. "Put Flame away, please."

"Yes, Papa," Mariah replied. She curtsied once again before going to the horse in the ring.

"This must be the pony you're selling?" Phillip asked, walking over to Marvello.

"His name is Marvello," Lucian said bitterly.

"Marvello, eh? Well, he looks well enough," Phillip said. He felt over Marvello's legs and examined his face. He looked inside his mouth at his teeth. "How old is he?"

"Ten since June," Lysander replied.

"How's his temperament?" Phillip asked, gently stroking Marvello's back.

"He's a gentle pony," Lucian said. "He never bites or kicks. He's the most patient, wonderful pony in the world."

Phillip smiled understandingly. "I can give you three hundred Simari for him. Now, you also wanted to buy?"

"Yes," Lysander replied, his chest puffing out with pride, "Lucian will be going to Charming Academy. He needs a white horse."

Phillip frowned, "I've only one white horse in my stables for sale, and he's an awfully big horse. I'm afraid he might be a mite big for Lucian as yet."

"Let's see him," Lysander commanded.

"Yes, sire," Phillip said, bowing. "Mariah, please bring Zephyr and the greys out."

"Yes, Papa," Mariah replied. She'd been standing at the gate waiting for instructions. She disappeared into the stable and soon returned leading three horses. Two were dapple grey and rather average sized. The third was incredibly large and the purest white. But he had a mind of his own. He pulled at the rope, causing Mariah to step back several times. "Zephyr, come," she said in a commanding voice.

The horse tossed his head and snorted in response.

"Here we are, sire. I've had other princes buy from me, so I know grey and white are accepted colors. Prospero here is a gentle ride, a little on the small size and older, but well-trained and very person friendly. Why don't you take him around the ring once, Prince Lucian?" Phillip suggested.

Lucian walked up to the horse Phillip had taken from Mariah. He mounted easily and clicked his tongue. Prospero began a slow walk around the ring. Lucian brought him up to a trot, which wasn't much faster than his walk. He came to the end of the ring and dismounted.

"What do you think of him?" Phillip asked.

"He's awfully slow. I think he's a bit too gentle," Lucian replied honestly.

"Not a problem," Phillip said. "Here we have Storm. He's not too old, but is also well-trained. A bit faster than Prospero, but I will warn you he's a cranky old fellow at times."

Lucian wrinkled his nose. "I don't really want a cranky horse."

"Understandably so," Phillip said. "Well, that leaves us with Zephyr. He's a free spirit; young and freshly broken. Not what I would recommend for a beginner, but he's a good horse. And, like all my horses, he's been blessed by the Fairy King himself to always be able to find his master if ever they should be parted. A valuable asset in a pet. Take him around the ring, why don't you? He has a smooth gait and a lively step."

Lucian wasn't at all sure that he wanted to take Zephyr anywhere, but he stepped up to the large horse. Zephyr sidestepped so that Lucian was no longer next to the saddle. Phillip held him still as Lucian tried to get himself in the saddle. He could barely get his foot in the stirrup. Lysander gave him a boost up and Lucian took the reins. However, it was soon very clear who was in control and it was not the prince. The more Lucian tried to pull back, the faster Zephyr went until they were doing a brisk canter around the ring. "Whoa, boy, whoa," Lucian said in what he hoped was a calm voice.

He had expected the horse to slow down and then stop, but that was not the case. Instead, and Lucian was not quite sure how, Zephyr firmly planted all four hooves on the ground which caused Lucian to rock precariously in the saddle. The horse whinnied and Lucian was quite sure that Zephyr was laughing at him.

"Well, what do you think of him?" Lysander asked.

"He's too big for me, Dad," Lucian replied. "He's a good horse, but he's too big."

"Nonsense," Lysander said with a dismissive wave. "You'll grow into him. Besides, you looked magnificent."

"Sire, if I might make a suggestion," Phillip interrupted quickly, "Prince Lucian does indeed look wonderful atop Zephyr, but he is a bit small yet. Why not buy Prospero for now and I'll save Zephyr until Lucian has the experience and height to handle him."

"No, Phillip, we'll take Zephyr now," Lysander said firmly.

"Very well, sire," Phillip replied, a resigned expression on his face. "He'll be a thousand Simari, but seeing as I owe you three hundred, you pay seven hundred and we'll both come out even."

Lysander paid Phillip before leading Lucian and Zephyr out of the barn. He mounted his own horse and the two of them headed to town to meet the ladies. They met at Priscilla's Café for lunch before heading back to their castle. As they unloaded their saddle bags and packages, Lucian cried, "Dad, we forgot to get the hunting hound!"

"No we didn't," Allegra said, a mischievous note in her voice. "Mom and I bought him for you. In fact, he's right here."

Lucian didn't know whether to cry in despair, laugh as though she were joking, or simply throttle Allegra then and there. In her arms was a tiny, rust-colored puppy. He was squirming around and licking at everything his little pink tongue could find. He looked at Lucian with big brown eyes and barked a greeting. Lucian just stared before saying in a deadly whisper, "Please tell me you're joking."

"No, I'm not," Allegra replied. "Isn't he precious?" She scratched behind his floppy ears and he barked happily.

"Allegra, it's a puppy," Lucian said, his voice rising with every syllable. "I can't show up at Charming Academy with an untrained puppy."

"He is trained," Allegra argued. "He's house-trained."

"I don't need a house-trained puppy," Lucian shouted. "I need a hunting dog. One that knows how to hunt!"

"They were going to kill him!" Allegra shrieked. "Just because he's the runt and has a limp. I couldn't let them do that."

"He has a limp? You bought me a lame dog?" Lucian yelled.

"Children, that is more than enough," Alexandra interrupted, causing them to jump as each had forgotten that their parents were there. "Lucian, you will simply have to train the puppy. You still have a month before classes start. I'm sure your father would be happy to help as he's trained several hounds himself." Lysander looked like he was going to argue, but thought better of it when the queen shot him a deadly glare while saying, "You will help him train the dog, won't you?"

"Of course, dear," Lysander said, knowing that she was not asking, but telling.

"Why can't Dad and I go buy an experienced dog and Allegra can keep the puppy?" Lucian asked.

"Don't be silly," Alexandra said. "What would she do with a hunting puppy?"

"Start a lame puppy protection agency," Lucian replied sarcastically.

"Lucian," Alexandra scolded. "You will take the puppy you have, or go without. Besides, training him will give you a leg up. Now, what are you going to call him?"

"Maybe I should let Allegra name him," Lucian said bitterly. But just as she was opening her mouth he continued, "Never mind! You've done enough damage already." He looked at the puppy. Allegra had just set him on the floor and he was hobbling over. He did have a limp in his left forepaw. He stood for a minute at Lucian's feet and then picked himself up so that his front paws were resting on Lucian's lower leg. Lucian bent over and picked him up. "How about Rusty since he's so red?"

"That's a wonderful name," Alexandra said with a smile.

As though recognizing the importance of what had happened, Rusty began barking merrily and then licked Lucian's face.

"Well, boy, it's going to be a long summer," Lucian whispered.

Rusty barked happily and continued licking Lucian's face.

Chapter 2

Prince Lucian and his parents left Maltisten early on the thirtieth of August. It was a full day's ride to the fairy capitol, Biberseth. They rode through the day, stopping only for meals and occasional breaks to stretch their weary legs. When they arrived in Biberseth, they stopped at The Glass Slipper for supper and to stay for the night. They didn't speak much, being too tired for conversation. Instead, they ate their supper and then retired to their rooms. Lucian had difficulty going to sleep. He was nervous and a little scared. He'd never been away from home for an extended period of time before. Now he was going to be away from home for four months before having a vacation. The idea was frightening. He'd never met any of the other princes before either. He would be in a place with no friends and no family. He wasn't sure he could pull this off, but by now it was too late to turn back. Lucian shifted restlessly and drifted into an uneasy sleep.

The next morning the royal family had a light breakfast before climbing back in their carriage for the short ride to Charming Academy. When they arrived at the castle, a tall fairy was waiting for them at the entrance. She had long, blue-violet hair and large eyes that were somewhere between blue and violet. She was wearing a long blue dress that seemed to float around her. Her iridescent blue and violet wings were similar in shape to a butterfly's wings although larger and thinner. "Good morning to you all," she said in a light, airy voice. "I am Calista Periwinkle. Welcome to Charming Academy for Boys. I'll lead you first to the stables where Prince Lucian's horse will be housed and your carriage horses will have rest."

"Thank you," Alexandra said.

Calista merely nodded and then asked, "Shall we begin?" She led them past the castle to a large, wooden building. Inside they met a pink fairy who was singing a cheerful melody as she brushed down a gleaming silver horse. "That is Phillipa Rosepetal," Calista said as they walked to an empty stall where Lucian led Zephyr. "She teaches our horsemanship classes. You won't find a better horsewoman in all of Sanalbereth."

The fairy turned and smiled at Lucian and then glanced at his parents and nodded her head in greeting. To Lucian's surprise, his father smiled and seemed to know the fairy. He didn't have time to contemplate the matter because Phillipa turned back to her horse and Calista was leading them out of the stable.

"Shall we continue?" Calista asked. She led them outside to a well-kept garden surrounded by several buildings. "At Charming Academy, we pride ourselves on having a well-rounded curriculum. Our students take the regular classes you would expect such as language arts and mathematics, as well as specialized classes that will help prepare them for their own quest. Out here we have the botany greenhouse and that dark building is our witches' hovel. I must warn you, we keep the witches on staff for disciplinary purposes. We share them with Fair Damsels Academy. When a witch is called, we have no control over the punishment chosen and are, therefore, not liable for curses or enchantments that may befall your son. If this is a problem for you, you may wish to reconsider his placement here." She paused momentarily, but when no response was made she continued, "Past the witches' hovel is our foreign language building. Our teacher is a mermaid which is why the building overhangs the lake. Your son will learn the languages of mermaids, dragons and unicorns; as well as some dabbling in gnome and dwarf. Gym classes are over there by the obstacle course as well as inside that building over there. Now we'll go inside the castle where the majority of classes are held."

She led them in through gilded oak doors that were magnificently carved with scenes of heroic princes. The outside of the castle was gleaming white and sparkled in the morning sunlight. Once inside, they saw a large staircase that split at the second level and continued to curve upward on either side. The walls were decorated in tapestries and paintings depicting Prince Charmings who'd gone years before. The hall was riddled with windows allowing the sunlight to stream through and light the hallways. Carpeted in plush velvet, Lucian couldn't hear anyone's steps as they walked through the halls. "On this level of the castle," Calista said, breaking Lucian's thoughts, "we have most of our specialty classes." A burst of flames, followed by a loud roar, shot through an open door on their right. "Dragon fighting, for example," Calista said as though nothing out of the ordinary had happened. She waved her wand and a rain shower appeared over the blaze and quickly put it out. "We also have fencing, spell breaking and alchemy on this level of the castle. This is also where our dining hall, infirmary, and common area are located. If you'll follow me, we'll head upstairs and continue the tour."

They followed Calista up the staircase. It was made of polished oak and carpeted with the same dark blue, velvet carpet as the floors below. As they reached the landing for the second floor, Lucian could see into one of the rooms. Had classes already started? A green fairy was lecturing on romantic poetry and he could see several boys taking notes. He also saw a few that were staring off at nothing in particular. Well, at least it would be like a normal school.

His father had noticed the class too and asked in a panicked voice, "Did we miss the first of the school year?"

"No," Calista replied," the older boys begin classes earlier. Our first year students start the fifteenth of September while our sixth year students begin August first. Each year begins a little earlier than the year before it. We do this to help ease the students' transition and to make time for parent orientation. Do you understand?"

"Of course," Lysander replied.

"Good. Now, on this level we have our academic courses. The class you can see is language arts, led by Airlia Willowlimb. On this level we also have mathematics, history, art and music. Also on this level are our teachers' offices. Each teacher has their own office which is used for meetings with students to go over strengths and weaknesses, trouble areas, or anything else the students may feel the need to discuss with their teachers. Now we'll head upstairs to our third floor."

They went up the left staircase and spiraled up to the next level. On this level, Lucian could see a few boys who appeared to be his age. His only disappointment was that it appeared they were all taller than he was. He shouldn't have been surprised. There was always someone taller than him; especially since he was short for his age. This level also had a very high, cathedral style ceiling. It appeared to be simply a long hallway and it only had three doors. Lucian's opinion was that this certainly wasn't a very interesting floor. Between the large, slanting windows hung more paintings depicting brave princes completing their quests. He did, however, find that he liked the windows because each one had a seat covered in blue velvet cushions and satin pillows.

"Here," Calista said, drawing Lucian's attention away from the windows, "we have the entrance to the dormitories to your right and the tower to your left. In the tower we teach orientation, hunting, etiquette and astronomy."

"How can you teach hunting indoors?" Lysander asked.

"The technique and ethics of hunting can be taught in a classroom. Our students also receive plenty of outdoor experience. But first they must understand safety and nature's laws. The third door," Calista continued, "is the door to my office. If you'll step inside for a moment, we'll complete orientation and you will have the rest of the day at leisure to see Lucian is comfortably situated in his room."

She held open the door as the three entered the spacious room. It was comfortably furnished with large golden chairs covered with blue cushions. There was a large oak desk neatly arranged with papers, pens and other necessities. The walls were pale blue and decorated with an oak bookcase, large chalkboard with a jar of chalk, and a large portrait containing several fairies, including Calista and the fairy king and queen. It appeared to be a wedding. Lucian noticed that Calista seemed to have the opposite problem he did. Everyone in the portrait was shorter than she was.

"It's a lovely picture, isn't it?" Calista asked.

"Yes," Lucian agreed. "Are you friends with the queen?"

Calista laughed, a merry sound like the babbling of a brook. "In a sense; the queen is my sister. She's a bit younger than I am, but we are great friends." She motioned for them to have a seat while saying, "Here at Charming Academy, we make every effort to make sure that your son is ready for his quest. This includes meeting his princess every quarter. I'm sure you'll agree that love at first sight is a romantic notion, but a myth."

"Not always," Alexandra replied, squeezing her husband's hand.

Calista smiled. "There are always exceptions. But in our experience, it does not happen often. It is for this reason you'll find that we have already selected a princess for Lucian based on the information you sent in your request." She pointed her wand at the chalkboard and the pieces of chalk jumped to life. Soon they had sketched a colorful picture of a little girl who appeared to be the same age as Lucian. Unfortunately for her, Lucian was hardly impressed. On the chalkboard was a smiling girl with dull blonde hair and watery blue eyes. Written above her head was Princess Moira of Lictthane. "As you can see, Princess Moira is a lovely girl." Lucian tried not to scoff. "She will begin attending Fair Damsels Academy this fall. Their first meeting will be in mid-October during our fall festival. Now do you have any questions?"

"When will we need to get Lucian?" Alexandra asked.

"We have a winter break starting after the celebration of the winter solstice," Calista replied.

"Does everything center around the seasons?" Lysander asked.

"Well, yes, Your Majesty. Nature is the most precious gift we've been given. We celebrate all its beauties," Calista explained. "You will need to pick Prince Lucian up on December twenty-third. He will be required back on January twenty-third. We give a full month for winter break. The school year ends on the summer solstice with a graduation ceremony combining the two schools which Lucian and our other princes will be required to attend every year. On that day we will meet together and we will then give you his certificate of completion, a grade card showing his mastery levels in each of his courses and a list of supplies for the following year. Any other questions?"

Lucian was tempted to ask if he had to stay there, but decided against it.

"No," Alexandra said. "Thank you."

"You are quite welcome. Well, I'm sure you want to spend some time with Lucian before you return home. You have a long journey ahead of you. Good evening," Calista said as she ushered them from her office.

It did not take long for Lucian to get settled in his room. There was a large golden plaque over the door that read "Prince Lucian of Maltisten" in sparkling blue script. When they walked inside, they found that Lucian's luggage had already been brought up. There was a large window in the room and next to it was an oak desk with candles for late night studying. A large oak wardrobe was standing near a huge four poster bed. It was concealed by deep blue curtains. On pulling them aside, Lucian discovered that the bed was very soft and covered in light blue bedding with multiple gold fringed, blue pillows at the head of it. He stepped away from it and looked around. The room was huge, larger even than his room at home, which seemed very surprising considering he was in a school and not his home. The furniture was all very comfortable looking and had the old and yet loved look that made him feel slightly more at home. Outside the door was a small letterbox. "I suppose that's where my mail will go," Lucian said quietly.

"Yes, it would be the proper place for it," Alexandra said. "Now you haven't forgotten anything, have you? You have all your clothes, your supplies, everything?"

"Darling, we checked five times before we left home. Everything is here," Lysander sighed. "You know how proud of you we are, don't you son?"

"Yes, dad, I know," Lucian replied.

"Well, your mother and I should be off then. Long way to go," Lysander said.

Lucian nodded. He wanted to go with them. He didn't want to be left here on his own. He didn't want to be special. He had to tell them. "Dad, I don't…"

"You'll be fine, son," Lysander interrupted. "Work hard, learn all you can. And remember, no matter what anyone else says; you'll always be a Prince Charming to me." He hugged Lucian tight before letting Alexandra say her goodbyes.

"Know that we love you, son. We'll write to you every week," Alexandra promised. "Now give me a smile before we go." Lucian attempted a smile, but it didn't quite work. "Oh now you can do better than that. Light up the room with it."

Lucian couldn't help but grin ear-to-ear at his mother's favorite phrase.

"That's much better," Alexandra said with a smile of her own. "Take care of yourself and remember what we've taught you." She hugged him close to her before letting him go. Then she and Lysander turned and walked out of the room, leaving Lucian alone, except for the sleeping puppy in the corner.

In the weeks before classes started, Lucian spent his time touring the castle and grounds. He also tried to meet some of the other princes his age. It was difficult to do not only because he was a little shy, but also because several hadn't arrived yet. He had been among the first to come for a new year at Charming Academy. One day as he was walking near the foreign language building, he heard someone behind him talking. "Mother, I don't want to stay here."

"Oh please. Don't make such a fuss. Moira had to go a week ago and she didn't complain," a woman's voice replied severely.

Lucian turned to see a tall, stocky boy with honey brown hair speaking to a rather intimidating-looking woman. She had dark brown hair which was pulled into such a tight bun it seemed to be pulling her face into an even longer, grimmer expression. The boy muttered something under his breath.

"What did you say?" his mother snapped.

"Nothing, Mother, nothing," he said quickly. "I suppose I'll see you in December. I love you."

The woman attempted a motherly smile, but it looked more like a grimace. "Yes, I suppose so. Goodbye, dear. I love you too."

The boy waited for the woman to stalk off before saying quietly, "Not as much as you love precious, perfect Moira."

"Hi," Lucian said as the boy came closer "Are you new here?"

"Yeah, I am," the boy said.

"Me too. My name is Lucian. I've been here for a few days," Lucian added.

"Adrian," the boy replied. "As you can see, Mother just left me here."

"I did see. Where's your father?" Lucian asked.

Adrian's face fell. "Dad died five years ago.

"Oh," Lucian replied, "I'm sorry."

Adrian shrugged. "It's okay. So, who's forcing you to come here?"

"Mom and Dad. Dad more than Mom. He didn't get to come so he feels like he's not really good enough for my mom," Lucian explained.

"Wow, that's sad," Adrian said. "I think Mom just wanted to get me out of the house. My twin sister is going to the girls' school so that she can get the prince she deserves." Adrian made a face. "The only prince I would wish her on is one who could turn her to stone or something equally silent."

"I know what you mean," Lucian said with a grim expression. "My little sister, Allegra, gets away with everything."

"Yeah. Did you say Allegra?" Adrian asked suddenly.

"Yes," Lucian replied.

"Where are you from?" Adrian asked.

"Maltisten." Lucian was feeling more confused by the second. "Why?"

For a moment Adrian gaped at him before saying, "Your sister is my princess."

"No way," Lucian said, "that can't be right."

"Unless you know of another Allegra of Maltisten, it absolutely is right," Adrian replied.

Lucian knew there wasn't another Princess Allegra. One was bad enough, but two? He would have gone insane. "I guess she is. I'm sorry."

"She annoying?" Adrian asked.

"She's a pest," Lucian said sourly before describing Allegra's latest escapade with his sword.

When he'd finished, Adrian asked curiously, "Who's your princess?"

"Princess Moira of Lictthane," Lucian replied.

"Wow, now I'm sorry," Adrian said. "Moira is my twin sister. She's the most horrid, conniving, evil girl on the entire planet. Maybe even in the whole universe!"

"That bad?" Lucian asked nervously.

"Yeah. Well, I guess we'll suffer together. You with my sister and me with yours," Adrian said, looking glumly brave about the situation.

"I guess so," Lucian replied. "I suppose somehow it could be worse."

"I don't see how," Adrian said doubtfully.

The next day, they both saw how things could get worse. They were wandering around the grounds talking when a gleaming carriage pulled up. Calista was standing in front of the steps as she had been when Lucian had arrived. The carriage was pulled to a stop, six golden horses panting after their long ride. Behind the carriage, a tall young boy was riding in on a brilliant white stallion. He was wearing the school uniform, but his jacket was dripping with medals and ribbons. A footman jumped from the back of the carriage and rushed to the door. "Presenting their royal highnesses, King Roland and Queen Angelique of Coleston and their son, Prince Kaelen of Coleston," the man said in a nasal voice before rushing to pull open the door with a sweeping bow.

Calista smiled as a couple exited the carriage and the prince dismounted his horse and stood next to his parents. "King Roland, it has been far too long," she said. "I've not seen you since you completed your quest and that has been many years ago."

"Yes, well, the pressures of ruling a province and all that," the king said heartily. "You understand."

"Indeed," Calista replied with a mysterious note of disappointment in her voice. "It would seem you missed our uniform policy. There is to be no ornamentation at this time."

"Well, surely a few awards can be overlooked," Queen Angelique said. "He is, after all, third generation."

"That is neither here nor there. In this school, all begin as equals. Surely King Roland remembered that." There was some spluttering from the king before Calista continued, "I'm afraid you will have to remove every ribbon and medal before you leave today. Charming Academy makes exceptions for no one. Shall we go to the stables? There your horses will receive some much earned rest and Kaelen's horse will be housed."

Adrian and Lucian watched Calista lead them away. "Can you believe that?" Adrian asked. "I've never seen so many medals on someone our age."

"Me neither," Lucian replied. "I feel badly for the fairies. He's going to be a handful."

"Yeah, well don't feel too badly for them; we're the ones who have to live with that snob," Adrian pointed out.

"Well, maybe it's just his parents," Lucian said hopefully. "He could be in the same boat we're in."

"You honestly think that kid isn't enjoying all the attention?" Adrian asked incredulously.

Lucian hesitated, "Well, he might not be so bad. It could just be an act he's putting on to keep his parents happy." They watched as Calista led the family past the witches' hovel and towards the castle.

"I hope you're right," Adrian said.

It didn't take long for them to find out that Lucian was wrong about Kaelen. He was every bit as selfish and arrogant as he had seemed that first day; and he was a bully. He was the best, the biggest, the strongest and the smartest in his not-so-humble opinion and you'd best remember that or else. Lucian and Adrian found themselves avoiding Kaelen whenever possible, but as the days wore on to the start of school, it became quite clear that avoiding him would not be possible. They very soon received their class lists in their mailboxes. Lucian and Adrian were thrilled to discover that they had all the same classes at the same time, but horrified to discover that so did Kaelen.

"Are you quite sure?" Lucian asked again.

"See for yourself," Adrian replied, handing him the copy of Kaelen's schedule he'd written down while Kaelen had been out.

Lucian took the schedule Adrian handed him and compared it to his own. What he read was disappointingly identical. There it was, black and white in front of him. There was no escaping it; Kaelen would be in their classes. He read off the list, wishing there was some way he could change it.

Class Schedule

Day	Time	Class	Teacher
Monday, Wednesday	8:00-9:30	Language Arts	Airlia Willowlimb
	9:30-11:00	Mathematics	Marius Hawkeye
	11:00-12:00	Lunch	
	12:00-1:00	History	Clio Stormcloud
	1:00-2:00	Hunting	Diana Foxglove
	2:00-3:00	Botany	Russett Snapdragon
	3:00-4:00	Foreign Language	Lorelei
Tuesday, Thursday	8:00-9:30	Physical Education	Achilles Stardust
	9:30-11:00	Etiquette	Gelasia Stardust

Friday			
	11:00-12:00	Lunch	
	12:00-1:00	Orientation	Honoria Peregrine
	1:00-2:30	Horsemanship	Phillipa Rosepetal
	2:30-4:00	Fencing	Raphael Peregrine
	8:00-9:30	Language Arts	Airlia Willowlimb
	9:30-11:00	Art	Stefanos Stormcloud
	11:00-12:00	Lunch	
	12:00-1:30	Beginner's Alchemy	Aurelia Sundance
	1:30-3:00	Music	Amadeus Comettail

On Friday evenings, Astronomy will be taught from 8:00-9:30 by Uralia Moonbeam

Adrian sighed, "I suppose you're going to say we may as well make the best of it."

Lucian grimaced. "That's exactly what I was going to say. We'll have to find a way of dealing with him. At least there will be ten other guys in these classes for him to pick on. Not that he should pick on anyone, but at least we're not the only targets."

"Yeah," Adrian said glumly. "At least we don't have to share rooms with anyone. Can you imagine having him as your roommate?"

Lucian nodded but said nothing as he tossed the copied schedule into the fireplace.

Chapter 3

When classes started, Lucian was more than ready. The two weeks with little to do had been torture, despite all the fun he had with Adrian. During the day, he and Adrian worked with Rusty, trying to teach him to hunt. Lucian and his father hadn't gotten very far with the playful puppy over the summer. Adrian's dog, Clover, was an older, experienced dog with enough love and patience to run with Rusty. She was a dark brown dog with a white patch over her heart resembling, vaguely, a cloverleaf. Rusty slowly improved, but still had trouble following basic commands. "He'll get it with practice," Adrian would often say in effort to reassure Lucian after a long day of working. "He's just having a hard time concentrating. This is a brand new place after all."

Lucian would smile and nod, but he was becoming more and more frustrated. Especially since Rusty would rarely come when called. But Lucian was pleased to find that Rusty limped less as the days wore on. He wondered if perhaps the puppy had been hurt while still a very small baby and was finally beginning to heal. Or perhaps it was being around the fairies that was healing Rusty's leg. Lucian wasn't quite sure which it was, but didn't particularly care. He found more and more each day that he loved that little puppy. Rusty was so loving and full of life. Lucian had even started letting Rusty sleep in his bed at night, mostly because it was nighttime that was hardest for him. Left alone with his thoughts, Lucian would dwell on how homesick he was. He missed his parents dreadfully. He even missed Allegra, though he would never have admitted it to Adrian. He began to look forward to Mondays when he received letters from home. He wrote back telling them about his progress with Rusty and, once school started, about his classes and teachers. Sometimes he drew little pictures to go along with the stories he told.

The week before the princes would meet their princesses in mid-October, Lucian was well used to his schedule. He already had favorite classes; he loved music and foreign language as well as astronomy. However, he hated hunting and horsemanship. The latter was due to how strong-willed Zephyr was. Lucian wasn't actually a bad horseman, but Zephyr made the lessons long and frustrating. It wasn't helped by the fact that Kaelen always had perfect control of his horse and pointed this out frequently.

"If you would learn to control your horse like I do," Kaelen said on their way to fencing Tuesday afternoon, "you wouldn't be struggling to learn how to ride."

"I know how to ride, Kaelen," Lucian said sourly. "Zephyr's just a free spirit. We haven't become a team yet."

Kaelen laughed in a superior manner. "You're not supposed to be a team. You lead and it obeys. That's the way it's supposed to work."

"Phillipa says we're to work with our horse," Adrian argued. "That means being a team."

Kaelen cracked his knuckles menacingly. "Are you saying I don't understand horsemanship?"

"Not at all," Adrian replied. He leaned over to Lucian as Kaelen walked ahead of them. "Just that you don't listen."

Lucian nodded but didn't reply. As the boys walked towards the castle for fencing, his thoughts had turned from the disaster that was horsemanship to the weekend. Phillipa had told them that they would be meeting their princesses that Saturday for horseback riding in the morning followed by a picnic lunch. He was not looking forward to riding his horse with the princesses there. It was humiliating enough to ride in front of the other boys, but to ride in front of the girls? It was a horrifying idea. He also hated the idea of missing a full day of working with Rusty. This thought caused him to think again of Monday afternoon's botched hunting class. In vivid detail, he recalled Diana Foxglove, their instructor, had been trying to help them learn to use silent signals with their hounds. It was difficult for the experienced dogs, but Rusty couldn't even follow spoken commands. Diana, a slender fairy with brown hair and golden eyes had come to Lucian and said, "Be firm with him. You must teach him that you are the master. Teach first with the spoken commands. Praise him as he comes. Try for me."

Lucian snapped his fingers and said, "Come, Rusty."

Rusty's ears perked up and he began loping over to Lucian. He could hear Lucian encouraging him, but just as he was halfway there, a butterfly flew past his side. He turned quickly and chased after the little insect, going in entirely the wrong direction.

"No, no, Rusty, come here," Lucian begged, but Rusty continued to chase the tiny butterfly through the field.

"You need to work with him on obedience," Diana said. "He should come when called."

She wandered away leaving Lucian angry and frustrated. He knew what Rusty was supposed to do. "Rusty, come here," he said angrily, snapping his fingers.

Rusty heard the sharpness in Lucian's voice. He whimpered as he hobbled over to Lucian, his tail tucked between his legs. He looked up at Lucian, his eyes sad.

Lucian sighed. He knew he'd hurt Rusty's feelings and he hadn't meant to. "I'm sorry, Rusty," he said, bending over and scratching behind Rusty's floppy ears. "I didn't mean to yell. Good boy, you came all the way that time. Thank you." Rusty barked happily and licked Lucian's face. "I guess I'm forgiven," Lucian laughed, picking Rusty up and hugging him. "Don't worry, boy, you'll get it soon enough."

"Yeah, when there's a snowstorm in July," Kaelen scoffed. "That mutt is worthless. You'd be better off flushing and tracking on your own and letting it shoot. Then you might actually catch something."

Lucian scowled, "Shut up, Kaelen. Rusty's a wonderful dog, he just needs to be trained. I'd rather have Rusty at my side than your flea-ridden mongrel."

Kaelen was about to say something nasty in return when Diana appeared. "Is there a problem gentlemen?" She looked sternly from one boy to the other.

"No, Diana," Lucian said quietly, "no trouble at all. Kaelen was just complimenting Rusty for coming."

Diana was hardly fooled by the lie, but replied, "Very well. Please pack up and get ready for botany."

"Yes, Diana," the boys said.

Lucian put Rusty back on the ground before turning to gather his hunting supplies. While his back was turned, Kaelen gave Rusty a well-aimed kick to the side. Hearing Rusty yelp, not only did Lucian turn, but Diana reappeared. "What did you do to my dog?" Lucian shouted.

"I'll handle this, Lucian," Diana said sternly. "Kaelen, it is against the laws of hunting etiquette to harm any living thing needlessly. You will apologize to Lucian and Rusty immediately. The rest of you will go to botany. Jacobi, please take this note to Russett and tell him that Lucian and Kaelen will be a trifle late."

"Yes, Diana," a short, red-headed boy replied, taking the small slip of brown paper from her. The boys walked towards the greenhouse, many whispering to each other.

"Kaelen," Diana said after a moment, "I believe I told you to apologize."

Kaelen stood in silent defiance while Lucian held on to his whimpering puppy. He stroked Rusty's fur gently, trying to soothe Rusty's hurt feelings. The poor puppy didn't understand why it had been hurt. He looked up at Lucian mournfully and whined softly. "It's okay, Rusty, I've got you."

Diana gave Kaelen one last opportunity to do the right thing. "Kaelen, I'm waiting to hear an apology."

"He insulted my dog," Kaelen replied smugly. "I won't apologize until he does."

Diana turned her gaze to Lucian. "Is that true, Lucian?"

Lucian nodded. "I'm sorry, Kaelen. I shouldn't have said that." He was embarrassed and angry. He shouldn't have let Kaelen get to him. Now it wasn't him paying the price, but Rusty.

"You've had your apology, Kaelen, now apologize to Rusty. He is a puppy and does not understand your aggression. You have hurt him not only physically but also emotionally," Diana explained.

"You just said it doesn't understand, so I don't have to apologize," Kaelen retorted.

"If that is your decision," Diana said, a deadly calm in her voice. She pulled out her wand and shot a piece of black paper from the tip. It flew to the witches' hovel and down the chimney. Within moments, a wild-looking figure approached them. Coming close behind was Calista Periwinkle.

"You called?" the witch asked in a hoarse whisper. She was wearing a ragged, deep purple gown. Her black hair was stringy and knotted as though it had never been brushed, except for a pure white strand near the front, which had been braided and was bound with a black leather strap.

"Yes, Morghana," Diana said. "We're having a little problem here."

"What has happened?" Calista asked. She looked from Kaelen to Lucian as Diana explained the situation.

"Lucian has admitted his mistake and apologized," Diana finished. "Kaelen has not."

"It would seem to me," Morghana said, turning to the two boys, "that Prince Kaelen needs a lesson in humility." Lucian instinctively stepped back from the witch. Her eyes were sunken and the darkest brown while her skin was withered and pale. Rusty hid behind Lucian's arm with a yelp. The witch smiled wickedly, revealing yellow teeth. "Step forward, Prince Kaelen." When neither boy moved, Morghana cackled, "Very well. Prince Lucian, please step to Calista's right side." Lucian wasted no time obeying the witch. He was utterly terrified. Morghana turned to Kaelen and said in a mystic tone while holding up the cane she had walked up with, "No words shall you utter nor with pen record until your apology is made by action and word." A violet light flashed from the knotted, wooden stick and wrapped about Kaelen's mouth and hands. Kaelen opened his mouth to speak, but no sound came out. "You cannot speak, young prince," Morghana cackled. "The only words you can say will be, 'I am sorry,' and that only when you have shown this boy and his dog that you are. This punishment will be as long or as short as you make it."

Lucian grinned to himself at the memory. Kaelen had come later that evening while Lucian was rubbing Rusty's sore ribs and stroked the little puppy. "I am sorry," he said. To Lucian it still sounded rather pompous, but he supposed that for Kaelen this was an improvement. Rusty had licked Kaelen's fingers.

"He says he forgives you," Lucian said, "and I forgive you too."

Kaelen had merely nodded and walked away.

Lucian was forced to return to the present as Raphael came into the room to start their fencing lesson. Raphael had a commanding voice and presence, his hawk-like eyes missing nothing that went on in his classroom. His long, golden-brown hair was neatly pulled back from his face in a ponytail that had been braided to prevent stray wisps getting in his face. Adrian believed it was so that he had a whip handy in case the boys got out of hand.

"What's he need a whip for?" Lucian had asked when Adrian had voiced this concern. "He's got a sword. He's fast enough he could run us through and have the sword clean before any of us knew he was mad!"

"Good afternoon, gentlemen," Raphael said. After a cacophony of response, he continued, "Please put on a mask and a shield then go with your partner to your exercise mat. Today we will be working on basic defense."

Adrian and Lucian grabbed their gear before going to the far corner they worked in. Going to the sword rack, each grabbed his sword before taking their stance. They'd been working for a while when Adrian asked, "Why is it you can do all this stuff so easily and I'm struggling to figure it out?"

"Dad taught me when I was little," Lucian replied. "As soon as he realized I was left-handed he started working with me using sticks, a wooden sword and teaching me to use a bow. Besides," he continued as he lunged, "you're getting better every day."

"Yes you are, Adrian," Raphael interrupted. "Please continue your exercise," he said as the two startled boys stopped to look at him. They continued and he watched for a while before saying, "Class, I want everyone to come see how Lucian is handling his sword." The boys gathered around the mat and Lucian felt himself blushing. Raphael looked at Adrian and asked, "May I borrow your sword?"

"Sure," Adrian replied, handing his sword over to Raphael as they had been taught to do.

"Thank you, Adrian. You did very well passing your sword safely. Now, Lucian, I am going to attack and I want you to block. Everyone, I want you to watch his hands. Oh, here, turn to this side so that everyone can see. I'd forgotten you were left-handed. There we are. Now, en garde." Raphael began a slow attack. "Watch how he holds the sword. He has a firm grip and is in total control, but notice how his hand is light. He has easy movement throughout his hand making him a better swordsman. You must learn this kind of control. Clutching your weapon restricts movement. Barely holding it can lead to fatal mistakes. Such control is difficult to master, especially when you are left-handed in a right dominant world. Excellent work, Lucian. Everyone return to your mats."

Lucian couldn't help beaming. Praise was so rare for him in many of his classes. This was the one class in which he was undoubtedly the best; much to Kaelen's chagrin. The fact that this class ended the day made it even better. He could carry the feeling of accomplishment on for the remainder of the day. Lucian was in total control in this class; he didn't have to rely on other students or on an animal that may or may not be on his side. He just had to rely on himself and his own skills. It also gave him one beautiful hour and half with no gloating from Kaelen since for once, Lucian was better at something. He couldn't quite push away a smug feeling of pride as he watched a scowling Kaelen return to his mat with his partner.

When class was over, Lucian and Adrian walked out to the open lawn with Rusty. "He is going to get this eventually, isn't he?" Lucian asked as Rusty ran off towards a tree.

"Of course he will. No dog is born perfect," Adrian replied.

"Yeah," Lucian said. "Rusty, come," he called snapping his fingers.

Rusty heard Lucian calling and started running over to him. He could hear the encouragement and excitement in Lucian's voice. He liked it when Lucian was happy. All of a sudden he caught scent of something in the bushes. He turned toward them and ran to see what it was.

"Well, he's a great tracker," Adrian said in what he hoped was a reassuring tone as a flock of birds flew out of the bushes.

"But I didn't ask him to track, I told him to come," Lucian replied miserably. "I'm never going to get anywhere with him."

"Don't give up," Adrian said firmly. "That'll only prove Kaelen right about him."

"As if he weren't already. Maybe we should call it quits for today." Lucian started to walk away and within moments Rusty was at his side. He picked the puppy up and scratched his head. "Promise me you'll try tomorrow," Lucian whispered.

Rusty barked at him and wagged his tail.

"Hey," Adrian said brightly, "let's go to the stable. I've got a treat for Stardancer. I even brought an extra for Zephyr," he added as Lucian looked about ready to argue.

Lucian laughed, "I don't know that Zephyr deserves it, but sure, why not? Maybe if I spend more time with him between now and Saturday he won't completely embarrass me when the princesses come. He still seems to think I'm the enemy."

"You're just not a team yet," Adrian replied. "I think he's starting to come around though. Just give him time. We're all still pretty new to this Prince Charming bit."

Lucian nodded as they walked into the stable. Luck had truly been with them when stable assignments had been made. Stardancer and Zephyr were right next to each other, making it easy for the two boys to continue talking as they worked with their horses. Stardancer was a light grey horse with a brilliant white star on her forehead. As Lucian walked into Zephyr's stall, the proud horse snorted. "Well, if you want to be that way fine, I can take my apple elsewhere," Lucian said with a grin, taking the apple from Adrian.

Zephyr snorted again and eagerly took claim of the apple in Lucian's hand. Lucian stroked Zephyr's neck with his free hand. "If only you'd be this still when I'm trying to get up," Lucian said softly. Zephyr snorted again. Lucian was quiet for a while and could hear Adrian talking in low tones to Stardancer. He stood on tiptoes to look over Zephyr's shoulder to see Adrian stroking the mare's neck and patting her. Lucian looked again at Zephyr who turned to look at him with that ever-present pride that got in the way of their being a team. "We could have that too you know," Lucian whispered. Zephyr shook his head about. Lucian sighed and thought, *Well, what did I expect?*

By Saturday, Lucian truly dreaded meeting Moira. Between Adrian's stories and the failed attempts to control Zephyr, Lucian was sure the day was going to be a complete catastrophe. When he woke up, he got dressed in his uniform and went downstairs for breakfast. Adrian was already down in the dining hall enjoying toast and eggs.

"Good morning, Lucian," Adrian said brightly. "Pull up a chair."

Lucian sat heavily and began eating. "How long are we supposed to do this meeting thing?"

"Ours is only four hours," Adrian replied.

"Lovely," Lucian said sarcastically.

"Hey, look at it this way, after lunch it will be over. Best make do with it. I heard Kieffer tried faking sick to get out of seeing his princess. Tallia caught him easily enough though. She didn't fall for the thermometer under the lampshade trick," Adrian said.

"Isn't Kieffer in his fifth year?" Lucian asked.

"Sixth," Adrian corrected. "If he doesn't figure out how to get along with that princess of his, his quest is going to be difficult at best. Tallia sent for the witches after whatever it was he said about his princess. He might be in for quite a bit of ridicule from her."

"I suppose somehow it could be worse," Lucian said.

"Sure it could," Adrian replied. "It could be raining. Of course, if it were raining, we wouldn't have to ride at all. Phillipa would have a conniption if we rode out in the rain."

"I just want today to be over," Lucian admitted. "I almost wish Allegra was coming because then at least I would see someone from home."

"Isn't she coming out to meet me?" Adrian asked.

"I don't think so because she doesn't start until next year," Lucian replied. "It's better for you this way. She's such a pain in the neck."

"That's sisters for you," Adrian said with a shrug.

He was interrupted from speaking further by Calista's voice piercing the air, though she was not shouting. The two boys turned to see who she was talking to, as did everyone else in the dining hall. There in the entrance was Kaelen, his jacket dripping once again with medals. "Prince Kaelen, it is incredibly regrettable to me that you have been informed of the dress code and have still chosen to disregard it. Never in all my years teaching has any student had the audacity to bedeck their jacket without prior consent twice. Indeed, few students have had the audacity to do so once. Do not make the mistake in believing that you are the only prince here to have been recognized for something. We allow such recognition to be kept in your room to serve as a reminder of past successes. But as you are incapable of following simple directions, all your awards and ribbons are hereby confiscated until the end of term." She waved her wand and the medals and ribbons decorating his chest disappeared.

"But you can't do that!" Kaelen shouted.

"As headmistress of this school, yes I can and if you continue to argue I will be forced to call the witches. I believe we already have one student meeting his princess with a tail, surely you do not wish the same embarrassing accoutrement. Am I correct?" Calista asked.

Kaelen scowled before muttering something incoherent and walking to an empty table.

"You know, I almost feel badly for him," Adrian said.

Lucian couldn't help but feel surprised. "Why?"

"Look at him. He hasn't got any friends at all. It must be lonely for him," Adrian explained.

"Well, if he wasn't such a snob he'd probably have friends," Lucian said. "But you're right. He's got to be lonely."

The boys were gathered outside at ten o'clock as the carriages the princesses were arriving in pulled into the grounds. The carriages were white with pink trappings and were pulled by silvery-grey horses. As the first carriage came to a stop, a fairy stepped out. She was wearing a dark blue gown which perfectly matched her eyes. Her long blue hair was wavy, an unusual characteristic since most fairies had straight hair. She walked gracefully to the group and said, "Calista, so nice to see you again; and these must be your princes. I see some new faces. How charming they all look."

"Melantha, as always it is a pleasure to welcome you and your ladies to our school," Calista replied, a bright smile on her face.

Several girls started exiting the carriages. Older girls were immediately going to their princes, some more enthusiastically than others. The younger girls were standing silently, looking around at the princes in front of them. Suddenly, Lucian heard a very familiar voice calling his name. "Lucian, Lucian over here!"

"Allegra?" Lucian asked as his sister moved around the body of girls and threw her arms around him.

"I've missed you so much!" she said as she pulled away. "I've been all by myself with nothing to do. Is this exciting or what?"

"Who are you and what have you done with my sister?" Lucian asked teasingly, though he was genuinely surprised at her fervor.

"What? Is it so wrong of me to be excited to see my brother?" Allegra asked, looking and sounding more like her old self.

"No, I'm just surprised to see you, I guess," Lucian said.

"Why? They said in my letter that there would be dates on which I would be required to come. Didn't you pay any attention when Mom read my letter?" Allegra teased, her hands on her hips.

"Considering how busy I was laughing at the look on your face, no, I wasn't paying any attention," Lucian retorted.

"First year ladies," Melantha called, preventing Allegra from having a chance to reply, "please come here and Calista and I will get you paired with your prince."

There was some confusion as Calista and Melantha sorted their students. It wasn't long before Lucian was standing next to Moira. She was exactly like the girl he'd seen on the chalkboard, minus the smile. Now she was scowling with her arms crossed over her chest. Worse, she was at least five inches taller than Lucian and looking down her nose at him. "Um, hi," Lucian said, trying to be friendly.

"Hi," Moira replied quickly.

When she made no effort to continue the conversation, Lucian continued, "I'm Lucian."

"I know who you are," Moira retorted.

Lucian was taken aback. He'd heard from Adrian that Moira was unpleasant, but this went beyond what he had imagined. "Are you feeling alright? You seem a little out of sorts, Moira."

"I'm fine," Moira snapped. "Let's just get this done with. I don't like horses and they don't like me."

Suddenly Lucian had the relieved thought that perhaps her contempt wasn't due so much to him as to her insecurity with their activity. "I'm sure you'll do fine," Lucian said, trying to reassure her.

"Whatever," Moira replied as they were led to the stables.

"Gentlemen, please get your horses and bring them here. Ladies, your horses will be here momentarily," Calista said.

Lucian left Moira outside the stable as he walked inside to retrieve Zephyr. He got out his saddle and bridle and began placing the tack on the large horse. "Please," Lucian whispered into Zephyr's ear, "don't embarrass me today. Just for today behave and then all next week you can throw me off for all I care. But please behave today." Zephyr snorted. Lucian wasn't sure if that was a good response or not, but he soon found out.

When Moira's horse was brought to her, Lucian could see why she struggled. The horse was a tall chestnut, as fiery in temper as she was in color. It took both Phillipa and another fairy to hold the horse still as Moira attempted to mount. Tired of watching her struggle to get a leg up, Lucian cupped his hands to give her a boost up.

"I don't need help," Moira said bitterly.

"Just step up," Lucian retorted, not bothering to keep the edge out of his voice. He was tired of the attitude. It was even worse than listening to Allegra whine at home.

Moira scowled at him and stomped down on his hands. She pulled herself up onto the horse and said tersely, "Thank you."

"No problem," Lucian replied, rubbing his sore palms. He walked up to Zephyr and pulled him to a nearby stump. Phillipa held him as Lucian pulled himself up into the saddle.

"You're getting better, Lucian," she said kindly, "he didn't fight as much as he used to."

"Thanks," Lucian replied. He walked Zephyr to Moira who was fighting with her horse.

"Cinnamon, hold still," she said. While she had been trying for a commanding tone, the quaver in her voice showed her fear.

Cinnamon whinnied and sidestepped. Zephyr seemed to catch Cinnamon's willfulness. He started pulling at the reins and stamping his foot. "Whoa, boy," Lucian said forcefully. He patted Zephyr's neck. "We'll be off soon enough, boy, just be patient."

Zephyr snorted. Patience was not his strength.

Soon Phillipa and the girls' riding instructor, who had been introduced as Augusta Horsefeather, led them away from the stables. They headed towards a tree-lined path going through the forest. It was a beautiful day. The leaves were beginning to change colors, creating a vivid display of red, orange, and yellow. There wasn't a cloud in the brilliant blue sky which was a welcome relief from the thunderstorms they'd been having in the last couple of days.

As they allowed other students to go past them, Lucian attempted to ease the experience for Moira. "You're giving her too much rein. Pull in a bit so she knows you're in control."

"I don't need your help," Moira snapped, though she pulled back on the reins as he'd said.

The farther they went, the more frustrated Zephyr became. He was used to taking this route at a brisk trot. Now he was plodding along in a very slow walk. He watched as other horses trotted past him. Showing his impatience, he tossed his head and snorted.

"Easy, Zephyr," Lucian said, leaning close to the horse's ear. "I know you want to go faster and I'd love to let you, but right now we need to be gentlemen. You're doing so well; just keep it up. I promise we'll go on a nice gallop tomorrow."

Zephyr snorted impatiently, but continued the slow pace. Perhaps it was the promise of a more exciting ride later that kept him in line.

Lucian looked ahead at the upcoming bend in the path. "Widow maker," he breathed as he watched a branch sway dangerously ahead of them. "Moira," he said, turning to look at her, "you'll need to move ahead of me now so we can get past that low-hanging branch. I'll be right behind you, so don't worry."

"Like it matters," Moira said bitterly as she pulled Cinnamon ahead. She knew the only people left behind her were Esmé and her prince. All through the ride she had heard Esmé talking rather loudly about how sad it was that some people couldn't ride. She was trying hard not to let it bother her, but she was reaching the breaking point.

"Oh this is ridiculous. If you can't make that nag go any faster, get out of the way so better riders can actually make it to the picnic sometime this millennium," Esmé said suddenly, trotting past on her palomino stallion.

Cinnamon sidestepped nervously as the other horse went past. "Whoa girl," Moira said, her voice breaking.

"You're pathetic," Esmé called over her shoulder.

Moira felt tears sting her eyes as she heard an unfamiliar voice call, "Wait up, Esmé. We're supposed to come in together."

Lucian looked back to see Kaelen moving past. "Moira, stay to the side so Kaelen can catch up to his princess." Too busy trying to calm Moira down, Lucian didn't see Kaelen pull out his riding crop and hit Zephyr smartly on the hindquarter. Zephyr half-reared and ran past Moira and straight into the branch Lucian had told Moira to avoid.

Suddenly, Lucian found the wind knocked out of him as he fell face first into a puddle of mud. The branch, now snapped, was sticking out of the mud next to him. He could hear Moira laughing and then suddenly screaming as Cinnamon bolted past Zephyr, who was now standing next to the puddle looking at Lucian expectantly. Lucian stood up, grabbed Zephyr's reins and ran out of the forest trying to see where Cinnamon had run to with his princess. He could hear other students laughing at him. He was covered in slimy mud, whereas Zephyr was as pristinely white as always. To his horror, he saw Kaelen leading a terrified Moira back atop Cinnamon. He could also hear him lecturing her on elementary horse safety.

"Everyone knows you can't make sudden noises while riding; it spooks your horse," Kaelen said pompously.

Lucian was pleased to hear Moira retort, "Stick a cork in it, snot." She looked down at Lucian and said sarcastically, "What was that about staying away from the branch?"

Before Lucian could respond, Phillipa and Augusta were in front of them. "I believe we need to have a little chat," Phillipa said.

The two followed the fairies into the forest. "What happened?" Augusta asked.

"Zephyr was spooked by something," Lucian replied.

"Lucian, we've been working on this," Phillipa said gently. "You were doing so well today, and I know you know better than to ride into a branch. I could see you were even helping your princess with instructions and for most of the time you were in control, not Zephyr. How did he get spooked?"

"I don't know," Lucian replied glumly. "He was fine until Kaelen and his princess passed us."

Phillipa's eyebrow rose but before she could say anything, Augusta had rounded on Moira. "Your prince was giving you instructions and you still lost control? How?"

Moira blushed. "I was laughing. The sound spooked Cinnamon."

"Your prince fell off his horse and you laughed at him? After he had been helping you keep Cinnamon in control you laughed at him?" Augusta asked, anger obvious in her face and tone. "How ungrateful!"

"Well, for once it wasn't me looking like the fool," Moira retorted sullenly.

Augusta's violet eyes flashed angrily. "If not for the fact that your horse ran away with you and provided embarrassment and punishment enough, I would call the witches right now. Melantha would not be happy if our celebration was spoiled by one of her young ladies, would she?"

Moira looked down at the ground. "No, Augusta," she said meekly.

"No, so I expect you to apologize to Prince, Lucian did you say?" Augusta asked. After Phillipa nodded, she continued, "Apologize to Prince Lucian and then we will go to the picnic. Phillipa will help Lucian get cleaned up."

Moira never looked up from the ground. "I'm sorry," she said quietly.

"It wasn't your fault," Lucian replied. "I probably would have laughed too."

There was no response from Moira. Instead, she followed Augusta out silently. Phillipa watched and looked at Lucian. "I am so sorry, Lucian."

"Will you be able to clean it?" Lucian asked, looking at the ruined jacket.

"Of course I will," Phillipa replied. "I wasn't referring to your clothing."

Lucian thought for a moment before it dawned on him that she was referring to his princess, not the accident. Afraid he wouldn't like the answer, but desperate to know, Lucian asked, "Do they ever change pairs?"

Phillipa frowned slightly. "We don't change pairs, Lucian. Love does not happen overnight. It's like working with Zephyr. You begin with trust, respect and then you become a team, friends and from there love is born. The only time a pair is changed is when one party fails a class, as you should know from your parents."

"I don't really know what happened," Lucian said quietly. "Mom and Dad never told me. I just know that Mom's prince failed his mission and Dad stepped in."

It was quiet for a moment before Phillipa said, "Come to my office tomorrow evening. You need to understand what happened. I can't tell you now because your princess is waiting for you. And gentlemen never make ladies wait." She smiled and waved her wand, causing the mud to instantly disappear before leading him back to the rest of the group.

Lucian soon found Moira sitting on a blanket with Adrian and Allegra. They were talking brightly as Lucian walked up. "Moira, are you doing better now?" Lucian asked as he sat down.

"I'm fine," Moira replied sharply.

Allegra looked up in surprise. Before she could say anything, Jacobi walked up and asked, "Do you mind if Clarissa and I join you?"

"Not at all," Adrian replied. "The more the merrier."

"Thanks," Clarissa said as she and Jacobi sat down. "Beautiful day, isn't it?"

"Yes it is," Allegra replied. "Are you a first year?"

"Not exactly." Clarissa explained, "I'm only twelve so I begin next year."

"That's great! I'm twelve too," Allegra said.

Their conversation was interrupted by the sound of Rusty barking. He ran to Lucian, tongue hanging out and wagging his tail. "Oh Rusty, I can't work with you today," Lucian said, scratching Rusty's ears.

Rusty looked at him for a moment before turning and seeing Allegra. He barked happily and jumped into her lap. "Good boy, Rusty. Look at how you've grown! You're such a smart puppy. Why did you say you can't work with him?" Allegra asked, turning her attention to Lucian.

"Adrian and I always work with Rusty after his lunch on Saturday. He thinks it's time for a lesson," Lucian replied.

"I told you he'd be the perfect dog," Allegra said proudly. "Didn't I say he'd be wonderful, even if he does have a limp?"

Someone sneezing behind them made them all turn around. "I'm allergic to dogs. You need to take that mutt somewhere else," Esmé said. She and Kaelen were standing together next to the group.

"Or you could go elsewhere, Esmé. It's not our job to keep you comfortable," Allegra said viciously. "That would be your prince's job."

Esmé sniffed and Kaelen asked, "What's that dumb dog doing here anyway? Haven't you embarrassed yourself enough for one day?"

"Dumb dog? Rusty's not dumb," Allegra retorted angrily. "He was the best dog I saw."

"It's okay, Allegra," Lucian said before Allegra could continue her attack. "Kaelen, you've already been in trouble once for hurting Rusty. Shouldn't you go before you make it twice?"

Kaelen blushed angrily and began pulling Esmé away as she started interrogating him about Lucian's comment. "You've been in trouble?" they heard her ask.

"I can't believe she was accepted," Allegra said, disgust in her voice.

"You know her?" Moira asked.

"Yeah, she's in the same dressage division I'm in, so I see her at competitions all the time. She's the most selfish person I know," Allegra replied.

"Well, she and her prince seem like a match made in heaven," Clarissa commented.

"I don't think they qualify," Adrian countered with a grin.

"Not to change the subject," Jacobi said quickly, "but where did you get Rusty?"

Allegra looked over and saw Rusty lying at Jacobi's feet, wagging his tail. "I got him at the kennel in Maltisten. Why?"

"That's why he looks so familiar. I know Rusty," Jacobi explained. "I was the first prince scheduled to arrive. I got here a week before Lucian did."

"How do you know Rusty? Outside of class, I mean," Lucian asked.

"I saved him," Jacobi replied, stroking Rusty's fur. "I saw a group of boys tie a rock to his leg and throw him into the river on the border of Maltisten and Calewall. I jumped in and pulled him out because I love dogs and it was simply the right thing to do. Dad said I couldn't keep him because I already had a hunting dog for school. So I told him we'd drop him off in Maltisten. We went to the kennel and the king was there asking about availability for a litter of whippets he was expecting in the coming month. He let me talk to the kennel owner while he was filling out some paperwork. He must have been listening to me because when I was finished telling them what happened, he awarded me a medal for showing humanitarian ideals in saving the puppy. Honestly, I was afraid to leave him there. I figured they'd kill him."

"They were going to," Allegra said. "Mother and I bought him for Lucian. I knew he needed a more experienced dog, but I just fell in love with Rusty the second I saw him. I couldn't let them do that to him."

"Wait, if the king gave you that award," Lucian interrupted, "you've met my father."

"King Lysander is your father?" Jacobi asked.

"Yeah," Lucian replied. "Small world."

"How about that, Jacobi saves the puppy destined to be Lucian's hunting dog and Lucian's dad gives him a medal for it. That's a story you don't hear every day."

The group laughed as the fairies brought baskets to each blanket. They passed around plates and silverware before then passing around deli sandwiches, apple slices, flasks of fresh apple cider, carrot sticks and little vanilla cupcakes. The meal was enjoyable, except for Moira sulking anytime the ride was mentioned. It didn't seem like long before Calista announced, "It is time for you to say goodbye to the lovely ladies of Fair Damsels Academy. Please remember there is no kissing when you say your goodbyes. We will meet again December twenty-second for our winter festival."

"Well, they don't have to worry about kissing here," Adrian said, his nose wrinkled.

"I couldn't agree more," Moira replied.

Lucian and Allegra exchanged glances, but said nothing. They didn't need to. Each knew from the other's expression their opinion of the announcement.

"Well, it was a pleasure to meet you," Lucian said to Moira.

"Yeah, likewise," Moira replied, though her sarcasm was not lost on Lucian. "I suppose I'll see you in December."

"Yeah, I guess so. Have a safe journey," Lucian said.

Moira didn't respond. Rather, she turned on her heel and joined the rest of the girls in line to return to Fair Damsels Academy. Lucian watched her go wishing Phillipa had said trades were allowed all the time. He would have much preferred Clarissa, although he certainly didn't wish Moira on Jacobi. Not even Kaelen was bad enough in his opinion. To his mind, the afternoon had been a failure.

"Didn't I tell you she was a piece of work?" Adrian asked, watching the carriages pull away.

Lucian just nodded as he fed Zephyr some of the leftover apple slices. "Thanks for trying today, Zephyr."

The horse munched happily on the slices while Adrian accused, "You didn't tell me Allegra was such a good rider."

"Oh yeah, riding's her passion. Well, that and glass blowing. She had a special art instructor while we were being homeschooled. Still does, actually," Lucian replied.

"Yeah, well, she's a lot better than me," Adrian said. "Let's head inside with Rusty. It's getting a bit chilly."

"We have to put the horses away first," Lucian replied.

"Then we'd best get moving," Adrian said. "We'll work with Rusty tomorrow."

Chapter 4

After supper on Sunday, Lucian climbed up to the second floor. He walked past the classrooms to the hall with the fairies' offices. There were golden nameplates on each door. He reached the one that read *Phillipa Rosepetal – Horsemanship*. He knocked on the door and soon heard a voice say, "Come in."

He walked into the office and saw Phillipa standing at her desk. She was wearing her normal riding habit and leather boots. "Good evening, Lucian," she said, looking up at him with large pink eyes. "I thought perhaps you might like to come help me in the stables as we talk."

"Okay," Lucian said. He looked around the office. There was a shelf filled with books on horsemanship and horse care. Another shelf held trophies and ribbons as well as a picture of a rose-grey horse standing in a grassy field.

"That's Shadow," Phillipa said, following Lucian's gaze. "She was my first horse. Your Zephyr reminds me of her. Same spiritedness and grace." She stood by the portrait a moment, her finger tracing the silver frame. "Anyhow, we should be going."

Lucian followed Phillipa silently as they walked to the stables. It was a clear autumn evening. There was the slight smell of rain left over from the afternoon's shower. "What do you want me to help with?" Lucian asked as they walked into the wooden building.

"Calista is going into town to see her sister. Tomorrow is her birthday, you see. She needs the carriage prepared. I'd like you to groom the horses while I polish the carriage," Phillipa requested.

"Alright," Lucian said. He grabbed a curry brush and went to one of the four charcoal-grey horses that would pull the blue and gold carriage.

They worked in silence for a while before Phillipa said, "I suppose I should begin telling you the story. I remember it like it was yesterday even though it happened many years ago. I should also tell it in true fairy tale format. Once upon a time, there was a young prince named Maximillion. He, like many others, graduated from Charming Academy and was sent out on his quest to rescue the fair Princess Alexandra. There were some who doubted Maximillion's abilities; he was not a very good student and barely scraped by in many of his classes. However, graduation came and his quest began. He searched for five full years for his princess and then met many obstacles when he found the location of the Forbidden Tower. Somehow he got through the forest of thorns, distracted the dragon; for I don't believe he actually defeated it. But he could not reach her."

"Why not?" Lucian asked.

"He was scared of heights," Phillipa replied simply. "The Forbidden Tower is so named because it is, as I stated, surrounded by barriers and it is well over one hundred feet to the small window that is the only way in or out. Princess Alexandra was blessed by the witches with hair that grew abnormally fast, was stronger than steel, and yet light as a feather and soft as satin. She was incredibly beautiful, not that I need to tell you. Beautiful in body and mind; she would not allow Maximillion to give up. She pled with him to keep going. She knew how difficult the climb was for him. But she continued to encourage him, calling down her love and her faith in him. But it was no use. Not even ten feet up, Maximillion, overcome by his fear, fled leaving her to her fate.

"Alexandra was heartbroken, doomed to remain in the tower for eternity. On the last day he could have saved her, her prince, her love had abandoned her. She cried late into the night, until she heard someone calling her name. Hope bloomed once again and she ran to the window, expecting to see Prince Maximillion there to save her. But to her surprise, it was not her beloved prince at the bottom of the tower. It was a young man she'd never seen before. He called up to her, 'Alexandra, let down your hair and I'll come save you.'

"'But you're not my prince,' she replied miserably. 'You cannot save me.'

"'Allow me to try,' the stranger said.

"Feeling she had no other choice, Alexandra threw her braid out the window and watched this young man, undaunted by the danger of his task, climb her hair to the window. Then she first laid eyes on her rescuer. His clothing was torn and his skin scratched by the forest of thorns he'd fought through. She could see burns from fighting the dragon. But she saw past these and into those pale blue eyes and immediately fell in love with him. In a story like no other, she had discovered love at first sight. She asked, 'What is your name?'

"He replied, 'Lysander, prince of Coleston.' Without waiting another moment, he kissed her and the enchantment was broken. A flight of golden stairs magically appeared and Prince Lysander led his newfound love down below where three fairies were waiting. Those fairies were Calista Periwinkle, Vulcan Firebrand, and me.

"Naturally we were quite confused to see Alexandra being led down by someone other than her prince. Maximillion was found and after speaking to everyone involved we were able to piece together what had happened. Your father had secretly been helping Maximillion with his classes since he was not able to attend Charming Academy himself. That's how he had come to know of Alexandra and of the dangers of rescuing her. He'd seen Maximillion flee, and unwilling to allow a princess to be left alone forever, he risked his own life to save her.

"It was determined that Alexandra and Lysander would marry, seeing as they were so in love with each other. However, it was also decided that the story would not be written because Lysander, though a Prince Charming in every sense of the title, had not graduated from Charming Academy. Prince Maximillion was stripped of his diploma and will never earn the title Prince Charming."

"But why wasn't the story written? It shouldn't matter that he didn't come to this school. He saved her didn't he?" Lucian asked, feeling angry that his father had been snubbed.

Phillipa sighed, "I don't have an answer for that, Lucian. In truth, it should have been, however I was not present for the final decision. Calista would know. Your father shouldn't have been able to get through those obstacles. So, in a sense, you are second generation and I hope you see what results from failure. While it was certainly good for your parents, Maximillion lost everything that should have been his. That's a horrible price to pay simply for a different bride."

Lucian was silent as he finished brushing the last carriage horse. He heard Zephyr whinny. He turned with a smile and walked over to him. "Are you feeling jealous?"

Zephyr snorted and pushed Lucian's chest with his nose.

"I owe you a gallop, don't I Zephyr?" Lucian asked with a laugh as he rubbed Zephyr's forehead. The horse whinnied and Lucian turned to Phillipa, "May I take him for a ride? I promised him yesterday we would go for a gallop since he was so good during our ride."

"I don't know, Lucian," Phillipa replied with a frown. "It's getting late and you still struggle with him."

"Please, Phillipa?" Lucian begged. "I made a promise and a gentleman never goes back on his word."

Phillipa laughed. "Using my own logic against me isn't fair, Lucian. Alright, you may ride. Put this in your pocket," she said as a piece of pink paper came out of her wand. "This way if Calista or anyone else sees you out they'll know you have permission to be out. Just be sure you put Zephyr back in his stall clean and fed."

"I will. Thanks, Phillipa," Lucian said.

She smiled before turning to Zephyr, "And you take good care of Lucian for me."

Zephyr whinnied as she patted his neck before leaving.

Lucian put Zephyr's tack on him before leading him outside to the pasture. The moon was rising as the sun fell towards the horizon, leaving a brilliant splash of color behind it. Zephyr's coat glowed orange as Lucian led him to the mounting block. He climbed up and clicked his tongue. Zephyr started off at a walk but needed little encouragement to stretch into a gallop. Lucian held the reins loosely, allowing Zephyr the freedom to go at his own speed wherever he wanted to go. As the world flew by, Lucian basked in the glorious sunset and the feel of the wind whipping his dark copper hair. Zephyr began to slow down after a while, working his way down to a brisk walk. Lucian looked about, his honey-brown eyes taking in the cool violets and blues that replaced the fiery sunset. He saw a group of sunflowers that had dropped their seeds. He dismounted and gathered them in his pocket. His mother loved sunflowers; if he wrapped them well enough, he could send them to her in his next letter.

Holding on to Zephyr's reins, Lucian walked about for a while, checking for more flowers that might be ready for picking. Ever impatient, Zephyr pushed his arm. "Are you ready to go home now, Zephyr?" Lucian asked, stopping to stroke the horse's neck.

Zephyr snorted and pushed Lucian again.

Lucian laughed, "Alright, alright, I get the hint. Come on; let's find a stump or something I can climb up on."

To his surprise, Zephyr knelt down, allowing Lucian easier access to the saddle. As Lucian climbed up, he patted Zephyr's neck. "I guess we're a team now, aren't we boy?"

Zephyr whinnied before beginning the ride home. The moon shone brightly around them, bathing everything in a silvery glow. Lucian listened to the sound of crickets chirping as he and Zephyr neared the stables. Zephyr began to speed up the closer they got to the cheery barn. Once they reached the pasture gate, Lucian dismounted and led Zephyr into the stables. He put the tack away before rubbing Zephyr down. Then he got his curry brush and brushed Zephyr's coat until it gleamed. After filling his box with oats, Lucian patted Zephyr's back before leaving the stables.

He hadn't gotten very far when he heard Kaelen's voice, "Well, if it isn't perfection himself out after hours."

"Leave me alone," Kaelen," Lucian said. "I have permission to be out. Do you?"

Kaelen waved off Lucian's comment. "I was just asking your buddy here if he was brave enough to go into the witches' garden." Kaelen was pointing to a skinny, terrified-looking boy Lucian recognized from class, but didn't know by name. "He could do it. I wonder if you can."

"Is there a purpose behind going into their garden, or is this just a show of guts? Honestly, I have better things I could be doing," Lucian replied, making to go around Kaelen.

"I knew you were chicken," Kaelen said.

"Am not," Lucian retorted. "There's a difference between being chicken and being respectful. We're not allowed in the garden. Everyone knows that."

"Nah, you're just chicken," Kaelen taunted. "And now everyone will know that you are a coward. It's going to be awfully hard to save your princess if you've got no spine."

"Fine," Lucian snapped, "I'll go into the stupid garden."

"Not so fast," Kaelen said, grabbing Lucian's arm. "You have to prove you were there. I want you to steal one of their herbs and bring it back to me."

Lucian scowled. "I hope they catch you," he hissed, wrenching his arm away and walking up to the gate. He could hear the witches chanting as he neared the house. He pulled the garden gate slowly, hardly daring to breathe as is creaked.

"What was that sound?" he heard one of the witches ask.

"Just the wind, Sister," another replied. "On with your lesson."

Lucian let out a silent breath of relief and slipped into the garden. He walked through the garden and looked at the tenderly cared-for plants. He couldn't spoil their garden. He knew enough of botany to know that some of these were very important for healing. His eyes fell on a bunch of weeds. Kaelen was so awful at botany he would never know the difference between a weed and an herb. He pulled up the weeds and then his eyes fell on a bare patch where someone had clumsily pulled out a plant. He felt horrible, even though he hadn't done it. If only he could replace it. A soft plop next to him made him look down. Lying on the ground was one of the sunflower seeds he'd gathered. Of course! His mother wouldn't miss a few seeds since she didn't know they were coming. But he couldn't plant them here. As they grew, they would block the sunlight. If he planted it under the window, though, it just might work. He tiptoed to the house and poked three holes into the soft, cold ground. He gently dropped a seed into each hole before covering it. In a voice that was barely a whisper, he said, "Please grow."

As he started to creep away, he heard a voice in the hovel say, "It's time to bless the garden, Sisters."

Frantically, Lucian began looking for somewhere to hide as he heard their door creak open. Seeing a large tree just outside the fence, he rushed to it, hopped silently over the fence and crouched behind the tree. Curious to see what was happening, Lucian peeked around the trunk. He saw five witches walking in the moonlit garden. It was difficult to say what they looked like. All were wearing dark colors, except for one who was wearing a blood-red gown. She had curly, fiery red hair that spilled about her shoulders. One appeared older than all the rest, her hair blue-white in the moonlight.

"Calypso, it is your turn to be the voice," a different witch said. "Everyone clasp hands in the circle."

A young-looking witch raised her face to the sky. "Blessed earth below hold our growing plants. Blessed water above rain upon our growing plants. Blessed air all around be gentle on our growing plants. Blessed fire in the sun shine down upon our growing plants. Make all that is good grow with speed and cast out wicked thorn and weed."

Together the witches chanted, "Blessed earth, blessed water, blessed air, blessed fire, keep care our garden dear." There was silence for a moment, before the five sisters returned indoors.

Lucian silently went around the garden and back to where Kaelen was waiting. "Here are your herbs," he said thrusting the weeds into Kaelen's hand. He then ran past him to the castle.

By November, Lucian had given up on Rusty truly becoming a hunter. He was smart and aimed to please, but still could not follow commands. While he understood sound signals, he had yet to master silent commands; though he did at least look in the direction Lucian pointed. As their hunting final loomed closer, Lucian was sure he would fail. The class period before the final, Lucian approached Diana. "I just don't know if Rusty can do this. Is there any other way to have this final?"

"I'm sorry, Lucian, but you know our rules. The final must be equal for everyone. Rusty will just have to do his best," replied Diana.

Looking at the ground, Lucian asked, "What if his best isn't good enough?"

"You'll be put on academic probation. We'll monitor your progress and if we see no improvement with one full school year, you'll be given a failing grade and then you'll leave Charming Academy," Diana explained. Then she smiled and tipped Lucian's chin so he was looking up at her, "Keep your chin up. Rusty has made great improvement and I don't expect perfection, especially not from a puppy."

Lucian nodded glumly and walked away. As much as he wanted to be at home, he did not want to fail. It simply wasn't an option. Not to mention his father would never believe him if he said he'd flunked out because of hunting. He would laugh and think it was a joke.

The day of the final dawned cold with a light blanket of snow covering the ground. "How do they keep that garden going?" Adrian asked as they walked past the witches' hovel with Rusty and Clover.

"They bless it every night," Lucian replied, looking at the garden. The sunflowers he had planted were blooming. There were now ten sunflowers lining the hovel's wall as well as a few wildflowers he had found. He and one of the other boys, Edwin, had been going to the boys Kaelen talked into going into the garden and asking for the plants they pulled. They took turns trying to replant the crushed seedlings. Sometimes they were successful and other times the damage had already been done.

Lucian and Adrian stopped short as a heart-stopping scream pierced the air. They turned back to the garden where the young, red-headed witch was standing in the garden shrieking, "Where's my silver hazel?"

"What are you screaming about, Lucretia?" another witch asked, appearing out of nowhere. She appeared older than Lucretia with long black hair that was pulled back from her face by a silver tiara decorated with five stones. The center stone was white and to the left were a ruby and sapphire while the right side held an amethyst and emerald.

Lucretia turned, her hair dancing about her head like a flame in a fireplace while her eyes burned vermillion. "Someone has stolen my silver hazel. I can't make the potion Tallia needs for the hospital without it; as you well know, Althea."

"Now, dear, calm down," Althea said soothingly, "I'm sure no one would steal your herbs. Some of our plants have turned up in the oddest places lately. Poor Maeve, as close to the Change as she is; I'm sure she's simply been misplacing them."

"But Maeve didn't plant this, I did," Lucretia argued, though her curly hair had settled about her shoulders and her eyes cooled to a warm chestnut.

"Let's look about," Althea suggested. "I'm sure it will turn up."

"Is there a problem, Althea?" Calista asked. Lucian hadn't seen her leave the castle as intent as he was watching Lucretia and Althea. He had half-wanted to show the witches where the silver hazel was. He had been the one to replant it after it had been plucked by one of the other boys. However, that would have meant admitting to having been in their garden and who knew what hot-tempered Lucretia might have done to him. He may have found himself finishing school as a newt.

"No Calista," Althea replied, interrupting Lucian's thoughts, "we've merely misplaced a plant."

"Liar," Lucretia hissed, her eyes glowing.

Calista ignored Lucretia's comment and said, "On that note, you have a lovely flower garden. I don't recall you ever having one before. Is this Maeve's idea?"

"No, Calista, we don't know who has given us a flower garden," Althea admitted. "Someone has been immeasurably kind. These flowers bring my sisters and I much joy. Partly because their oils can be used in many of our potions, but also because of the beauty they bring to our home. We would like to thank them."

Lucian blushed to the roots of his hair and grabbed Adrian's arm. "Let's go," he whispered. "We're going to be late for our final."

The boys ran with their dogs to the clearing where hunting was held. Phillipa was there with their horses. There were also several older boys. Lucian and Adrian exchanged glances but said nothing as they gathered with the other boys their age. Soon Diana said, "Gentlemen, today as you are all aware, is the winter final for hunting and horsemanship. These finals are all about teamwork; being a team with your horse as well as being a team with your hound. You will be given two hours to complete the final. You are required to demonstrate silent commands with your hound, flush out a flock of birds as well as catch one land animal. Phillipa will give you her instructions, but before she does, understand that your success now will greatly impact your supper tomorrow."

Phillipa started speaking before Lucian had long to consider how embarrassing this was going to be. Getting the ground animal shouldn't be too hard; he had really good aim. Finding a bird would be harder since Rusty was so easily distracted. "Your final," Phillipa said, interrupting his thoughts, "will consist of an obstacle course you'll have to go through on horseback. First years, we have not yet trained your horses for hunting, so you will need to dismount and then use your signal to call your horse back to you. Second years, I expect you to hunt from the saddle."

"Your two hours begin now. Good luck," Diana said.

Lucian pulled Zephyr to a nearby stump, Rusty close at his heels. "Please don't embarrass me," Lucian whispered to Rusty before stepping on the stump and mounting his horse. He watched as older boys gave their hounds silent directions and went off into the forest. With a last silent plea for help, Lucian pointed and clicked his tongue. Zephyr took off on a brisk walk and Rusty ambled along beside him instead of going left as directed. This was not going to go well.

An hour into the final, Lucian was one of the few left out in the course. He'd about given up on accomplishing anything for the hunting final. He'd already completed the obstacle course. Zephyr was now patiently waiting by a tree enjoying the last shoots of fall grass. Lucian's only comfort was that he would at least pass his horsemanship final. Suddenly, Rusty started creeping towards a bush, nose to the ground. He turned and looked at Lucian before beginning to bark excitedly. A flock of birds flew into the air and Lucian wasted no time in grabbing his bow and arrows. Soon he had a nice pile set up to take. "Good boy," Lucian said, patting Rusty's head. He then scooped up the birds into his hunting bag and followed Rusty through some underbrush leading to a small thicket. Rusty suddenly began barking and a couple of rabbits leapt from their burrow. It wasn't long before Lucian had added them to his bag. He tried to call Rusty back by swiping his hand past his leg, but Rusty didn't come. Lucian sighed and slapped his leg. Rusty immediately came over. He then whistled the three-note sign he'd taught Zephyr. Soon Zephyr was trotting to him. He mounted and was soon back with Phillipa and Diana.

"And you thought you'd fail," Diana said kindly, handing him a slip of paper.

Phillipa took Zephyr's reins. "Don't worry about clean-up; I'll be taking care of that with some help from the older boys. You did well."

Lucian simply beamed at them before walking over to Adrian. "Open it and tell me how you did," Adrian said excitedly.

Smiling, Lucian opened the folded paper and read aloud:

Excellent work with Zephyr. You've shown great improvement. Continue working on teamwork; at times Zephyr took control. Be firm. Phillipa

Great work with Rusty, continue working silent commands. More practice will help you both. As always, you are an excellent shot. You never missed. I'm very pleased with your progress. Diana

"Well, that's good; what are your marks?" Adrian asked.

"I don't know," Lucian replied. He scanned the page and at the bottom found a grading scale and his grades. It read:

Grade Scale
E – exceeds expectations
A – above average
P – proficient
I – improving
F – failing

Grades

Horsemanship
    Teamwork with horse   *I*
    Riding Ability   *A*
    Overall   *P*

Hunting
    Silent Commands   *I*
    Teamwork with hound   *A*
    Ethics   *E*
    Bowmanship   *E*
    Overall   *A*

"You got an E for bowmanship? That's better than Kaelen got. Trust me, he's been bragging about having bested the rest of us by getting an A. But you beat him!" Adrian exclaimed excitedly.

"That would be called beginner's luck," Kaelen said pompously. "Or rather, a mistake. Everyone knows Lucian's dog is worthless. Lucian probably just waited around for someone else's dog to be successful and shot their catch."

Lucian had listened to such comments with little rebuttal since the start of school, but this was the last straw. "Listen you no-good, arrogant jerk, I'll have you know that I've been hunting since I was five. Just because you can't accept that I'm better than you at something is no reason for you to attack my honor. Rusty proved himself today to be just as capable as any dog here. Your attitude is going to cause you to fail. You'll be just like the no-good coward that failed my mother, a failure." With that, Lucian swiped his hand past his thigh, the silent command for come. Instantly, Rusty was at his side and the two walked toward the castle for fencing.

Several boys watched them leave. "Diana, was that Rusty?" a prince asked.

Diana, though angry that Lucian had left without permission, smiled as she replied, "Yes, Elijah, that was Rusty." She turned to see an older boy walking out of the thicket leading his horse, his own head bowed. "Donavan, where is your hound?"

Donavan didn't look up, but merely shrugged. "I don't know," he said miserably. "He ran off."

"Why didn't you ride your horse?" Phillipa asked.

"He threw me," Donavan replied, his voice becoming quieter with every word.

Diana sighed, "Donavan, this is exactly what happened last year. We don't want to fail you, but you're leaving us with no choice. The only improvement is that you caught something."

"Actually, Thunder stepped on it," Donavan admitted, referring to the crushed squirrel in his bag. "I didn't want to come back empty-handed again, so I picked it up."

Diana and Phillipa looked at each other. Phillipa then said, "Diana and I will speak with Calista. Your lack of improvement could force us to give you a failing grade. As you are already on probation, you know what this means."

"It means I get sent home just like Charles was," Donavan replied.

Diana nodded before turning her attention to Phillipa and they addressed the older boys. As the fairies gave some recognition to the older boys, Adrian was deep in thought. He didn't want to see any boy leave the academy, especially if they felt the way Donavan seemed to. He waited until class ended with Diana saying, "The final is over. You may now go to your next class. First years to fencing, second years to language arts. Hunting will continue in the tower as an ethics/theory course until March. We will occasionally work with your hounds as well. Now off you go."

Adrian waited until everyone else had gone before going to Diana. "I'll help Donavan with his hound and I bet Lucian would too. Don't fail him."

Diana smiled sadly at Adrian, "You have a kind heart, Adrian, but this is the second year this has happened. I can't even tell if he's really trying."

"But you saw how miserable he was," Adrian argued. "Please let Lucian and I help him. We could even help him with his horse. Please."

Sighing, Diana said, "We'll see, Adrian. Now hop to, you're going to be late for fencing."

Adrian dashed away, Clover at his heels. When he arrived at fencing, it was just before Raphael began instruction. "Where were you?" Lucian hissed.

"I'll explain later," Adrian whispered back. As soon as Raphael told them to get to work, Adrian told Lucian about Donavan.

"That's awful," Lucian said after Adrian finished.

"I know. I don't think it's his fault either. I saw him a couple times in the forest. Those animals won't obey," Adrian replied as they worked through their warm-up routine.

"Maybe they need extra training like Rusty," Lucian suggested as he blocked Adrian's blow with ease.

"That's what I was thinking," Adrian grunted as he tried to block Lucian's attack. "I'm so bad at this."

"I keep telling you, you're not that bad. You just need practice. Besides, you've never been able to block that before, now you got in there just in the nick of time."

Adrian waved off the compliment. "You're just being nice. Is that why you get so frustrated with Rusty?"

"Is what why I get frustrated?" Lucian asked.

"Well, you said your dad started working with you young. You're practically an expert and yet with Rusty you struggle," Adrian explained.

Lucian nodded. "It's hard having a lower grade because I'm struggling with my hound. But I have the same frustration with Zephyr. I guess I'll just keep plodding along until they both catch on."

Raphael stopped their lesson, interrupting the boys' conversation. "Please pack up. It's time for you to go. We'll continue this next time."

Kaelen walked towards Lucian and Adrian, fuming. How dare Lucian call him a failure! Well, he'd show him.

Lucian had his back to Kaelen as he and Adrian packed. "I should probably go apologize to Diana and Phillipa for leaving early. That was wrong of me."

"I don't know," Adrian said with a smile, "you should have seen Diana's face when Rusty obeyed your silent command. It looked like she didn't know whether to be angry or proud. It was…Lucian! Look out!" Adrian cried as he turned to see Kaelen behind Lucian sword raised.

His warning was too late. Lucian felt a sharp sting in his left arm as he turned. Kaelen was already moving in for a second attack, but Lucian tossed his sword to his right hand and blocked it. He couldn't fight back, not right-handed, but he could at least block Kaelen's fury.

"Enough," Raphael bellowed for the third time, pushing past boys and reaching the two battling princes. Lucian dropped his sword, while Kaelen slashed again, leaving a second, deep gash across Lucian's wrist. Raphael grabbed Kaelen's arm and shook it until the sword clanked to the ground. "What on earth is going on here?" Raphael demanded.

Lucian tried to focus on Raphael's face, but it was becoming blurred. He felt himself sway to the side as everything went black.

As soon as Lucian crumpled to the floor, Raphael changed his line of thought. "Mithulan, run and get Tallia immediately." He pointed his wand up and two slips of paper, one black and the other yellow, flew out the door. "Adrian, help me control the bleeding. The rest of you will sit down at once."

The boys sat quickly as Tallia flew into the room, Mithulan panting behind her. "What happened?" she demanded as she began wrapping the wounds.

"Kaelen attacked him without provocation," Adrian replied. "Is he going to be okay?"

Tallia looked up at him, worry in her turquoise eyes. "He should be." She tucked a strand of turquoise hair behind her pointed ear and motioned for the other fairy, who had followed her in while she'd been examining Lucian, to come forward. "We need to take him to the infirmary now." She waved her wand and a stretcher appeared. The two carried Lucian out as Calista and the witch Adrian recognized as Althea walked in.

"Good heavens!" Calista cried. "What on earth happened?"

There was a barrage of boys' voices until Calista shouted, "Enough!" Even Raphael fell instantly silent, a look of fear on his face. Calista had never shouted at anyone before. She'd never needed to. "Now, Raphael, would you be so good as to explain to me what has occurred?" she asked, sounding more like herself.

"I'm not entirely sure, Calista. I had just asked the boys to pack up and the next thing I knew Kaelen and Lucian were fighting," Raphael said. "Adrian was nearby though not involved."

"Adrian," Calista said turning to him, "what happened?"

Adrian took a deep breath. "Lucian and I were getting ready to pack up and I saw Kaelen coming. He just attacked Lucian with no warning. I suspect it stems from Lucian calling him a failure after our hunting and horsemanship final. But Kaelen started that too by saying that Rusty was worthless."

"Yes, I've already heard about Lucian's previous behavior. In fact, I was going to send for him to come to my office to speak about that once classes were done for the day," Calista explained. She was silent for a moment before then continuing, "Raphael, please dismiss all students except for Kaelen. Ask Tallia to return with Lucian if he can be moved."

Raphael snapped to attention. "Alright, lads, class is over for the day. Go to your dormitories. I'll be available this evening for questions." He ushered the boys to the door. "You too, Adrian."

Adrian looked up at him, "But…"

"No buts, Adrian," Raphael said sternly. He continued more gently, "Lucian will be fine. Come along." Adrian nodded and walked with Raphael out of the room.

Calista was silent. She looked down at Kaelen, a look of withering disappointment on her face.

"Calista," Althea said, placing a hand on Calista's arm, "might I call one of my sisters? I need some counsel."

"Of course," Calista replied, her eyes never leaving Kaelen's face.

Kaelen just stared back. If she was waiting for an apology, she was wasting her time. He had no intention of apologizing to Lucian now or ever. Lucian deserved what he got.

Neither noticed Althea close her eyes. Nor did they notice that the brilliant emerald in her tiara began glowing brightly. The glow diminished as an ancient woman entered the room, leaning heavily on a wooden cane. "You called, Sister?" the witch said. She was a tiny woman and brittle-looking as though the slightest touch might break her. She had flowing white hair and was wearing a green gown with a golden belt. Dangling at the end of the belt was a green stone, swaying like a pendulum with every step.

"Yes, Maeve, I need counsel from you on how I should deal with this young man," Althea replied.

Maeve turned to look at Kaelen. "He's a handsome, young thing. We could put him in the garden with the flowers. He'd be lovely next to them."

Althea smiled, "That's not exactly what I meant, Maeve. He is to be punished for an attack on another student."

They were interrupted as Raphael came in, followed by Tallia pushing a wheelchair. Lucian was still unconscious, his head lolling to one side. As she stopped, something fell from Lucian's pocket. No one noticed, except for Maeve who began slowly inching towards it while the others began speaking.

"How is he, Tallia?" Calista asked, still staring at Kaelen.

"He'll pull through," Tallia replied. "He's lost a lot of blood, which is why he's still out of it. He hasn't woken since he fell. I'm not entirely sure if he simply passed out from loss of blood or if he may have knocked himself out hitting the ground. He's got a nasty bruise on his head. However, it'll be at least a week, likely more, before he can do anything with that arm. The wounds are very deep. He's got stitches right now and I'll have to see him every day to change his wrappings and check on how he's healing. But, it is his left arm, so it shouldn't affect his work too badly."

"He's left-handed," Raphael said angrily, as though he'd said this at least once before, "it's going to affect his work dramatically. He will be unable to participate in most of his classes, including mine. It's a shame too, because he is by far the best student I've ever worked with."

"Kaelen," Calista said gravely, "I'm still waiting for an explanation."

"I don't need to explain myself," Kaelen replied. "I defended my honor. He got what he deserved."

"Then Althea will give you what you deserve," Calista whispered angrily.

Althea was silent and turned to Maeve. "If he can't behave as a gentleman, than make him something else," Maeve said as though this was the most obvious solution in the world. "Oh and Sister, look what I've found." She held out her hand and beckoned to Althea to look. Resting on her palm was a sunflower seed. "I do believe I've found our little gardener."

A single tear trickled down Althea's face. "This calls for thanks." She looked down at Lucian and her tiara glowed as she chanted, "No thorn nor bramble shall bar his way and beauty shall be wherever he stays." The glow streamed from the crown's white jewel and around Lucian like a white ribbon.

"An excellent gift, Sister, but I do believe Calista is waiting on us," Maeve said gently.

"Of course," Althea replied, turning once more towards Kaelen. No longer did she appear calm and beautiful. Her eyes had darkened to black and her hair billowed about her. "Until thy victim is well and whole, a maiden's part shall be thy role." The tiara glowed and Kaelen was hit by a flash of white light.

When the light faded, Kaelen wasn't sure why everyone was staring at him.

Raphael was beside himself. "Now see here!" he shouted. "You can't do that! He's, well, look at him. He's a she!"

Althea turned angrily towards Raphael. "According to the agreement made, punishment is to be decided by myself or one of my sisters. No one, not you, nor even Calista can interfere."

"She's right," Calista said to Raphael when he looked ready to argue. "Althea, please tell me this isn't a permanent change."

"Of course not," Althea replied. "Didn't you listen? It's only until Lucian is well again, meaning that he is fully healed. Luckily for Kaelen, that won't include scarring. If it did, then I'm afraid the punishment would be quite permanent."

Kaelen suddenly saw himself in one of the room's large mirrors, only it couldn't have been him. Where he should have been a skinny little girl was standing in his clothes. "What have you done to the mirrors?"

"Oh, I've done nothing to the mirrors," Althea said, wicked amusement darkening her tone. "What you see is you. You will remain a maid until Lucian has healed from his wounds. Maeve is right; if you cannot follow the gentleman's code, than you should not be a gentleman. Attacking without warning shows both hatefulness and cowardice. Neither is the trait of a gentleman. So, perhaps spending a few weeks as a girl will teach you to appreciate your place."

Before Kaelen could say anything, Maeve said, "Sister, you've forgotten the attire of a maiden." She held the green stone of her belt in her hand and mumbled something. The stone glowed and shot out a green light at Kaelen's uniform which instantly turned into a violently pink dress, complete with petticoats and a corset that cut into his ribs. "Oh, that's not quite what I wanted. Oh well," Maeve said cheerily.

The two witches were about to leave when Calista said, "Althea, we do have to also deal with Lucian for leaving class early."

"Shall we dismiss Kaelen?" Althea asked. "I don't believe he needs to be a part of this any longer."

"Of course. Kaelen, please go wait in my office. I shall be there momentarily to discuss your new schedule."

Kaelen, humiliated and seething, left the room, slamming the door behind him. There had to be a way to change this. Maybe it was an illusion. He reached up to his hair. No, this wasn't an illusion. His normally short hair had been replaced by long, curly tresses. The pink monstrosity swished about dainty ankles that certainly didn't belong to him. He sat down in Calista's office feeling mutinous and unfairly judged.

Lucian woke up in his wheelchair and looked about the room blearily. Where was he? A stinging pain went through his arm as he tried to get out of the chair. Slowly, his memory came back. Kaelen. That stupid, no-good, evil…

"Welcome back, Lucian," Calista's voice interrupted his angry thoughts. "How are you feeling?"

"I'm okay," Lucian replied, trying again to get out of the chair.

A pair of hands pushed him back. "Oh no you don't," Tallia said firmly.

"Lucian, we need to discuss your behavior," Calista began.

"I know," Lucian interrupted her, looking to see Calista, Phillipa and Diana standing together, "and I was going to go apologize to Diana and Phillipa once class got out but Kaelen attacked me. I tried not to fight back, I was just trying to defend myself. Honest, I didn't want to get hurt worse."

"We know, Lucian," Calista said. "Kaelen has been dealt with. However, your behavior was still inappropriate. Althea will set your punishment. But you'll have to excuse the rest of us. We have an important meeting to attend." She then walked out of the room, followed by the other teachers.

When they were alone, Althea said, "It is a small crime and so a small punishment will be sufficient. Bound by time for a week you'll be, never early nor late will you be." The tiara glowed and a white light bound his ankles then faded.

"What exactly does that mean?" Lucian asked.

"It means, Lucian that you cannot go anywhere any earlier or later than you should. Your feet are bound by time. On the bright side, you won't be late to class," Althea explained. "Come, Maeve, our work is done."

"Very well. He's very handsome too, our little gardener," Maeve said as the pair left the room.

"Gardener?" Lucian wondered aloud.

"Come on, it's back to the infirmary with you," Tallia said, turning his chair.

"Can't I walk? I haven't lost my legs," Lucian pointed out.

"No," Tallia replied firmly. "You are my patient and will follow my instructions."

Lucian sighed, but did not argue as Tallia pushed him down the hallway.

Chapter 5

In Calista's office, mass chaos had taken over the room as all the fairies stood about Kaelen. "Please settle down," Calista said in that voice that was quiet, yet piercing. When the chatter dissolved, she continued, "Now, obviously he must continue to attend classes, but there will need to be modifications made. Let's start at the beginning of the schedule and work our way down. On Monday we have language arts followed by mathematics, there's no reason to modify those classes. History, hunting, botany and foreign language are next. The only class that should need modification is hunting."

"Actually Calista," Russett interrupted, "young ladies would not deal with the plants I'll be working with in the next few weeks. I'll have to modify Kaelen's assignments. I'm sure I can teach him to dry flowers, pick the perfect bouquet; it will be fine. You'll see."

"Very well, Russett, but I assume you can take care of modifications within your class?" Calista asked.

"Of course, not a problem," Russett replied with a smile.

"Then that leaves us with hunting. Diana, what can Kaelen do during your class?" Calista asked.

"Nothing," Diana said sharply. "Young ladies don't hunt."

"You're a lady," Kaelen pointed out bitterly.

"I am a fairy and the daughter of a renowned hunter. It is expected that I also have that ability. That is the exception, but for you I will make no exceptions. The most I can offer is continuing work with his hound," Diana continued, turning her attention back to Calista. "We will be doing some indoor activities with them. Other than that, he's going to have to sit out. There's no reason for him to be placed elsewhere."

Kaelen scowled, but Calista ignored this and continued through to Tuesday's schedule. "Next up are physical education, etiquette, map and compass, horsemanship and fencing. Achilles, is there anything Kaelen can participate in?"

Achilles, a fairy with black hair and moth-like black wings, stood and said, "I've got nothing for him, her." He looked momentarily confused before continuing, "He, she couldn't be in the gym. She'd be too distracting. You'll have to find someplace else for her, him." Thoroughly lost, Achilles resumed his seat and began rubbing his ankle thoughtfully.

"That may prove difficult," Calista frowned.

"Oh no it won't," Gelasia countered, "He can have double etiquette with me. We'll do some needlepoint and calligraphy. Don't forget, I taught at Fair Damsel's for a number of years." Gelasia was the oldest fairy in the school. In fact, no one remembered her ever looking young, not even her son, Achilles. Her hair was snowy-white and her eyes the palest blue. She was wrinkled everywhere and the pointy tips of her ears were beginning to droop. Yet despite her comic appearance, she still seemed elegantly beautiful.

"Very well," Calista replied. She waved at the piece of chalk which had stopped writing and it sprang into action, writing Kaelen's schedule where it had left off. "Let's see, orientation is next."

"Kaelen can still participate," Honoria said gently. "Even girls need to know their way around."

"Excellent, horsemanship?" Calista asked.

"I still have a side-saddle; he can use that in my class," Phillipa said.

Calista didn't even have a chance to reply before Raphael interjected, "I will not have a girl in my classroom. Most unnatural and entirely out of the question."

"I suppose we can find something; perhaps sewing. Gelasia, would you have time?" Calista asked.

"It is during my fourth-year class, but I'll squeeze him in. He will need more than one dress," Gelasia replied.

"I'm not going to wear a dress," Kaelen interrupted hotly. "And not this hideous pink thing either."

"Well, you can't very well go about in your skin alone," Gelasia countered sweetly, "so you may as well make the best of it."

Kaelen started to argue again, but Calista stopped him saying, "You've already caused yourself enough trouble, don't you think?"

He scowled at her. "Just wait until my father hears of this."

Calista smiled calmly. "I've already sent word to him. It should arrive early tomorrow morning."

Now Kaelen gaped at her. He hadn't actually intended on telling his father anything. He just wanted to scare the fairies into changing him back. He now realized that for the first time in his life, he was not the person in control. The fairies were.

"Shall we continue?" Calista remarked. "Friday's schedule is language arts, art, music, alchemy and astronomy. Concerns anyone?"

"I'm afraid he'll have to sit out in art. We don't want to dirty a young lady's hands with charcoal. However, our class could use a model, so he doesn't have to leave the room," said a tall, broad-shouldered fairy with midnight blue hair and wings that were dark blue streaked with white.

"Thank you, Stefanos. Amadeus, your thoughts?" Calista asked.

The fairy with ice-blue hair said simply "He'll sing."

Calista sat a moment, as though expecting him to continue, but when Amadeus remained silent, she said, "Alright. Aurelia, what will Kaelen do in alchemy?"

Aurelia, a fairy with golden hair and eyes replied, "Kaelen will be my assistant. Generally, young ladies are taught to spin gold, but I haven't the equipment to do that. I'll need to contact Alantria at Fair Damsels to see if she has anything spare I could use."

"That just leaves astronomy. Uralia?" Calista asked.

"There needn't be any modifications made," Uralia replied, brushing a wisp of black hair out of her face. "Women love the stars just the same as men."

"Well then, Kaelen, this is your new schedule. You will be expected to perform at your best. You have quite a bit of humility to gain from this. Don't waste the lesson," Calista said seriously. "Go ahead to supper now."

Kaelen knew this wasn't a request but a command. Head up at a defiant angle, Kaelen stood to leave. Gelasia's frail hands were suddenly on his back. "Stand up straight, Kaelen. Fold your hands like this. There, now float as a lady should." As he walked to the door, teeth grit, he heard Gelasia sigh, "I suppose we'll work on that."

As soon as Kaelen was sure none of the fairies could see him, he began sprinting down the hall. It was awkward in a dress, but he kept running. If he went fast enough, he could get to his dormitory before the boys arrived from supper where everyone could see him. He would just stay in his room and not come out until he was a boy again. No one would ever know.

"Hey, you!" a voice suddenly called. "What are you doing here? Aren't you in the wrong school?"

Kaelen turned to see an older boy peering down at him. "No, I belong here," Kaelen snapped angrily, noticing his girlish voice.

The boy laughed, "You don't look much like a prince, little girl. Maybe a damsel in distress."

"I'm not a damsel," Kaelen shouted.

This just made the boy laugh harder. "A wench then," he said.

"If you don't shut that big mouth of yours, I'll shut it for you," Kaelen warned, holding up dainty fists which didn't belong to him. Fingernails poked his palms but he ignored it.

"Oh, I'm terrified, Thumbelina," the boy cackled.

Kaelen was spared further banter by Calista's arrival. "Xavier, that is no way to treat a lady and certainly no way to treat a classmate. Prince Kaelen is indeed where he ought to be."

A wicked grin spread over Xavier's face. "Prince Kaelen?" he asked.

"Yes, Prince Kaelen," Calista replied. "Now go to your dormitory." She then turned to Kaelen. "You should be at supper."

"I'm not hungry," Kaelen lied, although his growling stomach told a different story.

"I thought you might say that," Calista said. With a flick of her wand, a laden tray of food appeared in mid-air. "You may eat in your room tonight, but only tonight." She walked away, leaving Kaelen scowling behind her.

By the next morning, there wasn't a single person in the school who didn't know about Kaelen's fate. Catcalls and jeers followed him as he went, in the hideous pink dress, to find a table at breakfast. The only reason he was wearing it was Gelasia showing up at his room an hour before everyone else got up and dressing him. "There's no way you could do this yourself," she'd said. "You're too fidgety." Scowling and angry, he'd had to stand silently as she tied the corset strings tight in the back, cutting off half of his air supply. Then she'd pulled the pink dress over his head and laced it up.

"Can't you at least change the color?" he'd begged.

"I'm afraid not, dear," Gelasia had replied. "Fairy magic cannot undo the magic of the Sisters. They are far more powerful than we are."

So now, hair pulled into a glittering hairnet, face powdered and cheeks rouged, Kaelen sat in the pink dress eating his breakfast. He tried to ignore the comments around him, but it was hard. An unfamiliar stinging sensation pricked his eyes, but he blinked it away.

The day continued from bad to worse. Gelasia ensured that Kaelen went to all of his Wednesday classes. Other than whispers and snorts, language arts didn't go too badly. Then he went to mathematics where he had to listen to more whispers and laughter; especially when a confused Marius asked, "Are you lost?"

"No," Kaelen replied through grit teeth, "I'm supposed to be here."

Marius looked at him for a moment; golden eyes squinted. "Oh, yes," he said suddenly. "I forgot, Kaelen, your punishment. Yes, of course, well, take your seat then. Now, long division is a source of trouble for many of you so please take out yesterday's assignment."

Kaelen had always found it difficult to focus in class, but today it seemed impossible. He could hear the boys whispering about him and he felt incredibly stupid in the vibrant pink dress. In a strange way he looked forward to sewing with Gelasia. He would be able to wear a color besides pink.

Lunchtime came and he spent it sitting by himself and cracking his knuckles. He tried to avoid doing that because he hated looking at his hands. He tried biting the perfect, long fingernails, but Gelasia caught him. She slapped his hand away from his mouth and said, "A young lady never bites her fingernails." When other boys began snickering, she continued loudly, "And gentlemen don't bite their nails either." Several boys stopped laughing and hid their hands from the old fairy as she tsked her way to the staff table.

After lunch, Kaelen spent a dull hour in history before going to the tower for hunting. He sat down sullenly as Diana brought the class to attention. "Today we'll be going down to the grounds to work with your hounds. There's not much breeze today which will make being outside nice. Be sure to grab your jackets, because it's not very warm. Kaelen, you may participate in today's activities."

The class headed down the stairs and out into the field where their dogs were waiting. He watched Diana stroke Rusty's ears affectionately while other dogs ran to their owners. His dog remained near Diana, confusion in his big brown eyes. "Rex, come here," Kaelen called.

The dog turned and loped over to Kaelen. He barked happily and wagged his bushy tail.

"Will you cut that out?" Kaelen demanded as Diana began giving instruction for the day.

Rex whimpered and cocked his head to the side. Thinking that perhaps the little girl in front of him needed cheering up, Rex ran away to find a stick. He brought it back and dropped it at Kaelen's feet, tongue out and tail wagging. When Kaelen made no effort to pick up the stick, Rex nudged it closer with his nose. Kaelen tossed the stick over his shoulder and watched in disbelief as Rex bounded away after it, barking merrily.

"Rex, come back here now," Kaelen shouted.

Poor old Rex was terribly confused. This little girl looked like one of Kaelen's sisters, but she didn't want to play. Anna always wanted to play. What was wrong with her? He tugged playfully at Kaelen's skirt.

"Bad dog, stop," Kaelen said harshly.

Rex whined and lay down at Kaelen's feet, looking up at him mournfully.

"Diana, what's wrong with him?" Kaelen asked.

"You're a girl, Kaelen. Girls play with dogs, they don't work with them. Good boy, Rusty," she interrupted herself as Rusty brought back the ball she'd been tossing him. She scratched behind his ears and tossed the ball again. Unlike a normal ball, this one zigzagged through the air before landing. "Even playing can help hone in a dog's skills. Rex will respond better if you play the part you look."

Kaelen was furious. He didn't have time to play. He needed the dog to work. He glared at Rex who was now watching Diana and Rusty with a wistful expression. "It's not my fault, you know," Kaelen spat.

Rex sighed and lay down with his head on his paws. As another dog approached, he picked his head up and watched intently.

"Good girl, Queenie," a blonde-haired boy said, patting the dog's head as he took the stick from her. "Hey, I know you probably don't want any advice from me, but if you teach the dog to protect you as a, um, in your current state he'll protect you when you're yourself again."

"Yeah and how would you know, George?" Kaelen hissed.

"Look, Kaelen, I've got nine older sisters and each of them has a dog. Dad insisted on their having one to protect them since we live so close to the mountains. My sisters will tell you that there is no fiercer dog than one protecting the person it loves. The stick teaches them to be alert and to attack on sight. Love teaches them loyalty and devotion better than shouting." George threw the stick and Queenie sped away. "Think about it," he called over his shoulder.

Kaelen sat sullenly for a moment before contemplating the stick lying next to Rex's paws. He picked up the stick. Rex looked up at him expectantly. "You want the stick?" Kaelen asked, holding the stick higher. Rex jumped to his feet and watched the stick. "You really want it?" Kaelen asked, tossing the stick to his other hand. Rex barked happily and hopped to the other side of Kaelen. "Go fetch!" Kaelen shouted, throwing the stick as hard as he could. One day of play wouldn't hurt them. Rex bounded after the stick before bringing it back to Kaelen. When Rex returned, Kaelen tried to take the stick away. Rex shook his head and growled playfully. "Come on, boy, give me back the stick," Kaelen grunted as he pulled on the stick. Rex let go and Kaelen once again threw the stick. It was the only bright spot in his day. Despite himself, he had fun throwing the stick for Rex and watching him chase it around the yard.

As they left hunting, George gave him a look that said, "I told you so." The boys walked inside the greenhouse for botany. Russett was standing at the doorway holding a vase in one hand and pruning shears in the other. "Boys, you'll have to excuse me momentarily so I can give Prince Kaelen his assignment. The rest of you will kindly sit at the benches and wait for instruction." Some boys started snickering as Kaelen followed Russett. Russett turned suddenly, hitting Kaelen in the face with his dark red ponytail and causing Kaelen to run into him. "I'll not have anyone making fun of Kaelen in my class or I'll see to it that all of you spend a day in his shoes." The laughter died instantly and Russett turned sharply round again, leading Kaelen into the back of the greenhouse muttering under his breath. "Laughing at classmates just because they're being punished. Not in my class. Boys will be gentlemen in my class. I'm sorry Kaelen," Russett continued more loudly. "I realize this must be hard for you. But think of it this way, girls like gentlemen who appreciate the finer things. Trust me; my wife loves it when I do the flower arrangements."

Kaelen was hardly comforted by this thought, but continued to the table Russett motioned towards. On the table was an assortment of vases. "What am I doing?" he asked suspiciously.

"Basic flower arranging," Russett replied. "Every young lady needs to know how to arrange flowers by color, scent, and size of bloom. It's easiest to start with color. Warm colors like reds, oranges and yellows work well as do cool colors like violets, blues and greens. Pink and white can be either dependent on the shade." When Kaelen looked at him blankly, Russett continued, "Now that you're thoroughly confused, I'll leave you to it." Russett turned to walk away and then turned again and looked at Kaelen. "You're not colorblind, are you?" he asked.

"No," Kaelen replied.

"Good," Russett said. "Please feel free to use any flowers you want. Just make sure your colors work well together. I'll be back in a half-hour to check on you."

Russett walked away, leaving Kaelen behind. Bushes of flowers of all colors surrounded Kaelen. He walked around them for a while. The varying scents assaulted his nose and he had absolutely no idea where to begin. How could pink be both warm and cool? To that end, how was white either of them? White wasn't even a color, Stefanos had told them so in art class. A group of brilliant red poinsettias caught his eye. He took the pruning shears and clumsily lopped off a couple blooms before moving on. "Okay," he said aloud, "I have red. Now I need orange or yellow." Kaelen searched for something equally vibrant. Spotting some boxes of daffodils, he chose a few bright yellow blooms. Then he saw a group of marigold plants and decided to throw some of those in for good measure. He saw a pale pink rose bush and chose one to complete his ensemble. Laying the freshly cut flowers in front of the vase, he tried to decide how to arrange them. "I'll just wing it," Kaelen said. He began putting the flowers haphazardly into the vase. He plucked some of the poinsettias' petals to make room for the taller flowers. He stood back from it and looked at it. "That is the ugliest thing I've ever seen in my life," he muttered bitterly.

"I'm afraid I have to agree," Russett said from behind him. "You really can't arrange poinsettias and you didn't do yourself any favors by decimating the blooms. And that pink is a cool shade, it really doesn't fit with the others at all." When Kaelen looked more miserable than ever Russett smiled. "I've got ten minutes before I have to check on the others. Let's see if we can salvage this, eh?"

Kaelen nodded glumly. "Where should we start?" he asked.

"Well, these daffodils are lovely, let's start there," Russett replied. "The poinsettias can't be saved, I'm afraid, but I believe I have some tiger lilies in here that would work nicely. Go fetch three lilies and one more daffodil. It's one of the cardinal rules in arranging. Do things in threes. I don't know why it works, but it does. The only time you want something to be single is when it's going to be the only thing in the vase, apart from water. Anyway, off you go."

Kaelen went through the aisles until he found the box labeled tiger lilies. Then he got one more daffodil. Next to them he noticed some white daisies. He held the daffodil up to them. Carefully selecting three, he returned to where Russett was standing and held out his find.

"Oh, I wouldn't have thought of daisies," Russett said as he took the flowers from Kaelen. "That's a clever idea."

"Thanks." Kaelen couldn't help feeling proud of himself. He knew botany wasn't his strength and he appreciated the praise; especially compared to the first part of his day.

Russett smiled and looked at the vase for a moment. "Alright, Kaelen, you have several flowers the same height. What should you do so that all of the flowers are visible?"

"Um, I don't know," Kaelen replied.

"Think about it for a minute; if I leave all the flowers the same height, they'll crowd each other right?" Russett asked.

"I guess so," Kaelen said.

"So doesn't it make sense to vary the height?" Russett continued.

"Yeah, but how do I do that?" Kaelen asked.

Russett laughed, "You trim the stem of course; and when you trim the stem do it at an angle. This helps the stalk absorb the water. So now you have to decide, which flowers do you want to be tallest?"

Kaelen looked at the three types. "I like the lilies best."

"Okay, then that one we'll trim only one inch from each stem. Second rule of arranging, you should always follow some color scheme whether darkest to lightest, yellow to red, whatever you choose. So, my recommendation would be to make daffodils your middle height and the daisies shortest. This will add to the ambience of your arrangement," Russett explained.

"Ambi-what?" Kaelen asked.

Russett shook his head slightly. "Don't worry about it. Go ahead and trim the stems and get these arranged the way you want them and I'll be back at the end of class to check on this."

Kaelen didn't say anything. He started trimming the stems and setting them in the vase. As he worked, he was surprised to find he enjoyed the flowers. They were lovely and smelled so nice. Soon, Russett returned and Kaelen asked, "What do you think?"

"Much better. With practice you'll be very good at arranging. Let me write some notes for you and then I'll have these sent to your room," Russett said. "But now you need to head to foreign language."

"Okay," Kaelen said.

Once at foreign language, it didn't take long for Kaelen's bright spot to be completely shut out. Lorelei was perched on a rock within the lake dipping her tail into the water. As Kaelen entered the gazebo she asked, "Who are you?"

"It's Prince Kaelen," one of the boys said. "The witches turned him into a girl."

The rest of the boys laughed until Lorelei held up a hand. "Well, no one told me about the change. You will not have any excuses for not working. I expect the same work as before."

"Yes, Lorelei," Kaelen replied, grinding his teeth. The mermaid started their lesson and Kaelen sat taking notes while she wrote things on the floating chalkboard. Something poked Kaelen's back and he turned to see one of the other boys holding a stick. "Quit it," Kaelen hissed and then turned back to face the front. It wasn't long before something was poking him again. "Stop," Kaelen said a little louder than he had intended.

"Is there a problem, gentlemen?" Lorelei asked, her green eyes flashing dangerously.

"No, Lorelei," the boys said.

She looked at them for a while longer before continuing the vocabulary list she was writing on the board.

For a while, things were quiet until something sharp poked Kaelen's back. "Ouch," he cried. "Would you cut it out?" he shouted, rounding on the boys behind him.

"Kaelen, I will not have you disturbing my class any longer," Lorelei said angrily.

Outraged, Kaelen argued, "But they…"

"No buts, Kaelen," Lorelei interrupted. "You will leave at once. I want you to return tonight at five thirty sharp. If you are late or don't show, I will speak to Calista about punishment. Now you will leave." Lorelei pointed towards the gazebo's entrance, her green eyes still flashing dangerously.

Furious, Kaelen rose from his seat. "Fine," he shouted, gathering his things before stomping away. One of the boys, who had been poking him, stuck his foot out to trip him. Kaelen fell to his knees, dropping his notebook and supplies. He jumped to his feet and rounded on his assailant. "Just you wait till I'm back to normal," Kaelen hissed.

"Oh, I'm really scared," the boy sneered, "Kaelinda."

"Out!" Lorelei shrieked as Kaelen lifted an arm to punch the boy.

"I'm going," Kaelen retorted. He lifted the edge of his skirt and continued out. Humiliated, hurt and angry, Kaelen headed towards his room. He desperately wanted to be alone.

But that was not to be the case as Calista walked out of her office just as Kaelen pounded up the last two steps. "Kaelen, why aren't you in class? You should be in foreign language right now."

"Lorelei kicked me out," Kaelen replied.

"Why?" Calista asked.

"Because I'm a distraction," Kaelen spat.

"What were you doing?" Then distracted by Kaelen's disheveled appearance, Calista continued, "What on earth did you do to your gown?"

"I tripped," Kaelen said.

"Over what?" Calista asked.

"Nathan's big foot," Kaelen muttered.

"Nathan?" Calista looked thoughtful. Then she looked back to Kaelen and said, "Well, we can't have you going to supper looking like that. Come into my office for a moment and then I'll send you to Gelasia."

Feeling as though he lived in the office, Kaelen rather reluctantly followed Calista. He looked about glumly as Calista penned a note on a piece of lavender paper. She folded it before grabbing a piece of black paper. "What's that for?" Kaelen asked.

"I expect my students to behave as gentlemen," Calista replied simply. "Now take this note to Gelasia. I will speak to Lorelei about a time for you to make up your lesson."

"She said for me to be there at five thirty," Kaelen said.

"I'm afraid that will be impossible," Calista explained. "The rent to your gown will take a lot of time to fix as will cleaning it. For now you have a reprieve. Now, off you go."

Knowing better than to argue, Kaelen took the folded note and watched the black paper fly out the window. He secretly hoped as he walked down the hallway that Nathan would be turned into a toad or something equally slimy.

As Kaelen walked into the etiquette classroom, Gelasia looked up. "Hello dear, I thought…Good heavens! What on earth did you do to yourself?"

Kaelen blushed as the older boys turned to look at him and his shabby, pink dress. "I didn't do it on purpose," he said defensively. He handed Gelasia the note.

"Might have known, boys never can keep themselves out of trouble. Including older ones," she added loudly as several boys started snickering. She skimmed the note before waving it in her hand causing it to disappear. "Very well, Kaelen, have a seat. Once I finish this lecture, I'll be right with you. And as for you," she continued turning to her class, "a gentleman never laughs at a lady. Ever." She glared at the boys until it was quiet enough to hear a pin drop.

Kaelen sat in the back of the room, playing absentmindedly with the tear in his dress. The hole was jagged from landing on the sharp stones littering the floor of the glass gazebo. Mud and green slime was smeared across the skirt and, he noted, on his hands. Spying a basin of water in a corner of the classroom, Kaelen quietly got up and began rinsing his hands. As he scrubbed, he noticed several small scratches on his palms. They hadn't bled much, but they stung horribly and he again felt an unfamiliar pricking behind his eyes. He blinked it away impatiently.

"Let's get some bandages on those to take away the sting," Gelasia said gently from behind him.

"Okay," Kaelen replied. He followed her to her desk and sat patiently as she put some kind of ointment on his hands and then wrapped them with thin strips of white cloth.

"Better?" Gelasia asked. When Kaelen nodded, she continued, "Now, let's see what we can do about that gown of yours. First things first, take this robe and go behind the screen and change out of that mess."

"Can't you just wave your wand at it?" Kaelen asked as he pulled the gown over his head.

"Dear, you know I can't change the Sisters' magic. I cannot alter anything they've done. Not even to fix it."

Kaelen sighed, "So can you fix it?"

"Of course I can, and you'll help me. It can be our first sewing lesson," Gelasia said cheerfully. She took the ruined dress from Kaelen and continued, "Now, the first rule in sewing is to always work with clean hands and materials. Your hands are already clean, but this fabric needs to be washed. So we'll fill that basin with hot water and soap and start scrubbing." She helped Kaelen fill the basin and handed him a washboard. "You're going to have to scrub very hard to get those stains out. I have to work with my students so I'll leave you to it and check on you in a bit."

Kaelen watched Gelasia walk away and started scrubbing the stained dress. "Maybe if I scrub hard enough, the color will change," he muttered. He kept scrubbing until the water was muddy. As Gelasia walked up to him, Kaelen pulled the skirt out of the water.

"That's probably as good as it's going to get, dear," Gelasia said, looking at the skirt. There was still a brownish stain around the tear, but most of the mud had come out. "Now, let's get that dried. Since you can't very well go around in a night robe, we'll have to use something quicker than wind." She pulled out her wand and pointed it at the dress. A stream of hot air blew over the skirt, drying it instantly.

"How come you could dry it with magic?" Kaelen asked.

"I didn't use a spell to dry it; I used a spell to create hot air. The effect was not because of the spell so much as the air. Hot air dries things very quickly so I simply used a spell for hot air. Between the two of us," she continued, dropping her voice conspiratorially, "some of these boys could have done a better job."

Surprised by the fairy's joke, Kaelen giggled, "Really?"

"Oh yes, and we won't go into fairies I know. Sometimes I can be funny," Gelasia continued as Kaelen stared at her in disbelief. "Besides, you've been so sullen lately; it's good to hear you laugh. A lady should always be cheerful, as should a gentleman."

Kaelen frowned. "It's hard to be cheerful when everyone's out to get you."

"Nonsense," Gelasia retorted. "I'm not out to get you. Neither are the other staff members. As far as your peers are concerned, I'll just bet there's someone who wants to be your friend. You just need to drop the tough-guy act."

In the infirmary, Adrian was catching Lucian up on what he had missed that day. "I started working with Donovan and his dog. I think I know why they struggle so much."

"Really, why?" Lucian asked.

"The dog and horse don't actually belong to him. They were his brother, Brian's. Do you know how many brothers he has? Three and each of them came here and failed within four years. They've just passed the animals down from one to the next. Those animals have no loyalty to anyone because they don't know who to be loyal to," Adrian explained.

"That definitely throws some wrenches into our plan," Lucian said with a thoughtful expression. "Teaching an animal what to do is one thing. Trying to teach loyalty is nigh unto impossible."

"So what do we do?" Adrian asked.

"I don't know. Let me write to my dad about it. He'll be able to give us some good advice," Lucian replied.

"Um, how about I write the letter?" Adrian suggested as Lucian clumsily tried to get into his bag for a piece of paper and pen. Lucian sighed, but handed Adrian the supplies. "You just tell me what to say and hopefully your dad will get back to us soon. There are only four weeks until the end of semester and we still don't know if Calista will approve of us helping him."

The boys were just finishing the letter as Tallia walked up to Lucian's bed with a tray in hand. "Well, what are you two up to?" she asked.

"Nothing," the boys replied simultaneously.

Tallia laughed, "Surely I don't look that gullible. Alright, Lucian, let me see that arm." Lucian held it up and Tallia gently unwrapped the bandage to look at the two rows of stitches. "Well, you're looking alright. No infection or additional damage. We'll wrap that back up to keep it clean and keep it in a sling so you don't toss it about. No writing, fencing, hunting, tossing, throwing or any other activity I may have missed for at least one week."

"Is there anything I can do?" Lucian asked.

"You can sit still and listen to instructions," Tallia replied, pinching his uninjured arm gently. "Come back next Wednesday and we'll see how you're doing."

"You mean I can go?" Lucian asked.

"Of course, silly," Tallia replied. "You didn't think I was going to keep you here forever did you?" After finishing the bandage she patted Lucian's shoulder. "You're cute, but not that cute. Go on, if you're fast enough you'll get to supper on time."

"Okay, bye Tallia," Lucian said as he and Adrian left the room and headed down the hall. They arrived just as the first years were lining up to serve themselves up for supper. The noise prevented them from talking much as did interruptions from other boys welcoming Lucian back. "You'd think I'd been gone a month instead of a day," Lucian said in disbelief as Adrian helped him carry his tray to their table.

"A lot of people were worried about you," Adrian explained. "Besides, everyone here likes you. You're nice to everybody."

"So are you," Lucian argued. He didn't like the extra attention.

"Yeah, but I didn't get my arm slashed up," Adrian pointed out.

Lucian shrugged as he and Adrian sat down. They were about to start eating as Calista's voice rang out, "Gentlemen, please rise; we have a lady in our midst.

Adrian and Lucian stood up. Lucian looked around to see a blushing girl in a stained pink dress practically run to a table. "Who's that?" he asked.

"Oh, I forgot to tell you. That's Kaelen," Adrian whispered. "His punishment is to be a girl as long as your arm is out of commission. At least, I think that's what it was. There's been a lot of confusion, you see. Some guys were saying he'd be that way until the end of the year and others were saying until graduation. I think that's a little extreme since he still has to make his princess fall in love with him."

Lucian's response was interrupted by Gelasia's sweet voice, "Dear, they can't sit down until you say they can."

"Let them stand," Kaelen said bitterly.

"A lady never does that," Gelasia retorted. "You must tell them to have a seat. One punishment is rather enough, wouldn't you say?"

"Fine," Kaelen sighed. "You may have a seat."

Everyone sat and there was some snickering as a small boy carried a covered tray to Kaelen and then bowed before scampering away.

"Why can't I get my own food?" Kaelen whined.

"A lady does not serve herself but is waited upon. Surely your mother does not serve herself," Gelasia said.

Kaelen scowled but did not reply.

"He's a girl?" Lucian asked Adrian.

"Yeah. A lot of the fairies are really mad about it because he's going to miss out on instruction," Adrian explained.

"I can understand that, but at the same time he deserves it. What he did was cowardly," Lucian said.

"No arguments here, but still, being a girl would be awful. I suppose he'll have a greater understanding of his princess than the rest of us will," Adrian pointed out.

"Probably not. Somehow I don't think that Kaelen thinks like a girl, no matter what he looks like," Lucian replied.

As it happened, Lucian was right. The thoughts going through Kaelen's head were certainly not the ones that a lady would have. Upon sitting down, he heard the whispered jeers of his peers. More than once, Nathan's loud voice had interrupted his thoughts, "Poor, clumsy Kaelinda." Of course, Kaelen felt that Nathan had nothing to say on the matter. It soon became apparent that the witches had bound his feet together with an enchantment. Watching Nathan bunny hop through the line for seconds had been very gratifying; especially when he tripped over his feet landing face-first into his mashed potatoes.

However, now Kaelen sat alone listening to the teasing through grit teeth. His eyes were stinging horribly and despite his best efforts, he couldn't blink it away.

"Are you going to cry, Kaelinda?" Nathan sneered.

"Don't call me that," Kaelen retorted, his voice breaking.

"Oh, poor Kaelinda. All alone with no friends. That's because you're ugly, Kaelinda. Even the servants don't want to be around you," Nathan continued as the serving boy cleared Kaelen's place and scurried away. "Poor, ugly Kaelinda. Go back home where you belong."

Hot tears spilled down Kaelen's face as he jumped to his feet. "Shut your face!" he shouted.

Everyone turned and stared as Gelasia said sharply, "Kaelen, we do not speak that way. A lady or a gentleman is always soft-spoken."

"Tell him that," Kaelen said before turning and running out the open door. He ran down the hallway to the stairs where he stopped out of breath. The heavy skirts weighed him down and the corset was cutting off his air. He felt completely helpless and alone. Angry and horribly hurt, Kaelen started tearing at his skirt, starting with the row of unsteady stitches he'd patched the skirt with.

"Ruining your only outfit won't make you feel better," he heard Adrian say behind him.

"Shut up or I'll knock you out," Kaelen retorted angrily.

"Oh please," Adrian scoffed. "You probably couldn't even do that as a guy. I'm twice your size. The only reason I wouldn't flatten you before you tried to hit is because right now you're a girl. I don't hit girls ever, even when they deserve it." When Kaelen made no response Adrian continued, "Besides, I didn't come out here to make fun of you. I came to offer my friendship."

"Why?" Kaelen asked suspiciously.

"Because I'm a nice person," Adrian replied simply. "Everyone needs friends; even tough guys who think they're better than the rest of us."

"So why would you want to be friends with me?" Kaelen asked.

Adrian sighed. "Look, I have a twin sister. She's annoying as all get out, but I protect her because she's my sister. People are taking advantage of your predicament to get some cheap revenge. I don't think that's right. So, I'm offering to be your friend to give you some protection."

"You can't protect me," Kaelen muttered.

"Oh yeah? Name one person in this school who messes with me. If you can name one," Adrian challenged, "I'll take back my offer and you can deal with Nathan and everyone else on your own."

Kaelen thought. He couldn't think of a single person who picked on Adrian. Even he generally left Adrian alone. In spite of his good-natured personality, Adrian looked intimidating. "What would I have to do?" Kaelen asked finally, wiping the final tears from his face.

Adrian smiled. "Quit picking on Lucian and sit with us at meals and classes. That's all to start off with."

Sniffing, Kaelen looked down the hall towards the dining hall. He could hear laughter and cheerful chatting floating towards him. Though he wouldn't admit it aloud, he wanted to be a part of the fun he was always on the outside of. He turned back to Adrian. "Okay."

Chapter 6

The next morning, after Gelasia had helped him get dressed, Kaelen went to breakfast. He walked quickly towards a table. He hesitated only a moment before sitting down at an empty spot with Adrian and Lucian. He saw a slight look of surprise on Lucian's face. After he told everyone to sit down, Adrian and Lucian smiled. "Welcome to our table," Adrian said.

"Thanks for inviting me," Kaelen replied. He purposely avoided looking at Lucian as the serving boy came with his breakfast.

Lucian wasn't any happier with the arrangement than Kaelen. In fact, he'd seriously contemplated sitting with Jacobi and George. But the forgiving side of him had made him sit with Adrian. "I still can't believe you did that," Lucian whispered as he and Adrian headed toward physical education. They had already said goodbye to Kaelen who was going up to etiquette for sewing with Gelasia.

"Come on, he wasn't that bad," Adrian said.

"No, but he wasn't exactly talkative either," Lucian pointed out. "I realize it's probably because he feels some kind of remorse, but it would've been nice to have some conversation."

"Give him some time," Adrian replied.

Their conversation ended as they went into the gymnasium. Achilles was standing at one end, holding a large red ball in his hand. As the last straggler came in, Achilles said in his booming voice, "Alright all, I want four laps around the gym. First stretches." He blew a whistle that was hanging around his neck.

Adrian and Lucian quickly found their spots and started working out. It was awkward for Lucian to stretch with only the one arm. So far, Achilles hadn't said anything to him about stopping and he wasn't about to give him the idea. He worked quickly and silently knowing that while Achilles was a little scatterbrained, he was also very strict about his warm-ups. The boys found this rather boring, but knew better than to disobey.

As the last boy came to a wheezing stop, Achilles started instruction. "Alright, boys, today we'll be playing Poison Ivy." There were several groans. "Hey, I could make you run laps all hour," he threatened. When silence took over the gym, he continued, "As always you are avoiding the balls. If you are touched, you have to sit out until you are able to catch a ball and hit someone else with it. Remember we aim for legs not heads. Go!" He threw the red ball in the air as the boys scattered. Halfway down, the red ball turned dark green and split into several dozen smaller balls which zoomed to the ground before zipping towards the boys' feet.

"This would be a lot easier if the balls weren't magical," Adrian puffed as he jumped over a ball heading for his ankles before twisting around for another shot.

"Yeah, well, you make it look easy," Lucian said as he sat down. He hated Poison Ivy because it never took long for the enchanted balls to take him out. Harder than dodging the balls was catching one. Even if he was able to catch one, there was no guarantee that the ball would hit the right target instead of a wall or the floor or the balls' favorite trick of pulling a u-turn in midair and hitting the thrower again just because it could. Now it was twice as hard to catch one because he couldn't move his left arm at all.

"Whatever," Adrian panted. "I've just got quick reflexes."

"You've got something," Lucian agreed. He lunged sideways at a ball zooming past his right side and caught it between his arm and his chest. As he tried to aim at one of the few survivors, the ball writhed and wriggled in an attempt to be free. Even though

Adrian would have been an easy target, Lucian had never been able to throw the ball at him. Instead he aimed for Nathan, hoping the ball would hit him smack dab in the chest. "Bulls eye!" he shouted as the ball hit its mark. Free to jump up, Lucian said as much to his surprise as anyone else's, "That's for Kaelen."

"What on earth are you doing?" Achilles bellowed, shocking everyone. The balls which had been zooming around, suddenly stopped dead in their tracks and quivered in what seemed to be fear. Everyone stared as Achilles walked quickly to where Lucian was standing. "You are not supposed to do any physical activity and you know it, young man. I can't believe you did… and I let you! Tallia's going to kill me. Tallia. Well, we are just going to march you up to the infirmary right now."

"But Achilles, I didn't use my bad arm," Lucian argued.

"I'm not interested in what you didn't do," Achilles said, taking his good arm and steering him towards the gym door. "It's what you did do. The rest of you keep playing." The balls zipped back to life as Lucian was towed away by Achilles. When they got outside the infirmary door, Achilles stopped and smoothed down his ponytail. He then knocked on the door.

Tallia opened the door, "Achilles, this is an interesting surprise. Lucian, what are you doing back here?" Suddenly she whirled on Achilles, her turquoise eyes flashing, "What did you do?"

"I…I, um, I didn't do anything," Achilles stammered. "He, he…"

"It was my fault, Tallia. I was playing Poison Ivy with the other boys. But I promise I didn't use my left arm at all. You can ask Adrian."

"And you just let him do that I suppose," Tallia directed at Achilles as she ushered both of them into the room. She started taking the sling off␣Lucian's arm.

"Now see here, I've got a whole room full of boys. I didn't see him until I caught him jumping up after throwing a ball," Achilles argued, sounding much like a teenager caught out after hours.

"You were letting him throw? Oh you can be so, so, argh!" Tallia growled. She looked over Lucian's arm. "And you, young man, you know better. I told you absolutely none of that. Just because he can't figure it out doesn't mean you can take advantage of that. You may have torn your stitches out or caused bruising around them."

"I'm sorry, Tallia," Lucian said softly. "I just couldn't sit there while everyone else was playing."

"Oh yes you could have," Tallia retorted. "You," she continued, turning to Achilles, "you better start watching him and making sure he's not doing anything he's not supposed to or so help me, I'll, I'll, well, I'll think of something horrible to do to you."

"I'm really sorry, Tallia," Achilles said gently. "You're right, I should have been watching him more carefully."

Lucian stared at Achilles in disbelief. He'd never once heard Achilles admit to being wrong about anything. Of course, he'd also never seen Achilles look at anyone the way he was looking at Tallia.

Tallia looked up at him from Lucian's arm. Achilles was smiling at her and she couldn't help but smile back. "I might forgive you this time. There was no harm done. Both of you, back to class now." She pushed them out of the room.

Kaelen was not there to see Lucian defend him or the trouble that Lucian had gotten himself into for it. He was now battling another row of blue stitches in the dress Gelasia was helping him make. It was the fourth time he'd had to do that row. The satin slid in his hands and despite the valiant efforts of his thimble, he'd pricked his fingers more times than he could count. When he finally finished the row, he looked at his work. "I hope I never have to make a living as a tailor; I'd starve," he said glumly.

"It's not so bad," Gelasia countered. "I've seen much worse. In fact, when I was first starting I'm sure I did much worse. Satin is terribly difficult to work with. Perhaps I should have given you something easier to start with."

"I chose this fabric, remember," Kaelen said through a mouthful of pins.

Gelasia chuckled, "I suppose then I should have warned you. Well, don't worry Kaelen, we'll get you through these and when you're done the gown will be lovely." Gelasia looked over the stitches again. "These will do. In fact, I don't think anyone will ever notice these. They're all on the inside so they won't be visible. As you keep at it, you'll get better. Oh, look at the time! It's time for you to go to your next class. Let's see, next you have oh, silly me; next you have etiquette. Well, if it's alright with you, I'll let you keep working on that until the rest of your class gets here. Then you'll join them for the lesson."

"Alright, I'll get this row right if it kills me," Kaelen said.

"That's the spirit, dear," Gelasia said as she got up and headed for the door to welcome in the rest of the class.

"Hey, Kaelen," Adrian said as he and Lucian came in. "What are you working on?"

"Dress," Kaelen replied through his pins.

"That's a nice color for you," Lucian said smiling.

Kaelen looked up from his work. "What's that supposed to mean?"

Lucian couldn't help but laugh. "Well, it's blue right? That's almost the same color as our uniforms."

"You don't think it's girly?" Kaelen asked suspiciously.

"No, I'd wear that color. I think it's a nice shade. It matches your eyes," Lucian added for an extra compliment.

"Oh, thanks," Kaelen said, surprised at the kindness Lucian was showing. A guilty feeling was settling in his stomach.

"You should probably come have a seat now. Gelasia's coming in," Adrian said.

"Alright, let me finish this row. You guys go ahead and have a seat," Kaelen replied. He finished the row carefully and then put the pieces down in the basket Gelasia had given him for his sewing projects. Then he walked to his seat just as Gelasia sat down on the seat next to her desk.

"Today we're going to have a class discussion," Gelasia said after taking roll. "I've been quite disappointed in the behavior of many of my gentlemen in the past couple of days. Specifically yesterday. Tell me, how should a gentleman behave in the presence of a young lady?"

For a while it was quiet, then Kaelen timidly raised his hand.

"Yes, Kaelen?" Gelasia asked.

"Well, a young lady is supposed to always be cheerful, so I suppose a gentleman would do things that would make her feel happy," Kaelen replied.

"Can you give me a specific example?" Gelasia asked.

Kaelen thought for a moment. "He would be kind to her, like offering to be her friend."

"Very good, what else?" Gelasia asked, turning to the rest of the class.

Adrian raised his hand and waited until Gelasia called on him before saying, "A gentleman would treat her with respect. He'd offer help rather than ridicule."

"A very good point, Adrian," Gelasia said with a smile. "What else?"

Lucian raised his hand. "At home, my mother always tells me that a gentleman compliments young ladies. Anytime Allegra, my sister, had a competition, I had to tell her at least one good thing I had seen her do. Like the time she won her first blue ribbon; I got her some roses out of our flower garden."

"Perfect, Lucian. That is a very gentlemanly thing to do," Gelasia agreed. "Although, I do hope you asked your mother first," she continued with a smile. "I want this to be a full class discussion. What else should you do? Or perhaps I should ask what should you not do?"

More of the boys started participating and Kaelen noticed that some were turning a bit red in the face. Gelasia allowed the discussion to continue until people were running out of ideas. "You have all given excellent examples. Now, since I can tell you all know how to behave like gentlemen, who would like to explain to me why so many of you have treated Kaelen with such animosity?"

The room was quiet enough to hear the snow falling outside. Many of the boys were staring at their hands or at the floor, trying to hide their shame from Gelasia.

"No one? Perhaps I can explain it to you," Gelasia offered. Kaelen felt himself go red in the face. While being the center of attention was not something he feared he certainly didn't want this kind of attention. "Many of you have allowed yourselves to forget the gentleman's code. Granted, it can be easy to forget, as it is not written down anywhere. You are expected to simply know it and follow it. That code applies to how you behave around everyone. Even young ladies have a set of rules that are to be followed. Kaelen has the wonderful opportunity of having to follow both at once. He must still keep himself to the gentleman's code while at the same time learning and following the rules a young lady is expected to obey. How difficult that must be for him! Imagine trying to learn two sets of rules, which can, at times, be contradictory. He must be the perfect gentleman and the perfect lady at once.

"Your attitude and the way you treat him will either strengthen his ability to do this or be horribly detrimental to it. Surely not one of you would purposely make his princess cry and yet, you have done this to your classmate." Kaelen could feel his face heating up worse as Gelasia continued, "Not a single one of you would dare to treat any of Melantha's ladies in the appalling manner you have treated Kaelen, and yet here we are. I should not have to have this conversation with you. I've taught you better and I am sure that your parents have taught you better. Instead of making this experience as hard as you possibly can for Kaelen, you should be looking for ways to ease this burden. Yes, he is being punished for his behavior, but none of you has the authority to punish him further. You are classmates, here for six years. By the time you leave, many of you will be very close friends, closer than brothers. Let's not spoil the opportunity by behaving as miscreants."

Silence fell over the room. Kaelen wished desperately he had somewhere to hide. He'd never needed anyone to protect him before. Having Adrian offer to be his friend was one thing. Adrian was at least a tough-looking guy. Gelasia was an ancient fairy who wouldn't be able to frighten anybody. Not only was she a fairy, she was a girl. It was embarrassing.

"Now," Gelasia said, interrupting Kaelen's thoughts, "it's time for you to go to lunch. I expect better behavior from all of you. Class is dismissed."

"Wow, she was serious," Adrian said as he walked down the hallway with Lucian and Kaelen.

"Let's just not talk about it, okay?" Kaelen interrupted. "That was really embarrassing."

"Don't worry about it, Kaelen," Lucian said. "I don't think that was her intention. She just wants to make sure we're all behaving like gentlemen. She wasn't trying to embarrass you. Besides, I think some of the guys were just as embarrassed as you were. That was like getting a lecture at home."

"Whatever," Kaelen sighed as they walked into the dining hall. He was glad they were some of the first into the room. There weren't as many guys in the room to gawk at him as he walked to his table. "Where should I sit?" he asked Adrian quietly.

"Pick a spot, we'll find you," Adrian whispered back.

Kaelen found a table that normally he saw Adrian and Lucian sit at. He sat down and then invited everyone else to sit down as a serving boy came over with his tray. "Can't I get my own?" he asked.

"I'm sorry, mi…sir, I have to bring it to you. That's my job," the boy replied before scurrying off again.

Kaelen sighed. Soon Adrian and Lucian arrived at the table. As they were sitting down, Nathan walked by. "Kaelinda, you're at the wrong table."

"Actually, Kaelen is right where he belongs, Nathan." Adrian said seriously. "However, you aren't where you belong so why don't you leave us alone?"

Nathan scowled and walked away, but not before throwing over his shoulder, "See you around, Kaelinda."

"Someone didn't listen in etiquette today, did they?" Lucian asked as Nathan walked away.

"Obviously not," Adrian said. "Oh well, let's eat."

No one said another word about Nathan as they ate their lunch. It wasn't long before the serving boy showed up again to take Kaelen's empty tray. After Adrian and Lucian cleared their places, the three walked out and upstairs to the orientation classroom.

They were almost up the stairs of the tower when they heard George running up behind them. "Hey guys, guys wait up!" George panted.

Adrian turned around. "What's up, George?"

George stopped when he'd caught up and started breathing heavily. "Give me a minute…to catch my breath." He stood there for a moment and then continued, "You will not believe what happened after you guys left lunch. It's never happened before; all the older boys were talking about it."

"Well, what happened?" Lucian asked.

"Come on, I'll tell you as we walk. So, you know how Nathan's been a bit of a jerk recently?" George said.

"Yeah, so? That's not any different than any other day of the week," Kaelen pointed out. "He's almost meaner than me."

"I'm not touching that, Kaelen," George teased with a smile. "Anyway, so Gelasia must have heard him teasing you because she got really mad."

"Gelasia? Mad?" Adrian asked.

"Yeah, that's what all the older boys were talking about. The weird thing was half of us didn't realize that anything had happened until that one really pretty witch, you know the one who hates all of us and thinks we're stealing her flowers or whatever?"

"You mean Lucretia?" Lucian asked.

"Yeah, the really pretty one all the guys like. She came in looking really confused and walked up to Calista and asked if there had been a mistake because she'd just been called in by Gelasia," George explained. "Gelasia then said there was no mistake and told Lucretia what had happened. Have you guys ever seen her mad? Have you?"

"Yeah, not an experience I'd care to repeat," Adrian said.

"She is so scary when she's mad, but it's kind of pretty too. Except for the vermillion eyes, that's really freaky. But her hair started billowing out everywhere and that necklace she wears started glowing red as she was chanting something at Nathan. And now? Oh, you'll never believe what he's doing now," George said as they walked into the room.

"What happened?" Kaelen asked, hoping that Nathan was now something embarrassing. Maybe not a girl, he wasn't sure he'd wish that on anyone; but something terrible.

"He can't talk right at all. He keeps garbling his words in sentences and adding funky endings to words where they don't belong. It's the weirdest thing. Especially when he started trying to tell her off for the punishment. Then she got really, really mad," George said, cowering at the memory.

"What did she do then?" Adrian asked. "She's pretty hot-tempered."

"He's now a really awkward shade of purple. He looks sick or something," George replied. "It's almost like an eggplant."

The other three boys looked at each other for a moment and then all of them starting laughing. "What is so amusing today, gentlemen?" Honoria asked as she walked into the room.

"Nothing," they replied in unison.

"I don't think I believe that," Honoria said with a smile, "but I won't press the matter. Make sure you have spare paper. You have a test today."

The boys groaned and Lucian looked at his arm. "Um, Honoria, how am I going to take my test? I can't write anything yet."

Honoria looked up at him. "Oh that's right. I'd completely forgotten. I suppose you can take your test orally. I'll have to see if someone has a break right now to watch the rest of the class." She flicked her wand and a silvery piece of paper flew out the open door. "There, someone should be up shortly. Calista knows everyone's schedule and would be able to send someone to help out."

She turned around and Lucian noticed for the first time that her silver hair was not down and flowing about her as it normally was, but braided and bound with a golden ribbon. "Your hair looks nice today," he said. "Normally you leave it down."

Turning again, Honoria smiled, her silver-grey eyes sparkling. "Thank you, Lucian. Raphael braided my hair for me this morning. He did a very nice job." The sparkling silver dress she wore wisped about her as she returned to her desk and sat down.

The boys quickly found their seats as the rest of the class came in. Everyone was already seated as Nathan, who was trying his very best to be invisible and failing miserably, slipped into the room. There were several snorts and even some badly covered laughs. "Is something amusing?" Raphael asked as he walked into the room.

The boys turned in unison and in one voice said, "No, Raphael." Then a barrage of whispers started as the students tried to figure out why he was in the wrong classroom. "It's not even like we're on the same level of the castle," one boy said as Raphael, undaunted, walked to the front of the room and kissed Honoria's cheek.

"Calista said you needed an extra pair of eyes today," he said as he took a seat near the chalkboard.

"Yes, Lucian needs to take his test orally today and I can't very well be in two places at once," Honoria replied with a smile. She returned her attention to the class to take roll. "I hope you all remembered to study for your test. Raphael is here to watch you while I take Lucian outside to take his test. I shouldn't have to remind you that since this is a test there is to be no talking and you will need to put your notes away. We all know what will happen if you should break the rules." When there were nods of acknowledgement, she continued, "If you need to get extra paper or writing utensils, I will give you three minutes to do so. Once everyone has returned to their seat, we will begin."

There was a flurry of activity as the boys started going through their bags to get out the supplies they needed. Kaelen was digging through his bag looking for a pencil. "Shoot, I must have left them in my room."

"Here," Lucian said, pulling one out of his own bag. "You can use mine. I won't need it."

"Oh, thanks," Kaelen replied. He took the pencil and then sat back in his seat.

Once everyone had settled down, Honoria passed out the test papers. "Please do not write on the test itself; that's why you have your own paper. When you have finished, hand your paper in to Raphael and set the test on my desk. You will then sit quietly at your desk for the remainder of the period. You may take out your textbook and start reading the next chapter. Good luck!" She walked to Lucian's seat. "Come on out into the hall with me, Lucian."

Lucian followed silently as the others began working on their test. He didn't think any of the boys in the room would try cheating. Raphael's hawk-like eyes never missed anything. Honoria led him down to her office on the second floor. Inside was a plain oak desk with comfortable blue chairs on either side. There was a shelf with several pictures. Some were obviously family pictures and then there was one of her wedding day.

He turned his attention to Honoria as she said, "What we'll do is I'll read the question to you and you answer me orally. For the map section, I'll point to an area and you simply tell me which province or landmark it is. I'll write in your answers and then grade it with the rest of the tests later. Make sense?"

"Yeah," Lucian replied.

"Then let's begin," Honoria said as she pulled out a test from one of her desk drawers.

Time seemed to crawl for the boys as they filled in their tests. It seemed like forever before Lucian had returned to the room with Honoria. She walked to where Raphael was standing in front of the desk and kissed his cheek gently. "Thanks for standing in for me," she whispered.

"You're welcome," Raphael replied. He kissed her forehead and then walked quietly out of the room. None of the boys saw him turn at the door and wave before leaving.

When the hour was finally over, the boys walked downstairs to go to horsemanship. After leaving the building, they walked quickly through the snow to the stables. "Maybe we'll be lucky and Phillipa won't make us ride," Adrian said through chattering teeth.

"Yeah right," Lucian replied. "If the snow isn't falling she'll have no problem sending us out in it. It's only when there's stuff falling that she has us stay inside."

Kaelen secretly hoped that they wouldn't be riding today. He hadn't gone to see Lightning since the riding final. He knew the spirited horse was easy enough to handle when he was himself, but as a girl? He didn't know if he could handle Lightning's willfulness.

"Good afternoon, class," Phillipa said as she turned from the horse she was grooming. "Are we all here?"

"Herely be everbodies evenish Kaelen," Nathan garbled.

"I beg your pardon?" Phillipa asked, looking very confused. "All I got out of that was Kaelen and I can see that he is here."

"We're all here. Nathan can't talk properly; he was punished by Lucretia," Jacobi replied.

"Ah, that explains the purple. That's been her favorite color recently," Phillipa said, a thoughtful expression on her face. "Well, in that case, Nathan, I'd ask you to refrain from speaking in class. I'm afraid I don't understand you." Nathan turned an even brighter shade of purple while everyone else turned to face Phillipa as she started their instruction for the day. "It's not horribly cold out, so I was thinking a brisk trot through the forest would be nice."

"Um, Phillipa, have you been outside?" Adrian asked. "It's freezing."

Phillipa frowned, but stepped outside. "Freezing? It's not that cold, Adrian. Just a little nippy. Besides, you all need to learn to care for your horses in all types of weather. Oh, Kaelen, follow me and I'll get you a sidesaddle you can work with. It should fit Lightning perfectly."

Kaelen sighed, but did as he was told. Everyone else went straight to their horses and started putting their tack on. He could also see Lightning looking about for him. At least he wouldn't start playing like Rex had. Then a worse thought came to him as he remembered Lightning's reaction to meeting his sister, Anna. He sighed again. This was going to be a catastrophe.

"Why so gloomy, Kaelen?" Phillipa asked as she handed him an old, but well-polished, sidesaddle. "You love riding."

"Um, could I borrow a different horse? I, um, I don't think Lightning will take it well if I ride him like this," Kaelen said.

"Why on earth not? You're still you. You just look different," Phillipa replied.

"Lightning doesn't, um, he doesn't like girls," Kaelen explained quietly.

"What makes you say that?" Phillipa asked. Kaelen's reply was so quiet she couldn't make out anything he'd said. "What was that?"

Kaelen sighed. "He charged my sister when I brought him home; and when she tried to pet him a few days later he bit her. Badly."

"Oh," Phillipa said, looking surprised. "Well, I've never had a problem with him. I'm sure you'll be just fine. Tell you what," she continued when he looked doubtful, "we'll see how today goes and then we'll decide from there. Lightning has to be worked, even when you're a girl."

Nodding, Kaelen started walking towards Lightning. Most of the boys were already standing outside with their horses. He could see Lucian and Adrian watching him. Blushing, Kaelen walked up to the large horse. He seemed bigger than normal, but then Kaelen was sure that his punishment had also cost him at least three inches in height. As he walked into the stall, Lightning snorted and flattened his ears against the back of his head. "Easy boy," Kaelen said, his voice quavering to his annoyance. "It's me, Kaelen. I just look funny today."

Lightning snorted again and started stomping his foot.

Kaelen turned to Phillipa. She merely nodded at him, holding the reins of her own horse, a palomino mare. He gulped and walked to Lightning's side with the saddle. Lightning turned and tried to bite, but Phillipa grabbed his bridle. "No," she said firmly. "Hurry and put his saddle on him, Kaelen. I'll help you lead him out." She turned her attention to Lightning as Kaelen worked. "You listen to me, Lightning and don't pretend you don't understand me. You will behave as a gentleman today. Understand?"

Lightning snorted again. He pawed at the ground and tried to toss his head.

"I mean it Lightning," Phillipa said, still using a firm tone. "You know better." She turned to Kaelen. "Go ahead and take the bridle. You have to show him that you're the boss. If you can be just as commanding as you normally are, you shouldn't have any problems with him."

Kaelen nodded as they walked outside. He tried to step up into the saddle, but missed. "Um, how am I supposed to get into this thing?" he asked.

"I'll help you up," Phillipa replied.

"Kaelen horsey getting upto cantaloupe," Nathan guffawed and then covered his mouth as the other boys started snickering at him.

"I believe I told you to refrain from speaking Nathan," Phillipa said sternly. "Luckily for you, whatever snide remark you were trying for was so jumbled no one understood it. The more you speak, the more foolish you appear." After helping Kaelen up, she mounted her horse and said, "Alright class, let's head out."

The boys headed out into the forest behind Phillipa. Kaelen was struggling to control Lightning who absolutely did not want a girl riding him. He tossed his head angrily. "Whoa, Lightning, easy," Kaelen said sternly.

Adrian and Lucian followed close behind Kaelen. They rode in silence as they tried to listen to Phillipa instructing them on their course. At one point she had all of them stop. "Everyone gather around me. Who can name one of the dangers of winter riding? Kaelen?"

"Ice patches. The horse can slip on them just as easily as we can," Kaelen replied.

"Excellent. What is one way of protecting your horse from that danger?" Phillipa asked.

Adrian raised his hand and waited to be called on. "If you use special shoes with a better grip, it helps the horse maintain balance while walking on ice. An easier way is to watch carefully for ice patches and avoid them."

"Very good point. The best horsemen are very observant. They know what is ahead of them, what is directly around them, and what is behind them. Other dangers?" Phillipa asked.

George raised his hand. "This kind of goes along with ice patches, but there are also icy stones or fallen icicles that can get lodged in your horse's hooves. The best way to prevent that is observation. If your horse does start to limp, you should have a horse pick in your pack at all times so you can dislodge any unwanted objects."

"Excellent, thank you, George. You should always be prepared for anything," Phillipa said. "Having the necessary tools for basic first aid or to prevent injury is essential. Your horse will be far more loyal if you are taking good care of him than if you neglect him. Other ideas?"

"One time I forgot to put a blanket on my horse at home," a boy in the back said. "He got really sick because I hadn't taken care of him. When you get back from your ride, you should always rub them down and then give them a warm blanket to keep them from getting sick."

"That is a wonderful example. Even though horses are blessed with long winter coats, they still need that extra warmth when they've been out just like you do," Phillipa explained. "Giving them a blanket will help them stay warm and healthy. Let's continue on our path."

The boys clicked their tongues and the horses began moving again; except for Lightning who stubbornly stood still by the tree. "Come on, boy," Kaelen begged, not sounding commanding at all. The horse snorted and flattened his ears, but did not move.

Adrian turned to see Kaelen still sitting there. He rode Stardancer up to Lightning's side. "Go on, Lightning," he demanded, hitting Lightning's flank lightly with his riding crop.

Lightning reached around and bit at the crop, but still refused to move. Frustrated, Kaelen kicked Lightning hard in the side. Lightning whinnied and half-reared before bolting past Phillipa and everyone else, causing Kaelen to squeal in terror. "Whoa, boy!" he shouted, pulling back on the reins. His skirt was flying up around him and the sidesaddle was hard and unyielding as he bounced around trying to slow Lightning down. "Whoa!"

"Lightning, stop," Phillipa's commanding voice came over the rush of wind blowing past Kaelen's ears. Lightning quickly planted all four hooves on the ground and Kaelen, already off balance, fell unceremoniously out of the saddle and onto the ground. "Are you alright, Kaelen?" Phillipa asked as she hopped down from her own horse and came to his side.

Kaelen stood shakily and brushed the snow off his skirt. "I think so, I landed on my ankle, but it doesn't hurt too badly."

"Here, you ride Dawn and I'll ride Lightning back to the stable," Phillipa said gently. "She's already got a sidesaddle and she's very gentle. It's hard not being in control, isn't it?" she asked as Kaelen tried to brush tears away without her noticing.

Kaelen nodded, but didn't speak as Phillipa boosted him up into the sidesaddle. This one wasn't any more comfortable than the other, but at least Dawn didn't squirm around or try to bite him. He could hear Phillipa speaking almost harshly to Lightning. To Kaelen, he seemed as smug as ever. Kaelen could only hope that Lucian healed quickly so that he would soon be back to his normal self.

The rest of the class went by quickly and soon the boys were on their way up to fencing. "Are you okay, Kaelen? You're limping a little," Lucian said as they walked into the castle.

"I'm just sore. I don't know how girls do it," Kaelen replied. "I hurt in places that never hurt before when I was riding. My ankle is really sore though. I might go see Tallia after sewing. Anyway, you guys need to get to fencing. I'll see you later."

"Bye Kaelen," Adrian said. Lucian waved and then the two of them walked down the hall to the fencing room.

The two boys walked past Raphael who was standing at the door greeting them as usual. He frowned as Lucian walked in. "I'm afraid I have nothing for you to do, Lucian. Unless you'd like to try learning right-handed."

"That's okay, Raphael. I'm so left-dominant I'd be more of a danger to myself than my opponent," Lucian replied with a smile. "I'll just sit out today. If you need me to get any materials for you, I'd be happy to do so."

"Well, I hate to see you sit out, but very well," Raphael sighed. He ushered the last few students in before closing the door and beginning their instruction for the day.

Lucian had never experienced a more boring day in fencing. He normally loved fencing; it was his favorite class. Now he was stuck sitting on a stool watching everyone else. The only bright spot occurred after watching Adrian try to work with Nathan. Adrian was much better than Nathan, even though he rarely fought right-handed. It didn't help that Nathan kept trying to talk to people.

"What are you mumbling about?" Raphael asked him as he observed the two work.

"Blading he's quickerly toos mesee forlorn," Nathan whined.

Raphael looked at Nathan as though he'd grown another head as the boys in the room started snickering. "What did you say?"

Nathan took a deep breath. "Adrian swordfish meals tooly quicksome forty."

Laughter burst through the room and Raphael was beginning to give Nathan a withering glare. "I've never seen such a blatant lack of respect in my life."

"Raphael," Lucian interrupted, "it's not exactly Nathan's fault. He's being punished by the witches. He can't talk properly because of a spell. He's not trying to be rude. I think he was trying to say that Adrian is too fast with his sword for Nathan to keep up. But I think the problem is that Nathan's not holding his sword firmly enough. See how loose it is? I think he needs to tighten his grip; then he could move faster."

Raphael looked at Lucian and then at Nathan. He thought for a moment and then said, "In that case, Nathan I apologize. Perhaps it would be best if you didn't speak. Lucian, I'd like you to help me observe. You needn't sit out just because you can't participate. You can be my assistant until you are able to work again."

Lucian agreed and began meandering about the room, stopping to help where he saw problems. While he couldn't fight right-handed, he knew how to hold his sword. It felt good to help his fellow students. He wished his dad could be there to see him.

Unbeknownst to Lucian, King Lysander was indeed standing in the doorway watching him, a smile on his face. He'd received Lucian's letter the same day as the letter from Calista informing him of Lucian's accident. Between wanting to give his son advice and Alexandra's panicked belief that their son was dying, he'd decided to come up to Biberseth to see Lucian in person.

"You have a wonderful son," Calista said, standing next to Lysander. "He never misses a chance to help the other boys. They are all quite fond of him."

"All except this Kaelen boy," Lysander corrected.

Calista gave an understanding smile before saying, "Even Kaelen is coming around. He's having to learn a difficult lesson."

Lysander kept his thoughts to himself. To his mind, Kaelen deserved whatever it was he'd gotten and probably worse. But, as a gentleman, he couldn't bring himself to voice that opinion. His thoughts were interrupted as the tawny-haired fairy teaching the class brought it to a close and dismissed his students. Lucian walked out with another boy, surprise written all over his face. "Hello, son."

"Dad," Lucian said, hugging his father with his good arm, "what are you doing here? I can explain my arm, it's fine really..."

"Your mother and I already know about your arm, which is part of why I'm here. Your mother was convinced you were dying," Lysander said with a laugh. "The other part is to follow up on the letter you sent me about your friend Donovan."

"Oh, great," Lucian said. "Oh, and this is my friend Adrian."

"Pleased to meet you, King Lysander," Adrian said, shaking his hand.

"Likewise," Lysander replied. "Lucian speaks very highly of you in his letters."

"Well," Calista interrupted, "we should probably reconvene in my office."

"Good idea," Lysander said. The three followed Calista upstairs to her office.

As they were walking in, Kaelen walked past. "Hi guys."

The two boys waved and Lysander stared after him as he walked into the dormitory tower. "Who is that little girl?"

Adrian and Lucian looked at each other before looking back at the king. They were each stammering until Calista said, "That is Prince Kaelen. As I told you outside the class, he is learning a very difficult lesson. If you recall, I have no control over the punishments assigned by the witches. Sometimes their spells are harsher than what I or the other teachers would have done. However, that is their right as our disciplinary arm." Lysander raised his eyebrows, but said nothing. Calista closed the door to her office and continued, "Now, as I understand it, the boys have written to you concerning Donovan, one of our students. So you are aware, the fairies and I have not as yet come to a decision about his fate. There are some fighting quite strongly for him to remain while others are just as determined that he should go."

"I've come because I have a proposal to make. From what my son has told me, Donovan does not own the animals he is using. They are hand-me-downs from previous attendees. As I'm sure you can understand, he is having difficulty securing the animals' loyalty and as one who works with animals every day I can tell you that at this point, he will not gain the loyalty of his animals," Lysander explained. "Therefore, I am proposing that he be given at least to the end of this school year to prove himself. I raise whippets and have a litter just old enough that he could train one and keep it for himself. I was thinking of giving one to Lucian, but I understand from my daughter that he has become quite attached to little Rusty. I can also secure him a very good horse. If his parents approve, he will come to Maltisten with me and I will work with him over winter break to train his puppy and fine-tune his skills. Then when term begins, he will have to show that he has learned from the experience."

Calista looked thoughtful for a moment. She looked at Adrian and Lucian, "What do you think, boys?"

"I think that's a great idea, Lucian and I can help him during the school year to get better," Adrian said. "I know he can do it, he just needs confidence."

Lucian hesitated a moment. "I'm willing to help him with his hound, but, well, I think Kaelen should help him with his horse." When everyone stared and looked ready to argue he continued, "Look, Kaelen is one of the best horsemen in the school, I've heard Phillipa say it. I'm good with horses, but Zephyr and I aren't exactly the ideal example to follow. We're still working out our relationship. Kaelen has a good horse and is an excellent rider. If we're going to give Donovan the best chance of success, he has to work with Kaelen on his horse. Adrian and I can help him with his hound. But I really think Kaelen should help him with the horse."

"Very well," Calista said, "I think that's everything. The fairies and I shall discuss your proposal, King Lysander. In the meantime, you boys may continue working with Donovan. At the end of term, we will discuss with you our decision. Thank you, King Lysander, for coming down to speak with us on the matter. I appreciate your concern not only for your own son, but for our other pupils. That shows great character. Unfortunately, I do have other matters to attend to, so I will bid you good afternoon. Feel free to stay for supper."

"I appreciate the offer, but I promised Alexandra I'd head home as soon as I could. I will however stay to talk to Lucian for a bit before I leave," Lysander replied.

"Of course, have a good afternoon and a safe journey home," Calista said as she ushered them from her office.

King Lysander waited a while before saying, "So, is there a reason you chose not to inform your mother and I of what happened in fencing?"

Lucian blushed to the roots of his hair. "Well, I didn't think you needed to know. I mean, the fairies took care of everything and I didn't want to upset you or mom. I know how much she worries."

Lysander laughed heartily. "That is very true. However, you should have known that your mother would have immediately recognized that the letter you sent wasn't written by you." They laughed and he continued, "So, Kaelen has been changed into a girl? How long is that going to last?"

"I think until my arm is healed. Some of the boys are more vindictive and think it's permanent. However, I don't think the fairies would let the witches get away with something like that," Lucian replied.

"No, probably not," Lysander agreed. They had been walking towards the entrance of the castle. When they reached it he turned to the boys. "I want you to know how proud I am, of both of you. Offering to help someone not even in your age group is very much what a gentleman would do. You have both exhibited 'great character' as Calista said. You are to be commended for your generosity. Adrian, I hope your parents know what a wonderful son they have."

Adrian smiled, "I'll let my mother know."

"Just your mother?" Lysander asked.

"Dad, his father died when he was young," Lucian said, as though reminding him.

"Oh, I'm sorry," Lysander said. "In that case, he must already know. I'm sure he'd be very proud of you, Adrian."

"Thank you," Adrian replied.

"Yes, well I should be going. It was wonderful meeting you, Adrian. If you boys need any other advice, feel free to write me," Lysander said. "Lucian, your mother sends her love and I love you too. Allegra can't wait for winter break. She's finding being the only one at home difficult; especially when she gets herself into trouble."

Lucian laughed. "I miss her too; but I have to admit that I don't miss getting in trouble for her."

"I won't tell her you said that," Lysander teased. "Anyway, I do need to be going. I love you, son."

"Love you too, Dad," Lucian said, giving Lysander another awkward, one-armed hug. "I'll see you at the end of term."

"See you then," Lysander replied. "We look forward to having you home again."

Lucian waved and watched his father leave. He and Adrian then walked to the dining hall for supper where Kaelen was already waiting.

Chapter 7

Friday was a long day for all the boys, but especially long for Kaelen. While he was able to be in class with all of his peers, his modifications put him on the spot more than once. Airlia's class had gone very well as it was language arts and there were no modifications to his instruction. However in art, Stefanos had insisted that he sit in front of the class holding a bouquet of flowers. Nathan would giggle and garble off a random string of nonsense, which, thankfully, took the attention away from Kaelen and to Nathan's ridiculous predicament. It wasn't made any better by Stefanos constantly telling Kaelen to quit fidgeting. "You young men are all alike. Can't stand still for a moment," he said as he rearranged Kaelen's hair for the third time and twisted him back to the position he'd been in originally. "Now, stop wiggling so much. You're making this very difficult on your peers."

Kaelen had sat sullenly until Stefanos told him that a lady should be smiling. He pasted a smile on his face. He knew it didn't look like much of smile. Of course, if he had been honest, he would have admitted that Lucian wasn't having a much better time than he was. He had needed to sit at his desk in both classes doing nothing since he couldn't use his arm at all. Guilt swept through him again. It didn't matter that Lucian had forgiven him or that he was being punished for it, he still felt bad for it. Strange how that had happened. Perhaps it was the kindness Lucian had showed him despite his cruelty; or maybe it was the beginnings of humility creeping into his character.

The boys went to lunch and then to alchemy. Aurelia was waiting beside the door, her sunny smile greeting them warmly as they came in. As Kaelen walked by she said, "Kaelen, I have wonderful news. When I told Alantria of your predicament, she immediately sent me a spinning wheel. So, you won't have to be my assistant at all. You'll find your materials in the corner. I'll show you how to use the wheel and then leave you to it. It's really not all that complicated. I'm sure you'll catch on quite quickly."

Later, Kaelen bitterly thought that Aurelia's idea of quickly and his were polar opposites. In the time he'd been sitting at the wheel he hadn't managed to turn any of his straw to gold. He hadn't even gotten it to change to bronze, which was supposedly even easier than gold. Instead, the same pile of straw, slightly kicked about while Aurelia wasn't looking, was still sitting in the corner. His only achievement had been in getting several blisters and making one bundle of straw look slightly shinier. Of course, he thought that was probably more from being rubbed raw than transforming to a golden thread. "Here," Aurelia said as he left, handing him a book, "read this by next class. It'll help you understand the process a little better. You'll soon get the hang of it."

After alchemy, the boys headed over to music. Kaelen hated music normally, but being the only singer in a chorus of off-key recorders was awful. Amadeus was also known for being exceptionally picky. He stopped the boys over and over again, making them retune their instruments. He also stopped Kaelen. "No, no, you're singing an A, that should be an A sharp. You need to stretch your voice a little higher. Not another word, Nathan! No one understands that jibber-jabber!"

When Amadeus finally allowed the boys to leave, Kaelen was reaching the breaking point. "I hate that class so much!" he fumed as the three headed for supper.

"It could always be worse. Besides, he actually let you get through that one song all the way through without stopping," Lucian pointed out.

"Yeah, after ten times of playing bits and pieces," Adrian said miserably.

"Well, maybe if we all practiced a little more," Lucian began hesitantly.

"Practiced?" Adrian asked in astonishment. "Oh come on, Lucian, how often do you take that thing out and practice?"

Lucian didn't respond. Instead he said, "I wonder what we're having for supper."

This started a new line of conversation, which continued through the meal and up until supper was over. Then each of the boys headed to their respective rooms, except for Kaelen who went outside to the gazebo where Lorelei was waiting.

Lucian went to his room and pulled out the wooden recorder. No one would know if he practiced it now. Amadeus had refused to allow him to play during class because of his arm. It wasn't that he liked the recorder any more than any of the other boys did. He just wanted to start the habit of practicing now so that when they got to the more interesting instruments like the lute or viol that he'd already have the habit set. Whatever the other boys may have thought about music, Lucian had always enjoyed it. Some of that had been his mother's influence. She was a wonderful harpsichord player and sang beautifully. She'd always sung lullabies to her children to help them sleep. At night, Lucian would imagine the soft notes of the instrument and hushed tones of his mother's voice. It made him feel close to her even though he was so very far away. So despite not liking the instrument much, Lucian did practice his recorder every night. Thankfully, as yet Amadeus had never noticed his playing above that of his peers. He wasn't sure he wanted to receive praise in that class.

Night fell and the boys headed to the tower for astronomy. Uralia was waiting patiently outside the door of the observatory turned classroom. She was soft-spoken and smiled gently as each boy walked in. When class started, she led them out to the balcony. "We'll be taking a bit of a quiz for class today. I want you to identify and locate the constellations as we go along. I hate doing this by paper, so it'll be one quiz for the whole class. However, if you don't participate, I will not give you points no matter how well your peers answer for you. I will either tell you a constellation or show you the location. You will need to locate it by pointing or name the constellation depending on which type of question I ask, so pay attention. Let's begin."

Adrian secretly loved this class. One of the few memories he had of his father was going out on an overnight campout. It had just been the two of them. "No ladies tonight, eh?" he remembered him saying. They'd gone out to a meadow some distance from the castle and had set up mats and blankets to sleep under the stars. He remembered it being a warm summer night. There had been just enough breeze to keep them comfortable and not a single cloud in the sky. They had stayed up for hours it had seemed to the young boy, talking and gazing at the stars. His father had told him the story of every constellation they found. He showed him the brave warrior and the beautiful princess he'd saved from the terrible sea monster, her mother sitting on her throne, and then the horse who had run so swiftly he'd begun to fly, earning him wings from the fairies. Young Adrian had fallen asleep to the sound of his father's voice those many years ago, not knowing that within a few short weeks, he would be gone. Now as he gazed up at the starry skies, he could hear his father's voice as a whisper through the years. "Find the hunter, Adrian. Did I ever tell you about the hunter?"

He blinked back a tear from the memory. Now was not the time to be sentimental. He refocused on Uralia and the constellation she was asking them to locate.

At the end of class, Adrian started out the door with the other boys when Uralia stopped him. "Could I speak with you just a moment please?"

"Sure," Adrian replied, confused. "I'll see you guys tomorrow," he said to Lucian and Kaelen. He followed Uralia back into the classroom. "Is there something wrong?"

"No, no, it's not that you've done anything," Uralia reassured him. "Quite the opposite, you have a very good knowledge of the skies which may come in very handy for you. No, I wanted to ask you if you were alright. While stars can cause eyes to glitter, normally they don't make you blink and clear your throat."

Adrian blushed. "I was hoping no one had noticed that."

"I'm afraid I did notice. Is anything troubling you?" Uralia asked.

"No, not really." Adrian explained, "My dad died when I was young. My only real memory of him was going camping and stargazing with him. It was the last thing we did together before he died."

"I see," Uralia said gently. "I just wanted to make sure you were alright. I don't suppose there's anything I could do to make things better?"

"No," Adrian replied. "It's just a bit tender for me, that's all. I miss him a lot right now."

"Okay, well, you best head to bed, Adrian. And don't worry, you're not alone. Your father still loves you very much," Uralia said knowingly.

Adrian nodded and walked out the door.

The next weeks passed unbearably slowly for Kaelen and Lucian. For Kaelen, it was a matter of living as a girl. Between double etiquette and fencing-turned-sewing, Kaelen managed to get three dresses sewn and two small samplers completed. He also learned to properly set a table, oversee kitchen staff, write the perfect invitation, write a proper thank you card, pay a compliment, take a compliment, do his hair properly, powder his face and learned that patience was never going to be his strength. In botany he learned to arrange flowers and dry them. He now had several vases of flowers in his room and he would never admit to anyone that he actually liked the arranging. Part of it was Russett made it so easy to enjoy, but the other part was he actually liked the flowers. He still didn't like botany, but he at least could enjoy the beauty of a well-planned flower arrangement. After two weeks of failure, Aurelia had let him take the spinning wheel to his room to practice daily. By the third week he was managing to spin gold about half the time. When classes were almost finished, he was usually spinning gold and if not gold, bronze. This was another unexpected pleasure. It was especially gratifying when Gelasia allowed him to use the golden thread to embroider the green dress he made when the blue one was finished. One of the best things had been the fact that Nathan was still talking in a garbled fashion, leading many boys to believe his punishment was permanent.

Lucian had found classes a complete waste of time since he couldn't do anything in most of them anyway. He still enjoyed fencing because even though he couldn't participate, he could at least help the other students. Once Tallia took his arm out of the sling, he was even able to start doing little bits to demonstrate as long as Raphael didn't catch him. Russett still allowed him to work with the plants, but only with a partner. The classes where he had to do a lot of writing were the first that he could return to. Tallia allowed him to start writing again during the second week after the attack. She still refused to allow him to do any physical activities which made physical education a disaster. If Achilles even so much as thought that Lucian might use his arm, he immediately escorted Lucian to Tallia. Lucian was beginning to feel that this wasn't because Achilles was actually worried about Lucian but more that Achilles wanted to see Tallia. This thought was encouraged when Santiago fell in class and got a bloody nose. While Lucian had offered to take him to Tallia, Achilles had insisted on going himself.

The Monday before classes were to end, everyone got a barrage of mail. Xavier, the first year students' mentor, told them that this was normal. "Everyone always gets a ton of mail at the end of semester. Parents telling you how proud they are, the fairies giving you the new schedules, and if you're really lucky, you get something from your princess. Although, I suppose some people wouldn't think of that as lucky."

Lucian found himself sitting amidst of pile of letters. There was the usual letter from his mother and three from Allegra telling him how much she missed him and the last detailing her first art show. That letter also included a small ribbon with a tag Allegra had labeled as being an honorable mention ribbon she'd earned on one of her projects. He also had two letters from the fairies, one containing his spring schedule and the other containing a supply list. Surprisingly, he had a letter from Clarissa telling him that she was sorry he'd been injured and that she hoped he was soon well again. At first, Lucian couldn't figure out how she'd known, but then Jacobi admitted to telling her about it. "You write to your princess?" Lucian had asked.

Jacobi blushed. "Yeah, George does too."

George blushed just as deeply and said, "I like her. I want to know what's going on."

Kaelen was also surrounded by letters. One of them was from his princess, but there wasn't a single good thing to be found. He went to where the others were standing. "I never thought I'd say this, but I need help."

"I don't think we're qualified, Kaelen," Adrian teased with a smile. When Kaelen didn't laugh he said, "I'm just kidding Kaelen. Hello? Are you okay?"

"What's going on, Kaelen?" George asked.

Kaelen read his letter out loud:

> Kaelen,
>
> There's a rumor going around that you wear a pink dress! Please tell me that's not true. I'm about to die of embarrassment. My prince wearing a dress! Well, you can imagine what all the girls are saying. They're saying all sorts of terrible things. You better not be wearing dresses, Kaelen, because that is quite unacceptable. My parents would never approve! Not to mention that's highly unusual. Just what do they teach you at the school of yours anyway?
>
> Please let me know soon what's going on. I can barely look my friends in the eye!
>
> Esmé of Altheirian

"What am I going to do?" Kaelen asked. "A gentleman never lies to a lady. I'm still a girl. It's true that I wear dresses. What am I supposed to tell her?"

"Well, you know, Kaelen, you are a girl," Lucian said.

"What's that supposed to mean?" Kaelen demanded.

"If you're a girl, than the gentleman's code doesn't apply. You don't have to lie necessarily, just don't tell her the whole truth," Adrian suggested.

"How?" Kaelen asked.

"Easy," George said. "I've got lots of sisters and they lie all the time. The thing is, it's okay to tell a lie if it'll save another lady from embarrassment. It's like when Phyllis asks Sarah how she looks. Sarah will never admit that Phyllis looks hideous. So, she makes up some kind of compliment and then suggests something to make it better. Usually that helps make Phyllis look better and it prevents hurt feelings."

"Yeah, besides, Kaelen, you haven't worn a pink dress in weeks," Jacobi said. "Whatever happened to that anyway?"

"It mysteriously vanished," Kaelen replied through grit teeth. "So what should I say?"

"If it were me," Lucian began, "I'd say, 'Dear Esmé, I'm sorry you've been embarrassed by such a silly rumor. I do not wear a pink dress. I hope this makes things better for you. Kaelen.'"

"Yeah, that's good," George said. "Besides, there's not a single lie in it!"

Kaelen sighed. "Alright, I guess that works. I can't believe they know over there. How would they have found out about any of it?" He looked at Jacobi and George suspiciously.

"Don't look at us!" Jacobi said. "I might write to my princess, but I would never tell her that you wore a dress. I think I merely said you'd been punished when I told her about Lucian. Besides, even if I had told her, Clarissa would never start a rumor like that. She's too sweet."

"Eleanor wouldn't have either and I know I didn't tell her about your punishment. Someone else must have said something," George added.

"Well, I suppose the damage is already done. No sense getting upset over it. Write your princess and tell her you don't wear a pink dress," Adrian said as Kaelen looked ready to start seeking revenge. "That'll stop any further damage better than getting into more trouble."

"That would be easier to believe if I'd turned back to a boy. The festival is in three days. If I don't change before then…" Kaelen's voice trailed off. "I don't even know what I'd do," he finished at last.

"Well, I'm supposed to get the last of my stitches out tonight. In fact, I'm supposed to be down at the infirmary right after supper," Lucian said.

"Can I go with you?" Kaelen asked.

"If you want to," Lucian shrugged. "Adrian can tell you, it's really not all that interesting. She just washes my arm and looks at it. The last couple of times she's been able to take some of the stitches out. Today the last ones are supposed to come off as long as Tallia doesn't see anything wrong."

"Well, as interesting as your arm is," Adrian said, "I'm starving. Let's go have supper."

The boys laughed and headed downstairs to the dining hall. Before leaving, Adrian tried to stuff his envelopes back into his mailbox. How the fairies had managed to do it was beyond him as the letters scattered across the floor. Lucian stooped to help him pick them up. "My sister wrote to you too?"

"Oh, yeah, I guess she was really excited about that art show. She wrote three pages about it; front to back," Adrian laughed.

"Oh," Lucian said simply. He shrugged and continued out with everyone else. They found one of the larger tables so all five of them could sit together.

During the meal there was laughing and talking and Kaelen finally realized what he had missed out on all those months of being selfish and stuck-up. He still thought he was better than most of the people here; but the friendship and companionship of the other boys his age made things worthwhile. Before he could stop himself he suddenly interrupted the conversation they'd had going and said, "Thanks."

"Thanks? We were talking about how Uralia has really pretty eyes and you say thanks?" Jacobi asked.

"Oh, no, not about that. I wasn't really paying attention to that. Thanks for being my friends. I didn't really know what I'd been missing out on by being such a jerk. I don't know, I guess, it's nice to have friends," Kaelen tried to explain.

The other boys looked at him for a moment. "Who are you and what have you done with Kaelen?" Adrian asked teasingly.

Everyone laughed and they continued chatting until Lucian said he needed to go see Tallia. He and Kaelen walked silently down the hallway to the infirmary, the only sound the pattering of shoes and the green skirt swishing around Kaelen's ankles.

They heard talking outside the door as they walked up. Curious, the two stood outside the door listening. "There really is something in my eye."

"Really, Achilles," they heard Tallia say, "if you wanted to come see me that badly, why didn't you just come without an excuse? In the last two weeks you've had every minor ailment you could think of and then some. I wouldn't object to you coming just to see me."

"I know, but there really truly is something in my eye and it kind of hurts," Achilles replied.

Tallia laughed. "Go rinse your eye out in the sink and try blinking. If that doesn't help I'll take a look at it." There was silence for a moment and then she asked, "Why do you keep coming to see me? And I want the truth."

There was some stammering over the sound of water rushing. Kaelen and Lucian looked at each other, noses wrinkled. Deciding they'd eavesdropped long enough, Lucian walked into the room. "Tallia, I came for you to take the stitches out of my arm. Or at least to look and see if you can take the stitches out yet."

Tallia looked up in surprise and blushed faintly before saying, "Of course, come on over, Lucian. Kaelen, what brings you down here?"

"I just wanted to come and see how he's doing," Kaelen replied.

"Alright, don't get in my way," Tallia said. She unwrapped Lucian's arm and peered at the last remaining row of stitches. She gingerly touched around them. "I think they're ready to come out. This might sting a little."

Lucian nodded but didn't say anything. Tallia worked quickly with a small pair of scissors removing the last of the stitches. As she worked, Achilles slipped from the room. When she was finished she looked up at Lucian. "How's your arm been feeling lately? Sore at all, any pain, stinging, achiness?"

"It feels unused," Lucian said honestly.

"Yes, well, it's probably good that you'll have a break from school soon. You'll be able to gradually work your arm back to full use. Now, I still want you to be careful. There's still the possibility of ripping those scars. They're just barely healed; any overzealous behavior could land you right back here. I don't want you participating in your more physical activities yet. However, I think that you are well on your way to recovery. Come see me again Thursday morning before the princesses arrive. I'll take a look just to be sure," Tallia said with a smile.

"Thanks, Tallia, for everything," Lucian replied.

"It's what I'm here for." Tallia smiled and then ushered them from the room saying, "Go on now, it's about time for you to be heading to bed."

As they walked Kaelen kept looking at himself oddly. "What's the matter?" Lucian asked.

"I should be a boy again. She said you're healed. You don't have stitches anymore. Why haven't I changed yet?" Kaelen asked impatiently.

"I don't know," Lucian replied. "Maybe it's one of those things where you wake up different."

"Maybe," Kaelen said thoughtfully. "Yeah, I bet that's it. I'll be a boy again by morning!"

But the next morning, Kaelen was not a boy. He was still the blue-eyed blonde he'd been the day before. He just didn't understand it. There had to have been a mistake.

When Lucian healed, he was supposed to turn back into a boy. The witch had said so herself. What if there had been a mistake? What if he was doomed to be a girl forever? He didn't think he could live with that. Surely though he wouldn't be. After Gelasia came into the room to help him dress he asked her about it.

"Dear, I'm sure you'll be yourself again soon. These things take time. Until Tallia says that Lucian is well and whole, you're going to stay that way," Gelasia explained.

"You mean she just has to say those words? That's all?" Kaelen asked. "Does she know that?"

"Kaelen, you mustn't get so worked up about it. You'll be yourself before the princesses come. I'm sure of it. If you're not, well, we won't worry about that," Gelasia said cheerfully.

Kaelen stared at her in disbelief. To him the idea of still being a girl when the princesses came was absolutely something to worry about. He kept his thoughts to himself as Gelasia finished lacing up the back of the second blue dress he'd made. He was thinking of giving it and the other two dresses to his sister, Anna over the break. They would look very nice on her considering her complexion. Certainly he wouldn't have use of them after Lucian was declared well and whole.

Thursday dawned cold with a gentle flurry of snow. Once again, Kaelen awoke as a girl. Anger, frustration and horror caused him to scream with all the lung power he had. "What on earth is going on in here?" Gelasia asked, bursting into the room.

Angry tears streaming down his face, Kaelen cried, "Look at me! I'm still a girl!"

"Now, dear, that's nothing to scare the life out of me for," Gelasia said, clutching her chest.

"Are you insane? Look at me! I can't face Esmé and the other girls looking like this. What would I say? I'm sorry, dear, I lied to you. I do wear dresses because I'm a girl. Maybe they'll take me with them because look I'm a girl. Obviously I'm at the wrong school," Kaelen shouted.

"Now, don't you get that tone of voice with me, young man," Gelasia said firmly. "Now, let's go get Lucian and then go see Tallia. We'll get this mess straightened out." She took Kaelen's arm and firmly led him down the hallway, still in his nightshift. Lucian was walking down the hallway away from them. "Lucian, dear, would you be good enough to wait for an old fairy."

Lucian turned and smiled. "Certainly, Gelasia. Kaelen? I thought you'd be a boy by now."

"There's been a slight hiccup," Gelasia said sweetly.

"Well, I'll just escort you to the infirmary. I assume that's where you were headed," Lucian replied.

"How very kind of you," Gelasia said. She released her hold on Kaelen's arm and took Lucian's outstretched elbow. "Come along, dear," she directed towards Kaelen. "I'm sure this will all play out just fine. You may even come to laugh about it someday."

"Yeah right," Kaelen muttered under his breath.

"What was that, dear?" Gelasia asked sweetly.

"Nothing," Kaelen said aloud. "I'm sure you're right."

Gelasia laughed knowingly. The three walked down the hallway and down the stairs slowly. "I'm afraid these old bones aren't as swift as they once were," Gelasia said with a smile.

"It's alright, Gelasia. You can take your time," Lucian said.

Kaelen did not speak but his eyes shot daggers at Lucian's back. He didn't want Gelasia to take her time. He wanted her to speed it up so they could get him back to normal. However, as much as he wanted to be a boy again, he had come to appreciate Gelasia's warmth and kindness, so he tried to muster what little patience he had to slowly walk behind them.

When they got to the infirmary, Tallia opened the door. "Lucian, and Gelasia, what a pleasant surprise. Kaelen, also a surprise. Well, come on in. Let's take a look at that arm." She ushered Lucian to a table. "So, Gelasia, what brings you down here?"

"Kaelen is quite distraught over still being a girl. I wonder, would you say Lucian is well and whole?"

"Well," Tallia began, examining Lucian's arm, "there will definitely be scarring. There's nothing I can do about that. But, as far as regaining full strength and usefulness, yes he'll be just fine."

"That's wonderful news, but I really need you to say the words," Gelasia replied sweetly.

"Which words?" Tallia asked.

"Well and whole," Gelasia said.

"You want me to say that Lucian is well and whole?" Tallia asked, her eyebrow raised.

"Yes, dear," Gelasia replied.

"Okay, Lucian's well and whole," Tallia said, confusion in her turquoise eyes.

The room filled with white light, temporarily blinding everyone. When the light dimmed, Kaelen looked in the room's mirror. His boyish face looked back at him with his usual short hair. He felt his face and his hair just to make sure it was real. "I'm a boy again."

"Indeed you are dear. Now, where did you put your pink dress?" Gelasia asked sweetly.

Kaelen blushed. "I, um, it's, well, gone."

"Oh dear. That's a shame because now it would be your uniform in pristine order as it was when you were first transformed. You'll have to explain to your parents why you need a new uniform," Gelasia explained.

"I'm sure they know," Kaelen said with disappointment in his voice.

"Yes, well, you'd best get back to your room and dressed for the day. It wouldn't do to be in a girl's nightgown when the ladies arrive now would it?" Gelasia asked with her same sweet voice.

"You too, Lucian, you'd best get dressed," Tallia said.

As the boys were leaving, Lucian heard Gelasia ask, "I wonder, dear, if you have my potion ready for me? I'm beginning to run low."

When the princesses arrived, it was business as usual. Lucian put on a cheerful expression as Moira walked toward him. "Hello, Moira. It's good to see you again."

Moira attempted to smile back. "Hello, Lucian."

Lucian was sure this wasn't going to be any better than their previous meeting, but valiantly vowed to make the best of it. At least he didn't have Esmé. He could hear her shrill voice shredding Kaelen. "How could you allow such a rumor to start? Do you have any idea how humiliated I've been? Don't interrupt me," she snapped as Kaelen started to open his mouth. "It was cruel! A horrible, cruel joke at my expense and I shall never forgive you."

"Really, Esmé, I have no idea who would have started such a silly rumor. As you can see, I'm not in a dress so would you just knock it off?" Kaelen retorted.

Lucian and several others stared as Esmé swelled and turned a vivid shade of red.

"Esmé," Clarissa interrupted as Esmé began to shriek, "what a lovely gown. Where did you get it?"

Esmé's normal color quickly overtook her anger as she turned and said in her snobbiest tone, "My mother's seamstress designed it. She only works for my mother and me. This one is quite beautiful isn't it?"

A steady flow of chatter diffused the situation. Lucian could see others talking and looked over at Moira who was fiddling anxiously with her skirt. It was a lovely shade of blue that matched her eyes perfectly. "You look nice today, Moira," he said, hoping this would start a conversation.

Moira blushed and looked at him. "Do you really think so?"

"Yes, that dress really brings out the color in your eyes. It's very pretty," Lucian replied.

"Oh," Moira said. Then returning to her normal self she continued, "Well, thanks."

The following pause was broken by Calista's voice announcing breakfast. The tables had been arranged in long rows. Lucian, Adrian, George, and Jacobi along with their princesses quickly found spots at a table where they could sit together. Kaelen looked momentarily confused until Esmé started dragging him towards a different table. "Come along, I see Roseanne and Melinda."

Watching him go, the other boys noticed the disappointment on Kaelen's face. They looked at each other, but didn't say anything as Calista stood and motioned for quiet. "For our younger princes I'm going to briefly explain how today will work. Following breakfast, we will have three hours of games and activities in the gym. We will have a staggered lunch schedule so that princes between first and third years can meet with me in my office while Melantha meets with the princesses in Airlia Willowlimb's office. At five o'clock we will have a great feast with the parents of all our students from each school. After supper, years one through three will go home and we will see you again in January."

Cheerful chatter took over the room as the tables were served. Moira, while not as sullen as the last time Lucian had seen her, did not speak to him except in one-word answers. Lucian found this incredibly unfair since she would speak to the other princesses and even some of the other princes. He felt very left out as he looked about. George and Eleanor were speaking excitedly with one another as were Jacobi and Clarissa. Even Allegra was avidly telling Adrian about her glassblowing while Adrian attempted to look interested. "If it isn't just so, I throw it in our family's old well."

"How interesting," Adrian replied in a noncommittal tone. Lucian knew he wasn't actually listening, but Allegra didn't seem to notice.

Lucian sighed after his latest attempt to engage Moira in any kind of conversation failed. A horrible mental image came to mind. There they were, married at supper. Lucian was on one end of a thirty foot table with Moira at the other end. No matter how hard he tried to talk to her, she wouldn't hear him. He hoped she would open up as they went to the gymnasium for the games and activities. He looked around and noticed that Nathan's princess, Leticia, was trying desperately to show interest in his garbled discussion. He felt badly for her, especially since her twin sister, Eleanor, had a prince like George. He rather felt that Leticia had gotten the very short end of the stick.

The gym had been transformed into a winter wonderland with icicles and snow gracing pine trees and the walls. Decorations of silver, blue and violet added to the illusion of a snowy night. Lucian let Moira choose the games she wanted to play. He noted with dismay that not a single one was a get-to-know-you activity. Instead, they played several board games in awful silence. This was worsened by the fact that no matter how well Lucian played, Moira always beat him. Lucian tried to compliment her skill, but she always shrugged it off. Lucian had never been so happy to hear lunch announced. He escorted Moira, or rather attempted to since she refused his arm, to the dining hall. Lunch went much the same way breakfast had. On their way up the stairs and into the dormitory tower to wait for their interviews, Lucian pulled George and Adrian aside. "Alright, George, you have older sisters. What am I doing wrong?"

"What do you mean?" George asked.

"I have done everything I could think of to start a conversation with Moira but she just won't talk to me."

"Did you compliment her?" George asked.

"George, I gave her every compliment I could except, 'My Moira, you're looking exceptionally tall today. Did you grow again?'"

Adrian laughed, "If you said that she'd squish you like a bug."

"Yeah, Eleanor told me Moira's very self-conscious about her height. She's taller than all the girls her age and most of the girls just older too. Not to mention she's gaining on the oldest girls," George explained. "Adrian, what are Moira's interests?"

"Interests?" Adrian repeated. "How should I know?"

"You're her twin brother. Who would know better?" George asked incredulously.

"In case you haven't noticed, Moira and I don't exactly have a stellar relationship. The only person she said less to today at meals was me," Adrian retorted.

"You are useless," George said, emphasizing each word in frustration.

"Hey, it's not my fault," Adrian said defensively. "When Da…" he hesitated a moment. "Our relationship got so bad, Mom separated the living quarters. I don't know what she does; she's in the tower all day."

George and Lucian stared at him. Lucian sensed this wasn't the whole story, but didn't have a chance to press the matter as George asked, "Well, what about at meals? Surely she talks then."

"No. When she comes out of her room she looks puffy-eyed like she's been crying. That's all I know. Look, I don't want to talk about this okay?" Adrian pushed past the other boys as Calista called him into her office.

George patted Lucian's arm. "Sorry Lucian. Looks like you've got a depressed mute with no hobbies for a princess."

Lucian didn't reply. His thoughts had turned from his unresponsive princess to his best friend. Adrian had never gotten upset like that before. Yet Lucian knew if he tried to ask him about it, Adrian would ignore him.

He didn't have long to dwell on this because Adrian soon returned with a grin as though nothing had happened. "Your turn, Lucian."

Lucian raised an eyebrow, but didn't speak. He walked down the hallway to Calista's office. Calista ushered him into the room where King Lysander was waiting patiently, a smile on his face.

"This is a little different than I normally do," Calista said as she closed the door. "Parents aren't normally present for the first winter meeting, but since your father arrived early, I consented to make an exception. Go ahead and have a seat, Lucian." Doing as he was told, Lucian sat down next to his father. When Calista was seated, she continued, "I'm going to conduct this as though Lucian is the only one present. I hope you will not be offended, King Lysander."

"Not at all," Lysander replied.

Calista smiled and turned her attention to Lucian. "This has been a busy semester for you. All of the teachers tell me that you are a hard worker and doing well. Phillipa has said that while the semester started off rocky for you and Zephyr, she has seen great improvement and wanted me to say that she admires your patience. Diana likewise has mentioned that you have taken what could easily have been a disadvantage and made the best of it. She assures me that Rusty will be up to speed with the other hounds before you know it. Even Amadeus, who between you and I has never shown much optimism towards any of his students, has said you are quite talented. A few things to consider over break; Raphael wants you to slowly work your arm back to use so when classes resume in January you will be able to rejoin your classmates. Phillipa and Diana have requested that you continue to build teamwork with your animals. On a more personal note, I want you to know I admire the forgiveness you have shown. Not many people would have befriended Kaelen put in your shoes. The mark of a true gentleman is that willingness to extend an arm of brotherhood."

"It wasn't easy," Lucian said, blushing at the praise.

Smiling again, Calista said, "I'm sure it wasn't. That's why I was impressed. I look forward to next semester and continuing to watch you grow and learn. Now, if you remain here for a moment, I need to get Adrian and Donovan."

She walked out of the room and Lucian turned to his father. When he saw his eyes glistening with unshed tears, he asked, "What's wrong?"

Lysander cleared his throat and hugged Lucian. "I am so proud of you, son."

"Dad, it's only been one semester," Lucian said in a teasing tone. "What are you going to do when I graduate?"

Lysander laughed. "Oh, my son, you'll understand someday."

They were interrupted as Adrian, Donovan and Calista walked into the room. "Please have a seat," she said. When the two boys had sat down, she looked at Donovan. "The other fairies and I have been discussing what to do with you, Donovan. While you do very well in your academic courses, you are scraping by in your specialty courses and failing two of them."

Looking at the ground, Donovan said in a voice barely above a whisper, "It's okay if you expel me. My parents said they're used to it. Failure runs in the family."

Calista reached across the desk to gently lift Donovan's chin. "Donovan, if I was going to expel you, I would not have invited anyone else to be here."

Donovan looked up at her, tears in his blue eyes, "You mean?"

Smiling, Calista said, "We've decided to take King Lysander at his word. We've contacted your parents and they will not be coming to take you home. Instead, you will spend winter break as well as summer break in Maltisten with King Lysander and his family. King Lysander will teach you to train a new puppy which he has graciously provided as well as basic bowmanship. At Lucian's suggestion, we're going to ask Kaelen to assist you in your horsemanship."

Donovan paled. "Couldn't Lucian teach me instead? Kaelen doesn't know who I am. I mean, he knows my name, but he doesn't know that we're, that I'm..."

"His cousin?" Calista finished for him. When Donovan nodded, she continued, "While I don't like the way this situation has been handled by either family, I will do nothing to disturb your arrangement. Kaelen need not know of your relationship. However, Lucian made a very valid point. Kaelen is one of the best horsemen in the school, which includes our older boys. He has the knowledge to help you work with your new horse. King Lysander, and I'm sure Lucian, will help you over the breaks. However, during school you will do an hour every evening with Kaelen or I will be forced to fail you."

Looking as though he weren't sure which option was worse, Donovan said reluctantly, "Okay. I'll work with him."

"Good," Calista said. "Now, I must stress to you the importance of you improving. The decision to give you another chance was a difficult one to come by. There are some who feel you are apathetic."

"What?" Donovan asked.

"Apathetic, indifferent," Calista explained. "If the next semester and following semester do not show adequate improvement, we will have no choice but to expel you from Charming Academy. Believe me when I say that to lose you would be a waste of your potential and a true loss to our school. You are not your father."

Donovan nodded but said nothing.

Calista smiled. "Now, I would suggest that the four of you take some time to get to know one another. Adrian, your mother has consented for you to go to Maltisten to help Lucian and King Lysander work with Donovan. Lucian, would you please send Jacobi to my office?"

"Sure," Lucian replied.

"Thank you," Calista said as Lucian walked out the door. "And thank you once again, King Lysander," she said shaking his hand. "Your generosity is much appreciated."

"I'm just doing what I can to help," Lysander said kindly and followed the boys out of the office. "Well, why don't the four of us go down to the fencing room after Lucian gets back? Raphael was kind enough to say we could borrow it for a few moments before supper."

After Lucian returned from sending Jacobi to Calista's office, the four headed to the fencing classroom. They sat down on a couple of the benches in the room. King Lysander said, "Well, let's start with some basic introductions. Obviously you boys know one another, but I don't know Adrian very well and Donovan I only know by name. I'll start. I'm Lysander and you can just call me that. There's no need to use my title while we're in Maltisten. I'm sure the fairies will want you to do so while we're at the school, but in Maltisten, you are my guests and can use my name.

"A little background, I've been the ruler of Maltisten since I married Alexandra of Maltisten. I am an expert hunter and swordsman. I also do gardening on the side and enjoy taking my children to ride on the beach. Any questions?"

Donovan hesitated and then asked, "Why do you rule the province your wife is from? Usually graduates inherit their father's kingdom."

Lysander smiled understandingly. "I did not have the opportunity to attend Charming Academy. There was a prince who, as a younger son, completed his quest before his brother. By rights, the older would inherit their father's kingdom and so the fairies gave him the kingdom my father had ruled."

Adrian frowned, "Does that mean that princes who don't come don't get to rule a kingdom?"

"Not necessarily. The fairies prefer princes who have come to the academy because they already know they have the character, leadership and knowledge to rule a kingdom. However, there are always those who do not complete their schooling or their quests; or who do not possess the qualities the fairies desire," Lysander explained. "These princes are often kept at noble status, but do not inherit a kingdom. Princes who do not attend the academy are given a look over and may be given a kingdom lost by a graduate or prince who did not complete his schooling. Princes who graduate but do not fit the profile may be denied a kingdom. The truth is, ruling a kingdom isn't decided by how you were schooled, but what the fairies see on the inside of you. They look beyond the surface."

Donovan looked thoughtful and it was quiet for a moment. King Lysander then asked, "Why don't you boys tell me a bit about yourselves? We'll start with you, Donovan."

Blushing, Donovan looked at his hands. "Well, my name is Donovan. I'm the fourth boy of five children and I'm from Serfronia. I'm the youngest and the only one who hasn't failed, yet."

"Don't say yet," Adrian suddenly interrupted. "You put yourself down more often than anyone else. Have some faith in yourself."

"Absolutely," King Lysander agreed. "If you don't believe in yourself, others will lose faith in you too. We're all here to help you reach your potential. You have everything you need right here," he said pointing to Donovan's heart. "You need only reach for it."

"Yeah, well, I'm not an expert at anything. I don't know, I guess there's not much to tell about me," Donovan said quietly.

"Maybe you'll warm up later," King Lysander said. "Adrian, your turn."

"Well, I'm not an expert either. I'm one of two children. My family lives in Licthane. I enjoy hunting and most sports. Language is my biggest weakness. And water; I hate swimming," Adrian said.

"Well, that'll do for starting off with," King Lysander said with a smile. "Now here's what we're going to do when we go to Maltisten." He then proceeded to describe in great detail the curriculum he had devised for the winter to help Donovan. They discussed living arrangements and travel until they heard a barrage of steps going through the hall. "It must be suppertime. You boys will no doubt need to escort your princesses, so I'll let you to it. I'll meet you in the dining hall."

The boys disappeared to find their princesses. When Lucian found Moira, she was looking sadly up at a portrait in the hall. He walked towards her slowly and silently as she traced the bottom edge with a finger. Suddenly she cleared her throat and turned towards him. "It's about time you showed up. Everyone else is already on their way in," she said sharply.

Lucian bit his tongue before saying gently, "I apologize. I was detained." He then offered his arm which she once again refused, tilting her chin at a stubborn angle. He sighed inwardly. This was going to be much harder than he thought.

The feast was magnificent and filled to the brim with people. Not only were there fairies and the boys and girls, but all the parents were there as well. Allegra was sitting next to King Lysander demanding to know why their mother had not come. "She's not feeling well, dear," King Lysander explained gently. Lucian marveled at his patience. He was sure that if he had to listen to Allegra talk his ear off and then be so demanding, he would have found a good rag to stuff in her mouth. However, he also knew that somehow his father always knew how to be the perfect gentleman. Lucian sat next to Moira who was sitting next to her mother speaking avidly about how wonderful school was and how she had made so many friends.

"Is that your prince?" her mother asked.

Moira turned to look at Lucian, "Oh, yes, Mother, this is Prince Lucian. Lucian, this is my mother, Queen Lavinia."

"It's good to meet you," Lucian said taking her hand and kissing it the way he'd been taught. "And thank you for allowing Adrian to come stay the winter with my family."

"You and Moira get along?" Queen Lavinia asked, ignoring Lucian's thanks.

"Oh yes, we get along quite well," Moira said before Lucian could reply with all honesty that he didn't know that they were capable of getting along since Moira didn't speak. He listened, dumbfounded, as Moira gushed on and on about him, leading her mother to believe that they were, of course, perfectly suited.

Knowing better than to make it obvious that he was confused, Lucian pasted a smile on his face and lied, "We have a great relationship."

This seemed to satisfy Queen Lavinia and Lucian ate the remainder of his meal completely perplexed.

When the feast was over, the princes said goodbye to their princesses and then Adrian, Lucian, Donovan and Allegra followed King Lysander out to his carriage to start the long journey back to Maltisten.

Chapter 8

Winter break passed in a flurry of activity. King Lysander set a challenging schedule with specialty work almost every day. Their arrival in Maltisten had been greeted by a small whippet puppy whom Donovan had named Snippet. Snippet learned quickly and soon Donovan had lost his timid demeanor and began to show slow, but steady, improvement with his hunting. On New Year's Eve, King Lysander took the boys to town to go to Phillip's Stables.

"Ah, King Lysander," Phillip said as Mariah led them into the barn. He was brushing a small, cream-colored pony. "What a pleasant surprise! To what do I owe this great honor?"

"Phillip, I'm in need of another horse for Charming Academy," Lysander replied.

"Oh? Surely there is nothing wrong with Zephyr!" Phillip exclaimed in disbelief.

"No, no," King Lysander assured him, "quite the contrary. We are very pleased with Zephyr. No, we're here with Prince Donovan of, where did you say you were from?"

"Serfronia," Donovan replied quietly.

"Yes, and he is in desperate need of a new horse. The one he has simply won't do," Lysander finished.

"I see, well, if you'll follow me, young prince, we'll get you set up with the perfect horse. I just got a new batch in the other week and I'll warrant there will be at least one who catches your fancy." Phillip smiled kindly and waved for Donovan to follow him. Donovan turned back to Lysander, who nodded encouragingly. He then followed behind the horseman to a different area of the barn. Adrian and Lucian followed King Lysander in the same direction where they found a multitude of horses ranging from charcoal grey to snowy white. "I've a friend in Danderleigh who has just retired. He specialized in raising horses for the academy and sent me his remaining horses for quite a fair price. These are all sure-footed and exceptionally trained. Just take your pick, Prince Donovan."

Donovan walked up and down the aisle of the barn slowly. He'd never been able to choose for himself what he wanted. He stopped in front of several horses, but always moved on just as Phillip or Lysander would get ready to praise his choice. It wasn't until a soft nicker further down caught his attention that he stopped longer. In front of him was a beautiful, silvery mare with white dappled up and down her as though snowflakes had been magically glued in place. Her mane and tail were the purest white and soft as silk. Her eyes were a warm, chestnut brown that looked trustingly back into his own. "Can I have this one?" he asked in a voice that spoke fear of losing her.

"I think that would be an excellent horse," Lysander said kindly.

"Indeed," Phillip agreed. "She's as smart as they come and gentle as a lamb. My friend didn't name any of his horses so you'll need to do that while His Majesty and I take care of some business."

King Lysander followed Phillip away while Donovan stared at his new horse, gently stroking her muzzle.

"Well, how about it?" Adrian asked impatiently. "What are you going to name her?"

"I hardly know," Donovan replied honestly, still not looking away from the mare. "I've never needed to name anything. I can't think of anything that fits her."

"How about Blizzard?" Lucian suggested. "She looks like she got caught in one."

"No," Donovan said, "she's too gentle to be a Blizzard."

"Stardust then?" Adrian asked. "Stars are gentle."

"No, no." Donovan shook his head. As Lucian and Adrian continued to throw out suggestions, he looked more carefully at the mare as though perhaps she might tell him what her name was. Her pure white mane seemed to glow in the lamplight and outside he could see the beginnings of flurries fluttering down slowly. "No, her name is Snow Angel," he said suddenly as the name came to him.

"A perfect name for her," Lysander said from behind him. "Well, let's head home. The snow may look nice now, but it's going to get bad before it ends. Thank you, Phillip."

"Anytime, Your Majesty," Phillip said, "anytime." He ushered them from the barn with a bow and a smile.

The last night of vacation, Lysander saw Donovan standing in front of a portrait of the king and queen, painted to commemorate their wedding. Though he'd said nothing, Donovan seemed to sense his presence. "You were my father's friend, weren't you?"

"Yes," Lysander replied.

Donovan nodded. "I thought so. He never told me your name; he just talked about his best friend. He said he always thought he'd let you down. That's why he stopped talking to you. I suppose in the end it worked out for the best, right? You and Alexandra are a great couple and my dad loves Mom with all his heart. They suit each other perfectly, just like you and Alexandra. When he talked to me about going to Charming Academy, he told me he wanted me to do well. I'm his last chance for success I guess. I want to do well, I really do. I want to succeed so that he can have something to be proud of. This year he told me that he hoped I'd find a friend to help me out like he'd had. Then I got a letter from them at the end of term. I think Dad's given up on all of us boys. I have a little sister too. She's going to go to Fair Damsel's when she's old enough. At least, that's what Dad wants. Mom doesn't care. I don't think she realizes how much it means to Dad that someone be a Prince Charming or be the princess rescued in the story. I think he was jealous of you for a long time. He says he's not anymore. But I think sometimes he wishes he hadn't given up. Do you think if he hadn't, that things would be different? Maybe I'd be more like Lucian if he had been able to finish his quest. I could be brave and smart and talented."

When Donovan was quiet for a moment, Lysander put a gentle arm around him. "Donovan, my boy, your father had what he needed. I don't know why things happened the way they did. However, I do know that you are a very smart, very brave and very talented. You have what it takes just like Lucian does. What happened with your father is in the past and that's where it should stay. Don't let his disappointment cloud your abilities. Instead, let it encourage you to do your best. Be your best so that he can enjoy watching you succeed. I suppose he'll always live with a touch of regret, even though he loves your mother very much. But that shouldn't make you fear doing your best. You be your best so that he can smile and feel pride in you and in himself."

Donovan tried to wipe away his tears without being noticed. He nodded and then said quietly, "Don't tell the others please. I don't want them to know."

Lysander smiled. "You tell them when you're ready. Until then, I will not tell them anything."

Donovan returned his smile and then walked silently back to his room. As Lysander watched him walk away, he sensed that Donovan had renewed his resolve. He knew that in the end, Donovan would more than accomplish his quest. He would make a name for himself, and his family.

Early the next morning, the group woke up and began the long ride to Biberseth;

their horses following behind the carriage. There was laughter and talking the entire way. Upon arriving at Charming Academy, Calista greeted them warmly. "It is so wonderful to see you back safely. I trust you had a pleasant vacation?"

"Yes, Calista," the boys replied.

"Excellent," Calista said with a smile. "Donovan, I see you have a new horse. She's lovely. Why don't you boys take her and your other horses to the stables? Then come inside; you're just in time for supper. As always, King Lysander, we'd be pleased if you joined us."

"Thank you," Lysander said. "I think today I'll take you up on that offer."

"Be my guest," Calista replied before returning her gaze to the road where another carriage was making its way in the entrance gates.

It wasn't long before everyone got back into the school routine. Every weekend Adrian and Lucian worked with Donovan and Snippet, getting them ready for hunting to resume as an outdoor course. Donovan always looked forward to these lessons and enjoyed spending time with Lucian and Adrian, sometimes George when he wasn't studying or doing something else.

Lessons with Kaelen began soon after school and Donovan was not at all sure this was going to go well. Kaelen had met with Calista and Donovan and taken the job with mingled surprise and pride. Lucian and Adrian had told Donovan they would not attend these with him. "You need to give him a chance before you decide he's going to humiliate you. He's really changed, honest," Adrian had said. He didn't mention the hour-long lecture he and Lucian had given Kaelen about teaching with kindness and not pride.

Now, standing at the entrance waiting for Kaelen to show up, Donovan was beginning to feel nervous again.

"Sorry I'm running a little behind," Kaelen panted as he reached the doorway after barreling down the stairs. "I got caught up in my homework and lost track of the time. Let's head to the stables, shall we?"

"Yeah, I guess," Donovan replied. He followed wordlessly as Kaelen led the way.

When they arrived at the stable, Kaelen said, "Before I can begin helping you learn better horsemanship, I need to see how you're doing now. So, today will sort of be like a test. That way I can see where you actually need to improve and where you're already doing okay. Then starting tomorrow, we'll do actual lessons or that kind of thing. So, where's your horse?"

"Snow Angel is down there," Donovan replied, pointing down the aisle. "Do you want me to bring her out here?"

"Yeah, and then tack up. I want to make sure you're doing it right. Sometimes the biggest problem with riding isn't the actual act of riding, but preparing to ride," Kaelen explained. "Not putting the saddle on right can really cause problems."

Feeling slightly sheepish, Donovan walked down to Snow Angel and led her up to where Kaelen was waiting. He put the saddle on her back then put her bridle on. He checked the saddle again after that before looking at Kaelen. "Now what should I do?"

"Well, let's start riding. I don't need to help you with tacking up. You did that perfectly; especially since you checked the saddle after a bit. Some horses tend to take a deep breath so that the saddle isn't as snug as it needs to be," Kaelen said. "Lightning thinks that's his job. Let me tell you, falling out of the saddle in front of my father was painful, and not just to my rear."

Unable to help himself, Donovan laughed. Maybe this wouldn't be so bad after all.

The lesson continued much as it had started. Kaelen watched with an eye wary for mistakes or weakness. He made a mental list of what needed to be worked on. Biting his lip, he tried not to allow the prideful thoughts which had entered his mind come out of his mouth. Donovan's riding was fine for a beginner, but at his age should have been more refined. At supper with his friends he found himself venting his frustration aloud. "I'm sure I've seen kids half our age ride better than him. Why didn't his parents get him a proper animal to begin with? That's his biggest problem. He's so used to being thrown he hesitates to take command. Luckily that mare of his is a real sweetheart. I hate to think what this would be like if he had Zephyr; no offense, Lucian."

"None taken," Lucian replied, "but you have to understand where he's coming from. In Maltisten, we were just barely beginning to get him out of his shell. Yes, he's improving, but it's going to be a long, hard road."

"More than anything, it's confidence that he lacks," Adrian pointed out. "If we could just get him to believe in himself, he'd do fine. Once he starts to see improvement, I'm sure things will get better."

"Yeah, well I hope for everyone's sake he starts to see it soon. You two have the patience of a saint compared to me," Kaelen said honestly.

Time seemed to fly from January to March. Slowly spring warmed the frozen grounds of winter. Buds showed on trees and flower bushes. Sunshine streamed through the castle windows, warming the rooms with its glow. Gradually throughout this process, the boys saw improvement in Donovan's skills. They were even starting to look forward to the end of the year final when he could truly show Diana and Phillipa that he wanted to stay.

But as much as they worked with him, they also needed time for their own studies. The fairies didn't allow the spring fever, which set in almost immediately as the weather warmed, interrupt their schoolwork. If anything, the boys were sure the fairies had purposely added to their workload. One warm afternoon after getting out of fencing, Lucian said, "Let's do our homework outside today. It's so nice out and I'm sick to death of my room!"

"I second the motion," Adrian replied with mock seriousness. "Anyone who objects is overruled. Let's go!"

Kaelen grabbed Adrian's sleeve before he started walking for the door. "Don't you think you should get your books and stuff?"

"Yeah, Adrian," George teased, "it's hard to do your homework if it's still inside."

Adrian smiled mischievously, "I was hoping you guys wouldn't notice until we got out there so that we could really enjoy the spring weather and not by doing our homework."

"Nice try," Jacobi smiled as they walked up the stairs together. Each boy gathered his bag and books and then met in the hall before heading out into the sunshine. There was still a cool nip to the gentle breeze whispering through the budding branches, but the sun felt so good and warm, the boys hardly noticed. They settled down near a large maple tree by the lake and got out their supplies. They worked in peaceful silence, each concentrating on quickly finishing the tasks given by their instructors.

Jacobi was struggling through the last of their mathematics homework when Kaelen asked impatiently, "Aren't you done yet?"

Looking up from his paper, Jacobi could see that the others had already finished all their homework. He also noticed the others looking at Kaelen with exasperation clear on their faces. "Sorry," he said with an apologetic smile, "math isn't my strong suit. I'm almost done though. It'll only be a couple minutes. Five tops."

Kaelen sighed while Lucian replied, "It's alright Jacobi. Take your time and get it done right the first time. Rushing doesn't do anyone any good." He shot a pointed look at Kaelen who had finished before anyone else had gotten near to being done. Kaelen shrugged his shoulders at him and Lucian couldn't help but laugh. While Kaelen was certainly much better than he had been before winter break, there were some things that would obviously never change.

"There! I'm finished!" Jacobi exclaimed, shutting his book with a snap. "Well, now what should we do?"

"I'm voting for a game of tag," Adrian said. "Extra points if you get a boy outside our group." He stood and lunged at Lucian, "And you're it!"

The boys suddenly started running around. Calista watched from a window as the game continued. Soon, it wasn't just the five friends playing, but dozens of boys in varying age groups running around trying to catch someone. She smiled as she watched the forging and breaking of alliances. What fun they were having! It reminded her of days long ago when she was a child playing with her brothers and sisters. She turned away from the window and resumed what she had been doing before the shouts and laughter had caught her attention. Within a few days the boys would be meeting their princesses again and there was still planning to be done.

It wasn't long before the sun started to dip below the horizon and the boys returned indoors for supper. Panting, Adrian said, "I told you tag would be fun."

"You always think tag is fun," Lucian teased. "You're faster than the rest of us and we can rarely catch you."

There was laughter and chatter as boys of all ages sat down to eat. At the end of the meal, Calista rose and reminded them that their princesses would be coming that Saturday. "We will be engaging in a scavenger hunt of sorts. Recall that as gentlemen you should absolutely be on your best behavior that day. You will, of course, be partnered with your princess for the day and lunch will have to be found. I shan't reveal more now, but be prepared." She smiled and dismissed them from the room.

"What did she mean, 'Lunch will have to be found'?" George asked.

"I don't know. Maybe we have to hunt for our own lunch," Lucian suggested.

"That's ridiculous," Kaelen replied. "We don't have the equipment for each of us to cook our own meal. Somehow I doubt the girls do either. In fact, half of them probably can't cook!"

"Great, we're going to starve," Adrian moaned.

Jacobi laughed, "I hardly think she'll let us starve, Adrian. I'm sure it's part of the scavenger hunt. Maybe we have to find the serving utensils and such. I don't know."

"Whatever it means, we'll find out soon enough," Lucian said.

Saturday dawned with bright, warm sunlight streaming through the windows. Lucian woke up and stretched. Rusty looked up from the corner of the bed he slept at and yawned. "Well, you can go back to sleep," Lucian said to him when he looked at Lucian as though to accuse him of waking him. "Some of us have things to do this morning."

Rusty yawned again in response and stood up before circling his corner again and curling up to go to sleep. He sighed as Lucian rubbed the top of his head.

Lucian chuckled, "Lazy thing. You must be growing again." He got dressed before walking out of his room and downstairs to the dining hall for breakfast. George was already down there with Jacobi and Adrian. Kaelen had yet to arrive. Lucian sat down with them and soon they were chatting and laughing as Kaelen walked in. "What took you? You're normally one of the first ones here."

"I know, but Rex isn't looking very good. He wouldn't touch his supper last night and he really looks sick," Kaelen said, his eyebrows drawn together in worry.

"You should take him to see Diana or Tallia. One of them would know how to help him," George suggested.

"I don't know, maybe he's just having an off-day," Kaelen said hopefully. "Dogs have off-days too, right?"

"I really think you should do as George says," Adrian insisted. "Diana would definitely know if it was just an off-day or if there's really something seriously wrong. I mean, your dog is older than any of the rest of ours. He might be really sick. I'll go with you."

"No," Kaelen said firmly, "I'll go. Rex is my dog." Without eating so much as a bite of his breakfast he got up from the table and walked to the staff table where Diana was sitting, talking to Clio Stormcloud, the history teacher. Kaelen cleared his throat and they both turned to him. "I'm sorry to interrupt, Diana but I, I think Rex is sick. Can you come look at him?"

"Of course," Diana replied. "Please excuse me, Clio."

"Certainly. I hope Rex gets better soon, Kaelen," Clio continued kindly.

Diana followed Kaelen up the stairs to his room, stopping only long enough to get Tallia. The three walked into the room. Rex was lying on his bed, whining softly. Diana and Tallia bent over him. Frightened, Kaelen stood by the door. "Is he going to be okay?"

"How long has he been like this?" Tallia asked, not answering Kaelen's question.

"He wouldn't eat last night. At first I thought it was just that he wasn't hungry. Is he okay?" Kaelen asked desperately.

Diana stood and walked to Kaelen, putting an arm around him gently. "I don't know, Kaelen," she replied honestly. "We'll do what we can for him but," her voice trailed away.

Despite himself, Kaelen felt tears well up in his eyes. "I don't want to see my princess. I want to stay with Rex."

Diana smiled understandingly. "I'm sorry, Kaelen, but you know that isn't possible. Tallia will take him to the infirmary and you can go to him as soon as the princesses leave. But for now, you need to be strong. You need to be a gentleman." She wiped away the tears that slid down his cheeks. "Chin up, we'll do whatever is possible to help him."

Tallia waved her wand which gently lifted Rex's bed with Rex in it. She guided it down the stairs and into the infirmary. Kaelen walked next to Rex all the way down the stairs, rubbing behind his ears the way he knew Rex liked. Rex looked at him sadly, but with a trace of his old self. "It's okay, boy," Kaelen said. "Tallia will help you out and I'll be back as soon as I can. I promise."

When Kaelen returned to where the rest of the boys were, the princesses had already arrived. "You're late," Esmé said haughtily.

Biting his tongue from saying what he really wanted to, Kaelen replied, "I apologize."

"Well, let's go with Rosemary and her prince," Esmé said.

"No," Kaelen said firmly, "I need to talk to a few of my friends before our activity starts."

Esmé sputtered, "But Rosemary and whatever-his-name-is are our friends."

"They're your friends," Kaelen argued. "Right now I really need to speak to my friends. So, we're staying right here."

Esmé turned a horrible shade of purple and then suddenly began to shriek. Everyone turned to her in shock. It didn't take long for Calista and Melantha to appear on the spot. "What on earth is going on?" Melantha asked.

How anyone could understand what Esmé was saying was beyond Kaelen, but apparently the fairy took in every word. Calista did too, and asked, "Kaelen, is it true that you won't let her see her friends?"

"No, I simply said I needed to talk to my friends. My friends are over here. If she wanted to invite her friends to join us over here, that would be fine," Kaelen replied.

"Liar," Esmé sniffed. "You said they weren't friends and treated them awfully."

Kaelen could see that Melantha was used to such exaggeration, but that didn't save him from a firm lecture. Angry, he walked away from the rest of the group and towards Esmé's rather cold circle.

He didn't notice until a few moments later that the rest had followed him. "Hey, what did you need to talk about?" George asked kindly.

Kaelen turned to see him. "It's Rex."

"Is he going to be okay?" Lucian asked.

Kaelen shrugged. "Diana said she didn't know. Tallia has him in the infirmary right now."

Lucian turned his attention away from Kaelen when Moira suddenly said, "How was break?"

"Fine, we got a lot of work done. How was your break?" Lucian asked, surprised by his princess starting the conversation.

"Lonely," Moira replied sadly. Then as though she'd revealed too much, she quickly added, "I mean it was very quiet. I enjoyed the peace."

Lucian knew she was lying. "It's okay to admit you missed your brother."

"Whatever are you talking about?" Moira demanded. "I enjoyed being on my own." She turned her back to him and Lucian knew the short-lived conversation was over.

His attention returned to the front when Calista cleared her throat. "Good morning, everyone. Today's activity is a scavenger hunt. Throughout the castle and grounds are hidden various items. Each of you will be given a list which will check itself when you find the items. You can only work as partners with your prince or princess. Remember, the first pair who finishes and returns will get a special prize. Use good sportsmanship and have fun! You may begin!" Calista raised her wand and dozens of lavender pieces of paper zipped through the air and landed in the princes' outstretched hands.

Moira and Lucian scanned the list. "I think we should start inside and then go outside," Lucian suggested.

"No, look everyone is starting inside. It'll be crowded. No, if we start outside and then come in, we won't have as far to go to turn our list in to Melantha and Calista," Moira explained.

Lucian smiled. "Good idea." He and Moira walked outside and began searching for things that would definitely be outside. A certain tree in the forest, a plant in the witches' garden, a rock near the lake. They worked in silence, seeming to communicate without words as one led and then the other. Lucian couldn't think of a time when Moira had been more friendly or happy. There was a sparkle in those blue eyes he'd never seen before. For the first time, he noticed that she was very pretty. He blushed as this thought came. Moira was a girl! He didn't like girls.

Soon, they were inside the castle with only one item left. They knew other groups were close too. A competitive urgency filled them as they desperately tried to find "a hero remembered in the stars". They'd gone to the astronomy tower, to the library, everywhere they could think of. Suddenly, Moira exclaimed, "I know where he is!" Not waiting for Lucian to follow, she started sprinting down the stairs. Lucian desperately tried to keep up. Panting, he caught up to her. She was standing excitedly next to a portrait of a Prince Charming, sword brandished at a ferocious dragon, stars twinkling in an inky black sky. The paper seemed to warm in Lucian's hand. The final checkbox was filled in. "Hurry!" Moira cried. "Someone will beat us." Grabbing Lucian's hand, she started sprinting to the dining hall. They saw others heading the same direction. Lucian already felt like he was flying, but this challenge spurred Moira on to even faster paces until they finally reached Calista and Melantha at the table they were seated at.

"Here," Lucian breathed, handing the crumpled paper in his hand to Calista.

"Very good," Calista smiled.

"I do believe this is the first time we've had a first year couple win the hunt," Melantha observed.

"Certainly the first in a long number of years," Calista agreed. "Well, Lucian why don't you go get some punch for yourself and Moira and sit down for a while? I daresay you could use the rest."

Lucian nodded. He was breathing too hard to speak. He led Moira to a table and held her chair for her before going to the serving area where cups and a large bowl of punch were sitting on the serving counter. After filling two cups, he returned to the table where Moira was sitting. He handed her a glass before sitting next to her. "You were awesome," he said. "How did you figure out that last clue?"

A slight sadness touched Moira's voice as she answered, "The remembered hero is my dad. I found his portrait last semester. I simply remembered that there were stars in it." She was quiet for a while. "Good job keeping up with me. I was sure you'd trip over yourself."

Lucian laughed, "I'm surprised I didn't. Your legs are so much longer than mine it was hard to keep up." Moira flushed and Lucian knew instantly that was the wrong thing to say. "I'm sorry, I meant…"

"No," Moira interrupted, "it's okay. In any case we won." An uncomfortable silence fell over them until others joined them at their table. Lucian was internally kicking himself. He knew better than to mention Moira's height to her. He'd bumbled things when Moira finally seemed to have opened up to him.

As the clock struck twelve, lunch began; or rather they were sent out to find it. This scavenger hunt wasn't nearly as difficult as the other. They went out to the gardens and found tables with long tablecloths laid over them. Each tablecloth was a different color. "Before you can be seated, you must find the appropriate tables," Melantha said. "Your age must match the color."

"Age must match the color? How are we supposed to figure that out?" Moira asked.

Clarissa looked thoughtful. "Age must match the color. Age…Oh! I know! There's an old poem from way, way long ago. It talks about the tradition fairies had about color. Certain colors came first and so on. Let me think, um, blue was the oldest of the colors, so that would probably be the sixth year students."

"I think I know what you're talking about," Eleanor said excitedly. "Green was next to fill the earth with serenity. So that's the fifth year students. Then red, the color of life."

"Yellow next to warm the planet," Clarissa continued. "Violet then to add nobility and passion."

"Orange to bring in the day and herald night! We're orange!" Eleanor exclaimed. She grabbed George's hand and the group followed her to the long table with the orange tablecloth. Others slowly filtered their way and when finally the fairies explained the clue, everyone else was seated. Lunch was served to them and the group ate ravenously. The search had really brought out their appetite. Only Kaelen seemed uninterested in eating. "Come on," Adrian said between mouthfuls. "Everything's delicious. Eat up!"

"He's right," George agreed. "Besides, starving yourself won't make Rex better."

Kaelen merely nodded and kept pushing the food around his plate. He ate a bite here and there to appease his friends, but he didn't at all feel hungry. He hardly paid attention as Calista announced that Moira and Lucian had won, earning them each a basket of goodies for them to keep in their rooms. He barely heard Melantha gather her princesses. He didn't say goodbye to Esmé who was sulking over the fact that they'd lost. Kaelen didn't care. Once everyone was gone, he went to the infirmary to check on Rex.

When he got there, Diana was sitting cross-legged on the floor next to his bed, trying to coax him into eating. "Come on, boy, just a bite. For me?"

Rex whined and turned away.

"Is he any better?" Kaelen asked.

"I'm afraid not," Diana replied. "I've been in here all morning trying to get him to eat."

"Haven't you eaten?" Kaelen asked.

Diana smiled but didn't respond. Kaelen suddenly knew the answer. He remembered not seeing her at the staff table either at breakfast or at lunch. He scratched Rex's ears before leaving the room again. He walked into the kitchen where a short, mauve fairy was attending the stove. "You're not to be in here, young prince. What do you want?"

"I'm sorry. I just wondered if I could take a tray to Diana. She hasn't eaten because she was taking care of my dog while the princesses were here," Kaelen explained.

"That Diana doesn't have her head on right. Take care of animals before herself," the fairy muttered. "Take care of students before herself. Take care of everything and anything before herself. I tell you that if it weren't for the fact that she'd die, I doubt that fairy would ever eat." She handed Kaelen a tray. "Now don't be coming in here again."

"I won't," Kaelen promised. "Thank you!" He walked back into the infirmary and handed the tray to Diana.

She looked mildly surprised, but merely said, "Thank you. I was feeling a mite hungry."

"I'll try to get him to eat," Kaelen said. "You take care of yourself."

Diana gave him a half-smile and carried the tray to a table to start eating. She watched Kaelen silently. The genuine worry and concern touched her. It was nice to see this human side of Kaelen. She watched him stroke the dog's head and even manage to get him to eat a few bites. She heard motion at the door and turned to see Tallia motioning for her. Quietly getting up, she walked over. "Well?"

"Lucretia says that the plant I need is one of the ones that disappeared last semester," Tallia said.

"Surely they've replanted," Diana replied.

"Of course they have, but the new plants aren't mature yet," Tallia explained. "Althea promised to bless them, but even with that it could be a week, probably two before they're ready."

"Two weeks? Rex may not have two days of strength left in him. He needs that potion," Diana whispered anxiously.

"I know," Tallia said gravely. "But it's the best we can do."

Diana turned to where Kaelen was. He was now lying on the floor next to Rex's bed, stroking his side while the old dog slept. She sighed. She very much doubted that Rex would survive to hunt again.

Four days later, the five friends met with Diana out in the woods with Rex. His body was wrapped tightly in his favorite blanket. Kaelen was clutching it, silent tears coursing down his face. He had taken Rex's passing surprisingly well. No shouting that it wasn't fair, no pleading. He'd just rubbed the dog's ears and softly whispered, "Goodbye, boy. I love you."

Now as they dug a shallow grave for him, Diana tried desperately to keep her own emotions under control. Losing a pet was difficult under any circumstances, but when it was the first one, it seemed a million times harder. She watched as Kaelen gently placed Rex in the hole and helped Adrian recover it. He had carved Rex's name on a medium-sized stone and placed that over the freshly covered grave. "I'm so sorry, Kaelen," she said, putting an arm around his shoulder.

"He's not sick anymore," Kaelen replied. "Now he can be better wherever it is dogs go when they die." He was quiet for a moment. "I'm really going to miss him. He was a good dog. My dad gave him to me when I was little. He was just a puppy then." He looked around and saw other stones in the area. "Are those?"

"Yes," Diana replied, answering the unfinished question. "Many princes have lost a dog while in school. It is a hard time for all of them, especially when it is their first pet. Some even lost horses through accident or illness. This is where we bury them, so that they can be in a place of peace and beauty. You can come here anytime you need." She squeezed his shoulder before walking away, leaving the friends behind.

"I'm sorry, Kaelen," Adrian said.

Kaelen shrugged. Part of him wanted to be alone, but he was glad his friends had joined him. "Thanks for coming with me."

"That's what friends are for," George said.

A light rain started to fall, as though the world were mourning with him. "I guess we should head inside," Kaelen whispered.

"We probably should," Lucian replied. He understood Kaelen's reluctance. He'd lost a pet dog too once. His dad had given him the runt of a whippet litter. Despite Lucian's most valiant efforts, the puppy didn't survive past three months.

"Come on," Jacobi said gently, placing a hand on Kaelen's shoulder. "Let's go."

Silently, the five left the small graveyard in the woods. As Kaelen left, he thought he heard the haunting sounds of dogs barking and horses whinnying. Perhaps Diana was right. Here, the cherished pets and beloved companions of princes gone before could find peace and rest in that beautiful glade. He turned and thought for a moment he saw Rex standing there. He seemed to smile and then bounded away into the trees. *Goodbye, Rex*, Kaelen thought as he continued into the castle with his friends.

Chapter 9

"I just can't do this," Donovan said for what must have been the fifth time.

Kaelen sighed. It was a beautiful spring day and he could think of much better things to do with his time than sit here with the obstinate prince. "Yes you can," he insisted. "You're not trying hard enough. Keep your legs tight."

Donovan squeezed his legs a little tighter. He was starting to improve, he knew he was. But he still felt awkward and timid in the saddle. Snow Angel stepped up to a trot and then Donovan relaxed and Snow Angel slowed down.

Exasperated, Kaelen said, "Stop, stop." When Donovan pulled Snow Angel to a stop, Kaelen rode over on Lightning. "Look, Snow Angel is not going to throw you. She's not going to bite you. She's not going to kick you. I doubt she even knows how to lay her ears back. You've got the sweetest-tempered horse in the world. What are you so scared of?"

"I don't want to hurt her," Donovan replied quietly.

"She's a horse! Look at her, she's not fragile," Kaelen snapped. "She's big and strong. You wouldn't be able to hurt her unless you pulled your legs straight out in a split and kicked down as hard as you could. Snow Angel needs you to lead. She's not going to follow that dressage course on her own. You have to lead her. You are the master, not Snow Angel. Keep your legs tight, take firm hold of the reins and lead Snow Angel through the course. Your final is in one week. You have to get this before then." Kaelen took a deep breath. Donovan looked about to cry which was not what Kaelen had intended. "Look," he continued in a more gentle tone, "you are a fine rider. You've got the knowledge; you know how to do it. Just take control and do it. Watch me on Lightning and then I want you to do exactly the same thing I do, okay?"

Donovan nodded.

Kaelen led Lightning around the course and then pulled over to the side where he had been before. He watched as Donovan bit his lip before clicking his tongue at Snow Angel. She immediately started to walk. Kaelen watched with apprehension as Donovan got to the bend he kept messing up at. "Yes," he whispered as Donovan pushed Snow Angel into a trot around the large circle and kept her at it. He saw Donovan's face light up as he continued through the course. Up to a canter, circle at extended trot, and then around to the finish. "Yes!" Kaelen cried, pumping one fist in the air. "You did it! I told you you could. Wasn't that easy?"

"Yeah, I think I get it now," Donovan replied.

About time, Kaelen thought but said aloud, "Good. Now, keep practicing that and the final will be a breeze!"

"Yeah," Donovan said, a look of confidence spreading over the once timid face. "Can I do it again?"

"Absolutely," Kaelen answered. He watched Donovan go through the course again and then a third time.

"You should be proud of yourself, Kaelen," Phillipa said suddenly from behind him, causing him to jump. "I've been working with him for two years and have never seen such progress."

"He just needed confidence, that's all," Kaelen replied, blushing at the praise.

"I suspect a less than patient teacher might have helped as well," Phillipa admitted with a smile. "I don't know that I would have given him the lecture you did, but it seems to have done the trick." She smiled once more at Kaelen before calling to Donovan, "Bravo Donovan. I look forward to seeing you at your final."

Donovan flushed and smiled. "Thanks Phillipa."

Phillipa returned his smile and then walked away before saying to Kaelen, "I'm proud of you. You've been a great help."

The next week the boys were busy with finals. The weather was as stormy as the boys' attitudes. The horsemanship final was held in the indoor arena and then the hunting final was held in the gym. "Obviously," Diana said as they were gathering, "you won't be hunting for any animals. Instead, you'll be working with targets and as usual proving your hounds." She then explained the final to them. Lucian was disappointed that they couldn't have the final outside. Rusty had improved as much as he had grown and was as good as any of the other hounds at understanding and following silent commands. Kaelen had yet to receive his other hunting hound, despite multiple letters sent from Kaelen, Diana and even Calista. For his final, Diana had arranged for him to work with one of her hounds. "It's not necessarily fair since all of my hounds are so well-trained, but the important part is your understanding, not theirs," she had told him.

Kaelen hated every moment of the final. He wanted his hound, though Diana's hound was indeed exceptionally well-trained and followed his every command in a flash. The target practice was better and he didn't feel quite as frustrated. In fact, the opportunity to shoot was rather relieving to him. When the final was finished he went over to his group of friends and said, "Well that was fun. How'd you do?"

"I've got an A overall, with E's in bowmanship and ethics. How about you?" Lucian asked.

"A overall," Kaelen replied. "I wish Knight was here. He's the hunting hound I left at home when I came. Obviously I only needed one dog, not two."

"Why haven't your parents sent him out?" George asked incredulously. "You need a dog out here and it's been weeks since, well…"

"Since Rex died," Kaelen finished with a grim smile. "I'm okay with it now. It's still hard, he was my first dog. But," Kaelen shrugged and didn't finish the sentence.

Adrian smiled understandingly, "Well, let's head inside and check our mail. We should have something today. Schedules for next year, notes from princesses and so forth."

The boys headed inside and sure enough, the neon pink mail fairy was finishing up her rounds. "Good afternoon boys, how's school treating you?"

"I hate finals," Adrian groaned.

"Other than that not too bad, Laria," Lucian said more cheerily.

Laria laughed cheerfully, "That's life for you. Even these fairies had to take exams you know." She was different from any other fairy the boys had ever met. Her pink hair was cropped short and always seemed windblown unlike the other fairies long, straight tresses. She also had her own flair in style and address which was completely different from anything the boys had ever seen. "Well, must be off. Lots of deliveries yet to do today. Have a great summer. I'll miss seeing you."

"We'll miss you too, Laria," George said smiling.

She waved cheerily and fluttered away.

Kaelen opened his mailbox and found several letters including one from his parents. Setting the other letters aside, he ripped open the envelope. As he read, anger filled him and he stormed away from the group, despite their repeated questions. He marched into Diana's office and threw the letter down on her desk. "I'm not responsible enough for a dog," he yelled as she looked up at him with a puzzled expression.

"I beg your pardon?" Diana asked.

"Read it," Kaelen said through grit teeth.

Diana picked up the crumpled letter and read, her eyebrows furrowing as she read on.

> *Dear Kaelen,*
>
> *Please refrain from sending these incessant notes about wanting Knight to come to Charming Academy. It is quite clear to your father and I that you cannot handle the responsibility of two animals at school. You have not mentioned any problems with Lightning so we must therefore assume that you are spending too much time caring for him. This lack of balance is what led to Rex becoming ill. Your irresponsibility will not be rewarded with another to neglect. You will simply have to show over the summer that you can handle caring for two animals before your father and I will consider sending Knight with you for fall term. I am disappointed in your lack of understanding.*
>
> *Love,*
> *Mother*

Tears of anger and frustration filled Kaelen's eyes. "She thinks I just let Rex die. How would she know? She wasn't here. She didn't see me taking care of him. She wasn't the one begging him to eat. Or holding him while he wheezed and whined. Her heart wasn't broken." Kaelen stopped.

Diana had been sitting in silent fury. She couldn't reveal to Kaelen her true feelings of his mother's cold response. "May I request that you follow your mother's command?" When he looked about ready to explode in indignation she continued, "I believe this is a matter that Calista and I will have to clear up. I am well aware that you have not neglected your animals. In fact, you are a very observant master and were most caring during Rex's final days. Leave this matter to Calista and myself. You must be a gentleman now and respect your mother's wishes. It is what an obedient son would do." Diana put a comforting hand on Kaelen's shoulder as he nodded. "May I keep the letter?"

"I don't want to see it again," Kaelen muttered angrily.

"Thank you. Now, I suspect you have friends anxious to know what has happened," Diana observed.

Kaelen nodded and stormed out of her office. Diana rose and walked up the stairs to Calista's office and rapped on the door. When she heard Calista's welcoming voice, she walked in. Diana frowned and said, "I know you are busy with end of year letters and such, but we have a serious problem."

The end of term came with graduation for the older boys. All the students both from Charming Academy and Fair Damsels Academy were present for the ceremony as well as the parents of each student. While one may have thought it would be quite crowded, the castle felt as comfortable as it had ever been and the boys didn't really feel any difference. Lucian and Moira continued in the same awkward relationship they'd always had while Allegra chatted non-stop to Adrian about how excited she was for the upcoming summer dressage tournaments. Soon Melantha stood and welcomed to the stage her graduating princesses. "For our new students, I have to explain part of what is going to happen today. As you know, Prince Charming cannot simply walk across the stage and take his princess by the hand and say, 'I'm done!' Life is not that simple. Some of our princesses, though they've done nothing wrong, will experience sudden departures due to the nature of their prince's quest. Have no fear, they are perfectly safe and we will see them again sooner than you may think."

Lucian hardly paid attention. It was a rather short ceremony and at the end of it, most of the princesses had magically vanished upon receiving their diplomas. Next Calista stood and bequeathed upon each prince his quest. The younger princes found this part far more interesting, especially as they watched some of the boys they were more familiar with. "Do you think Kieffer's princess will ever reappear?" Adrian whispered to Lucian as Calista handed Kieffer a rolled parchment.

Lucian shrugged his shoulders. As far as he knew, Kieffer and Samantha were still at odds with one another. He just hoped that somehow he wouldn't end up the same way with Moira.

There was encouragement and advice given before Calista and Melantha invited their guests to enjoy in their graduation feast.

"Can you believe someday that will be us?" Adrian asked Lucian during a pause in Allegra's chatter.

Lucian shook his head but was interrupted by Donovan's voice. "King Lysander, King Lysander!"

Lysander turned around. "Donovan, dear boy, how are you?"

"I passed all my exams! I can stay!" Donovan replied beaming, a badge gleaming on his cerulean jacket.

"Excellent!" Lysander said with a smile. "I knew you could do it."

"I couldn't have done it without your help," Donovan admitted. "Anyway, I just wanted to let you know. I've got to go find Kaelen and tell him. He got me through horsemanship and I've just got to tell him!"

Lysander smiled as Donovan scampered away. "You boys really have done well by him. I'm proud of you."

"He's still coming for summer break isn't he?" Lucian asked.

"Yes, as are Adrian and Kaelen, but they'll all have to go back home two weeks before school starts up again for you boys so that they can get their materials and such at home," Lysander replied.

"It's so good being here during a more social event," Alexandra said with a smile. "I was so sorry to have missed the winter get together."

"It's alright, Mom, we understand," Allegra replied.

Chatter and pleasant conversation continued well into the afternoon. At three o'clock the fairies bid their guests farewell with promises of mailed schedules and supply lists. Kaelen said an abrupt goodbye to his parents before joining Adrian, Lucian and Donovan with King Lysander and Queen Alexandra. The boys enjoyed the long trip into Maltisten and all of them looked forward to the adventure of summer.

Year 2

Chapter 1

Summer was a golden time for the boys. Days were alternated between lazing about the castle and grounds and working with Donovan to continue improving his skills with Snippet and Snow Angel. One morning King Lysander gathered the boys together shortly before the visiting princes would be returning home. "Come on, we're going on a campout. The weather is gorgeous."

The boys eagerly packed their bags and headed out with their horses. King Lysander led the way towards the shoreline on the farthermost border of the kingdom. They tied the horses and spent a day by the beach, laughing and playing in the water. King Lysander sat back and watched the boys play. He remembered earlier days when he was a young prince, playing in the fields of Coleston. The boys soon pulled him into the fun as well and in late afternoon, they set up camp. They cooked over a fire and then told stories as the sun was sinking below the horizon over the waves. As the twinkling stars began to fill the darkening sky, they talked about school and going back.

"I'm not afraid anymore," Donovan said suddenly. "I know I can do it. But I could never have gotten here if it weren't for you all helping me."

"We did what any good friend would have done," Adrian shrugged.

The boys laughed late into the evening. The next day they'd be going to their own kingdoms to prepare for the beginning semester. "Crazy isn't it?" Lucian asked. "Summer just seemed to fly."

"Time does that, my son," Lysander laughed.

"My dad always said that you know when you're having too much fun because the time speeds up. This has been the best summer ever," Kaelen declared.

"You bet!" Adrian agreed.

"I have to admit though, I'm kind of glad I'm going home. These hems are getting embarrassing," Kaelen admitted.

"You can talk," Adrian replied. "I've been wearing high-waters for the last two months. Even with Queen Alexandra rehemming these."

"Well, I think you should all consider yourselves lucky," Lucian said miserably. "I haven't grown so much as an inch."

"Oh you look a little taller," Donovan said in an effort to be comforting.

"Please, Lucian grows slower than a tree in ice," Kaelen retorted, then flushed. "Sorry, that came out meaner than I meant it."

"It's alright." Lucian shrugged. "I guess I just haven't hit my growth spurt yet."

"Don't worry son, I was short at your age," Lysander said, placing a hand on Lucian's shoulder.

"That's not what Grandma says. According to her, she couldn't keep you in clothes longer than a month from the time you turned thirteen until you were sixteen," Lucian argued.

"Well, I was short for a while," Lysander said sheepishly.

Soon yawning had replaced talking and the group got into their sleeping bags to fall asleep under the starry sky.

On the first of September the friends were reunited at Charming Academy. Kaelen saw Lucian when he first arrived and asked, "Okay, you're a diplomatic person, what do I do about my parents?"

"Hello to you too, Kaelen," Lucian said in confusion. "What about your parents?"

"They won't send Knight up with me. You remember me talking about him, he's my other hound," Kaelen explained.

"Yeah, I remember, is he sick?" Lucian asked.

"No, he's perfectly healthy. They just don't think I'm responsible enough to care for both a horse and a dog because Rex died while I was here," Kaelen replied. "I don't know what to do. I'm about to just throttle them, but that won't help either."

Lucian thought for a moment. "Have you talked to Calista about this?"

Kaelen nodded. "I talked to her and to Diana last year. Well, I talked to Diana, she talked to Calista. They promised to do something about it, and I know your dad wrote a letter to my parents about how I was doing at your place over the summer. I thought surely that would prove that I could handle it."

"Hmm. Maybe you should talk to them again. I don't understand why they haven't sent him up here with you. I mean, without your hound, you'll fail your classes," Lucian pointed out. "Don't they know that?"

Kaelen shrugged. "I'm going to go talk to Calista and Diana again like you said. Maybe they can figure out what's going on." He turned and walked down the hall to Calista's office. As though Diana had already known he needed to talk to both of them, she was sitting in the room with her. "I need to talk to you."

"Which one of us?" Calista asked with a smile.

"Both of you, actually," Kaelen said. "I have a problem. I know you've written to my parents and I know Lucian's dad wrote to them, but, well, they still won't send Knight with me. He's sitting at home, not being used, not being trained and I'm stuck here about to start losing out on instruction. I mean, I know you'd let me work with your hounds to a point, but I have to have my own dog and I know that. Eventually, you'd have to refuse me that adaptation."

"That is true. Part of the class is training and working with your own dog," Diana agreed. "Your parents didn't send Knight with you?"

"No, I even tried sneaking him into my bags," Kaelen replied with a blush. "I, I just wondered if you could talk to them again. I hate having to ask for help, but I've done all I can think of."

Calista looked at Diana and there seemed to be a silent conversation, "I'll see what we can do, Kaelen," she said at length. "Why don't you go get ready for supper? It'll be ready soon."

Kaelen nodded. He had a terrible feeling that even Calista wouldn't be able to fix the problem. Maybe he should just go into town and buy a new puppy. His dad had given him plenty of spending money.

Unbeknownst to him, Donovan had been standing outside the office listening. He walked in before Calista and Diana had started speaking. "Who have you been addressing in your letters?" he asked before they could even ask what he needed.

"Donovan, I really don't think that's any of your concern," Calista said.

"It is, if you're dealing with the wrong parent," Donovan retorted. "I know who decided to shut out my parents, and it wasn't Uncle Roland. He's full of himself and arrogant, but he's not cruel. If you want anything, you have to go through my aunt. Everyone knows that. If you're writing to Uncle Roland, he'll just go along with whatever Aunt Angelique says. I know it's ungentlemanly of me to say…"

"Then don't say it," Calista interrupted, giving him a stern look. "Thank you for that information. But I really do believe this is a matter that we should handle."

"Yes, Calista," Donovan replied, his cheeks flushing.

As he walked away, Diana looked at Calista, "That was revealing. What are we going to do? I don't know the queen at all and I came here shortly after Roland graduated so I can't even say I know him well."

"We'll have to speak with Melantha. This is going to be disappointing to her," Calista said.

As their classes resumed, the boys soon fell back into the routine. While Donovan talked about changes to his schedule, the younger boys didn't see much change at all. They had all the same classes as the year before only they were at different times. Lucian didn't find this surprising at all since they couldn't very well be in the same classes as the first years. Several of the boys were curious as the new first year boys came to the castle. Lucian's curiosity was drowned out by realizing that most of the new boys were taller than he was.

A couple weeks after Kaelen had spoken to Calista and Diana, King Roland arrived at Charming Academy with Knight. Calista had asked to see him privately in her office while he was there. When he did leave, he was sputtering and his face was red and looked like he'd swallowed a lemon. Kaelen saw him as he was leaving and tried to go up to him, but the look on King Roland's face said he didn't want to speak to him, or anyone. Kaelen couldn't help feeling that he'd deserved whatever Calista had said to make him look that way, but simply waved goodbye and after his father nodded back, turned to go into the dining hall for supper.

"I saw you had a new dog with you earlier, is that Knight?" Lucian asked as they sat down.

"Yeah," Kaelen replied, pushing his father out of his thoughts. "To tell you the truth, I was about to go to town and buy a new dog. I was actually about to leave as the carriage pulled in."

"Good thing you waited," Adrian said. "You would have had a tough time with two dogs."

Kaelen shrugged, "I probably would have just sent the puppy home with Dad to give to Anna."

"Who's Anna?" George asked.

"My little sister. She's eleven this year," Kaelen replied.

"Do any of us not have little sisters?" Adrian asked.

"I don't," Jacobi said. "I'm an only child."

"I don't either," George added. "All my sisters are older than me. I haven't talked to some of them in a while, quests and all that."

"So, the princesses have no contact with their families when they go missing?" Lucian asked.

George shook his head, "I don't think they're allowed. I know we were really starting to worry about Naomi because her prince didn't find her until the end of the fourth year after graduation. You're only allowed five to complete your quest."

"That must have been hard," Jacobi said.

"Not as hard as the one right now." George stopped momentarily before then continuing, "Samantha is my sister."

The other princes stared at him for a moment without understanding until memory suddenly caused Kaelen to say, "Samantha is Kieffer's princess. They…"

"She likes him well enough, but she said he always seemed to have his eye on someone else. My parents are having a harder time with her disappearance than they did with the others. To tell you the truth, I'm having a hard time with it myself," George admitted. "We don't know that he's really going to try to find her."

They were prevented from having any further discussion as Calista stood to announce that there was going to be a temporary staff change for orientation. "Honoria and Raphael are expecting their first child and she needs this time to prepare for that event. For the remainder of this year, Pagoma Snapdragon will teach the orientation classes. Please join me in welcoming her."

The boys clapped as a pale lavender fairy stood and waved to them. She resumed her seat and the dining hall was filled with chatter as the boys talked about this new development. "Do you think we'll see Honoria at all this year?" Adrian asked.

"I'm sure we'll see her at meals. All the fairies live nearby," Jacobi said.

"I wonder why she can't teach up until the baby is born," George commented. "Do you think she's sick?"

"Maybe she just wants some time to herself. As much as she enjoys teaching, this is probably a challenging experience since it's their first baby," Lucian said. "I don't know though."

"I suppose we could ask Raphael, but he probably wouldn't tell us anyway," Adrian added.

Kaelen said, "I don't think we should worry about it. It's not like Calista said she was dying or anything like that. She probably just wants some privacy and that sort of thing."

The next day, the boys found little difference in their orientation class. Pagoma was sweet-tempered and as knowledgeable as Honoria. They enjoyed her teaching style and the ease with which she taught them. "It's like she's done it before," George said one afternoon after class.

"Well, that's really not all that surprising," Kaelen commented. "After all, these fairies probably don't stay here their whole lives. I'm sure there are a lot of fairies who have once taught here."

"Right you are, Kaelen," Gelasia said, surprising all of them by appearing behind them. "Pagoma taught here before she and Russett started their family. Now that their children are grown, she's happy to come and teach as needed. I myself used to teach at Fair Damsels before coming here. I'm sure if you asked your parents, you would discover many names you are not at all familiar with."

"See," Kaelen said triumphantly as Gelasia walked away.

"Yeah, we get it, Kaelen," Adrian laughed.

The boys went outside to work on their homework. It was a beautiful autumn day. The sun was shining, but there was a cool breeze to keep it from getting too warm. Lucian looked out over the lake. It was beautiful. He almost wished that Allegra could see it right now. She was so good at art and would have been able to easily capture the beauty of the water rippling in the gentle breeze. He had always been a little jealous of that talent, but he didn't worry too much. He could do things that Allegra couldn't. The more he thought about her, the more his thoughts strayed to home. Having already finished his homework and knowing that others were still working on theirs, he decided to write a letter to his parents. He started by telling his parents about school and the new fairy who was teaching them. Then he told them about the rest of his classes. He then wrote:

> *I can't wait until next year. That's when I'll start my specialty classes. Donovan is starting his and is really moving forward. You did a great job with him, Dad; he's not the timid boy he was last winter. He's really coming through. I heard Diana saying that*

she's never seen such a turnaround before. Donovan told me that his dad was really proud of him. He said they had a big celebration when he went home after spending the summer with us. He's looking forward to continuing to prove that he belongs here; especially in Dragon Fighting. Can you imagine Donovan fighting a dragon? You were right, Dad. He already had everything he needed.

Soon the others pulled his attention away from his writing and he closed the letter with a little cartoon of Donovan fighting the school dragon. He then got up and walked with the rest of his friends into the castle for supper.

The weeks continued into October. The weather had grown dark and stormy for weeks. Horsemanship was taken to the indoor arena and the horses, like the boys, were starting to show signs of cabin fever. Lucian found Zephyr particularly willful. "It's not my fault boy," he said sharply one day after class as he put the proud stallion back in his stall. "I want to get outside as much as you do."

Zephyr snorted at him as though he didn't believe him.

Lucian couldn't blame him either. He and his class had come into the barn looking like a bunch of drowned rats. Now that his clothes were almost dried, he was going to be sprinting back into the pouring rain. He rubbed Zephyr down and brushed his coat until it gleamed. "At least you don't look like something the cat dragged in," Lucian said. "You look as clean as always."

Zephyr turned and whinnied. Lucian was sure that Zephyr was laughing at him.

"Yeah, I know," Lucian replied, shaking his head as he poured some oats into the box before walking out of the stable. He listened as Zephyr started crunching down on his supper.

"You'd have thought I got wet on purpose," Kaelen said as he joined Adrian and Lucian.

"I got the same response from Zephyr," Lucian admitted. "I can't wait for the sun to come out again."

"Don't look for it too soon," Phillipa said with a disappointed sigh. "The weather isn't going to change for a while."

"Great," Adrian moaned.

"Well, let's get back to the castle before it starts getting any worse," Lucian replied. "Bye Phillipa."

"Have a good afternoon, boys. Go quickly!" Phillipa encouraged.

The boys nodded and sprinted out after the rest of their class. When they reached the castle doors, several boys were standing outside pounding on them. "What's going on?" Adrian demanded, somehow being heard over the shouting around him.

"Someone's locked the doors," Mithulan shouted.

Lightning split the sky as deafening thunder rumbled around them. "They're never going to hear us over that noise," Lucian yelled. "We're going to have to think of another way in."

"Are you mad?" one of the boys asked. "There is no other way in."

Lucian refused to give up so easily. He walked away from the doors and started running from window to window, hoping that someone would see him. It seemed forever that he was running around the castle, drenched through and cold. Finally he reached the fencing room where Raphael was conducting class. He started waving his arms around desperately hoping the fairy would turn and see him. He could see older boys pointing at him and then to his relief, Raphael turned. The window opened and Raphael demanded, "What on earth are you doing?"

"The front doors are locked and we can't get in," Lucian panted through chattering teeth.

"That's impossible," Raphael argued. "Calista would never lock the doors while there were students out."

"I don't know who locked them, but they're locked and we can't get in. Please send someone to open the doors." Lucian was now shivering violently.

"Of course," Raphael said. "Go to the front doors, quickly now."

Lucian nodded and began running back to the front of the castle. The rest of the boys were still pounding on the doors. "I told you so," the boy said as Lucian came up.

"Raphael is on his way," Lucian shouted triumphantly.

The boys had never been so grateful to see their fencing master as they were when he finally got the doors opened. Streams of water followed the boys into the hallway as they entered the castle. Several fairies were standing around with blankets and towels. "Get dried off," Calista ordered. "Then I want you to tell me who did this."

"I can tell you," Mithulan said as a fairy was rubbing his hair with a towel.

Calista raised an eyebrow. "Yes?"

The boys looked at each other. Mithulan then returned his attention to Calista. "Nathan was the first one to leave and the only one of our class in the castle. He's the only one who would have been able to do it. Everyone else is in class."

The fairies looked at each other then at Calista. "Very well," Calista said. Her voice was calm, but there was a flicker in her eyes that most of the boys found slightly frightening. "Boys, please go to your dormitories. Hot water will be brought up for you to bathe. We need to get you dry and warm. Go on now. I'll deal with Nathan. Raphael, please have Russett help you make sure that all the boys get fresh towels and warm blankets."

"Right away," Raphael replied. He sent a tan piece of paper to the greenhouse which seemed to shudder before flying out a nearby window.

The boys went upstairs without noticing the black paper that had flown from Calista's wand. As they climbed the stairs Adrian asked, "You know, I've always wanted to know how those messages manage to go out the windows like that."

"Fairy magic," Raphael replied as he followed them up the stairs. "Our magic can allow something as seemingly solid as paper go through something just as solid like a window."

"But how?" Adrian asked. "I don't get it."

Raphael laughed. "Wait until you get into spell breaking with Althea. She'll explain it much better than I could."

"That'll be a whole year from now," Adrian whined.

"Are you whining at me?" Raphael asked.

"No sir," Adrian said as they reached the top floor.

Russett was standing at the top of the stairwell. "Seems you have a bunch of drowned kittens, Raphael. What can I do to help?"

In Calista's office, Nathan was sitting, looking smugly triumphant. He really hadn't needed to get the whole class. Just Kaelen. He'd spent four long months talking like an idiot and it was Kaelen's fault. He wasn't sure what Calista was waiting for and he really didn't care. It wouldn't matter what the witches did to him. Being out that long in the rain; he knew most of the boys would be sick. "Can't I go to my room so I can do homework while you wait?"

"If you honestly think I'm going to fall for that excuse, you're sadly mistaken," Calista said, not bothering to turn to look at him. "I've heard from many of your teachers that you do not do homework. You will not leave until we have discussed your behavior."

Nathan shrugged as Phillipa stormed into the room. Droplets of water ran down her hair and she looked furious. Seeing Nathan, her frown deepened and Nathan was sure he'd seen sparks fly from her wand which was clutched in one hand. "Calista, I need to speak to you about Nathan."

Calista turned to look at her. "What else has he done?"

"Else?" Phillipa asked. Then she shook her head, "Never mind, I don't have time. Look, I don't care what the witches do to him, but he is banned from horsemanship for the next two weeks."

"Really?" Calista said, a look of surprise on her face. "What did he do?"

"It's not what he did," Phillipa said, fury in every syllable, "but rather what he didn't do. He was in such a rush to leave class that he didn't take care of his own horse. When I went through the barn to ensure all the horses were adequately fed, I found Misty Shadow, still in his tack, not clean, not fed; nothing had been done to make him comfortable. The look of misery on his face…" Phillipa stopped, as though the memory was physically painful. "This is the last time he neglects that horse in my class. I will tolerate it no longer. I expect the boys to occasionally forget a blanket, or give too little feed to their horse, but to completely disregard it…" She paused as though looking for the right words. She took a deep breath and then continued, "I believe I've said enough. He will not be allowed in the stable for a fortnight. However, there is no need to place him in another classroom. He is to write me a fifteen page essay on the importance of proper equine maintenance. He will not be allowed in the barn until it is completed or the two weeks have passed, whichever is last."

Calista looked at Nathan and then returned her attention to Phillipa, "Very well. He can spend horsemanship in my office working on your assignment."

Phillipa nodded and left the office as Calypso entered. "You called for me I believe?"

"Actually, I thought I had called for Althea," Calista said.

Calypso shrugged, "She has been called to Fair Damsels. I came in her place, but if you'd rather wait," she continued, turning towards the door.

"No, that won't be necessary, thank you for coming so promptly," Calista replied.

"What was the crime?" Calypso asked as she turned back towards Calista. She was tall and lanky with a flowing blue gown. Her hair was so dark a brown, it looked nearly black and seemed to have a bluish hue in the shadows. Her eyes were slate blue, like the ocean in a storm. As Calista recounted Nathan's behavior, Calypso absentmindedly played with the shell bracelets around her wrists. "I see," she said when Calista finished. She turned to Nathan. "And you have no apology to make?"

Nathan just stared at her in obstinate refusal.

A wicked smile spread over Calypso's face. "Your choice. Neglected as you neglect, Wetter than those you wet, Locked from your own, Is the punishment you get." The shells on the bracelet glowed and a stream of blue light wrapped itself about him. An instant storm cloud appeared over his head, drenching him in seconds. "Don't worry Calista, you'll find your rugs as dry as ever. Enjoy the rain, Nathan." With a laugh, she walked out the door and was soon seen walking through the thundershower outside.

"I suggest you go to the dormitories and get ready for supper, Nathan," Calista said.

Soaked, Nathan got up and walked away. He should have expected something like this. Oh well, it was worth it. He tried to wipe the raindrops away from his eyes so he could see where he was going, but it didn't seem to be helping. When he reached his dormitory, he couldn't get the door open. He desperately tried to wipe his hand on his pants, thinking perhaps it was simply because his hand was wet. When he tried again, the door wouldn't budge. He shrugged away the temporary panic and walked down the stairs for supper; he was starving.

When he got to supper, he went through the line, ignoring the students around him; not that he needed to. They were avoiding him and his raincloud. By the time he reached his seat, his plate was drenched by the water. He considered complaining and getting a new plate, but knew it wouldn't do him any good. He started eating, but found the more he ate, the hungrier he felt. He went up again for seconds and then thirds with the same results. Truly feeling panicked, he walked up to Calista. "I'm hungry."

"Then get something to eat, Nathan," Calista replied, as though this were obvious.

"I have been, but I'm still hungry," Nathan argued.

"You must not have fed your horse. You are now feeling the pangs of neglect," Calista said simply. When Nathan continued to stare at her, she continued, "Perhaps you should learn to listen when people are talking to you. I suppose next you'll tell me that you can't get into your room."

Realization hit Nathan and he gaped at Calista. "But they can't do that, they can't lock me out!"

"Actually, it would appear that they can. The witches' magic is extremely powerful and should not be taken lightly; especially not by our students," Calista said seriously.

Lucian and the others watched Nathan stalk away from the staff table. "That didn't look pleasant," he said.

"No, but he deserves it," Jacobi replied. "Half the class is sniffling and it's only a matter of time before people get really sick."

"Well, he couldn't have chosen a worse time," George moaned. "The princesses are still coming next week, even if we all sound like toads."

"Maybe if we were all really sick they'd cancel," Kaelen said hopefully. "After all, they wouldn't want the ladies to get sick, right?"

"Yeah right," Adrian snorted. "Calista would probably just ask the witches to put glass bubbles around our heads so we couldn't breathe on them. Let's face it, we're going to see the princesses whether or not we're healthy."

"You say that like it's a bad thing," Jacobi said quietly.

"Don't get me wrong, I like her well enough, it's just that I'd rather be healthy than sick when I see her," Adrian said quickly.

"You like her?" Lucian asked, his nose wrinkled.

Feeling very much like a fish out of water, Adrian sputtered, "Oh come on, Lucian. If I said I didn't like her you'd have a conniption fit because she's your sister. I say I like her well enough and you're looking at me like I just confessed to writing love bonnets to her." He paused as Jacobi snorted. "What's so funny?"

"I think you meant to say love sonnets," Jacobi replied as the other boys started to giggle.

"I said that, didn't I?" Adrian asked, looking confused.

"No, you said love bonnets," George snickered. "A bonnet is something that girls wear to protect them from the sun. A sonnet is a poem, often romantic in nature."

"Oh," Adrian said with a sheepish grin. "Well, I don't write those either."

The boys laughed together and soon Adrian's true feelings for Allegra were forgotten, much to Adrian's relief.

By the next Saturday, many of the second year boys were in various stages of colds ranging from occasional coughing and sniffs to staying in the infirmary for a night to recuperate. Tallia spent all her time running back and forth between the witches' hovel and her office, brewing potions to help the boys recover faster. Most showed immediate improvement, although when Nathan came, still pursued by his raincloud, he never showed any improvement. Tallia finally told him to stop coming when he didn't seem to be getting any worse either. "Apparently this is part of your punishment. I'm wasting potion that I need for the other boys in giving it to you. I'm sorry, but you're stuck like that until your punishment is over."

As Adrian had predicted, promptly at ten o'clock the princesses arrived from Fair Damsels, despite some of the boys' fondest hopes that the meeting would be postponed, or better yet cancelled. As Melantha and Calista got the first year students sorted out, the other princesses quickly found their princes as was expected of them.

"Good morning, Moira," Lucian rasped as she curtsied properly.

"You sound terrible," Moira said, looking down at him. Much to Lucian's chagrin, Moira had grown a few more inches over summer break.

"I'm getting over a cold, but don't worry it's not contagious anymore," Lucian explained.

Moira raised an eyebrow but didn't respond.

The silence didn't last long as Allegra eagerly embraced her brother. "I'm so glad to see you," she said. "Thanks for writing to me. It makes me feel less homesick."

"You're welcome. I'm glad you've been writing back. I've…" Lucian was interrupted by a coughing spasm.

"Wow, you really sound awful. Maybe you should be in bed," Allegra said, looking at him with a mix of concern for him and fear of catching it.

"No, I'm fine, really," Lucian replied. "I'm not contagious or anything, just recovering from a cold."

When they heard another bout of coughing, Moira asked, "Is everyone here getting over a cold?"

"Just the second years," Adrian replied. "Someone thought it'd be funny to lock us out in the rain."

"Oh," Clarissa said, appearing with Jacobi. "That explains the raincloud following Leticia's prince."

Eleanor and George arrived shortly after and Eleanor looked with concern at her sister who was trying to engage Nathan in conversation. "It's just not fair," she said softly, not seeming to realize that she'd spoken aloud.

"What was that?" George asked.

Eleanor quickly smiled, "Oh, nothing. It's nothing." She smiled again when George looked like he didn't believe her. Laughing, she took his hand and said, "Don't worry so much. I'm fine."

George was prevented from pursuing the subject when Melantha stood. "Now that we're all organized, we'll tell you what we'll be doing today. Since the weather prevents our usual picnic, we'll be doing an indoor activity. Now, normally we don't do things like this, but Calista and I agreed this would be most beneficial. The fairies will be recreating some of the most famous fairy tales for you. We will adjourn to the dragon fighting room and you will be seated. Understand that you are in no real personal danger. Some of you may recognize the stories from your parents or grandparents. As in any performance, we ask that you not speak. Enjoy the show!"

Lucian offered Moira his arm. She hesitated only a moment before gingerly placing her hand on his arm and allowing him to escort her to the dragon fighting classroom. Lucian had never been in this room before and was shocked at the immensity of it. The walls were riddled with windows which made the huge room seem even larger. What surprised him most was that the room was actually built like an arena. There was a huge sand pit at the bottom surrounded by arena seats. Lucian allowed Moira to sit first before taking his place next to her. Soon the room was filled with students and large drapes were pulled across the windows before Calista pointed her wand at the ceiling and a spotlight appeared in the center, shining down into the pit where she was standing. "We'll begin shortly. Now again, understand that you are in absolutely no danger. We have everything under control, so don't be afraid. Enjoy!"

The spotlight disappeared and when it reappeared a fairy was standing in the center. They began the show, fairies taking the places of princes who had gone before. There were occasional whispers as students recognized the stories they'd heard throughout their childhood. Lucian sat in rapt attention. He watched as one by one, the fairy princes defeated their foe. He watched as Russett struggled through a forest of magical thorns. He recognized Raphael dueling. At one point he saw Honoria down, lying silently as though dead until Raphael's magic kiss brought her back to her feet. He gasped with everyone else when a huge dragon came into the arena. He watched as a fairy he knew only by name began the epic battle. Hearing a choking sound next to him, he looked over at Moira. Silent tears were coursing down her cheeks. He turned to his other side where Adrian was sitting and saw his friend struggling to restrain his own emotions. Understanding dawned on him as he watched Vulcan battle the ferocious dragon under a magical starry sky. They were watching their father's story. Wanting to comfort his princess, Lucian gently placed his hand over hers. She started and pulled at her hand, but Lucian held it in place. When she turned to look at him questioningly, he squeezed her hand and whispered, "It's okay. I'm just trying to help."

Moira stared at him, not sure what to feel. Rather than draw attention to herself, she simply turned back to the defeated dragon and watched the unknown fairy kiss his waiting princess. When Lucian moved his hand back to his own lap as the next act began, she was surprised at the disappointment she felt. She shook her head; she couldn't think that way. Returning her attention to the show, she tried to pretend nothing had happened.

After the fairies finished their performance, the students clapped and then followed them to the dining hall where lunch, delicious steaming soup in toasted bread bowls, was waiting for them. There was laughter and chatter throughout the meal. As she had at their first meetings, Moira spoke with everyone at the table except Lucian. When the time came for the princesses to leave he said, "I'll see you in December."

"Yeah, sure," Moira retorted. She looked preoccupied. Worse, she looked upset.

Once the princesses were out of earshot, Lucian turned to Adrian, "What did I do?"

"I have no idea," Adrian replied. "She wasn't that upset when she got here. What did you do?"

"I don't know," Lucian said, exasperation in his voice. "Things were fine this morning. Granted, she was looking down at me the whole time, but who doesn't?"

"I'm sure you'll hit a growth spurt soon. I mean, you can't stay that height forever," Adrian said hopefully.

Lucian didn't have time to respond since George came up and said, "Well, we'd best do our homework now. I know nobody did anything yesterday. We were all trying to get healthy again."

"Not that it worked," Jacobi said miserably. "Poor Clarissa seemed terrified to be near me even though I told her that Tallia assured me I wasn't contagious anymore."

Adrian laughed, "Well, life goes on. Let's get some work done."

The boys separated on their way into their own rooms. Lucian went to his desk. Rusty loped over and put his head in Lucian's lap. "Hello boy. I just don't know what to do. I have a princess who doesn't seem to know what she wants."

Rusty yipped softly and pushed Lucian with his nose.

Lucian laughed and scratched behind Rusty's ears. "Yes, I know boy. I love you too." He sat contemplatively, scratching Rusty's head for a while before getting out his books and starting to do his homework.

Chapter 2

The storms that had flooded the grounds of the academy and filled the lake behind the castle seemed to last eternity. It wasn't until one day in botany that a sudden, warm ray of light caused the boys to run haphazard out of the greenhouse and into the sunshine as though they'd never seen it before. "Would you boys come back to class immediately?" Russett demanded as boys whooped and ran outside, their arms outstretched as though to embrace the rays. He couldn't help but smile as the boys, reluctant to leave the sun's warmth, came back into the greenhouse. "I know it's exciting to have sunshine again, but we really must finish class before you enjoy the rays."

After what seemed hours, class was over and the boys ran back out into the sunshine. "Doesn't that feel good?" Adrian asked as he tipped his face towards the sun.

"Yeah, but if we don't hurry we'll be late to fencing," Lucian replied.

"Raphael wouldn't mind. I'm sure he'd understand," Jacobi said.

"Not even," Kaelen retorted. "You know how he feels about punctualness, or whatever it is."

"I believe you mean punctuality," George said as they walked into the castle.

"Yeah, that one," Kaelen said.

They walked into the classroom and worked through the hour. It seemed to go slower than any other class had before. When classes were finally done for the day, the group of friends went back outside to enjoy the sunshine. The trees were already beginning to drop their leaves, and the grounds were picturesque in red, orange and gold. The grounds were still soggy and the earth smelled of rain, but the boys enjoyed being outdoors for a little while before returning to their rooms to do the homework they'd been assigned.

As Lucian worked on conjugating verbs for Lorelei, he resisted the urge to throw the book across the room. Working with the mermaid language was difficult, and more than a little boring. He looked out the window at the setting sun and sighed. He knew soon it would be too cold to spend a lot of time outdoors. The days were growing shorter and colder. Shaking his head, he tried to return his focus to the list of verbs Lorelei had given them. He didn't have long to concentrate because soon a knock at his door reminded him that it was getting close to suppertime.

"Do you plan on eating tonight?" Adrian asked as Lucian opened the door. "We've been waiting five minutes for you to come out!"

"Sorry, I was trying to get through the mermaid pages," Lucian replied.

"I gave up on those," Adrian said shrugging. "I mean, seriously, when am I ever going to have to talk to a mermaid?"

"Every Monday and Wednesday between two and three," Kaelen pointed out.

"That doesn't count," Adrian retorted. "Most of the time she speaks to us in our language rather than that gibberish."

"You know you're asking to have to talk to mermaids in their language on your quest, right?" Jacobi asked teasingly.

"Oh no, they're not sending me anywhere near water," Adrian said.

"You're digging yourself deeper," George commented with a chuckle. "Why don't you quit while you're behind?"

The boys laughed and continued into the dining hall where supper was waiting. They went through the lines before sitting at their regular table. Conversation flowed easily between the friends and they were soon talking about their classes and what they hoped to have the next year. "I really hope I'm in dragon fighting. That just sounds like a lot of fun," Kaelen said.

"Fun? You want a giant reptilian beast breathing fire down your neck?" Adrian asked.

"Hey, that dragon won't get anywhere near me," Kaelen retorted saucily. "I'm too quick. A dragon would be really slow because they're so huge."

"Obviously you weren't watching the fairies very well when the princesses were here," Lucian said. "Vulcan was moving like lightning and still missing sometimes."

Kaelen scoffed, "Please, that was all part of the show."

"Whatever, Kaelen," Jacobi laughed shaking his head. "You tell us how fun it is when you come back from class burnt and scraped."

"You'll see," Kaelen insisted. "That dragon won't know what hit him."

"Tell us next year when you've actually fought it," George replied. "I don't think they'd let us actually be in any real danger though. After all, we do have to graduate in one piece, right?"

Everyone laughed. "I doubt the fairies would allow us to be dismembered. But at the same time, I bet Vulcan would hold out until the last possible second before jumping to our aid," Adrian replied. "We have to learn somehow."

"You should ask Donovan about it," Lucian added. "I saw him the other day and asked how things were going. If you can believe it, that's his favorite class."

"He's like a whole new person," Adrian agreed.

After supper, Lucian went back to his homework. When he finally finished he stretched and Rusty came over to his side. "Hello boy. I bet you think I'm neglecting you," Lucian said as he scratched Rusty's favorite spot behind his ear. Rusty panted and looked perfectly content with the world. Lucian laughed. "Well, maybe neglect is too strong a word. Come on boy, I've got to write some letters, but I'm not doing it at the desk. I've been here too long." He grabbed some paper and lay down on his bed, patting the spot next to him. Rusty jumped up onto the bed and circled around before lying down next to Lucian. Lucian scratched behind his ears again before beginning to write a letter to his parents. When that one was finished, he got a fresh page and started a letter to Allegra. He wrote:

> Dear Allegra,
>
> Sorry I didn't write Monday. I had a lot of homework and I just completely lost track of the time. How are your classes going? Mine have been busy! They give us so much homework. I think they do it on purpose so we don't have time to think about anything else.
>
> The rain finally stopped and all of the second year boys are finally well again. Seemed like forever! Nathan, the boy who locked us out, has finally lost his cloud too. He's still sniffling and probably will be for a while. Anyway, enough about that. I wish you could see the grounds here. Fall looks so beautiful. The leaves have all turned and the forest behind the stables looks like it's on fire! The air is crisp and smells of rain and earth. I know you could capture the beauty of it on paper better than I ever could.

Well, I hope this week goes great for you! Isn't it funny that we absolutely didn't want to come to these schools at all? Now I'm really glad that Mom and Dad sent us here. I'm having a great time and have made so many friends I never would have met otherwise. I'm still not sure I'm cut out to be a Prince Charming, but I'll do my best.

With Love,
Lucian

When he finished the letter and put it in an envelope he suddenly felt the urge to write a letter to Moira. "What do you think, Rusty? If I write to her do you think I'll be able to get to know more about her?"

Rusty looked up at him and woofed softly.

"You're right, it's worth a shot. After all," Lucian said, scratching behind Rusty's ears again, "what's the worst that could happen?"

Fall slowly faded into winter and finals were looming before the boys again. The horsemanship and hunting finals were combined again as they had been the year before. Lucian looked at the row of nervous-looking first year students. He could hardly believe that was him last year. Of course, no one would have believed that Rusty last year was little more than a puppy at the final. This year, fully grown and trained, Rusty was among the better hunting dogs there. He still walked with a limp which Lucian was sure he would have for life. However, it wasn't as bad as it had been when he was a puppy. While at home, King Lysander had taught Lucian how to properly groom Rusty's long coat. "He must have some setter blood in him," Lysander had said at one point, commenting on the long, silky red fur.

Now Lucian made the silent command to go and Rusty went off exactly as he should. Lucian followed behind on Zephyr. They'd been training to hunt on horseback in horsemanship. Lucian wasn't sure how Nathan would pass his final since he hadn't been in class during their three week training session. But he didn't think on it long. He had his own final to worry about. He guided Zephyr through the obstacles, following Rusty who had his nose planted to the ground and seemed to have caught scent of something. Rusty crept up to a bush and after looking back at Lucian started loudly baying. In no time, Lucian had a few pheasants in his bag. "Good boy, Rusty," he said as he patted him on the head. He called Zephyr who immediately came and he hopped up, trying to do it without a stump. Sighing, he pulled Zephyr to the nearest log and gave himself a boost up. "Someday I hope I can do that on my own," he muttered as Rusty began his search again.

When Lucian returned to where Diana and Phillipa were waiting, he was walking, leading his horse in. "Lucian, you've had problems before but Zephyr's never thrown you," Phillipa said in surprise.

"He didn't throw me," Lucian replied, a proud grin on his face. "I just didn't think I'd fit with the buck." He moved so she could see his catch.

"Bravo, Lucian," Diana said with a smile. "Venison is always such a nice addition to our dinner the night of hunting finals." She handed him a slip of paper with his scores on it. "Good work."

He walked over to where Kaelen and Adrian were standing discussing their grades. "So, did you get an A this year?" Adrian asked.

Lucian opened the paper and his jaw dropped. "You didn't get a P did you?" Kaelen asked nervously.

"I got an E," Lucian said, dumbfounded. "That can't be right, you look. I have to be seeing things."

Stuffing the paper in Adrian's hand, Adrian skimmed it and whistled with Kaelen looking over his shoulder. "Wow, you really did awesome! Diana said she's only seen that kind of turnaround once. I bet we all know who she's talking about. Turnaround may be too strong a word though, you were always a good hunter; Rusty just needed to catch up to you."

Lucian scratched Rusty's ears. "You did it, boy." Rusty just panted and seemed to smile as they waited for Jacobi and George to come out. When they joined the group they sat and talked until all the rest of their class and the first years had finished. Phillipa and Diana congratulated them on doing so well and Phillipa said. "Now is the time that the second years will remember from last year. We give out medals beginning in your second year for improvement and outstanding achievements."

"I don't remember that," Lucian whispered.

"You left early last year, remember?" Adrian asked.

Lucian nodded and returned his attention to the fairies. "Our best improvement award goes to Lucian of Maltisten. Last year he had a puppy that couldn't seem to follow even the most basic of commands," Diana said with a smile as Lucian flushed. "Now he has a hunting hound worthy of his own skill." She motioned for Lucian to come forward which he did reluctantly. "Congratulations Lucian on a job very well done," she said as she pinned the medal to his jacket.

"Thanks," Lucian said, "but I couldn't have done it without Adrian. He helped train Rusty as much as I did."

Diana simply smiled and they continued through their medals.

Kaelen was recognized for his continued show of expertise in horsemanship. When they pinned the badge on, Kaelen looked almost nervous. "Am I allowed to leave this on?" he asked.

Phillipa laughed. "Yes, Kaelen. Those awards won at the school are to be a reminder on your uniform to help encourage you and the students younger than you."

Beaming, Kaelen returned to the group. "Congratulations," George said with a smile.

"Thanks," Kaelen replied. They listened until the awards were finished before heading to the greenhouse for botany. Several of the boys were now sporting small medals on their uniforms. Each felt he was walking on air as they went to work with the plants preparing them for their final.

By the time classes were done for the day, Lucian couldn't stop smiling. It had been a perfect day, despite the chill in the air. When he hung his jacket up in his closet, he couldn't help but trace the edges of the medal he'd gotten. He still felt that Adrian had deserved one for being so helpful. Then he thought about his dad; he should write to him and let him know about it. He grabbed a handful of paper and lay down on his bed, patting the side so Rusty would join him. Writing feverishly, he soon finished the letter home and then wrote a letter to Allegra. Unable to stop himself, he then started writing a letter to Moira. So far, she hadn't answered any of his letters; but he refused to give up. There had to be some way of getting to know her better than he did. He also sincerely hoped that she hadn't grown at all during the semester. He figured he'd grown about an inch judging by where his pant legs fell. That would make the height difference more like seven inches rather than eight; assuming that she had stayed the same height throughout the semester.

Looking at his wall clock, he realized it was almost time for supper. He walked outside to see George perusing a letter. George looked up as Lucian walked out. "Hey," he said. "Just waiting on everyone else before suppertime. Mail came."

"Thanks," Lucian replied. He opened his mailbox and found a letter from his parents and one from Allegra. He opened the one from Allegra first.

> Dear Lucian,
>
> It's always so good to hear from you! I know we don't always get along at home, but I truly miss seeing you. School is going well. I'm not sure you could define me as a damsel in distress. I have a little too much spunk for that. But, I suppose they'll find some way of taming me.
>
> I've made lots of friends. Clarissa and I get along really well and we're friends with the twins in the age group above us. I think you know Eleanor and Leticia. They're both really sweet. I think everyone in the school likes them. Except maybe Esmé, but then she doesn't get along with anyone except those in her little clique. Oh well, we won't go there. You already know how I feel about her.
>
> Classes here are so different than at home. I really miss David, you know my art instructor at home. But, Rhianna is a really good instructor too. I just miss doing glass blowing. I can't wait until break when I'll be able to do it again. We're only doing pastels right now. I miss my paint set so much; especially when I look outside and see all the beautiful colors. I just want to capture it! This morning it was snowing and so peaceful out, I couldn't help but sketch it out during lunchtime. I sent it to you. What do you think of it?
>
> Anyway, I'm glad to hear Rusty is doing so well. Let me know how your final goes. I bet you'll be the best in your class!
>
> With Love,
> Allegra

Just as Lucian finished reading the letter and looked at the peaceful sketch of the castle blanketed in snow, Adrian and Kaelen emerged from their rooms. "We're waiting on Jacobi now, huh?" Adrian asked.

"Actually, he said to go without him," George said, folding his letter and putting it back in the envelope. "He got a letter from home and was pretty upset. He said he wanted to be alone for a while."

"Is he okay?" Lucian asked.

George shrugged. "He didn't want to talk about it. He said he'd come down later, but right now he's not feeling very hungry."

"Well, I guess we'd best go ahead then," Kaelen said. The boys walked downstairs after George and Lucian had put their letters away. They chatted about the final weeks of school and meeting their princesses again.

As they were almost finishing their meals, Jacobi arrived looking depressed and anxious. He sat down after going through the line for his meal. "Sorry I didn't come down with you," he said as he began pushing his food around the plate.

"That's alright," George said. "Is everything okay?"

Jacobi shrugged. "I'd rather not talk about it. It's personal."

The others sat in silence for a while before Lucian asked, "Have any of your other sisters returned home, George?"

"Mom and Dad wrote that Camilla is getting married during winter break. I think her prince set a record for our family. It was only a year and a half," George replied. "As far as the other two, they're still waiting for their Prince Charming to show up."

"I know you told me once how many sisters you have, but how many have finished school and been rescued?" Kaelen asked.

George took a deep breath. "Sarah, Naomi, Phyllis, Andrea, Tabitha and now Camilla have all finished school and been rescued. The first five are married now and Camilla's waiting until I get home for break so I can be her ring bearer or something like that." George rolled his eyes. "I've been a ring bearer five times already, you'd think my sisters would come up with something more creative. Anyway, Samantha just went out last spring and Susan has been out for three years now. Marissa graduates in two years."

"How do your parents keep track of them all?" Jacobi asked. "You'd be amazed how often I hear the dog's name instead of mine. And I'm their only child!"

"Let me guess, that happens when you're in trouble?" Lucian teased.

Jacobi nodded as George laughed. "My dad is really big into personalized jewelry. Each of my sisters has a locket with her name engraved on it and her birthstone. I think it's so he'll remember when their birthday is, but they tell me it's because he loves them. Maybe it's both. The sad thing is Dad had completely given up on having a son, so there's a locket at home waiting for my princess."

"Your dad bought you a locket?" Kaelen snorted.

"Hey, give him some credit," George said. "He got it before I was born."

"So, I guess the next question is do you and Eleanor have the same birthstone?" Lucian asked teasingly.

"Surprisingly enough, yes we do. She's two weeks younger than me," George replied with a grin. "So the birthstone will still help Dad remember which month she was born in."

"I hope it doesn't have a name engraved in it yet," Kaelen teased.

"No, Dad always waited until after the baby was born," George said with a smile. "So, when Eleanor is officially part of the family, her name will be engraved on it."

The conversation ended as Jacobi finished his meal and the five friends went upstairs to their own rooms. Lucian sat at his desk going over his homework to make sure everything was complete for the next day. When he was convinced that he hadn't forgotten anything he checked the grandfather clock in the corner. It wasn't that late but he felt exhausted. "What do you say we call it an early night, boy?" he asked Rusty.

Rusty looked up at him from his bed. The look he gave Lucian clearly read that Lucian had woken him up.

Lucian laughed, "Alright. Good night, Rusty."

Rusty yawned as Lucian blew out the candles and crawled in bed.

The weeks passed quickly to the end of the semester. The boys were glad when finals were over and despite himself, Lucian actually looked forward to seeing Moira. The last day of term came and Lucian woke up to gentle flurries fluttering past his window. He got up and dressed quickly. He now had two medals on his jacket; the one from hunting and one from fencing. Adrian had earned a medal in that class as well for showing the most improvement. Lucian was glad Adrian had been recognized for all the hard work he put in. It was hard learning left-handed and Lucian had been thrilled when Adrian, although not left-handed, was ambidextrous and was able to be his fencing partner.

Arriving downstairs, he found his friends waiting. Each of them had won recognition from at least one of their classes. Jacobi now had a medal of improvement in mathematics and George had a medal of continued excellence in alchemy. The friends waited for their princesses to arrive before going into the dining hall. It would be easier this way. As the ladies entered the castle, Lucian kept an eye out for Moira and Allegra in hopes that he'd be able to talk to his sister. However, when Allegra spotted him and came closer with a bright smile, his heart plummeted to his shoes. "You grew," he said, almost accusingly.

Allegra grinned that saucy smirk she always did when she outdid him. "I know. Medea had to teach me how to make flounces for my dresses because they were becoming embarrassingly short. What do you think of this one? I did it myself."

She spun around for Lucian and he looked at the delicately embroidered ruffle she'd added to her favorite green gown. "It's lovely, Allegra, but you're taller than me."

"I know, and I plan on enjoying it while I can," Allegra replied, tilting her chin in a teasing manner. "Adrian, it's good to see you again," she continued as Adrian stepped up behind Lucian.

Lucian saw his sister blush as Adrian returned her greeting, but decided to save the teasing for later. There'd be plenty of time for that over break. Spying Moira, Lucian turned his attention to his own princess. She was wearing a creamy yellow gown with the same lacey flounces he'd seen on his sister's gown. As she came closer, he was grateful to see that she didn't appear any taller. "Hello Moira," he said with a smile.

Moira flushed and nodded, but didn't reply. There was awkward silence for a while before she said, "Thanks. For your letters I mean," she continued when Lucian looked confused. "I, I enjoy hearing from you."

"You're welcome. I keep hoping that I'll hear back from you," Lucian admitted.

Stammering a little, Moira was saved from responding as Calista announced that breakfast was waiting for them in the dining hall. "After breakfast, we'll have an assortment of games in the gym." She continued speaking, making the same announcements as last year. There would be a staggered lunch schedule due to meeting with each prince and princess. Parents would arrive for supper and the first through third year students would be dismissed until January following the meal.

Lucian offered Moira his arm. She hesitated momentarily before accepting it and allowing him to escort her to the dining hall. Each table was already set with flatware and steaming trays of food. After helping his princess to her seat, Lucian served first her plate and then his own. Conversation around the table was swift and lighthearted. Kaelen had been dragged away by Esmé to sit with her friends. Leticia had convinced Nathan to sit with Eleanor and George. While Nathan wasn't any better than normal, Leticia was a welcome addition to the table. Softer-featured than her sister, Lucian imagined that Leticia had the look of a nymph with her titian hair and fair, freckled complexion. Eleanor was darker-haired, though still with strands of red. Her face was childlike and youthful, with a spattering of freckles across her nose. Only in personality and their eyes were they identical; brilliant, sparkling green eyes that held joy and laughter.

When the meal was over, the students went to the gym. Like the year before the plain space had been transformed into a mystical, winter wonderland. Also like the previous year, Lucian allowed Moira to pick the games. "I have an idea," Lucian said when they sat to yet another board game.

Moira looked at him suspiciously. "What's that?"

"If you win, you get to ask me any question you want about me, where I'm from, or anything else. If I win, I get to ask you a question. The person answering has to give an honest answer," Lucian said. "That way we won't be engulfed in silence like we were last year."

Looking thoughtful, Moira considered this. "Alright," she said at length. "Winner asks a question. Loser has to answer. But you seem to forget, Lucian. I won every game last year," she finished with a competitive edge to her voice.

"I'll just have to play better then," Lucian retorted.

Smiling impishly Moira said, "You've got a deal." They set up the pieces and Lucian paid closer attention to the plays than ever before. While they were wrapped in silence, Lucian didn't feel uncomfortable at all. He matched Moira's every move and as the game wound down, it would have been impossible to guess who the winner would be. "No!" Moira cried as Lucian found the loophole he'd been hoping for and won his first game.

Lucian smiled and looked at her. "Fair's fair. Alright, I'll go with an easy question first. Who's older, you or Adrian?"

"Adrian is older than me by fifteen minutes. He used to call me his baby sister," Moira added reflectively.

"Why did he stop?" Lucian asked.

Moira shook her head. "You're only allowed one question. Come on, let's play again."

Not willing to argue, Lucian reset the board. By the time the second and first year students were sent to lunch, Lucian had learned very little about Moira. He knew that Moira was the younger of the twins and that she often designed her own dresses. On the other hand, Moira had found out quite a bit about Lucian. He was left-handed, enjoyed fencing, often went to the beach with his father, and other tidbits. "She is ruthless," Lucian told George as they were waiting for their turn in Calista's office. "I'm telling you, I almost think she let me win those two games. All the rest of them were hers."

"Hey, at least she's starting to talk to you," George replied. "That's a vast improvement over last year."

"True. But I think she hesitates to get to know me. It's almost like she's scared of me," Lucian said.

George shrugged. "Maybe she's just not boy crazy yet. Marissa didn't start talking to her prince until last year. Now that's all she talks about." George imitated a high girly voice. "Xavier is so handsome. Xavier sent me a letter about school. Isn't Xavier wonderful?" Returning to his usual voice, "You have no idea how irritating it is. They've all hit that stage. I wonder how my parents have survived it!"

They laughed until Adrian came out of the office and said, "Your turn Lucian."

After meeting with Calista, Lucian walked downstairs to wait for Moira. She still hadn't had her meeting yet. While waiting, Lucian tried to engage her in conversation, but she simply flushed and seemed to have crawled back in her shell. As he looked around, he saw Esmé smirking at her. "Are you okay?" he asked.

"I'm fine," Moira snapped.

Taken aback, Lucian spied Allegra a little ways away. "Well, I'm going to go talk to my sister. If you need anything…"

"I won't," Moira interrupted.

Lucian walked over to Allegra, fuming. "It isn't her fault," Allegra whispered urgently.

"What?" Lucian asked.

"Come on," Allegra said. She grabbed Lucian's arm and pulled him farther down the hall where they wouldn't be overheard. "Moira's not talking to you, it's not her fault."

"What do you mean it's not her fault?" Lucian asked incredulously. "She's the one not speaking."

"Would you just be quiet and listen?" Allegra demanded, putting her hands on her hips. "Look, Moira's really sensitive about boys. I talk to her a lot at school because she's friends with the twins and I'm friends with the twins so we all hang out together. I mean, I think Adrian's really sweet and Eleanor absolutely loves George. We commiserate with Leticia because she's got that oaf for a prince. Clarissa talks about Jacobi all the time. But Moira never talks about you. At least, not a lot. When she does, she acts like she's said too much and she backs away from the subject."

"So, why has she suddenly decided to stop talking to me since she was fine this morning?" Lucian asked.

"Because before you came up, Esmé was teasing her dreadfully about liking you," Allegra explained. "She got really embarrassed and didn't seem to know what to say."

"Well, she's supposed to like me. I'm her prince," Lucian said.

"Not necessarily. You don't think Leticia actually likes Nathan do you?" Allegra asked. "And I've heard some of the things Esmé has said about your friend Kaelen. Just because you're destined to be together doesn't mean you like each other." She paused and Lucian considered what she was saying. "Look, I know it's got to be frustrating for you, but just give her some space for today. I don't know why this is such a touchy subject for her, but it is. Your job is to make her comfortable, not make things worse for her."

Before Lucian could respond that he wasn't trying to be difficult, Allegra walked away. Feeling like nothing he did was right, he kicked at the carpet. When that didn't relieve his frustration, he walked downstairs and started meandering the halls. Parents had been filtering in for a while and he found that he wished his own parents were there. As though hearing his silent request, Lucian heard a voice call his name from behind him. He turned to see his mother there. "Mom!" he called and went to hug her.

"Hello, dear," Alexandra said, kissing the top of Lucian's head. "Looks like you've grown a little bit. We'll have to get your hems lowered."

Lucian beamed and then looked around for his father. "Where's Dad?" he asked.

"Oh, milling about the hallways. He said he wanted to find your friend Donovan for some reason," Alexandra replied. "Wouldn't say much really. So, I got your letter about the medals. Let me see them," she said. As Lucian puffed out his chest so she could see the gleaming medals, she smiled. "I knew you'd do well. You're so like your father."

"Not always," Lucian admitted. "Dad always seems to know how to fix things and I'm afraid I just blunder them worse."

"What makes you say that?" Alexandra asked, concern in her eyes.

Lucian shrugged. "I'm just struggling a little with my princess, that's all. But don't worry, I've got four and a half more years to get it figured out," he finished with a smile.

"You'll have to tell me more about it later. This isn't quite the place for such a conversation," Alexandra replied. "Where's Allegra?"

Lucian led his mother upstairs and they arrived at the landing just as Melantha and Allegra walked out of Airlia Willowlimb's office. "Mom!" Allegra cried, rushing to her mother's outstretched arms.

"Oh, I've missed you so much," Alexandra said, hugging Allegra close. "How have you enjoyed school?"

"Better than I ever thought I would," Allegra replied, beaming.

Soon it was suppertime and Lucian went to find Moira. She refused his offered arm as they walked into the dining hall. Lucian tried not to feel frustrated, but it was difficult. It seemed that for every step he took forward, she pushed him back three more steps. He was glad his parents were there and he spoke with them as they sat to eat. "You must be Lucian's princess, Moira," Alexandra said, taking Moira's hand. "He tells us so much about you."

Moira flushed, "Thank you. You have a wonderful son. I'm sure he exaggerates."

"I doubt it," Lysander replied heartily. "Lucian is a terrible liar."

Queen Lavinia seemed to have heard them talking and quickly engaged Alexandra in a conversation about Moira and her many gifts. Lucian pulled Adrian into their own conversation. "I wish she talked about me that way," Adrian whispered.

Lucian tried to smile understandingly, but the truth was he didn't understand. His parents had always shown equal love for both of their children. Never had he been shadowed by Allegra nor Allegra by him. They were each held up for their unique abilities.

When supper was over, the friends parted, promising to write at least once during the month long break. Allegra and Lucian climbed into their parents' carriage with them and began the long ride home to Maltisten.

Chapter 3

During winter break, Lucian spent his time doing things with Allegra, working with Rusty and Zephyr outside on days it wasn't too cold out and practicing his fencing with his father in the large room his father had converted into a fencing hall. The walls were filled with shelves of swords and safety equipment as well as mirrors to allow those working in the room to watch their own progress. As the month progressed, Lucian asked to work with the rapiers as well as his usual epée. "I don't really have one built for your hands, son," Lysander had pointed out. "But you're welcome to borrow one of mine,"

Lucian wasn't interested in whether or not the swords were built for him, though he knew that would make handling it easier. He just wanted to try them out. He borrowed one of his father's rapiers and soon wished that his hands were not as small and delicate as they were. He looked at his father's broad, strong hands and hoped that one day he would grow into the swords his father cherished. "How did you learn to fight with both hands?" he asked one day as they were putting their swords away. "I know you're not left-handed."

"Your grandfather insisted that I learn with both hands. He said to me, 'You never know which hand your foe will fight with. If you can fight equally well with both hands, you'll never lose.' He taught me first right-handed and then when I'd mastered that left-handed. Someday I'll start working with you right-handed," Lysander said.

"Well, I hope I won't disappoint you. I know how left-dominant I am," Lucian replied ruefully.

Lysander laughed, "Don't worry son. You'll catch on well enough. I suspect you'll always be more comfortable left-handed. I've always favored fighting right-handed. It's easier for me."

"So why did you work with me left-handed?" Lucian asked.

"Because I knew that if I tried to force the issue it wouldn't work out well to my benefit or yours. I spent many evenings with your grandfather thinking of how best to teach you. He said you always start with the dominant before moving on to the other hand. It gives you the knowledge and skill that will make using your other hand easier. Not easy, but easier," Lysander explained.

"Wouldn't it be easier to just learn the one and not worry about the other?" Lucian asked.

Lysander laughed. "It would, but being able to fight with both hands is a valuable asset, especially for a Prince Charming."

Thinking of this made Lucian think of Moira. "Dad, do you think I'm doing something wrong?" He explained the problems he'd had with Moira. "She's really pretty and I kind of like her," Lucian admitted. "I just don't know how to get to know her better. Every time I think I'm close, she backs away from me."

"I don't know what to tell you son," Lysander replied. "I didn't really have to woo your mother. Ours was one of those once in a lifetime things. Love at first sight is very rare. Perhaps with time, Moira will come around. I suppose that's why the fairies spend six years throwing you together."

"What if she never comes around, Dad?" Lucian asked. "What if we're always at odds with one another?"

"Don't worry about it son," Lysander said gently. "You're both so young and you have so much time ahead of you. Whether you see it or not, I'm sure in her heart, Moira thinks you're handsome. She probably even 'kind of' likes you. Give her time." Clapping his shoulder, Lysander continued, "Now, let's see what your mother has arranged for lunch."

They went to the dining hall where Allegra and Alexandra were already waiting. "Well, my dear, that took you long enough," Alexandra said in a teasing tone.

"I apologize love, we lost track of the time," Lysander replied, kissing her cheek before taking his seat at the head of the table.

After lunch, Lucian went to his room and started writing letters to each of his friends. As he was about to get out a sheet of paper to begin writing to Moira, Allegra came to see if he'd play a game with her. Leaving the paper untouched, he decided he'd get back to it later. But as the day progressed, he soon forgot all about it.

The afternoon before they left, Lucian received a surprise letter from Moira. He opened it eagerly.

> *Dear Lucian,*
>
> *I just wanted to write and say that I've missed hearing from you. I guess I got used to getting your letters every week. But I understand that you must be busy at home, catching up with your family. They seem very kind. Mother hasn't stopped talking about your mother since we left the school. Could you tell her thank you for me? Mom has few friends and I'd like to think that they really got along well.*
>
> *I also wanted to apologize to you. I was very short with you at the end of the day before supper and that wasn't fair of me. I hope you'll forgive me.*
>
> *Well, I think that's all I wanted to say. Enjoy the rest of your vacation.*
>
> *Sincerely,*
> *Moira*

Unbeknownst to Lucian, Lysander had been looking over his shoulder. "I told you she'd come around," he said, causing Lucian to jump.

"Yeah, I guess she was just having a bad day," Lucian said. He reread the letter and then folded it neatly and put it back in its envelope. "Where's Mom?"

"In the sewing room with Allegra," Lysander replied.

Lucian went down the hall and knocked on the door. When he heard his mother's voice, he went in. He could see Allegra standing on a box while Alexandra was hemming a new dress for her. "Do you like it?" Allegra asked.

Looking over the pale blue gown, Lucian smiled, "It's very pretty on you. Mom, I wanted to show you something. If you have a moment that is, I don't want to interrupt."

"Give me just a moment, darling," Alexandra said through a mouthful of pins. "I'm almost finished." Waiting patiently, Lucian sat down on a stool while Alexandra finished the row of stitches. "There you are, dear, all finished. I must say that is a lovely color. I'm not sure I would have chosen it myself."

Allegra hopped off the box and spun in a circle so the skirt would fly around her. "It's perfect. And no flounces!"

"Yet," Alexandra chuckled. "Go on now, show your father and then take it off so we can get it packed with your trunks for school."

Allegra seemed to float from the room as she spun this way and that.

Shaking her head, Alexandra turned her attention back to Lucian. "Now, what was it you wanted to show me?"

Lucian handed her the letter. Alexandra skimmed it and smiled. "That's very sweet of her. Where do they live again?"

"Lictthane," Lucian replied. "That's only about three hours from here."

"You've been paying attention in geography," Alexandra said with a smile.

"Orientation, Mom," Lucian corrected. "Anyway, I thought you'd want to see that."

"Yes," Alexandra said thoughtfully. "I might have to arrange a day trip out there to see her. Of course, I'd write first to let her know that I was coming. Well, is there anything you need hemmed or patched up before you go back to school?"

Remembering his short pants, Lucian nodded and left the room, taking his letter with him. On arriving at his own room, he placed the letter in his trunk before getting out his trousers. He took them downstairs to the sewing room where Alexandra was waiting patiently. He stepped repeatedly behind the large screen in the corner as he changed into different pairs of pants for his mother to pin and hem. When she finished the last one she said, "I hope you don't grow too much more during the semester. I don't think those can be rehemmed again. We'll have to buy you new trousers for next year."

"Well don't say that too loudly," Lucian replied. "I may not grow at all."

Alexandra laughed, "Darling, just because your father grew constantly from thirteen to sixteen doesn't mean that everyone does. Why, I grew ten inches in one year and another three the next."

"Really?" Lucian asked.

"Yes," Alexandra said, her gaze far away as though remembering. "I went from being the shortest person in my class to the tallest within five months. And I didn't stop growing there. Luckily there were a couple of other girls who also had late growth spurts. Flounces were very popular that year. I remember one girl, Molly of Rendorlin who didn't grow at all, but added flounces to her gown to make people think she had."

Lucian laughed with his mother. "Well, maybe I'll grow like you."

"Oh I hope not, dear," Alexandra retorted. "How on earth would we keep you in clothes? You can't add a flounce to trousers."

"I suppose not," Lucian said, instantly seeing in his mind a pair of pants with lacey flounces off each leg. He wrinkled his nose at the thought.

"Well, these are all done for you. Finish packing and then come to supper. We're going to call it an early night because we have a long trip tomorrow," Alexandra said.

"Can I go see Zephyr before supper?" Lucian asked.

"Certainly, just be swift about it," Alexandra replied.

Lucian nodded and went to his room with his newly hemmed trousers. Secretly, he hoped he'd grow at least another inch during the spring term; two would be better. After neatly folding the pants and putting them in his trunk, he went to the kitchen for a carrot and then went out to the stables. He walked past Sunset Rose, Allegra's dressage champion, the carriage horses and to Zephyr who was happily munching oats. "He's a proud young thing, Master Lucian," the groom said as he added hay to another stall.

"I know," Lucian replied. He opened the stall door and walked in next to Zephyr. "Hello boy. I've brought you a treat."

Zephyr turned and looked at Lucian. He nosed around Lucian's pockets until Lucian pulled out the carrot. He took it and ate it happily before returning to his oats. Lucian laughed and grabbed a curry brush. As he brushed Zephyr's back, he talked to him about school and everything else that would be going on. When Zephyr's coat gleamed, he put the brush away and said, "Well, you're enjoying your supper. It's about time I enjoyed mine. I'll see you in the morning, Zephyr."

Zephyr snorted and continued to eat.

Very early the next morning, the group set out for Biberseth. Fair Damsels was only a few miles from Charming Academy and they had decided to drop Allegra off first before going to take Lucian. Lucian hugged his sister after going with her to take her horse to the stables. "I'll see you in the spring."

"Keep writing," Allegra commanded with a smile.

"You too," Lucian replied. He got back into the carriage with his parents and they rode the remaining miles to Charming Academy.

As always, Calista was waiting at the door for them. "Welcome back," she said with a smile. "I trust you had a good break?"

"It was great," Lucian replied with a grin.

"Excellent. Once you've put your horse in the stables, you can join us for supper. You're right on time," Calista said. "If you can spare the time, you're welcome to join us," she directed to Lysander and Alexandra.

"I appreciate the thought but we have reservations in town," Alexandra replied. When Calista merely nodded, she turned to Lucian. "Have a good semester love, and keep in touch."

"I will Mom," Lucian replied, hugging her. "I love you."

After hugging Lysander and watching them go, he went inside and joined his friends for supper. "How was your break?" George asked as he sat down at the table.

"Busy. Dad started teaching me rapiers because I wouldn't quit pestering him about it," Lucian replied.

"No wonder you're so far ahead of the rest of us," Jacobi laughed.

"Well, that's not all I did," Lucian admitted with a grin. "I worked with Rusty and Zephyr too. I just want to be at my best here."

"No arguments here. If my dad was any good with a sword, I'd have him help me," Jacobi said. "But I think there's good reason he never needed to use it on his quest. He does okay with beginners, but even I'm starting to outmatch him."

"I thought every prince needed to do fencing throughout school," Adrian countered.

"It depends on your quest I guess. Dad finished fencing his third year. I'm guessing princes who are definitely going to use that go through school with it," Jacobi shrugged.

"Yeah, my dad talked about having fencing but he also had double botany when he got to his later years here," George said. "He had some kind of magical forest he had to battle through."

"I would die if they put me in double botany," Kaelen groaned. "I'm bad enough at it just once; let alone twice!"

Adrian laughed. "Well, we won't have to worry about double anything until next year at the earliest."

The boys continued chatting until supper was over before going to their own rooms. When Lucian walked into his room, he looked over his schedule. The times really weren't changing much from last semester.

Class Schedule

Day	Time	Class	Teacher
Monday, Wednesday	8:00-9:30	Mathematics	Marius Hawkeye
	9:30-11:00	Fencing	Raphael Peregrine
	11:00-12:00	Lunch	
	12:00-1:00	Botany	Russett Snapdra-

gon

	1:00-2:00	Hunting	Diana Foxglove
	2:00-3:00	Foreign Language	Lorelei
	3:00-4:00	Orientation	Pagoma Snapdragon
Tuesday, Thursday	8:00-9:30	Horsemanship	Phillipa Rosepetal
	9:30-11:00	Physical Education	Achilles Stardust
	11:00-12:00	Lunch	
	12:00-1:00	History	Clio Stormcloud
	1:00-2:30	Etiquette	Gelasia Stardust
	2:30-4:00	Language Arts	Airlia Willowlimb
Friday	8:00-9:30	Music	Amadeus Comettail
	9:30-11:00	Beginner's Alchemy II	Aurelia Sundance
	11:00-12:00	Lunch	
	12:00-1:30	Art	Stefanos Stormcloud
	1:30-3:00	Language Arts	Airlia Willowlimb

On Thursday evenings, Astronomy will be taught from 8:00-9:30 by Uralia Moonbeam

Lucian was glad to see that fencing had been moved to the morning. Having the long afternoon had been difficult for many of the boys. After checking his bag to make sure all his supplies were available that he would need, he decided to call it an early night. After blowing out the candles, he crawled in bed and let sleep take him.

Winter was mild that year, allowing them to go outside with hunting and horsemanship more often. Lucian enjoyed horsemanship more than he ever had before. Zephyr was still several inches too tall for him, but he was also a natural dressage horse. He went through the courses Phillipa set up with ease and grace. His only weakness was the proud streak which often made him go his own way rather than follow Lucian's commands. Lucian shook his head at the end of class one day and said, "We almost had that perfect, you know."

Zephyr snorted and leaned into the place Lucian was scratching.

"Yeah, I know, you're right and I'm wrong," Lucian laughed, continued to scratch Zephyr's neck. "Well, next time could you be right in the way I tell you?"

Snorting again and munching happily on the carrot Lucian offered him, Lucian was fairly sure Zephyr had just ignored him. He shook his head again and after making sure Zephyr's coat gleamed, he had plenty of water, and his tack was polished and neatly put away, Lucian left the barn with everyone else to go the gym. On arriving, they were surprised to find the door closed and Achilles nowhere in sight. "Normally he's waiting here for us," Lucian commented.

"He's probably inside," Kaelen said, grabbing the doorknob confidently. "Let's go."

When they walked into the gym, they saw Achilles sitting with Tallia in the corner of the gym. "What are you doing here?" he asked the boys as they filtered in.

"It's time for class," Jacobi pointed out.

Tallia flushed and said, "Well, looks like you're busy. I'll see you later."

Achilles looked unfazed and told the boys to start stretching. "Ten laps around the gym."

"I bet he's doing that because we caught him with Tallia," Adrian whispered bitterly.

Lucian nodded but didn't speak. He went through the stretches and started running around the gym. He had seen Tallia around the gym more and more often as the days progressed. He'd heard the older boys talking about how Achilles had been secretly eying her for a while. "It's only a matter of time," one had said. Lucian couldn't help but wonder, a matter of time until what?

When classes were over for the day, the boys decided to go outside with their homework. It was a mild February afternoon. There was a cool crispness to the air, but the sun was shining brightly, warming them as they sat around their favorite tree. "Spring's almost here," Adrian observed. "The grass is starting to actually look green again."

"Wouldn't it be great to have an early spring?" George agreed.

"We could certainly spend more time outside rather than cooped up indoors," Lucian pointed out.

"Let's just hope the fairies don't overload us with homework this year," Jacobi said.

"Yeah right," Kaelen scoffed. "They always give us more homework when the weather's nice. I think they do it on purpose."

The boys laughed. "You think they do everything on purpose," George chuckled.

"Well, let's head back inside. It's getting a bit too nippy for me," Jacobi admitted.

Everyone agreed and they walked back inside just in time for supper. After dashing up the stairs to put their bags away, they went running back down the stairs for supper. They continued to chat long into the evening. After finishing supper they went into the commons and sat near one of the fireplaces just talking and laughing together. When Gelasia came in to remind them that they needed to get to bed, they tried to argue with her. She laughed, "Morning comes awfully early, gentlemen. You've already stayed up well past ten o'clock. Go to bed, you'll all still be here in the morning and you can chat then." She then left them.

Reluctantly, Kaelen said, "I guess she's right. We should head to bed."

"Yeah," George agreed with a yawn.

They walked up the stairs and then into their own rooms. As Lucian crawled under the covers, he contemplated the day and everything that had happened until sleep silenced his thoughts.

The boys were surprised the next morning as they walked into the fencing classroom to find Vulcan standing at the door rather than Raphael. "Um, where's Raphael?" Mithulan asked as they walked into the room.

"He's taking care of a family matter," Vulcan replied, his deep voice seeming to echo through the room. "I'm standing in for him." He took roll and then set the boys to work. "Don't think for a moment that because Raphael isn't here you've got the day off," he said, his orange eyes seemed to dare them to slack off. "I've got explicit instructions and I am watching you."

Under his fiery gaze, the boys picked up their lessons where they'd left off the day before. Lucian didn't worry in this class; he knew he was equal to the challenge. But he also had the distinct impression that Vulcan was watching the class, looking for those who were succeeding and those who were struggling. Lucian supposed that Vulcan probably had some sort of say on who entered his dragon fighting classes and who didn't.

When the class was over, the boys went to lunch, hoping to learn more about why their fencing master was gone. "I bet Honoria had her baby," Jacobi said as they walked through the line. "It's got to be about time, right?"

"Maybe he's just not feeling well. Even fairies get sick sometimes," Kaelen suggested.

As lunch started, a hush fell over the room as Calista's soft voice carried over the noise. "I have an announcement to make," she said. "Raphael came just a few moments ago to inform me that their new daughter, Theodora Peregrin was born early this morning. Mother and baby are doing just fine, but he is taking the rest of the day off to be with his family. Your classes will continue as scheduled with Vulcan Firebrand standing in his place."

As she sat down, a buzz of chatter sprang up. "I told you so," Jacobi said triumphantly.

"I wonder what's happening with the dragon fighting classes," Lucian said. "I mean, surely he has some today."

"Maybe he doesn't," Adrian replied. "I bet he has to have a day or two to rest in the middle. I certainly would if I had to care for that beast."

After lunch, the boys went outside to the greenhouse for botany. Russett was waiting for them at the door as usual. When the boys walked into the room, they were surprised to see the plants they'd been working with had disappeared. Instead they had rows of clay pots and several seed packets. "Russett, what are we doing?" a tall, dark-haired boy asked suspiciously.

"You boys are getting a taste of gardening this month," Russett replied cheerfully. "I've had a rather large order of flowers made with the request that you boys plant them. So, with some help from Lucretia who will come in after you're done each day, you'll be growing flowers. Now, you need to get into groups of five. You have ten seconds to arrange yourselves before I start picking groups for you." In no time, Lucian was surrounded by his friends. After the boys were set up the way Russett wanted them, he continued, "Each group will be assigned a different type of flower. You will plant them, weed them, water them and see to all their needs. These are very special so don't neglect them. You'll disappoint someone you all know and love."

"Who, Russett?" a freckled boy asked.

"That will be revealed later. For now, it's time to get started! Potting soil is available over there," Russett said pointing, "and everything else is in your area."

"Did you do any planting last year, Kaelen?" Adrian asked hopefully.

"No, I just picked them," Kaelen replied glumly.

"Guys," Lucian laughed when they all looked miserably at the pots. "It's not that hard. Let's read the back of the packets. My dad gardens all the time; they always put the instructions on the back." He picked up one of the seed packets. They were growing white garden roses. "Okay, first thing, we're going to need bigger pots. These are way too small for rose bushes. Uh, Jacobi, why don't you ask Russett if he's got some bigger pots that we can use? Adrian, why don't you grab a bag of peat moss and George why don't you get the potting soil? Kaelen, you help George, we're going to need a lot of soil. I'm going to ask Russett about fertilizer, this isn't very clear."

The boys readily accepted Lucian's directions and soon they were back together with the largest pots Russett had available and everything that they could possibly need. They each filled their pots with soil and then groaned as Lucian told them to take two feet of the soil out and mix it with the peat moss. They watched Lucian put this mix back in and then poke an inch and a half deep hole in it. He gently placed a seed in and then started on the other pot. After Lucian had planted his seeds, the others did the same. They carefully watered each pot and then set them on a shelf nearest the windows. They watched another group put their pots nearby. "What are you growing?" George asked.

"Larkspur," Mithulan replied. "You?"

"Roses," Jacobi replied.

"There's no way those will grow in just a month. Roses take years to grow," one of the boys said.

"I know that, Jared," Russett said from behind them. "That's why Lucretia will be coming. She can bless the plants so that they'll mature much faster than if they were allowed to simply go by their own course."

When class was over, the boys were dirty but satisfied with their work. As they were walking, they saw Lucretia heading towards the greenhouse. They avoided eye contact with her as she still seemed to hate all of them. Instead they focused on their own conversation. "I bet Lucian's will sprout first," Kaelen said. "He's like an expert."

"I'm no expert," Lucian insisted. "My dad's the expert. He grows his own hybrid roses. I should know more about them, but gardening has never been as interesting to me as it is to my dad."

"Well, Adrian's certainly not," George teased. "He had a hard enough time getting soil into the pot."

Lucretia watched the tallest boy stick his tongue out at one of his friends. Wicked amusement flickered in her eyes. *If a frog you wish to act*, she thought, *then a frog you'll be. Until your princess releases you went it's you she sees.*

The boys didn't notice Lucretia's necklace glow, nor the faint red light that swirled around Adrian like a ribbon. Frustration caused Lucretia to stamp her foot. Her silent spells weren't working like they used to. It was the Change; she could feel it altering her. She shrugged. While he wouldn't change today, he would eventually. The magic glow around him proved that her spell had hit its mark. And even with that, she knew once the fairies found out they'd make her take the spell back. She wasn't supposed to do magic on the boys unless she was called. But since when did a witch have to follow directions?

A knock at Calista's door made her look up from the paperwork she'd been going over. "Come in," she said.

"I'm sorry to interrupt you," Diana said, "but I have a question for you."

"That's fine, I could use a break anyway," Calista replied with a smile. "What did you need?"

"Is Adrian being punished for something?" Diana asked.

"Adrian?" Calista repeated. "Not that I know of, why?"

"He's glowing," Diana replied. "He's been hit with some kind of spell, and I couldn't imagine that he had done anything to warrant punishment. He's such a nice boy."

Concerned, Calista asked, "Is his behavior any different? Does he act like he's under a spell?"

"That's the strange thing and why I didn't say anything to him," Diana explained. "He's acting as though nothing happened. He's not a strange color, he doesn't have any unusual tics, he's just plain Adrian with a magic glow around him."

"Thank you for telling me," Calista said. "I'll speak to the Sisters about this and see if I can't figure out what's going on."

Diana nodded and left the room. Calista sent a piece of lavender paper through the window. Soon the Sisters were in her office. "You called all of us, Calista. Is something wrong?" Althea asked.

"I've just been told that Adrian is glowing," Calista said. "Is there a reason for that?"

Althea remained calm though she could see that Calista was angry. "I'm afraid I'm not as familiar with your students as you are Calista. Who is Adrian?"

"One of my second year students," Calista explained, pointing her wand at the blackboard behind her. The chalk sprang to life and began drawing Adrian's portrait as she continued. "You wouldn't be familiar with Adrian because he's never been in trouble."

Lucretia giggled darkly as the portrait finished. Everyone turned to look at her and Althea's eyes darkened. "Do you have something to say, Lucretia?"

"That's the frog prince," Lucretia replied with a malicious smile. "Quite charming isn't he?"

"Frog prince?" Calista repeated angrily. "Why? You know you are only to use your spells when you are called. I know you weren't called because I would have been notified. You have breached not only my trust, but the trust of every parent with a child in this school and at Fair Damsel's Academy. Do you realize the consequences which could arise from this?"

"You profess to teaching gentlemen," Lucretia argued. "A gentleman does not stick his tongue out. It's unsightly and unbecoming."

"That is neither here nor there," Calista replied. "Change him back."

"She cannot," Maeve said suddenly. "It is written in the stars. His quest has been altered. There is nothing we can do at this point except wait and see."

"There, you see," Lucretia said as though this vindicated her.

Calista eyed Maeve suspiciously. "Are you quite sure?"

"Oh positive," Maeve said sweetly. "I was looking just before receiving your summons. You see, Lucretia tends to come home upset when a spell goes awry. I could tell something was bothering her and so I took to my charts. Adrian's transformation will take three years, perhaps longer, to be complete. He probably won't even notice for the next year and a half. I'm afraid I assumed that she'd been called which is why I didn't come to see you."

"Maeve is never wrong about the stars, especially when we're close to the Change" Calypso added. "I would believe what she has told you."

"However," Morghana rasped, "Lucretia must be dealt with. She has breached the trust of the fairies and broken our code by deceiving her Sisters. Althea, you know what must be done."

For the first time since entering, Lucretia felt frightened. "You wouldn't." Althea turned towards her and merely held out her hand. "No," Lucretia hissed. "I won't give it to you."

"You can give it willingly, or I can take it by force," Althea replied. "It's your choice."

Lucretia's eyes glowed and her hair billowed about her like a flame. "I won't," she screeched. Her necklace glowed.

Althea closed her eyes and the ruby in her crown glowed, brighter and brighter each moment. The necklace rose slowly over Lucretia's head as though invisible hands were playing tug-of-war with it. As Lucretia screamed in anger, Althea said calmly. "You have chosen this. You are stripped of your powers for the next two months."

"You can't do this to me!" Lucretia sobbed angrily. "I have to be able to care for my herbs!"

"You'll do so as a mortal would," Althea replied coolly. "Maeve will take your place in botany blessing the student's flowers."

As Lucretia cried, Calista asked, "Isn't that a bit harsh? You and the others will have to take on her duties."

"As you said, she has breached the trust of many. Her punishment may have been shorter if she had willingly given up the necklace. She is young and vain and must learn this lesson," Althea explained. "However, I believe you still have things you need to do, so we will bother you no longer. I'm sorry for this misunderstanding, but have faith that it will turn out alright in the end." She stood and the others followed her, Lucretia weeping bitterly. "Enjoy the rest of your day," Althea said kindly before leaving with the others.

Calista could still hear Lucretia's anguished cries as she sent messages to all the fairies on staff and a longer note to Lorelei explaining the situation. When they had gathered in her office, she said, "We have a bit of a problem. Adrian is quite slowly turning into a frog."

There was a barrage of voices until Calista raised her hand for silence. "I don't understand," Airlia said when Calista motioned towards her. "Why is he being punished? Adrian's such a good boy."

"There's been a slight hiccup with the Sisters which has already been dealt with," Calista replied. "However, in talking to them, I feel it would be best not to say anything to him at present. Human eyes can't see the glow of magic, therefore it will be some time before he or his peers notice anything."

"Shouldn't he be told?" Achilles asked. "This will affect his ability to do his quest."

"Exactly," Gelasia said before Calista could explain. "He will see this as leading to imminent failure. He must continue on as though nothing has happened if we are going to be able to teach him all that he needs to succeed on his quest. That is the only way he'll be able to succeed. Imagine someone telling you that you were going to eventually turn into a frog and yet you still have to make a girl fall in love with you. Even you wouldn't be up to the challenge. No, Calista's right. We mustn't tell him yet."

"For now," Calista continued when Gelasia had finished speaking, "there will not be any changes made to his schedule. It would be unnecessary and raise his suspicions. I just hope that none of you will mention to this to him. As Gelasia said, it would destroy his own confidence in his abilities. I believe if we do everything we can to make this an easy transition for him, that he will be able to make his quest work. Perhaps not in the way we planned it, but to a happy ending nonetheless."

Chapter 4

Winter melted into spring with bright sunshine and cool, refreshing breezes. The flowers the boys had been growing in botany were growing beautifully, for the most part. Some of the boys had struggled with their plants. But with Russett's patient help, most of them had been able to still grow beautiful flowers. Lucian couldn't help a sense of pride in his rosebushes; though he had noticed with some confusion that not a single bush had thorns on it. In looking at the other boys bushes, he knew it wasn't the type of rose. Their rosebushes all had thorns. He simply shrugged and put the thought behind him as he pruned it and breathed in the delicate fragrance. He looked about the greenhouse. There were white rosebushes, bright blue larkspur, delicate forget-me-nots, and irises ranging from bright blue to darker blues.

"They are lovely, aren't they?" Russett asked, noticing Lucian's line of vision.

"Yeah. I think I know now why Dad spends so much time in his garden," Lucian replied.

Russett laughed, "There's something very soothing about working with growing things. My mother always said they bring peace to the soul."

When the boys were sitting at supper, Calista got up and made an announcement. "As you all remember, this weekend is when we will meet with our princesses. However, due to special circumstances, the meeting will be held at Fair Damsel's instead of here at Charming Academy. We will leave the castle promptly at seven thirty."

"Why do you think we'll be going to their school?" Kaelen asked. "They always come here."

George shrugged, "I'm sure we'll find out soon enough."

Kaelen was prevented replying by Russett appearing at his shoulder. "Can I speak to you after supper? Come meet me in the greenhouse," he said, handing Kaelen a deep red piece of paper.

"Am I in trouble?" Kaelen asked.

"No, you're not in trouble, silly. I just need to talk to you," Russett replied, clapping his shoulder. "After supper is fine, don't rush yourself."

"What do you suppose that's about?" Lucian asked.

Kaelen shrugged. "I don't know. Maybe I forgot to water my rosebush and he wants me to take care of it myself."

After supper, Kaelen said goodbye to his friends and walked outside to the greenhouse. When he walked in, Russett was arranging several of the flowers the boys had grown in a vase. "I hope you finished eating before coming out here," Russett said, barely looking up from the arrangement he was working with.

"No, I mean, yes I finished dinner. I didn't come out hungry," Kaelen replied. "What did you need to talk to me about?"

"I have a secret for you that you cannot share with the other boys. I had to beg Calista to let you in on this," Russett began. Kaelen listened eagerly. He liked being one up on everyone else. "As I'm sure you've observed, Tallia and Achilles are very close."

Feeling very disappointed, Kaelen said, "Yeah, so?"

Russett laughed. "So, they're getting married Saturday. That's why we're going to be going to Fair Damsel's for the meeting. Tallia's sister works there as the art instructor. Now, I'm sure you can imagine that a wedding demands lots of flowers and flower arrangements."

Kaelen was starting to feel suspicious. "I'm still not sure why you need me."

"You're the only other person in this school who knows how to arrange flowers.

It would be too much of a hassle to have your classmates do it," Russett explained. "You were a quick learner. Some of them would probably rival your first arrangement. For a wedding, that's not acceptable. I'd like you to help me create the flower arrangements for the tables and specifically for the trellis they'll be married under. All of the flowers that were grown by your classmates and some that I've been growing are going to be used for this. Are you up to the challenge?"

The tone in Russett's voice raised the competitive streak in Kaelen's nature. "Absolutely," Kaelen replied.

"Excellent," Russett said. "Every evening after supper come out here and we'll work on the arrangements. The nice thing is I can keep these fresh until the special day comes. And don't worry about the transportation. I'll be taking care of getting them there. In fact, by the time I'm done, no one will know they were planted here except you boys. Ready to start?"

"Yeah," Kaelen said, feeling anticipation build in him. He hadn't told anyone, but he'd missed working with the flowers and their month of gardening had been a welcome relief to him. He looked at the whitewashed trellis Russett had told him he'd be working on. He looked at it for a while and then knew exactly what he was going to do.

Saturday morning, the boys mounted up to go to Fair Damsel's Academy. Most of them had never been there before. Lucian had been outside, but had never gone inside the castle. In the early morning sunlight, the gray stones seemed to shimmer. The grounds were similar to those of Charming Academy. As they arrived, Melantha greeted them with a cheerful smile. "Welcome to Fair Damsel's Academy," she said as they entered. "Please, come find your princess and have a seat for breakfast and we'll begin the day's festivities."

It didn't take long at all for Lucian to find Moira. She was head and shoulders above her peers. He didn't say anything to her about the fact that there was now a second layer of ruffles on her skirt and she had widened the gap of their height difference. He hoped most sincerely that he would have a growth spurt soon. He didn't think he could live with having a princess who towered over him forever. "Hello Moira. You look nice today."

"Thanks," she said. "I enjoyed your last letter."

Remembering his promise, he pulled from behind his back a single white rose from one of his rosebushes. "As promised," he said, handing it to her as she blushed.

She smelled it and smiled. "Thank you. But, how did you get all the thorns off? I've never seen a rose with no thorns."

Lucian shrugged. "I really don't know. None of my bushes had any thorns."

"How unusual," Moira said as they walked together into the dining hall.

As they walked, Lucian looked around. Where blue was the primary color at Charming Academy, everything here was a shade of pink. Despite absolutely detesting the color, he had to admit that the effect at the school was quite lovely. He still would never use the color himself, but he supposed that for a girl it was probably very nice. "It's very pink here," he found himself saying aloud.

Moira laughed. "I don't really like it much either. The first weekend I was able to get to town I bought new bedding to replace all the pink in my room."

"Really?" Lucian asked, surprised at this revelation. Moira never spoke of herself.

Moira nodded and they sat down at a table. Soon all of their friends were gathered around them as well; except Kaelen who was being pulled to the table Esmé had set up with her friends. Conversation was fast flowing and breakfast seemed to go insanely quickly. It was strange for Lucian not to serve himself. Serving maids scurried back and forth between the tables and the kitchens, bringing refills as necessary and clearing plates nearly as fast as they were being used. As one flitted by, she looked vaguely familiar, but he didn't have time to think on it as he was pulled back into the conversation.

When breakfast was finished, Melantha rose and announced that everyone would be reconvening outside. "We have a very special occasion to celebrate."

Kaelen got a look on his face that plainly read he knew something the others didn't. "What special event?" Adrian asked him. "And don't try to tell me you don't know."

"I haven't the faintest idea," Kaelen replied nonchalantly, though his grin told another story. "And even if I did, do you think I'd be allowed to tell you?"

"In other words, you do know, you're just not telling," Lucian said with a laugh as they walked outside. When he looked ahead of himself, he gasped. Over the door was a giant floral swag with roses, larkspur and forget-me-nots, trailing down in ferny tendrils around the doorframe. The railings of the stairs were similarly decorated with garlands wrapped about them. There were rows of chairs set up, some already filled by fairies. Ahead was a trellis, lavishly decorated with climbing white roses and blue morning glory. The top of it was covered in greenery and fragrant flowers Lucian recognized from class. He could see the larkspur, forget-me-nots, roses and irises. Underneath the trellis, Achilles stood nervously rubbing his ankle with his foot. Instead of the normal loose attire he wore in gym, he was wearing a fresh, white doublet and formal trousers.

As they arrived to their seats, the students didn't sit, but stayed standing. In the row in front of him, Lucian saw Honoria and Raphael standing together. Cradled in Raphael's arms was a tiny baby, her eyes closed in sleep as the breeze played with a tuft of aqua blue hair. He saw a look of tenderness on Raphael's face that he'd never seen before. Honoria whispered something to Raphael which made him smile as they turned their attention to the couple coming down the aisle. Lucian also turned and saw the fairy king and queen walking towards the trellis, their silver crowns sparkling in the light. The queen wore a long, glittering green gown that matched her pale green eyes. The king wore white, which made a stark contrast to his bright blue hair which was pulled half back. When they reached the trellis, the queen was seated in a large silver throne which Lucian was quite sure hadn't been there a moment ago. She soon rose again as Tallia emerged from the castle. Lucian was sure she had never looked more beautiful. Her turquoise eyes sparkled as she walked to the trellis, carrying the bouquet Russett had arranged from the boy's flowers. Her normally loose flowing hair was curled into a crown, wreathed in flowers with blue ribbons trailing down her back. The light turquoise gown she wore shimmered in the sunlight with every step she took, the back trailing far behind her. When she reached the trellis everyone was seated.

The fairy king welcomed them. "Today is indeed a special one. The spring equinox to be so joyously celebrated in the form of a wedding; the beginning of a new step in the walk of life. When earth is in balance with time and nature, everything seems more beautiful. A marriage must likewise be balanced, with love, laughter and life."

He continued for a long time, talking about the joys of marriage and the hardships. Lucian tried to pay attention, but it was such a beautiful day and the scent of flowers was making him feel drowsy and peaceful. When the king held Achilles and Tallia's hands together, he found himself focusing more. "A union of hands, a union of hearts. Achilles Stardust, do you before these witnesses promise to walk through the seasons of life with this woman? To walk through the newness of spring and the harshness of winter? The storms of summer and the harvest of autumn?"

Achilles looked directly into Tallia's eyes and smiled. "I promise."

"Tallia Robinwing, do you before these witnesses promise to walk through the seasons of life with this man? To walk through the newness of spring and the harshness of winter? The storms of summer and the harvest of autumn? To leave behind the name of childhood and take on yourself the name of your husband?"

Tears glittered in Tallia's eyes as she replied, "I promise."

"As there are no objections I pronounce you husband and wife. You may kiss your bride, Achilles," the king said with a smile.

A cheer rose as Achilles kissed Tallia tenderly. They turned as the king announced them and soon people were rising from their seats to congratulate the new couple. Tears were in many girls' eyes and Lucian decided that it must be a girl thing to cry at weddings.

Luncheon was soon served out on the lawn, tables appearing out of nowhere and the chairs that had once been in neat rows, now surrounding them. The friends sat together and chatted cheerfully as they ate. "Doesn't Tallia simply look radiant?" Eleanor asked brightly.

"I love her hair," Allegra agreed. "I'm going to do my hair just like that when I get married."

The girls were soon off and running with the wedding topic; except Moira who sat looking nervously thoughtful. "Are you okay?" Lucian asked her.

"I'm fine," Moira replied, trying to soften the sharpness of her tone with a smile. "Just thinking," she added when Lucian continued to look at her.

"You look upset, that's all," Lucian said.

"That's ridiculous," Moira scoffed, though her cheeks reddened. "Why would I be upset? We just watched a gorgeous wedding and it's a beautiful day."

Lucian couldn't think of a single reason why Moira might be upset about anything. "Alright, I was just concerned."

"You needn't be," Moira retorted. "I'm perfectly fine." She then spent the rest of the meal ignoring him.

A small band of fairies began playing instruments in a soft, romantic tune. Achilles led Tallia to the center of the garden. Lucian never would have believed their gym teacher could be so graceful. The couple seemed to float across the grounds, twirling and dipping as though swayed by the wind. When the song ended and a new one began, other fairies and even some of the older students joined the dance. Calista could be seen speaking happily with her sister. Honoria and Raphael twirled about, taking turns holding Theodora. She giggled as they spun her and held her close.

After another hour of merrymaking, the princes were told it was time to leave. They watched Achilles and Tallia leave in a white phaeton, Tallia waving out behind them. "Where are they going?" a boy asked.

"Well, they certainly aren't going to honeymoon at the academy," Calista replied, though no one seemed to remember her being behind them. "For the next two weeks you won't have physical education and Selena will be running the infirmary in Tallia's absence. I'm sure you'll all miss them."

"We'll definitely miss Tallia," Kaelen agreed when Calista had moved on to the front of the group. "But I'm not so sure about Achilles."

Lucian nodded. He couldn't really say that he'd miss physical education very much. In fact, he probably wouldn't miss it at all. He said goodbye to Moira who merely nodded and walked away, the same slightly sulky expression he'd seen at their first meeting. He sighed. He'd been trying so hard to be a gentleman and get to know her, but she always backed away from him, as though if he knew her, he'd hurt her. The most frustrating part was that he had no idea why she seemed to feel that way. He sighed again.

Would things never work out between them?

It seemed like no time at all before the boys were studying for finals. Tallia and Achilles returned, and physical education classes resumed. They spent most of their evenings enjoying the beautiful sunshine and spring weather while going over pages and pages of notes. They practiced fencing in the yard with sticks rather than their swords as Raphael absolutely forbade the use of their weapons outside of class. In fact, once the swords went into the classroom, they didn't come out until break, if then.

One afternoon after orientation, the boys went out to the stables to practice for their dressage final. Phillipa was coming out quickly just as they were nearing the doors. "Boys, I'm afraid you can't ride right now."

"But we need to practice for the final," Adrian said. "We'll stay out of your way."

"I'm sorry boys, I don't have time to explain, but you cannot ride right now," Phillipa said. Without another word or giving them a chance to ask what was wrong, she was continuing on her way to the castle.

"Let's go see what happened," Kaelen said.

"No," Adrian replied, grabbing Kaelen's sleeve. "She looked really worried. We shouldn't go in."

"Oh come on, we're just going to get our horses," Kaelen argued.

"Adrian's right," George insisted. "We don't know what happened. I think we should go get our books and study for our math final instead."

Kaelen looked ready to continue arguing but Lucian interrupted, "Come on, Kaelen, we'll come back after supper. There will still be enough light for a couple hours of work with the horses."

Reluctantly, Kaelen turned to follow them out. He watched as Tallia, and a few other fairies followed Phillipa to the barn. When Kaelen started to get that curious gleam in his eyes, the others grabbed his arms and steered him into the castle. "I'm sure if it's something that concerns us, Phillipa will tell us tomorrow."

But the boys didn't have to wait that long. When they went to supper, they saw an older boy hobbling through the line on crutches, Tallia carrying a tray for him. He looked absolutely miserable and Lucian had a bad feeling that it wasn't because of the injury to his leg which was tightly bound in a cast.

After dinner, the boys went out to the stables. Phillipa was standing with Diana speaking in low tones. Lucian approached cautiously. "Um, Phillipa?" he said quietly.

She turned to him. "Yes?"

"We, uh, we were wondering if we could practice for our final now, with our horses?" Lucian asked. He was fairly sure she was going to tell him no.

A sad look passed over her face. "Lucian," Phillipa paused. She looked at Diana who touched her arm gently. She then turned back to Lucian and sighed, "Yes, you may, but not in the indoor arena. There was an accident and, well, we haven't been able to remove the body yet." When the boys' eyes widened she continued, "It's not a student. It was his horse. He was practicing for his final too, but took the jump at the wrong moment. There was nothing we could do for Duchess except ease her passing."

"Is the student going to be okay?" Jacobi asked.

"His leg is broken and I imagine his spirit as well, but he will recover both." Phillipa smiled gently. "Now, if you'd like to use the outdoor circle, I can have it set up for you while you get your horses."

"No thanks," Kaelen said suddenly to everyone's surprise. "At least, not for me. I'm going to go talk to the guy. What was his name?"

Diana smiled understandingly. "Rodrick is probably with Tallia in the infirmary. However, I'm not sure that right now he wants company. He is hurting physically and emotionally and needs rest. Of everyone here, I know you understand his pain, but for now, let him rest. Tallia will give him a sleeping potion so that he will have peace tonight. Visit him tomorrow. For now, train for your final. That's the best thing you can do."

Kaelen nodded and followed his friends into the barn. He couldn't resist the urge to look into the indoor arena. Lying against the sand was a pure white mare, an arrow sticking up from her chest. He shuddered, knowing the accident could have been much worse. They could have lost Rodrick too. But he wished that somehow they could have saved the long-legged mare now lying in the sand as though she'd merely decided to take a nap. He went to Lightning's stall and put his tack on before leading him outside to the dressage circle Phillipa had set up.

The boys were quiet as they went through the dressage movements they'd been learning that semester. As the light began to dim, Phillipa called to them, "Alright boys, it's time to go in."

They led their horses back inside. Lucian scrubbed Zephyr down, removing the sheen of sweat glistening on his sides and brushed him for far longer than was necessary to clean his coat. "I know we're not always best friends," he said as he poured oats into Zephyr's trough, "but I love you all the same."

Zephyr whickered softly and nuzzled Lucian's hair. His big brown eyes seemed to say that he loved Lucian too.

"I know boy, I know," Lucian said, rubbing Zephyr's forehead. "I'll see you in the morning."

Kaelen spent a little of each afternoon with Rodrick, trying to help him deal with the sudden loss. "I've done that jump a million times," Rodrick said miserably one afternoon as they gazed out the infirmary window. "I've never missed it. Never. Duchess always knew precisely when to fly. But that afternoon, she seemed bothered. I should have let her rest. I'm the best in my class; I didn't really need the extra work. Maybe I pushed her too hard.

"You can't blame yourself," Kaelen insisted. "It won't make her loss any easier."

Rodrick eyed Kaelen suspiciously. "You're different than I thought you'd be. No offense, but you always seemed a little stuck on yourself."

Kaelen shrugged. "I probably am," he said with a grin. "Anyway, I need to study. Get better soon."

Rodrick merely nodded and continued to look out the window.

Joining the other boys out under their favorite tree, Kaelen studied with the others in preparation for their finals. The coursework certainly hadn't gotten easier over the last year. Had it really been a year already? Soon they'd be going home to their own castles, seeing their parents and doing all the summer things. He'd be able to see Anna and Sarahbeth. Of course, he really didn't look forward to seeing Sarahbeth, she was snobbier than he'd ever been. But Anna was always fun to be around. She'd loved the dresses he'd made the last year. In fact, she had almost seemed disappointed when he didn't come home with any new ones at winter break. So, unbeknownst to any of his peers, he'd secretly asked Gelasia if he could sew another dress. "Whatever for, dear?" she'd asked. "You hardly need one now. I doubt you'll be doing anything to be turned into a girl again."

"My little sister liked the ones I brought home so much that I want to make her another one. I like seeing her smile," Kaelen had replied.

Gelasia had laughed. "Oh Kaelen, you are full of surprises, dear." She'd helped him choose the right material and now, waiting in his trunk, was a lavender gown with silver embroidery. He couldn't wait to see Anna's face when summer came and she'd get a brand new dress to start school with.

"Kaelen? We've asked you the same question twice now," George said, breaking through his thoughts. "Are you listening?"

"Sorry," Kaelen replied. "My mind was elsewhere."

"That was obvious," Adrian retorted. "Thinking of a beautiful young lady with ruby lips, perhaps?"

"Ew! I wouldn't think of my sister that way!" Kaelen exclaimed.

The boys laughed and then returned to their studies.

The finals passed quickly and the day soon came for their final meeting with the princesses for the year. Similar to winter semester, the boys had individual meetings with Calista, this time with their parents so they could discuss the changes that would be occurring the following year. While Alexandra was meeting with Melantha and Allegra, Lucian and Lysander sat in Calista's office. "You've done very well this year," Calista began, smiling at Lucian. "Next year, however will be very different. You will begin your specialty classes which will build the foundation upon which your quest will be built. On Monday and Wednesday, you will have your regular classes with the rest of your classmates. Mathematics, language arts, that sort of class. Tuesday and Thursday will be your specialty classes and Friday will continue to be a day for fine arts. However, even in those classes there will be differences. You will find yourself in much smaller classes as your peers go through different training. Some of your classes may even be one-on-one instruction with your instructor. You may not have that next year, but as the years progress, your coursework will become more individualized. Don't believe for a moment that things are going to get easier for you, Lucian; they are only going to become more challenging. Your class days will become longer as you must fit more courses into the day. I'm sure that you are up to the challenge. You are a very bright boy."

"So, am I going to get my schedule now?" Lucian asked hopefully.

Calista laughed merrily. "Yes, Lucian, I'll be giving you a copy of your schedule and your supply list for next year. I hope you have a wonderful summer. King Lysander, do you have any questions?"

"No, I think you covered everything," Lysander said with a smile.

"Very well, Lucian here's your schedule. Again, have a great summer. Oh, and before I forget," she stood and pinned a small badge to Lucian's chest. "For successful completion of two years at Charming Academy." She smiled as he beamed up at her. "Now, please send Jacobi and his parents in."

When Lucian got to the hall, Adrian was waiting impatiently. "Okay, I want to see if we have any of the same classes. I keep hoping someone will commiserate with me."

Lucian opened his schedule.

Class Schedule

Day	Time	Class	Teacher
Monday, Wednesday	8:00-9:00	History	Clio Stormcloud
	9:00-10:00	Physical Education	Achilles Stardust
	10:00-11:00	Mathematics	Marius Hawkeye
	11:00-12:00	Lunch	
	12:00-1:30	Language Arts	Airlia Willowlimb

	1:30-3:00	Etiquette	Gelasia Stardust
	3:00-4:00	Foreign Language	Lorelei
	4:00-5:00	Orientation	Honoria Peregrine
Tuesday, Thursday	8:00-9:30	Spell Breaking I	Althea
	9:30-11:00	Horsemanship	Phillipa Rosepetal
	11:00-12:00	Lunch	
	12:00-2:00	Double Fencing	Raphael Peregrine
	2:00-4:00	Double Botany	Russett Snapdragon
	4:00-5:30	Dragon Fighting	Vulcan Firebrand
Friday	8:00-9:30	Intermediate Alchemy	Aurelia Sundance
	9:30-11:00	Music	Amadeus Comettail
	11:00-12:00	Lunch	
	12:00-1:30	Art	Stefanos Stormcloud
	1:30-3:00	Language Arts	Airlia Willowlimb
	3:00-4:00	Foreign Language	Lorelei

On Monday evenings, Astronomy will be taught from 8:00-9:30 by Uralia Moonbeam

"Dang, I was hoping you'd have physical education with me Friday afternoon. Ugh! I can't believe I have that on Friday. That's just not fair," Adrian complained.

"It could be worse; I've got foreign language Friday afternoon. Why do I need that?" Lucian asked.

Lysander put a comforting hand on each boy's shoulder. "This is all to help you with your quest. You may not see it now, but I'm sure as you're on your quest, it'll make sense to you why you have these classes."

"Explain amphibian studies to me," Adrian muttered.

Laughing, Lysander led the boys downstairs. "Come on, your princesses are waiting on you. Besides, I'm sure that will probably help you later in spell breaking. You know, using bits of toad and such in your spells."

At the bottom of the stairs, Allegra and Moira were chatting excitedly while Alexandra and Lavinia were discussing something else. When the gentlemen joined them, Alexandra turned and said, "What do you think dear?"

"Well, if I knew what you were talking about I'm sure I could give a very good thought," Lysander said in a gently teasing tone.

"Lavinia was just telling me that she grew up by the ocean and hasn't been to the beach in years. I proposed inviting her and her children to spend a few days with us at the castle on the beach. You and the boys could go camping, we could go shopping," Alexandra explained. "What do you think?"

"Sounds like you've got everything planned beautifully, my love," Lysander said with a smile. "You arrange the details and I'll say yes."

They walked together into the dining hall which was filled with people. The graduation ceremony seemed somehow longer this year. Kaelen watched Rodrick hop across on his crutches to receive his quest, looking somewhat better than he had before. It would be some time before he would be able to begin his quest. His leg was still healing from the breaks. But he was no longer mourning Duchess. His parents had come out soon after the accident with a new horse and had spent a few days nearby to help him begin his way to recovery. He was glad as Calista announced, "Normally, a prince is given only five years to complete his quest. During an unfortunate accident, Rodrick broke his leg and it will be months before it is fully healed. In consideration of this, the fairy council has granted Rodrick an extra year in which to complete his quest in order to allow him the time to heal physically and revitalize his strength. Use that year wisely, Rodrick."

Rodrick nodded and continued back to his seat. His mother took his crutches from him and kissed his cheek.

When the ceremony was over, supper began. Moira had been very quiet and Lucian decided to try once more to engage her in a normal conversation. "So, you and your family will be visiting this summer. Do you like the beach?"

"I don't really know," Moira admitted. "I've never been to the beach. What's it like?"

"Maltisten is beautiful in summer. The ocean surf is aqua blue and the sands are warm and inviting," Lucian began. He painted a picture with words describing his homeland. The more he talked about it, the more he realized he missed it and was looking forward to going back. He described searching for seashells and swimming in the ocean. He talked about the colorful, shimmering sunsets as night fell over the sea. Moira seemed to catch his enthusiasm and asked more questions about Maltisten and Lucian finally felt like he was making headway. "What's Lictthane like?" he asked.

Moira faltered for a moment. She was fine listening to Lucian talk about his home, but she hesitated to speak of her own. Finally, she began describing the hilly plains she'd grown up on. "It's really pretty," she finished, looking away for a moment.

Not wanting to have spoiled yet another conversation, Lucian asked, "Do you know when you'll be coming out?"

Moira shook her head. "No, Mother never tells me the details. She always saves it for a surprise." She smiled. "It's like she thinks of everything as a present. If she were to tell me, I wouldn't like it as much."

Far too soon supper was over and it was time for them to head home. As they were walking outside, Adrian said, "I can't wait to see you this summer! It's going to be just like last summer!"

"I hope so," Lucian said with a smile. "Last summer was awesome."

Just before he got in the carriage with his parents and Allegra, Moira's voice made him turn. She ran up next to him. "Please write to me this summer," she said. Then as though afraid she'd sounded too anxious, she finished, "If you want to that is. You don't have to."

Lucian smiled. "I'll write if you will."

Moira hesitated, then held out her hand. "Deal," she said.

Lucian shook it with a smile and then got in his parents' carriage. This was definitely going to be the best summer ever.

Year 3

Chapter 1

Alexandra had arranged for Lavinia and her family to come in early July. Lysander had told Lucian that he and Adrian could ride out to the beachside castle ahead of the rest. Zephyr and Stardancer seemed to catch the boys' eagerness, racing against the wind towards the beach. As they neared the small summer castle, they slowed the horses. Zephyr tossed his head eagerly. Lysander had always called it their seaside cottage, though Lucian had never seen a cottage with towers and banners anywhere else. It was much smaller than their regular home. It only had fifteen bedrooms and a small dining hall. Lucian was sure that when he completed his quest that his parents would retire out here. Lysander would begin a new garden full of beauty and peace. Alexandra would develop a new sewing room and a music room.

"I don't remember us coming here last year," Adrian said as he looked at the grey sea-stone castle, breaking through Lucian's thoughts.

"We didn't," Lucian replied. "This is our summer retreat. Dad didn't want to spoil it by working so hard. Mom and Allegra came out here for a while."

Upon reaching the castle, the boys dismounted and took their tired horses to the stable. It was refreshingly cool inside. They scrubbed the horses down and brushed them until their coats gleamed. Ensuring they had plenty of grain and water in their troughs and lots of hay covering the ground of their stalls, the boys put away their tack and grabbed their bags before leaving the stable. They walked up to the castle doors and walked in.

"So, where do we stay?" Adrian asked.

"That's the best part of arriving first," Lucian said with a grin. "We get first pick! The only room off-limits is the master bedroom." Lucian dashed down the hallway to his favorite room. It was decorated in greens and blues, reminding him of the ocean surf outside. The best part of the room was the large window looking directly out over the beach. He had the best view in the entire castle. After setting his bag on the bed, he found Adrian standing outside his door, still holding his bag. "Come on," Lucian said. "I'll show you around." He led Adrian through the castle, showing him the rooms and talking about what they normally did. When they got to the bedroom next to Lucian's which had a similar oceanic theme and lovely view, Adrian set down his bag.

Just as he did, they heard Allegra's voice in the hallway. "We can get the best rooms, if the boys haven't stolen them already." She stopped in front of the room Adrian and Lucian were standing in. Her eyes narrowed. "I should have known," she said slowly. Then she shrugged and smiled. "Oh well, there are plenty of other rooms we can stay in. Come along, Moira."

That afternoon, everyone went to the beach. Lucian tried to be content staying in the shallows with Adrian, but the ocean surf seemed to beckon to him. "Go ahead and swim, Lucian," Adrian said understandingly.

Lucian smiled gratefully and stroked out to the deeper water. How he loved to swim! He was good at it too. He remembered the first time he'd ventured into the deeper water, his dad holding his hands and pulling him as Lucian kicked his little legs. He'd never understood Allegra's fear of the water. It was so cool and inviting. He dove under the water, the glass goggles allowing him to see the underwater utopia. Fish darted between rocks and plants. Sunshine rippled through the waves, brightening the ocean floor where shrimp scurried and starfish patiently waited for a meal. He came up for air and then swam back to where Adrian was splashing in the shallows. "You sure you won't go out?" Lucian asked.

"Yeah, I'm sure," Adrian replied.

"Well, at least borrow my goggles and stick your head in the water. You're missing a whole different world," Lucian said eagerly.

"No, really, Lucian, it's okay. I'm much happier with my head above water," Adrian insisted.

Lucian shrugged and then walked up to the beach, shaking the salt water out of his hair. He grabbed his towel and walked to where Allegra and Moira were sitting. He saw Moira looking longingly at the water. "Moira, do you want to go for a swim?" Lucian asked.

"Oh, yes, you must if you want to," Allegra said as Moira looked torn between saying yes and staying where she was. "It's so selfish of me to keep you up here to myself. Please, go swim if you'd like to."

"If you're sure," Moira said, rising slowly.

"Yes, yes, go enjoy the water," Allegra encouraged. "Lucian will keep me company while you're away."

"Here, you can borrow my goggles. Salt water stings horribly," Lucian said, holding them out to her.

Moira took them hesitantly. "Um, how do you use these?" she asked. "I've only swum in fresh water."

Lucian helped her get the goggles on and adjusted them under her ponytail. "There, you're all set," he said kindly.

Smiling, Moira went out into the water. Lucian watched her go and Allegra quickly noticed the look on his face. "So, just how much do you like her?" she teased.

"What?" Lucian asked, blushing to the roots of his hair. "I, I don't like her. I mean, she's nice and all, but…"

"Oh yes, she's very nice," Allegra interrupted impishly. "And she's pretty, and talented…"

"And tall!" Lucian exclaimed miserably. "If I don't grow soon she'll be a foot taller than me."

"Oh rubbish," Allegra scoffed. "You're not that short. She's about five nine right now and you're what, five two? That's only seven inches."

"Easy for you to say," Lucian moaned. "You're five five."

"Yes, and you wouldn't believe how excited Moira was when I reached that at school," Allegra replied. "You'll catch up to her soon."

"I hope so," Lucian sighed. "I have a feeling she's embarrassed by how short I am."

"She's not embarrassed by the fact that you're short, Lucian," Allegra explained. "She's more embarrassed because she's tall. You have to understand, there are now only two girls at school taller than she is. She's eye to eye with some of the shorter fairies. It's hard for her and she gets teased horribly. Every time she grows, even a fraction of an inch, it upsets her."

Lucian thought for a moment. "Well, maybe she's done growing? Yeah, I mean, five nine is really tall for a girl. I bet she won't grow at all anymore."

Allegra just smiled. They sat in silence for a while and then she said. "Moira does like you, you know." When Lucian looked at her, disbelief clear on his face, she continued, "She does. I can tell. I know you can't see it. You're falling for her tricks. I don't know why, but she doesn't want you to know. Truthfully, I'm probably not supposed to know either. But it's true. She likes you probably as much as you like her. Maybe more. You'll see."

Instead of responding, Lucian looked out over the waves. He could see Moira swimming out where he'd been earlier. Part of him felt like he was running out of time. He laughed at himself silently. What was he thinking? There were still a few years of school left, he had plenty of time. Maybe Allegra was right and she was just hiding her feelings. But why?

Lucian's thoughts were again interrupted as Alexandra said it was time to go in for supper. "I'm sure by now Cook has a fabulous meal waiting for us and we know how she hates to let it get cold." Lucian helped gather the towels and baskets they'd brought with them from the castle. He walked with Adrian talking about the campout they'd be going on the next day. As they walked, his only slight disappointment was that no one had remembered that it was his birthday. Granted, he'd had a wonderful time anyway swimming and playing on the beach. He'd even found a few new shells for his collection. But it would have been nice if someone had remembered. Even Alexandra had said nothing and she had never forgotten anyone's birthday before.

On reaching the castle, they quickly put their things away before going into the dining hall. Lucian gasped as he walked in. There were streamers and ribbons everywhere and a huge cake that he was sure Cook had spent all day on sitting in the middle of the table. "Happy birthday, darling," Alexandra said, kissing his cheek. "You didn't think we'd forgotten did you?" she asked mischievously.

"You tricked me," Lucian accused with a smile. He went to his seat and they began eating their supper which was placed wherever it would fit around the large, four-layer cake. Lucian figured that thirty people could probably have each had two good sized slices and there'd still be extra. It was decorated with blue frosting, accented by frosting seashells. On top were fifteen small candles, not yet lit. Even having not tasted it yet, he could tell it was his favorite. Cook never forgot. He could smell the vanilla and lemon which tickled his nose while they ate the rest of their meal. There was laughter and chatting as the night wore on. When the plates were cleared and dessert plates set, Lysander lit the candles. "One for each of your fifteen years. Make a wish, son."

Lucian considered the candles for a short while before blowing them out. As the others cheered and smoke curled around the blackened wicks, he sincerely hoped that his wish would come true.

Early the next morning, Lysander woke Adrian and Lucian so they could head out for their campout. They packed their bags, bows and a quiver of arrows before going to the stables and tacking up. Alexandra was up with them in a dressing gown, her long, red hair curling down about her shoulders. "I hope you boys have a wonderful time. We'll miss you."

"I'm sure you'll find lots to occupy yourself my love," Lysander replied teasingly.

"I never said I wouldn't," Alexandra retorted with a smile. She stood on her tiptoes to kiss him before saying, "Do have a good time."

"We will love," Lysander said. "Enjoy the shops."

She hugged Lucian and even Adrian before waving as they mounted their horses and rode away.

When they were out of sight of the castle, they spurred their horses on to greater speeds. Wind salty with sea air whipped past their faces as they rode down the beach. As they came closer to the spot they'd camped at last summer, Lysander motioned for them to slow down. Zephyr tossed his head willfully. "Hey," Lucian said. "I'd think you'd be tired after that run."

Zephyr snorted impatiently as though to say he wasn't in the least bit tired, though his sides heaved with each breath.

Lucian laughed as they dismounted and tied the horses to a post. They set up camp and went to the beach, spending long hours in the sunshine. Lucian spent some time swimming out in the shallows and farther out. He wore his goggles and searched the ocean floor for seashells. He found several, but the best was finding a rare clam shell. He picked it up and examined it under the water, it was only one half. Cupping it in his hand where it wouldn't get direct sunlight, he swam back to shore.

"Find any good ones?" Lysander asked as Lucian went to the small bag he kept his new seashells in until he could take them home.

"Yeah, I found a sunset clam," Lucian said excitedly.

"Are you sure?" Lysander asked, coming over. He looked into Lucian's cupped hand. "Well, wrap that one twice to keep it out of the sun. Congratulations son, you've been looking for that one for quite a while."

Adrian looked at the shell too. "That's cool. How do you find them?"

"Well, I always look in the water, but sometimes you can find shells washed up on the shore. This one though reacts with sunlight and fades, the colors turning dull. That's why I have to keep it well-wrapped so it'll keep the bright colors."

"I guess I'm never going to find one then," Adrian laughed. "I wouldn't be able to stay underwater to find it!"

In the late afternoon, they left the beach to go to the small woods nearby, bows and quivers ready. As the sun was setting over the aqua waves, they cooked their catches over a fire.

"I'm surprised, Dad," Lucian said at one point. "Normally you catch more."

Lysander laughed. "I'm not perfect, Lucian. Even I miss occasionally." He turned the spit thoughtfully. "Besides," he added with a mischievous note in his voice, "perhaps I was just letting you and Adrian get them."

"Whatever," Adrian laughed. "We're getting pretty good."

"Yes you are," Lysander replied, chuckling. "The fairies have taught you well."

"You too, Dad," Lucian added, not letting Lysander leave himself out. There was a distant expression on the king's face which troubled Lucian. When Lysander looked at him, he tried to search his face, looking desperately for a reason for him to look into the fire the way he had been.

In an instant, Lysander was smiling as usual, removing the expression which concerned Lucian so much. "Ah, my son, I believe you are biased."

He soon turned the conversation to other things, but Lucian couldn't help feeling a bit worried. There was something troubling him. However, he also knew that his father had closed the topic without it ever being brought up.

Morning came and they went back to the woods for some target practice, using old targets from the last summer. Whatever had been bothering Lysander seemed to have taken care of itself, or at least Lucian didn't notice anything unusual. They went swimming at the beach and Lysander showed them how to use their arrows as spears to catch the fish. "It's harder than using a spear, but sometimes you don't have many options," Lysander said as he stopped a fish with seeming ease. "The biggest key is remembering that the water distorts what you see. The fish may look like it's in one spot, but it won't be."

The smell of fish wafted from the fire that night, causing the already hungry stomachs to growl impatiently. At one point, Lysander said, "It's a good thing we'll be shopping for your new list with Mother next week. You've outgrown your pants."

"They are looking a little short. I just wish I had grown more," Lucian said. "I'm going to be the shortest person in my class."

"There's nothing wrong with that," Lysander said kindly.

"Besides, Mithulan is still shorter than you. Or at least, he was before we left for summer break," Adrian pointed out.

"That's not very comforting," Lucian replied grimly. "I've got to be the shortest prince on record."

"No, you're not. There was a prince only a few inches tall," Lysander said.

"Dad, we all know that's just a myth," Lucian argued. "I bet the fairies exaggerated to make the story more interesting."

Again, a slightly distant expression flicked across Lysander's face before he smiled it away. "I suppose that's very true son."

Late that night after Adrian had fallen asleep, Lucian looked at his father. He could tell he wasn't asleep. "Dad?"

"Yes son?" Lysander replied.

Lucian hesitated. "Dad, is there something bothering you?"

"No son, why do you ask?" Lysander said, though Lucian noted he didn't sound as firm as he usually did.

"You just have seemed preoccupied lately. I mean, you're a better shot than I am, but you've been missing a lot the past couple of days. Is something wrong?" Lucian asked.

Lysander was quiet for a while. "I'm getting older, Lucian," he said at length. "My reflexes aren't what they used to be."

"Is that it?" Lucian pressed. He had a feeling his father was hiding something from him. "I mean, Dad, you're not that old."

Lysander chuckled, "Thanks for that assessment, son."

"That's not what I meant, Dad," Lucian said exasperated.

"I know, son," Lysander said seriously. "Don't worry about me. I'm just a bit off my game right now. It's nothing to worry over. We all have those times in life. Now, go to sleep. We'll be getting up early tomorrow to meet the ladies back at the castle. She's a beautiful girl, son."

"Who is?" Lucian asked, trying to act like he didn't know.

"You know who I'm talking about, Lucian. You can't hide your feelings from me," Lysander replied with a laugh.

"She is beautiful," Lucian admitted. "I hope she'll warm up to me soon."

"She seems to be coming around," Lysander said comfortingly.

"Yeah, I guess," Lucian said. "Well, good night, Dad."

"Good night, son," Lysander said, turning back to stare at the shimmering blanket of stars above him.

Late in the morning after getting camp cleaned up and everything packed, they began riding towards the beach where they would be meeting the ladies. When they arrived, Lucian had barely gotten off his horse when Allegra walked up to him and demanded, "Prove it to her, Lucian."

"I missed you too," Lucian teased.

"Lucian Alexander, this is serious," Allegra retorted. "You prove it right now."

"Prove what?" Lucian asked.

"That you're a better swimmer than she is. She won't believe me," Allegra said, pointing to Moira who was standing on the beach, her arms crossed defiantly.

"Well, Allegra, I can't very well jump into the water in my clothes. They'll get ruined," Lucian said calmly. "Besides, why does it matter who's the better swimmer?"

"It matters," Allegra said through clenched teeth, "because I happen to know you're the best swimmer in Maltisten. There's no way she's a better swimmer than you are."

"And just how long have you been arguing about this," Lysander stepped in.

"All morning," Moira replied, also joining the fray. "I'm sure Lucian's a great swimmer, but I'm better than him at everything. I'm the better swimmer."

Lucian felt himself blush. "You are not better than me at everything."

"Really?" Moira asked, her eyebrow rising. "Name one thing you can do better than me."

"I can hunt, shoot, fight," Lucian listed off.

"Those don't count. They're things only boys do anyway," Moira retorted.

"Okay, I'm a better rider," Lucian pointed out.

Moira stammered for a bit. "That doesn't count either. You've, you've been riding longer than I have."

"Well, I've probably been swimming longer too, Moira. I grew up in the water," Lucian replied.

"Children," Lysander said quickly before Moira could say anything, "there's an easier way to determine this. We'll just have a race. Winner is the best swimmer. I'll mark off the distance. Get into your bathing suits."

Chin set at a defiant angle, Moira sneered, "I'll enjoy beating you."

"Try it," Lucian said. He went into one of the little shacks where he could change in privacy. Calista would probably have had a fit if she'd heard speak to Moira that way. In fact, he'd probably deserve whatever punishment the witches gave him for speaking so rudely. But he wasn't going to back down. He'd been swimming as long as he could remember. There was no way a girl born and raised in the country would be able to beat him on his own turf. He wouldn't let her.

They walked to a rock Lysander was standing on near the edge of the water. "Alright, you two, we'll do two lengths. Touch the rock down the way and then back here. First one is the winner. Are you ready?"

"Definitely," Moira replied.

Lucian nodded, but didn't speak. He was focusing on the water.

"Get in position then," Lysander said.

Preparing himself to dive, Lucian listened to the count off and on the word go, dove cleanly into the water. He knew a gentleman would give Moira a head start, but he wasn't feeling much like a gentleman at the moment. Instead, he stroked harder. To his surprise, Moira was matching him stroke for stroke. Despite being impressed, he didn't let it bother him. He kept his focus on the rock ahead of them. He knew if he reached it first, he could get enough speed going to make up for her kickoff. Being as tall as she was, she did have the advantage in a kickoff. He gave a burst of speed, reaching the rock and quickly kicking off and on the return. He couldn't hear Allegra shouting for him on the beach, nor Moira's mother encouraging her. All he could hear were the strokes of his arms and legs and the pounding of his heart. He could tell Moira was gaining on him and he urged his limbs to move faster. He was cutting through the water like it wasn't even there. Just a few more strokes and he would make it to the rock. With a last ditch burst of energy he sped away from Moira and to the rock, ending the race and proclaiming himself the best swimmer.

"We have a winner!" Lysander cried. "Well done, Lucian." He gave Moira a hand up and said, "Well done, Moira, not many people can challenge Lucian like that. You gave a valiant effort."

Moira didn't say anything, but turned to walk over to where her mother was standing on the beach with a towel.

"I'm not sure that was such a good idea, Dad," Lucian said, reflecting on how competitive Moira was.

"Humility hurts sometimes, son," Lysander replied. "Don't worry, she'll get over it soon enough. That was a good race. She nearly had you a couple of times."

Lucian nodded but didn't speak. He walked over to Moira and her mother. "Good job, Moira. You almost caught me."

Moira looked about to say something nasty, but seemed to see her mother and change her mind. In a tone that quavered with unspoken anger she replied with as much of a smile as she could muster, "I'm sure I wouldn't have. You're a very good swimmer, Lucian."

Knowing when it was best to bow out, Lucian nodded and walked over to Allegra who was squealing with delight. "I knew you'd win!" she cried.

"And you never doubted for a second, did you?" Lucian asked.

"Of course not!" Allegra retorted as though the very idea were a crime.

"I just hope this will have been worth it in the end," Lucian said quietly, looking where Moira was now swimming in the water away from the shallows where Lysander, Adrian, Alexandra and Lavinia were splashing. He could tell she was trying to prove to herself that she could swim just as well as Lucian.

Allegra looked thoughtful. "Oh, Lucian, I hadn't even thought of what it might do to your relationship. But I wouldn't worry. I'm sure in many ways she'll respect you more now. You're better than her at something that she's very good at."

"How is that a good thing?" Lucian asked.

"Because this gives you common ground. You're both excellent swimmers. Granted, she'll probably never forgive you for being a better swimmer, but, it's a start," Allegra pointed out.

They stayed at the beach all day and late into the evening, Cook bringing their dinner out to the beach for them. The next morning Lavinia would go home with her children. Alexandra and Lavinia were talking about the shopping they would need to do for their children's school supplies. "Lucian always has such an unusual list," Alexandra said. "This year armor, a lute, fire proof trousers and doublets; the strangest things."

"Oh yes, Adrian's list was quite unusual too, but Moira's list is always so much easier to take care of," Lavinia replied. She continued talking about Moira's school lists and classes.

Lucian saw Moira sitting on her own away from the group and decided to take a chance and go talk to her. Adrian and Allegra were talking near the fire. Lucian knew his best friend would never admit it, but he did like Allegra, more than just "well enough". Surprisingly, Lucian was happy for him. He felt a bit protective of his sister, but also knew that with Adrian as her prince, she'd be just fine. "It's beautiful isn't it?" Lucian asked, looking out over the sunset that was sinking below the crashing waves.

Moira started and looked up. "Yeah, it is," she replied, turning back to the waves.

"Look, I, I just wanted to say, no hard feelings about earlier, right?" Lucian asked.

"Whatever Lucian," Moira said, not bothering to look at him. "You won, fair and square. There's nothing for me to have hard feelings about."

They were silent for a while and Lucian said, "I got something for you while we were out camping."

"You did?" Moira looked at him, a surprised blush creeping into her cheeks.

"Yeah," Lucian replied, reaching into his pocket. He pulled out the small, pinkish orange shell from his pocket. "I wish it was both halves, but I found this while we were swimming the other morning. I thought you might like to have it. You can start your own seashell collection with it. See, it's a type of clam that only lives here in our waters. It's really rare and hard to find. You have to keep it out of the sunlight, or the colors will fade. But if you keep it somewhere it won't get bleached by the sun, it'll stay that bright forever, like a sunset that never ends."

He handed Moira the shell and she looked at it in the fading light. "It's lovely, but don't you want to keep it?"

Lucian waved his hand, "Me? Oh, no. I've already got one." He hoped that she wouldn't be able to tell he was lying. He'd never been able to find that type of shell before.

"Your sister's right about you," Moira said quietly. "You're a terrible liar. You've never found one of these before, have you?" When Lucian blushed and didn't reply, she continued, "So why give it to me?"

Shrugging, Lucian said, "I wanted to. I thought you'd like it since you seem to love the beach so much. It could remind you of the fun you had out here."

For a long moment Moira was quiet. She sniffed after a while and Lucian was fairly sure she was crying. She asked softly, "Why are you so nice to me?" Before Lucian could reply, she got up, walked to the others and said she was going to bed before running to the castle.

"Now what did I do?" Lucian asked himself. He rejoined the others long enough to say he was going to bed too before going into the castle and going to his room. He stared out the window at the beach. Stars were beginning to twinkle in the twilight. It had seemed like the perfect gesture, giving her a seashell he'd always wanted. Now he half-wished he'd kept it for himself and just let her alone.

"So, what did you do to make Moira run off like that?" Lysander asked, causing Lucian to jump. "Sorry I startled you."

"That's okay," Lucian said. "I didn't hear you come in."

"Well, after Moira ran off and you said you were going to bed, we thought perhaps it was time to call it a night," Lysander said gently. "So, what happened?"

"I have no idea," Lucian sighed. "I gave her a seashell."

"Hmm," Lysander said. "Did you say anything to her?"

"I just checked to make sure there were no hard feelings about the race and then gave her the seashell and she started crying," Lucian replied. They were both quiet a moment and Lucian asked, "Dad, do you think she avoids getting to know me because her dad died when she was little? I mean, maybe she's afraid of getting close because she thinks I'll die young or something."

"I can't tell you, son," Lysander said, putting an arm around Lucian's shoulders. "Emotions are difficult to understand, especially when you're dealing with the opposite gender. Perhaps it's that, perhaps it's something else. I'm not the right person to talk to about that."

"Who is?" Lucian asked.

"Moira is the only one who can explain to you what she's feeling," Lysander replied.

"I was afraid you'd say that," Lucian said. He sighed. "Maybe I'm not cut out for this."

Lysander turned so that he and Lucian were looking straight at each other. "Don't say that, Lucian. You can't give up so easily. I know what you're thinking. You've been trying for over two years now to get to know her, but Lucian you're only fifteen. From what I understand, she won't be fifteen until the middle of August. You're both young and this is a hard time for both of you. Life is changing in so many ways, many that you don't understand. You promise me, right here and now that you won't give up; that you won't quit on Moira or on yourself."

There was an urgency in Lysander's eyes that concerned Lucian. "I won't Dad, I won't let you down."

"Don't worry about letting me down. Don't let Moira down," Lysander said gently.

"Dad, are you sure there's nothing bothering you?" Lucian asked.

"I'm fine, son," Lysander said firmly, closing the subject. "Well, I should let you go to bed. Keep your chin up, Lucian. Everything will work out fine, you'll see."

The next morning, Adrian and Lucian rode together back to the family home. They rode slower than they had coming out to the seaside castle. They talked about school starting again and various other little tidbits. "I wish we didn't have to go back. This has been a great break, even with Mom and Moira," Adrian said.

"Adrian, why don't you guys get along?" Lucian asked. "I know there's more than you're telling me. What really came between you?"

Adrian flushed. "I, I don't know what you're talking about. We don't get along because we don't."

"Come on, Adrian," Lucian insisted.

"No, alright," Adrian snapped. "It's none of your business why we don't get along. Why do you need to know?"

"I'm sorry, I'm just," Lucian started, but never finished. Adrian spurred Stardancer to a gallop and rode ahead of him. Zephyr pulled at the rains. "Not this time, boy. I think he needs some space." Lucian sighed, "I just keep screwing things up."

Zephyr snorted at him.

"Gee thanks, Zephyr. That made me feel tons better," Lucian said sarcastically.

Whinnying, Zephyr seemed to be telling him that it wasn't his fault that Lucian was having problems.

Lucian rolled his eyes and let Zephyr speed up to a brisk trot. They arrived at the castle just before the carriage with the others did. He didn't have a chance to really talk to Adrian before they arrived. However, when he did get to the castle, Adrian was acting as though nothing had happened. "I'll miss seeing you," he said.

Surprised, Lucian replied, "Yeah, me too. But it's only for about a month. Then we'll be back at school."

"Yeah," Adrian said. The others pulled up and soon they were busy getting things packed into the other carriage, making sure that no one had forgotten anything and getting the horses taken care of.

"I'll see you in the fall," Lucian told Moira as he helped her get the last of her bags onto the carriage.

"Yeah," Moira said, the same preoccupied tone in her voice that she often had when talking to him. "Bye." She disappeared into the carriage before Lucian could say another word. Adrian waved out the window at him as the carriage disappeared down the drive.

"Well," Alexandra said after a while, "let's get our things put away and then we've got shopping to do. I just know if I wait any longer I'll forget all about it."

Allegra and Lucian sincerely doubted their mother would forget, but knew better than to argue. They grabbed their bags and took them into their rooms. Lucian didn't take long unpacking. Most of it needed washed anyhow. When he pulled out his bag of shells, he put each new one on the shelves with the others he'd gathered over the years. There were starfish, clam shells, sand dollars, and other shells of all colors and shapes.

"Aren't you done yet?" Allegra asked. "Mom's waiting."

"Just be patient," Lucian replied.

"So, where's my new seashell?" Allegra asked with a smile.

Lucian laughed. "I wondered when you'd ask." He motioned for her to come closer. "This one is yours," he said, handing her a small starfish he'd found by the beach their first night out.

"As always, it's lovely," Allegra said. "I'll put it with the rest of my collection." They stopped by her room before going downstairs where Alexandra was indeed waiting. "Where's Dad?" Allegra asked as they started to go outside. "Isn't he coming with us?"

"He has some things to take care of here," Alexandra replied with a smile. "Don't worry, we'll be able to get everything sorted without him. Now, you each have your list, right?"

Allegra assured their mother that they did, while Lucian considered what would keep their father from coming with them. Then again, if he had a choice, he wouldn't go on the shopping trip either. Lucian hated shopping. As they got back in the carriage, Lucian allowed his thoughts to wander. Allegra and Alexandra spoke excitedly the whole way into town. When they arrived, Alexandra took their lists. "Alright, we're going to go to each store one by one. This would have been easier with your father, but oh well. We'll start at Maude's for your paper supplies and then continue our way down the list."

They walked into a shop and while Alexandra spoke with Maude about paper, pencils and pastels, Lucian wandered the store aimlessly. It was filled with the smell of ink and paper. Books lined several shelves and there were rows upon rows of parchment and fresh papers. Pens of every color and variety were stored in wire racks. Art supplies were on one wall where Allegra was pleading with Alexandra while Maude gathered supplies. Lucian breathed in the inky smell of the shop. It was a comforting smell like being at home or near the ocean. It was the smell of a thousand good memories and clever ideas.

Lucian reluctantly left with Alexandra and Allegra. They went to the tailor's shop to pick up some dresses the girls had ordered earlier and order Lucian's new uniforms. "I wondered when I'd see you again, young prince," Tom said as they entered the shop. "I do believe you'll need more than a hem lowered. You've grown."

"Tom, I'm so glad you're in. Lucian needs all sorts of new things for school and I haven't the faintest idea where to look," Alexandra explained. "Of the things he needs to wear, could you tell me what you can do?"

"Well, now, let me see," Tom replied, scanning the list. "I can do the uniforms, of course, and I just received a new shipment of fireproof material, so I can cover that too. The armor I'm afraid is far out of my arena, Your Highness. I would recommend going to Angus for that. He's excellent with armor and such. And of course you'll go to Bill for the new sword. There's none better than Bill. Now, Miss Allegra, if you'll step behind the curtain, we'll fit these gowns to you one last time just to be sure everything's proper."

Allegra eagerly darted back and forth between the curtain and the small stool Tom had her stand on. He fixed all the hems to perfection and fluffed the skirts for her. As she spun around in a buttery yellow gown, Gabriella was taking Lucian's measurements. She disappeared as soon as she had finished and Allegra looked up at Lucian. "Well, how do I look?"

"Like a little sister," Lucian teased.

Smacking him while Alexandra wasn't looking Allegra said, "That's not what I meant. I'm serious."

Lucian laughed, "You look beautiful. Adrian won't know what hit him."

Blushing, Allegra smiled. "You think so?"

"Unless he goes blind in the next few weeks," Lucian replied with a smile.

"Alright you two, let's go. We've still got lots of stops before lunchtime. Thanks again, Tom," Alexandra said with a smile.

"As always, it was a pleasure," Tom replied, bowing them from his shop.

Shop after shop they went in and out, each time with more bags and packages to add to their carriage. The last stop was Lucian's armor. They walked into the steaming blacksmith's shop. It was miserably hot and Lucian wished he could go back outside. A great bear of a man walked out from a back room. He had bushy eyebrows and a scraggly beard and a booming, deep voice as he said, "Well, Queen Alexandra, what a pleasant surprise. What can I do for you?"

"I've been told that you are excellent with armor. Lucian needs a set of armor for school," Alexandra replied.

"Well then, lad, come up here please," the blacksmith commanded. Lucian obeyed quickly. Angus was intimidating, but as he took measurements and asked questions, Lucian soon discovered that despite his gruff appearance, he was just as kind and gentle as Tom. "For someone as young as you, I'll do a special armor. It'll be loose fitted so you have room to grow this year. I'll also use a light weight metal which will be easier for you to wear and carry. But have no fear; my metals are always tough as dragon scales." He discussed some particulars with Alexandra before saying, "Enjoy the rest of your afternoon."

Finished with their shopping, Alexandra treated the children to lunch at a small, open air diner. They talked about school and everything that would be going on. "I do hope you'll both continue to write home as often as you have in the past. It's always so nice to receive your letters," Alexandra said.

"Only if you keep replying," Allegra replied. "I can't wait for the dressage tournament next weekend! Three weeks of competing and I've been practicing extra so that I can do really, really well. Clarissa and the twins will be there too. Moira even said she'd come to cheer us on," she added with a significant look at Lucian. Lucian pretended not to notice, though he could feel his face warming and it had nothing to do with the sunlight.

Alexandra's face fell. "Yes, about the tournament. Well, your father won't be able to make it dear."

"What?" Allegra exclaimed. "Why? He can't miss it! He's never missed a competition before. He promised! I can't go without him."

"Don't be silly, dear," Alexandra said, trying to smile, "of course you can go. Your father just needs some rest. Lucian and I will be there though."

"Then I'm not going," Allegra pouted. "It's just not the same if Dad's not there. He's always there. Always."

"Darling, we've already arranged everything for it. We'll be taking you to the tournament and at the end you and I will take Lucian to school. You'll have a whole week to tell Dad all about it," Alexandra explained.

"I'm not going," Allegra said stubbornly. "It wouldn't be right."

"Please, Allegra, you have to go," Alexandra pleaded. "He would be so disappointed if you didn't. This is hard enough on him as it is. Please don't make it harder by being so stubborn. He would want you to go and do your best just the same as if he could be there. Please, don't say anything to him and don't give up just because he won't be there. Please, Allegra."

It took some more convincing, but Allegra relented and the next weekend they were packing their largest carriage with all of Lucian's things as well as everything that Allegra and Alexandra would need for their time in Altheirian. They were almost ready to go when Lysander came out with a packed bag and set it with the others. A silent conversation passed between king and queen while Allegra and Lucian watched. For a while, they weren't sure who was winning until Lysander said quietly, "I've never missed a competition. I'm certainly not going to start now."

Alexandra sighed and allowed him to hand her into the carriage where Lucian and Allegra were already sitting, trying to pretend that they hadn't noticed anything.

As she opened her mouth to say something, Lysander interrupted with a smile, "You can say I told you so later."

Unable to stop herself, Alexandra laughed and leaned her head against his shoulder as the carriage pulled out of the drive. The travel time wasn't long and the journey was filled with cheerful chatter about the tournament. Lysander and Alexandra were sure that Allegra would sweep the competition easily while Allegra modestly argued that there were others just as talented as she was.

Upon arriving, they went through the procedures of having Allegra and Sunset Rose checked in. A veterinarian went over Sunset Rose to make sure she was in perfect health before they could put her in a stall. A judge looked over all the tack to make sure it was within regulation. He finally said, "Everything looks good, Princess Allegra. You and your family can go to your lodgings and then be back here at six o'clock sharp for the opening competition. That's how we'll determine where you'll start out."

"Yes, sir," Allegra replied, a slight note of nervousness in her voice. The family then left in their carriage to a nearby inn. The inn was full of women, girls and their families all in the area for the tournament.

Soon they saw Clarissa and the twins. "Oh, you made it!" Leticia said as Allegra gave each of them hugs. "We were hoping to see you soon."

"Thanks. Have you seen Moira?" Allegra asked. "She told me she was going to try to come to cheer us on."

"I haven't," Clarissa said. "But, if she doesn't make it we'll still have Eleanor."

"I thought you were competing too," Allegra said, turning to Eleanor.

"Oh, no. I'm pretty good at dressage, but not like Leticia. Besides, it would be awful competing against her. We decided early on that we would never go into the same things so that we wouldn't have to compete against each other for anything. No, I'm a jumper instead," she added with a conspiratorial smile. "Unfortunately only boys are allowed to compete in jumping. They think it's too dangerous for girls."

"What do your parents think?" Lucian asked.

"Oh, Daddy's the one who taught me," Eleanor replied. "Mother didn't really approve, but I told them I didn't want to do dressage so that Leticia and I wouldn't be competing against each other. He's been trying to get a ladies' division started, but it's slow going. Perhaps someday, but for now, I'll just stick to my art competitions."

"You're very good there," Clarissa said kindly.

The group of friends was soon joined by their parents and it was decided that they would have lunch together after Allegra's family had a chance to get situated in their rooms. As Lucian ate, he was pretty sure that when George and Jacobi found out that he spent three weeks with their princesses that they were going to be pretty jealous. In talking to the girls, he realized that none of them had informed their princes about the competition. "I couldn't do that to him when I'm not sure he'd be able to come. I'm sure he wants to spend time with his family," Clarissa had said when Lucian asked.

"I'm not going to be competing anyway," Eleanor had added.

Leticia hadn't responded, but Lucian was sure that she and Nathan weren't on writing terms. Even if they were, Lucian didn't want to spend three weeks with that slime and he was sure from Leticia's expression that she didn't need him ruining her concentration.

Two weeks into the competition, Lucian had a secret that no one else knew. He had written to George and Jacobi and they were both going to come for the final week of the competition. Lucian had told them not to say anything to their princesses and he wouldn't tell either. So far, Moira hadn't shown up at all. While Allegra was warming up with Sunset Rose one afternoon, Lucian went to one of the small shops near the tournament. Allegra, Clarissa and Leticia were all competing together as was Esmé. The three friends were working hard to stay ahead of Esmé, but it was difficult. She was very gifted and had a wonderful horse. At the moment, Esmé was in the lead followed by Allegra and Leticia. Clarissa was farther behind. In all honesty, Lucian was afraid that if Jacobi didn't arrive soon, he wouldn't get to see Clarissa compete at all.

He cleared his thoughts as he looked at the trinkets being sold. His eyes fell on a small necklace with a tiny green colored pendant. It would go perfectly with Allegra's favorite hunter green riding habit. The shopkeeper followed his gaze and said kindly, "Those are always a favorite amongst dressage riders. If there's a special lady competing out there, you may want to get that for her."

"My sister would like it," Lucian replied. "But, I think I'll keep looking for a while."

Later that evening, Lucian was sitting with Eleanor in the stands watching the competition. Clarissa was in the ring at the moment. She was wearing a deep violet riding habit which created quite the contrast against her silvery dappled gelding. She was taking the course flawlessly. Just a few more turns. She glanced at the stands and her eyes widened. Lucian turned to follow her gaze and smiled. Jacobi was standing with a bright smile and single rose. Turning back to Clarissa in the ring, Lucian could see that she wasn't allowing him to break her concentration, but a trace of a smile and blush was evident on her face.

"You wouldn't have had anything to do with that now, would you?" Eleanor asked in a teasing tone as Jacobi worked his way to where they were sitting and the stands erupted in applause as Clarissa and Brilliancy finished the course and took a final bow before exiting the ring.

"Me?" Lucian asked innocently.

"Yes, you, Prince Lucian," Eleanor said with a laugh.

Lucian just shrugged as Esmé rode into the ring on Midas. He was sincerely hoping that she would do something horribly wrong.

When the day was over, the standings had changed so that Esmé and Leticia were tied. Allegra was just behind them with Clarissa holding sixth place. For the next two days there wouldn't be any competitions so that the top ten horses and riders could prepare their final programs to determine the overall winner in each division. George arrived at the inn just as they were getting ready to call it an evening. "Now, why exactly didn't you tell me that you and your sister would be this close to Rendorlin?"

Eleanor sputtered for a while before Leticia said, "We simply didn't think you'd want to come when she's not competing. It wasn't that she was keeping secrets from you."

George smiled broadly. "Well, I'm here to keep my princess company and cheer for her sister. Besides, I had to get away from my sisters. They're driving me batty!" Everyone laughed and he looked at Eleanor, "I've got something for you."

Eleanor blushed deeply as George handed her a small box. She opened it to find a charm bracelet and smiled as George put it around her wrist. "Thank you, George. It's lovely."

Leticia looked like she was about to go upstairs and George stopped her. "Not so fast, the champion needs a gift too."

It was Leticia's turn to blush as George pulled a second box out of his pocket. "I asked my mom what kind of things you ladies are allowed to wear when you're competing and she said that girls love hairnets. Hopefully this will work out nicely for you."

Pulling out a glittering gold hairnet decorated with small blue stones she gasped, "How could you possibly have known that it would match my habit?"

Suddenly all the girls turned on Lucian at once. "You little sneak," Clarissa chided teasingly. "You told them didn't you?"

Before Lucian could attempt to deny it, George said, "Well, I suppose we could go home."

"If that's what they want," Jacobi added with a smile.

"No!" the girls said at once.

It was the final day of the tournament. Clarissa was wearing her violet riding habit and rubbing Brilliancy down one last time to make sure his coat gleamed, Jacobi talking to her in confident tones. Leticia was standing nervously in her blue habit with Eleanor and George near Moonbeam, her hair pulled back in the hairnet George had given her. Lucian could see Esmé standing with Midas, a servant polishing the horse's tack one final time while she made loud comments about how easy it would be to win the competition. Allegra was nervously fiddling with the skirt of her hunter green riding habit. Sunset Rose gleamed, her fiery coat shining golden-red in the sunshine. "If I mess up today…"

"You won't mess up," Lucian said confidently.

"If I mess up, cover Dad's eyes so he doesn't see it," Allegra said.

"Allegra, you've been doing near perfect the whole time. Don't worry so much, you'll do great. And whether you get first or last, Mom and Dad will both be proud of you," Lucian insisted.

Allegra nodded but didn't speak. She suddenly looked a little green. "I think I'm going to be sick," she moaned.

"Breathe," Lucian said. He modeled deep, calming breaths and she breathed with him, the green tinge around her lips leaving slowly, though she was still pale.

"I don't think I can do this," Allegra admitted quietly.

"Yes you can," Lucian replied, "and this will help." He pulled from his pocket the gleaming pendant. As Allegra sputtered and tried to find words, he continued, "Consider it a good luck charm. I was going to save it for the end of the competition, but I think you could use it now."

The judges told them to line up and Allegra smiled nervously at Lucian. "Well, this is it."

Just as they were about to leave, Moira and Adrian came running up. "Don't line up yet!" Moira called to her and jumped Allegra with a hug. "Sorry we're so late. Mom's been sick for the last week and a half and we couldn't get away until today."

"It's alright," Allegra said, suddenly looking a million times better. "I'm glad you could make it."

"Good luck out there, Allegra," Adrian said with a smile.

Allegra blushed. "Thanks. Now, you guys get out of here so I can go get where I'm supposed to be."

Moira, Adrian and Lucian went up to where all the parents were sitting and sat with Jacobi, George and Eleanor. They watched nervously as the competitors went through their programs. Esmé went first and, to their glee, made a few mistakes. "I hope those were big enough to lose her major points," Lucian whispered as a rider they didn't know entered the ring. "Right now she still has a pretty good lead. Our girls are going to have to ride perfectly."

Soon Clarissa was in the ring. It seemed to be going perfect until the middle when Brilliancy started limping and she stopped and dismounted. They could see tears in her eyes as she picked up Brilliancy's hoof to pick out a small, jagged stone. She got back on Brilliancy and finished the program, but she knew, as did her friends, that she had lost the competition.

Leticia rode out after her and had a flawless program. "This will put her ahead of Esmé for sure," Lucian said.

The last rider was Allegra. Lucian watched with bated breath as Allegra went through her routine. Even though Lucian had seen it several times over the last couple of days, he was nervous for her. He kept his eye on every turn and every move, looking for the slightest flaw. When she finished, he cheered more than anyone. The program had gone perfectly. It was going to be between Leticia and Allegra. Esmé would probably come in third. Clarissa, he feared, wouldn't place at all.

That evening at dinner, the families all celebrated their ladies' performances. Leticia had taken first followed closely by Allegra. Clarissa had surprised everyone by receiving best horsewoman of the competition, though she hadn't placed. "Not many riders would have stopped mid-program to help their horse," the judge had said as he handed her a bouquet of roses and small trophy. Perhaps the best news had been when Esmé had been disqualified for cheating. Another rider had turned her in for putting the stone in Brilliancy's hoof. Someone else had heard her complaining about putting it in the wrong horse's hoof. She'd been trying to sabotage Leticia's horse. Since there were two witnesses, the judges had stripped Esmé of third place and banned her from competitions for two years.

King Julian, Leticia's father, suddenly stood. "I propose a toast to our ladies, for being the best horsewomen in all of Sanalbereth."

"And to our princes, for being the best support we had," Leticia added, also standing.

Lucian couldn't help smiling as everyone toasted and finished their meal together. He was sad summer was ending, but looked forward to a new school year with his friends.

Chapter 2

When classes started again, the boys waited impatiently for Tuesday afternoon when they would have their first dragon fighting class. Monday seemed intolerably long and Tuesday also seemed to drag. Their first class was spell breaking with Althea. The class was held in a small classroom directly in front of the witches' hovel. In fact, there was a door leading from the classroom straight into their garden. The room was filled with cauldrons, dead animals in jars of formula, dried and drying herbs and plants. The room was dank and dark and smelled musty, yet there was a hidden power in the room, one that made many of the boys feel nervous. "Good morning," Althea said calmly as the boys sat down. "I am Althea, though some of you already know me." Her eyes seemed to linger on boys who had unfortunately been punished by her at one point or other. "In this class I will teach you the basics of spell casting and, of course, spell breaking. You will learn the art of healing and power to destroy. A Prince Charming faces many dangers before finding his true love. He must deal with both good and evil. To face these dangers, a prince must be always on his guard and needs to have every possible advantage. That is the purpose of this class. To begin with, these are your textbooks." Althea raised her arms and stacks of books floated through the air, landing on each prince's desk. "Tonight, you will need to read chapter one."

A boy opened his book and gasped, "Chapter one is over fifty pages!"

Althea turned to look at him with a flash of a smile. "I never said the assignment would be easy. It is however important that you read carefully. You will be expected to know it well enough for a class discussion Thursday. For now, we will be discussing what you already know. Who can tell me the difference between fairy magic and the magic held by the Sisters?"

Kaelen raised his hand and was called on. "Fairy magic is less powerful. It can't undo what you or one of your sisters has done."

"Very good, Kaelen," Althea said. "Anyone else?"

Lucian raised his hand and waited for Althea to call on him. "Well, I think the fairy magic only has specific things it can be used for. Even in anger, the fairies don't use their magic, so I guess their magic would only be able to do things that are constructive or helpful, not destructive."

"An excellent observation, Lucian," Althea replied. "The magic of the fairies is indeed limited to certain abilities. They cannot destroy, though in times of anger many of their wands have been seen to spark or smoke. That is part of why the Sisters are here as the disciplinary arm. Our magic is not restricted to helping. We have the ability to harm as well.

"Another difference is how the magic is created. In one aspect, fairy magic is more powerful because it does not need an incantation. All magic performed by a witch or warlock has an incantation, whether or not the incantation is spoken. This is something that can hinder a witch, so if you should chance to have one on your quest, keep that in mind. You have a few seconds head start. And I do mean, a very few," Althea added. She called on a boy raising his hand.

"How do you know if a person is a witch or not?" he asked.

Althea smiled. "It is nearly impossible to tell merely by looking at someone whether or not they have magic powers. However, in reading chapter one, you will be able to begin the power of discernment. For example, all witches and warlocks have some sort of talisman in which their power is stored. For example, my crown holds the powers of the four elements plus my own unique powers. Without the crown, I would be on an even playing field as any mortal. I would have no magic to assist me. Determining where a witch's power is stored can be very difficult. It is sometimes a mere trinket that seems of little or no value that they store the magic in. In fact, it is often something of little value so as not to be suspected."

The class continued on and at the end of it, the boys walked outside to the stables for horsemanship. Phillipa greeted them as usual and they continued on in their lessons as they always had. They went to lunch and after that went to fencing. As usual, Raphael met them at the door. After an hour of fencing, Raphael dismissed everyone except Lucian. When the others had gone, he turned to Lucian and said, "I suppose you're wondering why you're the only student in here."

"Yeah," Lucian admitted.

"You are an excellent swordsman, Lucian. One of the best I've ever worked with, if not the best," Raphael began.

"Thank you," Lucian said, wondering what this had to do with him being the only student.

Raphael held up a hand. "Let me finish. You are very talented. However, you are also, unfortunately, very left-handed. For the safety of the other students I've requested that you be in this class by yourself."

Lucian didn't like where this was going. "What do you mean?" he asked.

"It's time, Lucian, for you to learn to fight right-handed. For the next two years, longer if necessary, you'll have double fencing and the second half will be right-handed instruction.

Lucian's heart plummeted to his shoes. "Oh," he said.

"Don't worry, Lucian," Raphael said confidently. "As talented as you are, I'm sure you'll take to right-handed fencing like a fish to water. Now, en garde!"

It was clear by the end of the hour that whatever his skill with his left hand, it didn't transfer to his right. He dropped the sword several times, hearing its echoing clang against the floor in the near-empty room. He swiped in all the wrong direction several times and wondered bitterly how he'd ever managed to block Kaelen during their first year.

"Well, that wasn't too bad," Raphael said at the end of class. Lucian knew he was just trying to make him feel better, but it didn't work.

"That was awful," Lucian moaned.

"Cheer up lad," Raphael replied heartily. "Today was just a test run, to see where you are. Now I can truly fit the instruction to best fit your needs. Why, in no time at all, this will feel completely natural. Now, off to your next class."

Lucian trudged to the greenhouse meeting Adrian on the way. "You have no idea how disgusting toads are," Adrian said with his nose wrinkled.

"Nice to see you too," Lucian teased.

"How was fencing?" Adrian asked.

"Terrible," Lucian replied. "He's trying to teach me right-handed."

"Who else is with you?" Adrian asked.

"For their own safety, no one. I'm in class by myself," Lucian said bitterly.

"Ouch," Adrian said. "If it makes you feel any better, I'm the only person in amphibian studies. And trust me, you don't want to be alone with Salvador Mottleback. He's the most boring fairy alive and looks like he's coated in moldy mud."

Lucian laughed as they walked into the greenhouse. Russett greeted them as always. The class seemed to fly by and then about half the students were dismissed. Jacobi, George and several others waited for Russett to continue their instruction. "Alright, gentlemen," he said as the last straggler left, "you boys are in here to learn about magic seeds. Most of the plants we'll study are quite harmless, but some won't be. So, we'll be studying plant safety this week."

The class seemed to drag until dragon fighting. Lucian was sure most of it was that the boys were so excited about their new class. Some of it may also have been the fact that they'd studied plant safety the first week of every year at Charming Academy and as far as Lucian could tell, the lecture hadn't changed in the last three years. As the boys walked into the arena-like classroom, Vulcan Firebrand was standing in the pit. "Come to the front row and have a seat, lads," he said. When everyone had taken a seat, Vulcan got things started. "Dragon fighting is a very serious matter. Any horseplay or tomfoolery will be severely punished. There's no room for it in my classroom and I'll not tolerate it. Am I clearly understood?"

"Yes, sir," the boys replied.

Vulcan eyed all of them with fiery orange eyes. "Good. Now, understand that in this class, you are not actually in any serious danger. However, if you let your guard slip while fighting a dragon, it may well be the last thing you ever do. This class will prepare you in body and mind to take on the dragons that may or may not be in your future quests."

As though on cue, an enormous dragon entered through a gate at the other end of the classroom. It seemed to eye each boy through yellow-orange reptilian eyes while its green scales shimmered in the sunlight pouring through the windows. Smoked curled from its nostrils and its fangs glistened. "A pitiful lot this one. May I eat them, Vulcan?"

The boys jaws dropped as Vulcan replied, "No, Draconus, you can't eat the students. They have to be taught."

"Pity," Draconus said. "They look tasty and I've not had supper yet. Except for that one," he continued looking scornfully at Adrian. "Looks rather sick doesn't he? All that green."

"I warned you already about that, Draconus," Vulcan barked.

The dragon snickered, "So sorry, couldn't resist."

"I look green?" Adrian whispered to Lucian.

Lucian shrugged as one of the other boys squeaked, "It talks!"

Draconus rolled his eyes. "Three thousand years I've been at this place, teaching these princelings and every single year they say the same thing. 'It talks!'" he mimicked. "No wonder my brothers eat them. Highly unoriginal, the whole lot of them. Of course I can talk, young princeling. All dragons can talk."

"But dragons only speak their own language," Kaelen retorted. "Lorelei said so."

Flames burst from Draconus' mouth as he laughed. "You believe that fish? It's true that most dragons only speak in our tongue. It's hardly worth the effort of learning the languages of your prey. Then you become attached to it and mother always says you shouldn't play with your food." Draconus looked hungrily at Kaelen. "However, since I owe Vulcan my life, I've given up the taste of men. Cattle taste so much better; especially rare and still mooing." He snickered again as he licked his lips with a forked tongue. "As I have to be able to assist in training you I must be able to speak to you. And since you butcher my own language, it was less painful to learn your rather vulgar tongue."

"We're not that bad," Kaelen snapped, his pride wounded and several boys nodded, sharing the sentiment.

"Are you sure I can't eat that one? I'd even give him a head start, make it sporting," Draconus hissed hungrily.

"Yes I'm sure you can't eat him," Vulcan replied, as though this was an argument they'd had several times over the last few thousand years. "Kaelen, even the most skilled of linguists trip over Dragon. We lack the forked tongues that aid in proper pronunciation." Turning to the rest of the class, he continued, "As Draconus said, he has been with the school three thousand years. He will do most of the instruction in this class as he, being a dragon, can best prepare you for the encounters you will face. I would advise all of you to take note of what he says."

Draconus seemed to smile and said, "Right then, shall we begin, little princelings?" For the rest of the class, Draconus droned on and on about the different types of dragons, the history of dragons and anything else that came to mind concerning dragons. He didn't allow the boys to ask questions and didn't even seem to need to stop for breath. It was the most painfully boring hour and a half the boys had ever sat through.

"And we didn't even get to try fighting him!" Kaelen complained as they walked to supper. "Talking isn't going to prepare us for anything."

"You're just mad because he wanted to eat you," George said teasingly.

"He's got a point though," Adrian admitted. "If all we do is lecture, and very biased lecture at that, we'll never learn anything."

"I suppose we'll learn their weakness," Lucian said with a grin.

"And what might that be?" Kaelen asked.

"Vanity," Lucian replied simply. "He's so absorbed in himself and dragons as a race that it would be to our advantage to use that against him. Other dragons are probably very similar."

"Well look who knows so much," Kaelen said bitterly.

"Oh come off it, Kaelen." Jacobi rolled his eyes. "You've been like this all day. What's eating you?"

"Nothing," Kaelen muttered.

They went to supper and were surprisingly quiet throughout the meal. When Lucian arrived at his room, he got busy doing his homework. He tried to assess what would take the longest and decided it would definitely be spell-breaking. As Rusty hopped onto the bed next to Lucian, he scratched behind his ears as he read the first chapter. Whoever wrote it certainly didn't want to make it interesting. The content of the pages were as dry as the book itself. When Lucian caught himself drowsing for the third time, he shoved the book aside and got out the homework from the other day that he hadn't finished yet. He noticed Rusty looking outside wistfully. "What is it boy?"

Rusty whined and looked out the window.

Lucian went to the window and tried to find whatever it was Rusty was looking at. "I'm still not getting it, boy. What do you want?"

Rusty seemed to roll his eyes and walked over to the door and started scratching it with his paw.

"I wish you could just tell me that you wanted to go outside," Lucian said, feeling exasperated.

Rusty woofed as the two walked downstairs. They got out into the yard. It was late evening. Crickets were chirping as Rusty loped around the yard and came back with a stick. Lucian laughed as he threw it as far as he could while Rusty chased after it. He shielded his eyes from the evening sunshine. The sun slowly sank towards the horizon and Lucian whistled for Rusty. "I know you're having fun, but I've got to finish my homework before it gets too late."

Rusty whimpered and turned his big brown eyes at Lucian.

"That's not going to work," Lucian held out, though he knew that Rusty knew he'd give in eventually. "Oh, alright, but only five more minutes." He threw the stick as hard as he could, watching it fly through the air. Rusty barked happily and continued to go after the stick. Lucian could see stars beginning to twinkle in the darkest parts of the sky. There would still be sunlight for a while. Long enough to finish the homework due the next day and still get to bed at a reasonable hour. When the five minutes were up, he patted Rusty's head. "It's time to go in now. And don't give me that look; it's not going to work a second time."

Rusty woofed and panted as they walked back up to Lucian's room. As soon as Lucian opened the door, Rusty made a beeline for his comfortable bed in the corner.

Lucian just laughed and shook his head. He took his books and papers back to his desk and got back to work.

By the time Friday rolled around, every third year student hated dragon fighting and thought Draconus would do well at a barbeque as the main course. "We've only been in two days and in that time there hasn't been a single fight. He just sits there talking the whole time. We can't even ask questions because if we raise our hands he ignores us," George complained as they sat at breakfast Friday morning.

"Just be glad that none of us have to deal with him again for five whole days," Lucian said. He couldn't help agreeing with his friends. The class had been a waste. He was sure that Donovan must have been joking when he said dragon fighting was his favorite class. How could anyone enjoy listening to Draconus, nicknamed rather unaffectionately Dronecus by the boys, for an hour and half?

"I can't wait until we actually get to use weapons in that class," Kaelen said through grit teeth. "I'd like to shish kabob him."

"I don't think it'll be that easy," Adrian groaned.

They continued chatting about other things until it was time to go to their first class of the day. Their arts classes went by quickly and soon they were each separating to go to their Friday afternoon special course. Lucian and George walked out to the gazebo for foreign language. They were the only two in that class.

When they arrived, Lorelei was sunning herself on a rock in the middle of the lake. "Oh, good afternoon boys," she called. "Have a seat." She dove into the water and swam to the large rock inside the gazebo which she sat on during instruction. "Well, you boys are the lucky two. We will be doing intensive, in-depth study of Dragon. Then perhaps you can teach that lizard some manners," she said with a steely glance at the castle.

"Um, Lorelei, why do you and Draconus hate each other so much?" George asked tentatively.

"I have no idea what you're talking about," Lorelei replied with a dismissive wave of her hand. "Now, Dragon is a particularly difficult language to learn because of the forked tongue. Obviously I'm not going to split your tongues, but I can teach you a few tricks to help you properly pronounce the words in three different dialects of Dragon; Eastern, Sea Serpent, and Common." She said the last with a slight giggle which gave George and Lucian every reason to believe that Draconus fell in the last category. "Let's begin with the trill, shall we?"

For the rest of the hour, George and Lucian trilled. Lorelei would stop them and demonstrate before making them start again.

"How are you supposed to trill 'l'?" George asked in frustration as they walked back to the castle. As they got closer, they could hear a heated argument between Achilles and Tallia.

"You nearly drowned him," Tallia shrieked.

"What was I supposed to do? The boy has to learn to swim," Achilles argued. "He wouldn't get in on his own."

"So you thought it'd be good idea to just toss him in at the deepest end of the pool? Do you even use your brain?" Tallia demanded.

Achilles was sputtering as Calista came outside. "Perhaps you'd best finish this discussion later. Tallia," she continued as each blushed and Achilles stormed off, "how is he?"

"Still in shock. His color is returning to normal; well as normal as it can be," Tallia replied.

George and Lucian walked up the stairs after rounding the corner. Calista saw them and said to Tallia, "Good, go make sure everything else is alright."

"It's Adrian isn't it?" Lucian asked.

"How long have you been listening?" Calista asked calmly. Tallia stood still, suddenly looking as though she'd been caught saying something she shouldn't have said.

"We heard shouting as we were coming back from foreign language," George replied.

"Yes, it's Adrian. You can come up with me and see him," Tallia said. She nodded to Calista and the boys followed her inside.

When they arrived at the infirmary, they found Adrian sitting on a bed, his teeth chattering. "He tried to kill me," Adrian said as they sat on the bed across from him. "They want me to learn how to swim. I can't swim. Tell them I can't swim, Lucian." Panic showed in Adrian's eyes as he looked at Lucian.

"Well, this must be part of your quest," George said in an effort to be reassuring. "You'll figure it out."

"Well, I quit then, because the only person who hates water more than me is Allegra and I doubt she'll take kindly to being told we have to swim somewhere," Adrian retorted miserably.

"That's ridiculous," Calista said from behind them. The boys all jumped and turned to look at her. "I'll not hear you mention quitting again, Adrian. You have far too much potential for such a poor attitude. However, as we were unaware of how far behind you are, Achilles will be modifying your lessons. Don't worry. I'm sure you'll be a fine swimmer. Now, why don't you and George head to supper? I need to speak with Lucian for a moment."

The two looked at Tallia. "Yes, you can go silly," she replied with a smile. "You'll be fine, Adrian."

They left and Calista turned to Lucian. "You didn't answer my question earlier. How long were you listening?"

Lucian took a deep breath. "Long enough to know there's something wrong with Adrian's color," Lucian said.

"Why do you say that?" Calista asked.

"Draconus has mentioned Adrian's color every day in class. And then Tallia said his color was as normal as it could be. What's going on?" Lucian demanded.

Calista looked thoughtful. "You're going to miss supper if you don't hurry," she said at length. "Run along." Without another word, she left the room, leaving Lucian alone and feeling mutinous. Why did people keep brushing him off?

When Lucian got to supper, he took a good look at Adrian. He looked perfectly normal. His hair was messy as usual, his green eyes sparkled and laughed as he spoke, he still had the same dimpled smile. Lucian decided he must have heard Tallia wrong. *And Draconus?* a nagging voice in his head asked. *Well, Draconus is a dragon. He probably sees things differently than we do.* However, soon Lucian's thoughts were replaced by the conversation flowing around him and their laughter and chatter made him forget what he had been worried about.

It did not take long for the boys to get into a regular routine. By September, they were well used to their classes; though Adrian still dreaded going to swimming Friday afternoons.

Dragon fighting had become more tedious than ever. Even after a month, they were still only doing lecture. Finally, one Thursday afternoon, Kaelen snapped. "This is a waste of time," he said, rising from his seat.

Adrian was desperately trying to pull him down by his arm as Draconus turned his yellow-orange gaze towards them. "I beg your pardon?"

"You're such a joke!" Kaelen shouted. "You hide behind stupid lectures instead of letting us fight you. If you're so wonderful and unbeatable, why don't you prove it?"

"I don't have time for distractions," Draconus drawled lazily turning away. "Now as I was saying…"

"You're afraid," Kaelen accused. "You're nothing but an overgrown, ugly lizard."

The boys gasped as Draconus' eyes narrowed. Smoke rose from his nostrils and Vulcan started to say something but Draconus cut him off. "Very well, princeling. If you think you're ready, we'll see how long you survive. Come to the pit."

Kaelen strode down as confident as ever. Vulcan helped him put on his armor and gave him a sword and spear. "We don't go for death strikes," he said, more as though reminding Draconus than Kaelen.

The other boys watched anxiously as Kaelen tried to take on Draconus. The dragon was wickedly fast, dodging Kaelen's blows almost before he'd moved to strike. He shot fireballs at him, which Kaelen avoided with his shield. The temperature in the room was rising and Kaelen was becoming more and more agitated. "Come along, princeling, I'm just toying with you," Draconus taunted. "Is that the best you can do? Kaelen rushed at him and Draconus swiped him up off the ground in one paw. His scales were like molten metal and Kaelen felt like he'd been buried in hot coals, but refused to show any fear. "If this was a real fight, boy, I'd have eaten you by now."

"Why don't you, Dronecus?" Kaelen retorted angrily.

Draconus bared his fangs, steamy saliva dripping from them. "Tempting, but you're rather puny as yet. And my name is Draconus. Don't mistake it again." He set Kaelen down on the ground roughly before turning to the rest of the class. "Starting next week you'll all have your chance to prove yourselves. It's time for a more practical approach."

As the boys were leaving class, Adrian said, "Of all the stupid things to do! He could have killed you."

"But he didn't," Kaelen retorted, "and now we'll actually start learning in there."

The others shook their heads as they walked to supper. Suddenly Lucian said, "I bet he wanted someone to do that."

"What?" George asked.

"Draconus," Lucian clarified. "I bet he was just waiting for someone to lose it in there and challenge him. It's the perfect way for him to prove his point. He had to know we were all getting frustrated by the lectures. He was probably just biding his time knowing that eventually someone would lose control and challenge him. He knew we wouldn't be able to beat him this soon into the class."

"Well," Kaelen said stubbornly, "one of these days, he's going to lose."

They continued to chat through supper, comparing their specialty courses. George and Lucian talked about having foreign language Friday afternoon and their extra hour of botany. Kaelen had an extra hour of botany Friday afternoon and double etiquette. "What?" he demanded when the boys smiled. "I don't know why I have it again. Gelasia said I'm usually very good."

"Okay Kaelen," Jacobi smiled. "At least your extra classes make some sense. I'm in art twice. I also have a weird class about observation. I can't remember what Arden calls it."

"I wouldn't say that all of our classes make sense. I still have no idea how amphibian studies is supposed to help me," Adrian said. "And I can't believe they're forcing me to learn to swim."

"Well, look on the bright side," Lucian said. "The next time you come to Maltisten you can go swimming with me."

Soon they were forced to cut their conversation short so each of them could get their homework done. The mountains of homework hadn't gotten much better since the beginning of the year. If anything, there seemed to be more of it. Lucian worked long after the sun had set. Candlelight flickered over his desk and the grandfather clock against the wall chimed. When he finally finished, he stretched blearily. Rusty was already asleep in his corner. Lucian changed into his pajamas and blew out the candles before climbing wearily into bed.

October came and soon it was time for their first meeting with the princesses for the year. Lucian sincerely hoped that Moira's relationship with Cinnamon had improved. They were scheduled to go on the traditional ride through the forest. Last time they'd gone Zephyr had been spooked and Lucian had landed in a mud puddle while Cinnamon had bolted with Moira. While he knew he and Zephyr would be just fine, he wasn't sure about his princess.

As the gleaming carriages from Fair Damsel's arrived, followed by the girls' horses, the boys were standing on the steps waiting. Calista and Melantha got the first year students sorted while the other princesses went to their princes. "Hello Moira," Lucian said as she came up. "I hope you enjoyed the rest of your break."

"It was nice," Moira replied quietly.

Lucian had hoped she'd say more but was tackled by Allegra in a tight hug. "Isn't it terrible?"

"Isn't what terrible?" Lucian asked.

"Haven't you heard yet?" she asked, concern in her eyes. When Lucian continued to look at her blankly, she continued, "Oh dear, your letter must have gotten lost in the mail. I'm sure Mother would have told you." Allegra seemed out of sorts and was wringing her hands nervously.

"Told me what?" Lucian demanded. He felt horribly confused.

"Dad's sick," Allegra replied. "Very sick. Mom didn't say too much about it, but I could tell by the way she was writing. Lucian, I think Dad's dying."

Time stopped and Lucian felt as though someone had plunged an icy dagger into his heart. When he found his voice he said, "We should go home."

"No, we can't, we mustn't. Mom made me send her a letter promising her that I wouldn't leave school," Allegra explained. "You know how important it is to Dad. He wouldn't want us to go."

"But we can't just stay here and do nothing," Lucian cried. "What are we supposed to do?"

Tears filled Allegra's eyes. "We have no choice, Lucian." She threw her arms around him again and Lucian tried to comfort her, but he felt numb all over. He hardly heard Calista announce the activity. He let Adrian take Allegra to her horse, knowing that she'd be taken care of. He then led Moira to Cinnamon and held the horse while Moira mounted.

As he mounted Zephyr, Moira said, "I know what Allegra told you. She told me about the letter as soon as she had received it. I, well, I just wanted to say that if you want to talk about it, I'll listen."

Lucian felt angry. "Why didn't anyone tell me about it? I'm being pushed off by everyone. The fairies won't tell me anything, my own parents won't tell me anything."

"I'm sure your mom wrote to you. Allegra's probably right and your letter was simply lost in the mail," Moira replied calmly.

They were silent for a while as they rode into the forest. Lucian didn't feel much like talking and Moira didn't seem willing to start a conversation. She kept Cinnamon in control, though her riding was not as refined as some of her peers.

The silence continued long enough that Moira finally said, "It's beautiful isn't it?"

"What?" Lucian asked.

"The forest," Moira clarified. "It's beautiful at this time of year. So vibrant."

Lucian looked about at the fiery leaves. Normally, he would agree with Moira; he loved fall. But his heart was far away. "I guess," he admitted.

"I know what you're thinking," Moira said after another long pause. "It won't fix anything."

"How do you know what I'm thinking?" Lucian demanded.

Moira's eyes narrowed. "Perhaps you've forgotten, but I've been where you are before. I know what it feels like. Sometimes I wish I had been far away, so I wouldn't remember the way he looked when he was sick. I was so young, I only remember him when he was sick. I have few memories of when he was healthy," Moira's voice trailed off as though she were trying not to cry.

"Maybe I actually want to be with my father," Lucian said coldly.

"Do you think I don't?" Moira asked angrily. "Do you think I don't miss him every minute of every day?"

"You said you hardly remember him. Obviously he wasn't that important to you," Lucian spat. As soon as he said it, he wished he could take it back. Moira's eyes filled with tears and she looked as though he'd slapped her. She spurred Cinnamon and galloped past everyone, including Phillipa and Augusta. Augusta promptly followed after her. Lucian knew he was in trouble and he also knew he deserved it.

It didn't take the fairies long to send Lucian to Calista's office. Maeve was called. "Lucian, I don't think I have to say how disappointed I am in what you have done. How could you say something so heartless to Moira?"

Lucian didn't have a good answer for her. "I spoke without thinking," he said at length.

"That," Calista replied, "was obvious. I expect much better from you, Lucian. You are one of our best students and normally quite the gentleman. Whatever is going on in your life, there is no excuse for what you have done. Maeve will set your punishment and then you will return to the activities. You owe Moira an apology." Calista left the room, leaving one last look of disappointment on Lucian.

Maeve rose and tottered a bit before saying while clasping the stone on her belt, "To fix the wrong and make it right, In her shoes you'll walk a fortnight." A faint green light issued slowly from the stone. "Go on," Maeve said coaxingly, to which it split and shot at Lucian's heart and feet. "Oh not again," Maeve sighed, disappointment on her face. She shook her head, muttered something about "the Change" and walked away, leaning heavily on a cane.

Lucian's feet felt pinched and when he looked down, he was wearing a pair of very feminine, blue slippers. Everyone was going to laugh at him. Tears stung his eyes and his cheeks flushed. One thing he knew, Moira may have been taller than him, but her feet were definitely smaller. How long would he be stuck with these? A fortnight? He was going to be a laughingstock. Miserable tears fell from his cheeks as he walked down the stairs. Before going outside, he desperately tried to pull his pant legs down over the dainty slippers. When that didn't work, he tried his best to be invisible until he reached the blanket where his friends were sitting. Allegra and Adrian were sitting on either side of Moira, Adrian patting her back while Allegra rocked her back and forth as she cried. When Allegra saw Lucian, she gave him a look of deepest loathing. Adrian stood and grabbed Lucian's arm before hauling him away back into the forest. He glanced about to see if anyone was watching before punching Lucian square on the eye.

"Ow!" Lucian cried, "What…"

"Don't you every make my sister cry again," Adrian spat, "or so help me I'll do something worse to you. Do you have any idea how hard this summer was on us? You have both your parents and we only have the one. I don't care how sick your dad is or if he's dying or anything else. You have no right to take it out on Moira. She cries all the time because she misses Dad. She doesn't like to ride horses anymore because she used to do it with Dad and it's just not the same anymore. She may be annoying and snobby and Mom's precious, perfect princess, but she's also my sister. I'm not going to let anyone hurt her, especially not my best friend."

Adrian looked close to tears and Lucian was already crying enough for both of them. "I'm s-sorry," Lucian choked. "I sh-shouldn't have s-said it. I, I wasn't thinking."

"Obviously," Adrian retorted before storming away, leaving Lucian alone.

More tears fell as Lucian miserably walked back towards the picnic. Phillipa found him before he'd gotten very far. "Lucian," she called.

"Are you going to yell at me too?" Lucian interrupted.

"While the thought had crossed my mind," Phillipa admitted, "no. I came to see what was going on and…Lucian, what happened to your eye?"

Lucian looked away. "I walked into a branch," he lied.

"Adrian did that, didn't he?" Phillipa asked. Lucian hesitated a moment too long. She sighed, "I'll have to call the witches."

"No!" Lucian cried, "you can't. I deserved it. If he'd said to Allegra what I said to Moira, I would have done the same thing."

"That's no excuse, Lucian," Phillipa said gently. "A gentleman does not beat people."

"He didn't beat me and a gentleman always protects the ladies in his life," Lucian argued. "I'll be fine. It's just a little sore, and everybody hates me," he sobbed.

Phillipa looked at Lucian quizzically. "Your punishment must have affected your emotions," she said.

"No," Lucian sniffed, "it put me in these terrible shoes."

One eyebrow raised, Phillipa looked down at Lucian's feet. "Oh, that's an interesting punishment. Lucretia?"

Shaking his head, Lucian said, "Maeve."

"Oh. Well," Phillipa said, "you'd best get something to eat. Go on now."

Lucian walked back to where his friends were sitting. He sat down next to Allegra who scooted away from him as though he were diseased. Tears coursed down his face and he didn't even attempt to speak to anyone. He didn't think it would have mattered though; they all seemed to be pretending he wasn't there, except Nathan who smirked, "Nice shoes."

Leticia gently smacked Nathan's arm. "Leave him alone," she warned.

Nathan looked daggers at her, but she simply glared back. Finally, glowering, Nathan looked away and continued to eat his lunch.

As the princesses were leaving, Lucian tried to talk to Moira. "Can I speak with you? Just for a minute?"

"You've said quite enough for one day," Moira snapped and turned away from him.

Lucian grabbed her arm. "Please, Moira, I just wanted to say that I'm truly sorry for what I said. There's no excuse for it, it was cruel and ungentlemanly and, well, I'm sorry."

Moira looked into his eyes. He could see pain and anger swirling in the brilliant blue depths. "Sorry," she whispered at length, "doesn't take the words back, Lucian." She yanked her arm away and got into the carriage with Allegra, Clarissa and Eleanor.

Leticia hung back a moment. "I shouldn't talk to you; girl rules being what they are," she said quietly with a short laugh. "But you need to give her time and space. Deep wounds like that take a long time to heal; especially when they reopen old wounds." She then entered the carriage, leaving Lucian standing by himself.

Chapter 3

Lucian had a rough time in his classes following Saturday's incident. He would burst into tears at random moments and he constantly felt embarrassed; especially as boys snickered at the slippers on his feet. He couldn't even take them off at night to sleep. The teasing was made worse by a sudden growth spurt that left his pants two inches too short, even after Gelasia hemmed them, and the slippers painfully tight and awkwardly visible. Classes were torture; especially fencing where he had to be on his feet the whole time and his right arm was so weak he didn't feel he was progressing at all. "I'll never be able to get this," he sobbed one afternoon.

Raphael rolled his eyes while Lucian had covered his face with his hands. He tried very hard to be understanding, but he was losing patience. Since meeting with the princesses, Lucian hadn't gotten through a single class without bursting into tears over something. "Lucian, you'll get it. It takes time and hard work to learn fencing with your weak arm. Even I didn't get it overnight." He waited for Lucian to at least smile and finally with sigh said, "Look, the only way you'll progress is if you keep working. Now, on your feet. Let's give it another go, eh?"

When that class was over, he'd gone to dragon fighting where Draconus had tormented him about his girlish slippers and tears. "You should add yourself to the witches' garden as a waterfall. No doubt their herbs would grow faster under your care." This had spawned renewed strength and anger in Lucian and he'd redoubled his attack, though he was still defeated anyway.

Later that evening, Lucian checked his mail and had a letter from his mother. He opened it quickly and read:

> My Dear Lucian,
>
> I heard from Allegra that somehow your letter was missed. I do apologize for that. However, I am also very disappointed in your behavior towards Moira. We've raised you better than that. I expect my son to be a gentleman under all circumstances. That said, I'm sure the fairies took care to setting an appropriate punishment and I'll not say another word on the matter.
>
> Lucian, I suppose I owe both you and Allegra more details. Your father has been ill for quite some time. It began midway through last year. Of course, we naturally assumed that it was simply getting older and we thought nothing of it until nearer the end of last school year. As he weakened, I forced him to see a physician. The doctor's prognosis was bleak. He told us that with more rest and care, your father might recover some of his former strength. But the illness is gradually eating away at him. Your father, being who he is, has not necessarily kept to the rules given by the physician. He insisted on continuing in his regular routine, though it weakened him. Now he is bedridden and unable to leave

the room. I feel that some of this is unrelated to the illness. We both know how he desperately desires your success and sees himself as less than he is. His spirit is weakened more than his body. (Although I would ask that you not tell Allegra that. She has not been privy to that aspect of your father's personality.)

It is for this reason that I have contacted Queen Lavinia about winter break. I don't want you and Allegra to see your father like this until it is clear he can go no further. Perhaps by getting adequate rest over the break, his strength will be renewed and he will once again be his old self. I have not yet received an answer from Lavinia, but as soon as I do, I will inform you and Allegra of your winter plans.

My dear son, know that I love you. I am sorry that your letter was missed. I hope that you will make amends with Moira. She is a wonderful girl and deserving of a prince like you. Stay true to who you really are. Your father would want you to be at your best, as you always have been. Keep that sunshine in your smile. The day may come when you will need it.

All My Love,
Mother

Though he had been sure he had already cried every tear he had, fresh tears streamed down his face. His father was dying and he didn't have a friend in the world to lean on. Allegra hadn't written to him since that Saturday and the letter he'd sent to Moira had been returned. Adrian wasn't speaking to him and the others avoided him as well. The fairies wouldn't help him and truth be told, Lucian was beginning to blame the illness on them anyway. Why hadn't they written the story? Couldn't they see the hurt that had been caused?

While he had been crying, Adrian had come up the stairs. At first he'd wanted to continue on to his own room, but his heart softened as he saw Lucian standing there. "What's the matter?" he asked.

Lucian looked at Adrian sullenly. A strange resentment filled him and he couldn't keep the bitterness from his voice, "Suddenly speaking to me again?"

"Oh come off it, Lucian," Adrian snapped. "We've both behaved as children. I, I should apologize for ignoring you the way I have. Now, are you going to tell me what's wrong or should I leave you to drown in your tears?"

Too choked up to continue speaking, Lucian handed Adrian the letter.

Adrian read silently. When he got to the end he said quietly, "I had hoped that Allegra was exaggerating. Lucian, I'm sorry."

"It's not your fault," Lucian sniffed.

"Well, let's head down to supper. I know you're probably not hungry," Adrian continued when Lucian looked ready to argue, "but some food will do you good. I'll write to my mother and see what's going on this winter, okay?"

Lucian nodded but didn't speak. It felt good to rejoin his friends at their regular table. He was still sniffling and tears leaked down his cheeks. Adrian explained what was wrong and the boys expressed condolences. "It might not be so bad, Lucian," Jacobi said kindly. "Maybe he just needs a rest during winter and when you go back in summer, he'll be good as new."

The others tried to sound as hopeful, but Lucian knew they were all thinking the same thing. From what his mother said, it sounded pretty hopeless. It almost seemed as though he was just giving up. Lucian suddenly felt angry at him. He couldn't just abandon them like this. Didn't he know that they needed him? What would Mom do without him there? Lucian played with his food, but didn't eat much. He also avoided talking to Adrian. He was surprised by this change in himself. Adrian was his best friend, and yet Lucian felt a type of resentment towards him, like he reminded him of a painful memory.

When he returned to his room, Lucian attempted to work on his homework, but it just didn't seem to matter anymore. Finally, exhausted and upset, he blew out the candles and crawled into bed before crying himself to sleep.

The next week passed tolerably enough, despite frequent emotional breakdowns. It was well into a third week that Lucian realized his punishment hadn't ended yet. He continued going to his classes, thinking that perhaps he'd simply misheard Maeve and he didn't give it another thought for some time. He was helped by a trip to town, which many in his age group had needed, to buy trousers. At least people weren't laughing at his high-waters anymore. It wasn't until the beginning of a fifth week of slippers and tears that Lucian felt somewhat panicked. He was sure Maeve hadn't said a month or a semester. He went up to Calista's office to ask her about it. When he entered her office, she looked up from her desk and asked, "Lucian, can I help you with something?"

"I'm still wearing Moira's shoes and crying all the time," Lucian said. "I was only supposed to be punished for a fortnight."

"Oh," Calista said, as though there weren't a problem. "Maeve's spell must have been more potent than she intended. That happens when they're this close to the Change. Althea has said it will happen within the next six months, although she won't be positive until the day before. I hope it occurs during winter break while you boys are away."

"But what are you going to do about my punishment?" Lucian asked. "I've worn these slippers for over a fortnight and all that's happened is they've gotten tighter and I'm constantly an emotional wreck."

"Lucian, as you well know, there is nothing I can do about your punishment. Think about the words Maeve used. Sometimes even though they set a time limit," Calista explained, "there are other things that might preclude that. Did she say anything other than the two weeks?"

Trying to remember, Lucian said, "Something about making wrong right and walking in Moira's shoes."

"Well, that certainly explains the slippers and the mood swings. Girls can be very difficult during this stage in their lives. That's why I prefer working with boys," Calista admitted. "You'll have to make things right with Moira."

"Great, then I'm going to be stuck in her shoes for eternity because she hates me and will never forgive me," Lucian muttered bitterly.

"Nonsense," Calista said. "You just need to ask her forgiveness."

"I've sent her a letter apologizing every single week. Sometimes I've sent two letters. Every letter I've sent to her has been sent back," Lucian said angrily. "She doesn't want to hear that I'm sorry."

"Try again," Calista said simply. "Perhaps through this you've learned that words can cut far deeper than swords."

Anger filled Lucian and he shouted, "Well this is all your fault, so why don't you fix it?"

Calista looked shocked. "I beg your pardon?"

"I wouldn't have said what I did if I hadn't been worrying about my dad. I wouldn't be worried about my dad if he wasn't so sick, if I had known before Moira came. My dad is dying and it's all your fault," Lucian yelled, banging his fists on the table as he stood up. "He's giving up because nobody at this stupid school thought he was worthwhile. Oh yeah, you let him marry my mom, but nobody knows his story. There's no painting of him in the hallway. Nobody reenacts him rescuing my mom. He's not considered a Prince Charming even though he's better than any stupid prince who ever went to this school. He's going to die thinking he was just second best because of you. He'll think my mom was disappointed in him because of you. You caused this. It's your fault!" Lucian sobbed and slumped back into the chair, shaking like a leaf in a thunderstorm.

For a long moment, the only sounds were Lucian's sobbing and the soft pattering of raindrops against the window. "Lucian," Calista said at length, calmly and gently, "this is not my fault."

"It is your fault," Lucian insisted between sobs. "You couldn't let him be what he wanted. You couldn't let him live his dream. You rejected him."

"I'm not talking about your father, Lucian," Calista said. "You can't blame anyone but yourself for what you said. You can't blame me or your father or anyone else. You said those things, not me. The situation with your father is complicated. I'm not the only one responsible for that decision. There were many things to be considered. He didn't go to our school."

"You wouldn't let him!" Lucian cried.

"Let me finish," Calista interrupted firmly. "He was never a student here. Yes, he managed to get through every obstacle, but at a price. One of our students was denied what should have been his."

"He gave up! My dad had the courage to save her, not Maximillion. I know what happened, Phillipa told me," Lucian said angrily.

Calista considered Lucian for a moment. "Lucian, I can't say that I'm surprised that Phillipa told you. However, I must say that I wish you would look at this from our perspective. It doesn't look good when someone who is not from your school rescues the princess while your student flees. Right or not," she continued before Lucian could interrupt her again, "it was not deemed appropriate to write the story. Your father is a wonderful man; deserving of every happiness life has to offer."

"Then give this to him," Lucian begged. "Don't let him die thinking he wasn't good enough."

Silence fell over the room. "You need to go back to your dormitory. Get your homework done and write to Moira. I don't want any more teachers saying that you haven't completed your homework again." Calista paused before saying, "Your father would want you to do your best, especially in his condition."

Lucian swiped at the tears on his face. "I'm sorry I yelled," he whispered.

"Under normal circumstances, I would have sent for one of the Sisters to deal with your behavior. A gentleman knows better, and I believe I can say quite confidently that you are indeed a gentleman. However, considering the stress you must be under and the heartache you are feeling, I'll let it slide this time. However, do not expect to be able to speak so disrespectfully to me again," Calista replied.

"I won't," Lucian said softly. "I am sorry."

"You needn't be," Calista said gently. "You made some very valid points, even if not in the appropriate manner. Consider yourself forgiven and go do your homework."

As Lucian left the office, Calista got out a piece of paper and began writing.

As the semester wound to a close, Lucian's mother had written him to say that he and Allegra would not be coming home and that she expected each of them to be on their best behavior while in Lictthane. Allegra had finally written to him saying that she was sorry she'd ignored him and that she'd forgiven him for being so cruel. "I suppose I hadn't thought of it from your perspective," she had written. She'd then continued on to say how she was looking forward to spending winter with Moira and Adrian, though she would miss being home.

There was also a spring schedule and supply list. Luckily he already had everything he needed, though he was sure that he would have to take a trip to the store to buy another new pair of trousers. The ones he'd bought recently had also become too small. Gelasia had measured him and said, "Well, you're certainly catching up to everyone. You're nearly five seven now."

"Terrific! I only need to grow two more inches to be the same height as Moira," he had said.

Gelasia had laughed, "Well, my dear, you're assuming that she hasn't grown again."

This was met by a flood of tears and Gelasia had gently reassured Lucian that she was sure no matter what Moira's height, she would still like him and appreciate him as the charming prince that he was.

Moira also had written to him. He tore the letter open eagerly and was slightly disappointed to read:

Dear Lucian,

I forgive you. Please return my slippers; those are my favorite pair.

Moira

"Great," Lucian said aloud as the slippers disappeared off his feet and he felt a flood of normal emotions fill him. "She didn't forgive me because she's actually forgiven me. She just wanted her shoes back. Well, she can have them and welcome; they're awful."

"Talking to yourself again? Must be crazy," Adrian teased as he stopped by Lucian's door.

"I just got the longest letter ever written," Lucian replied sarcastically, showing Adrian the missive.

"Yeah, well, Moira never did mince words," Adrian retorted. "So are you going to send the slippers back?"

"I can't they disappeared after I read her letter," Lucian explained. "She probably already has them."

"I hope so," Adrian said as they walked to supper, "because if she doesn't get those slippers back, you'll be back where you started."

At supper the boys sat with their friends, discussing the upcoming meeting with their princesses. "I hope you don't blow it this time, Lucian," Kaelen said in the tone he had picked up over the last few months. The others had two possible reasons for this. Most of the boys believed that it was simply that his growth had sky-rocketed in recent weeks. Kaelen was growing faster than any of them and had filled out considerably, his body taking on the look of a man. Between the trips to town for new clothes, teasing about his voice cracking, and all the other changes that came with growing, the boys believed he was simply becoming moody because of it. The second, and more likely in Lucian's opinion, was that he had discovered that Esmé was very beautiful. He often pointed out that she was the most beautiful girl at Fair Damsel's, which the other boys contested. But it was clear that her ebony locks, emerald eyes and perfect figure had stolen Kaelen's heart. He refused to even allow her to be equal with the other girls, saying that she outshone them all.

"Kaelen," George chided, "knock it off, would you? Lucian has apologized to Moira and set things right. Otherwise he'd still be a water fountain; no offense, Lucian."

Lucian shrugged, "None taken. Anyway, I doubt I could make things any worse with her. I mean, I've hit rock bottom so the only way to go is up, right?"

"Yeah," Jacobi agreed optimistically.

Supper soon ended and the boys went outside for a little while, enjoying the fresh blanket of snow. It was cold outside, but bundled in their coats and scarves, it didn't seem as bad. They went out to the barn to visit the horses and watched the sun set over the horizon, casting a pinkish glow on the whiteness surrounding them. When they got too cold, they returned inside, going to the common room and warming up by the fire. They stayed there, talking late into the night. There were older boys working on homework at some of the desks and younger boys playing games. It was a peaceful place, despite the buzz of activity around them. They laughed about things that had happened and talked about more serious matters. Adrian was glad to see Lucian talking and really laughing again. The most disconcerting part of Lucian's punishment was that he had become very much like Moira, constantly upset over the smallest thing. It had also hurt that Lucian had seemed to avoid talking to him. He had even talked to Gelasia about it, though he wouldn't have admitted it to anyone. Gelasia had assured him that Lucian would eventually be his old self again. "Growing up is hard to do, Adrian dear," she had said gently. "He still knows who his best friend is. Don't worry so much. He'll come around."

As seemed to always be the case when they were truly enjoying themselves, Calista appeared and told them it was time to head to bed for the night. "You've got finals in the morning. You'd best get plenty of rest before then. I expect all of you to perform at your best."

The boys reluctantly followed her advice, chatting their way up the stairs until they separated at their own rooms. Rusty was asleep in his corner when Lucian came in. He changed quickly into his pajamas. Now that he thought about it, he was exhausted. He blew out the candles and fell asleep.

The finals they took left Lucian feeling tired and somewhat discouraged. Though he had done as Calista had told him after his outburst, he still felt as though he'd fallen behind. He was now desperately trying to reach where he thought he should have been all along. Shame filled him as he thought of what his father would have done if he'd heard that Lucian had decided to simply quit. The one class he really wanted to do well in was dragon fighting. Draconus had become more boorish than ever while Lucian had been punished. Now that he wouldn't burst into a fit of girlish tears, Lucian was sure that this time he could beat him.

The boys entered the arena-like classroom at the end of the day. Vulcan reminded them that they were not to go for death strikes. "A dragon's soft spot is at the base of the neck; however, you will thrust your point between his arm and body."

"Please, like anyone will get that close," Draconus drawled. "Well, let's get this over with. I'm having veal for supper tonight and I can hear it calling." He licked his lips hungrily.

"I don't hear anything," Adrian whispered as the first boy went into the arena.

"I think he has better hearing than the rest of us," Lucian replied.

"Certainly I do, waterfall," Draconus said as the boy missed another blow. "You and his greenness had best be paying attention."

Adrian scowled. The jokes about his color had worsened throughout the semester. He wouldn't have minded so much if he'd been wearing any green, or if he'd been turned green by a witch as punishment, but the only green there was about him were his green eyes. Surely that was no call for teasing. Lots of people had green eyes.

Lucian could tell Adrian was frustrated and tried to smile reassuringly, but he was concerned about the teasing too. It had to stem from something. He was forced to push his thoughts aside as Draconus defeated yet another boy and it was his turn to try.

"Ah yes, the waterfall," Draconus sneered. "This should be easier than the last boys. But I see your slippers have gone. What a pity, such a nice shade for you."

Lucian blocked his attack with his shield and struck out with his sword. He heard the clang of the metal against dragon scales. Even Draconus looked surprised; so far no one had been able to touch him. His eyes narrowed into reptilian slits and he spouted fire, which Lucian once again blocked. He struck again and again, missing most of the time, but every now and again hearing the satisfying ring of sword against scales. He leapt away from spurts of flame and Draconus' snapping jaws. He could feel himself wearing out, but he refused to be beaten. Not this time. He wouldn't fail this time. Spying an opening, he thrust for Draconus' arm, but didn't see his tail snaking along the room until it was too late. He had flicked Lucian's sword away and pinned Lucian to the wall before Lucian could take the stroke.

"You are supper, my little waterfall," Draconus hissed, though he seemed nearly as tired as Lucian. "A valiant effort, but you must constantly be on your guard. Dragons are as quick with their tails as they are with their tongues."

"A mistake I won't make next time," Lucian panted angrily, staring straight back into the dragon's eyes, still pinned between Draconus' thick, scaly tail and the arena wall.

A flicker of a smile seemed to flit across Draconus' face. "Bravely spoken," he said before he sent Lucian off and the next boy was brought into the arena. At the end of class, Lucian was brought forward to receive a medal for improvement in the class. Lucian thought this unwarranted since Draconus had remained undefeated by the end of the day, but kept it to himself. There was no reason to seek to offend the already easily offended dragon. Besides, he couldn't help but enjoy, even just a little bit, the look of jealousy on Kaelen's face. While he was not as bad as he had been when they'd first met, Kaelen's arrogance and pride had worn down the bonds of friendship they'd forged.

As they left class, the boys headed first to the infirmary. George had a pretty nasty burn on his hand where his shield had broken during his final. Draconus had immediately ended the battle, but it hadn't been early enough to prevent the already sent blast of fire. George's hand and arm had gotten the worst of it and his clothing smoked a little. As soon as he'd finished with George, Vulcan had led him to the infirmary.

George smiled as his friends entered. "Wouldn't you know it? I would lose my writing hand."

"Tallia didn't cut your arm off did she?" Jacobi asked in wide-eyed panic.

"Of course I didn't," Tallia replied with a smile. "I merely put a burn relief potion on it and bandaged it. I believe he meant he couldn't use his arm, not that is was permanently gone." She turned back to George. "Come back in the morning so I can apply a fresh bandage and round of potion on it. Good thing you're done with finals." She suddenly frowned. "You are done with finals, right?"

"Yeah, I'm done," George replied with a smile. "They did our fine arts finals last week so that Friday could be the meeting with the girls. I'm going to meet Eleanor one handed."

"I'm sure she'll think you just as dashing. Besides, they always say that girls love a man with scars," Tallia said with a wink. "Now, off to supper all of you. I've got lots to do." She shooed them out as Achilles stepped in the door with a wide grin on his face.

"Those two fight like cats and dogs and yet still love each other," Jacobi said, shaking his head as they walked out the door.

"Probably because Tallia has the patience of a saint," George added.

They went down to supper and sat together talking about winter break. Lucian remained quiet and reflective. He hadn't heard that week from his mother and he was starting to feel very nervous. What if the next letter he got was to say, "I'm sorry Lucian, Dad died."? He didn't think he could take it.

His friends didn't allow him to stay somber long. They soon pulled him into a conversation about princesses and dragons and quests, laughing and talking about how they would look back on school someday. "I bet we'll still remember all the fairies here," George said.

"Are you kidding? They'll all still be here. I bet Gelasia will still be tsking around the school if she catches boys biting their nails or being rude," Adrian replied.

"And Calista will definitely still be here. She can sneak up without anyone knowing she's there. And I'd love to be able to get a room's attention by merely starting to talk. She never raises her voice. It's like our hearing gets better to pick it up," Jacobi said.

"I bet it's part of that fairy magic," Lucian agreed. "She can make us hear her without straining her voice at all.

"Can you imagine Raphael in thirty years?" George asked. "I bet he won't have changed a bit."

"Not a chance," Kaelen through in. "He'll still be exactly the same. Although, since he's got a daughter now, maybe he'll let girls in the classroom."

"Bite your tongue!" Adrian laughed. "He'd have to be dead before he'd let a girl walk into that room, his daughter or not. Even Honoria never goes in there. That's like his sanctuary."

"Dronecus will be here too, tormenting years of students yet to come," Kaelen added ruefully. "Good job today, Lucian, you hit him. I wish I could say I'd done it."

Lucian shrugged, "I think I managed to hit him more because he wasn't a blur of tears than because I'm really getting any better. We've all still got a long ways to go yet."

The laughing and chatter continued late into the evening until they were once more told by a fairy that it was past their bedtime. The boys said goodnight and trudged to their own rooms before each going to bed, dreaming of what the next day would bring.

Friday morning dawned with soft snow flurries drifting past the castle windows. Lucian dressed quickly, excited for the day; until he remembered that his parents wouldn't be coming to see him. He frowned, for only a moment before forcing himself to put a smile on his face. Today he was going to be the perfect Prince Charming, just like his dad. Since he'd woken up early, he'd taken time to write to his parents, telling them he'd miss them over break, about the fight with Draconus, his new medals and the rest of his finals. He sealed the envelope and put it in the mailbox to be taken out before heading down the stairs and waiting with his friends for the princesses.

As the gleaming carriages pulled up to the door, Calista warmly greeted their guests. The girls walked in and shrugged off winter cloaks into the waiting hands of other fairies. Allegra immediately hugged Lucian tightly, traces of tears in her eyes. "I'm sorry I was so awful to you. Can you ever forgive me?"

Lucian couldn't help but laugh, "Allegra, I forgave you a long time ago; or did you miss my letter."

Smiling her impish grin, she said with some seriousness, "It's much easier to write it than to say it. I just want to be sure."

Soon, Moira joined them and Allegra backed away to speak to Adrian and give Lucian and Moira a chance to talk to each other. Lucian could see in Moira's eyes barely hidden traces of hurt. But better, he noticed that he was now about an inch taller as she said, "Hi."

"Moira," Lucian said, "I'm so sorry for what I said."

"I already told you that I forgave you," Moira replied quickly.

Lucian shook his head. "What I said was cruel and heartless and I don't want you to think that I'll always treat you that way. I normally would never…"

Moira put a finger to Lucian's lips. "Don't, Lucian," she said, her voice slightly strained by emotion. "I know that was out of character for you. I'm sure when you read my letter you thought it was just to get my shoes back, which by the way I can't wear anymore because you stretched them out so badly," she added with a teasing grin; one of the first he'd ever seen. "I truly meant it when I said I forgave you. It wasn't just for the slippers. Let's," she sighed. "Let's just not talk about it again, okay?"

Unable to find his voice, Lucian nodded. Moira's touch had been so gentle and her voice so soft. She looked away, the dark blue depths of her eyes hidden behind her eyelashes. As his heart skipped a beat, Lucian suddenly knew what it felt like to be in love.

He didn't have time to contemplate this newfound emotion as the boys led their princesses into the dining hall. Moira reluctantly accepted his arm as they walked. When they'd had a seat and Lucian had served them both, there was chatter and laughter around the table. They each spoke avidly with their friends. Moira and Adrian were describing vividly the wintry plains of Lictthane to Allegra and Lucian found himself listening as Allegra smiled appreciatively. Leticia then grabbed his attention by saying, "Lucian, I was sorry to hear from Allegra about your father. He's a very kind man; I hope he is soon well."

Lucian smiled. "Thanks, Leticia. What are your winter plans?"

"Eleanor and I will be staying at home for the winter. There's an art contest during break which Eleanor will be entering. Do you know if Allegra has made up her mind about it?"

Grinning sheepishly, Lucian replied, "While my sister and I have a pretty good relationship, I don't necessarily remember everything she's told me. I'm really not sure if she will be or not."

Leticia laughed; a pleasant sound that reminded Lucian of Calista's laugh. "That's alright. Even as Eleanor's twin I don't always know what's in her head."

"I don't think siblings ever really know what is going on in the other one's head," George added. "Or maybe it's just that I'm a boy surrounded by girls and I never know what they're thinking."

Laughing, Eleanor replied, "I don't know that I believe that, George. You read people very well."

Breakfast continued with laughter and chatting about the table. Allegra revealed that she would be entering the contest, but refused to say what she was entering. "It's a surprise," she said with a mischievous twinkle in her eyes. They quieted as Melantha told them about the day's activities and they adjourned to the gymnasium.

The fairies seemed to have outdone themselves in decorating. The gym was a sparkling wintry fairyland with snow encrusted pine trees and fragrant cedar boughs crackling in the magical fireplaces. There were pale blue and lavender armchairs in front of the fireplaces where they were allowed to sit together. Some older couples were hogging most of them, but Lucian saw one available. "Do you mind if we just sit and talk for a while?" he asked. When Moira looked ready to refuse he added, "If it starts getting too personal we can go play silent board games or whatever. I just really want to talk to you for a bit. Just talk."

For a moment, Moira looked like she was going to say no. There seemed to be an inner conflict, but at last she said, "Alright, we can talk."

Lucian led her to the last available fireplace and held her chair for her. She was wearing a satiny lavender gown with a purple ribbon tied in her hair. "You look lovely this morning," he said as he sat down.

Moira blushed. "I just threw myself together really. I woke up late," she admitted.

"Well," Lucian laughed, "you threw yourself together pretty well. I'd still have bed head if I'd woken up late.

"What did you want to talk about?" Moira asked. She looked nervous and fidgety and Lucian got the sense that she was uncomfortable.

"This may not be a good way to start, but I wanted to talk about you and Adrian," Lucian said hesitantly. "Why don't you get along?"

"You're right, that's a bad way to start," Moira replied. She looked about to get up from her seat, then settled back saying, "There's a lot between us, Lucian. And it's very complicated. I'm not ready to talk to you about that. If you ask Adrian, he'll tell you the same thing. The truth, well, the truth is that we see eye to eye more often than we argue. But," she hesitated, looking as though she'd revealed too much. "I really don't want to talk about that. You wouldn't understand."

Lucian bit his tongue to keep from saying that she wasn't letting him try to understand. Instead, he asked her about Lictthane. "I couldn't help hearing what you were telling Allegra. I really appreciate you taking her mind off things like that. She needs it right now."

Moira smiled gently. "Like I've told you, I've been there before. Lictthane is prettiest during the winter I think. There's always snow." She continued talking about the plains, describing sledding down the hills behind their castle, taking her pastels out to capture the gently rolling slopes of snow.

"Allegra likes to do that, only she prefers paint," Lucian said.

Laughing, Moira replied, "I know, we had an argument once over which medium was better. We had to agree to disagree."

They were prevented continuing by a sudden shout, "If I wanted your opinion I'd give it to you."

Everyone turned to stare at Nathan and Leticia. Leticia was holding her ground; her head tilted at defiant angle and said calmly, "I was merely making a suggestion. There's no need to shout."

"I don't need your suggestions," Nathan retorted, backhanding her.

There was a collective gasp and then a roar of anger as one of the older boys tackled Nathan to the ground. Eleanor was desperately trying to pull him away as Leticia stood rooted to the spot, tears welling in her eyes, her cheeks red with embarrassment and the one throbbing with pain. "Please, Benjamin, no. Stop!" Eleanor was crying, still trying to no avail to pull him away.

"Don't you ever hit my sister again," Benjamin growled, punctuating each word with a well-aimed blow to Nathan.

"Benjamin." Leticia's voice was barely a whisper, but it carried over the entire room as the fairies swarmed in to pull the fighting boys apart. He turned to her. "I know you're just protecting me, but he is not worth your efforts. Leave him to the witches."

"But look what he did to you," Benjamin said, touching her cheek gently as angry tears rolled down his cheeks.

She covered his hand with hers. "I know, but the pain will stop, and the fairies will take care of this. Don't stoop to his level. You're too good a person to do that."

Calista looked furious. "Normally, Nathan," she said as everyone was still watching, "I try to take care of punishment and discipline privately. But you have committed your last offence in my school." As Althea entered the room she continued, "After Althea has set your punishment, you will gather your belongings and leave Charming Academy, never to return. I will not tolerate the abuse of our princesses within my walls. Never in over three thousand years of existence has this school ever been so shamefully represented. What kind of example are you setting for the younger boys? I cannot afford for them to believe that such behavior is ever acceptable. What kind of message are you sending the princesses who visit? I cannot afford for you to fill their hearts with fear and distrust and pain. You have disgraced my school and the teachers within it. More than that, you have disgraced yourself. Althea," she said turning to the witch, "he is yours to do with as you see fit."

Althea looked darkly at Nathan. "We meet again, prince. In all our years, the Sisters have never had a prince that each of us have had to punish multiple times. In all your punishments, you have yet to learn the lesson. You are still the same uncouth child you were upon your arrival. Every word of anger, every act of malice, every feeling of loathing," she said, her hair billowing as the white stone on her crown began to glow and her eyes darkened to coal black, "will be shown as a scar on your body. Every lash of the tongue a lash on your back. Every evil thought a pockmark on your face. Every hurtful act a source of pain to you forever."

Blinding white light surrounded Nathan and several princes shielded their princesses from the glare. Lucian turned Moira away, not knowing what would happen, but sure that he didn't want her to witness it. Many covered their ears as howls of pain emitted from where Nathan was standing amidst the blinding light. When the light faded, no one would have recognized Nathan in the hideous form before them. He howled again before running from the room, his gait lopsided and limping.

Calista, once Nathan was gone from the room, stopped Althea from leaving. "We have another student to deal with."

"Please, Calista," Leticia pleaded. "Don't punish Benjamin. He was trying to protect me, as a gentleman would protect the women he loves. I'm not saying that his actions were right, but they came from good intentions and a loving heart."

Smiling slightly, Althea said, "A gentleman does indeed protect and revere the women in his life. But he must also show self-restraint. Have no fear; your brother's punishment will be small in comparison to your prince."

Benjamin put a gentle hand on Leticia's shoulder. "My actions were out of control. I deserve punishment. But I appreciate you standing up for me."

Leticia smiled through tears. "You're my brother. I'll always stand up for you."

Calista and Althea walked out with Benjamin while several of Leticia and Eleanor's friends surrounded the sisters. Moira hung back with Lucian. "Why did you turn me away?"

"You have enough bad memories in your life," Lucian said simply. "You didn't need another."

"His screams will be etched on my mind forever," Moira admitted, shivering slightly.

Lucian put a gentle arm around Moira, causing her to flinch. He moved and then said, "Well, let's sit by the fire and get you warmed up."

"No," Moira said, a competitive gleam in her eyes, "I'm going to beat you at checkers."

Laughing, Lucian replied, "We'll see."

Soon the tone in the gym returned to normal as people continued to play and talk together. Lucian knew no one would forget the fate Nathan had brought upon himself. He was sure he'd have nightmares of the scarred, hideous face that had glowered at them as Nathan had run from the room. He was glad that at least Moira wouldn't have to remember that face. Allegra wouldn't either; Adrian had pulled her close to him so that all she had seen was his jacket. Neither girl would admit it aloud, but they were grateful for the protection their princes had offered them.

As the gym emptied slightly while first and second year students went to eat lunch, the group of friends sat together in front of one of the fireplaces, having exhausted the games they wished to play. Eleanor was sitting close to Leticia. They had left long enough for Eleanor to help powder Leticia's face. Even with the dusting of rouge and powder, the bruise Nathan left was still visible. No one mentioned it to her and she did not bring it up; no one wanted to. When it was time for the rest of the students to go to lunch, Benjamin and his princess, Grace, sat with Leticia, Eleanor and their friends. No one mentioned the unsightly wart on Benjamin's nose. They knew it would go away soon enough. A silent conversation passed between brother and sister. Lucian knew that Leticia was assuring her brother that she really was alright. Laughter soon spread over the table. Benjamin was much like his sisters; kind, smiling and full of laughter. The meal continued pleasantly and then the third year students, as well as Clarissa and Allegra who were told that since their princes were third year students, they would follow their schedule, went upstairs to wait for their interviews. Most of the parents had begun arriving. Queen Lavinia was there and showered Moira with praise before greeting Adrian rather stiffly. "Looks like you've grown again," she said, her voice strained. "We'll have to go to the tailor for new trousers."

"Yes, Mother, Lucian will need to come too," Adrian replied.

She nodded as Calista called both Adrian and Lavinia to her office for their end of semester interview. Lucian looked curiously at Moira who shook her head, warning him not to ask about it. Instead, Allegra began talking to Moira about how they would get to Traifloran for the art competition. "Don't worry," Moira said, patting Allegra's shoulder, "I've already talked with Mother about it. We'll all be going up. I was thinking of entering anyway, so I told Mother to take care of both our fees."

"How could you have known I would decide to enter?" Allegra asked. "I just made the decision this morning."

Moira laughed, "I'm your best friend, that's how. I knew you couldn't resist the temptation, especially with everything going on."

Soon Adrian left the office, but Lavinia stayed behind for a while. "What's going on?" Moira asked.

Adrian shrugged, "Calista said she needed to speak with Mother privately for a moment."

Not long after, Lavinia left the room, looking as though she'd swallowed a lemon. Thankfully Moira was called to go to the office Melantha was borrowing and she took her mother with her. Lucian wasn't given time to ponder this as Calista called for him.

As she shut the door behind them, Calista said, "I'll be having our conversation recorded so that I can mail it to your parents. I do wish that they could be here, but understand that under the circumstances they need to be where they are." A pen on Calista's desk was busily writing every word she said on a piece of lavender parchment. "Not every word. Wait until I start the interview," she scolded. The parchment was suddenly wiped clean and the pen seemed to be looking innocently at Calista despite not having eyes or a face. She looked at it sternly before saying, "Now, Lucian, how would you say this semester has gone?"

Lucian had to think for a while. "It's been hard," he admitted at length. "I allowed myself to get discouraged, but then I thought of what my dad would want. It helped give me the strength to really do my best. I'm still a little behind, at least I think so. But I'm working hard now."

"According to your teachers, you are doing remarkably well, despite your lapse in work. I've heard only positives from all of them. Raphael says that you are making progress in your right-handed work, even if you're having trouble seeing it. He requests that you spend some time over the break practicing. I believe Adrian will be able to work with you. Vulcan says he expects you to continue to do extremely well in his class," Calista added.

"Really?" Lucian asked. "I didn't think anyone was doing well. I mean, no one has beat Drone…I mean, Draconus at all."

Calista laughed, "I see he's earned his nickname once again. Back to the topic though, my understanding is that you are getting closer than your peers to being able to actually beat him. Vulcan did say to beware of anger. Attacking in anger allows the dragon to have the upper hand. It distracts you. Keep your mind clear while you're fighting." Lucian nodded and Calista smiled. "I'm proud of you, Lucian; you have done very well in spite of the challenges that have faced you this semester. You have continued to show that you are indeed where you belong."

"I'm only here because of Dad," Lucian said, hoping that the pen would continue writing. "Dad was the one who saw the Prince Charming in me. I think it's because he's a Prince Charming himself, underneath it all."

Calista smiled and picked the pen up before setting it, motionless, back on the desk. "Nicely phrased, Lucian. And your point has been taken. I do hope that during the break you will take the opportunity to better acquaint yourself not only with your princess, but also with Adrian. I realize that you are already best friends, but there is much that you can still learn about each other. Perhaps this winter, you'll be able to solve some of the puzzles you've been dealing with." When Lucian stared at her in disbelief, she continued, "The fairies know a great deal about the dealings of the families our students come from. We have to in order to best design your quests. Now, have a wonderful winter and I'll see you again in January."

Lucian left the room and after sending Jacobi and his parents to the office, went to find Adrian. He was sitting with Allegra outside what was normally Airlia's office. "Have you had your interview yet?" Lucian asked as he sat on Allegra's other side.

"Yeah, same old same old," Allegra replied smiling. "It was nice though that she was recording the interview for Mom and Dad. They'll appreciate getting that, even though they weren't here."

"My interview was recorded too," Lucian replied.

Lavinia and Moira soon left the office and Lavinia said, "I know normally we would stay for the dinner, but I'd really like to get home as soon as possible. Are you boys packed and ready?"

"Yes, we are," Lucian replied.

"Alright, I'll get the carriage and you'll have five minutes to say goodbye to your friends. Girls, I believe your things have already been taken out," Lavinia added. She looked troubled and Lucian wondered what had been said to her during her interviews.

Moira was looking at the floor. "Well, I'm going to find the girls and let them know we're leaving." She looked up at Allegra. "Don't worry, we'll ask Leticia at the contest what's going to happen for her now. I'm sure they wouldn't expel her because of her prince. It wouldn't be fair."

After saying goodbye to their friends and promising to write during break, the boys took their belongings out to the carriage where Lavinia and the girls were waiting. Lucian watched out the window as the castle shrank in the distance. He still wanted to go home and be with his father, but he knew that Moira was right. He wouldn't be able to magically fix anything; it would be better for him to have the opportunity to rest. As Allegra pulled him into the conversation, he couldn't help smiling and letting his worries slip away.

Chapter 4

Upon arriving at Lictthane, Lavinia showed her guests to their rooms as Moira and Adrian took care of their own belongings. Allegra and Lucian had been placed in rooms right next to each other's. "I hope this arrangement will work out well for you two. I thought with being away from home, you'd probably wish to be close to each other for comfort. However, there are many, many rooms and we can move you if that is your wish."

"No, thank you, Queen Lavinia," Allegra said kindly. "I'd much rather be close to Lucian. It'll be almost like home."

Lavinia smiled. "Well, get yourselves settled and refreshed. Supper will be served within half-an-hour."

Lucian started organizing his things within the spacious guest room. It was well decorated with green furnishings and large, cherry wood furniture. He walked to the window and looked out over snow-covered fields. It was exactly as Moira had described it. He heard a noise behind him and turned to see Allegra standing in the doorway. "Can I come in for a bit?"

"Of course," Lucian replied with a smile.

Allegra walked in and sat on Lucian's bed. She looked near tears and he sat down next to her and put a gentle arm around her. "I'm so scared," she sobbed against his shoulder.

"I know," Lucian said gently. "I am too."

There was a long pause as Allegra cried against Lucian. "I want to be with him, Lucian. And yet, I don't. I don't want to see him so weak. Does, does that make me a terrible person?" she asked, heartbreak coloring her voice in shades of sorrow.

"No," Lucian reassured her, "that doesn't make you a terrible person. You're the most understanding person I know. I'm sure everything will turn out alright in the end, you'll see."

"How can you be so sure?" Allegra whispered.

"I'm not," Lucian admitted. "But I have to try to believe it anyway."

Allegra nodded. "I know."

"Come on, wipe your eyes and let's go to dinner," Lucian said with a smile. "Otherwise they'll think you're depressed."

"Maybe I am," Allegra half-teased. She hugged him before they got up. "Thanks Lucian."

"What are big brothers for?" Lucian asked.

Together they walked to the dining hall where Lavinia, Moira and Adrian were waiting. The conversation was very one-sided; Lavinia did most of the talking, telling them about the schedule she'd prepared and the things she had planned for them to do. "Moira told me about your art contest and so we'll all be traveling for that. Before we do though, we'll stop by the shops in town to make sure everything is in order for school. That and you boys simply must get new trousers. It's disgraceful walking around with so much of your leg showing. I shan't take you anywhere before you get new trousers. You're hardly fit to be seen. Of course, girls, we'll buy some new gowns for you as well. All those flounces, you must have grown inches at school!"

As Lavinia kept talking, Lucian noticed that Adrian was focusing a little too much on his plate. Lucian could see an unreadable expression on Adrian's face. He couldn't tell if it was anger, annoyance or hurt. The more he thought about it, the more he was sure it was a combination of the three. When he looked at Moira, he saw a different expression. She was looking at Adrian with what seemed to be a mix of envy and pity. He realized that their home life was more complicated than he'd ever suspected. Moira was obviously Lavinia's pride and joy while Adrian seemed to just be there; an afterthought.

When the meal was over, Lavinia had said she was going to bed. "Lights out within half an hour," she said before going up the stairs.

Moira walked with Allegra to the room Allegra was staying in. Lucian and Adrian stayed behind for a moment. Adrian was quiet for a moment before saying, "Lucian, whatever you see here or hear while you're here, please don't tell the others."

"What do you mean, Adrian?" Lucian asked.

Adrian sighed. "Look, you have the perfect family. I know you and Allegra fight sometimes and you're parents get mad at you and probably even argue with each other occasionally. Our friends come from similar families. My family, we're complicated. You'll probably learn things here that, well, I just don't want the other guys laughing at."

"They're your friends, Adrian," Lucian said. "They wouldn't laugh at you."

"Kaelen would," Adrian pointed out. "I know you're trying to be a good friend, and I appreciate that. But I'm serious. There are things that happen while I'm at home that I don't want everyone else knowing about, okay? Nothing super bad or anything like that, it's just…it's just stuff they wouldn't understand. Promise you won't tell them anything?"

Lucian put a friendly arm around his friend. "I promise Adrian. Are you sure you don't want to talk about it?"

Adrian shook his head. "No, you'll figure things out soon enough." He then said good night and left the room.

Lucian stayed for a while before heading down the hallway to his room. He was confused by the mysterious promise he'd just made to his friend, but decided not to worry it over too much. It was late and he needed to get to sleep. As he neared his room, he could hear Moira and Allegra talking. Unable to stop himself, he listened for a while. "Look, I know you've got Lucian right next door to you, but if you need to talk or anything, my room is just around the corner of the first stairway. Don't worry about waking me up. I'm here if you need me."

"Thanks, Moira," he heard Allegra say. "I appreciate it."

"I'm just glad we were able to convince Mother to let you two stay. Unfortunately she probably listened to me more than Adrian, but that's neither here nor there. Both of us were pulling for you," Moira replied.

"Moira, why does your mother treat Adrian the way she does? It's like he's not even there sometimes," Allegra said.

"I can't talk about that right now," Moira's reply came after a moment of silence. "It's, it's complicated. I'm sure you'll figure it out on your own. But don't ask me about it, okay?"

"Okay, Moira," Allegra promised. "Good night."

"Good night," Moira said.

Lucian could hear her moving towards Allegra's door and he quickly ducked into his own room before she'd notice him listening in. He listened as her footsteps got farther away and then stopped before continuing away from him. He looked outside his door and could see her form going up the stairs. It didn't make sense. Adrian had told him their first year that Moira had been put in the tower. However, sleepiness cleared his thoughts and soon he got in bed and fell asleep.

The next few days he spent with Adrian outside riding horses, throwing snowballs at each other, and hunting in the forests behind the castle. Clover and Rusty worked well as a team, flushing flocks of geese and searching for hares. When it was too cold to be outside, Adrian showed Lucian his fencing room and they practiced both left-handed and right-handed. "It feels weird being better than you at this," Adrian admitted one afternoon.

"Trust me, it's weird for me to be beaten," Lucian retorted.

They continued working until Adrian said, "Well, suppertime. Let's see how long I get ignored tonight." Then, as though he hadn't meant to say it out loud, he added, "I mean, you know, how long the girls talk to each other."

"Adrian, I already figured out that dinner doesn't quite go the way you described it and that Moira's not the one in the tower," Lucian replied gently.

Blushing, Adrian said, "I'm sorry, Lucian. I didn't really want to lie to you; it's just hard to admit that my mother seems to wish I'd just disappear."

Lucian nodded and said, "Well, I won't ignore you if it's any consolation." They laughed and the two walked to the dining hall where they continued to talk about how things were shaping up with Lucian's fencing.

Later that night, Lucian was lying silently on his bed, staring at the ceiling while the rest of the castle slept. He felt restless and frustrated. Since arriving, he'd rarely been able to talk to Moira. If anything, she seemed to avoid being near him except at meals where she would often talk and laugh, as though more for her mother to see than to actually communicate with Lucian.

Unable to sleep, he threw the blankets off and slipped into his slippers before wrapping a robe around himself and silently walking out of his room after lighting a candle for himself to see by. He poked his head into Allegra's room. She was fast asleep. Unwilling to disturb her, he silently closed the door again before walking up the stairs. Adrian hadn't really shown him around the castle and he thought maybe some walking about would do him good. He wandered about hallways, really not sure which direction he was going. He neared the castle's large tower and he opened the door slowly, hoping that no one would hear it creaking. Closing it behind him, he continued down the hallway. It was dark; the only light coming from the moonlit windows and the small flame of his candle. He continued up a flight of stairs until he came to an open room. It seemed to be a shrine dedicated to someone. There were several portraits of the same person along the walls. A suit of armor stood in one corner, still black from fiery blasts of a dragon's breath. A sword glinted on the wall above the armor. There was a saddle in another corner and a desk covered by letters and other memorabilia. He looked around at everything and then stopped in front of one of the portraits. He gasped. It was Adrian, only older and more distinguished. But it was the same face, the same sandy brown hair, same sparkling green eyes. The man even had the same smile.

"I see you've met my father," a voice said behind him.

Lucian nearly dropped his candle as he whirled around. "You startled me," he accused as his eyes tried to adjust to the dimness.

Moira stepped out from the shadows she'd been hiding in. "I'm sorry, I wasn't trying to." She walked closer to the portrait. "That's my dad."

"Adrian looks just like him," Lucian said, unable to think of anything more intelligent to say.

"Painfully so, yes," Moira replied sadly.

"Adrian wasn't banished to the tower because you fight," Lucian commented.

Moira shook her head. "No. Our relationship, while certainly not as good as yours and Allegra's, was never that bad either. When Dad died, Mother took everything that had ever reminded her of him and threw it out. Adrian and I salvaged what we could, bringing it here. His favorite sword, the armor he saved Mother in, his portraits, the letters he wrote her; anything we could. Adrian, bless his heart, has always been the spitting image of Dad. Mother couldn't simply throw Adrian out, so she sent him to the tower. She does the minimum that she must with him and otherwise lets him be to himself. It's," she sighed, "it's hard, on both of us. The energy and love she should show him is thrust on me. She lives for every little thing I do while Adrian rarely, if ever, hears a word of praise."

"Is that why you won't let me get near you?" Lucian asked.

"What?" Moira asked, looking taken aback.

"I get it, you're afraid that I'll die young, right?" Lucian said. "That you'll be left alone."

"That's, not," Moira was stammering over her words.

Lucian continued before she could finish, "In the three years since we've met, I've tried everything I could think of to get to know you. I've tried talking about myself. I've desperately tried to win games in the hopes of winning a question. I've gone out of my way to be nice to you and still you hold yourself back."

"I can't get to know you," Moira said.

"Why not?" Lucian demanded; his voice strained from trying not to shout. "We're supposed to fall in love with each other. I don't know anything about you. I don't know what you like to do, what you hate to do, your favorite vacation, what you hope to do when we're old and gray; I don't even know your favorite color! How am I supposed to get you to fall in love with me if we never get to know each other?"

"I don't want to fall in love with you," Moira cried.

Lucian took a step back from her as though she'd slapped him. "What?"

Moira was now sobbing. "I'm sorry, Lucian. I can't fall in love with you. Look at what happened to my mother. She lives as recluse within herself. She shuns her own son because he looks too much like the love she lost. She has no pictures in the house, no letters kept; nothing to remind her of him because she's still so in love with him that he might have died yesterday for the pain it causes her. All because she fell deeply in love. I don't want to become my mother. I can't. I can't." She slumped against Lucian's chest, throwing her arms around him.

Unsure why he did it, Lucian ran his fingers through Moira's hair. It was soft as satin and flowed like golden, silk threads between his fingers. He held her while she sobbed against his chest. Tears filled his own eyes. So this was it. This was how it was going to be. Moira wouldn't fall in love with him because she didn't want to become her mother. They would never have happily ever after because she was afraid of banishing his memory should something happen to him.

"It's no use, Lucian," she said, rising to meet his gaze as she regained some control of her emotions. "You've broken every defense I've put up just by being you. You're so handsome, so good, so kind and true. Please, don't try any harder. I'll tell you anything you need to be able to complete your quest. I'll do whatever I have to so that we can be happy. Just don't ask me to fall in love with you, please. I've already fallen harder for you than I ever wanted to. Let's just be really good friends. And after your quest is over and you rescue me, we can be really good friends that get married. Please."

Lucian stepped away from her and took her hand in his. He brought it gently to his lips, the only kiss they were ever allowed to share with their princesses. Althea had taught them in spell breaking that only love's first real kiss would break a spell. A kiss on the hand was admissible, though some boys took that to an extreme. "I'll respect your wishes," he said at length, "though if I may say, you don't strike me as being like your mother. However, that said, I'll stop trying. We can be friends."

Moira smiled and seemed to breathe a sigh of relief. "Thank you, Lucian."

He tried to return her smile, despite his heart shattering within him. "Good night, Moira," Lucian said, turning away from her.

"Lucian," Moira called.

Hoping she would take back what she had just said Lucian turned to face her again. "Yes?"

Moira smiled, "My favorite color is lavender."

The next day, the group went into town so that they could buy their supplies for the next semester of school. Lucian and Adrian both got new trousers as well as new doublets and jackets. Adrian had long outgrown his and when they picked them up later that afternoon, he couldn't stop showing Lucian that the sleeves actually fell at his wrists and his trousers were actually to his feet.

Lucian laughed, "Yes I can see that your clothes fit. Mine do too. It's a nice change."

The rest of the day was spent preparing for the trip to Traifloran. When they had finished, Adrian and Lucian spent some time in the fencing hall practicing. "You seem preoccupied," Adrian commented. "Anything bothering you?"

"Nothing out of the ordinary," Lucian replied. It wasn't technically a lie; he had often worried about his relationship with Moira. However, he didn't want to share with Adrian the conversation he'd had with Moira the night before.

"You know you're the worst liar I know," Adrian said. He set his sword down. "Seriously, what's bothering you?"

"You're going to get mad at me," Lucian warned.

"No I won't, just talk to me, okay?" Adrian said.

"I made Moira cry yesterday. Not on purpose," he added hastily as Adrian scowled. Lucian sighed. "I couldn't sleep last night so I just kind of wandered around and I found the tower with your dad's things in it."

"Moira was there wasn't she?" Adrian asked. Lucian nodded and Adrian continued with a sigh, "Look, Lucian, we're only fifteen, right? I know right now Moira's worried that she'll end up like our mother. It hurts both of us. When Dad was alive, my mother was the happiest woman alive. After he died, she sort of pulled into herself. Anything that reminded her of him was shunned, even me. But, I don't think when it comes down to it that Moira will continue holding off from you. I mean, is there a prince at Charming Academy more charming than you? Seriously?"

"George," Lucian offered with a teasing smile.

"Okay, point," Adrian admitted with a laugh. "But I think in the end, Moira will come around."

"She told me last night that she doesn't want to fall in love with me," Lucian said sadly. "She just wants to be friends."

"What did you say?" Adrian asked.

"What could I say?" Lucian demanded. "I couldn't very well force your sister to fall in love with me. She's so independent, it'd be an insult to her and then she'd hate me forever. I told her I'd respect her wishes."

"You don't want to though," Adrian said, seeing through his friend.

Lucian shook his head, "No I don't. I never thought I'd fall in love, with any girl. Much less Moira. I mean, she's a beautiful girl, but she was always so reserved and frankly abrasive. And really, fall in love with a girl? It seems like yesterday that we were both talking about how gross love is and that we'd never ever love anyone."

"Pretty naïve of us," Adrian laughed. "I know it hurts, Lucian. But I think you're doing this the right way. She'll see her own strength before the end. She may think she can resist you now, but it won't last; especially with how hard you've fallen for her."

"You think so?" Lucian asked with a smile.

"Oh yeah, trust me," Adrian said, clapping Lucian's shoulder. "You just keep being the perfect gentleman you've always been and she'll fall in love with you on her own. Then she only has herself to blame. Now come on, you've almost got me with that weak arm of yours. Let's give it another go."

They continued practicing until Allegra and Moira came in. For a while they didn't notice the two girls standing in the doorway. It wasn't until Lucian felt an intense pair of eyes watching him that he turned and saw Moira looking at him, a far away smile on her face. She flushed and said as the boys lowered their swords, "Mother said supper is nearly ready and to get you if you plan on eating tonight. Oh, and you may want to clean up before you come, Nana is here." She smiled even broader and then left with Allegra.

When they arrived at supper, Lucian met a woman who, if twenty years younger, could easily have been mistaken for Lavinia. Nana was tall and had the same face, though her hair was silvery white and flowed about her shoulders rather than kept up in the severe bun Lavinia favored. She also appeared to be a picture of optimism, her face lit with a beautiful smile that Lucian was sure Lavinia probably shared. "Well, if it isn't my favorite grandson," she said as Adrian walked in.

"Nana, it's so good to see you," Adrian replied, eagerly enveloping himself in his grandmother's outstretched arms.

"Oh, it's good to see you too. My, my, you must have grown a foot since last I saw you," Nana replied with a smile.

"Only five inches," Adrian corrected with a smile.

"Close enough," Nana laughed. "Now, you must introduce me to your handsome young friend here."

Adrian turned and waved Lucian over. "Lucian, this is my grandmother, the dowager queen Bethany. Nana, this is my best friend Lucian. He's going to be Moira's prince when they finish school."

"Ooh," Nana squealed, with a significant look at Moira, who blushed under her grandmother's scrutiny. "Well, you certainly got the luck of the draw, Moira. He's very handsome indeed. Where are you from young man?"

"Maltisten," Lucian replied, taking Nana's hand and kissing it. "It's a pleasure to meet you."

"Oh I despise formality, Lucian," Nana retorted and pulled him into an eager hug. "Welcome to Lictthane. You must tell me what you think of it. I've always preferred Fallcrest, being my home province, but it is quite nice here."

Lucian caught on to Nana's infectious optimism and laughed. "I like it very well here, though I do miss the ocean."

"An ocean boy, yes, I could see it in your build." Nana turned away from him and spied Allegra. "And who might this be?"

"I'm Allegra," she replied with a smile. "Lucian is my older brother. When Adrian graduates, I'll be his princess."

"This is so delightful." Nana clapped her hands together before clasping Allegra in a tight hug. "Lavinia, dear, you didn't tell me what a beautiful family your children were marrying into. They are really quite darling. Over supper you must tell me everything there is to know about you. After all, if you're marrying my grandchildren someday, I simply must approve." She winked at Lucian and Allegra before the group sat at supper.

It was the most entertaining meal they'd had since their arrival. Nana brought a life and energy to the melancholy home that no one, not even Lavinia, could resist. When the meal was over they sat in the large parlor having dessert and Nana talked about everything under the sun. "Now Lavinia dear, whatever happened to that family portrait that used to be in here? I haven't seen it in ages and it was a beautiful likeness. I don't think you've seen any pictures of their father," Nana continued turning to Allegra and Lucian, "but he was quite handsome. In fact, Adrian looks just like him." She turned again to Lavinia as though waiting an answer.

Lavinia hesitated a moment before clearing her throat. "It was unfortunately destroyed, Mother. There was a flood several years ago. Everything on the first floor had to be replaced."

"What a pity," Nana replied, not seeming to catch the lie in her daughter's voice. "I'm sure I could you bring you a new portrait for your parlor. I have two excellent portraits from when the children were young."

"No, really, Mother, that's not necessary," Lavinia said quickly. "You would miss it far too much. I, I'll just have to contact the artist and see if he can make a replication."

Adrian and Moira were looking nervously between their mother and grandmother as the conversation about their father continued. Lucian caught Adrian's eye and decided to take a chance. "Queen Bethany," he began.

"Lucian, dear, I've told you I despise formality," Nana interrupted. "Simply call me Nana."

"What was it like in Fallcrest?" Lucian asked with a smile.

With that topic in her mind, Nana was off like a racehorse. She spoke long about the province she'd grown up in. The fire was dying in the fireplace and the candle light flickering as she continued her tale. Everyone was captivated by her story. She was able to weave a tapestry of words that was almost visible to her rapt audience. They could see the landscapes she painted and hear the mountain breezes whispering in their ears. After a long while she suddenly said, "My goodness. Listen to me chatter on like this, just like an old mother hen. You must all be exhausted and we have a long journey ahead of us tomorrow. Go on now, off to bed my precious ones. We'll have all day to chat." She hugged and kissed each child before watching them leave the room. "You have such wonderful children, Lavinia," they heard her say as they left the room. "You should be proud of them."

"I am, Mother," Lavinia replied.

Nana made the ride to Traifloran fun and enjoyable as she continued to keep each of the occupants busily engaged in conversation. Lucian instantly took a liking to her. She was as giddy as a child and yet held the elegance and sophistication of an adult. Even Lavinia seemed more relaxed and happy with her mother there. Lucian almost wished that the older woman lived with his friend's family. He was sure that Nana's bright optimism could easily overcome the dark shadows of Lavinia's grief. Adrian was relishing in his mother's attention as she tried to show equal attention to both of her children. It was obvious to Lucian that Lavinia was trying to keep her mother in the dark about how they lived when she was gone, though it was clear that she was unused to spending so much of her time on Adrian. Her smiles on Moira were always true, while she seemed to hesitate on Adrian.

On arriving in Traifloran, Eleanor and Leticia immediately found the travelers and said excitedly, "You're staying at our house." Then they giggled as they realized they'd spoken together.

"It's good to see you again so soon," Allegra said, hugging each girl in turn. "What do you mean we're staying at your house?"

"Mother and Daddy agreed that you could all stay with us for the competition. It's only for a couple days anyway, and they'd be happy to house you," Leticia replied.

"Yes, and we've even had rooms prepared for you, so you can't refuse," Eleanor added with a smile.

Lavinia had heard them as well and said, "My mother surprised us with a visit. Will that be a problem?"

"I'm sure we can have another room arranged," Leticia said graciously.

"Nonsense," Nana retorted. "I'll stay with Lavinia. I get the feeling I need some one-on-one time with my little girl."

"Mother, I haven't been your little girl in many years," Lavinia said with a teasing smile.

"Darling, even when you're as old as the dust, you'll still be my little girl," Nana replied.

"Well, it's settled then," Eleanor said brightly. "Come on, we'll show you to the castle as soon as you've both set up your exhibits."

"You have to show us yours now," Leticia told Allegra.

"Not a chance," Allegra retorted. "I'll have it covered until tomorrow. It's to be a surprise."

As they walked, Lucian asked, "Will George be coming?"

"No," Eleanor said, "I invited him, but it seems another of his sisters, Susan, has been found and is getting married. He's got to be there so he can be the ring bearer. I think he'd like to have told her no, but you can't refuse your sister can you?"

They laughed and when they arrived at the judge's table, the two girls entered their pieces. Allegra had insisted that they wait farther back so they wouldn't hear the title of her piece. Once she had been told where to set it up, she walked away, carrying the cloth-bound artwork. Lucian felt insatiably curious as to what his sister had done, but she wouldn't even tell him. They then followed Eleanor and Leticia to their family home. It was a large castle built at the base of a large mountain range. Snow covered trees surrounded the grounds like silent citadels. On going inside, they found King Julian and his wife waiting. "Welcome to our home," the queen said. She had the same elfin looks that made Leticia different from Eleanor. "I don't know that we've all been acquainted. I'm Queen Rebekah and of course you know my girls, Eleanor and Leticia. This is our son, Benjamin and my husband King Julian."

"It's a pleasure to meet you," Lavinia replied. "I'm Queen Lavinia and I believe you met my children, Adrian and Moira, and Lucian and Allegra during summer's dressage competition. This is my mother, the dowager queen Bethany."

"We're glad you could stay with us," Julian said. "Rebekah will show you to your rooms. If you boys are interested, Benjamin and I were about to go on a short hunt. We'd be pleased to have you join us."

"That would be great!" Lucian replied.

"We'll wait for you here then," Benjamin said.

After getting settled in their rooms, the boys followed Julian and Benjamin outside to the forests behind the castle. "We've had lots of game birds recently," Julian said quietly as they stepped through the snow. "Hopefully we'll catch some to take home for supper."

"If only I had Rusty with me," Lucian said.

It turned out that the king's hunting hounds did near as good a job as Rusty would have. The men soon had caught several birds before heading back inside. They rejoined the ladies and the afternoon and evening was spent together in laughter and talking.

"I hate to bring up something painful," Allegra said, "but I have to know. What's going to happen with your schooling, Leticia?"

Frowning slightly, Leticia replied, "I'll continue going to Fair Damsel's like the rest of you. Melantha didn't make things very clear, but it sounds like they'll just let me continue to go to school and then set up a suitable match after graduation. Don't worry though, I'll still be at school and all the visits just as though nothing had happened. I just won't have a prince anymore."

"I can't say that I'm very sorry, Leticia," Julian said. "He was never well-suited to you."

Leticia was too much the lady to agree aloud with her father, but Lucian could see in her eyes that she agreed. There was a barely covered greenish tinge on her cheek where Nathan had struck her. The wart on Benjamin's nose, while it had shrunk, was still visible. It would be a long while before the emotional pain completely healed.

"Anyhow," Rebekah said, interrupting Lucian's thoughts, "enough of sadness. Now is a happy time. We're surrounded by friends and family. Lavinia, tell us more about Lictthane. I don't believe I've ever visited there. Is it pleasant?"

The conversation continued to flow and swirl about the table like a happy breeze. When they retired for the evening, Rebekah asked everyone if they had enough blankets and bed warmers to be comfortable. Lucian could easily see where the twins had gotten their sweet demeanor. Rebekah was kindness itself and smiled often. When she was sure that everyone was taken care of and comfortable, she too retired to her room to sleep. Silence fell over the castle as sweet dreams carried its occupants to peaceful, quiet realms of contentment.

In the morning, the whole group went to the nearby art competition. It was within walking distance of the castle, once everyone had put on their winter clothes. On arriving, the girls separated themselves from the rest of the group, except for Leticia. She stayed with her parents and Benjamin, who had offered her his arm as they waited to be allowed to mill about. The others had gone to their pieces and were preparing them for inspection by the judges and attendees. At eleven o'clock sharp, the judges said everyone would be allowed to inspect the pieces. "Please do not touch anything," the raspy voiced, balding judge said as people began to move about. "We wouldn't want to spoil our ladies' hard work."

Lucian looked about at the pieces girls and women from various parts of Sanalbereth had created. There were paintings and tapestries, meticulously detailed urns and jars, glass projects that would have made Allegra green with envy to have created. Moira had a pastel piece she had done of the grounds of Fair Damsel's Academy. Lucian knew looking at it that it was a representation of Tallia and Achilles' wedding. "I hope you'll give it to them when this is over," she said as Lucian stopped to admire the piece.

"Of course I will," Lucian replied. "It's beautiful. You are quite talented."

She flushed. "Don't let Allegra hear you say that," Moira teased. "She might get jealous."

"Nah, she'd be mad at me if I didn't tell you that," Lucian replied.

"Well, you'd best continue on. I think Allegra's piece is down and around the corner a little ways," Moira said knowingly before turning her attention to another group who had come to view her piece.

Lucian stayed a while to listen as Moira described her inspiration and choice of colors and medium. He hadn't even thought to ask her why she'd chosen that. In fact, he hadn't asked any of the artists questions about their art. Was that how you were supposed to go about an art contest? He looked at Adrian who shrugged and they continued. They soon arrived at Eleanor's piece, a tapestry depicting a summery meadow with horses playing about a sparkling blue stream. He stopped to chat with Eleanor a while before moving on through the pieces. He hadn't been able to find Allegra yet.

Adrian was the first to spy Allegra. "Lucian, you've got to see this," he said.

Lucian turned and was sure that his jaw hit his shoes as his mouth fell open. Allegra was standing next to her painting. A bright smile, softened by tears, was on her face as she asked, "What do you think? If you tell me you like it than I can take last place and not even care."

For a long time, Lucian couldn't speak. In bright splashes of oil paint, Allegra had captured their father's daring rescue of their mother. Alexandra was at the top of a tower, her hair a shimmering ribbon of red braid draped out the window as Lysander bravely climbed to the top. But there was more to the painting. In one corner Allegra was standing with Adrian, hands clasped. The opposite corner showed Lucian and Moira, Moira held in Lucian's arms, love's first kiss breaking any enchantments between them. "Allegra, it's…"

"I called it 'Legacy'," Allegra replied softly. "Do you like it?"

"It's wonderful, Allegra. You captured everyone beautifully," Lucian said, hugging her. "Although," he added teasingly, "I really hope that painted kisses don't count for spell breaking. Otherwise I might be in trouble."

Allegra laughed and smacked his arm gently. "I highly doubt it, Lucian."

Leticia appeared with Benjamin soon and gasped, "Oh Allegra, that's beautiful. But that's your parents and there you are in the corner with Adrian and," Leticia turned a teasing smile to Lucian before saying, "and there's Moira and Lucian. Why, it's breathtaking, Allegra. No wonder you wouldn't show it to the rest of us. Now, you have to tell me the stories that you've made up for yourself and Lucian."

Later in the afternoon, the artists were allowed to visit the other contestants' pieces. Moira and Eleanor added their surprise and compliments to Allegra's piece. "Oh I hope you win, Allegra. That's so lovely," Eleanor said.

Moira flushed at seeing herself in the piece and said, "It's very nice, Allegra. You must have put a lot of work in this to capture everyone so accurately."

Allegra smiled and then they all went about looking at the other pieces while the judges were making their final rounds. There was an hour break for luncheon so the judges could deliberate. The group of friends went to the castle and enjoyed conversation and warm chicken soup before heading back to the competition for the announcement of the winners. When they arrived back, Allegra looked at Lucian and whispered, "There are so many talented women here; I doubt I'll place at all."

"If I were a judge, I'd give you first," Lucian replied.

"Ah, but you are biased," Allegra said with a smile. "You'd give me first no matter what."

"That's because I'm a gentleman," Lucian teased.

"That's because you're a big brother," Allegra retorted, but she smiled brightly. "Oh well, it's enough that I entered. I'm glad I did."

They listened as the same raspy voiced judge began the announcement of the winners. He first talked about how the decision had been very hard to come by because of all the talent that surrounded them. In fact, he spoke for nearly fifteen minutes just about the deliberation they'd gone over. Lucian felt as though someone were pressing down on his eyelids. When he took a side glance at Adrian, he could see that he was sitting with the same droopy eyed expression. Finally he began the announcements. Moira received honorable mention in the pastel division and Eleanor received second place in tapestry.

Allegra wasn't mentioned during the paint division and everyone shot her a look of shared disappointment and condolence. They almost didn't hear the judge say, "Our overall competition champion for beauty of subject and expertise in execution is Princess Allegra of Maltisten and her piece 'Legacy'. Princess Allegra?"

"That's you, Allegra," Adrian said suddenly. Allegra's jaw dropped and she stood slowly as though in shock.

"Ah, there she is. Come along, dear," the judge said. He was holding a large trophy. Applause burst over the crowd as Allegra slowly made her way up to the stage on which he was standing. She accepted the trophy handed to her as well as a large bouquet of red and white roses while another judge pinned a vibrantly colored ribbon to her gown. Even though Lucian couldn't hear her, he could see her stuttering her gratitude to the judges. "Once again, Princess Allegra of Maltisten!" the judge announced.

With the most brilliant smile Lucian had ever seen, Allegra curtsied deeply before returning to her seat as the judge announced that the gallery would be open for viewing for the rest of the day. "Artists, please pick up your pieces in the morning. Congratulations to all our talented ladies."

The group headed home and the whole evening Allegra expressed her disbelief in winning and her wish that her parents had been there. Congratulations were given to all of the participants and especially to Allegra. When the adults told them it was time to retire, Allegra came to Lucian's room. "If you're tired, I'll leave, but I couldn't possibly sleep now. I'm too excited."

Lucian laughed, "Come sit down." After she did he hugged her. "Congratulations again, Allegra. You really did a fabulous job. I knew you'd get something."

"That was just totally unexpected and there were so many women who deserved it much more than I did. I mean, I did okay, but really there were some fabulous pieces there," Allegra said.

"Yes, but yours had the most heart. And don't tell me I'm biased," Lucian interrupted before she could even begin to speak. "You must have worked on that for weeks to get it done that well."

"Two and a half months," Allegra admitted.

"See?" Lucian said. "You earned it. And now you can send Mom and Dad a beautiful letter all about how you won the competition hands down."

Allegra frowned. "I don't want to send them a letter. I want to tell them in person. I know we promised we wouldn't go home for break, but it's only three hours from Lictthane. We wouldn't stay long, just long enough to show Mom and Dad. Mom can hang it up somewhere and then we can go."

Lucian hesitated. It wasn't that he didn't want to go home. He did, but he also knew that he'd never gone back on a promise before. He didn't think now would be a great time to start. "I don't know Allegra. Let's see what Lavinia says when we get back to their home. It might be better to just send a letter for now."

Nodding, Allegra said, "I know. I miss them."

"I do too," Lucian admitted, hugging Allegra. "Now, go pretend to sleep, okay?"

"Okay," Allegra agreed. "I'll see you in the morning. Good night, Lucian."

"Good night, Allegra," Lucian replied.

She got up and started to walk out of the room. "Lucian?" Allegra said at the doorway. When he turned to look at her she smiled and said, "I love you."

"I love you too, Allegra. Get to sleep," Lucian returned.

Unsurprisingly, Lavinia turned down their request to go home. She'd agreed to mail a letter to their parents about the competition, including Allegra's ribbon, but Allegra shook her head. "No, I'll write it." However, as the days passed, the letter didn't get written. Allegra couldn't bring herself to write the words she longed to say in person. Lucian could tell she was becoming desperate and so spent more time with his sister than he did ordinarily to keep her mind off things. One afternoon as a snowstorm raged outside, there was a knock at the door. "I wonder who that could be in weather like this," Lavinia said as she opened the door. "Oh, please come in."

A tall, cloaked form entered. "Thank you, Queen Lavinia. I shan't be long," a familiar voice replied. "I'm here for Allegra and Lucian."

The two, who had been sitting with Adrian and Moira with Nana in the parlor heard their names and went into the foyer where Lavinia was standing with their visitor. Pulling back the hood covering her head, Calista turned towards the children. "We haven't much time," she said. "You must go home now. It's time."

Allegra choked on tears while Lucian put his arms around her, trying to hold back the tears stinging his eyes.

"We're coming too," Moira said suddenly.

Calista shook her head, "While I value your kindness, this is something they need to do alone."

"No," Adrian argued, standing at Moira's side. "We did this alone. We're not going to abandon our friends to do it alone as well."

Sighing, Calista said, "I haven't time to argue with you. If you insist on coming you must get ready now."

Gathering coats and scarves, the family got ready to go while Allegra and Lucian gathered their things quietly. Within minutes, they were in one of Charming Academy's carriages seeming to race the wind towards Maltisten. Lucian's mind was in a whirl. What if they arrived too late? What if his father was already dead? Why on earth was Calista there anyway? Calista was silent on the journey while Lucian tried to continue to comfort his sister. Moira was sitting on Allegra's other side, patting her arm. At one point, she lifted her eyes to meet Lucian's. As though he could hear her voice in her head, he knew what she was telling him. "I'll be here, for both of you."

Lucian smiled. "Thank you," he returned in the same silent manner.

Moira covered his hand with hers as the carriage rocked along the road.

On arriving in Maltisten, the butler opened the door. "Calista Periwinkle, and Master Lucian, Miss Allegra, what are you doing here?"

"I have business to conduct here. I brought the children to be with their father," Calista replied. "We've also brought some friends along. Please, it is urgent. Where is King Lysander?"

The butler frowned. "He's up in his chambers with the mistress." He looked at Allegra and Lucian with sorrow. "I'm sorry my young ones. The doctor says it'll be any day now."

Tears fell unrestrained from Allegra's eyes and the group followed the butler to the master suite. On opening the door, Alexandra looked up from the bed on which the king was lying. "Lucian, Allegra, what...Calista? I don't understand."

"I've come as a representative of the fairy council," Calista replied, entering the room and standing at the end of the bed while Alexandra embraced each of her children. They stood by Lysander's bedside. "Lysander, are you awake?"

Lysander nodded. "I am. What brings you to my home?" Lucian was shocked at the image before him. His father who had always been strong was now pale and thin, a pallid form against the sheets of his bed. His voice was raspy and drawn, as though the effort of speaking was too much for him.

Calista smiled. "I come bearing wonderful news. First however, I know your daughter has something she wishes to tell you."

Allegra choked again. "Oh Daddy!"

"What is it my star?" Lysander asked. "What would you like to tell me?"

"I, I," Allegra stammered. Her tears had cut her voice short and she threw her arms around her father.

"Allegra won the art competition in Traifloran, Dad," Lucian said, trying to curb his own emotions. He pulled out Allegra's painting. "This is what she entered. 'Legacy' is what it's called."

Lysander looked at the painting and stroked Allegra's hair. Alexandra had tears of her own as she looked from the painting to her heartbroken daughter. "It's perfect, Allegra. I'm so proud of you. Quite the lady now," Lysander rasped.

"I love you Daddy," Allegra sobbed. "I just wanted to capture your story."

"This leads me into my purpose for being here," Calista said gently. "After consideration of new information gathered by the council from various sources, we have changed the ruling we came to all those years ago. The story of Princess Alexandra of Maltisten and Lysander, Prince Charming of Coleston has now been written." Pulling from under her cloak a bound leather volume, Calista handed it to Alexandra. "Within the book, you will find an honorary diploma from Charming Academy and a copy of your quest and the record of your brave deeds as compiled by Phillipa Rosepetal, myself and other fairy historians. Congratulations, King Lysander, Prince Charming."

Tears filled the eyes of the sickened king. "You see, my love," Lysander said, turning to Alexandra, "you don't have to be stuck with second best anymore. You get the Prince Charming you always deserved."

Alexandra choked on her own tears. "Oh, Lysander, you wonderful man; I never thought you were second best."

"You didn't?" Lysander asked weakly.

"No," Alexandra replied. "It doesn't matter what these fairies have done. You have always been Prince Charming to me." She kissed him gently, their tears mingling together while their children cried on either side of the bed.

Calista smiled as a magical glow brightened the room. "Well, I must return to the academy," she said as everyone looked at her in confusion. "My work here is finished. Have a swift recovery, King Lysander. Lucian and Adrian, I'll see you soon at school." She then left the room.

"Well," Lavinia said after a while, "we should go too."

"Oh, no, please stay," Alexandra pled. "We'd love to have you stay to supper. I appreciate so much you taking the children for me so that I could take care of Lysander. It's only fair that you stay here. You've had a very fast trip unexpectedly."

Lavinia hesitated, "Well…"

"Please, Mother," Moira begged. "I'm sure Nana would love to get to know Lucian and Allegra's parents."

Nana smiled, "Oh yes, I must get to know all about you."

"And I want to hear the story," Adrian added. "Come on, Mother, we'll be the first in the whole world to hear the story. Please?"

A rare laugh escaped Lavinia. "I see I'm outvoted. I was going to say that we should allow you time to be together as a family, but I can see that everyone else is going to want to stay."

"Wonderful," Alexandra said. She turned back to Lysander. "Now, you are going to get some rest while I take care of everyone."

"You expect me to rest after all this excitement?" Lysander asked teasingly, trying to sit up. "Why I feel better already."

Alexandra pushed him back. "Oh no you don't. You're staying right here and resting until supper. Lucian and Allegra can speak to you after supper. For now, you're resting."

"Yes, Mother," Lysander teased, kissing Alexandra.

"I'm hardly your mother," Alexandra retorted before kissing him again and shuffling everyone out.

Once everyone was outside the room, Nana caught Alexandra's arm. "Now, my dear, you must tell me everything about yourself and your dear husband."

The others laughed as Nana, Lavinia and Alexandra walked downstairs together. Lucian led Adrian to the fencing room and then turned as he realized that Allegra and Moira were following them. "I know, we're not allowed to fight, but can we just sit and watch?" Allegra asked.

"Sure," Lucian shrugged. They continued to the fencing room.

"Wow," Moira said as they walked inside. "This is incredible."

"Swordsmanship is my dad's passion," Lucian replied. "Someday I hope to be as good as he is. Here Adrian, your hands are bigger than mine; this sword should fit you fairly well."

As the boys practiced their swordplay, the girls watched in silence until Allegra asked, "So, has anything happened since you talked to Lucian?"

Moira shook her head. While Lucian had been reluctant to share their conversation with anyone, Moira had been so overwhelmed that she'd immediately drawn Allegra into her confidence; spilling everything from the real reason she was touchy when speaking about boys to the reason Adrian got ignored so often. "No, he hasn't done or said anything. He's kept to his word."

"It's not going to be easy, you know," Allegra pointed out. "Eventually you won't be able to just be friends anymore."

"I know," Moira whispered in defeat. "But for now, I need to be distant. I need to know for myself that I won't become my mother. I think Lucian understands that."

"Lucian is pretty understanding that way. Always could read my feelings no matter how hard I may have tried to hide them," Allegra admitted.

"That's what scares me," Moira said.

"Well, give yourselves time. After all, you've both still got well over three years of school left," Allegra said with a smile.

"More like three and a half," Moira corrected. "And that half is going to go by faster than we know it."

"Well, you know what they say," Allegra teased. "Time flies."

Chapter 5

The next month did seem to fly. Lysander gradually got better, though Alexandra would not allow him to travel with Allegra and Lucian back to school. Instead, she arranged with Lavinia to have them travel up together so that she could stay behind with Lysander. On arriving back at school the boys immediately fell back into their school schedule. By February, they were well-used to their routine. One bitingly cold day, they shivered their way to the stables for horsemanship. When they arrived, Phillipa said, "Go back to the castle, boys, class is cancelled.

"What?" Kaelen argued. "But Phillipa, you never cancel class."

"I do when there's a blizzard on the way. Now come on, quickly, back to the castle," Phillipa replied, ushering them from the barn. Lucian could see her bright pink fairy eyes doing one last check on all the horses and equipment before she locked the doors and then whispered a fairy spell on the barn before following the boys inside. As they walked, the boys saw other classes coming from the gym and from the gazebo.

"Phillipa, how will Lorelei survive?" Lucian asked as they walked inside.

"Don't worry about Lorelei," Phillipa said kindly. "That lake is deeper than it appears. Her home is located near a thermal spring, so it is always quite warm enough for her."

"So then, the lake shouldn't ever freeze over, right?" Jacobi asked.

"Not exactly." Phillipa explained, "The thermal spring is near the very bottom of the lake. It only warms the bottom of the waters. It's not a very strong spring and so it doesn't necessarily reach up to the top waters; especially when we have a storm of this magnitude coming."

Upon going inside, Calista was standing at the door. "Anyone missing from your class?"

"No, Calista," Phillipa said. "Everyone is accounted for."

"Good, you'll find your usual emergency quarters ready for you," Calista replied.

"Thank you," Phillipa said before smiling at the boys and walking down a corridor they'd never explored. In fact, Lucian was quite sure it had never been there before.

Soon Achilles entered with his class and Lorelei's class. "Everyone's here, Calista," he assured her before the words left her mouth.

Calista smiled. "In that case, you'd best go to your emergency quarters. They're ready for you and Tallia." As Achilles walked away she turned to the boys in the hallway. Lucian could tell she was doing a mental headcount. Assured that everyone was indeed present, she said, "Now, for those of you who would normally be in class right now, you'll find an assignment in the common room for each class. They will pertain to what you have been learning. You may adjourn to that room until it is time for your next classes. Any other periods you have today or until this storm passes that would normally be in our outdoor areas, will be spent in the commons."

She had barely finished speaking when Russett entered the building alone. "I just checked the whole grounds. No one is left unaccounted for. There are no straggling boys from classes or simply out enjoying the frostiness."

"Thank you, Russett," Calista replied. "Go to the kitchen and get something to warm yourself."

The boys headed into the commons and immediately saw the stacks of assignments that Calista had referred to. Each class grabbed their own assignment and went to various parts of the room to work. For a moment Lucian wondered how they would possibly know if the boys did the work or not, but on looking up, saw Calista, Achilles and

Phillipa in the doorway watching. They weren't going to be fooled by pretended studying.

The blizzard lasted for almost a full week. Phillipa assured many worried boys that their horses would be perfectly fine and would not want for warmth or food. "The barn has been blessed," she told one hysteric first-year boy. "The horses will automatically be fed at the normal times. If they are cold, a blanket will automatically be wrapped about them. At the time you are normally in class, they will be allowed out of their stalls and into the indoor arena. When done there, they will be brushed down and cleaned and fed. It will be as though I myself am there to care for them."

Even with the loss of their outdoor classes, the boys weren't lacking in work to do. They were kept busy in their regular classes as well as having the assignments in the commons. When the blizzard finally blew to a close, they still had to wait for sufficient paths through the snow to be made. Midway through the week following the blizzard, the boys were finally able to go to their outdoor classes. Sunshine was blinding on the drifts of heavy white snow as they walked to their classes, following the trails that had been cut for them by the fairies. While walking to the gazebo with George Friday afternoon, Lucian saw that even the witches' garden had not been entirely safe from the storm. Lucretia and Maeve could be seen salvaging what plants they could and sadly discarding the ones too frozen to be saved. Lucian was glad to see that the flower garden he'd continued adding to had somehow survived the wintry blast. He wondered if it was because it was so close to the window and the witches were at least able to bless that part of their garden.

At supper the boys discussed the effect the storm had taken on their classes. "Oh the fairies are just loving this," Kaelen said bitterly as he piled food onto his plate. "They're trying to squeeze a week and a half into one or two days' work."

"Well, think about it Kaelen," George said logically, "we missed out on a lot of instruction. They have to get us back up to speed in order for us to be where they want at the end of the semester."

"Do you always take their side?" Kaelen asked.

George rolled his eyes and sighed, "I'm making a point, Kaelen. If you don't want to face facts that's fine, but don't get mad at the rest of us when we say we understand what's going on."

Kaelen scowled but didn't reply. The rest of the boys ignored this. Kaelen's attitude after winter break had gotten more haughty and selfish. The boys were trying their best to continue in their friendship, but even Adrian was losing patience with the arrogance.

Later as they finished their meals, George asked Lucian, "Have you heard from home recently?"

Lucian knew what they were all hoping to hear and smiled broadly, "The doctors say that Dad has made a full recovery. He's still working himself back up to his old strength; the weeks of disuse have weakened his muscles. But he said that by the time I come back for summer, he'll be good as new."

Adrian smiled, "That's great news. Do you know what they did with Allegra's painting."

When the other boys looked at them in confusion, Lucian explained about the award winning painting and its subject. "Mom has it hanging in the main entrance of our home along with the trophy and ribbon Allegra won. I know she also promised to dry the bouquet Allegra was given. It was in sad shape when my mom got it from Allegra, but she promised to do the best she could with it."

"You know, I think it's so great that they wrote your dad's story," Jacobi said. "That's really exciting. I've never heard of anything like that happening before."

"I can't think of anything," George added. "But I bet the very first princes didn't come here."

"That's possible," Lucian admitted. "I don't know. But I know Dad's really happy with it. He's got the book on a special shelf in our library."

They continued to talk for a while before going to their rooms to study and do homework before bed. Lucian had kept to his promise of trying his very best. While at home, he'd had the opportunity to talk to his dad about everything. "I just got discouraged," he'd told Lysander. "You were dying and it didn't seem to matter anymore. And then, then I said the stupidest thing in the world to Moira, almost ruined my chance of ever getting her to like me. It took me a while but I realized that I needed to keep at it, to not lose focus."

Lysander had smiled weakly. "I wish I'd been there to help you, son. But I'm glad you pulled yourself together. You're a lot stronger than you think. How are things with Moira? She's growing lovelier every time I see her."

Lucian thought about the heartache on his dad's face as he described their conversation. He'd thought about not telling him, but knew that his father would have seen through a lie faster than Adrian had. Instead, he'd told him everything. The horrible thing he'd said at school and then the short conversation they'd had at school after Moira had forgiven him. The last thing he had talked about was their impromptu discussion in the tower. It had broken his heart to talk about it and he could tell it hurt his father too. But there had been another look in his father's eye, contemplative and thoughtful. It was a similar look that Lucian had seen when Lysander was considering a sword. He balanced it in his hands and then weighed it in his arms. Lucian was sure that Lysander was weighing and measuring every word that had been exchanged and finding a way to put it in a positive light to the advantage of both.

The chiming of the clock forced Lucian to refocus his thoughts. He stretched his arms over his head and looked at the page of half-finished homework on his desk. It was no use; he couldn't finish it with his thoughts straying as widely as they had been. He stifled a yawn as he got up from the desk and pushed the chair in. That assignment wasn't going to be due soon. He'd just gotten a head start on it. He changed into his pajamas and blew out the candles before crawling under the covers and allowing his mind to continue wandering until sleep silenced his thoughts.

In the morning, Lucian spent another twenty minutes working on the assignment before going downstairs to breakfast. Adrian was downstairs already. As Lucian sat down he said, "The others haven't come down yet. I waited for a bit, but I was starving, so hopefully everyone will forgive me for starting without them."

Lucian laughed, "That's alright, Adrian. I don't care. I've been up for a while; just trying to get some more work done on an assignment."

"You mean you didn't finish yesterday?" Adrian teased. "I'm shocked."

"Well, it's not due for another week," Lucian retorted. "I was just trying to get a head start on it."

Adrian laughed, "You are so much more dedicated than I am."

"Better get dedicated," Lucian warned teasingly. "Allegra would be very disappointed if you fell behind."

"Whatever," Adrian replied, blushing.

They continued to laugh until the others arrived, pulling them into the conversation as they came. Afterwards they walked together to the commons. It was too cold to go outside, but none of them wanted to do their homework alone; except Kaelen. He left them and went to his room. "If this is a stage he's going through, he better grow out of it soon," George said in frustration. "I don't know how much longer I can deal with it."

"I don't think it's entirely Kaelen's fault," Lucian replied. The others stared at him and he explained, "Look, he started going back to his better-than-everyone attitude after he discovered Esmé. I think all the time he spends with her when she is here and then constantly trying to impress her is bringing out the worst in him. I mean, honestly, Kaelen's always thought he was better than the rest of us."

"Yeah, but at least he used to pretend to hide it," Jacobi pointed out.

Lucian smiled, "I know, and believe me, I miss the old Kaelen. But, maybe what he needs is a dose of reality to set in so that he'll quit being so brutish."

"I sure hope it's soon," Adrian sighed. "We're not the only ones losing our patience. If he's not careful, he'll find himself on the wrong side of the witches and that's a dangerous place to be."

"Trust me," Lucian laughed, "I don't need reminding."

They continued to work on their homework for a while before deciding to go to their own rooms for a bit to read their mail, if of course there was any to read. When they got up the stairs they could see Laria, her shaggy pink hair more windswept than usual, stuffing the last of the letters into mailboxes. "Well, hello again, boys. Crazy weather lately, huh? Got all the mail fairies completely behind in their deliveries. Hope you can forgive me." She smiled at them, her neon pink eyes sparkling.

"Of course we forgive you," Jacobi said.

"Well, I just hope none of this was time sensitive. Have a great weekend," Laria replied before fluttering down the stairs.

Lucian opened his mailbox and was surprised by an explosion of letters falling from it. "How on earth did she manage to get all of that in there?" he asked as he watched his friends have similar reactions with their own mailboxes.

"Magic?" Adrian suggested, picking up a few letters that had fallen on the ground.

"Must be," Lucian said. He picked up his mail and walked into his room. He grabbed a few pieces of paper from his desk to write replies on before flopping on his bed with the stack of mail. Rusty looked up from his own bed and woofed softly. "Yeah, you can come up," Lucian said, patting the bed next to him. Rusty jumped onto the bed and circled around for a while before lying down again. Lucian scratched behind Rusty's ears as he read one of the letters from Moira.

Dear Lucian,

I'm sure because of the storm this isn't going to reach you for a while. But, I wanted to write anyway.

Over winter break, I promised to tell you everything you need to complete your quest. I don't know how much any of this will actually help you, but I've decided to start answering some of your questions.

Your first question was what I like to do. I've always enjoyed the arts, especially sewing. I design my own clothes often. In fact, if you remember the gown I was wearing the day of our winter meeting, that was one of my creations. As a child, I wanted to become a seamstress. Mother told me that as a princess, such an occupation would be unacceptable, but that hasn't stopped me from de-

signing and sewing.

I also very much enjoy spending time outdoors. As you saw during summer, I enjoy swimming. The shell that you found me was perfect and I have it on my bedside table. It's still as colorful as the day you gave it to me. There's something special about that, but I haven't quite placed in my mind why it's so special. Perhaps someday I'll solve that little mystery.

Well, there's your first answer. If you continue to ask questions in your letters, I'll continue to answer them. Nana told me over break that every relationship starts with trust and knowing about the other. So, I suppose I should take her advice. She was quite smitten with you, you know. She even threatened to steal you away from me. I don't think I have to worry about that.

Enjoy your classes and I'll see you in the spring.

Your friend,
Moira

Lucian smiled and opened the other letter. This one was shorter, a note saying she hoped he was warm and safe and that she'd hear from him soon. He was slightly disappointed that there wasn't more to it, but smiled anyway and read the rest of his mail before picking up a piece of paper and beginning a letter to Moira.

As March began, winter slowly retreated. The fields of snow melted away revealing, young, tender shoots of green grass. The breezes were still chilled by winter's frost, but the boys could sense spring around the corner. Sunshine began filtering through the buds of spring leaves on trees and bushes. Daffodils and spring tulips were blooming in the gardens Russett looked after. As they walked to their outdoor classes they could hear the sounds of birds chirping in the trees and animals were beginning to come out of their winter habitats.

The world around them wasn't the only thing changing. In spell breaking, many of the boys had noticed that Althea seemed to be aging, a streak of gray showing in her ebony hair. There were also frequent mishaps in spell breaking, some of them more dangerous than others. The Tuesday before the spring visit with the princesses, Althea didn't show up at all. Instead, they found her neat handwriting on the board detailing their assignment and her old black cat, Horus, sitting on the desk, his tail twitching. They knew he was there to ensure they did their work. They hadn't quite figured out how he was able to do it, but the cat seemed able to communicate with Althea. Anyone who chose to misbehave was immediately caught and dealt with. Even with Althea gone, the boys knew it would be best not to disobey her orders.

The rest of the day continued as it would have normally until supper when Calista rose to make an announcement. "For the next two days, you will not be allowed out of the castle. This is for your own safety as the witches go through the Change. Althea informed me this morning that Maeve has passed; the beginning of this process for them. Classes have been cancelled so that we can ensure that everyone stays safely within the castle while they pass through this ordeal. This is not something to be taken lightly. Their magic is outside their control and the fate of anyone foolish enough to go out will not be pleasant. When you finish your supper, you will go to your dormitories."

A curious gleam lit Kaelen's eyes, "We should watch from our windows."

"Are you nuts?" Jacobi asked. "Don't you remember what Althea told us in class about the Change? All of their magic is transferred about and the elements combine until separating into the new carrier. It's a form of magic so potent and ancient that the witches themselves are in danger of being lost to it."

"All the more reason to watch," Kaelen replied. "Or are you chicken?"

"Kaelen, Jacobi's right," Lucian said seriously. "There's no telling what may happen even from something as seemingly innocent as watching from a window. This time, take the safe road."

Kaelen scowled, "How'd I end up friends with a bunch of babies?"

The others looked hurt and something in George snapped, "Well, if you hate our company that much we'll leave." He got up and walked away, followed by Jacobi and Adrian.

Lucian hung back long enough to say, "Friends don't treat each other that way, Kaelen. When the old you comes back, the one we're friends with, let us know." He then walked with his tray to the table the others had moved to. While he didn't think it was a good idea to leave Kaelen to his own devices, he also didn't want to give Kaelen more opportunities to berate the rest of them.

Late that night, Kaelen was pacing his room while the rest of the castle slept. The fairies had put some kind of enchantment on the curtains and they wouldn't budge even an inch. He had to know what was going on. Esmé would think him so clever if he discovered the witches' secret. He'd prove the others wrong about the danger. What harm could come from watching by a window? Or, maybe he should play it up, just to make the others more in awe of him.

Making his decision, Kaelen slipped silently from his room and crept downstairs. He could see the shadowed form of a fairy by the entrance. He'd already guessed that the entrance would be guarded, but he'd thought of a better way. Waiting to see the fairy turn another way, Kaelen silently tiptoed around the corner and start heading for the spell breaking classroom. That would be the best place to watch from. There were windows in there viewing the witches' garden. He twisted the doorknob slowly and entered. When he did, the room was eerily lit by flashes of different colored lights. He crept past desks and shelves towards the windows, despite an ominous feeling of foreboding. At first he stayed by the window, trying to see what was happening. He couldn't see much. He could see each of the five witches, but he couldn't have told anyone who they were. They were unrecognizable, all of them had pure white hair which billowed and streamed around them and their faces were expressionless and turned upwards to the sky. Bursts of light flowed from one to the other and into a central ball that glowed brightly and seemed to pulse as though alive. He looked at the door and considered going back, but curiosity won out and he slowly pulled the door open.

The scene before him was both beautiful and terrifying. The witches' voices were blended together as one, and they were chanting in some language that Kaelen couldn't understand. Each of them was surrounded in a cloud of colors. It seemed to be transferring the powers of each between them. The five talismans the witches usually carried were hanging in midair around the central ball of power.

Kaelen was about to decide that he'd seen enough when he saw Horus at his feet. Before he could do or say anything, the cat hissed and the Sisters turned towards Kaelen. Their faces were expressionless and their eyes glowed white as they hissed in their one voice, "Intruder!"

Blinding bands of light wrapped about Kaelen's legs, preventing him from running. They wound up his legs and body like a vine around a tree. He screamed as they tightened around him, cutting off his air. He begged the witches to release him as the bands circled his neck and face, but they had turned back to their circle, seeming not to hear him. Panic filled him as the bands closed around his face. Still they tightened, cutting off his vision of what was happening until he saw no more.

Raphael, who had been guarding the front entrance, suddenly saw a blast of light from the end of the hall. "No," he whispered as he sprinted towards the light. He sent multiple tan notes from his wand to the others in the castle. When he reached the door, he could hear screaming. The powerful streams of magic and light were trying to break through the door. If he opened the door to save whoever was out there, the wild magic would enter the school, putting everyone in danger. He had but a split second to make a decision. Using all of his strength, Raphael used the magic in his wand to bar the door. Who could have gotten past him? As others arrived, they added their magic to his as they tried to keep the wild magic from getting into the castle.

"What happened?" Calista asked as she joined the others, her wand pointed at the door.

"I don't know, I've been watching this whole time," Raphael replied. "Calista, I think one of the boys is in there."

Calista turned suddenly, her violet eyes an expression of concern and sorrow. Others turned to look at her. "There's nothing we can do right now for him," she said at length, sadness causing a tremble in her voice. "We must protect the others. When the Change is complete, we'll do what we can for him. Russett, go search among the boys. Find out if there's anyone missing. Perhaps it's just an animal that got trapped in the middle of it." While she was trying to sound hopeful, everyone knew she didn't believe what she'd said.

"Alright," Russett said. He turned and left, his wand still hovering in air, trembling from the effort of holding the magic at bay.

Gelasia closed her eyes and began a different chant. Perhaps she could save the stranger's life. She put all of her energy into putting what protection she could around the being she couldn't see.

Russett returned soon. Calista turned to him, "Is anyone missing, Russett?"

"It's Kaelen, Calista," Russett replied sadly. "He's the only one not in his room."

"Is there nothing we can do?" Honoria asked desperately as piercing screams turned to howls.

"No," Calista said firmly. "We must protect the others. Kaelen is a strong young man. The most we can do is hope he survives and then do what we can for him from there."

At dawn Friday morning, when the danger was past, Raphael opened the door of the classroom that the fairies had guarded for the past day and a half. They were all exhausted and their magic all but spent. Calista had broken from the group long enough to help Tallia slip a drop of sleeping potion into every boy's mouth. It would cause them to sleep for two full days. None of the boys would remember Wednesday or Thursday happening, but the fairies would never forget. Broken jars and scraps of parchment were scattered around the room, still glowing from the residue of powerful magic. Calista searched the room and on seeing the wide open door leading into the witches' garden, gingerly stepped around bits of broken glass and outside. The classroom hadn't been the only thing affected by the surge of power around it. Several of the plants in the garden were suddenly much different than they had been. Calista saw the five witches standing in a circle. "Althea?" she asked somewhat timidly.

Althea turned with a sad smile. Her hair was streaked with silver and her normally black gown had been replaced by one in deep violet. "I'm sorry Calista, I'm no longer the head of the Sisters. I believe you wish to speak with Calypso. She is now our head and can best help you."

"Is the Change finished then?" Calista asked, approaching the five Sisters.

Calypso, her once brown hair now black as a raven's wing, turned and said, "Yes, Calista, it is finished. Unfortunately, we have found a victim of the Change we were not expecting."

The Sisters stepped aside as Calista stepped closer. She gasped as she looked at the body lying on the ground. It had to be Kaelen, and yet she wished it weren't. A large, fur-covered beast lie motionless on the ground wearing the tattered remains of a school uniform. "Is he alive?" Calista asked.

"Barely," Althea replied.

"We had hoped to be able to reverse the magic that caused this," Calypso said. "However, as you well know, the Change has greater power than even the five of us combined."

Calista looked at each of the Sisters. It would take time for her to put the right names with them again. Maeve was now a young, beautiful blonde wearing the ruby necklace and flaming red gown. Lucretia's hair had darkened to auburn, which created a lovely contrast against the blue gown she had inherited with the shell bracelets. Calypso stood in the crown, signifying her place among the Sisters, and black gown. Morghana's hair was white and wild around her shoulders and she wore the green gown that had once been Maeve's. Calista sighed, "Well, let's take him to the infirmary. Could you please help us move him? We've been barring the door for so long, I'm afraid none of my staff have the strength to carry him."

Calypso smiled and raised her hands and Kaelen was lifted from the ground. She directed him to the infirmary. The others followed her. When they arrived, Tallia waved to an empty bed and Calypso followed the silent command, gently placing Kaelen upon it. "We'll stay with you until he awakes. He will have questions that will need to be answered," Calypso said.

"Thank you," Calista said. "Tallia, is there anything you can do for him?"

Stifling a yawn, Tallia replied, "I can do my best. I hardly know where to begin. It's been years since I've dealt with this sort of problem. Actually, I don't think I've ever dealt with something this serious."

"May I?" Morghana asked. "Each Sister has her own unique gifts that follow her no matter what her rank in the Sisterhood. Despite my wild appearance, medicine is my specialty."

"Of course," Calista replied. "How could I have forgotten?"

"Well," Morghana rasped with wicked amusement, "I don't think I need to remind you how long you've worked here. This is hardly the first Change you've seen." Then in a more gentle tone she added, "You're also exhausted in mind, body and spirit. Take some rest, all of you. I'll get him awake soon enough. In fact, Calypso, why don't you have Maeve look at the star charts."

"Me?" Maeve asked, her voice young and unsure. "But, I can't, I don't know how."

"My dear," Althea said, patting her hand gently, "it will come naturally to you. As healing is Morghana's gift and Lucretia's is in growing things, your gift is in the stars. Take a look at the charts and they will speak to you."

"Are you sure?" Maeve asked, looking at each of her Sisters in turn.

"Of course," Calypso replied. "Each of us has a special gift. Yours is indeed reading the stars. Go to the charts, Lucretia will show you where they are kept."

Lucretia led Maeve away and Althea turned to Calista, "You really should take some rest. Morghana will be able to take care of Kaelen."

The boys were just going to breakfast as the fairies trudged into the dining hall. After eating, Calista rose and announced that classes would be canceled for the day. "Please don't forget that the princesses will be visiting tomorrow. And before you ask if I made a mistake, I didn't. It's Friday morning and the princesses will be here tomorrow. For today, I would ask that you all enjoy the sunshine and take the time to get your homework finished for next week. The fairies will not be available in their offices until after lunchtime as we need time to rest after the ordeal of the last few days. Enjoy your time off."

It didn't take long for a buzz of conversation to flow over the dining hall as boys wondered what had happened. It also did not take long for Lucian to realize that Kaelen was nowhere to be found. "Have you seen Kaelen?" he asked the others.

"No," George said. "Why?"

Adrian frowned, "I think we discovered why the fairies are so exhausted. I don't know what happened with him, but I bet that's why the fairies look like they've been up for two days straight."

"They have been up for two days straight," Jacobi said suddenly. "Calista just said that it's Friday. When we went to bed, it was Tuesday. They've been protecting the school for over two days. No wonder they look dead on their feet."

The boys considered this. "Well," Lucian said at length, "we may as well take her advice and go enjoy the sunshine."

Kaelen woke up in the infirmary late that evening. His bed was surrounded by fairies and the witches. "How are you feeling, young prince?" Maeve asked him. Wait, that wasn't Maeve, it looked and sounded more like Morghana.

"Tired," Kaelen replied in a voice that was more like a growl. He raised a hand to his throat and was horrified to see that where his hands should have been were paws with talon-like claws and golden-brown fur, the color his hair normally was. "What have you done to me?" he demanded.

"Your transformation was a result of the Change," Calypso said. "Quite frankly, you're lucky to be alive at all. However, there are many things we must consider. The Sisters and I cannot change you back to yourself. Neither can the fairies. This transformation is going to completely alter your quest. You are a beast now Kaelen; you won't be able to do what was originally set forth."

"I'm a beast?" Kaelen shouted; his voice was thunderous and frightening even to himself.

"Fitting isn't it?" Lucretia asked wickedly.

"Lucretia," Calypso chided, "you are not helping. Keep your opinions to yourself." Lucretia blushed slightly, but said nothing. Calypso then turned back to Kaelen. "Yes, Kaelen you are a beast. We have already tried to undo this magic, but it is beyond us. Maeve, have you read the star charts?"

"Yes, I have," Maeve replied. "It was amazing how easy it was, just as Althea said. I just looked at it and it was all right there. It was the easiest thing in the world."

"Would you kindly tell us what you read?" Calypso requested.

"Read where?" Maeve asked.

"The star charts, Sister," Calypso repeated. "What did you read?"

It was clear that even as the youngest, Maeve had a habit of rambling and getting off subject. "Oh," she said, "of course. How silly of me. The transformation Kaelen has gone through cannot be undone by any of us. Only the maiden who is a true princess at heart will be able to rescue him. He must be able to fall in love with her and win her love for him spoken in word and deed before this magic will be undone."

"What kind of stupid thing is that?" Kaelen asked. "Seriously, the stars told you?"

Maeve's eyes flashed a venomous green color as her blonde hair billowed out around her. "Do not insult the stars, prince. You have only seven years to win the love of this maiden as it is. Do not tempt me to shorten your time considerably."

"Sister," Calypso said sharply, "control yourself."

Maeve's hair returned to normal and her eyes faded back to their normal aqua green. "I'm sorry, Calypso. Anyhow, according to the stars, he has seven years for this maiden to fall in love with him. I cannot say more about it, the stars forbid it."

Calypso turned to Kaelen and Calista, "Well, there's your answer. We've done all that we can. I would recommend that Kaelen be put in double spell breaking as soon as is possible. He will need the extra instruction in order to meet this challenge with the best possibility of success. We'll leave you now."

Calista sighed, "Very well. Thank you, Calypso. I'll be in touch with you soon about how we'll proceed with things. In the meantime," she directed at Kaelen. "The meeting with the princesses is tomorrow. We'll have to groom you the best we can so you look your best for your princess."

"I'm not seeing Esmé like this," Kaelen cried. "What would she think of me? She would never understand. Worse, she would think it a joke at her expense."

"Kaelen, your princess has to be able to fall in love with you," Calista replied. "That means she needs to see you. Secrecy does not help love grow. Besides, Esmé should be mature enough to understand when we explain the situation to her. You are both well within your third year at our schools. She is as well-acquainted with the dealings of the witches as you are."

That evening at supper, the boys discovered Kaelen's fate. Several of the younger boys squealed in terror as Kaelen entered the dining hall. For the second time in his life, he wished he could become invisible. It was difficult to get through the line for his supper; the tray was slick in his paws and the claws didn't help. The fairy serving them fainted when he showed up, causing giggles among some of the boys until Kaelen started growling. A different fairy started serving the boys and placed silverware on Kaelen's tray as she watched him struggle to get some onto the tray. "Thanks," Kaelen muttered before heading to the table Lucian and the others were sitting at. "Can I sit with you guys?"

"Pull up a chair," Adrian said kindly.

"So which one of you wants to say 'I told you so' first?" Kaelen asked miserably.

"We may have thought it, but I don't think any of us planned on actually saying it to you, Kaelen," George replied. "None of us are that rude."

"Well, you can say it. If I ever deserved it, I do now," Kaelen said. He told them as much as he could remember about what had happened. Most of it was a blur to him, he couldn't remember anymore than they could about the last couple of days. "It was like living in a nightmare," he said at length. "I couldn't tell if I was awake or asleep half the time. The light was so bright I couldn't see anything at all."

"So, what are they going to do?" Jacobi asked nervously. "We meet with the princesses tomorrow."

Kaelen growled, "The fairies are going to help me get groomed and looking as handsome as possible and then I'll be meeting Esmé. Maybe Calista's right and she'll be okay with it."

The other boys looked at each other nervously. None of them thought for a minute that Kaelen's princess would take his transformation well. In fact, they were all sure that tomorrow was going to be the greatest disaster that they had ever had with the princesses.

Chapter 6

When the princesses arrived Saturday morning, Kaelen was waiting for his princess along with everyone else. He saw Calista stop the girls before they entered and explain something to Melantha. He could see her frown and turn and relay a message to her girls. As the girls began entering, some screamed in fright at the sight of Kaelen. Others gasped, but held their composure as they walked to their princes. When Esmé entered the castle she screamed before collapsing in a dead faint. Melantha and Calista rushed to help her back to her feet and get her comfortable. Kaelen walked nearer to her. Her eyes fluttered open and she looked about herself. "What happened?"

"You swooned, dear," Melantha said. "Esmé, we need you to be strong. Kaelen is slightly altered from the last time you saw him."

Slightly? Kaelen thought. *That's certainly a matter of opinion.* Aloud he said, "Esmé?"

Esmé turned to Kaelen, her green eyes widening in fright and then narrowing in fury. "What did you do?"

Kaelen began stammering. "What he did is unimportant," Calista interrupted him. "The important thing is that together you must overcome this obstacle. He is going to need you, Esmé."

"That hideous beast?" Esmé cried angrily. "Absolutely not! That's not Kaelen. You tell me what you've done with Kaelen you monster!"

"Esmé, I am Kaelen," he said. He wasn't surprised by her disbelief; he didn't sound like himself at all. His voice was a low growl, harsh and wild sounding.

"You did this on purpose didn't you?" Esmé shouted. "Did you want me to be a laughingstock? Look at yourself, you're not a boy and you're certainly not a man; you're a monster. You did this to humiliate me. Well, it's the last straw, Kaelen. I've never been so humiliated, so insulted in all my life." She sniffed as though crying, though Kaelen could see that her emerald eyes were as dry as ever.

"Esmé, I didn't do this on purpose. I never meant for this to happen. I need you to stand by me, you're my princess," Kaelen pleaded.

"I?" Esmé asked, her voice biting and superior. "No, Kaelen, I am not your princess. Nor will I ever be. I refuse to join myself with a monster."

"Esmé," Melantha interrupted, "don't you understand? Together you must solve this if Kaelen is to return to himself. If you refuse to help him, you doom him to a terrible fate."

"Not only that, but you doom yourself to a life of solitude," Calista added.

A cold laugh escaped Esmé's lips. "You think I need Kaelen? My mother has already said that she could find a more suitable match than you were able to procure. I hardly need any of you to come up with a match. Who would refuse me? I'm beautiful, I'm rich, and I'm the only child of a very influential man." She turned to Kaelen. "Enjoy your life as a monster, Kaelen. We will never be." She then turned on her heel and walked out of the castle.

Hushed whispers filled the hall and Kaelen felt heartbroken and humiliated. She couldn't even have waited for the hall to clear before shredding him like an old piece of paper. He ran up the stairs to his room as Calista turned to Melantha. "What do we do now?" she asked.

Melantha frowned. "Perhaps with time, she'll come to understand. She will be punished for her behavior of course, but perhaps," she sighed. "Perhaps Esmé will see her role in all this."

Despite the warmth of the sunshine and beauty around them, the others felt that a form of darkness had fallen over the day. The group of friends spoke in hushed voices around their table during the outdoor picnic. The scavenger hunt had been won by Jacobi and Clarissa, yet they didn't feel like celebrating. "What will happen for Kaelen now?" Adrian asked.

"Well, maybe Esmé will change her mind," Clarissa said hopefully. Everyone looked at her and she sighed, "You're right. Esmé never changes her mind about anything."

"I'm sure the fairies will think of something," George said. "I mean, they're not just going to let him live out his days as a beast."

"But they can't force Esmé to fall in love with him," Lucian pointed out. "So unless there's a girl we don't know about in Kaelen's future, things look pretty bleak for him."

"You of all people should know that we don't have all the answers," Leticia said gently. "Look at your parents. Your mother wasn't left to spend eternity in a forbidden tower. Life will always find a way to make things work out. Even if it's not what the rest of us expected."

While the students were trying to enjoy the festivities prepared for them, Gelasia followed Kaelen to his room after telling Calista her intentions. When she knocked on the door, she heard him growl, "Go away." Nonchalantly, she opened the door and entered. "I told you to go awa…Oh, Gelasia," Kaelen said in a softer tone when he turned and saw that she was standing in the doorway, a sweet smile on her face.

"I must have misheard you dear," Gelasia said gently, "I thought you'd said to come in."

Kaelen sighed with a smile, "I'm glad you'll cover for me when I'm being a brute."

Gelasia smiled, "Growing up is a painful process, dear. I came to see that you were alright."

"Do I look alright?" Kaelen snarled. "Esmé's right, I'm a monster."

"That spoiled brat is certainly not right about you," Gelasia said firmly. Kaelen was surprised at the unladylike tone her voice had taken. She took a deep breath before continuing, "Kaelen, you mustn't believe the things that will be said about you. The next years are going to be the hardest you have ever faced. But, if you can face them as the strong prince I know that you are, then the rewards will far outweigh the sorrows. You must be strong."

Tears pricked Kaelen's eyes. "How? Look at me. Who would fall in love with me now?"

"Well," Gelasia said with teasing wink, "if I were four thousand years younger…"

"Gelasia!" Kaelen gasped with a laugh.

"Alright, so I'm out of the question," Gelasia said, sharing in Kaelen's laughter. "But you must remember, that there is more to a person than physical appearance. You may look like a beast, but you are so much more than that; and I believe you know that as well as I do. For the remainder of school, we will work very hard to bring forward those best parts of your personality, but it won't be easy Kaelen. This is going to be difficult. Humans are so easily led by their eyes; they often forget to follow their hearts. But don't fret, you're not beyond hope."

Kaelen nodded. "But Gelasia, what if Esmé never comes around? What if she refuses to love me?"

"There's more than one way to interpret any enchantment, my dear. You must promise me you will not despair, no matter what," Gelasia replied. "I will help you in any and every way that I possibly can. But, I can't help you if you don't know within yourself that things will work out."

"I won't give up," Kaelen said.

"That's the spirit," Gelasia smiled. They chatted for a long while until Gelasia commented, "Now, would you be a dear and escort me to luncheon? I believe we're both missing it."

Kaelen stood and bowed before offering Gelasia his arm. "It would be my pleasure, my lady." She laughed merrily as she took his arm.

They walked down the stairs and outside to the picnic lunch that was being held on the grounds. Kaelen started to lead Gelasia to the staff table and then hesitated. "Since my princess is unavailable, I'd be pleased if you'd join my friends and me."

Gelasia smiled brightly, "I'd be happy to, dear."

Leading her to the table he saw the others at, he held her chair as she took her seat. The others stared for a moment until Kaelen said, "Ladies, this is Gelasia Stardust. I'm her escort this afternoon."

"Are you going to be okay, Kaelen?" Eleanor asked.

Nodding, Kaelen replied, "Things will work out somehow."

"We were just talking about a secret Moira's been keeping from the rest of us," Leticia said to Gelasia. "Did you know she's quite the seamstress?"

Gelasia turned to Moira with a bright smile. "Are you really?"

"I enjoy sewing, yes," Moira replied blushing.

"There's a design competition in Biberseth next month and we're trying to get her to enter it," Clarissa explained.

"She's trying to hold out on us," Allegra added.

"Hmm," Gelasia said thoughtfully. "What do you think she should do, Lucian?"

Lucian had been trying to stay out of the conversation. He turned to look at Moira. She was looking at him with an almost challenging expression. "I think she should do what she wants," he said at length. "I agree that she is very talented, having seen some of her designs. I recognize her work and she's very good. But, maybe the reason she's hesitant is because she wants to continue working at her own pace. If she wants to enter, I'll support her one hundred percent. If she doesn't, I'll still think her the best seamstress I've ever met."

For a brief moment Moira and Lucian looked at each other and the rest of the world was lost until Gelasia said, "Wise words, Lucian. I agree with you."

Blushing, the two returned their attention to the rest of the group. There was laughter and chatter, especially with Gelasia there. Lucian hadn't spent much time with the fairy, but appreciated her sweetness and the light she brought to the afternoon. He could tell that Kaelen was still upset and hurt, but Gelasia's gentle demeanor and kindness had obviously helped to lessen the pain.

Suddenly, a short, blonde girl who looked so much like Kaelen that it was obvious they were related ran to the table. "Kaelen, is that really you? I'll believe you if you tell me it's you, but I hope it's not."

Kaelen frowned. "I'm sorry, Anna, it is true. I am Kaelen."

Tears welled in Anna's bright blue eyes. "Oh, Kaelen, what happened?"

"I did something incredibly foolish and I'm paying the price," Kaelen replied with a shrug. "But don't worry, somehow this will all right itself in the end."

Anna was still crying. "But Kaelen, what will Mother and Father say when they see you? Can this be fixed?"

"Of course it can," Gelasia replied, patting the young girl's hand. "Why, sooner than you know it, Kaelen will be back to himself. What a lovely gown you're wearing."

"Thank you," Anna gushed, wiping her eyes and looking down at the lavender gown with gold embroidery. "Kaelen," she paused suddenly as she saw Kaelen's eyes widen and then continued, "bought it for me. It was a gift. I think he chose just the right thing, don't you?"

"Indeed, the color fits you perfectly," Gelasia said sweetly with a wink. Soon Anna's prince had pulled her back to their table and friends.

The rest of the group continued to talk. The girls enjoyed Gelasia's company so much that when the day ended, they asked her to write them when she had spare moments.

"Of course, dears," Gelasia said graciously. "Just be sure you write back."

"We will," Eleanor promised.

As the boys led their princesses to the carriages, Lucian took Moira aside. "I've really enjoyed getting to know more about you from your letters. I hope they'll continue."

Moira smiled. "They'll continue as long as you keep writing. I've thought a lot about what happened over winter break and, well," she paused.

"It's alright, Moira," Lucian said before she could continue. "We'll take this one day at a time. Have a pleasant journey back."

Before she could say another word, Lucian was hugging Allegra and saying goodbye to the others before looking once more at her and waving. Moira noticed a smile on his face, one that he didn't share with the other girls. It was different. She blushed as she realized that it was a smile meant only to be shared with her. She smiled in return before getting into the carriage, hoping that the other girls wouldn't comment on her rosy color.

For the last half of the semester, Kaelen was put into alternate courses, while maintaining those of his regular courses that he could. His schedule was completely rearranged. In hunting he worked with Knight to build trust and teamwork. It took a while for Knight to come to him without whining or scampering off to hide behind Diana's legs. The first time he'd gone to horsemanship after the transformation, Lightning had bolted at the sight of him and even Phillipa hadn't been able to call him back. No one knew where the horse had gone and Phillipa had said kindly, "I'm sure he'll come back at some point. Horses have to eat after all and this is where he's fed." But because he no longer had a horse and he made the other horses nervous, for horsemanship he stayed with Gelasia and worked on improving his fine motor skills. After the transformation it had become incredibly difficult to eat properly, hold his pens and write legibly. He admired the old fairy's patience because he knew most would have given up on him. Raphael had moved him to an individual class. "I'm just afraid that until you learn your own strength and size, you'll be a danger to others," he'd explained. Kaelen thought that was ridiculous. He could barely grip the tiny handle of the rapier he'd brought with him to school.

The other boys tried to sympathize, but they were all busy with their own classes. As spring warmed the grounds, the fairies seemed to add to the homework. The group of friends often worked together on their homework out under their tree. It was a tall maple tree with a large, thick trunk. It spread its branches towards the sky, bright green leaves hiding most of the branches from sight. Sitting on the grassy ground beneath, the boys had ample shade to make doing their homework easier as well as giving them protection from the sun's rays. Their dogs played together under the branches, close enough to come immediately to their masters when called, but far enough to not distract the boys from their studies. The boys also invited Kaelen to watch them as they rode. "I'm not trying to make this worse, but our horses have to become accustomed to being around, you know," George began.

"Hideously frightening beasts?" Kaelen finished for him.

"Well, that wasn't quite how I was going to put it," George said quickly.

When Kaelen laughed, it still sounded harsh and angry. "I understand George, yeah I'll watch you guys work. I'll even give you some pointers and stuff," he added. The boys were relieved that he understood their need and didn't say anything else as they walked to the barn. Kaelen ducked his head in. Lightning still hadn't shown up. Kaelen wondered if the strong-willed horse had run all the way to Coleston to get away from him. He couldn't blame him. It had been foolish for any of them to believe that the horses would react well to Kaelen's transformation. Even being a girl had been better; at least Lightning had eventually adjusted to Kaelen's new form. Now not only had his own horse been spooked, but he also scared the other horses.

Lucian was riding the ring with Zephyr and Kaelen said, "Hey Lucian, I think you're reining him in a little too much. He'll go better if you give him a little more freedom. Not too much, but a little."

Loosening his hold on the reins, Lucian called back, "Thanks Kaelen. Does he look better now?"

"Perfect," Kaelen admitted.

The evening practice continued until the sun was dipping low beneath the horizon. The boys put their horses away and then went inside to their own rooms. Lucian stopped by his mailbox before walking into his room. There was a new letter from Moira, as well as letters from Allegra and from home. He flopped onto his bed with paper and pens for replies while Rusty hopped onto the bed next to him. He opened the letter from Moira and read.

Dear Lucian,

I hope that things are getting easier for Kaelen. I'm afraid he won't be seeing Esmé again. Please don't tell him what I'm about to tell you. Melantha swore all of us to secrecy and I frankly shouldn't even be telling you. Apparently Melantha had another meeting with Esmé to discuss the situation with Kaelen. Her punishment after the meeting was two weeks of a furry face. It was actually rather attractive on her, though I suppose you know me well enough to know that I'm not saying that as a compliment. Anyhow, after that punishment ended, Melantha spoke with Esmé again about Kaelen and her responsibility to him. There was a lot of shouting which of course drew everyone's attention. I've never seen all five witches called before. When the witches arrived, Esmé was standing in the front hall. They tried to have her go into another room, but she refused. The witches have cursed her to look on the outside what she is on the inside...forever. Now she's been expelled from the school. I don't really know why we aren't to tell Kaelen, so please do not break this confidence. I know you would never do so intentionally, but even as his friend, you must keep this to yourself. I suppose they think that it would affect his ability to do his quest if he knew that his princess is no longer anything that he remembers.

And now, I will answer your last question: my favorite place to go. I love the stars. Dad used to take Adrian star gazing because the stars were what helped him on his quest. So, on warm nights when everyone is asleep, I like to sneak out of the castle and go into the fields nearby, lie on my back and just search the stars. It's like being close to Dad, even though he's not here anymore. When I can't go outside, I like to go to the tower and be with Dad's things. It helps me to remember him as he was. It's also quiet there and gives me lots of time to think. I think about school, about family, everything and anything that I need to. Sometimes, I even talk to Dad while I'm there. He never answers, but it's a way of being close, like looking at the stars.

I hope you'll understand when I say I was really jealous of you and Allegra after winter break. At first, it didn't seem fair that your dad got better, but mine was taken away. But, the more I thought about it, the more I realized that fair has nothing to do with it. It just is. Life happens and eventually so does death. I guess the point is to try to make the best of what you have. I'm not jealous anymore and I think it's great that your dad is getting better.

Well, I hope that you enjoy the rest of the semester. It's going by swiftly. I hope you're not disappointed that I chose not to enter the competition. I considered it, but in the end you were right. I want to be able to just design for myself and those who are nearest me. I don't want to have people suddenly asking me to design something for them. In some ways, Mother is right; I'm a princess, not a seamstress. I'll still sew and design for myself, but probably not outside that.

Good luck with your homework and finals. Let me know how things go. Allegra always seems to find out before me. Of course, since she's your sister, I guess that makes sense. I'll see you in June.

Your Friend,
Moira

Lucian folded the paper and put it back in its envelope before putting that in a small box that he kept all of Moira's letters in. How could she think he was disappointed? It was her choice. He pulled out a piece of paper and began to write her a return letter. He told her that he wasn't disappointed at all in her decision.

> You don't have to enter a competition to impress me. I've seen some of the dresses you've designed. You have a lot of talent, but I won't think any less of you if you

choose to sew for yourself only. You couldn't possibly have time to sew for everyone!

When he finished writing, he put that letter in an envelope and set it aside to be sent to her before opening Allegra's letter. Her letter also mentioned Esmé's fate as well as the threat that if he told anyone she'd kill him. He laughed to himself and then stopped laughing as his heart sank. How many of the other princes had received letters telling them what had happened to Esmé? If Clarissa told Jacobi and Eleanor told George, it would be okay because the secret would be safe with them. But what about the other boys? What would they do if they heard about Esmé? They'd probably run to tell Kaelen thinking it would make him feel better. He sincerely hoped that Moira and Allegra were the only ones who had broken Melantha's trust by telling him.

As the weeks past, none of the princes said anything to Kaelen about what had happened to Esmé. Lucian had talked to his other friends at a time he knew they wouldn't be overheard by other princes, or worse Kaelen. They had each heard from their princesses what had happened and were under the same oath not to tell Kaelen. As far as they knew, none of the other boys had heard about it. They didn't have a lot of time to worry as they were soon busy with getting ready for their finals. Like in winter semester, their Friday arts courses held their finals the week before the princesses' summer visit. Late Friday afternoon, George and Lucian went to the gazebo for their final. When they arrived, Lorelei was lying on her favorite rock in the middle of the lake. Upon seeing them, she swam back to the gazebo. "Good afternoon boys. Each of you will have an oral exam and then there is also the written exam which is on the board. Your test sheets are on my desk. Lucian, why don't we start with you for the oral exam?"

"Sure," Lucian said, though he would much rather have told the mermaid no. He walked to the front of the classroom while George picked up a test sheet and took it to his desk before beginning the written exam.

"What I want you to do is have a brief conversation with me in Sea Serpent about the lake, then I want you to tell me about your favorite class in Common and lastly you can pick a topic for your Eastern dialect," Lorelei explained.

Lucian tripped over the three dialects before switching with George. He felt slightly better when it was obvious that George was struggling with it as much as he was, but the feeling didn't last as he took the written exam. It was harder to explain how the three were different on paper than to speak in any of them. As the two walked back to the castle for supper George said, "I think she enjoys listening to us trip over it."

"Well, considering her relationship with Draconus are you surprised?" Lucian asked.

"No," George replied with a laugh. "I definitely would not want to put those two in a room together. She'd get fried and he'd be drowned." They laughed as they went to supper. When they got there, Adrian was already waiting. "So," George asked, "how was your swimming final?"

Adrian grimaced. "I passed, sort of. Achilles said I need to practice more and really try. But, I managed to get through it okay. I'm still breathing."

"Maybe this summer you can come visit and we'll go swim at the beach," Lucian suggested.

"Yeah, maybe," Adrian replied.

Their other friends soon joined them and they talked about all they had done throughout the day. Everyone was looking forward to the weekend, though they'd need to spend some time studying during the two days free from classes. Kaelen seemed unusually tense, playing with his food and not really joining the conversation. "Is something bothering you?" Jacobi asked.

"No," Kaelen lied. When the others looked at him in obvious disbelief, he sighed, "Okay, yes."

"You want to tell us about it, or are you just going to sulk?" George asked in a teasing tone, though Kaelen knew he was serious.

"I haven't heard from anyone since this happened," Kaelen said, referring to his transformation. "My parents haven't written me, Esmé hasn't written to me and I'm worried that they're taking this badly. I mean, it's not permanent, right? I'll be myself again soon enough. Esmé just has to fall in love with me and you know, the whole quest thing, and I'll be good as new."

"Sure," Adrian replied confidently, though a silent look had passed between the others while Kaelen had been looking at his plate. "Maybe they're just trying to think of the right thing to say, you know not wanting to hurt your feelings or that sort of thing."

"Maybe you're right," Kaelen said.

"Of course we're right," Jacobi teased. "We're always right!"

The conversation turned to happier topics and soon Kaelen's worries were forgotten. They talked about the rest of their finals and set themselves a study schedule to follow for the next couple of days. When supper was over, they walked out to their favorite tree, sitting under its leaf-laden branches enjoying the warm, spring air as they watched the sunset. As the stars started twinkling overhead, they decided to call it a night. Lucian returned to his room and got ready for bed. Even though it wasn't particularly late, he was extremely tired. Rusty loped over to the bed as Lucian was getting in it and nudged Lucian's hand. "You've got your own bed, boy," Lucian said with a yawn.

Rusty turned big, puppy brown eyes at him and whined softly.

"You know I can't share a bed with you forever. Eventually you'll have to learn to stay in your own bed all the time," Lucian said. When Rusty continued to just look up at him, he gave in. "Oh alright, but this is the last time, Rusty. You're getting too big to do this."

Lucian blew out the candles as Rusty settled down at the foot of Lucian's bed. Normally, Rusty didn't sleep on Lucian's bed at all. But every now and again he'd come sit by Lucian's bedside staring up at him and whining until Lucian would let him onto the foot of the bed. Lucian would never tell Rusty, but it was nice having him down there because his feet were always kept nice and warm. It also reminded him of when he first started school and Rusty slept at the foot of his bed every night. His thoughts retreated as sleep played dreams in Lucian's mind.

Finals week passed in a blur of activity. The boys seemed to be shuffled from one test to the next. Kaelen's schedule had been altered so much that he hardly had any finals to do and so spent most of his time with Gelasia when she wasn't teaching, trying to regain the nimbleness his fingers had once had. "Gelasia," he said one day as they were sitting in her classroom.

"Yes, Kaelen?" Gelasia looked up from the embroidery she was working on.

"Do you think my friends are right? About my family I mean," Kaelen explained. "They think the reason I haven't heard from them is because they're trying to find the right thing to say, but I'm not so sure. What if they're taking this badly?"

Gelasia sighed, "I'm afraid my dear I don't have a good answer for you. I don't know why your parents have chosen not to write to you. Haven't you still gotten letters from Anna?"

"Only one, right after the meeting," Kaelen replied. "But she hasn't written since

April. It's June now. What if," he paused before admitting his fear to her, "what if my parents hate me now and won't let me come home?"

"That's silly, Kaelen," Gelasia said cheerfully. "After all, you're still you. It doesn't matter what the outside of you looks like."

"Maybe," Kaelen said doubtfully.

Gelasia smiled. "Listen to me, Kaelen. Things right now probably look bleak and hopeless. I know it's hard right now, but you have to believe that in one way or another, things will work out the way they're supposed to. After all, no one became Prince Charming in a day. It takes time and hard work. I'm afraid, dear, you'll probably have a harder time of it than your peers, because you're not the one on the quest. This time, she's on a quest. A quest to rescue you. It's a strange reversal of the roles, don't you think?"

"Yeah," Kaelen said with a slight laugh. "I guess that's a first isn't it?"

"No, we've had other princes who for whatever reason were not the ones going on a quest. Rather their princess was sent to rescue them. I doubt you'll even be the only one in your class to have that reversal," Gelasia replied knowingly.

Kaelen looked at her suspiciously. "Do you know something I don't know?"

Laughing merrily, Gelasia teased, "My dear, I know a great many things you don't."

They laughed and continued to chat until suppertime when Kaelen met the rest of his friends at their usual table. "Well, you certainly look happier than we've seen you in a while," Lucian commented as Kaelen took a seat with them. "Feeling better?"

"Yeah," Kaelen replied. "Gelasia really knows how to make you feel better about things."

"She's incredibly understanding that way," Adrian agreed.

"Well, I'm just glad that finals are over," Jacobi said. "I still don't think I did very well on that math final."

"You've been saying that since yesterday," George sighed. "I'm sure you did just fine on it."

"Yeah, you always think you've failed the math final and yet each time you do really well. In fact, last semester you did better than all the rest of us," Lucian pointed out.

"I guess so, but that one really bothered me," Jacobi held out stubbornly.

George laughed, "I guess you'll just have to wait until tomorrow to find out. I'm sure Calista will say something to you if your scores weren't perfect."

The next morning Lucian awoke early and quickly changed into his uniform for the day. He was a little depressed; after the big growth spurt last winter he had hoped that his growth would continue. Instead he was trapped at a hair more than five nine. He shook his head to clear his thoughts and put his jacket on, straightening it and looking at the gleaming medals he'd earned. His thoughts strayed to the graduation he would watch that day. In only three years he'd be the one graduating. Would Moira disappear off the stage as so many girls before her had done? Would she still insist upon them only being friends? He sighed as he double-checked that all his things were packed and ready to go before leaving the room and going downstairs.

When he got down there, his friends were all waiting and there were parents milling about to find their children. Kaelen was standing in the new uniform Gelasia had helped him make. It had been difficult when all he had were the tattered remains of his old uniform. The others could tell he was looking for Esmé and his parents and were relieved when Melantha asked Kaelen for a private word. None of them wanted to tell him that his princess was no longer a student. "Kaelen," she said when they were a ways apart from the other students, "I'm afraid Esmé will no longer be coming to these meetings. Her feelings as yet have remained unchanged and so she has been expelled."

"But, what will happen to me?" Kaelen asked, panic in his voice. "I can't stay like this forever!"

"Of course you won't stay a beast forever. How very silly of you to think so," Melantha replied as though they were discussing the weather. "You'll continue in your classes as always and then when the time comes you'll be sent to discover your princess. I just wanted you to hear from me and not from the students. They have a tendency to," she paused, searching for the right word, "exaggerate the facts."

"Will I ever see her again?" Kaelen asked.

"Perhaps," Melantha said. She smiled and continued, "Well, we have meetings to attend and a graduation ceremony to begin. Go sit with your friends and don't worry about what tomorrow will bring. Life has its ways of fixing things." She patted his shoulder before walking towards the dining hall where things were being set up for the graduation ceremony.

Kaelen rejoined his friends and told them what Melantha had said. "Did any of you know about this?" he demanded.

"Well, we knew that something happened," George admitted, "but we were also sworn to secrecy. You wouldn't want us to break our princesses' trust would you?"

"I guess not," Kaelen replied gloomily.

"Don't worry," Lucian said as Adrian came out of Calista's office with Lavinia and Nana. "I'm sure everything will work out." He walked to Calista's door. "My parents are still meeting with Melantha and Allegra. Would you like me to send Jacobi and his parents in and you can interview me after you've finished with them?"

"That would be very kind of you, Lucian," Calista said with a smile.

Lucian found Jacobi standing with his parents and told them that they could take his spot. "My parents are still meeting with Melantha. I think Dad forgot that Allegra and I tend to have our meetings at the same time. You go on ahead and they should be done by the time you finish."

"Thank you," Jacobi's mother said.

Before any of them could move, Kaelen had found his parents and sister and they were now marching to Calista's office, Queen Angelique in the lead. "I demand you explain this immediately," she cried upon reaching Calista's door.

Calista looked taken aback. "I believe I already sent you a letter regarding the unfortunate accident in which Kaelen was transformed. At the moment, I am about to meet with another student and his parents. You will simply have to wait."

Angelique started to swell up as Jacobi's mother graciously said, "Calista, why don't you go ahead and meet with them? I'm sure waiting another few minutes won't hurt any of us. We still need to be here for a while anyway."

Calista smiled gratefully at her before saying, "Very well, please come in. Although, I believe your daughter could wait outside. There's no reason for her to be present for this."

"I can wait here," Anna agreed with a hopeful smile.

Angelique nodded and then swept inside with King Roland and Kaelen. "Why has he been transformed?" she demanded before Calista could even ask them to be seated.

"Again, I wrote to you directly after Kaelen's transformation. I am also under the impression that Kaelen has written repeatedly concerning this unfortunate matter. I fail to see where you have been misled or uninformed." Calista's voice was calm and even, though Kaelen detected a note of carefully masked anger and frustration.

"Frankly I thought this was another of Kaelen's bouts for attention. His first year you claimed he was turned into a girl, last year you pestered us to no end about bringing the dog to him, no doubt because Kaelen was pushing you," Angelique said dismissively. "Naturally when I received the letter that he'd been turned into a beast I dismissed it as another story."

"King Roland, is that what you believe?" Calista asked, interrupting the queen's rant.

Roland spluttered for a moment, looking from Angelique to Kaelen to Calista and back around again. "Well, you know, boys will be boys; they're prone to exaggeration."

Kaelen looked hurt. "You think I've been lying to you?"

"Oh please, Kaelen, you've always sought attention in the wrong ways," Angelique said. "Now," she continued, turning to Calista, "is this permanent?"

"That depends on a number of things," Calista replied. "He has seven years in which to complete his quest for the princess true at heart. While this is not necessarily a permanent change it will take time for he must get her to fall in love with him."

"Than what you're really saying is that this is a permanent change. No woman of any decent breeding will fall in love with that animal," Angelique sneered.

"Queen Angelique, I must remind you that you are speaking of your son and he can hear you," Calista said. Her voice had become a deadly calm.

"That is not my son," Angelique retorted, rising. She looked directly at Kaelen as she continued coldly, "I have no son."

Angry tears spilled from Kaelen's eyes. "You're my mother. If you won't love me, who will?"

Not bothering to answer him, Angelique walked to the door. "Come Roland, we've no business here."

"But, dear, can't we," Roland began, looking at his heartbroken son.

"Don't argue, Roland," Angelique snapped.

"I warn you now, Queen Angelique," Calista said, causing Angelique to stop in her tracks, "your actions will bring dire consequences to you and your family. You have already been the cause of much pain and hardship in this family as is."

"Are you threatening me?" Angelique asked in an angry whisper.

"I am a fairy," Calista replied, her head high. "We do not make empty threats. You can consider this a warning. Your actions will come back to haunt you and you will regret them."

Angelique glared at Calista before continuing out the door. Kaelen followed her. "Mother, please."

She continued, taking Anna's hand as Anna got up, "Come, we're going home."

"But, Mother, what about Kaelen?" Anna asked, pulling her hand away.

Angelique looked at Kaelen and then at Anna. "You have no brother Kaelen. We're leaving, now."

Anna ran to Kaelen and hugged him fiercely, tears streaming down her face, "No! It's not fair, Mother. He's my brother. We can't just leave him!"

Pulling Anna away from Kaelen, Angelique spat, "Stay away from him! No daughter of mine will be seen with that monster."

"No, Mother, please," Anna begged as she was pulled down the stairs, her other hand still reaching for Kaelen. "Let me say goodbye. Please!"

There was no doubt that Angelique heard every sobbed request, but she listened to none of them. Pulling Anna along with Roland following meekly behind, Kaelen's family left the castle amongst the throngs of others watching. Kaelen stood rooted to the spot, too hurt and shocked to move at all. He barely felt Lysander's gentle arm around his shoulder as he said, "Don't worry, Kaelen, you'll always have a home with us."

"It's not the same," Kaelen replied, in a voice barely above a whisper. "But I appreciate your generosity." He then turned to go to his room.

Calista's voice stopped him. "Kaelen." He turned to look at her, tears falling from his face. "Kaelen," she said as she neared him, "I am so sorry about all of this. Please, come back to my office with me. We have much to discuss."

His head held high Kaelen said, "No, Calista, you have other students and parents to meet with. When you have finished with them, I will come to your office. For now, I need a few moments to myself."

Calista nodded in understanding and put a gentle hand on his arm. "As you wish," she said gently as he turned again to go to his room.

Outside, a king had followed the leaving family. "Roland, Roland! Don't pretend you can't hear me."

"You are never to speak to us," Angelique replied, not bothering to turn and look at the speaker.

"I wasn't addressing you, Angelique," the man replied coldly. "I'm speaking to my brother." Roland turned wearily. Before he could say anything the man continued, "Roland, you can't do this. He's your son, your only son. Forget what that lying snake has said to you. You cannot simply abandon Kaelen to his fate. It's bad enough you have abandoned me and my family. Don't cast Kaelen out as you have done me."

"I'm sorry, Max," Roland whispered. "I have no choice."

"For once in your life, be a man," Maximillion growled. "Be the strong person you were before you married. Stop letting that pretentious woman make the decisions."

"It's too late," Roland replied, turning his back to his brother and getting in the carriage. Maximillion shouted after it long after it had disappeared from sight.

When he finally came to himself, Maximillion walked back into the castle and straight to Calista's office. Lucian and his parents were about to enter as he arrived. "Lysander, I hope you'll forgive this interruption, but I must speak with Calista."

A silent look of understanding passed between the old friends and Lysander finally smiled and said, "Of course. Calista, I hope this won't put you too far behind schedule."

Calista sighed with a smile, "It's already all backwards. Don't worry, I'll make it all work out in the end. King Maximillion, if you could bring your son in, we'll do your meeting with him; unless this is a matter best discussed in private."

"Donovan knows the story behind everything. I have no problem with him being present," Maximillion replied. Donovan hadn't been far and quickly entered the office with his father. As soon as everyone had been seated Maximillion continued, "I understand that King Lysander has generously offered to take Kaelen this summer and at any other times necessary."

"That is correct," Calista replied. "As of yet, Kaelen has not accepted that offer, however, I'm sure being close to his friend will do wonders for him. Have you a better suggestion?"

"No, I'm thinking of when he graduates. His parents will not take him back; I just tried to speak reason with my brother. I will not see Roland's son fail. He is far too good for that. I've seen enough of failure to wish it on anyone," Maximillion admitted sadly. "For this reason, I am offering our old summer castle for Kaelen's living accommodations whenever he desires them. We hardly go there anymore, but it is well-kept and in such a location that he would not draw unwanted attention. I realize that this may cause difficulties in his quest, but I believe having a place of solitude for him to think and reason with himself would do him good. If he's anything at all like my brother, I know it would be helpful."

"I see," Calista said after Maximillion had finished. "And, would you like to make this offer? I believe considering the circumstances, it is best that the secrecy of your relationship be undone."

Maximillion faltered. "It is not that I don't wish Kaelen to know that he still has family to support him, but I think it would be best for now that nothing be said of that. Tell him that a family friend has offered it. After all, before Roland married he was the closest friend I had other than Lysander."

Calista frowned. "I do not like secrecy; however, I will follow your wishes. I would recommend that at some point, this barrier needs to come down. But that is all I will say on that right now. Thank you, your offer will certainly bring Kaelen some peace of mind."

"Right now, that's what he needs," Maximillion agreed. "I think keeping the secret a little while longer will help in that. He's had enough surprises and shocks for one day."

When all of the meetings had concluded, everyone met in the dining hall for the graduation ceremony, followed by supper. Kaelen sat with Lucian's family as well as Adrian's family. He could hear Alexandra and Lavinia speaking about the summer plans for another week long trip to the castle by the sea. After meeting with Calista and discussing his options, he had decided to go with Lucian's family. He stayed quiet through everything, too numb from everything that had happened to feel much like talking. His princess had abandoned him, his parents had abandoned him, taking poor Anna away before he could even say goodbye to her. Sad tears pricked his eyes as he went with Lucian's family to their carriage. They'd almost gotten there when a feminine voice stopped him. Lavinia was standing in front of him. She hugged him gently and whispered in his ear, "To complete the hug your sister was denied. Don't worry, I'm sure you'll see her again."

Kaelen nodded, surprised at the warmth of friendship that so many had extended to him. There was Lucian's family, Lavinia, and then an unknown friend who had offered him a place of his own whenever he might want it. A smiled tugged at his lips. Perhaps hope was not lost after all; he was not entirely abandoned.

Year 4

Chapter 1

It wasn't long after arriving at Lucian's home that they were leaving for the summer castle. Lavinia had promised to meet them there with Nana, Adrian and Moira. As the carriage rolled in, Lucian could see a cloud of dust that meant his other friends were on their way. Lucian led Kaelen to the room with the best view and told him that he could stay there. They unpacked their things and then everyone went to the beach for the afternoon. Kaelen sat on the beach for a long while, away from everyone else. He could see Adrian and Lucian swimming around with Lysander giving Adrian pointers and lessons. The three women were playing in the shallows while Allegra and Moira sat near the water, though not in it. Every now and again Moira would wade out into the shallows and splash for a bit before returning to Allegra. He could tell that everyone was having a good time. He sighed. It wasn't that he didn't want to be part of the fun, but it was awkward. Everyone here had family with them; everyone except him.

"Kaelen?" a gentle voice asked. He looked over to see Adrian's grandmother smiling down at him. "Kaelen, dear, I believe you should join the rest of us in the water. Some swimming will do you good."

"Thanks, but I'd rather stay up here," Kaelen replied.

"I don't think either of us believe that, dear," Nana said with a smile. "Come, sitting up here brooding over everything won't make it change. It won't fix anything either. Enjoy the sunshine and the water. It'll help take your mind off of things."

Nana's smile was so inviting and the water seemed to add to her beckoning. Finally, Kaelen stood up and walked down the beach with her after offering his arm to Nana. "I suppose you think I'm doing this just because you asked me to," he teased with a smile.

"Naturally," Nana retorted with a grin. "Everyone always does what Nana wants them to. That's the joy of being Nana."

Kaelen couldn't help but laugh as they waded into the water. The warm ebb and flow of the waves seemed to wash his worries away. Soon Adrian and Lucian joined everyone else.

"Where's your father?" Alexandra asked suspiciously.

Lucian turned with a frown, "He had been right behind us."

Suddenly Alexandra squealed as Lysander came up from behind her, picking her up out of the water amidst laughing from everyone else. "Hello my love," Lysander said with a grin. "Did you miss me?"

"Lysander Paul, you put me down this instant," Alexandra demanded, though she was giggling.

"As you wish," Lysander replied, dropping her back into the water. As Alexandra came back up there was a water fight that even Allegra couldn't resist joining. The waves churned around them as each splashed at anyone and everyone they could.

"Well, it's nice to see that children never grow up, isn't it, Mother?" a voice from the beach asked loudly, somehow breaking over the sound of the waves.

"Indeed," a woman replied with a smile as everyone turned to see them.

"Grandma and Grandpa!" Allegra cried running out of the water and into Grandpa's outstretched arms.

"Well, well, how is my little girl?" Grandpa asked heartily, hugging Allegra tightly despite the sea water dripping from her. "Quite the young lady now, aren't you?"

Allegra beamed up at them and started pulling them towards everyone else who had gotten out of the water to greet them. "Adrian, Moira, Kaelen, these are my grandparents, Paul and Marsha, emeritus king and queen of Coleston."

"Better yet, we're just Grandma and Grandpa, aren't we darling?" Grandma replied with a smile.

"Right as always, dear," Grandpa replied.

After everyone had introduced themselves, the group headed back to the castle while Lysander asked his parents what had prompted the visit. "I was so worried about you and couldn't bear the fact that we were away the entire time you were sick," Grandma said. "So, we decided it was time for a visit to see if you were doing better. Of course I got your letters," she interrupted as Lysander tried to argue, "but a mother has to see for herself. Isn't that right, Alexandra?"

"Absolutely," Alexandra smiled. "But how did you know that we were here?"

"Oh we didn't," Grandpa replied. "But your butler told us that you were having a vacation at the seashore and we decided to crash."

There was much laughter and chatting as the sun-soaked group headed to the castle. They talked about everything that had happened in the last year, touching as lightly upon Kaelen's predicament as they could. "You've always been a generous man," Grandma told Lysander when they had a moment away from the rest. "You've done well."

"I couldn't just leave him there," Lysander shrugged. "He's one of Lucian's best friends. I couldn't imagine disowning Lucian that way. It was heartbreaking."

"Yes, I'm sure it was," Grandma agreed. "How sad. He didn't say where he was from."

Lysander hesitated only a moment before saying, "He's from Coleston, Mom."

"Coleston?" Grandma repeated. "But when the king and queen arrived they said their son had died in a terrible accident at the school. They wouldn't give any details at all, but they said he'd died. I thought that was why Princess Anna was crying so. How dreadful! I must tell Paul about this."

"No, Mom," Lysander pleaded. "Please don't. This is hard enough for Kaelen as is. Don't make things harder for him."

"My dear, you know that your father and I have no secrets between us," Grandma chided gently. "I'll be sure that we say nothing of the matter to Kaelen. And we won't spread it about the country either. This is going to be hard on everyone. Although, I suppose that explains why the funeral was held for family only. Funeral indeed," she said with distaste, "there was no body to bury."

They soon rejoined the group for supper and the laughter and talking continued late into the evening. Nana revealed that she had decided to move in with Lavinia. "It's not good to spend so much of your time alone," Nana said as they were sitting in the large parlor having dessert. "Besides, I can't stand living alone anymore either. It'll be better for both of us if we're together."

Adrian and Moira were thrilled at the announcement. "When will you be all moved in?" Moira asked eagerly.

"Oh, I have a few things to see to back at home, but within the month everything will be settled. The former king and queen will be moving into my palace, now that their son has finished his quest. I told them I've been wanting to move closer to my daughter for a while now anyway," Nana admitted. "If I remember correctly, their boy is marrying at the end of July, so I have until then to get my things all settled and arranged properly."

"Who is it?" Lucian asked curiously.

"Why, Prince Kieffer of course," Nana replied with a smile. "They only had the one son. Two girls a bit younger than he is, but he's the only boy."

"Kieffer," Adrian said thoughtfully. "Do you mean Kieffer and Samantha?"

"Why yes, that is his princess' name. But how did you know?" Nana asked.

"Samantha is George's sister," Kaelen explained. "George is one of our other friends at school. They'd been rather worried about her."

Nana smiled understandingly. "It's amazing what going on a quest can teach you. Of course, I'll have to be present for the wedding, traditions being what they are. That and the queen and I are good friends. Such a kind woman." Nana spoke for a long while after that describing the family that had taken her place in the kingdom and then talking of the wedding plans.

"I bet we'll all get a letter soon from George saying he's the ring bearer again," Adrian whispered as Nana continued her story.

It wasn't many days later when they did receive a letter from George. He talked about Kieffer finding his sister and the complete change there had been.

I never thought I'd see Samantha looking so happy. Better than that, Samantha has asked me to be groom's assistant. No more being the ring bearer! Kieffer is an only boy like me and all his friends are still out doing their quests. He's so different than he was at school. He told me that his quest taught him a lot about what's really important in life. I can't wait for the wedding. Samantha also said I could invite any of my friends that I wanted to, so all of my friends should be receiving invitations shortly. I hope you can make it!

See You Soon!

George

"Well, that should make him happy," Lucian said, handing his letter to Kaelen and Adrian to read. "He's not the ring bearer this time."

"Yeah, but what's a groom's assistant?" Kaelen asked.

"I don't know and I bet George doesn't care," Adrian replied.

The boys spent the rest of the day celebrating George's good luck. Nana explained that the groom's assistant basically helped take care of any minor details the groom had forgotten. "I'm sure George will make an excellent assistant from all you've said about him."

The day continued much as the others had. The families enjoyed time out at the beach. Lucian went searching for seashells, this time taking Adrian along with him. "I really don't like the idea of putting my head underwater," Adrian said nervously as they waded into a deeper section.

"Don't think about it so much," Lucian replied calmly. "Here are the goggles," he continued, handing them to Adrian. "Just put them on, take a deep breath and go under the water. It'll be easy. When you can't hold your breath anymore, just stand up. You'll do fine."

Adrian looked at him skeptically before reluctantly sticking his head under the water. He looked around and was amazed at the underwater visions swimming before him. There were fish and other creatures and everything was so colorful. He came back up almost immediately. "It's gorgeous under there."

Lucian laughed, "I know. Go on; see if you can find some shells. Just dig a bit at the sand. Not too much, but a little at a time."

Steeling himself to go back under the water, Adrian took a deep breath and went under. He brushed the palm of his hand against the ocean floor. Every so often, he'd get lucky and find a shell, but he was too hesitant to stay under long and often forgot where he'd found them at. He'd only managed to keep three of the shells he'd found by the time he decided he was done. "Well, that was rather pathetic," Adrian muttered.

"It's alright," Lucian said, "it can be hard the first few times. You'll get the hang of it." For a fleeting moment as Adrian took off the goggles and handed them to Lucian, his eyes seemed to be bugging out. But as Lucian tried to look closer, they appeared as normal as ever. Assuming it was just a trick of the light and the goggles reflecting funny, Lucian took them from Adrian's outstretched hand. After adjusting the goggles, Lucian dove under the water. He loved the feeling of being completely submerged. He continued along the floor as long as he could before rising for air. They had decided to swim in an area near where he'd found the sunset clam last year. With luck, maybe he'd find another one this year. He continued the search, finding other shells but never the one he was looking for. Despite his disappointment, he placed each new find in his bag.

Soon he gave the goggles back to Adrian, inviting him to try searching again. Adrian's trips underwater were always hesitant and much shorter than Lucian's, but he too was building quite the collection. As they heard Alexandra calling them back for supper, Adrian smiled. "I guess that's mom-talk for 'Fun's over.'"

Lucian laughed, "Probably. But supper should be excellent tonight; I saw Kaelen and Dad fishing a while back."

"I hope you know how lucky you are," Adrian said, suddenly serious. "Your dad is pretty awesome."

"Yeah, he is," Lucian agreed.

The two friends joined everyone else inside for supper. As at every meal, there was laughter and talk long after the table had been cleared. Grandma and Nana had immediately become good friends. When they finally left the table, Grandpa asked if there was somewhere the men could go to practice their swordplay. Lysander led them to the fencing hall. It was almost an exact replica of the one at their home, except slightly smaller and with fewer swords in it. Soon Grandpa and Lysander were busily practicing their form while the three boys watched.

Kaelen sighed, "I wish I could still use my sword."

"Sure you can," Adrian replied.

"Yeah right," Kaelen retorted with a harsh laugh, "These paws are too big to handle my sword."

"We'll have Bill make you a new one when we go to town for our school supplies," Lucian said kindly. "In the meantime, you might be able to use one of Dad's swords. He's always had big hands."

Suddenly their conversation was cut short by Grandpa interrupting, "Lucian, come show me what you've been learning. Your dad says you've been learning right-handed."

Lysander handed Lucian his sword. "Yeah, but I'm still not very good," Lucian admitted nervously.

"Nonsense," Grandpa scoffed before each took his stance. For a long while the only sounds were footfalls and the clanging of the swords. Finally Grandpa held up his sword to stop them. "You're doing very well for a beginner, Lucian. Very well indeed."

"I couldn't agree more," Alexandra said from the doorway. "However, gentlemen, it is time all of you were in bed." She strode into the hall and took the sword carefully from Lucian before handing it to Lysander. "Put them away and then straight to bed."

A challenging grin spread across Lysander's face, but the queen held her ground and he relented. "You heard her, boys, bedtime," he said as he placed the rapier back on its shelf. His father had already replaced the sword he'd been using. He then took Alexandra's hand in his and together they left the room.

"No one could say they didn't have happily ever after," Kaelen commented as the three boys left the room.

"It's a lesson I hope you'll keep with you," Grandpa said from behind them, startling the three as they'd forgotten he was there. "The story doesn't end when you finish the quest. Romance in your relationship with your princess should never die."

Summer continued in much the same way it had begun. When the week of the visit was over, Grandma and Grandpa left, Grandma being assured that her son was indeed well again. Lavinia also took her family home, promising to take Allegra to school if Alexandra and Lysander could take Adrian. "It'll make both our trips so much easier," she explained.

"Certainly," Alexandra said with a smile. "We'd be happy to take Adrian with us."

Once back in Lictthane, preparations were being made for Nana to move in. Nana's favorite room was being refurbished which took Nana and Lavinia to the shops several times. One day, as they were debating over curtains, Nana asked, "Why did you hug Kaelen at the end of the school year?"

Lavinia frowned. "I know what it's like to be rejected, Mother. The quest Martin went on was a wonderful quest. He had to find me among the stars and then battle the dragon keeping me there. But his quest was also swift; it didn't take him long at all to find my starry prison. His parents didn't think his quest worthy of him because it should have taken longer. They never accepted me and when Martin made it clear he would marry me with or without their consent, they disowned him," she recalled sadly. "They've never come to see the children. They never visited, never forgave. They didn't even come to Martin's funeral. I couldn't let Kaelen be abandoned that way."

"Though you do it to your own son?" Nana asked. Lavinia blanched and Nana continued, "I've never been fooled by your actions when I've visited, dear. I didn't say anything before because I had hoped you would overcome this yourself, but it has to end now; especially in light of what has happened to Kaelen."

"You don't seriously think I would disown my own son, do you?" Lavinia asked defensively.

"I know you wouldn't, my dear, but what I know and think is unimportant. It's what Adrian thinks," Nana said.

"Adrian knows I'd never disown him," Lavinia said weakly.

"Does he? I'm not sure he does, Lavinia," Nana admitted. "You must not have seen his face as Kaelen's parents left him there. But I did. I saw fear, a fear he wouldn't have if you showed that you loved him."

"I do love him," Lavinia replied. "It's just so hard to be near him because he is so like his father. It's like having Martin there and yet knowing he isn't."

"Martin is dead, Lavinia," Nana chided gently. "You have to let him go."

Tears filled Lavinia's eyes. "I can't. He's the only one who loved me. He risked everything and gave up so much for me."

"Then honor him by loving his son," Nana said.

"But it hurts, Mother," Lavinia admitted.

Nana patted Lavinia's hand. "Even the most beautiful rose has thorns, my dear. Adrian needs to know that you love him. He needs to know that if something happens to him, you won't leave him to fix it himself. He needs you, Lavinia."

"How do I undo what I've done?" Lavinia asked; pain in her voice.

"One step at a time, dear," Nana replied. "You could always start by moving him back into the family quarters."

Lavinia nodded quietly. "This will take time," she said at length.

"I know, love, that's why I'm here," Nana said gently. "Now, I really think these yellow draperies are just the thing to bring some light into that room, don't you think?"

Laughing, Lavinia agreed and they continued with their shopping. When they arrived back at the castle, Lavinia asked to see Adrian alone for a moment in her art studio. As he walked in, Lavinia remembered the way Martin looked. Adrian had the same build and soon would be the same height Martin had been. His face was baby smooth, just as his father's had always been; Martin had rarely needed to shave. There were the dimples, hiding now because Adrian wasn't smiling. Lavinia felt as though someone had stabbed her. She couldn't do this; it was too late. The damage had already been done. For a long time Adrian just stood there and Lavinia stared at him, noticing every feature that was like Martin's. The green eyes, sandy hair, stocky build, round face.

"Mother? Did you want to see me?" Adrian asked when they'd been there for about ten minutes.

"I, I was just thinking," Lavinia started. She stammered over the words, trying to get them out. "I was thinking, Adrian, that I think, I think it's time for you to move back into your old room. The tower, it's so drafty and, and, well, I just think that you should move back into your old room, that's all." She could see his surprise and a trace of a smile lit his face.

"Really?" Adrian asked, hardly daring to believe what he was hearing.

"Yes, Adrian," Lavinia replied. "I think that you and Moira are mature enough to be in the same wing of the castle now."

The smile faded slightly as Adrian said, "Oh, okay. Should I start moving my things back then?"

"Yes, I'll have Jameson move your furniture," Lavinia said. "But anything smaller you can start moving." Adrian simply nodded and started out of the room. Lavinia took a deep breath before calling to him, "Adrian?" He turned and faced her. She smiled; a true smile, though it was shaded with sadness. "I love you."

Adrian smiled in return. "I love you too, Mother."

As he walked down the hall, Nana stepped into the studio and hugged her weeping daughter. "Well done, my dear," she said gently. "Well done."

When July was almost over, the family went to Rendorlin for the wedding. The invitations had said that the wedding would be held in the bride's home province and a week later would be the coronation ceremony in Haldersee, where Kieffer had grown up. When they arrived they soon met with Lysander and Alexandra, who had brought with them their children and Kaelen. On seeing Moira, Lucian smiled. "It's good to see you again so soon. That dress is lovely by the way, did you make it?"

Moira smiled, "Yes I did. Nana also had me make her gown. It's still missing something I think, but…"

"It's lovely," Lucian interrupted, handing Moira a long stemmed, pale lavender rose.

"Lucian," Moira gasped, "where on earth? I didn't think roses grew in lavender."

"They only do in Maltisten where there's a king who thinks roses are everything. This is one of the hybrids he's been working on. This time I helped him with it. When we finally got a bush to flower and it was what we wanted, he let me name it," Lucian added with a knowing smile.

"Oh really?" Moira asked teasingly. "And what name did you give it?"

"Moira's Star," Lucian replied, smiling at her.

Moira couldn't help flushing and said with a teasing smile, "You do remember that you were supposed to not be trying, right?"

"Must have slipped my mind," Lucian retorted with a smile. "But I seem to remember someone saying that her favorite color was lavender and that she really liked the first rose I gave her."

"I have no idea what you could be talking about," Moira replied innocently. Lucian thought she'd never looked more beautiful as she smiled radiantly while sniffing the rose.

Their conversation was interrupted by Nana saying, "What a beautiful rose! Lucian, have you been keeping secrets from me? It's quite naughty to keep secrets from Nana, you know."

"I would never keep secrets from you, Nana," Lucian replied, hoping she wouldn't notice how pink he was. He noticed that Moira was blushing too, which only made him blush more. "My dad's more of a gardener than I am."

Nana laughed knowingly, "I do believe, dear, that you have quite the green thumb."

"What makes you say that?" Lucian asked.

"Oh, just a feeling I get," Nana replied mysteriously. She then wandered away to greet Alexandra and Lysander.

Lucian turned back to where Moira had been, but she was gone. Searching the crowd, he saw her standing by Allegra, showing her the rose and talking excitedly. *Well, at least she's not crying*, Lucian thought before joining Adrian and Kaelen. "So Adrian, how does Nana seem to know so much?"

"Hello to you too," Adrian laughed. "The story is that Nana's great-great-grandmother was a fairy who fell in love with a human. She gave up a fairy's lifespan to live a life similar in length to what we live. Nana says the reason our family is so tall is because of the fairy blood. She also gets feelings and senses things, magic things. I think she's been looking at me more, but I can't figure out why. There's nothing magical about me."

"So do you get feelings like that?" Kaelen asked.

"Me?" Adrian repeated. "I don't think the fairy blood made it into my senses. I'm so unobservant it's pathetic. I wouldn't know a magical thing from an ordinary thing unless someone told me which was which."

Suddenly the innkeeper started trying to shove Kaelen out the door, "I'll not have animals in my establishment. Shoo!"

"Hold on there," Lysander said, suddenly appearing. "Kaelen is one of my guests and I'll not have him treated so shamefully."

"You know this creature?" the innkeeper asked, disgust in his voice and face.

"That 'creature' is a prince and you will treat him as such," Lysander replied coolly. There was an icy fire in his eyes and he was standing at his full height. "If you have a problem housing Kaelen, we will take our business elsewhere."

"I don't allow animals in my inn," the innkeeper said stubbornly, though he had backed away from Lysander.

"Then we have no further business here. I do not work with simpletons," Lysander retorted. He then took Alexandra by the hand and walked out the door, motioning for Allegra, Lucian and Kaelen to follow him.

As they walked out, Lavinia too approached the innkeeper, "We won't be needing your rooms after all." She then left as well, taking her family with her.

Nana stayed behind only for a moment and said, "What you do to others will be done to you."

It took the families a couple of tries before they were finally welcomed into The Dancing Fairies. The elderly woman running the inn showed them to a few comfortable rooms. "I don't get very many customers," she said, though her voice was still cheerful and pleasant, "so you've got pretty much the whole inn to choose from. Not that there's much, but I'm sure you'll be quite comfortable in any of the rooms. And for you, sir, I think you'll like this room," she said to Kaelen. "It's very roomy and quite comfortable." She opened the door leading to a large, spacious room, cheerfully decorated with fresh flowers in a vase on the bedside table and homemade quilts and bedding.

"This will be great," Kaelen replied, trying to stifle a yawn. The group had already spent much of the day traveling and the added distance trying to find an inn that would accommodate Kaelen had been exhausting.

"I thought you'd be pleased," the old woman replied, patting Kaelen's arm. "I can have supper ready for everyone in an hour so you'll have time to freshen up. Oh my dear, would you like a vase for your rose?" she asked Moira. "I have many in my cupboards and would be glad to let you borrow one."

"Yes, thank you," Moira replied. "That's very kind of you."

"Don't mention it," the woman replied with a smile. "I'll be back up in a few minutes with that vase and then again when supper is ready. For now, rest your feet a while and get yourselves settled." She then turned and walked down the stairs, leaning heavily on the banister for support.

"A woman her age shouldn't have to work so hard to earn her bread," Alexandra said sadly. "So kind and generous; I'm going to go downstairs and see if I can't help her in the kitchens." Before anyone could argue with her, Alexandra was heading down the stairs after the woman.

The rest of them went into their rooms and got their things unpacked and ready for the next day. Even with her showing them all of the rooms, there weren't enough for everyone to have their own room. Adrian and Lucian had agreed to share a room while Moira and Allegra had said they would share a room. Nana had strongly suspected that the woman had given up her room for them and insisted upon staying with Lavinia. "That will leave a room available for her to sleep in. I do believe she has given Kaelen hers; so Kaelen, do be careful not to tear anything."

Kaelen nodded. He figured if he slept on the floor, he definitely wouldn't have to worry about it. But he also knew that if he did, somehow the kindly woman would know and be disappointed. She reminded him of Gelasia.

When supper was served, Alexandra helped the woman set the table and serve everyone up. Lucian could see flour on his mother's nose and some of her hair had fallen loose from the style she'd worn it in. But she also looked happy and there was a sparkle in her eyes as she poured stew into a bowl for him and handed him a fresh baked roll. As they ate there was much laughter and chatting. The boys talked about the classes they would be taking. "I'm in double amphibian studies," Adrian groaned. "Double! Wasn't one bad enough?"

"It could be worse," Kaelen pointed out. "You could have double spell breaking."

"I do, hey, when is yours?" Adrian asked. "Maybe we have it together. It won't be nearly so bad if there's someone else in there. It's bad enough I'll be in double swimming and diving by myself."

"You have double swimming?" Lucian asked.

"Yeah, my guess is Achilles didn't think I improved enough to have it just once," Adrian replied. "I have double swimming and on days I don't have swimming, I'm in diving."

"You'll get the hang of it," Lavinia said confidently.

Adrian smiled at her. He wasn't sure what had brought about the change in his mother's demeanor towards him, but he liked it.

"Well," Lucian said, breaking his thoughts, "I've got double fencing, double botany, double foreign language and beginner's healing."

"Healing?" Kaelen asked. "What would you need healing for?"

"I don't know," Lucian replied. "But apparently I'll need it because I'm taking it."

"Do you girls get any weird classes?" Kaelen asked Allegra and Moira.

"I suppose that all depends on your definition of weird," Allegra replied. "Most of them are the same as they have been. Although, this year they added a water-life studies class and best of all glass blowing."

"I don't know that I have anything I would consider truly unusual," Moira said at length. "I have all the general classes that the other girls have had. I'll be in Allegra's glass blowing class. Oh, the only weird one I have is dream interpretation class with Calypso. That one is at a weird time too, because she does spell breaking at Charming Academy during most of the day."

"I wonder why she doesn't have one of the other Sisters teach it," Adrian said. "Surely she doesn't have to teach all of the classes.

"Calypso has always taught dream interpretation," Nana explained. "It's her special gift. Each of the Sisters has one. Lucretia's gift is in the growing things of the world. Calypso understands dreams and their meanings. Althea has a magical bond with animals. Morghana is able to heal almost any ailment. Maeve can read the stars. Although, I suppose they're not in the same order they were in while I was in school."

"They just went through the Change," Kaelen replied. "That's why this happened to me."

"Well, don't you worry, I'm sure everything will turn out alright in the end," Nana said gently.

When everyone had finished eating, Allegra and Moira took the dishes into the kitchen and started washing them before the older woman could begin to protest. "Really, I shouldn't allow my guests to do all the work," she said at length.

"My dear," Nana said, leading her away, "consider us family for today. Now, you go rest your old bones. We'll manage just fine."

"No, I couldn't do that. It simply wouldn't be right," the woman argued.

But Nana would not take no for an answer. She gently prodded the other woman into the room they'd left open for her and then went to the kitchen to see if they needed any help. It had taken longer to get the older woman to her room than Nana had expected for when she had returned to the kitchen, the work was finished. Giving it a nod of approval, Nana suggested that it was time for everyone to go to bed. No one even tried to argue. Instead they walked into their rooms and promptly fell asleep.

Very early the next morning, the families left to go to the wedding. Before they left, Nana had restocked the woman's kitchen and Lysander had left far more money than what was owed. Lavinia also left a generous amount and the two families left after ensuring that they had done everything they could to make less work for the old woman who ran The Dancing Fairies.

When they arrived at the castle in Rendorlin, there were doormen waiting to take their invitations. Another servant announced their arrival and they were led to their seats inside a grand hall, decorated with fragrant, yellow roses and white, summer daisies. Garlands of greenery were draped about, mixed with flowing cuts of sheer fabric and ribbons in yellow and green. Kieffer was standing at the end of the hall with George standing next to him, straight and tall with a bright smile on his face.

"I wonder how much I would have to pay someone to just say Nana instead of announcing me like that," Nana complained as they had a seat. Despite asking the young man announcing everyone to say that she was Nana of Haldersee, the man had continued with her proper title.

"You can be announced however you'd like at my wedding," Adrian whispered with a smile.

"That could be a dangerous promise, my love," Nana replied with a wink.

They quieted as everyone rose from their seats as the fairy king and queen walked down the aisle, heads bowed respectfully before looking up again. Soon, Samantha was walking down the aisle, one hand on her father's arm while the other held a bouquet of roses and daisies. Her dress was a pale, summery yellow and there were green and yellow ribbons tied with roses and daisies intertwined through her tumbling bronze curls. She was a picture of loveliness and joy. As she reached the front, they saw Kieffer smile warmly. Though her back was to them and he couldn't see her response, Lucian knew she was smiling brightly in return.

The friends didn't talk while watching the ceremony. It was very similar to when they had seen Tallia's wedding during their second year. When Kieffer kissed his bride a cheer went up. They walked together out of the castle and onto the lawn where a large banquet complete with outdoor tables and chairs had been arranged. Kieffer and Samantha were seated and then everyone was invited to find their seat. George was sitting with his family, but the others were able to sit together. Lucian wasn't sure whether to blame George for the seating arrangements or Samantha. Each prince was seated next to his princess, except Kaelen who was seated instead next to Nana. At first Lucian was worried that this would mean another meal in awkward silence; but Moira surprised him. "They really look happy together don't they?" she asked.

Lucian glanced over at them. He could see the couple giggling and blushing. He was sure neither was aware of the conversations going on around them. "Yeah, they do," he replied.

Moira was quiet for a long while which wasn't too bad because Nana was telling everyone at the table about her wedding. "In the middle of winter," she said; a wistful expression on her face. "It snowed all that week, but the day of the wedding there was not a cloud in the sky. The world was a blanket of sparkling white under a sunny, blue sky. I wore a blue gown, they're lucky you know, and had a bouquet of winter flowers and berries. Alistair was so handsome. It was a perfect day; one I'll never forget.

"Will you wear blue?" Lucian asked Moira without thinking.

Blushing brightly, Moira sputtered, "I, um, I haven't thought much about it."

"Oh, I'm sorry," Lucian started, also blushing to the roots of his hair, "I didn't…"

"Do the fairy king and queen always preside at weddings?" Allegra interrupted, saving Lucian from trying to cover himself.

"Only graduate weddings," Alexandra replied, "Any couple who both graduated from the academies is married by the fairy king."

"So who married you and Dad?" Lucian asked.

"Phillipa Rosepetal," Lysander recalled. "She got special permission from the king and queen."

"Wouldn't that be difficult?" Adrian asked.

Lysander laughed, "I can't claim to know Phillipa well, but she seems the type who gets her way. She doesn't back down."

Soon it was nearly time to leave. George broke away from his family long enough to say hi to everyone before they prepared to leave. Samantha and Kieffer thanked them for coming. "I wish you could stay for the rest of the activities," Samantha said, "but I understand that you must travel home. Have a safe trip."

After everyone had said their goodbyes, the two families headed to their own provinces. Lucian listened to Allegra babble the whole length of the trip of what her wedding would be like. He tried to point out that Adrian may not agree with everything. "Don't be silly," Allegra retorted with a dismissive wave of her hand. "Boys never care about the details of the wedding so long as there is in fact a wedding. Isn't that right Daddy?"

Lysander, who had long since stopped listening, mumbled, "Of course, Allegra."

"See?" Allegra said triumphantly.

Lucian was about to argue that his answer didn't count because he didn't even know what they were talking about, but caught his mother's eye. There was an amused twinkle and she just barely shook her head. *Of course Mother is right*, Lucian thought. *It's not worth the argument.*

It was very late in the evening when they arrived home. After a light meal, the family retired to their rooms for the night. When Lucian got to his room, his head had barely hit the pillow before he was fast asleep. His dreams took him to faraway places and then in front of a familiar castle, though for some reason he couldn't place where it was. He was standing in front of a large group of people. Soft music was playing and a breeze ruffled his hair. In the distance, he could see a girl walking towards him. People stood as she walked by, but while she seemed to be walking closer, she appeared to be getting farther away from him. Clouds gather overhead and rain began pouring down, washing away the scene as though it were drawn in chalk. Lucian reached out for the girl, now so small and faded he could barely see her, until a large, wet raindrop landed on his outstretched hand.

Lucian rose with a start. "Moira," he whispered. He looked around himself in the dark. It had only been a dream, but why was his hand wet? A soft whine near the bed made him look over. "Oh, hello Rusty. Did I wake you up?"

Rusty put his paws on the bed and looked up at Lucian, whining again. Even in the dark, Lucian could see concern in Rusty's big brown eyes.

Scratching Rusty behind the ears, Lucian sighed, "I'm alright, boy. Just a bad dream, that's all. You can go back to sleep now."

Jumping onto the bed, Rusty curled up over Lucian's feet.

"I meant on your bed Rusty," Lucian whispered.

Woofing softly, Rusty refused to budge, even as Lucian tried wiggling his toes under him to get him to move.

Too tired to care that Rusty wasn't a puppy anymore and certainly didn't need Lucian's feet to sleep, Lucian lay back down and tried to forget the images from his dream, falling into a restless sleep.

Lysander entered Lucian's room early in the morning to get him up so they could go to town for his school supplies. He was surprised to see Rusty sleeping on the end of the bed, his own bed left empty in the corner. "Lucian, it's time to get up," Lysander said gently while rubbing the top of Rusty's head. As Lucian groaned, Lysander looked down at Rusty who seemed to be smiling at the attention. "You're a bit old to be sleeping at the foot of the bed, don't you think?"

Rusty yipped quietly and hopped off the bed.

Lucian slowly got out of bed as Lysander asked, "You don't let him sleep there every night do you?"

"No, normally he stays in his own bed," Lucian replied. "I think sometimes he has nightmares and feels safer at the end of the bed."

"Do you think that's why he joined you last night?" Lysander asked.

"He wasn't the one having nightmares last night; I was," Lucian explained. He told Lysander about the dream.

When Lucian finished, Lysander scratched his chin thoughtfully. "Rusty is very loyal; it's common in setters. He's also very aware of your feelings, Lucian. He probably sensed that you were upset and came to protect you. He's a good dog, son."

"I know," Lucian said, stepping out from behind the changing room he'd been in. "But why do I wake up with him on my feet when I haven't had bad dreams?"

"It's as you said earlier," Lysander replied. "Perhaps Rusty has nightmares. He had quite the traumatic experience as a puppy. It's possible he has dreams that remind him of that. However, it could be something totally unrelated. No one could claim to fully understand animals."

No one except Althea, Lucian thought, remembering the conversation with Nana. Perhaps it would be good to seek her council about Rusty.

After going downstairs for breakfast, Lucian and Kaelen went with Lysander to do their school shopping. As they went to the various shops, Kaelen was surprised by how warmly he was received. No one balked at his size or his looks. He was served with the same cheerfulness and kindness as Lucian was. Bill, in fact, was overjoyed to work with him. "I love a good challenge," Bill said as he took measurements. "All right then," he continued when finished, "I'll have both orders ready for tomorrow."

"Well," Lysander said as they left the shops, "looks like you both will be ready to go to school tomorrow."

Chapter 2

After picking up Adrian in Lictthane, Lysander's carriage made the familiar trip to Biberseth. Calista was waiting in her usual place by the doors. She greeted them cheerfully as they came up, "Welcome back. You look like you've gotten some sun. I hope you have everything you need."

"Yes, Calista," the boys replied.

As the boys went to their rooms to put their things away, Lucian couldn't help but feel excitement at a new school year. They saw familiar faces of friends and caught up with them as they waited to go to supper. Lucian also spent some time in his room getting things unpacked and organized the way he wanted it. He moved Rusty's bed from its usual corner to a place at the side of his own bed. He hoped that by moving him closer, Rusty would gain comfort from the nearness and not feel the need to sleep on the end of the bed as he had been doing recently.

As evening fell, the group of friends went over their schedules together. As Calista had predicted in years prior, their courses were becoming more individualized. They still had their math, language arts, and other core classes together. However, many of their specialty classes were different. Adrian and Kaelen had both been dropped from dragon fighting. Adrian looked slightly disappointed as he said, "Well, I suppose that means I won't have to fight any dragons on my quest."

"I'd consider myself lucky if I were you," Jacobi replied. "I wish I had gotten out of that one. I don't think I'd stand a chance against a dragon. I've got that observation class again. What am I going to have to do? Tell Clarissa apart from a look-alike?"

The boys laughed and continued the comparisons as supper started. George and Lucian still shared the foreign language class while Adrian and Kaelen had double spell breaking. Jacobi seemed to always end up in specialty classes by himself.

"If it makes you feel any better, I'm in that second fencing by myself so I don't accidently kill someone," Lucian told him.

"Oh good!" George said suddenly. When everyone looked at him, he continued, "I was afraid I was the only one in a second hour of fencing by myself. I'm glad I'm not alone. Raphael says that I'm not quite at a point that he could safely allow other students in while I learn left-handed."

"That's why I have it, only to learn right-handed," Lucian replied.

"I wonder why you'll need that," Adrian said.

"Hopefully it won't be because somebody chops my good arm off," George retorted with a grin. As the boys laughed he said, "I can do fencing left-handed, but I doubt I could learn to write well left-handed."

The meal continued with laughter and chatting. Kaelen thought it was great being back at school. The regular routine would certainly be a help to him as it would keep him busy. He wouldn't really have time to contemplate his predicament. He found himself thinking of Anna often, wishing that he'd been able to properly say goodbye and tell her that he'd always be there for her whenever she needed him. His last comforting thought before he and the boys were told to head to bed was that he'd at least be able to see her at the quarterly meetings with the princesses.

Within a couple weeks of school starting again, the boys were continually busy with school work. They often brought their homework under their favorite maple tree while the weather remained warm and pleasant. Often during these times, Lucian would contemplate going over to the witches' hovel and asking to speak to Althea. Over the past week, Rusty had refused to sleep in his own bed every day, curling up on Lucian's feet and refusing to budge; even if Lucian's tone became frustrated. Finally one afternoon, finished with his outside work, Lucian decided it was worth the trip.

"Where are you going?" Jacobi asked.

"I'm going to go talk to Althea about Rusty," Lucian replied.

"Are you sure that's a good idea?" George asked. "Nobody ever goes to the hovel willingly."

"Oh come on, guys, I go there every week for my healing class," Lucian said.

"But you're not going to class," Jacobi pointed out. "You're just going to go."

"It's not like I'm in trouble," Lucian replied. "I just have a question."

"Couldn't you ask Diana?" Kaelen asked.

Lucian sighed, "I don't know that she can help me anymore than she's already tried. I talked to her about the problem last week and there hasn't been any change. If anything, Rusty's gotten worse. Althea is my only other option." Without another word to the group he walked confidently over to the hovel and knocked on the door. He heard a faint, "Come in."

He opened the door and looked inside. Lucian had never actually seen the inside of the hovel. From its gloomy outward appearance, he had expected similar on the inside. However he was surprised as he saw a comfortable sitting room with rocking chairs and a crackling fire in a well-kept fireplace. A large cauldron was bubbling and frothing over the fire, yet he didn't feel nervous or apprehensive. The room was as inviting and comforting as being in his own living room at home. It even had a slightly homey smell, although the herbs were a little more overpowering than the soft potpourri his mother made.

"Prince Lucian," Althea said, breaking his thoughts, "this is a pleasant surprise. To what do I owe the honor of a visit?" She was sitting close to the fire, Horus purring on her lap as she gently stroked his silver-tinged black fur.

"I came because I was hoping that you could help me with Rusty," Lucian said, not feeling that this was a time to waste on small talk.

"I see," Althea replied. "What seems to be the problem?"

Lucian pondered for a moment before explaining, "He won't sleep in his own bed. I've done everything I can think of. I've moved him closer to my bed, given him extra blankets, everything. I don't understand why his behavior has changed."

Althea looked thoughtful. "Is anything else different about him?"

"Well, he's reluctant to leave me at all, honestly. It's almost like he's afraid I'll disappear if he's not there," Lucian said.

"Bring him here tomorrow evening," Althea requested. "I'll have a chat with him and see if I can't figure out what's bothering him."

"You can do that?" Lucian asked.

Althea laughed gently, a strangely pleasant cackling sound. "My dear, I am a witch. I can do a great many things that are, shall we say, unconventional." She smiled as he blushed and repeated her request. "Bring Rusty tomorrow and I'll see if we can't work out this puzzle. How are your classes going?"

The change in subject surprised Lucian, but he continued chatting with her for a short while before saying, "I should probably get back now. Thanks for helping me."

"Anytime, dear," Althea said and turned backed towards the fire.

As Lucian walked out of the hovel, the other boys were waiting anxiously. "Well, what happened?" George asked.

"What do you mean what happened?" Lucian asked as they walked toward the castle for supper. "I just talked with her. It's not like they punish people for talking to them."

There was a strange ribbeting and they all looked over. Adrian blushed. "Oops, hiccups I guess. Must be hungrier than I thought."

The boys laughed and continued to chat as they got in line for supper, the meeting at the hovel all but forgotten. As they ate their dinner, they talked about their classes and decided which ones were tolerable and which were simply boring or a waste of time. Adrian won out on most boring class after his description of the two hours of amphibian studies. "I'd rather fight Draconus a thousand times than take that class one more time. I might just find out if it's possible to die of boredom."

"I'm really sorry, Adrian," Jacobi said. "Unfortunately, I don't think it'll be that easy to get out of. Salvador would probably just bring you back to life and give you extra homework for the trouble."

"I know," Adrian moaned. "Oh well, maybe by next year I will have gained what I was supposed to and he won't bug me anymore." A strange buzzing filled Adrian's ears and he looked around the table as the conversation continued around him.

He couldn't find a source, so turned his attention back to the group as Kaelen asked, "How's your swimming going?"

Adrian groaned and related the latest of his swimming classes. It was difficult because his eyes always felt funny after class, as though they were bugging out. The other problem was that Achilles had grown testier over the break and even more impatient. "I didn't think it was possible for him to become less patient. He was already the most impatient teacher we have. Now it's like he's running a marathon and can see the finish, but can't quite get there. Or rather he thinks I'm running a marathon and on the verge of losing."

"I'm sure it'll get better as you continue to improve," Lucian said confidently.

"I hope so," Adrian moaned. "I'm really trying the best I can. It's not easy diving into the water when you're terrified that you won't come back up."

"You just need to have confidence in yourself," George replied, "that's all. Once you believe that you can do it, I'm sure it'll get easier."

"He's right," Jacobi agreed. "Just have a little faith in yourself."

"Thanks guys," Adrian said with a smile. "Unfortunately that's easier said than done."

"Well, if Gelasia were here, she'd tell you that everything worthwhile takes effort and is always easier to say than to do," Kaelen added.

The boys continued to chat late into the evening in the common room until Gelasia told all the boys in the room that it was time for them to be going to bed. Lucian went up to his room where Rusty was pacing by the door. As soon as he walked in, Rusty came over and he scratched his head. "You'd think I neglected you, boy," Lucian said teasingly. He walked over to his bed and Rusty jumped up onto it. "Not tonight Rusty," Lucian said firmly. "You have a bed and it's a very comfortable one. I've even given you my favorite blanket. You don't need to sleep by my feet."

Rusty began whining and turned his big brown eyes at Lucian, hoping that Lucian would give in.

"That's not going to work this time. I'm not going to suddenly disappear in the middle of the night," Lucian replied. "On your bed. If I need you I'll call you."

Whimpering, Rusty hopped off and curled up on his own bed. He continued to whine at Lucian as he watched Lucian get ready for bed and blow out the candle.

"Rusty, neither of us will be able to sleep if you keep that up," Lucian said sleepily as Rusty continued to whine. "I'm fine and you're fine. Go to sleep."

With one last soft whimper, Rusty quieted and Lucian drifted off to sleep. Rusty however was listening to Lucian's breathing. When it slowed to the deep, steady breathing of someone sleeping, Rusty quietly hopped onto Lucian's bed and curled around his feet. He lay there for a while looking at his master before finally closing his eyes to sleep.

After his classes were done the next afternoon, Lucian led Rusty to the witches' hovel. He was surprised to see Althea standing outside waiting for him. "Hello Lucian. If you'll wait here, I'll talk to Rusty inside. It's easier if you're not around, he'll be more open to discussing his problem. After I've talked with him, I'll let you know what you can do."

Lucian nodded as Althea waved Rusty into the building. Rusty briefly glanced at Lucian before following the witch indoors. As he waited, Lucian watched Lucretia work in the garden. She really did have a knack for growing things. He watched as she tenderly picked weeds from around young sprouts and the more mature plants. Lucian understood better now why his father spent so much time in the garden. There was something innately satisfying with working in the soil and bringing something as small and ordinary as a seed to life.

Lucretia looked over at Lucian a couple of times before coyly saying, "You wouldn't know who keeps leaving me gifts on the garden gate, would you?"

"Um, no," Lucian lied, knowing exactly who left things on the gate. No longer confident that he could get in and out of the witches' garden unseen, Lucian had begun leaving wildflower seeds that he found in small paper packets on the gate. Today Lucretia was lovingly planting the seeds with the others in the flower garden. Then she would gently train the young tendrils of plants up and around a trellis arbor near the gateway.

Walking closer to the gate and batting her eyelashes, Lucretia persisted, "You're sure you don't know?"

"Yeah, I'm sure," Lucian replied haltingly.

She looked him up and down. "Hmm, I suppose if you're sure. You seem especially *gifted* with botany."

Lucian blushed, "I do as well as anyone else I suppose."

"I don't think that's quite accurate," Lucretia countered. "Yes, I can tell. You're very good with plants. Why, I'll bet you've never met with a thorn on any plant you've grown. Quite a gift. You're quite the gardener aren't you?"

Slightly unnerved by the way Lucretia was looking at him, Lucian replied, "Yeah, I guess so. Um, I'm going to just, uh, sit over there and do my homework."

Lucretia shrugged and turned back to her gardening, though every now and again she cast a curious glance Lucian's way as he sat with his back against the hovel wall. He got out his books and some paper and began working, trying to put the conversation with the young witch out of his mind. *How does she know that my plants never have thorns?* he thought as he wrote the paper for Russett about the difference between magic vines and ordinary vines.

It was nearly an hour before Althea came back out with Rusty. When Rusty and Althea stepped out, he immediately stood and walked over. "I'll speak to you for a moment inside," Althea said before Lucian could say anything. Once they had both gone inside, she motioned for Lucian to have a seat. When he had, she sat down and began, "I believe you'll find Rusty to be more willing to leave your side now. He had several concerns he needed to address which is why it took so long."

"Were you able to find out what was wrong?" Lucian asked.

"Of course," Althea replied. "The problems are simple. One, he has nightmares from his trauma as a puppy. Being nearly drowned isn't easily forgotten. It unfortunately creeps into his subconscious while he's sleeping and occasionally gives him nightmares.

The other problem was one I could more easily remedy. He was concerned that you, like your best friends, would be put under a spell."

"Wait, friends? Kaelen is the only one under a spell. He was turned into a beast," Lucian replied. "Everyone else is perfectly normal."

"You've not been told?" Althea said, as though she'd revealed something she ought not have.

"Been told what?" Lucian asked.

Althea looked as though she weren't sure how to proceed then shrugged. "I suppose you'll find out soon enough anyway. Kaelen is not the only one of your friends undergoing a transformation. Adrian is as well."

"Adrian?" Lucian repeated. "Adrian can't be; he never gets in trouble."

"While it is true that Adrian is a very well-behaved young man, he has been in trouble once; though he unfortunately was not privy to that fact." Althea explained, "You see, young witches, like young boys, can be reckless and act without thinking. It would seem that Adrian was caught being less than gentlemanly and was punished without his knowledge or anyone else's. The matter has been dealt with accordingly, however it does leave Adrian in a predicament. Surely you have noticed some of the changes. He's getting shorter, he probably complains of hearing insects when there are none to be seen, his eyes are probably affected by being underwater; he may even be turning slightly green, though I myself wouldn't be able to tell. He's appeared green to me for close to two years."

"Are you telling me that Adrian is being turned into a lizard?" Lucian asked incredulously.

"Not a lizard, dear, a frog," Althea replied, as though this were obvious. "Now, before you do anything rash, it is apparent that the fairies have chosen not to tell anyone about this. I would recommend that you do the same. I realize this is quite a burden to place on you, but for Adrian's sake, you mustn't say anything. Not even to your princess."

"Well I couldn't tell her anyway," Lucian said slowly as he allowed what he had been told to sink in. "Moira is Adrian's twin sister."

"Then she may already have suspicions, but you cannot say anything one way or the other to her regarding this," Althea insisted.

Lucian sat for a moment dumbfounded. Adrian was slowly turning into a frog and somehow that had affected Rusty. "This may seem a stupid question," he said, "but how does that affect Rusty?"

"No question is stupid, Lucian. Animals see far more than humans do," Althea replied simply. "Rusty, like myself and the fairies, can see the glow of magic around Adrian and Kaelen while the rest of you remain oblivious to that. You can see the results of the magic on Kaelen and soon you'll see them on Adrian. Rusty sees it already and was afraid that you would be transformed as well. He's quite a loyal animal and loves you quite dearly."

"I know," Lucian said. If anything, he knew that about his dog. "I love him too. So, will he be able to stay in his own bed now?"

"He should be able to," Althea said kindly. "I've assured him that there are no present dangers for you being turned into anything. You're a true gentleman, Lucian. We don't see many of those in the world, even here."

Lucian blushed at the praise. "Thanks. And thanks for talking to Rusty and finding out what was bothering him."

"My pleasure, Lucian. Enjoy the rest of your afternoon," Althea replied, rising and showing Lucian to the door.

"You too," Lucian said as he walked outside. Rusty joined him and he walked with the dog towards the glade near the school to play fetch. It would be good to take a break from schoolwork and try to allow his thoughts to clear. He picked up a stick and began throwing it for Rusty, enjoying the sunshine and the time with his dog. He certainly knew that Rusty was loyal; he had been from the very start. It had been wonderful watching the awkward puppy grow into a handsome and well-trained dog. Lucian was grateful that he had kept with Rusty and not insisted on getting a more experienced dog. He found that he couldn't imagine life without the cheerful, red setter.

"Hey Lucian," George called. Lucian turned as his friend came closer. "Do you plan on eating tonight? 'Cause it's almost suppertime."

"Oh, is it?" Lucian asked. "I guess I lost track of the time. I just wanted to enjoy some time outside."

"I can understand that," George said as the two boys and Rusty headed towards the castle. "Adrian, Kaelen and Jacobi are already at a table."

"Alright, I'll meet you guys there after I get Rusty back upstairs to my room," Lucian replied.

"See you in a bit," George said as he walked into the dining hall.

"I guess I should pay more attention to the clock, eh boy?" Lucian said as he and Rusty went up the stairs.

Rusty woofed softly and eagerly went through the door as Lucian opened it for him. Lucian watched him curl up in his bed and promptly close his eyes. Laughing to himself, he headed downstairs to join the others for supper.

"Took you long enough," Kaelen teased as Lucian sat down with his tray.

"Sorry, I was enjoying the outdoors," Lucian retorted.

"Oh, you missed the announcement Calista made before supper started," Jacobi said as they were eating. "She told us that all of us in our fourth year will be starting a new class Tuesday evenings after supper."

"Did she say what type of class?" Lucian asked between bites.

"No, she just said that we all need to be there promptly at eight o'clock to begin our new lessons. She said the class will start next week and it will affect future meetings with our princesses. The meeting coming up will be the typical ride through the forest and picnic lunch afterwards," Jacobi explained.

"I bet it's going to be a new etiquette class. Gelasia is always trying to give us better manners," Adrian said.

"I doubt she needs extra time to do that. Most of the boys try not to cross her," Kaelen replied.

"I suppose we'll find out soon enough," Lucian said. "But, first we'll meet with our princesses."

"Maybe I'll have a moment to talk to Anna," Kaelen said hopefully.

"She's your little sister, right? The one who was trying to hug you at the end of last year?" George asked gently.

Kaelen's face fell. "Yeah. But, hopefully I'll be able to see her Saturday when the princesses come visit. Then maybe we can find a way that we can keep talking to each other."

"I hope so," Adrian said kindly. "Not to reopen wounds, but have you heard from your family at all?"

Laughing harshly, Kaelen replied, "Adrian, when my mother makes a decision, it is final. I can pretty much guarantee that I'll never hear from either of my parents or my older sister again. Anna's probably the only one that would maybe still talk to me. And that'll only be if she can do it without Mother finding out." He sighed. "It's not fair, but that's life."

"Well, hopefully Saturday will be as beautiful and sunny as today. There was a bit of a nip in the air though," Lucian said, knowing that for Kaelen's sake there needed to be a change of topic.

Kaelen smiled gratefully at Lucian as the others continued chatting about the meeting. It was hard talking about his family and made him feel a mix of anger and sadness. It wasn't fair what was being done to him. It wasn't entirely his fault. Okay, maybe it was if he really admitted that he'd been in the wrong sneaking out to watch the Change last year. But even so, he wished his family had stood by him; or at the very least his princess. As it stood right now, he was doomed to be a beast forever.

"Hey, Kaelen, we've asked you the same question twice. Are you still on the same planet as us?" Jacobi asked teasingly.

"Huh?" Kaelen asked. "Oh, sorry, I guess I was out in space for a while. What did you ask?"

The boys laughed and continued talking as they finished their meals. Unfortunately, because of homework, they had to cut the conversation off when they were done eating. Lucian went to his room and Rusty sat on the bed with him as he worked on finishing his homework. He had been able to get quite a bit done while Althea had been working with Rusty. After about an hour, he stretched and scratched Rusty's favorite spot behind his ears. "What do you say we call it a night early, huh boy? I'm beat."

Rusty woofed quietly and hopped down off the bed and curled up in his own. As Lucian blew out the candles, his mind swirled around the different things he'd heard today. Lucretia seemed convinced that he was more than just a little good at botany. Of course, Lucretia was also talking to him like he was human which was a far cry from how she had treated the boys before the Change. Lucian wondered if she was the young witch who was behind Adrian's slow transformation. That was another thing to think about too. How had no one noticed that Adrian was being transformed? Were people really that oblivious to the world around them? And how was he going to keep from saying anything to anyone? He couldn't even talk to Allegra because Adrian was her prince. *Oh no, Allegra*, Lucian thought. Allegra absolutely hated frogs and really any type of amphibian. They scared her. How was she going to handle Adrian being turned into a frog? If Adrian had to rely on her kissing him, he'd best get used to being a frog. Lucian couldn't see Allegra agreeing to pick up a frog, let alone get close enough to kiss it. He sighed wearily. All he could think as he fell into a restless sleep was that he had two of his best friends in worse situations then any prince on record had ever been dealt before.

Saturday morning dawned sunny and pleasant with a crisp breeze. Lucian wasn't at all surprised to see that the girls were wearing cloaks against the chilly wind. He was rather grateful for his jacket. He almost envied Adrian who had needed to roll up the bottom of his pants. "Someone must be playing tricks on me," Adrian had said that morning when Lucian had asked why his pants were rolled up. "None of my pants fit anymore. They're all too long. After the princesses leave I'll have Gelasia help me hem them up."

Moira smiled as she saw him. "Good morning, Lucian," she said, breaking through his thoughts.

"Good morning. It's a bit chilly this morning, isn't it?" Lucian asked.

"A bit," Moira admitted, "but the cloak takes the edge off. How have your classes been going?"

"Pretty good," Lucian said with a smile. "Raphael seems happy with my progress in my right-handed fencing class, so that's certainly a good thing."

Moira laughed, "I would imagine so."

"How are your classes?" Lucian asked. He was enjoying the pleasant banter back and forth. Moira usually wasn't this open right away and he wasn't going to waste the moment. He listened intently as Moira described her classes to him. She became so animated talking about the classes she enjoyed and barely skimmed over the ones she didn't.

After a while the conversation was interrupted by Calista and Melantha telling them to mount up and prepare for their ride. Lucian no longer had to offer Moira a hand up to mount Cinnamon, but he held the reins for her as she mounted. He then mounted Zephyr and they were soon enjoying an ambling walk through the fiery autumn glade. They were quiet for a moment, each enjoying the beauty of fall. "I love this time of year," Lucian said as they looked around at the fall foliage. "It's always so pretty."

"It is," Moira agreed. "And peaceful. Everything quiets down, like wintertime."

Lucian nodded. They continued for a while and he said, "Your riding has really improved. Are you and Cinnamon getting along better?"

Moira laughed, "I'm not sure it's so much that as we have an understanding. Allegra's been very helpful. We've been working more on my technique and such. I'll never be as graceful as she is in the saddle, but I'm beginning to see why she enjoys it so much."

"I rather enjoy riding," Lucian replied. "Although, Zephyr and I didn't really start on such good terms; he seemed to think he was the boss."

Zephyr tossed his head and Moira giggled. "It would appear he still does," she teased.

"Sometimes," Lucian admitted. "But once we came to an understanding, we've been doing much better. We've started learning some basic jumping in horsemanship and Zephyr just sails over the fences. I'm sure as we continue he'll become even better."

"I've been dropped from horsemanship," Moira admitted. "I don't mind much though, since it never was a gift of mine. But Allegra and I sometimes go on trail rides through the glade near the school. She enjoys it so much, I could hardly tell her no."

Soon they came to the end of the ride and Lucian wished it could keep going. He had enjoyed the conversation; especially since Moira had rarely opened up so much before. He helped Moira down from her horse after dismounting Zephyr. Then they walked together to a picnic blanket where the rest of their friends were waiting.

As they began eating, the friends chatted easily. It was strange that they still ended up somewhat coupled since Kaelen no longer had a princess and Leticia didn't have a prince. However no one commented about either situation. The day was too nice to ruin it with bad memories. They sipped from steaming mugs of cider as they enjoyed toasted deli sandwiches and warm apple turnovers. "They always seem to know exactly what we need," Allegra said as she nibbled the end off her turnover.

"It must be a fairy thing," Jacobi agreed.

Kaelen found it hard to concentrate on the conversation. He'd been looking all day for Anna but hadn't seen her. He hoped that his mother hadn't done something drastic like pull Anna from school. Then he suddenly found her. She was sitting a few blankets away. "Would you excuse me for a moment?" Kaelen asked as he rose from his spot.

"Sure, do you need anything?" Adrian asked.

"No, just need to walk around a bit," Kaelen replied. He walked towards Anna's blanket. "Hi Anna," he said as he stopped.

Anna blanched and stuttered, "Kaelen, I'm, I'm not supposed to talk to you."

"Mother's not here, she'll never have to know. Please, Anna, I just want to say hi," Kaelen pleaded.

Tears filled Anna's bright blue eyes. "Kaelen, I'm so sorry. I've missed you so much. It's horrible what Mother's done."

"What do you mean?" Kaelen asked.

"Everyone in Coleston thinks you died in an accident out here," Anna explained sadly. "Mother told them. She even made us hold a funeral to bury an empty coffin so that people would believe that you were dead. Kaelen, you've no home to come back to." Anna stopped as she started crying more. "It's not fair, Kaelen. I wish I could make it go away, I really do."

Kaelen sighed, "I know Anna. Listen, I know you're probably forbidden to do it, but could you maybe write to me every once and a while, just so I know I'm not totally abandoned."

Anna got a defiant look in her eye; a look he knew he had had several times before. "I will never abandon you, Kaelen. Not ever. I can't send the letters myself, but I'll talk to some of the other girls who write to their princes and see if I can get some messages to you that way."

"Talk to Eleanor, Moira and Allegra. They all write to their princes and they would get the messages to me. Thanks, Anna," Kaelen said. "I know this is hard."

Nodding, Anna said, "Well, I suppose I should let you get back to your friends. I'll send a note with one of those girls." She suddenly grabbed his arm and slipped something into his hand after reaching into the pocket on her cloak. "I've been hanging onto this for you. Thought you might like it. I wish I could have saved more from your room before Mother trashed everything."

Opening his hand, Kaelen saw the signet ring that his grandfather had given him upon his acceptance to Charming Academy. Grandfather had died less than a month later. Because the huge ring hadn't fit his small hands, Kaelen had left the ring at home where it would be safe. Now he was glad he had it with him. "Thank you, this means a lot to me," Kaelen said.

Anna smiled, "I knew it would. Mother was furious when she couldn't find it," she added with an impish grin.

Kaelen smiled and then walked away, leaving Anna with her prince and her other friends. He looked at the ring. His grandfather, the ultimate hero, had left him with a precious gift. "It's not just a ring," he remembered his grandfather confiding as Kaelen had sat next to him on the bed. "It's got a special magical gift bestowed on it. A witch blessed it you see, when I helped her get her cat out of a tree. When you are in the direst of need and feel the loneliest, it will bring to your mind a vision of the one you wish most to see. It helped me many a time on my quest and since your dear grandmother passed, I've been able to have some comfort."

Now as Kaelen looked at the ring, he realized what a unique gift his grandfather had given him. He could see Anna anytime he wanted to. He held the ring in his hand for a while before attempting to fit it onto his finger. Now that his hands were so much bigger, just maybe it would fit. While he couldn't wear it on his ring finger, he was able to get it onto his pinky.

"That's a nice ring, Kaelen," Eleanor said as he sat down again. "I don't remember you having it before."

"It belonged to my grandfather," Kaelen replied. "Anna brought it to me. Grandfather gave it to me when I got accepted into Charming Academy. I couldn't wear it before because it was too big, now it's almost too small."

"Well, you have, um, grown recently," Clarissa said gently.

They continued chatting until Melantha began gathering the girls. Lucian led Moira back to the group. "Lucian, I really want to talk to you about what happened last winter."

"Moira, I'm doing the best I can to stay true to my word," Lucian replied with a strained laugh. "It's not easy."

"No, I mean, yes, I understand that. But Lucian, that's not what I mean, I..." Moira began, but was interrupted as Melantha began shuffling girls into the carriages.

"You'd best go," Lucian said kindly. "Write to me about it."

Exasperated, Moira snapped, "Boys always make things so complicated." She then turned on her heel and marched into an open carriage with the others not far behind. Would he never just listen to what she was really trying to say?

"I think I just messed up again, Adrian," Lucian admitted as they watched the carriage go.

"You sure have a knack for it," Adrian teased. "Don't worry, what happened?"

"She was trying to tell me something and I think I took it the wrong way. I just don't get girls at all," Lucian moaned.

Adrian clapped him on the back. "Do any of us?" he asked as they walked back into the castle.

The next Tuesday, the boys in their fourth year met in the gym after supper to begin their new class. There was a lot of confused chatter as the boys tried to puzzle out what it was they were supposed to be learning. They already had fighting classes, etiquette classes, and their regular classes. What could there possibly be left to learn? The other question was why had this class been reserved for midway through the semester rather than beginning at the start of the year with the rest of their classes. The confusion did not lessen when they saw the row of stationary mannequins lined against one wall. "Are they going to turn us into mannequins too?" one of the boys asked.

"Don't be dumb," another boy said. "Those are all girl mannequins. We're probably going to learn how to do some sort of spell-breaking."

"But we already have a spell-breaking class," a different boy replied.

Lucian and his friends were standing together not taking part in the conversation. They were just as curious about the new class, but there didn't seem to be any way of discovering the purpose until one of the fairies came and announced to them what they would be doing. Instead the boys listened to some of the other comments, at times trying not to start laughing at their peers' wild ideas; like the hopeful boy who thought they'd be learning how to kiss properly.

"Oh yeah, because the fairies are going to teach us how to kiss," Kaelen whispered, unable to keep the comment to himself. "I mean, really? Why on earth would they need to teach us that? It's not like kissing can possibly be that hard. You stick your lips together and congratulations; you've just kissed."

George started giggling, "Somehow I think there's more to kissing than just sticking your lips together. But you're right; the fairies aren't going to need to teach us how. I'm pretty sure that'll come naturally."

"Besides," Jacobi added, "they certainly wouldn't teach us how to kiss two years before we're allowed to try it for real. That would just be asking for trouble."

The chatter stopped as Gelasia entered the room followed by Raphael and Honoria who was holding Theodora's hand. The little toddler fairy looked around at all the boys and tried desperately to hide behind her mother's skirt, which unfortunately didn't give her much protection from the view of the boys in the room. Lucian smiled down at her and waved. Her turquoise eyes looked up at him shyly and she gave him a half-smile before ducking behind her mother again as they stopped in the middle of the room.

"Gentlemen," Gelasia began, "I'm sure you're all very curious about what you'll be doing in these classes. Before I reveal the intention of the class, let me remind you that it is imperative that each and every one of you attend every single time. There's not much time before you'll be using what you learn. I can assure you that the ladies will be very disappointed if you do not take this class seriously." There was some shuffling about as boys moved to be able to better see their speaker. "In this class," Gelasia continued when it quieted again, "you will be learning the art of dancing from Raphael and Honoria. Let me tell you, they are beautiful dancers and if you pay close attention, you'll be able to sweep your princess off her feet; quite literally in fact."

The reaction to this news was mixed. Some looked mildly disgusted while a few looked genuinely excited about the news. But many boys looked as though they'd just been told they were flunking every class. Before the whispering could get out of hand, Gelasia waved her wand and the still mannequins at the side of the room suddenly came to life and began walking towards the boys. As the mannequins neared the boys closest to them, they stopped in front of a boy until each boy had a dancing partner. Kaelen found it vastly unfair that as undoubtedly the biggest person in the room, he had the shortest and most delicate mannequin of the whole group. He didn't have a chance to ask if he could change partners because Gelasia was already walking away, taking Theodora with her. Kaelen noticed a rocking chair in one corner by which were several toys. Obviously they wouldn't be leaving the room, just watching in the corner.

His thoughts were interrupted as Raphael began instructing. "Now, the first thing you'll need to learn is proper positioning. You bow to your partner and then take her right hand like so and place your left hand on her waist." He demonstrated with Honoria. "Before we let you have a go, I will warn you; these mannequins do not take kindly to fresh behavior. Your left hand should be on the young lady's waist, no lower or higher. Now you give it a go."

Several boys looked at each other before turning to the mannequins they were to be practicing on. Kaelen eyed his mannequin suspiciously. He was fairly sure his hands were big enough that even with perfect placement he would be over-reaching the appropriate boundaries. Just what would happen if you went too far? His question was soon answered by a loud smacking sound and a boy's yelped, "Hey!" He turned to see that one of the boys was rubbing a sore spot on his cheek. The mannequin had crossed her arms over her chest and had her head tilted to an offended angle.

"Oh, she slaps you," Kaelen muttered. "Terrific."

"You're going to have to ask forgiveness and try again, Robert," Raphael said to the boy. "She won't work with you otherwise and we've got another hour and a half before you boys are done."

There was some groaning that met this announcement. Kaelen turned back to his mannequin. Her eyeless face seemed to be anticipating him to do something. Feeling immensely foolish, he bowed. To his surprise, the mannequin curtsied. He took her delicate hand in his and then gulped as he attempted to place his hand on her tiny waist. "Please don't slap me," he begged. The mannequin didn't move as he gingerly laid his left hand on her waist. "Thank you," he breathed. There was no response from the mannequin. He half-wished that it could speak to him. He felt like a fool speaking to an inanimate object.

Once everyone was in position, they were given more instruction, this time by Honoria. She explained the steps and the importance of counting. She waved her wand and a slow waltz began. "We'll demonstrate the steps and then you join us. If you wait too long, your mannequin will begin without you," she warned. They watched as the couple began the steps. Then slowly, the boys began following suit. It wasn't long before another smack was heard.

"Hey!" Jacobi cried bitterly, "my hand was where it should have been."

"You must have stepped on her foot," Honoria said gently as they came to where he was. "Ladies don't appreciate being stepped on."

"I bet Clarissa is more forgiving," Jacobi muttered before apologizing to the offended mannequin and attempting to pick up the steps again.

By the time their first dancing class was over, most of the boys had crimson spots on their cheeks where their mannequin had shown disapproval for wandering hands or clumsy feet. Even George hadn't been immune to the mannequins' knack for catching mistakes. Poor Jacobi looked as though he'd been slapped at least a dozen times. "I'm a klutz," he said miserably as they walked out of the gym after the rather disappointing announcement that they would be seeing Honoria and Raphael again the next Tuesday to continue their lessons.

"You'll get the hang of it soon enough," Adrian said confidently. "After all, you're trying, right?"

Surprisingly, Kaelen had not once run the wrong way of his mannequin, a feat that Lucian complimented him on. "I hope you won't be offended, but I figured you would have had the hardest time," Lucian said. "After all, your mannequin was half your size. I was afraid you wouldn't even be able to touch her without getting slapped."

"I was too," Kaelen admitted.

"Size doesn't matter in dancing," Gelasia said sagely from behind them, startling the boys since they didn't realize she had followed them out of the room. "It's a matter of grace and manner. None of you did terribly."

Jacobi looked at her surprised. "I got slapped fifteen times," he said in disbelief. "I was terrible."

"Nonsense," Gelasia reassured him. "It'll come to you with time. Just remember to count the steps and you'll do just fine. Besides, you've only got to work on being more graceful. Some of those boys need to work on that and their manners." She smiled and turned to go a different direction as the boys continued up the stairs to their rooms.

"Can you believe that?" Jacobi asked when he was sure they were out of earshot. "She doesn't think I did terribly. I think she's being overly nice."

"Not really," Adrian said. "It's like she said; once you've got the beat down, you'll do great. And if it makes you feel any better, I wasn't far behind you in slaps for stepping on toes; my mannequin slapped me eleven times." He didn't tell them that one of the times he'd been slapped was for randomly sticking his tongue out. Of course, he wasn't sure what exactly he would tell them. He couldn't explain to anyone, including himself, why he had done it. It had just sort of happened, like an odd tic some people got. In fact, weird things had been happening more and more often to him. Swimming was almost painful because his eyes seemed bugged out at the end of the class. He constantly heard buzzing in his ears, like there was a fly nearby that he couldn't see and couldn't get rid of. The weird part was that hearing the buzzing made him feel hungry. Then there was the fact that Lucian was the same height he was and yet, he didn't seem to be growing. It was unfair of him to think that way; Adrian knew Lucian was still hoping to gain some more height before the next meeting since Moira had grown again and was once more taller than he was, though only by two inches. If she didn't stop growing, she was going to be six feet tall! As it stood right now, Lucian was trapped at a hair under five ten. That was what made being the same height as Lucian so weird. Adrian knew that when he'd left home he had been six foot one, nearly six two. How was it that now he was suddenly three inches shorter?

His thoughts were interrupted as the other boys said goodnight. He determined not to worry about it. Maybe Lucian was growing after all and the other things were just his imagination. After all, it would be great if Lucian was catching up to everyone in height. It would certainly make Lucian feel better if nothing else. He patted Clover's head before crawling into his bed and going to sleep.

Chapter 3

"You need to concentrate more, Lucian," Morghana said as Lucian sat in the overbearingly stuffy classroom he had beginner's healing in. It was a room in the witches' hovel which made it even more uncomfortable. For some reason it felt like intruding on their privacy as he walked into the room for his classes. It didn't matter that the room had its own door from outside and did not lead into their home at all. He still felt weird knowing that he was inside the hovel on a regular basis. "Really concentrate on the ingredients," she continued, interrupting his thoughts. "If you do a haphazard job, the results could be disastrous."

Lucian bit his tongue to keep from saying that the overpowering smell of dried herbs was making it difficult to focus on anything. He'd spent the last several weeks with Morghana learning how to make different pastes and poultices for healing small wounds and infections. These were supposedly the simple ones. He couldn't imagine what the hard ones would be like. As he continued working, he was keenly aware of Morghana's intense eyes watching him. That didn't help him concentrate either. He was terrified that one day she was going to become totally exasperated with him and turn him into a rock.

"Well, I suppose that's all the time we have for today. Reread chapter fifteen before next class. I think that will help you," Morghana instructed a few minutes later.

"Okay, I'll see you next Thursday," Lucian said, feeling rather miserable about the whole thing. He wasn't sure he wanted to remember how many times he'd been told to reread chapter fifteen. So far it hadn't seemed to help him at all. He read it each time he was asked, but all it did was confuse him more. Maybe he just wasn't reading it carefully enough. He pulled his jacket around himself as he walked out into the lightly falling snow. Winter had descended on the school quietly with light snow flurries occurring on a regular basis. The effect was mesmerizing and he often enjoyed peaceful moments by his window just watching the flakes fall. He knew Allegra and Moira were enjoying some time drawing the wintry wonderland that had taken over the school grounds at Fair Damsels. Each of them had sent him a sketch of what they had seen. Both had been beautiful and unique. His sister was more detail oriented than Moira was, capturing the snow trapped in the cracks of trees while also showing the delicate frost patterns on windowsills. Yet Moira's picture had captured the peaceful tranquility of the snow-covered grounds at twilight in delicate, swirling lines of color. Coming into the castle, he shook the snow out of his hair, which seemed to take with it the thoughts he'd been enjoying. Instead his thoughts returned to his botched healing class. He sighed as he headed upstairs to his room to start on his homework.

"Aren't you coming to dinner?" Adrian asked, meeting Lucian on the stairs.

"Oh yeah, let me drop my stuff off at my room first," Lucian replied miserably.

"Class that bad?" Adrian asked understandingly.

Lucian sighed, "I really hope that my quest doesn't involve saving Moira from some weird disease. I think she might die if that's the deal."

Laughing, Adrian said, "I suppose it could be worse."

"How?" Lucian asked.

"Well, since you're learning about healing at least you wouldn't be able to turn her into anything. I mean, you couldn't turn her into a toad if you messed up," Adrian pointed out.

For a moment Lucian gaped at him, unable to say anything. It was becoming harder and harder not to tell Adrian what Althea had confided to him. But having given the witch his word, he didn't want to risk what might happen if he broke his promise. He was certain that being a frog would be the least of anyone's worries were that to happen. It was hardest because Adrian was starting to notice strange behaviors and changes and often confided in Lucian about them. Lucian would do his best to simply be understanding and offer comfort without giving the impression that he could explain anything.

"How was swimming?" Lucian asked, trying to steer the conversation away from amphibians of any nature.

"I swear one of these days Achilles is just going to zap me into oblivion," Adrian replied with a frown. "I don't know what his deal is. I'm doing the best I can, right?"

"I guess so," Lucian said as they continued to walk. "I mean, if you're trying your absolute hardest and making progress then he should be happy with it."

"You'd think I was purposely behind in this," Adrian complained. "I mean, what does he want from me?"

Without realizing it, they had started walking past the infirmary where a raised voice had spoken Adrian's name. The boys stopped to listen. "I can't get him where he needs to be because the change is happening too rapidly. I thought we had more time than this," they heard Achilles say, frustration clear in his voice. "Isn't there something you can do?"

Tallia's voice replied, "Achilles, you know very well that I can't do anything about the Sister's magic. Even the students know that. I realize this transformation is going faster than we anticipated, but you're just going to have to make the best of it."

Achilles growled in frustration. "What am I supposed to do? He's barely making progress at all. I still think we should have told him from the beginning but no one else agreed with me."

"Your own mother knew it was best not to say anything," Tallia retorted, obviously irritated. "How would you have reacted as a fourteen-year-old being told that you were slowly turning into a frog?"

Suddenly Adrian gulped, no longer listening to the conversation going on in Tallia's office. "They're not serious are they?" he whispered to Lucian.

Lucian tried to shrug innocently. "I wouldn't think so. And besides, maybe they're talking about someone else. I mean, you'd know if you were being turned into something right?"

Adrian eyed him suspiciously. "You know something don't you?"

"No," Lucian squeaked, knowing full-well that he couldn't lie to his best friend if pressed.

"I'm going to talk to Calista about this," Adrian said, determination in his voice. He knew Lucian was lying and it was making him mad.

"Talk to me about what?" Calista asked. Both boys jumped and whirled around, unaware that she had been standing behind them.

"Tallia said I'm being turned into a frog," Adrian blurted out. He had wanted the statement to come out sounding stronger, but instead it came out feebly as though he'd simply heard something wrong.

"Why would Tallia tell you that you were being turned into a frog?" Calista asked, trying to sound nonchalant, but startled that Adrian knew.

Adrian blushed. "Well, she didn't exactly tell me, I overheard her say it."

"You were eavesdropping?" Calista offered.

"No, not exactly, well maybe, yes. I wasn't doing it on purpose," Adrian said quickly. "I heard my name and started listening. But they said I'm turning into a frog. I can't be turning into a frog, can I? I've never been in trouble."

Calista sighed, "This isn't the way I wanted to do this."

"You mean I am turning into a frog?" Adrian asked, panic setting in. "I can't save my princess if I'm a frog!" He suddenly gasped, "Allegra. You have to stop this, you have to! I can't go through what Kaelen did. I can't watch Allegra leave me! I love her."

"Allegra won't abandon you like that," Lucian said comfortingly.

"Of course she won't," Calista agreed, "because Allegra will not know. Come to my office after supper and we'll discuss this."

"Why not now?" Adrian asked, trying to ignore the buzzing in his ear.

"Because we're late for supper as it is and I'm sure you're both very hungry," Calista replied as Adrian's tongue shot out of his mouth and he slapped a hand over it. "And yes, Lucian," she continued before he could ask, "since you have unfortunately become aware of the situation as well, I'll have both of you come to my office. In fact, things may be simplified with your knowing about this. But for now, we're going to eat and I would advise both of you to not say anything about this to your peers."

Calista walked away and they followed slowly. Adrian suddenly turned to Lucian. "You've known all along haven't you?" he accused.

"No, I haven't, I promise," Lucian replied. "I just found out a little while ago."

"When?" Adrian demanded.

"Remember when Rusty kept having problems and I went to talk to Althea about it?" Lucian asked. When Adrian nodded, he continued, "Well, Althea told me about it then. I couldn't say anything to you because she made me promise not to. I'm sorry, Adrian, I really am. I wanted to talk to you about it but I couldn't. I wasn't allowed to."

Adrian sighed, "I'm going to be the worst Prince Charming ever. I won't even get to rescue my princess."

"Cheer up, you don't want the others to see you like this," Lucian said. "Especially since we can't let them know about this."

"You don't honestly think I'm going to keep them in the dark about this do you?" Adrian asked. "It's bad enough that you had to keep it a secret from me. I won't tell them right now," he added when Lucian looked like he was about to argue with him, "but as soon as we finish talking to Calista about this, I'm going to let the others know about it too. I can't keep this a secret by myself. Besides, you guys will probably have to really help me out when I reach the point that I can't hide this from Allegra any longer. Be honest with me Lucian, do you think I even have a chance at this?"

"Absolutely," Lucian said confidently and was surprised to realize he truly meant it. "If anyone in the world can get Allegra to fall in love with a frog, it's you."

Adrian laughed, "I'm not sure if I should be offended or take that as a compliment."

"Well," Lucian replied, "I meant it as a compliment."

They stopped talking about it as they joined their friends at a table. Instead they talked about everything and anything else they could think of. They were helped by Kaelen excitedly describing his latest classes with Gelasia to improve his fine motor skills. "I finally held the spoon without bending it backwards. Gelasia is sure that within a few more weeks they won't have to give me these altered things anymore," he said, referring to the oversized silverware he'd been using since his transformation.

The topic soon changed to the meeting they would be having with their princesses at the end of the month. "You don't think we'll have to dance at this meeting, do you?" Jacobi asked hopefully. His dancing hadn't improved much over the past weeks of lessons.

"I don't know," George said doubtfully. "They wouldn't have started the lessons if we weren't going to be dancing at some point. Maybe it's for the end of the year banquet," he added when Jacobi looked miserably at his plate.

No one had the heart to disagree with George while Jacobi was there. Lucian was fairly sure that there wouldn't be a ball at the end of the year. After all, most of the graduating princesses would be disappearing during graduation. Surely they wouldn't have a ball when there would be girls missing. But he could easily see there being a ball after supper during their winter meeting. It made the most sense because all of the girls would be there.

After supper, Adrian and Lucian excused themselves from the group and went upstairs to Calista's office. She was waiting there behind her desk with Lucretia sitting at her side. She invited them to have a seat. "Please close the door first, Lucian."

Lucian did as he was told and then sat down in one of the comfortable chairs.

"Now," Calista continued when each boy had taken a seat, "we'll discuss what is going on. In your second year, Adrian, Lucretia saw fit to cast a spell on you. I'm fairly sure that she had intended for you to instantly become a frog, so you should consider yourself grateful that it has taken the better part of two years for this transformation to even become noticeable to you."

"Grateful?" Adrian said in disbelief. "I'm turning into a frog!"

Calista raised an eyebrow which instantly silenced the room. "Nevertheless," she said when Adrian was sitting back quietly, "it is going a little faster than what some of the fairies anticipated. We were under the impression that it would take a full three years or longer for this to complete. However, things seem to be speeding up, perhaps because you are a growing boy and that might be affecting the spell."

"Can I ask why this happened?" Adrian asked. "I mean, I've never once been in trouble."

"That is very true, Adrian," Calista replied. "However, this was not done because you were in trouble with any of the fairies on staff. Lucretia did this of her own choosing and will now explain to you her reasons and why we have done nothing to change it."

Lucretia looked at Adrian almost apologetically. "This may take some time, so bear with me," she began. "During your second year; well, I should start earlier than that. You will of course remember that I was the youngest witch during that time in your schooling. Much like Maeve who had difficulty controlling her magic because she was the oldest and the Change was already beginning to alter her, I too was at a vulnerable stage because I was the youngest. There was still much for me to learn. In fact, there still is much for me to learn," she admitted. "One of the traits of being the youngest is impulsiveness. They are also very easily offended, rather like teenage girls. However, you may also recall that each Sister has a gift and mine is with growing things. This is why Russett asks me to bless the plants grown by his students, especially when there is a time limit involved. I was asked that year to bless the flowers you were growing for the fairy wedding. Tallia and Achilles, wasn't it?" Lucretia asked. Calista nodded and she continued, "Yes, well, I was walking towards the greenhouse and you were walking with your friends back to the castle. The reason I put the spell on you is I caught you sticking your tongue out. While that is certainly typical boy behavior, it is not the behavior of a gentleman. So, being in a wicked frame of mind anyway, I cast a silent spell on you to turn you into a frog. Calista is quite correct in believing that it should have been an immediate transformation. However, the Change alters the magic of all the Sisters and it made what should have been a sudden change a long-lasting spell that would take time to come to pass. It was very frustrating to me because an immediate change is easier to fix than one that is going to last for several years."

"Why didn't you try anyway?" Adrian asked.

"I knew eventually the fairies would see the glow of magic and force me to undo the spell, so for the time I did nothing. As I said, the youngest witch is impulsive and can be vindictive," Lucretia replied. "When Calista was told and the Sisters were brought to her office, I honestly did have every intention of removing the spell; though I will admit that I would have done so a little reluctantly. But Maeve, even at her oldest and to you strangest, has a gift; she reads the stars. She told us that it would be impossible to remove the spell. Adrian, you never were going to be the one to go on the quest. It was writ in the stars that your princess, Allegra, would be the one to find and rescue you. The spell which I cast in a moment of frustration and bitterness was meant to be. As much as I would like to say that I can take it all back and return you to normal, I cannot. It is forbidden by the stars and that is a rule that no matter where in the Sisterhood I stand I cannot go against. I am truly sorry, Adrian," Lucretia finished. "But this is what is meant to be. And you should know that I paid a terrible price for my indiscretion."

"Thank you, Lucretia. You may go if you need to," Calista said.

Lucretia smiled and rose from her seat. She patted Adrian's arm gently and repeated, "I am sorry."

"Over the past couple of years," Calista continued as Lucretia left the office, "we have tried to add things into your schedule that will make this transition easier."

"Like the amphibian studies class and swimming," Adrian said, trying to keep up with what was being told to him, though his mind was reeling from Lucretia's revelation.

"Precisely. You see," Calista explained, "the reason I chose not to tell you when this happened is I wanted you to still have confidence in yourself and your ability to have a successful quest. I hoped to give you the longest time possible to come to terms with what is happening. Perhaps I should have told you sooner, but I was afraid that your knowledge would destroy your confidence. However, we do need to discuss how to deal with this matter in regards to your princess. In light of what happened to Prince Kaelen, I do not feel it would be prudent to tell her about this little hiccup in your plans. Instead, you will continue to go about as though everything is perfectly normal."

"How?" Adrian asked. "Eventually it's going to be obvious, right? She'll be able to see like anyone else that I'm not a person anymore."

"When the time comes that we can no longer hide the fact that you are changing, we will set up a meeting between myself, Melantha, Allegra and you. We may even invite Lucretia so that she can best explain to Allegra what is happening. However, for now you are just as normal as any of the other boys, at least, I think so. Lucian, is Adrian green at all to you?" Calista asked. "I'm afraid having fairy eyes can sometimes be a disadvantage."

"No, Adrian really isn't turning green right now," Lucian replied. "He's just shorter than he used to be and has a habit of ribbeting at inopportune moments."

"Well then, she won't notice that you're any different. I'll have Gelasia make you some shoes that will put you back to the height you were without being horribly noticeable. When you reach the point that it is obvious something is happening, then we'll meet again to discuss how to proceed," Calista said. "For now, I would suggest you continue in your coursework and personal life as though nothing has changed."

"Calista, I have a question for you," Lucian said before she could continue. When she looked at him expectantly he asked, "Can we tell our closest friends about this? I think having the support of our friends will make this easier on Adrian and be of help in determining when we need to talk to his princess."

Hesitantly, Calista replied, "I'm not sure that's a very good idea, Lucian. While I understand the need for support, word travels far too quickly around a place like this and it would be very difficult to keep your entire class from saying anything to their princesses or to others in general."

"I'm not keeping this to myself," Adrian said defiantly. "I need my friends to help me with this. I'm going to tell them with or without your permission. I trust each of them; they won't repeat what's been told to them if they have given their word. They are all true gentlemen. I have no reason to believe that anyone outside our circle will know what is happening."

Calista eyed Adrian and Lucian for a moment. Then she smiled and said, "Very well, Adrian. It will be as you wish. You may tell Kaelen, George and Jacobi. However, I would stress that it is vital not to tell anyone else."

"I won't," Adrian promised.

"Well, it is late now and you both need to be getting to bed. Have a good night boys," she finished, holding the door of her office open. As Adrian walked through the door, she said, "Don't worry, Adrian. Everything will work out just fine. You'll see."

Adrian knew that despite the multitude of questions he still had, the meeting was over and there would be no continuing it tonight. "Good night, Calista," he said quietly. Feeling as though he'd been defeated by thirty dragons in a row, he walked away from the office with Lucian following close behind.

"You going to be alright?" Lucian asked as they went up the stairs.

"I guess," Adrian replied. Without bothering to say good night, he walked into his room and went to bed.

The end of the semester came faster than the boys were ready for. Their finals had gone by quickly and soon it was time to meet their princesses before winter vacation. Adrian had told the other boys about the slow transformation into a frog. "That explains the ribbeting," Jacobi had said.

"Thanks for making me feel better," Adrian had replied miserably.

The boys had put their heads together and were doing what they could to try to help Adrian have a smooth transition. Of all the boys, Kaelen was probably the most helpful having actually been transformed into something else. But even there, his situation wasn't very comforting. His princess had left him to remain a beast for all eternity. Adrian could only hope that Allegra would have a better reaction when it finally came out that he was turning into a frog. After all, eventually Allegra would be able to tell by just looking at him.

He tried to keep those thoughts out of his mind as the princesses arrived for breakfast. He smiled at Allegra who smiled back. She was looking beautiful in a light green gown with little golden flowers. "You look lovely," Adrian said.

Allegra blushed. "Thanks, Moira helped me with the embroidery. She's very talented."

Moira had stopped long enough to say hello to Adrian before turning to talk to Lucian. "Is there something different about Adrian?" she asked.

Lucian tried not to look guilty as he lied, "No, what makes you think so?"

"I don't know," Moira replied. She was looking at Adrian as though he were a puzzle missing a piece that she couldn't find. "He just seems different somehow, not himself. Oh well," she continued, shaking her head and returning her attention to Lucian with a smile, "I suppose it's because I don't see him very often."

"That must be it," Lucian said with a smile. "You look very nice today. Did you make the dress?"

"Yes I did. I'm glad you like it." Moira smiled, looking down at the delicate, lavender gown. "Did you see Allegra's dress? She did most of that herself."

"But I bet you helped didn't you?" Lucian teased.

Moira smiled impishly, "Maybe a little. But the design was all hers; except for the sleeves. I told her flutter sleeves would work best on it."

Lucian smiled as Moira took his arm and allowed him to lead her into the dining hall. As they walked he said, "You told her just the right thing; it looks beautiful on her. You have quite a gift."

Blushing, Moira said, "Thanks." Lucian held her seat for her and soon they were surrounded by all their closest friends. Chatter flowed about the table lightly and easily as they caught up from the last time of seeing each other.

"Oh, Kaelen, I have something for you," Clarissa said, reaching into the pocket of her dress. "It's from your sister. I'm sorry I didn't send it in a letter like I normally have, but she just gave it to me last night. I thought you may feel better getting it now rather than waiting for next semester to start."

"Thanks," Kaelen said, taking the folded piece of paper from her. For the past several weeks each of his friends had made similar deliveries of notes that their princesses had sent to them. He took a moment to read the short note.

> Dear Kaelen,
>
> I wanted you to get this just before winter break since I know I won't be able to write to you then. I hope that things are going well in your classes. The girls have been so kind in giving me the letters you send. Don't stop. I miss you horribly. I'm not going to try to see you during this meeting in hopes that Mother won't find out that we've been in contact. In fact, I've left all of your letters at school in a hidden place so that she won't ever know about them.
>
> School has ended well for me. I'm doing very well in all my classes. Melantha says that I have great talents. That makes me feel really good since Mother is so picky.
>
> Well, I need to keep this short. Have a wonderful winter break! I'll write again when school starts.
>
> With Love,
> Anna

Kaelen refolded the letter and placed it gently in his jacket pocket. "Thanks again, Clarissa. I appreciate it. Really, I appreciate all of you for helping me stay in touch with her."

"That's what friends are for," Eleanor said gently. "You would do the same for any of us. It's a pleasure to help you out. I just wish there were an easier way for you two to talk to each other."

"Me too," Kaelen admitted.

They were interrupted by Calista stopping by their table. "Kaelen, may I have a moment please?"

"Sure," Kaelen replied. "Excuse me," he said to the group before getting up and following Calista out into the hall. Melantha and Gelasia were waiting there as well. Kaelen nodded his head towards them.

"Kaelen," Calista began, "I have a strange request for you. But I would like Melantha to explain the situation before I make that request."

Melantha smiled sadly at Kaelen. "I'm very sorry, my dear," she began. "I received a letter from your mother stating that Anna is to have no contact with you. In fact, I suspect that your mother assumes you have been expelled from the school. Rather, she demanded it in the letter. Of course, why she sent that to me and not the headmistress of your own school is yet to be seen. However, she has stated that if she finds that there has been contact between you and Anna that she will pull Anna from Fair Damsels. I'm sure I don't need to tell you how heartbreaking that would be for your sister. She is one of my best students and a true lady. I would hate to lose her to someone as," she paused, trying to find the best word, "bitter as your mother is. Now, I happen to know that you have both been sneaking messages to each other. I will not ask you stop that communication; I think Anna needs to hear from you. I will do what I need to in order to ensure that your mother not find out about it. But I would urge you to use caution in sending those messages."

"I don't understand," Kaelen said, turning to Calista. "You said you had a request. If you're going to allow me to keep writing to her, which I appreciate, I don't see what the request is."

"Yes, Kaelen," Calista replied, there was sadness in her tone and in her eyes. "I need to have you stay away from the activities in which your sister could be involved. Most especially, I need you to be in your room while the parents are here so that there is no chance of your parents seeing you. I hate allowing others to dictate what happens at my school. However, in your best interest and in Anna's, Melantha and I agree that it would be best to appear to be following Queen Angelique's wishes. I am so sorry, Kaelen. I know this is already a hard situation for you."

"It's fine, Calista," Kaelen interrupted, wishing he could remove the sorrow from the fairy's eyes. "I understand. If you feel that this is the best way to ensure that Anna and I can finish school, then I will comply. Gelasia, I assume that you were going to offer to stay with me?"

Gelasia smiled sweetly. "That was indeed my intention if my company would be of comfort to you."

Kaelen returned her smile warmly, "Gelasia, you are always welcome and always a comfort." He turned again to Calista, "Can I finish breakfast with my friends and explain the situation to them? They'll miss me if I just disappear."

"Of course you may," Calista replied. As Kaelen walked away, she couldn't help but feel a surge of pride in her student. She cleared her throat and dashed a tear from her eye. "Well, Gelasia, he has certainly grown since coming here hasn't he?"

"Indeed he has, dear," Gelasia replied, patting Calista's arm. "Indeed he has. Calista, while he finishes breakfast, I'm going to go speak to Maeve."

"Whatever for?" Calista asked.

"I think there's more to Kaelen's story than perhaps we are aware of. Let's be honest, dear, many do not see much hope for him at all. His family has disowned him and his princess has abandoned him to a cruel fate," Gelasia explained. "I think it's time we revisited the stars and see what is truly in Kaelen's future. I can't believe that there is no hope for him. I just can't. He has grown and matured far beyond what any of us would have imagined when he first arrived. So, with your permission, I'm going to ask Maeve if she can get us more details on this situation. Then, after his parents have left with Anna, I suggest we have a meeting with him again to discuss our findings."

"As always Gelasia, you are a fount of wisdom," Calista replied with a smile. "Go speak with Maeve. Perhaps there is some hope after all."

Once Kaelen had returned to the dining hall, he told his friends about the meeting in the hallway, mentioning only that he would be upstairs for the remainder of the day. He didn't want to further depress them by telling them that it was because of his mother that he would probably spend every meeting this way.

"How awful!" Clarissa said. "That's so horribly unfair."

Kaelen just shrugged. "Don't let it ruin your day."

The others looked at him as though to say, "Too late," but no one did. Instead, they picked another topic of discussion and continued as best they could as though nothing had changed. When breakfast was finished, Kaelen excused himself and led Gelasia up the stairs and towards his room.

"Dear, may I recommend that we convene in my classroom?" Gelasia requested as they came to a stop at the top of the stairs.

"Your wish is my command," Kaelen said genially.

Gelasia giggled merrily. "I always knew there was a gentleman in you. Even from the very beginning."

Kaelen couldn't help but laugh as well. "I'm sure for a while you were the only one. I'm afraid I really botched things in the beginning."

"Well, my dear, no one is perfect," Gelasia replied with a smile. "Now, before we go inside, I insist that you close your eyes. I have a surprise for you."

"For me?" Kaelen asked.

"Unless you know a Kaelen I don't," Gelasia retorted teasingly. "Go on, close your eyes." Kaelen did as he was told and allowed Gelasia to lead him into the room. "Not yet, not yet, and now you may open them."

Kaelen did and blinked a couple times. In front of him was a spinning wheel and carefully bound bundles of straw. Sitting on the seat of the wheel was a sewing kit with oversized needles, thimbles, scissors and spools of thread. "Gelasia, this is, wow! Thank you."

"You're very welcome, my dear," Gelasia replied with a smile. "I know as much as you may not want to admit it to your peers that you enjoy the more delicate tasks. And I thought that during those times when you can't be with your friends, this will give you something to do that will be enjoyable and bring you happiness."

Hugging Gelasia carefully, Kaelen said, "This is the best present anyone has ever given me! Can I start on something right now?"

Gelasia laughed, "Of course you may, dear."

A slightly sad expression crossed Kaelen's face. "I wish I could do a dress for Anna. I know she'd like it."

Smiling sadly, Gelasia said, "I know, dear. Better than that, why don't you make her a handkerchief? That's something that she could carry with her always to remember you. Every good young lady of breeding needs a beautiful handkerchief. I would make sure it got to her without your parents knowing who the benefactor was. Anna will know because she knows you and your style, but they would be none the wiser."

Kaelen smiled, "That's a perfect idea. I better get some gold thread going."

For the rest of the morning until lunchtime, Kaelen worked on spinning gold and embroidering a delicate handkerchief for Anna. He wanted it to be something richer and more beautiful than anything his mother had ever had. But more than that, he wanted it to express to Anna how much he cared for her. She was the only one of his family who had stood by him. He had a feeling that even if things got back to where he was himself again that Anna would be the only one to come see him. He banished any sad thoughts while he was working; they made it difficult to concentrate. All too soon there was a soft knock at the door. "Calista asked us to bring this up for yourself and Prince Kaelen," an unfamiliar voice said. "Enjoy."

"Thank you, dears, how very thoughtful of you. Well, Kaelen," Gelasia said as a couple of fairies brought in two steaming trays of food. "It's lunchtime. Best stop what you're doing for now."

"It's almost finished I think," Kaelen replied as the other two fairies left the room. "What do you think of it?"

Gelasia looked over the delicate embroidery. "It's beautiful, Kaelen. Now take a break and eat. You can finish it after lunch is over."

While Gelasia and Kaelen were enjoying their private meal, the others were in the dining hall trying to enjoy their lunch. "It's so unfair that Kaelen can't be here with us," Jacobi said as they were eating.

"I'm sure the fairies have good reason for doing that," Leticia replied. "After how his family reacted to his transformation, I'm sure it's for the best that they have him not participating in this."

"I hadn't thought of that," Jacobi admitted. "But you're probably right."

"Well, Kaelen wouldn't want us to talk about it or be sad because of it," Lucian said. "What is everyone doing for winter break?"

"We're visiting our grandparents over the break," Eleanor said. "We haven't seen them in a while and Grandma's health has been declining recently."

"I'm sorry to hear that," Clarissa said gently. "My family doesn't really have any plans. We're just doing things at home."

George rolled his eyes. "I'm doing what it seems I do every break; I'm in yet another wedding. Susan finally got rescued just in the nick of time. I guess Samantha is the only one willing to give me a different job; I'm back to being the ring bearer. We'll be going to wherever he's from. I can't remember now, but it's somewhere east of where I live."

"I suppose it could be worse," Adrian said kindly.

"Yeah, I could have even more sisters," George retorted with a grin. "As it is the only one left is Marissa who graduates this spring."

Adrian laughed. "Well, I don't think we're going anywhere for break. At least, Mother hasn't told me anything."

"Not that I know of," Moira added. "I think Nana had said in her last letter that she wanted to just enjoy a quiet vacation at home with her grandchildren."

"There's nothing wrong with that," Allegra commented. "I think we're staying at home as well. We haven't been told yet."

They continued to chat until it was time for them to each meet with their parents. Most of the parents had been arriving throughout lunch, including Allegra and Lucian's. They spent some time sitting together talking before they split to get ready for their individual meetings. Lucian and Lysander continued up the stairs to wait outside Calista's office while Allegra and Alexandra stopped by Airlia's office. "How has your semester been going?" Lysander asked as they waited.

"It's been going fairly well. I was able to solve Rusty's problem with some help from Althea," Lucian replied.

"Is she one of the teachers? I don't seem to remember that name," Lysander commented.

"No, she's one of the witches," Lucian explained. "But her special gift is with animals, so I asked her to see if she could find out what was bothering him. He hasn't slept in my bed since talking to her."

"That's good. I'm glad you were able to get that sorted out," Lysander said.

They were prevented talking further by Calista coming out of her office and waving them in. After she'd shut the door and they'd sat down, she said, "As usual Lucian, you are doing very well. Many of your teachers have been impressed with your progress in their classes. I understand from Lorelei that you are doing incredibly well with learning to speak dragon."

"Really?" Lucian asked.

Calista laughed merrily, "Yes, and coming from Lorelei that is high praise indeed. Even though we both know that she has no love of dragons, she is a very picky teacher and expects perfection of her students. She is very impressed with you and asks that over the break you try to find some time to continue practicing your Sea Serpent. She said that's the one dialect you're still a bit backwards on. George it seems also struggles with that dialect. Now I realize that he will be very busy over break with his sister's wedding, but it might be wise for you to attempt to start studying together when school reconvenes in January."

"Alright," Lucian said.

"Now, I have your schedule for next semester and a list of supplies as well. King Lysander, do you have any questions for me before we adjourn?" Calista asked.

Lysander shook his head. "I don't believe so. I am correct in assuming that we will need to stay overnight due to the nature of this evening's program, yes?"

"Indeed you are. We have arranged for housing at The Glass Slipper in town," Calista explained. "I believe you know where that is?"

"Yes, Alexandra and I have stayed there many times," Lysander replied. "Thank you."

"It's the least we can do when we have so many who have long journeys that will be delayed," Calista said graciously. "Now, if there is nothing further, I'll meet with you again next spring."

"I have a question for you Calista, but I, um," Lucian began stuttering. He didn't want to ask with his father there, but also did not want to force him to leave.

Lysander picked up on the hint and smiled. "I'll wait outside for you, Lucian."

Once Lysander had closed the door behind himself Lucian asked, "Calista, can I tell Dad about Adrian, or should I keep this to myself."

"Because Adrian is your sister's prince, it would be wisest not to say anything," Calista replied. "I understand that you and your father have a very close relationship and that is a wonderful thing. In fact, I wish all my princes had that kind of relationship with their father. It is a precious gift that you should never take lightly. However, I also know that he is very close to Allegra and that his relationship with your mother would prevent him from keeping the secret to himself. I think you'll agree that it is best that your family not know what is happening to Adrian. In some ways I wish you had not become privy to it. I know it will be difficult for you not to say anything, but I do believe that it will give Adrian the best possible chance for success."

"I thought you'd say that," Lucian said a little glumly. "But I understand your reasons and will keep this to myself. Thanks, Calista."

"You're welcome, Lucian. Enjoy your winter break," Calista said with a smile before ushering him out of the office and asking for the next student and his parents.

As they began their end of semester feast, Melantha rose to make an announcement. "For those in your fourth year, and for my ladies if your prince is in his fourth year, you will need to stay after supper. There will be one final activity before we part for the year. For the rest of you, we sincerely wish you a pleasant break and a safe journey home."

Supper continued with chatter around the tables as parents caught up on what their children had been doing over the semester. The table Lucian and his family sat at was a buzz of activity as they also had with them Adrian's family and Jacobi's family. The other friends' families hadn't been able to fit at their table and so were at a table nearby. There was discussion of what they had planned for their winter holiday as well as what they should do during the summer. Where Lucian and Lysander were sitting, topic soon turned to Kaelen. "Where is he? He hasn't left the school has he?"

"No, he's here," Lucian replied quietly. "I think the fairies have sent him elsewhere because of his family. I'll explain later."

"Disgraceful way to treat your son," Lysander muttered, but allowed the topic to change as conversation flowed around them.

Soon supper was over and the fairies spent some time bidding farewell to the younger students who were leaving. As they did that, other fairies were causing the tables and chairs in the dining hall to relocate themselves closest to the walls, leaving a wide open space in the middle. "Oh no," Jacobi moaned.

"What's the matter?" Clarissa asked.

"They're going to make us dance," Jacobi said miserably.

Clarissa laughed gently, "I take it the lessons haven't been easy for you either?"

"You've had a hard time learning to dance?" Jacobi asked hopefully.

"Well, it certainly hasn't been the easiest of my classes," Clarissa replied kindly. "But don't worry, I'm sure you'll do just fine."

Soon Melantha came back into the room. "Tonight, we will be having our Winter Ball." She waved her wand and the room suddenly was transformed into a magical fairyland with snow encrusted pine trees and softly fluttering, glittering snowflakes that disappeared instantly on touching something. Silver and blue streamers surrounded the tables and ran along the walls of the hall. It was one of the most breathtaking sights any of them had seen. "Let's enjoy ourselves."

A small fairy band arranged themselves on the stage where the teachers' tables normally were. As they began the soft strains of a romantic waltz, slowly the dance floor filled with couples. Even parents were taking part in the music and going out to dance. For a moment, Lucian just watched as his father led his mother in a graceful waltz about the room. He hadn't really seen his parents dance together often, but he couldn't help but feel jealous of their grace and the love that was so obvious on each face. Finally he turned to Moira and cleared his throat. "Shall we join them?" he asked with a bow.

For a moment she looked reluctant, then smiled and curtsied. "Yes, I'd like that."

As Lucian tried to keep the rhythm of steps in his head, he also tried to engage Moira in conversation. While she had been polite throughout the day and even pleasant at moments, there was a reserve in her behavior that he hadn't noticed the last time they had met. Trying to think of a way to broach the subject, he commented, "Your letters have been somewhat shorter recently."

Moira looked surprised. "Really? I guess I haven't had much to say."

"Are you sure that's it?" Lucian pressed.

"What else would it be?" Moira asked, a stubborn tone sneaking into her voice.

"Well, I know I kind of flubbed things at the last meeting," Lucian said.

"I don't know what you mean," Moira replied, trying to sound like she meant it.

"Oh come on, Moira," Lucian retorted, trying to keep the edge off his voice, "we both know you left mad. I just wanted to make sure I hadn't said anything that offended you."

Moira nearly came to a stop in the dance floor, though the music was still playing. "You really have no clue do you?"

"About what?" Lucian asked.

Shaking her head, Moira said, almost bitterly, "Boys really are blind."

"Then help me see," Lucian replied, exasperation clear in his voice, despite his attempts to hold it back. "I'm really not trying to be stupid here though obviously I'm succeeding."

"I did not say that you were stupid," Moira said. Though he could tell she was still mad, her tone was gentler. "Look, I was frustrated because I've tried a couple of times to tell you something and you seem to think you already know what I'm going to say. You don't let me finish."

"Well, why didn't you write it to me?" Lucian asked in an attempt at a teasing tone. "I can't interrupt a letter."

"Lucian," Moira said seriously, coming to a stop in the middle of the floor, "this isn't the kind of thing I wanted to say in a letter. Yeah, some things you can say in a letter and it's just fine. I can tell you what I like and what I don't like in a letter. It doesn't matter if you're there in person to hear it. But there are some things that a girl wants to say in person. That she doesn't want to write down because it's just not the same in a letter. Besides, I can't see you from a letter and you can't see me. I needed to say it to your face, where I could see you."

Lucian considered this for a moment and then said, "Okay, so what did you want to tell me?"

Moira hesitated. "I, I want to talk about last winter. And don't just assume that I'm going to tell you that you're not doing a good enough job. You've done a fine job of being my friend and I appreciate that."

"Well, what then?" Lucian asked. "If I'm not breaking my word, I don't understand what there is to talk about."

"Oh, Lucian, you really are clueless," Moira laughed nervously. "And that's not making this any easier to say. Lucian, I, I don't want to just be friends anymore."

Lucian was sure he had heard her wrong. "What?"

"I don't want us to just be friends. I know I said that's what I wanted and maybe for a while I was telling the truth, but not really. I've never just wanted to be friends, but I thought that would be the best way to prevent myself from getting heartbroken. But then, after seeing your parents and then with things that have happened at home with Mother. I mean, she's actually happy now and she does things with Adrian. I think it's still a little strange to her, but she's there doing it and trying," Moira explained. "With everything that's happened, I realized that it wouldn't matter if I tried to just be your friend. I," she paused. "I already like you. Not just as my friend, but as my prince."

"So, we don't have to just be friends anymore?" Lucian asked, hardly allowing himself to believe what he was hearing.

Moira laughed. "No, we don't have to just be friends."

Despite the fact that music was still playing, for a moment Lucian and Moira just stood under the soft candlelight. For the first time in his life, Lucian was tempted to kiss a girl; and not just a kiss on the hand or a kiss on the cheek. He wanted to really kiss her. Moira seemed to sense this and looked away, breaking momentarily the spell that had seemed to hold them captive. They once again heard the music, though it was coming to a close and other couples were already leaving the floor. Blushing, Lucian offered Moira his arm. She took it and he led her back to where Leticia was sitting watching everyone. She had a knowing smile on her face as she watched them walk towards her. "Enjoy yourselves?" she asked with a teasing grin.

"Yes, I believe we did," Moira replied, smiling at Lucian.

While the Winter Ball was beginning downstairs, Calista was meeting with Kaelen, Gelasia and Maeve in her office. Once everyone was seated, she said, "Before I ask Maeve to tell us what she's learned, I'd like to speak to you, Kaelen, about this semester. All of your teachers have expressed that you are doing well in their classes. We've seen a great deal of growth in you. You have taken an incredibly difficult situation and done the best you can with it. Next semester you'll have some slightly different classes, but for the most part they will remain the same, though perhaps at different times. Calypso did say she'd like you to read chapter fourteen about recognizing enchantments over the break. You missed several points that she says are vital to your success."

"So there is hope?" Kaelen asked.

Calista smiled. "There is always hope. In fact, that is why we've asked Maeve to join us. Gelasia felt our last meeting about your predicament left everyone feeling rather hopeless. So she asked Maeve to consult the star charts once again to see if we can glean a little more about what will be your quest. Maeve?"

Maeve had been staring out the window at the stars. "Don't fear, dear, you won't always be a wallflower."

"Maeve?" Gelasia said.

"Sorry," Maeve said, turning her attention back to the group. "The sky is so clear tonight and the stars have so much to say." She sighed and then continued, "However, after rereading the charts, I've discovered more that I can tell you. I'm afraid that while I do have a knack for reading them, I do sometimes rush myself and miss important details. So when Gelasia asked me to take another look, at first I saw no difference. Then Calypso told me to take my time and look deeper." Maeve rolled her green eyes at the ceiling. "She was right of course. There's more."

For a moment it was quiet. "Yes?" Kaelen prompted.

"You will have a quest," Maeve stated.

"That's it?" Kaelen said after she was quiet for another moment.

Maeve raised an eyebrow. "Isn't that what you wanted to know?" she asked. There was an impish innocence to her voice. Kaelen could hardly believe that the blonde, green-eyed witch in front of him was the same dotty old woman who had turned his uniform into a hideous pink dress his first year. This witch wasn't dotty, but more like a cat playing with a mouse.

"We're going to need you to be more specific, Maeve dear," Gelasia said, sensing both Kaelen and Calista's frustration.

"Well I certainly can't give you all the details, now can I?" Maeve asked teasingly. "It would spoil the whole thing. But I do understand that you need a little more information. Yes, Kaelen you will have a quest. The stars have guaranteed that there is a young lady for you to rescue. I can't explain to you the how and whom, but she is out there. Perhaps, Kaelen, the most important thing for you to know at this time is that your transformation did not actually alter your quest at all."

"What do you mean?" Kaelen asked.

"There was always going to be a transformation involved in your quest, Kaelen," Maeve replied simply. "We couldn't have known at the time what exactly that transformation would be. But from the very beginning, this has been a part of your quest. You have the same chance of success as any other prince facing any other challenge."

"So then, this was meant to happen to me?" Kaelen said slowly.

"Yes," Maeve said. "You were always going to face some challenge. Every prince does; yours just seems bigger and more difficult to overcome. But your chances are just as good as any boy here. Although, Calista, you do know that his schedule is going to have to undergo serious overhauls, don't you?"

Calista looked surprised. "Excuse me?"

"You heard me. The classes you have him in now are nowhere near sufficient," Maeve repeated coyly. "Although, I think Kaelen has been separated from his friends long enough. I suggest he return to the festivities and we can continue this discussion in private. Have a pleasant evening, Kaelen," she finished with a smile.

Kaelen looked at Calista for a moment, unsure of whether or not he was actually dismissed. "Yes, Kaelen, you may go. Enjoy yourself," Calista said kindly. As soon as he was out of the room and the door closed she said, "What do you mean his classes aren't sufficient?"

"I don't think you fully comprehend the nature of his transformation," Maeve explained. "He is going to go through a complete transformation."

"He has gone through the transformation. He's a beast," Calista replied. "Well, a beast in body."

"Precisely," Maeve countered. "His transformation is not complete. The magic of the school is the only thing preventing his full transformation. When the time comes for him to leave the school on a permanent basis, the rest of the transformation will occur; quite rapidly I might add."

Calista was confused. "I'm not following you. What exactly are you saying?"

Maeve sighed impatiently, "I'm saying that he will undergo a transformation of self. He will no longer be a gentleman at all. Right now he looks like a beast, but he's still very much Kaelen. He's still human. When he leaves the protection of the school permanently, he will become a beast in body, mind and action. He will hardly be the Kaelen that you are teaching."

"Then there really isn't any hope," Calista said sadly.

"As you so eloquently put it earlier, there is always hope," Maeve replied. "Where Kaelen lives after school will be the only place he can be. He will be unable to leave. Yes, he has a quest, but the lady will come to him rather than the other way around. He, like every boy here, has a princess."

"But Esmé has abandoned him," Calista recalled. "And as I understand, she has been altered beyond repair."

"I don't believe I said that Esmé was his princess," Maeve retorted.

Calista thought for a moment, "But, I seem to remember that every prince has only one princess. Are you saying that Esmé was never Kaelen's princess?"

"While it is true that every prince has but one princess and vice versa, it doesn't work quite the way you seem to think," Maeve explained. "Esmé had the opportunity to be Kaelen's princess, but she gave that up. She chose to not have a prince and to be a hag for eternity just as Nathan chose not to have a princess last year and will be an ogre for eternity. There is indeed one who will be Kaelen's princess."

"Well, the only young lady without a prince is Leticia, is she his princess?" Calista asked.

"You are quite mistaken," Maeve said, "Leticia has a prince."

"But Nathan was her prince," Calista pointed out.

"He had that chance. He gave it up," Maeve replied. "But, Kaelen is not Leticia's prince anymore than Nathan is."

"But none of the other princesses at Fair Damsels are without a prince," Calista said, exasperation in her voice.

"I didn't say that the young lady in question was a princess at Fair Damsels," Maeve said, rolling her eyes. "You are taking yourself in circles with things you clearly don't understand. I'll tell Calypso to come see you tomorrow in order to help you reset Kaelen's schedule. There are many things you will have to do in order to not lose him entirely to the transformation. If you don't, then I'm afraid all will be lost and you'll have no one to blame but yourself. Now, if you'll excuse me, I have business elsewhere." Maeve rose to leave.

"I'm not finished with you," Calista said.

"Oh, but you are," Maeve replied with the same impish tone she'd had at the beginning of the meeting. "I cannot neglect my duties and the longer I sit here, the less I can accomplish."

"I can call Calypso," Calista warned.

Maeve smiled impishly. "Be my guest. But she would tell you the same thing. I have other business I need to attend to and you are delaying me. Enjoy your evening." She turned to leave and then turned back to Gelasia, who had been sitting quietly throughout the course of the meeting taking everything in. "Oh, Gelasia, the one you're concerned about? You needn't be. There is a happy ending there. Good night." She smiled before continuing out the door.

"I hate it when they're young," Calista sighed as the door shut behind Maeve. "They're so frustrating. That gave us absolutely nothing to work with."

"I don't think that's true," Gelasia countered. "We received a great deal of information."

"All she did was lead us in a circle that doesn't lead to a happy ending for anyone," Calista retorted, frustration in her tone.

"No, I think I understand what she's saying. It is a little complicated, but yes, I think I see. I need to go speak with her about this," Gelasia replied.

"You're not going to explain this to me either, are you?" Calista asked as Gelasia was rising.

"I'm afraid not dear," Gelasia said sweetly. "I believe there may yet be one more task for me to do before I leave."

"Leave?" Calista asked. "You're not leaving are you? I thought we had already discussed this; you'll be here, working."

"No, I don't think so," Gelasia replied. "We both know that my time here is very limited. I had been planning on one thing, but I think my plans may be about to change."

"But, you're staying here until that time, aren't you?" Calista asked, almost desperately.

Gelasia shrugged. "I'm not sure. I really must speak to Maeve about this. There's something else for me to do. I'm not meant to finish my days at the academy. Good night, Calista." With that, Gelasia walked out the door leaving Calista feeling more confused than ever.

"Old fairies aren't any better," Calista muttered before getting up and returning downstairs to the ball. She tried to make sense of everything she had been told, but couldn't seem to make heads or tails of anything. Kaelen had a princess; but apparently she, whoever she was, didn't go to Fair Damsels. Leticia had a prince, but he didn't seem to go to Charming Academy because she didn't have any princes who were without a princess. How was it possible that the only two students who were without companions were not destined to be together? It just didn't make any sense at all. Then there was the business of Kaelen's transformation. How could there be any hope if he was going to be so altered by the transformation that he wouldn't be himself? No girl, princess or not, was going to be able to soften the heart of a true beast. She sighed as she tried to focus her thoughts on the dancing couples in the hall. Perhaps there was more to this than she could understand. After all, she never would have claimed to know everything. *I just wish I understood this*, Calista thought as she let the soft music enter her thoughts and clear her mind.

Kaelen went downstairs to the dining hall after finishing his meeting with Calista and Maeve. He wasn't sure he understood at all what he'd been told, but felt immensely better that there was hope for him after all. So he wouldn't be stuck as a beast as long as he could finish his quest. But, what would his quest be? He couldn't blame Maeve for not telling him that much. None of the princes knew what their quests were. It would have been unfair for him to know when no one else did. As he entered the room, he felt jealous of the couples dancing around the room. He could see Jacobi and Clarissa stumbling their way through the steps. Apparently, Jacobi wasn't the only one with a habit of stepping on toes. He couldn't help but smile. They'd get the hang of it eventually. And if they didn't, they would probably just skip having a ball at their wedding, or at any other time in their lives. He spied Leticia near the wall, her body swaying to the music though she was sitting down. Deciding to take a chance, he walked over to her. "I know I'm not your prince, but you look lonely. May I have the pleasure of this dance with you?" He bowed as he spoke.

Leticia smiled up at him and stood up. Curtsying, she said, "Certainly you may, Kaelen."

Kaelen offered his arm and they walked out onto the floor. He took her gently into his arms and began the slow steps of the waltz. For a moment it was quiet and they each just enjoyed the sound of the music. "That's a very pretty dress," Kaelen commented after a while.

"Thank you," Leticia replied with a smile. "It's one of my favorites. You're a very graceful dancer. I'm not sure I would have expected that."

Laughing, Kaelen said, "I doubt anyone would expect someone of my size to be very graceful at anything. But thank you."

"They all look so happy together, don't they?" Leticia asked as they saw other couples out on the floor.

Kaelen nodded. "They do. It makes me a little jealous to be honest."

Leticia laughed gently, "I understand how you feel. I suppose one way or other things will work out to the best for both of us. I'm sure there's a beautiful girl out there for you to rescue."

"Somehow I don't think she's the one who needs rescuing," Kaelen admitted with a smile.

"Touché," Leticia replied with a smile. "Either way though, I'll bet there's a happy ending for you."

"How can you be so sure?" Kaelen asked sincerely.

With a slightly sad smile, Leticia said, "Because I have to be. I have to believe that somewhere out there is a prince waiting to rescue me. If I can believe that you will have a happy ending, than it's easier to believe that I will too. After all, I think of the two of us, you have the greater challenge."

"I suppose I'd never considered that before," Kaelen said. "But you're a beautiful young woman. Any man would be lucky to have you as his princess."

Leticia blushed and looked away. "Thank you," she said quietly. The music came to a close and she smiled up at Kaelen again. "Thanks for the dance, Kaelen. I appreciated being able to enjoy the music. I like dancing."

"It was my pleasure," Kaelen replied. He bowed and led Leticia back to her seat. As much as he liked Leticia, he was sure that she was not the princess who would rescue him from his form. However, he couldn't let her sit by herself. Everyone needed good friends to stand by them; he of all people knew that. As more of their friends came to where they were sitting, they seemed to sense that Leticia had been feeling left out. In turn, each of the boys, except Jacobi, asked Leticia to dance.

"I would dance with you, but I think it would be more painful than enjoyable," Jacobi admitted to her with an apologetic smile.

"It's alright, Jacobi," Leticia had replied as George offered his arm. "Perhaps next time you'll be more confident."

The ball continued late into the night with dancing, chatting and laughter. When it was finally time for them to say goodnight, there was reluctance to see the princesses and parents leave. However, they knew that the next day they'd be going home and it would be a month before they'd have homework or be in classes again. As the exhausted boys went to their rooms, most were fast asleep before their heads even hit the pillows. Their dreams carried them into unknown realms as they fought dragons and battled evil to save their princesses and become the heroes the fairies believed each of them to be.

Chapter 4

Early the next morning, Adrian and his family began the trip back to Lictthane. Nana talked nonstop all the way home about what a delightful time she'd had the evening before. Nobody minded that she was doing so; they loved to hear Nana talk. As they were coming towards their castle, they noticed a carriage near the front entrance that was being led towards the barn. "I wonder who that could be," Lavinia said as they neared. "I'm not expecting anyone. Did you have someone coming today, Mother?"

"No, but I'm pretty sure I know whose carriage that is," Nana replied with a smile.

Adrian and Moira exchanged grins. They had a pretty good guess who the carriage belonged to as well. As soon as their carriage stopped, they ran into the castle. A tall, spindly man was standing in the hall where the family portrait Nana had brought from her old home was hanging. He turned. "Well, how are my favorite niece and nephew?"

"Uncle Sebastian!" Moira cried as she threw her arms around him.

Sebastian laughed heartily. "Well, well, my love, you've certainly grown since the last time I saw you. Turn about and let me look at you." He watched Moira spin about. "Yes, you're still the loveliest girl there ever was. And you young man," he said turning to Adrian, "well, you've hardly changed at all." Sebastian looked every bit Nana's twin. He had the same crinkled blue eyes surrounded by laugh lines. His hair hadn't grayed as much as hers had; there were still traces of black beneath the frost of silver. But they had the same face and the same cheerful disposition.

"Uncle Sebastian," Lavinia said with a smile as she came inside, "what a pleasant surprise. I didn't know you were coming; I would have had the guest room prepared for you." Her tone held a slight disapproval, though it couldn't mask her joy at seeing him.

"You know how I hate such formalities," Sebastian replied. "It's so much better seeing the surprise on your faces when I show up. Besides, spontaneity keeps you young and helps those you love stay on their toes. Hello again, Bethany."

"Sebastian, it has been far too long since you visited," Nana said almost chidingly as she hugged her brother.

"You know me," Sebastian replied with a grin. "Now, you two must tell me all about school and your future loves. I simply must know everything."

Sebastian led the two children away while Nana and Lavinia shared a glance and then laughed. "He always did like an entrance," Nana laughed.

"That is very true," Lavinia replied. "Well, I'd best go have the guest room prepared for him. I wish just once he would tell us when he was coming."

"Oh he'll never do that, dear," Nana retorted. "Besides, consider yourself lucky. He might have arrived yesterday and then we would have lost a full day of his visit. We never know how long or short his visits will be. He has a restless spirit."

"True again," Lavinia agreed. She then walked to find the housekeeper and arrange a room for Sebastian to stay in. She knew the housekeeper would be out of sorts with the news. While a kind-hearted woman, she had a very definite schedule and did not at all like surprises.

As Lavinia was making all the necessary arrangements, Sebastian sat in the parlor with Adrian and Moira discussing everything that had been going on in their lives. "Moira, tell me about your Prince Charming. What's he like?"

Moira blushed. "He's the perfect gentleman, Uncle Sebastian." She began describing Lucian in great detail. She told him about the letters they wrote back and forth, explaining all that she'd learned about him. "Unfortunately," she finished, "he's still a little shorter than I am."

"Well that's an easy enough fix," Sebastian replied with an impish wink. "Quit growing so much. And if that doesn't work, I could always cut your feet off at the ankles. That might give him the advantage."

"You would not!" Moira giggled.

"Best stop growing then, m'dear," Sebastian retorted with a teasing grin. "And now you, Adrian, what is your princess like? Is she as pretty as Moira?"

Adrian blushed. "Uncle Sebastian, that's an unfair question. If I say that Moira's prettier, you'll be mad at me because I should say that Allegra is prettier. But if I do say that Allegra's prettier, I risk offending Moira."

"I didn't ask if she was prettier," Sebastian said, winking at Moira. "I asked if she was as pretty."

"They are both beautiful in their own way," Adrian replied.

"Very delicately put, son," Sebastian said. "Now, tell me what this Allegra looks like. I like her already, beautiful name. Very musical somehow."

"Well, I don't actually know how musical Allegra is, but she is very artistic," Adrian added when Sebastian looked slightly disappointed. Sebastian smiled and Adrian continued, "She's very pretty. She has light brown eyes, almost the color of amber, and long, wavy auburn hair." He continued to paint a portrait in words of his princess as his great-uncle listened with rapt attention.

Moira was also listening intently. She'd suddenly realized something that she'd never noticed before. She supposed it was because she and Adrian never had been very close as well as the fact that she had recently been so full of her own inner conflicts that she just hadn't noticed. But now as she listened to Adrian talk about Allegra and how wonderful she was, Moira realized that her twin brother was in love. She smiled, knowing that he couldn't have given that love to a better princess. Being one of Allegra's best friends meant that she had already discovered Allegra's instant liking for Adrian. She listened for a while longer until Uncle Sebastian pulled her back into the conversation. They enjoyed a pleasant chat together until Lavinia arrived and announced that luncheon was ready. The three walked out of the parlor and as Adrian passed her, Moira again got the feeling that there was something different about him. He seemed to be shorter than she was. Of course, she had to have been mistaken; Adrian had always been the taller of the two. *Unless*, she thought miserably, *I have grown again*. Yet even as that depressing thought came, she was sure that wasn't it. She wasn't growing and yet, Adrian was definitely different somehow. Something had changed in him. She knew it and just couldn't quite put her finger on it. However, as they sat to eat, Moira's concerns were pushed away by the cheerful chatter around the table.

As the meal came to a close, the family went into the parlor and sat before the fireplace, listening to the crackling logs and Uncle Sebastian as he told them the latest of his adventures. Adrian and Moira were never quite sure how much of their great-uncle's stories they should believe. They knew that as soon as the kingdom he had ruled was turned over to a new ruler, Sebastian had dedicated his life to traveling Sanalbereth and discovering all he could about the land and its people. There wasn't a province in the whole country that he hadn't been to at least once. Many of them had seen him twice or more. Sebastian was an adventurer and possessed a vivid imagination which sometimes made his tales of travel far more exotic and wild than perhaps they actually were.

"Never have you seen such trees," Sebastian said stretching his arms towards the ceiling. "They seemed to be as high as the very clouds; reaching upwards forever and ever. I went into the forest to make sketches of the wildlife there. It was as dark as a stormy midnight; my only light was my lantern that I always bring with me on such occasions. The forest was filled with sounds of birds, insects, wild creatures. There wasn't a person to be found for miles around. I felt quite alone in that place. Yet, I often felt as though I were being followed; by man or beast I had not yet learned."

The story continued on with Sebastian facing a terrible panther deep in the woods. Moira still gasped in all the right places as she had since childhood, making the story even better for the listeners and the teller. He told of the epic battle and how he'd nearly become the meal of this fearsome predator; building the story until he finally reached the climax where he defeated the hungry beast with barely the strength to stand.

"I was so exhausted that I leaned against a tree nearby and soon fell asleep, the rustling of the leaves in the trees playing a soft lullaby to soothe me," Sebastian continued. "Despite the dangers in the woods, there was a peace there as well. In that quiet I slept until morning when I continued my journey to the heart of the forest where I discovered the ruins of an ancient fairy city in a small dell. The craftsmanship was strange and beautiful at the same time. There was a delicacy in it and yet it seemed also primitive. It was an interesting balance of the two. I spent many hours there, sketching and studying the remains of buildings. I estimate they haven't been used in thousands of years. They were built mostly of wood, but also of stone. I surmise the stone would have come from the mountains that were not far distant."

"Uncle Sebastian, how would the wood not have rotted?" Adrian asked.

"I asked myself the same question," Sebastian replied. "The best guess I have is that some of it is the magic of the fairies; we do know that they have always charmed their homes with protection from harm. I suppose also that some of it would be the protection from the elements. Not a lot of sunshine or water would be able to get through those trees. That might help prolong the life. Some of the buildings were built right into trees and these trees have simply adapted to the inconvenience. But there were places where the wood had indeed succumbed to its age. That's why I said the ruins of a city." Sebastian winked and for a long while continued his tale. He described the city and then a river that ran through the city and had led him to the mountains from which the ancient fairies must have quarried their stone. There was a large, rushing waterfall that flowed into the river. The mountains were riddled with caves and, of course, more dangers. But the adventurous Sebastian would not be stopped by these, but merely continued his exploration, facing the danger and finally reaching a small town in the province he'd been exploring. "And upon arriving there, I decided it had been far too long since the last time I had visited my niece and her children. Imagine my surprise when I found my sister staying here too," he finished.

"I wrote to you saying that I had moved," Nana said gently.

"Well, I haven't been home in nearly a year and a half," Sebastian replied with a smile. "I've been far too busy. I daresay there's probably a whole mountain of mail waiting for me to come and read it."

"You need to go home more often," Nana teased.

Sebastian waved a hand. "Home is boring and lonely. I'd much rather be out in the world than stuck at home twiddling my thumbs. Besides, if I'd been at home, I wouldn't have been able to bring such unique gifts with me." He rose and went into the hall where he'd requested one of his bags be left when the butler had taken his things to the guestroom. Coming back into the room, he sat down and began pulling packages out of the bag. "Let's see, one for Moira, one for Adrian, one for Lavinia and of course one for Bethany. Although, I had planned on delivering yours as my next stop, but you've made my job easier."

Nana laughed merrily as each of them began unwrapping the brightly colored packages. Moira pulled out a sketchpad and new set of pastels as well as another, long box. "How'd you know I was running low on paper?" she asked as she set the paper and pastels aside and turned her attention to the long box.

"Lucky guess I suppose," Sebastian replied.

Moira smiled as she pulled the lid off the box. Inside was a delicate crystal and gold necklace. She gasped, "This is so beautiful, Uncle Sebastian! Thank you."

"My pleasure. You're not a little girl anymore, it's time you had some real jewelry," Sebastian said with a smile. "Besides, I found that crystal in one of the caves that I discovered. What better way to remember a wonderful trip than to see you wearing it?"

Lavinia also had a crystal necklace and matching earrings. Nana was soon wearing a crystal brooch while Adrian pulled a dagger with tiny crystals in the hilt out of his box. It had a leather sheath with intricate craving on it. "Wow," he said, "this is awesome! Thanks, Uncle Sebastian."

"Just promise me that you won't get into any trouble with that," Sebastian teased with a wink. "I'd hate for your mother to take it away from you."

"I won't," Adrian promised.

Soon the cook entered the room to tell them that supper was ready for them. Moira asked Sebastian to help her put the necklace on before they went into the dining hall. "This really did turn out beautifully. I was sure the jeweler could do it, but I must say he did a perfect job. You're lovely, my dear."

Moira blushed. "I think you say that because I'm your niece."

Laughing, Sebastian retorted as they sat down, "I am bound to say only the truth, love. If you happen to be my niece, that's just a coincidence."

Later that evening after most of the castle was sleeping, Sebastian stood by his window looking out over the snowy plains of Lictthane. The moon was shining brightly overhead, casting a silvery blue light on the wintry world below. Stars twinkled in the heavens and everything seemed to be at peace. He stood in silence for a long while before saying, "Well, Bethany, shouldn't you be sleeping?"

"I could ask you the same question, Sebastian," Nana replied in a teasing tone, gently closing the door behind her.

Sebastian laughed as he turned away from the window. "That you could. So, what brings you to my room at this hour?"

"I knew you weren't sleeping and thought I'd come talk to you for a while," Nana said. "I don't get to see you nearly often enough. And with all your traveling, I rarely receive letters from you."

"You know me, I never could sit still for very long," Sebastian retorted with a grin.

"No, you couldn't," Nana admitted. "Even when Isabelle was alive you longed to travel."

"Yes, but then I could take her with me," Sebastian said sadly. "Now it's just me. It's a lonely way to travel."

"I would imagine so," Nana replied. "I suppose that's why you came to Lictthane; feeling a bit lonely out in the world by yourself."

"That's probably part of why I came," Sebastian said. "However I also felt that it was something that I needed to do. I know I was never as in tune to that fairy blood as you, but every now and again I do get feelings. I'm not sure why, but I felt that Lavinia and her children needed me. It got so strong I couldn't ignore it any longer. But on arriving, they seem as happy as ever; happier actually. I haven't seen Lavinia looking this content since Martin died. It's good to see her smiling and laughing again."

"It is," Nana agreed. "So why do you think you needed to come?"

"I was rather hoping that you would tell me," Sebastian teased. "Now that I'm here, I don't have the slightest clue why I felt I should come. Perhaps some of it is this is the hardest time of year for me. Maybe I needed to come for me more than for them."

"Perhaps," Nana said. "Does Adrian seem different to you?"

"Well, he's taller than he was the last time I saw him. But then again, it's been close to five years since the last time I visited. So really, I don't notice that much different. Why?" Sebastian asked. "Does he seem different to you?"

"He does," Nana admitted. "I can't quite place it, but he's changing. I think he may be under a spell."

"Should we tell Lavinia?" Sebastian asked.

"No, I don't think there's any need to get her worried over it," Nana replied. "After all, it could just be that old age is affecting me."

"Age has nothing to do with it, Bethany dear," Sebastian said. "If you don't think we should tell Lavinia than we won't. But Bethany, you've never been wrong about this sort of thing before. And I don't think either of us wants to admit how many years you've been at this."

Nana laughed, "No, I don't think we do."

"Are you sure we shouldn't say something to Lavinia?" Sebastian asked again.

"Yes, I'm quite sure. Whatever is going on I'm sure will manifest itself soon enough," Nana said.

"Very well," Sebastian agreed.

"So how are you doing, Sebastian?" Nana asked, closing the subject of Adrian at least for the evening. "And don't try giving me your routine answers. You know they won't work on me."

Sebastian chuckled, "Never could fool you. You think having been born ten minutes earlier means you get to know everything too."

"Absolutely," Nana retorted.

"I'm well, I suppose," Sebastian said after a long pause. "I'm starting to get old and a little tired. I can't do as much as I used to be able to. It's very depressing, takes all the fun out of life. And truth be told, I'm lonely. I don't like traveling by myself, never did. When Isabelle would go with me, we'd have fabulous adventures together. Then she got sick and no matter what I did for her, it didn't help. It's the only time that gift from the witch didn't work for me."

"It was her time to go," Nana said gently.

"Yes, but she was so young. It feels strange not having her here," Sebastian admitted. "Every time I travel, I talk to her as though she's there with me. I get her a memento even though she isn't there to receive it."

"And every summer you go to the ocean to send flowers to the sea maidens," Nana added.

Sebastian nodded. "Isabelle loved the ocean; I suppose that's why she was turned into a mermaid for my quest. And she had the most beautiful voice I've ever heard. It was her voice that led me to her you know."

"Yes I do," Nana said with a smile. "I've heard the story many times."

"It's my favorite story to tell," Sebastian said wistfully.

"It was a noble quest and I'm sure a wonderful adventure for both of you," Nana replied, patting Sebastian's arm.

"Indeed it was," Sebastian agreed. He turned to look out the window again. "I should let you get to bed. Old folks like us need our sleep after all," he added with a wink.

"And do you plan on going to bed?" Nana asked.

"Eventually yes," Sebastian said. "For now, I'm enjoying the beauty of the snow under the moonlight. It's quite enchanting; I don't see snow like this at home. I'm too far south. But you can go to bed, Bethany. I'm well and happy. I get to spend time with my family and that is what is important."

"How long do you intend to stay?" Nana asked.

"As long as I need to," Sebastian replied.

There was a mysterious quality to the way he said it that puzzled Nana, but she didn't ask about it. Instead she hugged her twin and said, "Well, good night then. Don't stay up too late."

"Would I do such a thing?" Sebastian asked innocently.

"Yes you would," Nana teased gently.

Laughing, Sebastian replied, "Well, tonight I won't. I promise," he added when she looked at him with disbelief clear on her face. "I'll be heading to bed soon myself. Good night, Bethany." He kissed the top of her head.

"Good night, Sebastian," Nana said and then walked out of the room.

When the door closed behind her, Sebastian turned once more to look out the window. It really was a beautiful night. The stillness outside calmed him and soon he did blow out the candles in his room. He got into the bed and whispered, "Good night my Isabelle." Then, with the memories of a cheerful day spent with the ones he loved most floating through his thoughts, he slowly drifted into a calm and peaceful sleep.

Late one night in Maltisten, Kaelen was sitting next to the window in his room, staring out at the moonlit lawn. There was a light dusting of snow on the ground with flurries fluttering down past the frosted panes from the heavy, snow-filled clouds above. Despite being enormously tired, he felt restless. He sighed as he continued to watch the peaceful world outside, wishing that he could bring some of it inside to his thoughts. The meeting with Calista and Maeve had left him with more questions than answers. While he had felt initial relief at being told he had the same chance as any of the other princes, he felt that something had been left out. There was something he wasn't being told and he wasn't sure what it was. He knew that Calista would never allow the witches to lie to him, so there must be a princess out there for him somewhere. But how could he rescue anyone as a beast? And who on this earth would fall in love with him? He knew that perhaps some of his problem was that his growth had not stopped with becoming a beast and he had his moments of teenage imbalance. He was still becoming taller; as though being head and shoulders above his peers wasn't enough. He was covered in ever-thickening golden-brown fur that became tangled easily and made grooming in the morning a painful task. His voice was deepening and becoming gruffer. Part of him didn't know if he would even recognize his own voice when he did become human again. The voice that greeted his ears anytime he spoke barely resembled anything human he'd ever heard before. There was also the matter of having strength that he could never quite control. He didn't want to remember how many vases he had broken in his floral arrangement class with Russett. It didn't matter that Russett was extremely patient and never got upset, but simply helped him clean the mess and got him a new vase; it was frustrating to Kaelen.

Rising from the window seat, Kaelen picked up the spell-breaking book he'd been reading to appease Calypso. It had become his habit when he couldn't sleep or just wanted something to do. What was he supposed to gain from recognizing enchantments? Obviously he could look at himself and see quite plainly that there had been an enchantment. Wasn't that enough? He opened the book to chapter fourteen as gently as he could. The claws that had replaced his fingernails often tore at the paper and binding, leaving his schoolbooks looking tattered and uncared for; especially the more he read them. With how many times over the break he had reread this section, he wasn't sure it would even still be attached to the rest of the book when he went back to school. Already he'd had to paste pages back in when in frustration he'd opened the book too roughly. He tried to focus on the words on the page, but he didn't seem to be gleaning anything new from what he was reading. "What does she expect me to learn from this?" he muttered in a low growl.

As the candlelight burned lower, he finally discovered something he had missed before. "Every enchantment casts a glow of magic around the individual or object in question," he read aloud. "Fairies, witches and animals will see this glow, but not necessarily recognize what the glow is from. Different types of enchantments leave a different glow. A curse will show up as either a green or violet glow. This will fade over time, but never disappear entirely until the curse is lifted. Protective charms and blessings show up as a white or golden glow. The glow left from these charms is very visible for the first few days, but will eventually fade until becoming almost unrecognizable, even to the most distinguishing eyes." Kaelen lifted his eyes from the page and thought for a moment. After he had been transformed into a beast, Adrian had always looked slightly green. Not noticeably so, but just a tinge. He suspected that it was due mostly to his being human trapped in an animal body. It would make sense that he wouldn't see the glow of magic as clearly as a true animal. But that made him think of his other classmates. Anytime someone was being punished, their color had looked off. He'd never mentioned it to anyone before because he had assumed that everyone saw them that way. His thoughts turned to Lucian. He had recently noticed that every now and again, he looked like he was in brighter light than everyone else. It wasn't much brighter, but a little. Was Lucian blessed for something? How could he find out what?

Determined to learn more, Kaelen turned back to the pages of the book and continued reading. He was disappointed to learn that he would never be able to determine exactly what the blessing was simply by looking.

Curses are often obvious to determine by a change in the behavior or appearance of the person or object that has been cursed. Blessings and protective charms are more subtle and often require more careful attention to determine their nature. When trying to determine what type of blessing or protection has been granted to an individual or object, one must invest quite a bit of time to observation. If time is of the essence, a few simple tricks can help aid in the discernment. First, recognize the glow of magic. Second, see if there are things that are different around the person or object. For example, if a gate has been protected to ward off intruders, one might see the gate, but not a knob or handle with which to open the gate.

So, Kaelen thought, *what is different about Lucian?* For a while he tried to think, but couldn't come up with anything. His eyes beginning to droop, Kaelen closed the book; growling when a corner of the page he'd been reading ripped off. He then blew out the candles and climbed into bed. Lucian's mother had been kind enough to give him a bed that had sheets and blankets that had been made of a stronger fabric which didn't tear easily under his powerful hands. He was grateful for all the kindness that Lucian's family had shown him. They had truly taken him in as one of their own. He doubted that he would ever be able to repay them for the charity they had shown, and yet hoped that somehow he could find a way to show his appreciation. With these thoughts, Kaelen finally went to sleep.

The next morning, Kaelen and Lucian practiced their swordplay in Lysander's fencing hall. Lucian had insisted on practicing right handed. "I'm getting better, I know I am," Lucian said as they took a short break. "It still feels really weird though."

"I can understand that," Kaelen replied. He wasn't feeling much better about his swordsmanship than Lucian was. "I suppose it'll get easier. You know what's going to be terrible though?"

"What?" Lucian asked as they started up again.

"I'm going to get so used to being a huge beast with super strength that when I do become human again, I'm going to feel like the weakest, tiniest person in the world," Kaelen said with a laugh.

Lucian laughed too. "I doubt you'll be tiny. You were a lot taller than everyone before the transformation. Well, everyone except Adrian."

"He's going to feel huge when he becomes human again," Kaelen said, after making sure there was no one nearby to overhear them. Lucian had made sure he told Kaelen that they couldn't talk about Adrian's transformation in front of his family. Kaelen had agreed not to talk about it unless it was just the two of them alone. Since they really didn't get a lot of opportunities to be alone, this was the first time either had mentioned it.

"Probably," Lucian agreed. "I guess the rest of us should feel really lucky, we don't have anything changing in us."

"Nope, you'll have an easy time getting Moira to fall in love with you. That is of course, if you haven't already," Kaelen teased.

Lucian blushed. "I don't know that I'd say she's in love with me. But at least we're not still under that 'just friends' rule. That just made everything complicated."

"Just friends rule?" Kaelen asked.

"Oh, I never told you about that. I guess the only person I did talk to about that was Adrian. You know how Moira and I didn't exactly get along during the first couple of years?" Lucian began.

"Yeah," Kaelen replied.

"Well, I guess Moira was afraid of getting close to me for a lot of different reasons," Lucian explained. "So she tried being unpleasant to make me not like her. Then when that wasn't working, she just tried to ignore me. I guess that didn't really work either. Anyway, last year when Allegra and I were staying at their house for the winter while my dad was sick, she told me that she just wanted us to be friends. She said she didn't want to fall in love with me."

"Ouch," Kaelen whistled.

"Tell me about it," Lucian said. "So I've been trying to live up to just being friends. It's stupid how hard that was. I mean really? It should be easy to just be friends with someone, right?"

"But you were already in love with her, weren't you?" Kaelen pointed out.

"Yeah, I guess I fell like a ton of bricks," Lucian replied with a rueful laugh. "But, long story short, at the ball last month, she told me she doesn't want to just be friends anymore. So like I said, I don't know that she's in love with me, but at least she likes me enough that the idea doesn't terrify her anymore."

Kaelen suddenly laughed, "You must not have seen the way she was looking at you."

"What?" Lucian asked.

"Trust me, Lucian, she's in love with you," Kaelen said. "Whether or not she'll admit it is a mute point, but she definitely likes you more than a little bit."

Lucian blushed and contemplated this for a moment. "You think so?"

"Oh yeah," Kaelen replied.

Slightly exasperated, Lucian sighed, "Why does everyone else see things before I do? I've got to be the most oblivious person on the face of the planet."

Laughing, Kaelen said, "I think all of us are pretty much oblivious to what's right in front of us. It's like Esmé and me. You guys probably all knew that Esmé was a snob and didn't actually like me at all. I didn't see that. I saw us as the perfect couple and I was going to be the best Prince Charming ever and she'd be my queen and the whole happily ever after blah blah blah. But I can tell that George and Eleanor are like the match made in heaven and Jacobi and Clarissa are the same way. Adrian and Allegra are so obviously in love that it's funny neither one has admitted it. Then there's you and Moira. You guys look complicated on the outside, but when you really look close, it was pretty obvious that you both liked each other."

"How did you become the observant one?" Lucian teased.

"Honestly? Not having a princess of my own made it pretty easy to start observing everyone else's relationships," Kaelen explained. "I bet Leticia probably feels the same way since she doesn't have a prince right now."

"I wonder what will happen for her," Lucian said.

Kaelen shrugged. "I'm sure things will work out for her one way or another."

They were prevented from speaking longer as Alexandra came in to tell them that lunch was ready. "Put your swords away properly and then come eat."

"Yes, Mom," Lucian said. The boys put their swords away and walked down the hallway to the dining hall. They joined everyone else for steaming bowls of soup and freshly baked rolls. Conversation floated around the table lightly and easily as they ate together. As a maid was removing the lunch dishes, Cook came in with a large tiered cake with a single candle on the top. "Happy Birthday, Your Majesty," Cook said with a grin as she set the cake down in front of Alexandra.

Alexandra smiled brightly. "You always remember that chocolate and raspberry is my favorite," she said to Cook. "I don't know what we'd do without you."

Cook simply smiled before returning to the kitchen.

Everyone wished Alexandra a happy birthday and watched her blow out her candle before they began passing plates of cake around. "Well, love, what did you wish for this year?" Lysander asked.

"I can't tell you or my wish won't come true," Alexandra replied.

"Well, you should at least give me a hint so that I can try to help it come true," Lysander teased.

Alexandra laughed, "I have everything a woman could possibly want. I have a wonderful husband, the two most beautiful children in the world, and I even received a second son who is wonderful in and of himself," she added, smiling down the table at Kaelen. "There's very little left for me to wish for."

"Well," Lysander said, a mischievous note to his voice, "I was thinking that maybe it was time we went on a second honeymoon. But if you already have everything you want…"

"Lysander Paul," Alexandra chided teasingly, "you know perfectly well that I wouldn't say no to a trip. What exactly did you have in mind?"

"I was thinking that you and I would go on a trip around the southern portion of Sanalbereth so we can warm up a little bit. We'd visit your parents and then come up and visit my parents, taking the longest route possible," Lysander replied, taking his wife's hand. "What better way to spend our silver anniversary?"

Smiling so brightly that it seemed to literally light the room, Alexandra said, "That sounds perfect, darling. When do we leave?"

"Tomorrow," Lysander said.

"But the children, how will they get to school? Where will they stay?" Alexandra asked.

"I've already arranged with Lavinia to come and get the children for school. She'll be taking them back when she takes her children. And all of them are old enough to be on their own for a while. Besides, Samuel will keep them out of trouble, won't you?"

"Of course, sire," the butler replied as he brought the mail in for the day.

"There you see? Everything is all taken care of. For a few weeks, you can just concentrate on being the most beautiful woman I know," Lysander said.

Laughing, Alexandra replied, "Well, I suppose I have no arguments left. Tomorrow it shall be."

It was still early when Alexandra and Lysander left the following morning, waving from their carriage. The sun was barely peeking over the horizon as Alexandra hugged and kissed each of them before leaving. "Now you be sure you behave and if you need anything at all, send word. And don't forget to make sure you go to town today to get any supplies that we missed for school. Oh and…"

"Mother, we'll be fine," Allegra interrupted with a smile. "Go on and enjoy yourselves."

As the carriage left, everyone else headed back inside. Allegra went into the parlor to work on the needlepoint she'd been working on over the break. The boys went to the fencing hall, but didn't feel much like actually practicing. Instead, they polished their swords until they gleamed and talked. Kaelen said, "Your dad said yesterday that this is their silver anniversary didn't he?"

"Yeah," Lucian replied. "Mom and Dad will be married twenty-five years this coming Wednesday."

"Why is there so much time from when they got married to when they had kids?" Kaelen asked. "Most of the parents we know had kids right away."

"Mom and Dad would have too, if there hadn't been complications," Lucian explained. "Dad said that Mom had a condition that made it very hard for her to have any children. They lost several babies before I was born. When they had Allegra the fall after I was born, they had hoped it would mean they could have lots of children like they'd always hoped for. But I guess Allegra was their miracle baby."

"Sounds like both of you were," Kaelen pointed out.

"Yeah, I guess so. But, that's what Dad told me when I asked him about it once," Lucian said. "He doesn't like to talk about it much. I think it makes them both sad. Mom always wanted a large family and Dad did too. But I guess it wasn't meant to be."

"Yeah," Kaelen said. "Well, I guess we should make sure we have everything ready for school. After all, Adrian's mom will be coming tomorrow afternoon to get us."

"Why does break always go by so quickly?" Lucian asked with a laugh as they left the fencing hall and each headed for their own room. They spent the rest of the day packing and making sure that there was nothing left to be gotten from town. After checking everyone's bags at least twice, they went into town with a list of things that they needed to pick up. Lysander and Alexandra had left a bag of money on the small table in the hallway for them to take to make any last minute purchases with. They took the smallest carriage into town and went to each of the shops they needed to. Allegra remembered needing to pick up a couple of new gowns for school from Tom's and Lucian needed to pick up his new uniforms. He'd started growing again and needed longer trousers. His jacket had become uncomfortably tight as his shoulders broadened. When he'd gone in with Lysander to make the order, he'd asked Tom if he could leave extra fabric in the hem.

"Certainly I can," Tom had replied. "Expecting to grow even more?"

"I hope so," Lucian had said.

As they stopped at the shop, Lucian paid for their purchases while Allegra had a last fitting to make sure the gowns fit properly. Tom's granddaughter worked with her while Tom took care of Lucian and Kaelen. "You look beautiful, Princess," Gabriella said as she smoothed the skirt on a soft pink gown.

"Thanks, Gabriella. I'll see you back at school. You'll still be there won't you?" Allegra asked.

Gabriella nodded, "Yes, I'll still be there. I'm just running a bit behind getting back." She paused as Allegra went behind a changing curtain to get back into her other gown. She continued when Allegra came out, "Melantha said there was something she needed me to pick up here before coming back and the shipment hasn't come in yet. I certainly hope it arrives soon. I've already written her to keep her updated on the situation. She said to just wait until it arrives."

"Well, I hope to see you soon. It's nice to have a familiar face there," Allegra replied as Gabriella handed her the gowns.

"It certainly is," Gabriella agreed. She then curtsied before disappearing into a backroom.

"Well, are you ready to go?" Lucian asked.

"Yes, I believe I am," Allegra said. "As always, Tom, they're lovely."

"You can't thank me this time, Princess," Tom admitted. "Gabriella did those for you. She insisted."

"Give her my thanks then," Allegra replied. Then she and the boys left the shop and continued to make the rounds about town before going back to the castle. They enjoyed a late luncheon and talked nonstop about what the new semester at school would bring.

Chapter 5

The day they were to be leaving, Sebastian insisted on taking all the children back to school. "It would be so much more convenient for me to go," he urged when Lavinia had tried to say she wanted to do it. "I plan on going on another adventure anyway. This way I can drop them off at school and then be on my way. I can even help you out with something before I go."

"But I was looking forward to taking them, Uncle Sebastian," Lavinia argued. "Please, at least let's all travel together. You can't be serious about wanting to leave now."

"Actually, it is indeed time for me to move on," Sebastian replied. "However, I suppose I can prolong my visit by a few days so that we can all make the journey back to school together. It's been ages since I was there. I'm sure all the fairies have long forgotten me."

"Don't count on it," Adrian teased. "They don't forget anything."

"Where are you going to go this time, Uncle Sebastian?" Moira asked.

"I just came from the mountains so I think I'll head south. There are some very interesting birds down that way at this time of the year. I think the birds are rather smart, moving to where it's warmer for the winter. I think my old bones could use some warm weather," Sebastian said teasingly.

"Oh you're not that old," Nana retorted. "You just think you're old."

"Heaven forbid!" Sebastian replied dramatically. "I certainly don't think I'm old. I merely said my bones were old. The rest of me is quite young I can assure you."

"Which province are you going to be going to first?" Lavinia asked. "If you'll be stopping in Rendorlin, there's a charming little inn there you could stay at. It's almost more like a bed and breakfast than an inn, but it's quite comfortable."

"I might have to look it up," Sebastian said. "What's it called?"

"The Dancing Fairies I believe," Lavinia replied.

"Yes that was it," Nana said. "The woman running the place is a sweetheart of a lady. I'm sure a stay there would do you good, Sebastian. You should stop there."

"Well, as everyone insists, I will indeed stop at The Dancing Fairies on my way through Rendorlin," Sebastian said with a teasing grin.

"Well, if we're going to get Alexandra's children on time, we'd best get going. Is everyone packed and ready?" Lavinia asked.

When everyone had confirmed that they were ready to go, they loaded up in the largest carriage they had and made the three hour trip to Maltisten where they picked up Allegra, Lucian and Kaelen before turning and making their way towards Biberseth. As the newest passengers got into the carriage Sebastian turned to them. "Why, you must be Allegra," he said upon seeing her.

"Yes," Allegra said, feeling a bit uncomfortable with having a complete stranger recognize her.

"I'm sorry, how very rude of me," Sebastian muttered as though more to himself than to her. "I'm Sebastian, Moira and Adrian's great-uncle. Adrian has told me a great deal about you in the last few weeks. He is quite right in saying that you are perfectly beautiful."

Lucian nearly began to laugh. He wasn't sure who had turned pinker, Adrian or Allegra. Both blushed to the roots of their hair. "Thank you," Allegra finally stammered. "I'm sure he exaggerated."

"No, if anything he didn't quite do you justice. Moira dear, I think it's a good thing that you know where you stand in my heart," Sebastian said teasingly. "Allegra is quite charming. But don't fear, you'll always be the most beautiful girl to me."

Moira laughed, "Uncle Sebastian, I do believe you're embarrassing her and Adrian."

"Well, Adrian needs embarrassed every once in a while. Get some color into those cheeks," Sebastian teased. "However, I shouldn't embarrass Allegra having just met her, should I?" When Moira shook her head, he turned his attention to Lucian. "You must be Lucian. I must say you seem a bit taller than Moira said you were."

Now Moira turned a furious shade of pink and Lucian said, "Well, in all fairness to Moira, I did grow over the break, so she wouldn't have known."

"She's told me quite a bit about you as well. Is it true that you bring her roses to match her favorite color?" Sebastian asked.

Soon the only people in the coach not blushing were Nana, Lavinia and Kaelen. For Kaelen's part, he was particularly glad that there was not another princess in the family; otherwise the teasing might have gotten around to him as well. But despite being embarrassed frequently by the older gentleman, everyone in the carriage took an instant liking to Sebastian. He was fun to be around and there wasn't a moment of the journey that they didn't spend in laughter and enjoyment. When they arrived at Fair Damsel's Academy to drop the girls off, Lucian and Adrian helped their sisters take their bags out. Sebastian stepped out as well and wrapped Moira in a tight hug. "You take care of yourself, my love. And keep drawing, the sketches you showed me over the break were beautiful. You have quite a talent."

"I will," Moira promised. "Please write to me from wherever you're going. You know I love to hear from you."

"I'll do my best," Sebastian said. "I won't make any promises though."

Moira laughed, "Your best is all I can ask for. Goodbye, Uncle Sebastian. Have a good trip."

"Goodbye, my dear," Sebastian said and hugged her once again. He then returned to the carriage where everyone else was waiting. He watched Allegra and Moira wave as the carriage pulled away before being ushered in by their headmistress. He couldn't recall the name of the fairy; it had been many years since he was a student at Charming Academy. But he remembered always thinking that her wavy, dark violet hair was very pretty.

His thoughts were interrupted as Nana said, "It seems yesterday that the children were too young to be in school, doesn't it Lavinia?"

"It does," Lavinia admitted. "I almost miss those days. Now they're very nearly grown."

"Children do that," Sebastian said with a laugh. "Now, Lucian, where did you say your parents were going for their second honeymoon?"

Lucian shrugged, "I really don't know many exact locations. I know they'll go to Cape Darshall where my mother's parents live and they'll be going to Coleston to see my dad's parents."

"None of your grandparents live in Maltisten?" Sebastian asked.

"Not anymore. Grandpa's health was getting pretty bad and his doctor recommended living further south so as not to irritate his lungs with the cold weather we get in winter," Lucian explained. "Since Grandma grew up in Cape Darshall, that's where they decided to go. They moved away when I was nine or ten. We go visit them when we can, but it is a long distance."

"Yes," Sebastian said, rubbing his chin, "Cape Darshall would be almost two days from Maltisten. I'm sorry that your grandfather is in poor health."

"He's doing much better now," Lucian replied. "In fact, the doctor knew exactly what he needed. Every time Grandma writes she says that Grandpa is healthy as a horse."

Sebastian laughed, "Sometimes a change in scenery is just what a person needs."

The carriage soon pulled to a stop at Charming Academy. Sebastian helped the boys unload their trunks and other items. "Well, if it isn't Prince Sebastian," Calista said with a smile as the four climbed the stairs. "It has been many, many years."

"Indeed it has, Calista," Sebastian replied, returning her smile. "I hope you are well."

"Quite well, thank you," Calista said. "Boys, I trust you have everything?"

"I sure hope so," Lucian said. "I don't think I could stuff more into my trunk if I tried."

Calista laughed merrily. "Well, do get your things inside and you're just in time for supper. Will you be staying with them or have you other places to be?" she asked, turning to Sebastian.

"I'm afraid I must be going," Sebastian said. "I'm spending a couple more days with my niece and sister and then I'll be on the road once again."

"Enjoy your travels, Sebastian," Calista replied before ushering the boys inside.

Once the boys had taken their things to their rooms, they met downstairs again for supper. It wasn't long before they found Jacobi and George and the five friends spent the meal catching up on what they had missed. "I don't know if it's just that Susan and I never did get along very well or what, but I don't think I've ever seen a longer, more boring wedding. And I've seen my fair share of weddings," George added with a grimace.

"That bad, huh?" Lucian asked.

George groaned, "It took forever. I think they listed off every single thing each of them has done from birth to the quest. And the quest part took forever as they talked about all the stupid things that he did when he was trying to find her." George rolled his eyes. "I don't think I've ever heard a lamer Prince Charming story in all my life."

The others started laughing. Jacobi said, "I'm sorry, George. I guess it could somehow have been worse, though I can't think of how. How was your break, Adrian?"

"Mine was great," Adrian replied enthusiastically. "My great-uncle Sebastian came and visited the whole time. We almost never see him because he's always traveling somewhere. In fact, you've all got to come by my room later to see the dagger he brought me. It's awesome!"

"He brought you a dagger?" Jacobi asked enviously. "My relatives never get me gifts that cool. I always get socks or something like that."

"Well, I suppose you can never have too many good socks," Lucian teased.

"Thanks a lot, Lucian," Jacobi retorted with a smile. "What did you two do over break?"

"Really we just practiced fencing and did a few things around Maltisten," Kaelen said. "There really wasn't anything special about our break."

"Although, you have grown some, Lucian. Are you taller than Moira again?" George asked.

"I think just barely; if I stand as tall as I can. Honestly, we're probably the same height, and she may still have a little bit on me" Lucian admitted with a smile. "I did have to get new trousers while I was at home, though. The tailor left extra material so I can grow more. Mom's afraid that I'm going to grow like she did."

"How'd your mom grow?" George asked suspiciously.

"All at once," Lucian replied. "I don't remember how many inches she grew in three months, but it was a lot. I'm not really sure that I want to grow like she did, but I'd be happy with a few more inches. Just enough so that I'm definitely taller than Moira."

"I guess we'll all see what happens throughout the semester," Jacobi said with a smile. "I have a feeling I'm going to be the short one in our group." He'd stopped growing the last year at just a hair under five eleven.

"Having been there, it's not too bad," Lucian said. "Besides, Clarissa is shorter than a lot of the princesses. To her, you'll be tall."

Jacobi laughed, "I guess that's true."

The chatter continued until everyone had finished eating. They then followed Adrian to his room where everyone admired the new dagger. Then they each went to their own rooms for the night. Lucian felt somewhat tired, but spent a little time going over his schedule again. His fencing class had changed times, switching spots with healing. That meant that in the morning his first stop would be the witches' hovel for class. Hopefully he'd do better now that he'd spent the break studying the chapter repeatedly. He'd even asked his dad to go over it with him in hopes that somehow something would magically click in his head. Yawning, he put the schedule back on his desk and blew the candles out. He rubbed the top of Rusty's head before lying down and going to sleep.

Morghana watched Lucian as he measured the ingredients for the poultice he was working on. She studied the way he worked, trying to find the best way to help him improve. While he was doing better than he had been before winter break, she still saw plenty of room for improvement. She was also aware that she had a tendency of making her students nervous because she watched them so intently. But if they only knew that the best way for her to help them was to carefully observe what they were doing and how they did it. She played absentmindedly with a lock of tangled white hair, twisting it around her finger as she watched. *No, no, that's not the way*, she thought as Lucian began heating the mixture over the small fire. "Lucian, you need to hold that up higher over the flame or the ingredients will burn. If they do, it will render your poultice useless."

Lucian sighed and lifted the small pan higher above the flame. He got the feeling that no matter what he did, it was never going to be good enough. In his mind he could just see himself working on poultices up until the day of graduation. Then Morghana would say there hadn't been enough improvement and he wasn't ready to be a Prince Charming. Moira would be stuck dying in some tower who knew where and he'd be stuck in this miserable little room trying to figure out the cure.

As though sensing Lucian's frustration, Morghana said, "Why don't you set that to the side for a while? A little break never hurt anyone." Gladly, Lucian set down the pan and sat back in his chair. When he had, Morghana asked, "How do you think you're doing, Lucian?"

Unsure quite how to respond, Lucian shrugged, "I guess I'm doing better. I just don't get everything."

"Well, dear, nobody learns this overnight," Morghana rasped gently. "Even my very best students have struggled with this part. It probably doesn't help that I am a bit of a perfectionist when it comes to this sort of thing. A lot of that is because I have to be. Even the slightest mistake can change a cure to a death sentence."

Great, Lucian thought, *I am going to kill Moira and not even be trying to*.

"Don't be too hard on yourself," Morghana continued, as though she had known his thought. "You really are improving a great deal more than you see. In fact, I do believe you're almost ready to move on to more difficult poultices. The reason that we spend so much time on them is because they are universally useful. There are so many applications for them. They can be used to heal people, sick animals; some can even help wilting plants, not that you face that problem," she added. Before Lucian could ask what she meant, Morghana had continued on. "The art of poultice making is a long and difficult process to master. In truth Lucian, you are one of my better students. I've only had a few who learned this process as quickly as you have and one of them had perhaps an unfair advantage."

"He'd had a blessing of some kind," Lucian guessed.

"Yes, he had," Morghana replied. "In fact I was surprised that they'd put him in the class. But while the fairies often recognize that a gift has been given, they don't necessarily know what that gift was. And in the long run, he'd needed the class to help him fine tune that gift and make it something he could use."

"So, I'm not failing?" Lucian asked hopefully.

"Dear heavens, no," Morghana laughed. "Believe me, child, if you were failing you would know it." Morghana glanced at a wall clock. "Well, we're out of time for today. I know you're tired of hearing it…"

"I need to reread chapter fifteen again," Lucian interrupted, unable to keep the misery from his voice.

Morghana smiled. "Actually, I think if you just read the section on heating the ingredients that should be sufficient. Read that section and perhaps the section on cutting them. You're still a little too choppy with some of your cuts. Then, we'll see how you do next time. Enjoy the rest of your day Lucian."

"You too, Morghana," Lucian replied. Then he walked out of the hovel and back towards the castle. He pulled his jacket closer about himself as he walked to block out the wind. It was bitterly cold which didn't really improve his mood much. At least he wasn't failing, but he really didn't think he could say that he was doing well either.

His thoughts were interrupted as he got inside and met with the rest of his classmates in Airlia's classroom for language arts. They were studying romantic poetry, which most of the boys found to be rather pointless. Lucian tended to spend much of this class in a bit of a stupor. He had never been particularly good in language arts, much less romantic poetry. He didn't think he was capable of writing anything properly romantic. Words just weren't enough. Then Airlia's voice interrupted him again. "You'll have to write a series of ten sonnets for your princess, two of which you will memorize and present to her at your next meeting. These sonnets are due at the end of the month. We will then revise and edit them until they are perfect. Your presentation will be graded, so think carefully about what you wish to write."

Her announcement was met with much groaning and suddenly Lucian wished he hadn't spent so much of the class daydreaming. How many sonnets? And what exactly was a sonnet anyway? As the boys filed out of the classroom to go to their next class, Lucian felt like his day couldn't possibly get any worse. Adrian looked about as miserable as he felt. "How are we supposed to write ten sonnets?" Lucian asked quietly as they walked through the door, hoping that Airlia wouldn't hear him.

"With paper and pen," Airlia replied sweetly.

"I'd like to know how we're supposed to memorize them and then present them," Adrian said when they were farther away from the fairy's classroom. "When during the meeting are we supposed to have time to do that?"

"I guess now that I think about it, the fourth years never do win the scavenger hunt. Part of their list must include stumbling through their poems or maybe they don't even get to do the scavenger hunt," Lucian said.

"That would be a bummer. I actually like doing that," Adrian replied. "So, what do you have after math?" he asked as they walked into the classroom.

"Besides lunch?" Lucian teased.

"Yeah, besides that," Adrian retorted with a grin.

"Part one of fencing," Lucian replied. "After that spell breaking and then dragon fighting."

"Hit Dronecus good and hard for me will you?" Adrian said.

Lucian nodded as Marius began their lesson. Even though Lucian usually kept Draconus' snide comments to himself, some of the other boys were quick to let Kaelen and Adrian know that the dragon had not forgotten them though they were no longer in the class. Lucian wasn't quite sure why the boys bothered to do that. It wasn't like Kaelen or Adrian could do anything about the dragon. Really none of them could do anything about it. Draconus remained undefeated in their classes, though Lucian knew he was getting close to finding the dragon's weakness. George was getting pretty good too. The two of them often hit the dragon, even if they didn't get close to the "death strike" Vulcan had taught them in class. Lucian also thought that some of it was that in their language classes they were getting a great deal of information about how dragons think and react, at least at a linguistic level. This could sometimes apply to their fighting class, but even there, it didn't give them much of an advantage over their peers.

As the boys went to lunch following their math class, they saw Kaelen looking over a piece of paper. "What's that?" George asked as they sat down at the table with him.

"My new schedule," Kaelen replied.

"New schedule?" Jacobi repeated. "Why do you need a new schedule?"

"I don't really know, but I've got some real delightful ones now," Kaelen said. He handed Lucian the schedule and then slowly began picking at the food on his tray.

"Wrestling, double botany, double fencing, portrait painting, double spell breaking, and of course all the regular stuff; triple etiquette?" Lucian read. "What's that all about?"

"You tell me," Kaelen replied miserably. "I can't do half that stuff. I mean, wrestling? Who am I going to wrestle? Even Adrian is puny compared to me. No offense."

"None taken," Adrian said. "Besides, it seems I'm getting shorter every time I turn around."

"I'm more confused about the triple etiquette. Last time you only had it twice and I know some of that was to help you with your coordination and stuff so that you could use normal utensils," Jacobi said. "Why on earth do you need it three times?"

"Maybe two isn't enough," Kaelen retorted. "I mean, I guess the double botany isn't too bad, I've been doing double botany, but the time on one of them changed, so I'm guessing that's different then what I have been doing. And the double spell breaking and double fencing aren't really different. And then portrait painting? I've got to be the worst artist in our class and I can't even hold a paintbrush right now."

"I guess you'll be using jumbo-sized brushes and in your third etiquette class, Gelasia will help you learn how to hold a regular-sized brush," George said comfortingly.

"That doesn't help with the artistic ability. Art in general is hard enough but portraits? That means I have to paint people. People!" Kaelen repeated miserably. "I don't know what I did to deserve this, but I'm never, ever doing it again."

"It looks like your next class is the first part of spell breaking, so that shouldn't be too bad, right?" Lucian said, handing him the schedule.

"I guess not," Kaelen replied. "Oh well, maybe things will turn out better than I think right now. Who knows? Maybe they'll hire me to paint the new portraits for the castle."

The friends laughed and continued to eat their meal as they talked about how their classes up to that point had gone. Soon, it was time for them to go to their next classes and they separated to go to the classes they had next. Adrian and Kaelen headed to the classroom for the first part of their spell breaking class. Calypso was seated behind her desk waiting for them. "Good afternoon, boys. I trust you had a pleasant break?"

"Yes," the boys replied.

"That's good to hear," Calypso said with a smile. "Now if you will get out your books and open to the twentieth chapter, we're going to be discussing how to break enchanted barriers."

While Adrian and Kaelen were in spell-breaking, Lucian was surprised to see George walking to the fencing hall as well. "Are you in fencing right now too?" he asked.

"Yeah, I've always had it at this time," George replied.

As they walked into the room, Raphael turned his attention to them. "Alright, lads, you've both improved enough that it's time you began working with another student at your own level. We'll flip a coin to see which hand we use first. George, heads or tails?"

"Um, tails?" George said as though not sure he meant it.

Raphael flipped the coin. "Sorry, George, it's heads. That means that today we'll start left-handed. Halfway through class we'll switch and work right-handed. Any questions?" The boys shook their heads. "Very well, get your protective gear and your rapiers and we'll begin."

About half an hour before class would end, Raphael had them go ahead and put away their things. "I want to talk with you boys for a while before we get going too far into the semester," he said. "Each of you has been working with your weaker arm for the better part of a year and a half now. The purpose behind this is twofold. One, it will give you a distinct advantage in an actual fight. I will grant you that your weak arm will never be as easy to work with as the one you are used to fighting with; nor will it ever feel as natural. However, having the skill to use either hand if necessary gives you an advantage over your adversary. As he becomes tired, you can switch hands and continue fresh. The second purpose is to prepare you to work with both hands simultaneously. This is another skill that will give you great advantage over your adversary, especially if you should happen to have more than one challenger at a given time. Because of this, I will need both of you to purchase a second rapier at some point, though not right away. Right now neither one of you is at a point that we could begin double-handed fencing; however we may reach that point sooner than I had originally anticipated. You are both doing remarkably well with your weak arms. To be honest I hadn't expected moving you into a class together so soon; though I am pleased that you have improved to the point that I've been able to do so. I will keep you informed as to what you will need. Just be aware that by mid-semester, we may need to make a trip into town to purchase new swords for each of you. If not, certainly by next school year you will need to purchase a second sword. Do you have any questions or concerns for me?"

"No sir," the boys replied.

"Alright then, I know we're still a bit early, but why don't you two run along now? You've done a magnificent job for one day. I'll see both of you tomorrow," Raphael said, opening the door to the fencing hall so they could go leave.

The two boys walked down the hall to the door to the dragon fighting classroom. They knew class was still going on inside. "I sure hope Draconus is in a better mood than he was before we left," George said as they were waiting.

"I don't know that I would count on it," Lucian replied. "He was like this last winter too. Maybe the cold makes him grumpier than normal."

George grinned. "Maybe he doesn't like his dinner cold."

Lucian laughed, "That could be. Although for someone who eats everything raw, he really shouldn't complain. He doesn't know how nice a warm meal is."

"You've got it Lucian! I can just see him, wishing there were a way to warm his meal. All he'd have to do is breathe on it," George said. "But, he's jealous because we get a warm meal for just about every meal and his is always shivering."

Still laughing Lucian retorted, "Well then he should learn to kill it first. Then at least the shivering would stop."

The boys' conversation was cut short as the last class exited the room and they were able to go inside. Draconus was curled in the middle of the pit, his tail flicking back and forth impatiently. "Well, well, here a bit early aren't we?" he hissed as the two headed for seats.

"Yes," Lucian replied simply.

"Couldn't wait to be beaten again, eh?" Draconus asked nastily.

The boys ignored him and sat quietly waiting for the rest of the class to arrive. As boys filed in, Draconus continued to dole out snide comments. Lucian and George looked at each other. Obviously, Draconus wasn't in any better a mood now than he had been at the end of last semester. If anything, he seemed worse. Once the last of the boys entered the room, he began a long lecture on where they were lacking from last semester. "If you boys have any dreams of defeating a dragon on your quest, you'd best shape up," Draconus snarled. "Some of you wouldn't last a full minute were one of my brothers to find you. Others of you are becoming lazy. This is not child's play, princelings. You need to be at the top of your wits, what little you have, every time you come to class. Only two of you seem to have shown any improvement at all. Though perhaps that's just luck," he added with a sneer towards Lucian and George. He continued his rant until the class time was over and the boys were finally allowed to leave. His parting shot was, "I want a ten page essay on the skills of dragon fighting due to Vulcan by oh, let's be generous, Friday afternoon. Until that time, you'll be sitting in lecture."

"So, that's how it feels to get raked over the coals," George said miserably as they left the room. "That was completely depressing."

"Yeah," Lucian agreed. "I wish we'd had that before fencing. What little feel-good we had from that class was totally blown away back there."

"Don't fret, boys," Vulcan's voice came from behind them, startling them both. "Draconus is always this way with his fourth year students. I don't think any of you are doing horribly, although a good wake-up call is sometimes just the thing you boys need to get yourselves motivated. He is right in saying that some of you have become very lazy in that class."

As Vulcan disappeared into another room, George said, "Was that supposed to make us feel better?"

"If it was, it didn't work," Lucian replied. "In fact, I think I'd call that a fail."

"A fail of epic proportions," George added.

The following day was the first with some of the major changes made to Kaelen's schedule, beginning with portrait painting. He went into the art classroom and was completely depressed to find that he was the only student in the room. Stefanos was standing near an easel, holding his paintbrush up as though measuring something in the distance. For a while, he didn't even notice that Kaelen had entered the room until Kaelen cleared his throat. Stefanos started and turned. "Oh, is it class time already?" he asked. "I must have gotten carried away with my work. That happens sometimes." He smiled and motioned for Kaelen to have a seat before putting his brushes and paints into a small wooden box next to his easel.

Kaelen looked at the painting Stefanos was working on and thought, *I sure hope he doesn't expect me to ever be that good.* The painting showed the forest behind the castle as though the painting were actually a window to the outside. Everything looked exactly as it did in real life. Even the tiny flecks of white that were supposed to be softly fluttering snowflakes looked real.

"Well, welcome to portrait painting," Stefanos continued when Kaelen had sat down. "As you can see, it's just the two of us, so you'll get plenty of my time for pointers and such. However, this is an art class and you need to be able to get in touch with your creative muses, so for as much of class as I can, I will not hover over your shoulder. This class will be fairly independent with some instruction. I will need you to read through this book before we can begin on any of your pieces." He handed Kaelen a delicate-looking book entitled *Beginning Portraiture: a Guide to the Human Face*. "This is full of excellent tips on how to best capture the look of a person as well as capturing personality," Stefanos explained. "I want you to try to have this read by the end of the week. Can you manage that?"

"If I don't shred the pages," Kaelen replied. "I have difficulty with books. Is there a more, um…"

"Resilient copy?" Stefanos finished for him. Kaelen nodded and he said, "I'm terribly sorry, this is the best copy they have. Just do the best you can with it. If it comes back looking a little shabby, I can fix that. Any other reason you wouldn't be able to finish?"

"Nothing that comes to mind," Kaelen said.

"Good, read that this week and by next week we'll get our hands dirty," Stefanos instructed. "Now, you won't just be learning to paint in this class. I'll also be teaching you how to make brushes, mix your own paints and where to find the minerals for certain colors. After all, you never know when inspiration may hit you and you want to always be prepared."

Kaelen didn't think it would be a good idea to tell Stefanos that art never inspired him with anything other than dread. Instead he listened quietly as Stefanos continued to give him an overview of what the class would be like. They wouldn't actually start with paint at all. Instead, Kaelen would fine-tune drawing faces in pencil and pastels before moving on to paint.

"But while you're doing your sketched portraits, we'll also spend some time beginning to make the materials necessary to begin your painting. We'll start of course with making the brushes and then move on to mixing the paints. When you do start your first painting, it will be with materials that you have made yourself. It makes the painting mean more to you when you've spent the time making everything. Besides that, it makes it more fun too," Stefanos added. Kaelen was fairly sure that he wouldn't find any part of this class fun, but kept it to himself.

By the time Kaelen met the other boys for lunch he'd had three of his new classes and all of them were individual classes with no other students. He discovered that his opponent in wrestling would be varied, but would start with Achilles and then when he was ready move to more challenging opponents, though Achilles wouldn't say who or what they were. His third etiquette class was also before lunch. In that class he was being taught how to properly manage and run an estate.

"Gelasia, why do I need this class but none of the other boys do?" Kaelen had asked. "After all, we're all going to be running kingdoms and stuff, right?"

"Well, of course we expect all our princes to succeed and eventually be ruler of their own kingdom, however this class isn't about running a kingdom, Kaelen," Gelasia had replied. "It's about running an estate. You're in a very unique position and we'll be working to prepare you for that."

George broke through Kaelen's thoughts by asking, "So how were your morning classes, Kaelen?"

"Pretty boring, really," Kaelen replied. He gave them the short version of what he'd gone through for the first part of his day.

"Maybe wrestling won't be so bad once you actually get started on it," Jacobi said.

"I'm the only student in the class," Kaelen argued. "That means I'm the only one that Achilles can get after for not doing it perfectly."

"He's not nearly the perfectionist that Raphael is," Lucian pointed out. "Besides, at least you were able to have a fairly light day today. Once things really get started is when they'll become harder."

"Thanks for making me feel better, Lucian," Kaelen said teasingly.

"Well, at least you know your next class isn't individual," Adrian said. "The others are in that botany too. I've got amphibian studies next." He made a face. "I sure wish there was some way out of that class. I mean, I already know I'm going to turn into a frog. Why does it matter what type of habitat salamanders prefer to live in? I'm not going to be a salamander. Shouldn't they just call it frog studies and I can study the life habits of frogs?"

"I guess they want you to have a well-rounded knowledge of all forms of amphibian life," George replied with a teasing grin.

"All I know is that amphibians are slimy and gross and that if you chase girls with them they squeal," Adrian retorted.

The other boys started snickering and Lucian asked, "Have you practiced this before?"

"What do you think? I have a twin sister," Adrian replied impishly. "Of course I chased her around with frogs and toads and any other slimy thing I could get my hands on. Although I will admit, the scullery maid was much more fun to chase around. Man could that girl scream," Adrian recalled with a mischievous smile.

"I bet that didn't go over well with your parents," Kaelen said as everyone laughed.

"When he was alive, Dad said it was just part of being a boy and never minded much. Mother though would have a fit and tell me to behave more like a gentleman," Adrian replied. "So I suppose it depends on which parent caught me how badly I was punished. I quit doing it when Mother got so fed up with it that she made my dad do something about it."

"What did he do?" Jacobi asked.

"He threatened to let the maid chase me around with a snake," Adrian admitted. "That was the only animal I could never really handle. They still give me the creeps. I think it's the whole slithering thing; it's just weird. Anyway, I doubt that maid would have deigned to be in the same room as a snake, let alone touch one. But I wasn't going to take any chances either."

The boys continued laughing and chatting until it was time to go to class. Adrian said goodbye as he headed to amphibian studies and the rest of them walked outside to the greenhouse for botany. It was bitterly cold outside with fat, wet snowflakes falling from a leaden sky. The greenhouse felt infinitely warmer as they hurried inside. "Well, boys, bit nippy out today isn't it?" Russett asked as they shivered and crowded together by one of the tables.

"It's freezing!" Jacobi stammered through chattering teeth.

"Well, give yourselves a few minutes," Russett said. "It's much warmer in here than it is out there. The wind is certainly talking out there."

"Howling is more like it," George muttered.

Russett laughed and after giving the boys a few minutes to let the warmth of the greenhouse sink in, started class. "We'll be doing some different things this semester. For one thing, you all need to know how to recognize dangerous plants. The first thing in doing that is by seeing them at each stage of growth from seed to full maturity. Sometimes a plant is only dangerous during a particular time in their development. For example, darted morning glory is only dangerous in the middle stage of development before the flower fully matures. During that stage, the bud spits poisonous darts which would be a lethal problem if you didn't recognize the plant for what it was."

"Russett, wouldn't it be lethal even if you did recognize it?" Jacobi interrupted. "If you get hit with a poisonous dart, you'll die."

"If you know what you're dealing with, then you can be prepared to prevent injury," Russett explained. "And if you did get hit with the darts, if you recognized the plant, you could easily use an antidote that will cure the injury. You might have to deal with some temporary pain, but you'll at least survive the encounter.

"Other plants," he continued, "are dangerous from the very start such as water hemlock or spiked hedgerow. Danger comes in many packages in the plant world. Some have poison, others throw spikes or thorns, and some try to wrestle with you. If you are not prepared, these will defeat you easily. However, that's why we're in this class; to teach you what to look for and watch out for. We'll also be learning cures and antidotes to use when dealing with these plants."

"Wouldn't it be better to avoid the plants?" George asked.

"It would always be better to avoid them," Russett replied. "But sometimes you don't have that option. If your princess is held hostage by a dragon, then he lives in a thicket of thorns. The interesting thing about thickets, is that they tend to favor all sorts of dangerous plants, not just thorn bushes. Really, all dangerous plants seem to like growing together. I suppose it's because misery loves company. So, yes, you could avoid the thicket; but then your princess is left in the middle with no one to rescue her. Are there any other questions?"

Kaelen paused for a moment before saying, "You said we'll be seeing these plants at every stage of development. What does that mean, exactly?"

"That means, Kaelen, that you'll be planting them and observing them," Russett said. "I have plenty of antidotes available if we should have problems in the class, but rest assured you're really not in any danger. The key to this class is learning the plant's full life cycle. That means you need to see it from seed to full maturity. I could have you read it in a book, but life doesn't come out of a book. Real, hands-on experience is the best teacher. With that in mind, it's time to start with our first plant; stinging thistle. Please put on a heavy set of gardening gloves and follow me."

By the end of class, the boys were wishing they'd had some kind of face mask too. The gloves protected their fingers from the spiny seeds, but they weren't prepared for the seeds to spit spines at them when they attempted to plant them in the soil-filled pots. Russett had given each boy a small tube of ointment. "Those will probably sting for a few days. Just put a little ointment over each one and you'll be good as new in no time. That's really the hardest part, getting it planted."

"You'd think the seeds would want to go in the soil," Jacobi complained, rubbing some ointment on a spot over his eye where a particularly nasty spine had struck him. The spot was now a bright red blister.

"Maybe they just don't like being touched," George said hopefully, though he wasn't much better off than Jacobi.

"I suppose I got off lucky," Kaelen added. "The spines just got stuck in my fur. Only one actually hit me."

"I don't know that I'd say you got lucky, Kaelen," Jacobi admitted. "You got hit in the lip."

Lucian tried not to engage in the conversation. He hadn't had a single spine spit from his seeds and he very much doubted that the others would feel pleased for him. Instead he was pretty sure they'd find him disgustingly lucky. He almost envied Kaelen's fur. At least if he was furry, the others wouldn't be able to tell looking at him that he hadn't been hit.

"Hey," George said suddenly, "where'd you get hit, Lucian?"

"In the chest," Lucian lied, hoping that he sounded convincing. "I guess my seeds didn't have enough oomph to reach my face."

"Ouch. Well, at least no one will be able to see it," Jacobi said comfortingly.

"Yeah," Lucian replied. "What's everyone got next?"

They continued to their next classes and Lucian was rather grateful to be going to foreign language where George would be the only other student. He wouldn't have to keep talking about the spiny seeds they had been working with.

"You didn't actually get hit by any of the spines, did you?" George asked as they walked towards the gazebo for their dragon languages class. Apparently he hadn't been fooled by Lucian's answer.

Lucian knew he wouldn't be able to lie and said, "No I didn't."

"Lucky," George admitted. They stopped chatting as they walked inside and sat down at the desks that had been placed nearest the lake. Every now and again a cold blast of air came through and the boys shivered.

Lorelei was sitting on her rock at the front of the room. If she was feeling at all cold like the boys were, she didn't let on. Instead she smiled and said in Sea Serpent, "Good afternoon, boys."

They responded in the same and the lesson got underway. Lucian and George had already decided that if they were going to keep the mermaid happy, then they were going to have to start practicing the dialects on their own as well as in class. At the end of the hour she asked, "Are you doing anything to study outside class?"

"We're setting up a time we can practice today," Lucian replied.

"Excellent," Lorelei said. "Please make sure you both work especially hard on Sea Serpent. Your accent is a little off and sea serpents don't take kindly at all to people mispronouncing their language."

Lucian wanted to say that he felt that dragons in general became offended for the sheer purpose of becoming offended. However, he saw no purpose in being disagreeable to the mermaid either. They had learned over the past four years that mermaids were easily offended too. While Lorelei couldn't burn them to a crisp, she had her own unique ways of showing displeasure and neither boy wanted to walk back to the castle soaked to the bone; especially since the snow was beginning to pick up outside.

When Lorelei dismissed them, the boys walked to the barn for horsemanship. They were grateful for the warmth of the indoor ring and their horses as they walked inside. Phillipa got them started on a simple workout as more boys filtered in. This class, like so many of their others, had been shrinking in size. It seemed that only hunting and their regular education courses had stayed with all the students. Everything else was becoming more and more individualized. In this class there were only about ten of the original students. Lucian was fairly sure that the number would probably drop again next year. He supposed that it made sense. After all, not every prince would need to face obstacles that required his horse. In fact, some of them may only use their horses as a way to travel and not have any difficulties at all. But he knew that Adrian missed the class. The truth was that Lucian missed seeing Adrian in the class as well. Adrian had a natural seat and worked so well with Stardancer that it seemed a shame for him not to be in a class that he enjoyed so much. But what would a frog need with a horse?

Lucian's thoughts were interrupted as Phillipa brought the class to the center of the ring and gave them the instructions for the low jumps course they were beginning. She had added a bar to each of the jumps they'd been working with previously. "It's time to begin challenging yourselves and your horses more. We'll take the course one student at a time. Remember to use proper posture and commands. Jacobi, let's begin with you."

Chapter 6

Within several weeks, the boys had fallen into a regular routine. They often met in the common room after supper to work on their homework, helping each other out wherever they could. Lucian and George spent a half hour each evening practicing their dragon dialects, particularly sea serpent since Lorelei kept insisting that their accent was still not what it should be. Neither was quite sure why she was focusing so much on that dialect rather than the other two. "Maybe she knows something we don't," George commented one evening when they'd decided they'd had enough of tripping over the strange words.

"I don't know," Lucian said as he stretched his arms over his head. He looked out the window. Spring was just around the corner. Soft shoots of tender, green grass were poking out of the grounds while buds were forming on the trees. It wouldn't be very long at all before they'd be meeting again with their princesses. Glancing at the wall clock, he suddenly said, "Shoot! I'm late!"

"Late for what?" George asked as Lucian got up from his seat and started shoving his books back into his bag.

"Gelasia was going to see if she could get one last hemming out of these pants. I sure hope she can, they've become really short again," Lucian replied.

"What are you eating that the rest of us are missing?" Adrian teased as Lucian started out of the room.

"Don't know," Lucian called over his shoulder, "but I like it!" He didn't hear any other responses as he ran up the stairs to the third floor tower where Gelasia's classroom was. Out of breath, he paused for a moment before knocking on the door. When he heard her reply, he walked inside. "Sorry I'm late," he said. "I was working on some homework and lost track of the time."

"That's quite alright, dear," Gelasia replied sweetly. "Get up on the stool and we'll see what we can do about these trousers of yours. This is the third time you've been in here in the last fortnight. Did they spike your food with growth powder?" she teased.

"I don't think so," Lucian said with a grin. "Everyone else would be growing too. But my mom said she grew this way."

"Yes, I remember helping Alexandra with quite a few flounces," Gelasia recalled with a smile. "Several girls actually."

"You were at Fair Damsel's then?" Lucian asked.

"Yes, dear," Gelasia replied. "I worked at Fair Damsel's for many, many years. I came to Charming Academy just after your mother's class graduated actually. I felt the gentlemen needed me. Well, I think we might be able to get this just long enough, dear; but if you grow anymore then you'll need to make a trip into town for new trousers. I'm afraid all the magic in the world won't add more fabric to this hem."

Lucian shrugged, "I didn't think they'd last the semester. Or rather I hoped that they wouldn't."

Gelasia laughed, "Ah, my dear, you must be careful what you wish for. Sometimes what we think we want isn't necessarily what we need."

"True," Lucian agreed. They were quiet and in no time at all, Gelasia had re-hemmed the trousers.

"That's you all done, my dear," Gelasia said kindly, straightening up. "Anything else you need?"

"I don't think so," Lucian replied. "Thanks for everything."

"Don't mention it, dear. Now back to your studies. I've heard that you are doing quite well in your classes. I wouldn't want you to falter on my account," Gelasia said.

Lucian blushed at the praise. "Thanks. I hope I'm doing well."

"I think it's going better than you realize," Gelasia assured him. "Now, run along."

Thanking her one last time, Lucian left the tower and headed back to his own room to finish his homework. He was trying to memorize his sonnets. If you asked him, they were absolutely terrible and there was no way he would happily share them with Moira. But since he didn't have a choice, he desperately tried to learn the horrible prose. As he stumbled over the words while pacing the room, Rusty yawned loudly.

"Hey, you try doing this," Lucian said miserably. "It's not easy and it's certainly not fun."

Rusty yawned again as though to tell Lucian that it wasn't his problem.

"Yeah, I know, you're a dog. You don't have to get anyone to fall in love with you," Lucian replied. He sighed as he sat down on the edge of his bed and rubbed the top of Rusty's head. "It's just not fair boy. Why couldn't the assignment have been, 'Have a ten minute conversation with your princess.'? I could probably manage that without totally offending Moira. My poetry is so awful she's going to hate me forever."

Woofing softly, Rusty leaned into Lucian's hand.

"I know, boy, I know," Lucian said. Tired from a long day, Lucian blew out the candles in his room and crawled under the covers. He let his dreams take him far away from dragons, mermaids, and awful love sonnets.

Lucian's mood hadn't improved much the next day. In healing he accidently caused an explosion by adding one of the ingredients too rapidly. Morghana had quickly put out the flames and Lucian had apologized at least five times, but it didn't save him from scorched eyebrows and a new assignment. "You will write a three page paper on proper safety while working with highly flammable ingredients," Morghana had rasped angrily, her dark eyes flashing dangerously.

When he got to language arts, Airlia still wasn't satisfied with his attempts at rehearsing his sonnets. "Your voice is so," she paused, looking for the right word, "soporific, Lucian; as though you were merely speaking of the weather. You need to really feel the words as you say them. Show some emotion. Let the love you feel for your princess enrich your tones and soften your edges."

On and on the day dragged going from bad to worse until Lucian was bottling up so much pent-up frustration that the others were afraid he might explode if they said hello to him. When Draconus began dragon fighting, Lucian was more than ready for his turn to fight the dragon. It didn't matter that this would probably end in defeat as it had every other time he'd been in the class. What mattered was that he could wail on Draconus and not have to worry about hurting him or breaking anything. As though Draconus sensed his eagerness, he seemed to drag out some of the other fights longer than he normally did, baiting the princes with taunts and his usual snide comments. Lucian just waited.

"Well, I believe that leaves you, young princeling," Draconus sneered at him. "Let's see if you have improved at all or if you're as pathetic as your classmates."

Lucian entered the pit with his armor on and his sword ready. Being wickedly fast, Draconus usually made the first move, leaving the princes constantly on the defensive. This time, though, Lucian was ready for him. He sprang into action, not really taking consideration of where Draconus was or what he was doing. At first the dragon seemed surprised, but soon began as always to anticipate Lucian's moves. "You're angry, princeling. That's good for me, but dangerous for you," Draconus warned with a sneer. "Perhaps you're feeling sorry for your beastly friend that he can't be in here. You should be happy for him. He would never survive a real battle."

Lucian continued to rage on, the ringing sound of sword against scales seeming to echo in the room. For what seemed hours he tried to reach the soft spot that would bring an end to the battle. Each time he thought he was close, Draconus would move with lightning speed, removing the opportunity almost as soon as it was there.

"And your little green friend, he would be all too easy to defeat," Draconus hissed. "No spine at all."

Furious already, Lucian charged the dragon angrily; narrowly avoiding being knocked down by a sideswipe of Draconus' tail. "He's braver than any boy here and has more spine than you have," Lucian snarled as he brought his sword crashing against Draconus' belly. Sparks flew from the impact and Draconus curled around with a blast of fiery breath. Blocking it with his shield, Lucian found the spot he was looking for and thrust his sword between the dragon's arm and body. Everyone gasped and Lucian hissed in dragon, "You're dead, Draconus. You've just been beaten."

Draconus' eyes narrowed to barely slits and smoke rose in tendrils from his nostrils. "You speak well for a human," he replied, speaking also in dragon. "But, you got lucky, princeling."

"That wasn't luck," Lucian retorted, his accent clear and pronunciation perfect. "That was vengeance. Leave Kaelen and Adrian out of your commentary. They aren't here to defend themselves and only a coward preys on the defenseless."

Hissing angrily, Draconus said, "Watch your tongue, Prince Lucian. It could well be the death of you." He then rose and turned his attention to the awe-struck classroom. "Well, we've had one success among dozens of failures. Class is dismissed." He watched Lucian angrily as he left the room.

"Draconus," Vulcan asked as the boys were leaving, "did you let him win?"

"When in the last three thousand years have I ever allowed a princeling to win?" Draconus returned shortly. "No, I did not allow him a victory. He managed to sneak past my defenses."

"More than that," Vulcan added, "he put you on the defensive. Few of our students have reached that stage this quickly."

"I am well aware of that," Draconus snapped. "I'm the one who gets defeated, remember?"

"You'd best watch yourself," Vulcan warned. "I don't think the death strike I taught him is the one he wanted to use."

"Of course it's not the one he wanted to use. These boys know what a real strike is and had he used that one, you and I wouldn't be having this conversation," Draconus retorted snidely. "None of your princelings ever want to use the false strike. But since they can't very well kill their teacher, they don't have much of a choice do they?"

"I realize that, Draconus," Vulcan said. "I'm just saying that he was very angry."

"Angry, yet controlled enough to use it to his advantage," Draconus said thoughtfully, with almost a hint of respect. "Most humans aren't capable of controlling their emotions at all. He'll be dangerous if he ever meets with a dragon in the future."

"You think so?" Vulcan asked.

Draconus didn't answer right away. When he did speak, it was not to answer the question. "You are keeping me from my dinner and I'm very hungry. All that fighting turns quite an appetite." He turned and walked through the large gate into the cave-like lair underneath the castle.

Vulcan considered the conversation he'd just had with Draconus as he left the room. He also considered what he had watched during the class period. When Lucian had first begun the fight, it was without any sort of plan or rhythm. He was just hitting in anger and hoping to get lucky. For having no actual plan, he'd done very well. Then something had changed; he had gotten himself into a rhythm and had managed to begin anticipating Draconus' moves. Sometimes he had miscalculated, but for the most part he had been able to follow the patterns Draconus was setting up and come in for a successful blow. He wondered what would happen if Lucian was put into a double portion of dragon fighting the next year. As of yet, there was only one student slotted for two rounds of the class. That one had been at Calista's insistence, though Vulcan had not argued. George was one of his best students and would greatly benefit from the double portion. However, he was beginning to wonder if perhaps it would be wise to have Lucian join the class as well. Vulcan had no doubts that Lucian could stand his own against a dragon if the occasion called for it. But he found that he wanted Lucian to be able to do better than that. Scratching his chin thoughtfully, Vulcan left the dragon fighting classroom and headed to Calista's office. Upon entering, he said, "I need to talk to you about Lucian's schedule next year."

"Anything wrong?" Calista asked. "We're still planning on him having the class."

"No, nothing's wrong," Vulcan replied. "But I was wondering if he could be added to the double portion of dragon fighting with George."

"Really? Why the sudden change?" Calista asked.

Vulcan related what had happened during the class and Draconus' response. "I think a double portion would be of great benefit to Lucian."

"That's highly unusual. You don't normally have fourth year boys capable of defeating Draconus," Calista commented.

"No, the last time was Prince Martin and that's been some years ago," Vulcan replied.

"Martin," Calista repeated thoughtfully. "Adrian's father. Yes, I recall he did quite well in your class. He was a very brave prince."

"All that aside," Vulcan said, "I think Draconus is holding back from us. He is, as I'm sure you can imagine, very put out at having been defeated."

Calista smiled. "I'm sure I can imagine. Let me talk to him. If you indeed feel that it would be best to put Lucian in a double portion, than perhaps it would be best to consult Draconus. If he won't speak to us, I'll see Maeve and see if we can't glean a little more information about this." She rose and they walked down to the classroom. As though walking into her own room, she entered the cave. "Draconus, I'd like a word."

The dragon glared at her. "What are you doing here?" he sneered.

"As headmistress I can go where I please, Draconus," Calista replied, not in the least bothered by Draconus' tone and temper. "I need to speak with you about Lucian."

"And just why would I wish to speak of that little princeling?" Draconus asked, a bored tone in his voice.

"I need to know what happened this afternoon," Calista instructed.

Draconus growled. "Why does it matter, Calista? The boy got lucky."

"From what I understand it was more than merely getting lucky, Draconus," Calista said seriously. "It is imperative that I know your opinion on what happened."

"Well, Calista," Draconus said snidely, "it would appear you've already been told about it. I haven't the time nor the desire to speak about the class. If you'd like to join my supper, or rather join me for supper, you're welcome to stay."

Calista's eyes narrowed. "Draconus, you are on dangerous ground. I will find out what happened, whether from you or other sources is irrelevant. However, as you are the one who works most closely with these princes as they learn, you are the most qualified to assist me in understanding the strengths and weaknesses my boys have. Since you are too tired to discuss it with me now, I'll call on you in a couple weeks. I expect a better reception." Without waiting for Draconus to have a chance to respond, Calista left the cave, followed by Vulcan. "I hate that dragon," she said as they moved out of the classroom. "I will consider your request. In two weeks I will come again and see what we can learn from him. If he is still being stubborn, I'll consult with Maeve regarding this matter."

At supper, Jacobi and George were excitedly telling the others about Lucian's fight with Draconus. "It was so awesome! I wish you guys could have been there to see it," Jacobi said after they had finished telling every detail they could remember. "Although, I'm not sure what exactly you said to him, Lucian," Jacobi admitted. "I didn't do very well in dragon when I was in foreign language."

"What did you say?" Adrian asked.

Lucian stayed quiet. He didn't really want to talk about the class. He knew that he had gone out of control and that he had been rather unpleasant to everyone throughout the day. It wasn't his friends' fault that he had been having a bad day.

"I know what he said," George said when Lucian didn't answer. "He basically said that Draconus was a coward for picking on you two when you're not in the class to defend yourself. I think that made him madder than the fact that you beat him Lucian."

"Well, yeah, considering he basically said if I didn't watch my tongue I'd die," Lucian retorted. "Guys, it really wasn't that great. I was mad and got out of control. If anything, I got lucky."

"For being out of control, you sure did well," Kaelen teased.

"Yeah, but I've been a jerk to everyone all day," Lucian said, looking down at his plate and not at the others at all. "I'm sorry."

"Lucian, we all have bad days," Adrian replied.

"Yeah," Jacobi added. "Growing up isn't fun sometimes. Throwing these classes into the mix just makes it worse."

"I guess that's true," Lucian said. "I still don't think what I did in dragon fighting was right."

"I think it was if it gets that overgrown lizard to leave us alone," Kaelen replied. "Somebody needed to put him in his place. Why not you?"

"Not to change the subject, but how are your sonnets coming?" Adrian asked. He could tell Lucian wasn't feeling any better about the class, though he secretly agreed with Kaelen's sentiment. "I don't know that I'll be ready for the princesses to come next week."

"Terribly," Lucian moaned. "I hope your sister is forgiving. Or maybe I'll give her earplugs before I start and then she won't have to listen to me. I hate poetry, it's so lame."

"It's not that bad. I've got mine down. I'll help you out with yours if you want," George suggested

Lucian smiled. "I appreciate the offer, but the problem isn't just memorizing them. They're pretty awful."

"All the more reason to let George help you," Jacobi said. "He can help you smooth out the rough spots as well as memorizing them. To tell you the truth, he helped me polish mine out a little bit."

"I'll think about it," Lucian said. "I just don't want to deal with it right now."

"Understandable," Kaelen replied, "but you've only got a week to have these down and perfect. Airlia doesn't take kindly to shoddy work."

"Yeah, I know," Lucian shrugged. "I just don't want to work on it right now. I've got a big paper to write for Morghana and I think I'll get that taken care of first. Airlia's a lot more forgiving than Morghana is and I really screwed up today."

"I was wondering what had happened, but didn't want to ask you at lunch. You looked pretty mad," Jacobi pointed out.

"The reason I have little eyebrow left is because I accidently blew up my poultice," Lucian explained. "I guess I wasn't paying as close attention to how fast I was pouring as I needed to be."

"I'm guessing that didn't make Morghana happy," Adrian said.

"Frankly I think I'm lucky she didn't turn me to stone," Lucian admitted. "I think if she could have killed me with a glance she would have. She was really, really angry. I'm almost surprised that she just gave me an assignment and didn't strap me with some punishment."

"Lucian, I'm pretty sure the assignment is the punishment," George replied. "She must have thought having a tail wouldn't teach you as well as writing a paper."

Lucian nodded. "That's probably true."

"Well, I think we all have lots of homework tonight," Kaelen said. "Let's head over to the common room and get busy. No sense putting it off any longer."

"Unfortunately I have to agree," Adrian admitted. "Let's go."

The boys left the dining hall and went into the common room. They gathered around their favorite fireplace and each got out their own assignments. Soon they were busily working and there wasn't a sound to be heard amongst them. Lucian was working on his paper for Morghana. For a while it was difficult to concentrate on the paper. He got out his book for the class and began reading over the pages talking about flammable ingredients. As he read he got more ideas of what he could write and soon was ready to begin the paper. He wrote out the three pages she wanted and then he turned to his homework for other classes. It didn't seem fair that the fairies would add on extra homework as soon as the weather was becoming nice enough to actually do things outside. He looked out the window longingly. It would be so nice to go outside, just for a little while. The sun was still peeking over the horizon, as though trying not to sink any lower. Lucian knew that before long it would be dark. He sighed. Maybe tomorrow he'd have time to go out.

When the boys had finally finished all of their homework, they spent a little more time talking before going to their own rooms for bed. On arriving at his room, Lucian realized he really wasn't feeling tired, so he got out some paper and a pen before sitting down on his bed. He patted the side next to him and Rusty hopped up to sit next to him. Rubbing Rusty's head as he wrote, Lucian told his parents about all that had been happening. Then he got out a piece of paper and started writing to Allegra. When that letter was done, he started writing to Moira. Then he thought about his parents again. He hoped that they were enjoying themselves on their trip. He'd got several letters from them about the places they had visited and the things they were doing. As he thought about the letters, he realized that he hadn't checked his mailbox at all that day. He left the room and went to his letterbox. Opening it, he discovered a letter from his mother. He went back to his room and opened it.

Dear Lucian,

 I do hope that classes are going well for you. Your father and I are now working our way back home to Maltisten. It's been a wonderful trip and I'm so glad he planned this for us.

 Yesterday we visited the province that he rescued me from. It's a beautiful place with forests and gently rolling hills. Allegra would probably draw it beautifully, but we both know that I was never much of an artist.

Both sets of grandparents send their love and wish you the best in all you are doing. They are all so proud of you. Keep being my ray of sunshine!

Love,
Mother

Lucian smiled as he put the letter back into its envelope. It was a shorter letter than some, but it was just what he needed on a day like today. "Well, boy," he said after stretching his arms above his head. "I think we should probably get some sleep. What do you think?"

Rusty woofed and hopped off the bed before curling around the blankets in his own.

"I thought you'd agree with me," Lucian laughed. He got up and blew out the candles before crawling under the covers and drifting into a peaceful sleep.

The next week flew by in a flurry of homework and late-winter snowstorms. Saturday dawned cold with lightly fluttering snow outside. While some of the boys had hoped that snow would cancel the activities, the princesses arrived nonetheless, perfectly on time as always. Lucian was glad to see Moira and Allegra. He hugged his sister and smiled as Moira said, "So, you defeated the great dragon, I hear. Congratulations."

"But I didn't write to you about the dragon," Lucian said.

Moira laughed, "No, you didn't. But, George and Jacobi both wrote to their princesses about it and you did tell Allegra who in turn told me because she thought I already knew." With a teasing tone she chided, "You really shouldn't be afraid of telling me things like that. I think it's wonderful that you were the first in your class to defeat a dragon. Not many princes get that distinction."

Knowing it might get him into trouble, Lucian asked, "Was your dad the first in his class?"

While she looked a little sad, Moira didn't get upset by the question. "Yes, I believe he was. He wrote to Mother about it while they were in school."

"Well, I'm sorry I didn't write to you about that. It had been a rather long day anyway," Lucian said with an apologetic smile.

"I understand," Moira replied. "So how are your other classes going?"

Soon their friends joined them and they all went in to have breakfast together. There was much laughter and chatting until Calista rose and began to announce the schedule for the day. "Due to the weather, we have had to alter our usual festivities just a smidge. There will still be a scavenger hunt; however it will only take place in the castle. Following that activity, we will have a soup and salad luncheon here in the dining hall." She waved her wand and dozens of lavender pieces of paper flew through the air and into the hands of the princes. Lucian looked over the list. "This is the weirdest scavenger hunt list we've ever had," he said.

"None of these are items," Clarissa added as the others looked at their lists.

"They're all assignments or places," George explained. "Look, there's the sonnet assignment and here's an art thing. I'm guessing you ladies are responsible for that one. I haven't had an art class since my second year. And we have to do them in a specific room. No wonder fourth year students never win the scavenger hunt. We're going all over the place and whether or not this gets checked off is determined by how well we do the assignments."

"Well, this year it's even more impossible," Adrian said gloomily. He pointed to the other princes "All of their things are indoors. It'll be a lot easier for them to find."

"I suppose there's no use complaining. We may as well do the best we can," Eleanor said.

"Kaelen, I think you and I are supposed to work as a team for this activity. You received a paper with my name on it," Leticia pointed out.

"Yeah, I did," Kaelen replied, looking down at his list. "Our list is different from theirs even, so I guess we'll see how we do."

"No time like the present," Leticia replied with a smile, accepting Kaelen's offered arm. "See you back here, everyone."

Lucian's heart seemed to be bouncing between his throat and his shoes. The sonnet assignment. He'd been so busy with his other homework that he'd nearly forgotten about that. He hadn't had George help him at all and now as Moira looked at him expectantly, he desperately wished that he had. "Well, erm, where shall we start?" Lucian asked.

"I don't believe we have a choice, Lucian," Moira replied, looking at the list again. "The instructions at the top say we have to do each item in the order presented. It looks like first up is sonnets in Airlia's classroom."

Gulping, Lucian offered Moira his arm. "Well, I guess that's where we'll start." *And finish*, he thought miserably as he led Moira up the stairs into the classroom.

"You seem tense," Moira commented as they got to the classroom door.

"I'm just, well, I'm," Lucian stammered. Moira was still looking at him expectantly and he sighed. "Look, I'm a terrible poet, okay. I'm not at all romantic. There's not a single romantic word or bone in my whole body. This is going to be really embarrassing. Can we just take the loss on this one?"

"Absolutely not," Moira retorted. "I don't believe one word of that, Lucian. Not one word." Without waiting for Lucian to do so, she opened the door and marched into the room.

Airlia was waiting inside and said, "Ah yes, I thought you were up first, Lucian. Although, Lucian, you know a gentleman always opens the door for a lady."

"That was my fault, Airlia," Moira said. "I didn't wait for him to open it."

"I see," Airlia replied. "Well, it's time for your sonnets. Lucian has written a collection of beautiful sonnets for you and has chosen two of them to recite to you. When he has finished reciting, I need you to fill out this card for me." She handed Moira a green piece of paper. "After that, you will give me the card and I will give you the collection of sonnets. Hopefully Lucian won't be embarrassed by that."

Lucian wasn't sure that embarrassed was strong enough a word for what he felt right then. He was downright horrified. Moira turned to him and for a long moment he just stood there. "Well?" Moira asked.

"Your princess is waiting Lucian," Airlia chided gently. "Go ahead."

Taking a shaky breath Lucian began stumbling through his first sonnet. The more he said, the stranger the look on Moira's face. He couldn't tell if she was trying not to laugh at him or if she was trying not to cry. If it was the latter, he didn't think it was because he had written so beautifully that her heart had been touched by his words.

When he finished Moira asked, "Was that it?"

"Um, yeah, for the first one," Lucian said quietly.

A knock at the door caused Airlia to get up and leave. "I'll be only a moment," she said as she walked out.

As soon as the fairy was gone and out of earshot, Moira hissed, "The next one better be really good, Lucian. That was pathetic. I can't help you pass this if you spout off that kind of, of, well, there isn't even a word for that."

"I tried to tell you I was no good at this," Lucian whispered back.

Moira spied Airlia coming back and put on as sweet a smile as she could muster and said, "Whenever you're ready for the second one, I would love to hear it."

Lucian did not miss the sarcasm in Moira's voice. Feeling hurt, angry and a bitter need to prove himself, Lucian cleared his throat and closed his eyes. The second sonnet was the one Airlia had suggested would be the best to recite. In fact, it was her personal favorite of anything he had written in class. When he reopened them, he looked into Moira's eyes and began,

> "Softly hedged in by thick golden lashes,
> My love's eyes are a mystery of blue.
> Swirled emotions like ribbons and sashes
> They dance in and out with varying hue.
> At times like the sea on a calm spring day
> They are bright and clear, full of light and joy.
> Blue forget-me-nots under morning ray
> Twinkling and beautiful, yet shy and coy;
> Till they change and darken in sorrow's grasp
> And her eyes are deep, an unfathomed sea
> Of darkest blue till when her hand I clasp
> To ease her sadness and bring peace. I see
> In her eyes that she is meant to be mine
> And will treasure her 'til the end of time."

It seemed an eternity that Moira just stared at him. She didn't say anything and Lucian couldn't quite tell what was going through her mind. Her expression had changed so drastically from the first sonnet that he wasn't sure whether this had been a second failure or if maybe he had somehow succeeded. He couldn't even bring himself to say anything to her or ask what she thought. He just stared back into the eyes that had inspired him to write something that his teacher considered somewhat romantic.

"Okay, you two, the mooneyes have to stop now," Airlia interrupted. They both blushed as she continued, "Moira, write your thoughts down on the card please and then I'll give you the rest of the sonnets. Lucian, why don't you wait for her outside?" She shuffled him towards the door. As she was closing it behind her she said, "You did very well on the second sonnet, Lucian. Very well indeed."

Lucian waited outside for Moira for several moments. When she finally left the room she was holding a stack of papers. He recognized his handwriting on them and said, "Seriously, if you just want to throw those out without reading them, I'd feel a lot better."

"I can't do that, Lucian," Moira replied. "I have to see if any of them are as good as that second sonnet you recited. I knew I shouldn't believe that there wasn't a romantic bone in your body. Although, with that first sonnet I started to doubt you."

Lucian laughed. "Well, then keep the good one and throw the rest of them out. I can guarantee you that the last sonnet I did in there is the best of the bunch," Lucian insisted.

"I'd like to find out for myself," Moira said stubbornly. "Now, where are we supposed to go next?"

Knowing that he'd lost the argument, Lucian sighed and looked at the paper. A checkmark had appeared next to the sonnets. "We're supposed to go to the gym. I wonder what we're doing there."

"Only one way to find out," Moira answered. They walked down the stairs and into the gym where Raphael and Honoria were still working with Jacobi and Clarissa. Others were in the gym as well. "Oh, we must be dancing," Moira said as she watched Raphael try to help Jacobi learn the proper counting.

"Well, no use holding everyone else up. That's good enough I suppose," Raphael said. "The rest of you get into your pairs and begin the waltz with the music.

Lucian took Moira into his arms and they began the steps to the dance. It wasn't long before Honoria and Raphael were watching them. Honoria soon said, "You're both doing very well. I wonder though, Lucian, if you could loosen up a little. You look a little stiff. Much better, wouldn't you say dear?"

"Yes, they both dance very well. Alright, you two may go to the next part of your test," Raphael said.

The paper checked itself off and Lucian and Moira walked out of the room. "This is a test?" Lucian asked.

"Makes sense," Moira replied. "These are things we're being graded on. What's our next stop?"

"Profiles in Stefanos' room," Lucian said.

"Well, then let's go," Moira said. She had her hand resting lightly on Lucian's arm as they walked down the hallway.

When they arrived, Stefanos was standing chatting with a fairy that Lucian did not know. She had long, dark green hair and there were streaks of gold through her butterfly-like wings. Her gown fluttered about her in shades of green. When she turned, she revealed gold-flecked green eyes. "Moira," the fairy said with a smile, "you know what is expected; two profiles. There is a desk there along with a silhouette shade available for the second profile picture."

"Thank you Rhianna," Moira replied.

The fairy smiled again and then turned back to Stefanos, continuing their conversation. Lucian and Moira headed to the desk. "Do you want me to do the silhouette first or the regular profile?" Moira asked as she sat down.

"Whichever is easiest for you," Lucian said.

"Let's start with the silhouette. That one will take less time. You're going to have to stand very still for me," Moira added after a moment.

Lucian smiled, "I think I can manage that."

"And no talking," Moira instructed. "It breaks my concentration."

Doing as he was told, Lucian stood silently behind the shade. There was a candle lighting it and he could see his shadow on the shade. He'd never seen anyone do a silhouette before and bit his tongue to keep from asking Moira about it. After a while, she removed the screen and told Lucian to sit down next to the desk. "Stay sideways," she said as he started to face her. "A profile is always done from the side. This one you really have to stay still for me or I'll mess up."

"And I shouldn't talk," Lucian added before she could say it. "Don't worry so much. I'm sure you'll do fine."

Moira smiled and then began working. Lucian tried not to fidget in his seat or say anything as Moira worked along. She would sketch a line and then erase it several times before she was satisfied. In fact, they were in the room for very nearly an hour before she finally was happy enough with what she had done to take the two pictures to Rhianna. "You're allowed to move now," she said with a teasing smile as she stood up.

"Good, I have an itch between my shoulder blades that's driving me crazy," Lucian replied.

Laughing, Moira took the profiles to Rhianna. "Very nice, Moira," Rhianna said as she looked at them. "You two can move on to the next portion."

The morning progressed through various classrooms as they were put through different tasks. Sometimes Lucian was the one challenged and sometimes it was Moira. By the time they had finished, they knew they were not the first to return to the dining hall. In fact, there was quite a crowd of students already returned from their tasks. Several of their friends were already in the hall sitting at a table together. Lucian and Moira joined them and they soon began talking again. "That was actually quite fun," Leticia said as they were sitting down. "At least, I enjoyed it."

"It was fun," Kaelen admitted.

"I don't think the first part of ours was fun at all," Lucian replied. "But I enjoyed some of it."

"What was your first part?" Clarissa asked. "I know ours took quite a while because it was the dancing."

"Lucian recited some beautiful poetry to me," Moira said.

"You and I have a very different idea of beautiful," Lucian teased with a smile.

"Well, our first part," Leticia said, "was doing profiles in the art room. How many of you knew that Kaelen was such a good artist?"

Even with the fur, everyone could tell Kaelen was blushing. "I'm really not that good. I was just trying harder, I guess."

Leticia smiled, "He's being modest. His profile was actually very good. I'd say his was better than mine, but I'm also not much of an artist."

"I'm glad I didn't have to draw anything," Lucian replied. "We'd still be in that room."

The friends laughed and the conversation continued even as lunch began. They were enjoying the time together and hardly realized that the time was quickly escaping them. All too soon, Melantha was gathering her princesses to return to the school.

"I suppose I'll see you at the end of the year," Moira said as Lucian helped her with her cloak.

"Yeah, I'll see you then. I've enjoyed your letters, keep writing," Lucian added.

"I will as long as you promise not to withhold information from me again. I want to know about your successes, even if they don't seem like a big deal to you," Moira said teasingly.

"Fair enough," Lucian replied with a smile. "You do the same."

"I already have been," Moira teased. For a moment they stood in silence, neither wanting to be the first to say goodbye. As others walked around them, Moira finally said, "Well, goodbye Lucian. I'll see you in a couple months."

Lucian smiled. "Goodbye Moira. Enjoy the rest of your semester."

Moira returned his smile and waved as she turned away. She headed out of the castle with the other girls and was hardly surprised when Allegra was at her side. "Well, things seem to be going much better for you this time then last."

Laughing, Moira replied, "Well, since I finally got him to listen to me, there's no reason for me to feel frustrated."

"So then I would guess that the 'just friends' deal is off?" Allegra asked with a smile.

"Yeah, it's off," Moira said. "I can't spend my whole life hiding behind my fear, right?"

"Right," Allegra agreed. "Well, let's see how everyone else is doing."

Moira laughed and the girls got into a carriage with their other friends and spent the rest of the trip to Fair Damsels talking about their princes and daydreaming of weddings yet to come.

Chapter 7

It was not long at all after the princesses had visited, that the weather seemed to catch up to the idea of spring. Flowers blossomed and there was beauty everywhere; everywhere but the greenhouse. One sunny afternoon, the boys were in the greenhouse desperately wishing they could leave. The seeds they had planted had now sprouted and were no better now than they were when the boys had first planted them.

"Ouch!" George cried as one of the thistle plants he was working with shot a sharp spine into his arm.

"Careful now, George," Russett said, moving over to where George was working. "You don't want to give those a chance to shoot you. It doesn't take long for a rash to develop around the hit area." He gently pulled the spine out with a pair of tweezers before handing George a bottle of cream. "Here, that will ease the stinging."

"They'd be easier to avoid if I had Lucian's plant," George muttered bitterly. "Why doesn't his plant have any spines on it?"

Russett didn't have a chance to answer as he was now helping Kaelen pull out several spines. His plant seemed particularly vindictive and had shot a volley of spines while he'd been listening to George and Russett talk. While Russett helped pull the last of the spines out of his arm, Kaelen noticed that George was right. Lucian's plant didn't have any spines on it. Come to think of it, he wasn't sure that the seeds had ever been a problem for Lucian either.

"What was the question, George?" Russett asked as he walked away from Kaelen after handing him a bottle of cream.

"Never mind," George replied. "It was nothing."

Russett continued the class as it had begun. After the boys put their plants away and left, he went to the witches' hovel. Lucian's plant didn't have spines. In fact, none of the plants they had worked with had posed any dangers at all to Lucian. The other boys' plants were just as they should have been as though pulled from the pages of a textbook. Lucian, however, had thorny plants that didn't have thorns, spiked plants with no spikes and spitting plants that didn't spit. How could he teach Lucian the dangers of these plants if his plants were so domestic?

When he arrived, Lucretia was out in the garden tending to her wildflower garden. "Lucretia, might I ask you a question?"

"Certainly," Lucretia replied. "Which boy needs punished?"

"No, it's not that kind of question," Russett said. "Do you happen to know if Lucian has been given a gift regarding plants?"

"You know we're not supposed to reveal that kind of information, Russett," Lucretia replied, her tone teasing and yet serious at the same time.

Russett sighed, "Yes, I know the rules. But he's in a class about dangerous plants growing plants that just aren't dangerous. Even if I switch his pots with someone else's, the plants never do anything to him. I need to know if he has been given a gift in botany so that I can alter his coursework to best fit what he needs."

Lucretia didn't answer right away. Instead, she held one of the flowers closer to her and breathed in the fragrance. "You'll have to talk to Calypso, Russett," she said at length, looking over the top of the flower at him. "She's the only one with the authority to answer your question. Besides, even if he does have a gift, and I'm not saying he does, I'm not the one who bestowed it and therefore wouldn't be able to say exactly what it was anyway."

She turned back to her gardening and Russett knew the conversation was over.

He sighed and knocked on the door. When he was told to enter he did. "Well, Russett, this is a surprise. Is there something I can do for you?" Calypso asked.

"I know you're not usually to divulge when a gift has been given, but I need to know if Prince Lucian has been given a gift. His plants aren't doing what they should and it can't just be luck or having the wrong seeds," Russett explained.

Calypso looked at him for a moment. "As you know, gifts are highly personal and tend to be secretive as a general rule," she said after a moment. "If I tell you the nature of the gift Lucian has, you are sworn to secrecy and cannot reveal the information to anyone, other than Calista."

"I am aware," Russett replied. "Then Lucian has had a gift."

"Yes, I believe so," Calypso said. She pulled out a large, leather-bound volume from the bookshelf. "In this book we record every gift and curse we place. It is part of the way we do things. Our magic is instantly recorded the moment it is performed. Let me think. I suppose we could start with his first year and work our way up." She flipped through pages and soon said, "Ah yes, here we are. Gift bestowed on Prince Lucian of Maltisten by Althea. 'No thorn nor bramble shall bar his way and beauty shall be wherever he stays.' What I would say, Russett, is that Lucian will not have any dangerous features in the plants he grows and works with."

"But then why is he in this class?" Russett asked. "If plants pose no danger for him, he shouldn't need the class at all."

"You know plants incredibly well," Calypso replied. "I'm sure you can see areas that would still be a challenge for him. You must also consider his princess. I highly doubt she's been given the same gift. Anyhow, I'm sure you have classes coming up soon and I have things to attend to. Have a nice afternoon. If you have any further questions, you'll have to speak to Calista about this. She of course can be made aware of the gift, if she isn't already." Calypso then ushered Russett out of the hovel.

Russett considered what he had been told and made his way up to Calista's office. She was walking out as he came up the stairs. "Russett, what can I do for you?" she asked as he came into view.

"I have to talk to you about Lucian's schedule," Russett replied.

"Oh, you as well?" Calista said. "I was about to go speak to the witches about Lucian. That insufferable dragon still won't tell me anything. It's quite frustrating. Well, what seems to be the problem for you?"

"Calista, are you aware that Lucian has been given a gift in botany?" Russett asked, dropping his voice so as not to be overheard.

"I seem to remember there being something, but I'm not sure what precisely it is," Calista replied. "Is it causing problems in his classes with you?"

"None of the plants are at all dangerous for him," Russett said. "I expected Kaelen's plants to react more violently to him than the others based on our staff meeting over winter break. However, I was not at all prepared for Lucian to have absolutely no problems at all with the plants. The strange thing is some of them are starting to flower that shouldn't."

"How unusual," Calista said thoughtfully. "Well, I have to speak with Maeve and Calypso about Lucian anyway. I'll discuss with you what is spoken about when we all meet to set the boys' schedules for next year. I really must go now. I'm sorry to be so short."

Russett smiled and said teasingly, "No one could accuse you of being short, Calista. However, I will let you get to your meetings. I'll wait until later to figure out what to do with him. I'm sure things will work out to the best for everyone involved. If you do discover something highly important, let me know before the meeting please."

"I will do that Russett," Calista replied with a smile. She then continued on her way down the stairs and out the castle doors. She took a deep breath as she walked outside. It had rained the day before and the world smelled fresh and new. She loved springtime; it was as though the whole world awoke and came back to life. The buds on the trees were now tiny leaves that would continue to grow under the sun's warm rays. She could hear baby birds in their nests calling to their parents. It was a beautiful and wondrous time of year. She took one last breath before knocking on the hovel door.

The door was opened by Maeve. "Why, hello Calista. I was not aware you were coming."

"I'm sorry to come without announcing myself, I've just spoken with two of the teachers and could really use your help," Calista explained.

Maeve flushed. "Really? What can I do for you?"

"I have a question regarding Lucian and his quest. We're trying to get his schedule set for next year and he has proven himself to be very capable in dragon fighting and seems to have an interesting problem in botany," Calista said.

"Problem?" Maeve asked. "He should do quite well in botany."

"Well, that seems to be the problem," Calista replied. "May I come in?"

Maeve seemed to suddenly realize that they were still standing in the entryway. "Oh, of course! How silly of me. I'm sorry."

When Calista entered, she saw Calypso and Althea sitting together discussing something. "They look busy," she said as Maeve led her to where the maps were kept.

"Not really," Maeve said. "They're just having their afternoon chat before Calypso goes to Fair Damsel's to teach dream interpretation."

Calypso looked up on seeing Calista and said, "Well, this is a surprise. Is there something wrong, Calista?"

"No, nothing wrong," Calista replied. "I just needed some guidance. Draconus is being extremely stubborn, even for a dragon. He refuses to tell me anything about Lucian's victory a couple weeks ago."

"Lucian beat Draconus?" Morghana asked, coming into the room leaning heavily on her cane. "When?"

"It's been a couple of weeks now," Calista said. "I'm afraid I don't remember exactly which day. But Vulcan is thinking that it would be wise to have Lucian placed in a double class next year to fine tune those skills. I'd like to have talked to Draconus about it, but it seems Lucian has deeply wounded his pride and he refuses to discuss the matter. So, I was hoping that perhaps Maeve could get me some extra information while consulting the stars and that I could have a little more information about a gift Lucian was given."

"I take it that Russett came and spoke to you," Calypso said.

"Yes, he did," Calista replied. "I just want information that will be useful in setting up his schedule. It's very difficult sometimes to place them in their classes when there are unknowns."

"But my dear, this shouldn't have been unknown to you," Althea chided gently, also joining the group. "You were present when the gift was bestowed."

"Well," Maeve interrupted Calista before she could respond, "I'm afraid you're going to have to tell me what you wish to know first."

Calista sighed, "I really need to know what happened with dragon fighting and if there's any reason with Lucian's quest that he should have a double portion of the class for next year."

Maeve smiled and looked at the chart. "Well, as far as the class is concerned, it seems that Prince Lucian was having a particularly bad day when he defeated Draconus. I do hope Sister that you weren't too hard on him, you know you are quite picky," Maeve directed at Morghana.

"I'm going to be picky on you if you don't stick to the subject," Morghana warned in a quiet rasp.

"Oh, I mustn't be too far off," Maeve teased with a sweet, impish smile. "Anyhow," she continued when Morghana's eyes flashed at her, "Lucian was very upset and I would say allowed his emotion to get the best of him. But he was able to control those emotions to work for him instead of against him. What a unique quality. It will be very useful to him in the future. Looking at his quest, oh my. Well, I'd say double dragon fighting is just what Lucian needs. You may also consider his botany classes. He must continue those. Both of them"

"How can he continue in a class for dangerous plants if the plants show no danger to him?" Calista asked.

"Well, dear, you are only thinking of the one part of the blessing. You, like Russett, are being very one-sided. It is true that Lucian will not have his way barred by thorns or brambles. Plants that pose those dangers to anyone else will be altered by his very presence," Calypso explained. "However, there is another part to it. Beauty will follow Lucian wherever he goes in the plant life around him. I'm sure that Russett has noticed differences beyond just the lack of dangers in Lucian's plants. If not, perhaps he should take a closer look at Lucian's plants."

"What did Lucian do to warrant such a powerful gift?" Calista asked without thinking.

The witches looked at each other before all turning to Calista. Calypso spoke, though there was a chiding tone to her voice. "Calista, we cannot reveal that to you; gifts are highly personal as are the reasons behind them. Suffice it to say that great kindness is rewarded in kind. As Althea was then the head of our Sisterhood, she had the greatest power of any of us. You must remember that as the head, we have not only our own unique power, but also a smidgeon of the power of our Sisters. By being the one to bestow the gift, Althea could give a gift of great power. Had it been myself or one of the others, the gift may not have been as powerful. However, it is not for us to say why the gift was given."

Calista blushed slightly and apologized, "I'm sorry; I suppose that was prying. Is there anything else that you can tell me?"

"Well, you'll want to give Lucian classes that will utilize the unique qualities of his gift. I believe Russett is quite talented when it comes to arranging," Calypso said. "And I believe Maeve made it clear that a second class in dragon fighting would also be wise. Beyond that I'm afraid we have nothing to add. Now you must excuse me, I'm late." Calypso opened the door and walked outside before disappearing.

Calista smiled at the others. "Thank you for your insight." She then left to return to her office. She had much to do and it was going to make some definite changes to Lucian's schedule. Then she recalled her promise to Russett and walked towards the greenhouse. He was working with a class of younger students as she walked in. She stood at the back and smiled as she watched the boys work. When the class was dismissed and the last of the boys left, she said, "The plants Lucian has grown, what all have you noticed about them?"

"It would be easier to show you," Russett replied. He motioned for her to follow him back into another part of the greenhouse. When they arrived, Calista could easily see which plants were Kaelen's and which were Lucian's. It was a night and day difference. "As you can see, the plants that Lucian has planted lack spines. It's almost as though his spines were transferred to Kaelen's plants, actually. I know that's not the case, but it does look that way doesn't it?"

"It does," Calista agreed. "Lucian's plants have some flowers on them, don't they?"

"Yes, as long as they are plants that he himself planted," Russett replied. "The plants that the other boys planted don't do anything to him, but even if he works near them, they don't flower."

"Part of Lucian's gift is centered around beauty," Calista said. "The witches recommended that he do flower arranging. But they also said he should stay in the dangerous plants class. I think it would be best if you put him in a separate class from his peers. It wouldn't do for them to become aware of his gift. And I'm not only concerned about jealousy."

"I agree," Russett said understandingly. "There's really not much I can do for this semester. But next semester we'll see what we can do. How can I teach him about dangerous plants if they aren't dangerous to him at all?"

"I don't know, Russett," Calista shrugged. "You'll have to figure that one out on your own. Anyhow, supper will be beginning soon. I'd best get back to my office and make some notes before that."

"Of course," Russett replied. "Thank you."

"You're welcome," Calista said and walked out of the greenhouse.

That weekend the boys were going to the shops of Biberseth. They had ridden in from the school because several of them needed new trousers, especially Lucian. He had tried to make the trousers from home last as long as he could, but they were now far above his ankles and it was past time to get new ones. In fact, he'd needed to write to his parents because he needed an entirely new wardrobe. Nothing fit him at all. Not only had he grown several inches in height, but his shoulders had continued to come in, making his jackets and shirts uncomfortably tight. The letter he received back from his parents had money sufficient for two new shirts, two pairs of trousers and a jacket. It had also included the command that he stop growing; at least until summertime. Lucian was beginning to hope that he'd stop growing. He was now well over six foot and definitely taller than his princess. In fact, he highly doubted she could top him again. The problem he faced now was that he towered over most of his classmates; even the ones who had always been taller than him. "Are you done yet?" Kaelen had teased one day. "Pretty soon you'll be taller than me, and I'm a beast."

"I hope so," had been Lucian's reply. This conversation had been followed by another two inches of growth, much to Lucian's dismay. Worse than that was the appearance of a reddish shadow across his chin and upper lip. Because the dress code insisted upon no facial hair, he was soon told that he would need to shave. "Um, I can't," a rather embarrassed Lucian had said when Calista approached him.

"Why ever not, Lucian?" Calista asked. "You've never had a problem before."

Blushing, Lucian replied, "I've, um, never needed to shave before."

For a moment Calista looked at him and then said, "Oh dear. I hadn't thought of that. I just assumed…well, no matter. Go talk to Raphael. He's taught many a boy to shave in the past. He'll help you."

Now as they were in a clothing shop, the others were sitting waiting while Lucian was having a final fitting in his new clothes. "That looks pretty good," the young seamstress said. "How do they feel, Prince Lucian?"

"Perfect," Lucian replied with a smile. "They're very comfortable."

"Well then, come over to the counter and we'll get this paid for and you can head back to school. Should I expect you again soon?" she asked teasingly.

"No, I think you left enough room in these to have the hems redone if needed," Lucian said. "Thanks," he added as he handed her the money for the clothes. "Do you mind if I just wear these out?"

"Not at all," the seamstress laughed. "In fact, shall I keep those old things for you to give to the second hand shop down the street?"

"That would be great," Lucian said. "Let me make sure I didn't leave anything in my pockets." He checked over the old clothes and got any last things out of the pockets and checked that he'd really taken off all the medals before handing them back to her. "Thanks again," he said.

"You're most welcome," she replied as she ushered the boys from the shop.

As they walked out onto the street they could see an ice cream cart not far from where they were. "I've got a little extra. Ice cream sound good to everyone?" Lucian asked.

"I won't say no," Adrian replied teasingly.

The boys headed over to the cart and bought some ice creams before slowly walking to the carriage they'd come in with Phillipa. Phillipa was standing next to one of the horses as they approached. "Got everything you needed and more I see," she teased as they came closer.

"Yep, we even got one for you," Lucian replied, handing her a cone.

"Oh, why thank you," Phillipa said. "You certainly didn't need to."

"Should we finish these outside the carriage?" Jacobi asked.

"That would certainly make me happier and keep the carriage cleaner," Phillipa replied. "Besides, it's difficult to drive one handed. I'm capable of it, but would rather not get ice cream down my front." They laughed and finished their ice creams while continuing to chat. When everyone had done she asked, "Are we all ready to go back to the school now?"

"Yep," the boys said and they got into the carriage.

Soon they were back at the castle and getting their things put away. Lucian wrote a letter to his parents thanking them for the money and telling them that he now had clothes that fit him properly. Afterwards, he put the envelope in his mailbox and then went back to his room to work on some of his homework. While he was working, Rusty brought him a ball and nosed it closer to him. "I've got to do my homework, boy," Lucian said. Rusty looked up at him and whined softly. "Can you wait for about ten minutes so I can finish this assignment? Then we'll go outside for a while."

Rusty picked up the ball and went to the window. Lucian shook his head and smiled as he turned back to his assignment. When he finished he got up and stretched before grabbing his bag and whistling for Rusty. When Rusty was at his side, the two went downstairs and out onto the lawn. Lucian saw Kaelen and George sitting under the maple tree. "Can I join you?"

"We're doing homework, but yeah, have a seat," George replied.

Lucian sat down and took the ball from Rusty before throwing it as hard as he could. As Rusty bounded away after it, he opened one of his books.

"Your dog wanted out too, huh?" Kaelen asked as Knight came running back with a stick.

"Yeah," Lucian replied. He watched Rusty find the ball and start loping back. "I can't say I blame him. It's nice out and I didn't particularly want to spend the day in my room."

"Me neither," George said. He rubbed the top of Queenie's head and took a ball from her before tossing it. "I figured Queenie and I could use a break from being inside."

For most of the afternoon the boys alternated between throwing things for their dogs and working on their homework. When the sun started slowly going down, the boys headed back inside, knowing that it would soon be suppertime. When they arrived inside, they joined their other friends for an enjoyable meal.

The end of the semester came rapidly. It seemed all too soon that the boys were in finals and that they were getting ready for the end of year meeting with their princesses. Adrian had shrunk again and Gelasia was desperately trying to make shoes for him that would disguise the lack of height as well as look somewhat normal. The biggest problem was that his skin was beginning to become paler and sometimes took on a greenish tinge, making him constantly look ill. The boys spent as much of their time outside as they could in hopes that they could tan away the odd color. When that didn't work, Gelasia taught Adrian how to powder his face with a tinted powder so that he would look normal. The worst change was that anytime Adrian heard buzzing, his tongue would shoot out. "You can't do that in front of Allegra. She will notice and she will become offended," Lucian warned the day the princesses were coming.

"I'm not trying to," Adrian retorted. "It's the bugs. They're buzzing and I just can't…" he was interrupted by his tongue shooting out again. "I can't help it. What am I going to do?"

"Just ignore the buzzing," George said. "Don't listen to it. Put all your attention on Allegra."

"If worse comes to worse," Jacobi added, "turn around when you hear the buzzing and then it won't be a problem."

"It's not that easy to ignore," Adrian said. "And I don't necessarily know when I'm going to stick my tongue out."

"Well then glue your mouth shut," Kaelen suggested. The others glared at him and he laughed, "I'm just teasing, guys. Adrian, you're going to have to concentrate on not doing it. Otherwise, Allegra's going to notice that there's something different about you."

Adrian groaned. "This is going to be a disaster. Even if she doesn't notice, someone's bound to."

Their conversation was interrupted as they saw the carriages from Fair Damsel's begin pulling into the drive. They waited patiently for their princesses. Kaelen excused himself to go up to his room. Calista had told him that, as with the winter meeting, he would need to spend this meeting in his room. He found that he really didn't mind too much. Since he didn't actually have a princess of his own, there was no real reason for him to be there anyway. But he did miss the time with his friends and their princesses. He was very fond of all of them and it made him feel less isolated when he was able to be with them.

The others waited for their princesses and were soon leading them inside for breakfast. The meal passed with pleasant conversation. Soon, parents were filtering into the building for the meetings with their children and for the graduation ceremony. Adrian was spared having much time to talk to Allegra as the ladies began planning their annual trip to the sea. "It's become a sort of tradition, hasn't it?" Lavinia asked with a smile as they chatted about what they could do.

"It has and we enjoy every minute of it," Alexandra replied. "I'm so glad that our children were paired together. I don't know that we would have met otherwise. And I enjoy your friendship."

"I think we've all gained from the experience," Lavinia agreed.

"Didn't you say there was a wonderful tailor in Maltisten?" Nana asked as they were continuing to make arrangements.

"Yes, I go to Tom for everything," Alexandra said. "He's getting older, but there's still no finer hand with a needle anywhere. And he has such an eye; always knows exactly what color should be used. His granddaughter is also quite good, but she's only there during winter and summer breaks. During the school year she works as a maid at Fair Damsel's."

"It must be lonely for him to not see her for so much of the year," Nana said thoughtfully.

"I'm sure it is," Alexandra replied, "but they need the income. And I know that the other shopkeepers in that area look in on him to see that he wants for nothing. He's quite well-liked."

"Well, during our visit we must go there," Nana insisted. "I need a few new gowns and as gifted as Moira is, she should work on her own wardrobe."

"I didn't know Moira sewed," Alexandra said. "I quite enjoyed sewing when I was younger. Every now and again though it's nice to have something you didn't have to make yourself."

"Moira is quite the seamstress," Lavinia replied. "She used to tell me that she wanted to do that when she grew up. I'm afraid I may have been a bit hard on her when I told her such occupations weren't for princesses."

"Yes, but what a gift to have for her own use," Alexandra said.

The conversation ended as the meetings with Calista and Melantha began. Lucian and Lysander waited together outside Calista's office. Lysander was looking at his son. "You weren't kidding when you said you'd grown a lot. I had hoped it was a bit of an exaggeration."

"I'm afraid not, Dad," Lucian replied. His pants were once again too short and he knew that he would soon need new ones.

"Your voice is deeper, you've been shaving and you certainly aren't short anymore," Lysander said with a smile. "I do believe you're taller than I am now."

Lucian laughed and told him about the sudden growth spurts and that he had been teased that if he continued at that rate he'd soon be taller even than Kaelen.

"I assume his parents haven't changed at all since last time?" Lysander asked.

Shaking his head, Lucian said, "No, they haven't. That's why he's not with the rest of us. Calista said that if we stay after everyone else has gone, we can take him home then. She knows it's a bit inconvenient…"

"Nonsense," Lysander interrupted. "There's nothing inconvenient about it. We'll simply enjoy some extra time at the school."

They stopped as Calista welcomed them into her office. When they had all sat down she began, "Well, King Lysander, I'm sure I don't have to tell you how pleased we are with how Lucian is progressing. He is one of our top students."

"Thank you," Lysander said as Lucian blushed to the roots of his hair.

"Lucian, you've been doing an excellent job this semester and throughout this year. Morghana is quite pleased with your progress and asks that you continue your study over the summer. I know that may be difficult with summer plans, but you may consider going over the book at least once, just to say you did," Calista said with a knowing smile and a teasing lilt. "Vulcan was highly impressed by your performance and has recommended that you be in his class twice next year. I have agreed to this as you will see in your schedule. All of the teachers had nothing but positives to say about you. You're doing remarkably and we are all quite proud of you."

Lucian wasn't sure that his face could get any redder, but he was sure it must have matched his hair by the time he finally stammered a quiet, "Thanks."

Calista smiled and continued, "Next year will bring many changes. Some of your more routine classes will be dropped. You are coming quite close to graduating. Only two more years left with us before you begin your quest. During these next two years we will truly emphasize your quest and the skills you will need to be successful. Use your summertime to continue honing the skills that you can at home. We of course will continue your instruction when you return. Do either of you have any questions?"

"I don't believe so," Lysander said. "Lucian?"

"No, well, yes," Lucian replied. "Does that mean I won't have math or those classes anymore?"

Calista laughed, "I suggest you look at your schedule, Lucian. That will tell you which classes you will no longer be taking and which you will still be responsible for. There is also a supply list of course so that you can get any new supplies you may need. Do have a good summer. King Lysander, I'm sure Lucian has probably already told you, but if you intend on taking Kaelen home with you again this summer, I'm going to have to ask that you stay after all the other parents have left. Particularly his own. It's tragic that it must be this way, but…"

"Lucian has apprised me of the situation," Lysander interrupted. "We have no problem waiting for him to be ready and for the appropriate time. I'm only sorry that he must be put through this."

Smiling, Calista said, "As always, King Lysander, you are a great man of fine quality and we appreciate your generosity and that of your wife. Extend our thanks to her as well."

"It would be my pleasure to do so," Lysander replied as they all stood.

"In that case, I will see you at the beginning of next school year. Have a very pleasant summer," Calista said.

The two replied in like and then they went downstairs to await the graduation ceremony. They sat together with the other families, taking note to sit close to their friends. As they watched their older peers cross the stage, Lucian couldn't help but be struck by how soon his own graduation day was coming. "Adrian," Lucian whispered leaning over, "in two years that will be us!"

"Scary, isn't it?" Adrian replied.

Eleanor and Leticia watched particularly as Benjamin walked across the stage for the copy of his quest. They listened as Calista commended him on his honor and wished him well. They cheered with everyone else and watched as he came back to sit with them again. As he did, Eleanor had a fleeting feeling that this would be the last time she saw her older brother. She frowned as the thought came and he winked at her. "Don't worry, sis, I'll be the best Prince Charming there ever was," Benjamin whispered as he sat between his sisters. He took each of them by the hand and squeezed them.

"I'm sure you will be," Eleanor replied with a smile, squeezing his hand back.

"Without a doubt," Leticia agreed.

They continued to watch in silence and watched as the princesses went through their part of the ceremony. Many of them disappeared as soon as the diploma touched their hands.

"Be safe, Marissa," they heard George whisper as a young woman who looked so much like him that it was obvious she was his sister disappeared from the stage.

"Were you two close?" Jacobi asked.

"Not as close as Samantha and I," George explained, "but yes, we're pretty close. We often get asked if we're twins."

"I'm sure she'll be fine," Eleanor said kindly, taking George's hand with the hand her brother wasn't holding.

George smiled at her and squeezed her hand before they turned their attention back to the graduation taking place.

When it was finished, the group of friends and families enjoyed a sumptuous feast filled with laughter and talking. Lucian watched one by one as each of his friends' families left. When asked why his family was waiting he would simply look up the stairs and the others understood. George leaned over and whispered, "But Kaelen's family was among the first to leave."

"Calista doesn't want to risk any of the others seeing him," Lucian replied quietly.

"Oh, I suppose that's wise. She doesn't want rumors to reach them," George commented thoughtfully. "Well, have a good break."

"You too, George," Lucian said. "I'll see you in August."

Year 5

Chapter 1

Summer began with Lucian's family going directly to the seaside castle. While it would be a few weeks before their friends would join them, they wanted to enjoy some family time there beforehand. At times, Kaelen felt a little awkward to be included in the family activities since he wasn't actually a part of the family at all. He found that as they had picnics by the seashore and went on outings he missed Anna more than ever. The secret notes she had sent him were all he had of her; other than a rather poor drawing he had done. He was still working on it, though Stefanos had said that it wasn't too bad. He continually tried to improve the sketch so that he could perfectly capture his sister's face. At times when he was alone in his room, he would sit with his grandfather's ring and think of Anna until an image of her smiling face appeared before him.

One afternoon as they were on a family picnic, Kaelen was sitting alone with Allegra. "Kaelen, Anna asked me to give this to you but to wait until after the semester was over," Allegra said, reaching into a pocket on her sundress and handing a folded piece of paper to him. "She said she hopes you're doing well."

"I wish she could tell me herself," Kaelen said, a bitterness darkening his tone.

"Someday she will, Kaelen," Allegra assured him. "You just have to be patient."

Kaelen laughed gruffly. "Patience never was my strength."

Allegra smiled and said, "Me neither. Perhaps that's part of your test; to gain patience. Anyway, there's her last letter for you from last school year. She said to wait until about halfway through the summer before giving it to you, but you've looked so miserable the last couple of days that I thought you could do with reading it now."

"Have I been that bad?" Kaelen asked.

"Not bad, you just look depressed and miserable," Allegra explained. "None of us can blame you. You're in a very difficult position and we understand why you'd feel sad. But I thought getting a last note from your sister might cheer you up. I'm sure you must miss her terribly."

"I do," Kaelen admitted.

"Shall I go join the others so you can read in privacy?" Allegra asked, motioning out where her parents and Lucian were splashing in the shallows.

"There's no need for you to leave," Kaelen replied, opening the letter. "I appreciate your company."

"Then I'll stay right where I am," Allegra said. She tilted her face towards the sunshine and sat silently as Kaelen read the note.

Dear Kaelen,

I'm sure this will reach you before the middle of summer. Allegra is such a wonderful person and reads people incredibly well. I hope that this will cheer you up and want you to know that I'm doing alright. I miss you, as I'm sure you already know. School ended on a high note; I got E's in all of my classes. Next year I'll be starting a portraiture class, just like you. I'm sure I won't be any good at all, but I'll certainly try my best.

Thank you for the lovely handkerchief. Melantha gave it to me during our last meeting. Mother and Father had no idea who it was from and so Melantha told them that it was from Ge-

lasia, the fairy at Charming Academy. She said she had too many and was giving them to some of the girls she knew from the meetings. Mother and Father believed her, but I knew looking at it that you had made it. It's absolutely lovely and I will keep it with me always.

Well, I'm taking quite a risk in writing right now. Mother isn't far away, so I'll close and get this to Allegra. I hope you are well and I miss you.

Love,
Anna

Kaelen folded the letter and placed it in his pocket before asking, "How was she able to write this?"

"Several of us girls stood around her making a show of talking to her so that she could write without drawing your mother's attention," Allegra replied. "She was so touched by the handkerchief you made that she wanted to write to you right away. She couldn't wait for the beginning of next year to thank you for it."

"So you know I made it," Kaelen commented, blushing slightly.

"Yes, Anna told us all about the dresses and then the handkerchief when she got it," Allegra said. "But don't worry, we won't tell the boys about your sewing. You are quite good though."

"Thanks," Kaelen said, "on both counts. I'm not sure the boys would find my sewing to be a very masculine hobby."

Allegra laughed, "Not all of your hobbies have to be tough and manly, Kaelen. But I agree that they might not understand why you enjoy it and I won't tell any of them. Besides, I think everyone has a secret hobby that they don't tell anyone about because they don't think they'll react well to it."

"Well, you know my secret hobby," Kaelen said teasingly. "What's yours?"

With a conspiratorial smile Allegra replied, "Fencing. I used to steal Lucian's toy swords and practice what I watched Daddy teach him."

"Do your parents know?" Kaelen asked, shocked that Allegra would even consider picking up a sword, let alone use it.

"Daddy does and he's probably told Mom; but if he has she has not said anything to me as yet," Allegra said. "You see, he caught me one day playing around with Lucian's sword and asked what I was doing. I may tease Lucian about being a terrible liar, but he isn't the only one, so Daddy soon found out what I was really doing. He said if I was going to learn swordplay that I had to learn it properly. So he's been secretly teaching me for years. I'm nowhere near as good as Lucian is, but it's a fun hobby nonetheless. Though much like your sewing, I doubt the other ladies would find it to be a good use of my time."

"You're lucky," Kaelen replied. "Our fencing master would have a conniption fit if you walked into his fencing hall. It's like his sanctuary."

"I'm sure most men would be shocked by such an indelicate hobby in a female," Allegra said. "But, I find I don't really care what most people think. After all, there's only one me and I only have one life to live. I'm going to live it to the fullest and enjoy myself along the way. If that means that I occasionally do things that are out of the ordinary, so be it."

"That's an interesting take on life," Kaelen said.

"It's a truthful one," Allegra replied. "If I can't be myself, who am I supposed to be?"

Kaelen didn't have a chance to respond as the others came in from the ocean's surf to join them for a picnic lunch. There was laughter and talking and Kaelen found himself enjoying the activity more than he would have otherwise. He was sure that part of it was the letter gently tucked away in his pocket. But he also thought that a large part of it was being surrounded by a family of friends who had made him one of their own. He didn't have to feel like a loner or that he was intruding on them. They thought of him as one of them; he belonged there as much as anyone else. With a smile, he joined in the fun and conversation for the rest of the afternoon.

The next week, Adrian's family came out to the beach. Adrian had been desperately trying to keep his family from noticing that he was starting to change. He'd noticed brown flecks in his eyes and hoped that his mother wouldn't notice. He wasn't as concerned about Nana, who he was sure already suspected something, or Moira who never really looked at him much anyway. But he knew that his mother would notice a change like that if he wasn't careful. After all, he'd always looked so much like his dad that if suddenly something was different, his mother was bound to notice. So he spent mealtimes looking at his plate and desperately trying to ignore the sound of bugs outside. They sounded so…tasty.

On arriving at the seaside castle, they were shown to their rooms and then both families went out to the beach. Kaelen and Lucian went with Adrian to a more secluded part of the beach where he could swim without people noticing how pale he had become. "I hope you brought some of that powder with you that Gelasia made," Kaelen said as Adrian got in the water.

"Yeah, but it's not going to cover all of me," Adrian replied. "I save it for when people are really going to notice that I look different." He ribbeted and then covered his mouth. "I wish that would stop. It was terrible the other day, Mother kept looking over at me like I was doing it on purpose. I tried to say it was hiccups, but I'm not sure she believed me. I know Nana didn't. Do you think maybe she knows already?"

"How would Nana know?" Kaelen asked.

Adrian related the story of Nana's great-great grandmother who happened to be a fairy. "She notices things that the rest of us don't," he explained. "It's not good, especially when I absolutely can't tell my family about this right now."

"Eventually they're going to find out," Lucian stated. "What are you supposed to do then?"

"I don't know," Adrian replied. "But when Calista met with Mother and I, she had Mother leave for a while so that she could tell me not to let my family know what is going on. I figure at the rate I'm going, I'll be lucky if Mother hasn't figured something out by the time summer's over. Look at my eyes!"

"They're green," Kaelen said.

"Yeah, but they've got brown flecks in them now and the green is starting to look yellowish," Adrian complained. "Mother absolutely loved Dad's eyes. She's bound to notice that mine aren't the same green anymore."

"Well, don't look her in the eye," Lucian suggested.

"Yeah, because that's real easy to do," Adrian scoffed. "Who does Calista think I'm kidding? I can't keep this a secret all summer. And I don't know what I'll do if Allegra figures anything out."

"We'll keep her from noticing," Lucian said.

"Just don't look deeply into her eyes anytime soon," Kaelen teased.

Adrian blushed, "I wouldn't anyway." The others looked at him, clearly disbelieving. "Okay, so maybe I like her, but I'm not going to have a mushy staring contest with her. She'd win too easily. Ribbet! Ugh!" Adrian moaned as his tongue shot out and then back into his mouth. "I think I just ate a bug."

Lucian and Kaelen started to laugh. "Come on, let's go for a swim," Lucian said. "Then you'll be a little farther away from the bugs."

The boys put on swim goggles and enjoyed the feel of the cool ocean water against their skin. Kaelen was enjoying the strange, yet pleasant, sensation of the water running through his fur. Like Lucian, he was a fairly strong swimmer and would spend long periods of time under the water. He scraped at the bottom looking for shells. It was almost amusing watching the fish dart away from him. To them he must have looked like an otherworldly monster with floating tentacles of hair. It wasn't until he realized that the fish were fleeing without seeing him that he started to feel a little nervous. He turned slowly and saw a large shark heading in his direction. Quickly kicking to the surface he called out to Lucian, "Shark!"

Lucian immediately turned, "Where?"

"About twenty yards that way," Kaelen said pointing.

"Okay, swim with the current towards shore without making too many sudden moves," Lucian instructed, also beginning to go towards shore. "How fast is it swimming?"

"I don't know; I wasn't paying attention!" Kaelen retorted, trying to downplay the panic he felt. "Where's Adrian?"

"He went to shore a while ago," Lucian replied, calmly continuing his swim towards shore. "He said his eyes hurt and they were really bugged out, so we thought some time out of the water would do him good." Lucian saw a fin slice through the water. That must have been the shark Kaelen had seen. "Okay, that shark is moving pretty quick, try not to panic, but keep moving towards shore."

"Don't have to tell me twice," Kaelen muttered. His eyes grew wide when he saw the fin disappear. "Uh, Lucian? Where did it go?"

"Swim faster, Kaelen," Lucian replied, his voice coming from behind Kaelen. "You're almost to shore and he thinks he can still get a bite. Hurry!"

Kaelen turned slightly to see that Adrian and Lucian were both standing on shore. He felt panic building inside him. He knew he was close to shore, but this part remained fairly deep almost to the shore itself. He felt something bump against him and jumped sideways, seeing the shark come to his side. He could barely hear Adrian and Lucian calling to him over the thunderous beating of his heart. The only way he was going to avoid becoming a snack was if he took the shark out first. Feeling rash, he dove under the water, ignoring Lucian's shouts to keep swimming. He saw the shark coming at him and charged at it, wrapping his arms around the shark's body. Crushing it against him, he fought to keep it from wriggling free. He was suddenly grateful for the silky fur that covered his body and protected him from the shark's rough skin. As the shark thrashed wildly, trying to break free, Kaelen concentrated on holding it tighter, not loosening his grip until the shark quit fighting.

"Kaelen! Kaelen, are you alright?" Lucian asked as he saw Kaelen come back to the surface. He had sent Adrian to go get his parents.

"Yeah," Kaelen replied, coughing up water as he pulled the shark to shore and threw it on the beach. "Yeah, I'm fine."

Lucian sighed in relief before spouting, "You idiot! Just because you're a beast does not mean that you can just take on a shark like that! You should have kept swimming. You were so close to shore."

"Hey, I beat it didn't I?" Kaelen pointed out stubbornly.

"That's beside the point, Kaelen," Lucian said, exasperation clear in his voice. "You could have been injured, or worse killed. How would I have explained to my mother that you decided to be fish food?"

Kaelen was spared answering as he saw people running towards them. "Oh my goodness, Kaelen, are you alright?" Alexandra asked as she and the others came running up the beach towards him. She wrapped a dry towel around him and started rubbing the water out of his fur. The others crowded around him as well, asking the same question.

"I'm fine, really," Kaelen said, almost embarrassed by the amount of attention he was getting.

"You're bleeding, son. Let me see that leg," Lysander demanded.

Kaelen hadn't even noticed that his leg hurt at all, but now he felt a rush of stinging as saltwater ran into the wound. "It can't be too bad, right?" he asked.

Lysander was shaking his head. "I don't know how you got so lucky, but apparently you don't taste very good. You've got a nasty bite here, but luckily he didn't take your leg as a souvenir."

"No, I took him," Kaelen replied, nodding to the dead shark lying on the beach.

Everyone turned and looked. "How did you manage to wrestle that thing?" Nana asked. "It's quite as big as you are."

Alexandra frowned as Lucian and Lysander helped Kaelen get to his feet. They had wrapped one of the towels around the leg to stop the bleeding until they got to the castle. "I'd like to know what the shark was doing in these waters. We never see sharks out here. At least, not that I can remember."

"I don't know dear," Lysander replied as they started heading towards the castle. "I suppose there wasn't enough food in its normal territory. Anyway, I'll send someone down for that shark. No use wasting a perfectly good fish."

"I guess I'm a pretty good fisherman," Kaelen said, trying to lighten the situation as Lucian and Lysander steadied him on their slow walk back to the castle.

There was some laughter and Lucian teased, "Yeah but next time you decide you want to catch a shark, use a fish as bait and not yourself."

Everyone laughed and they continued up to the castle. Upon getting inside, Lysander instructed for the cook's assistant to go and collect the shark from the beach before asking the butler to bring him some hot water and clean rags. "I'll also need the ointment in the back cupboard of my room," Lysander added.

"Right away, sire," the butler replied before leaving to do as he'd been asked.

"Alright, sit down, Kaelen," Lysander commanded. He got Kaelen's leg propped up and said, "Alexandra, dear, would you get me my shaving kit? I'm going to have to get rid of some of this fur to be able to see how bad this really is."

"Lavinia," Nana said, "why don't we take the girls out to the gardens for a while? I'm sure King Lysander has this well under control."

"An excellent notion," Lavinia replied. She and Nana then shooed the girls from the room, leaving Kaelen, Adrian, Lucian and Lysander in the room. When Alexandra returned with the shaving kit, she also left, joining the other ladies out in the gardens while the butler walked into the room.

"Here's the hot water and the rags, sire. I'm afraid though you've run out of ointment," the butler said.

"Wait, is it the anti-infection poultice that Mom uses when we get scraped on the coral?" Lucian asked as Lysander frowned.

"Yes, it is. We're going to need that to keep this clean and prevent it from becoming infected," Lysander replied.

"I know how to make it," Lucian said. "Please, if someone can get me the ingredients, I can make it up and then we'll have enough for this and to spare."

"Are you sure?" Adrian asked.

"Please tell me this isn't the poultice you blew up," Kaelen added.

Lucian rolled his eyes. "No, this was one of the basic poultices. I didn't have any problem with it at all." He turned back to his dad. "Please, I know I can do this and you need it."

Lysander looked at his son with pride. "Tell the butler what you need."

Smiling, Lucian ran after the butler and gave him a list of ingredients that he would need before then going into the kitchen to ask the cook if he could borrow the stove.

While Lucian was preparing the poultice, Lysander gently shaved around the bite before beginning to wash away the dried blood. He used a set of tweezers to gently pull out a tooth from Kaelen's leg. "Well, dinner isn't the only souvenir you get," he said with a lightly teasing tone. "You've got yourself a rather fine shark tooth, once I get the blood off of it."

"Really?" Kaelen asked. "That's cool!"

Lysander laughed and shook his head. "Only a teenage boy would think getting bit by a shark and having a tooth stuck in his leg was cool."

"I think it's cool," Adrian said defensively, looking over Kaelen's shoulder at the tooth.

"That just proves my point the more," Lysander chuckled. "You're a teenage boy."

"Well, I don't want to get bit by a shark," Adrian added.

They laughed and Lysander continued working. Some of the cuts were wide enough that Kaelen needed a few stitches. Lysander told Adrian where to find the emergency kit with thread and needle and began stitching up the bigger cuts when Adrian got back. As he was finishing the last one, Lucian came in with a poultice. "Here, it's ready."

"Alright, thank you, Lucian," Lysander said, taking it from him. "When I finish, put the extra in the ointment bottle please."

"I'll do that," Lucian replied.

"This is going to sting a little, Kaelen," Lysander warned. He gently rubbed the ointment over Kaelen's leg and Kaelen bit his lip to keep from crying out in pain. When he'd finished, Lysander wrapped clean rags around the wound and said, "There you are. You won't be able to go in the water until those stitches come out. But, you know Allegra always welcomes company on the beach."

Adrian went to get the others and everyone came inside. They decided, in light of Kaelen's injury, to spend the rest of the afternoon inside the parlor enjoying some friendly chatter. Nana offered to read aloud the latest letter she'd gotten from Uncle Sebastian. "It would seem," she said before beginning, "that someone hinted rather strongly that he doesn't write often enough."

Moira blushed as Nana gave her a significant look.

"Please do read the letter," Alexandra said. "We've heard quite a bit about your brother from Allegra and Lucian."

"Very well," Nana replied with a smile. She read:

Dear Bethany, Lavinia, Adrian and Moira,

I do hope this letter finds all of you in good spirits. I'm having a fabulous time down in southern Sanalbereth. It has been quite an adventure I can assure you. The climate here is so very nice. It's no wonder Lu-

> cian's grandparents decided to move down here. By the way, should you see him or dear Allegra, please tell them that I say hello. Anyway, I do love this area. It's quite beautiful and filled with interesting places to go and things to see. I rather think I could build a little cottage here and live out my days quite happily.

"No he couldn't," Adrian interrupted. "Uncle Sebastian hates staying in the same place long."

"Shh," Moira chided and Nana continued.

> This week I will be in Rendorlin. There's a very quaint little village in the very most southern tip of the province that has a most fascinating summer festival every year. I've been meaning to see it again for some time and decided that there is, of course, no time like the present. Per your recommendation, I am staying at The Dancing Fairies. The proprietress is a charming woman. But Bethany, you did not tell me all the details of your last stay. As soon as she found out I was related to you she told me all about your kindness and generosity. Really, sister, and you say I keep secrets. She has been most obliging and is quite an interesting person. There's something familiar about her but I can't quite place my finger on it. I need you here, Bethany. You and your fairy senses could probably help this old fool figure things out.
>
> Anyway, the last place I visited wasn't nearly as interesting as I had hoped. Though of course being by the southern mountains was quite a pleasant trip. The rain forests there are quite lovely and it is always a pleasure to hunt through them. Be watching your mail for a package to arrive. I've sent gifts for everyone and even a little something for my future niece and nephew. I suppose it may be a little early, but I consider them family already. They are really such charming people. I hope to meet their parents soon.

"Soon?" Moira asked. "Does that mean he'll be visiting us again later this year?"

"I haven't the faintest idea," Nana replied before finishing the letter.

> Again, I do hope that you are all well and happy. I expect you'll be going to the seashore again this year as you have told me about the last couple of years. Enjoy yourselves. If you see or do anything interesting, you must be ready to tell me all about it on my next visit. No, I shan't tell you when I'll come again. It would take all the fun out of it.
>
> Ever Yours,
> Sebastian

"He should sign them 'Your Mysterious Uncle'," Adrian joked as Nana folded the letter and put it back in its envelope.

"Well, that wouldn't make any sense at all since he addressed it primarily to me," Nana retorted with a smile. "He's hardly my uncle."

"Okay then, 'Your Mysterious Little Brother'," Adrian amended.

Everyone laughed and they chatted long into the afternoon about Uncle Sebastian and his many adventures until evening fell and Cook announced that supper was ready. They went into the dining hall where steaming bowls of shark fin soup sat waiting along with fresh-baked biscuits, a green salad with shrimp and a bowl of sliced melon. For a long while the only sound in the room was the clanking of silverware as everyone enjoyed their sumptuous meal. It did not take long however for the chatting to continue where it had left off.

"Now, you'll have to remind me Nana, is Sebastian your twin?" Alexandra asked.

"Yes, he is," Nana replied. "He is younger than me by ten minutes. He says that's why I always have to know everything. But we're quite close friends despite everything."

"Do twins run in your family?" Lysander asked. "You were a twin and then Lavinia, do you have a twin?"

"No, I came by myself. I think sharing is a little too difficult for me to have been a twin," Lavinia said teasingly.

"Twins do run in the family though," Nana said. "Quite rampantly, actually. Lavinia is one of the few not to have a twin. I must confess I was almost disappointed when she was born and there was just one baby. But she was such a beautiful little girl that I immediately forgave her. After all, it was hardly her fault. I expect though that Adrian and Moira will probably carry on the tradition. But who's to say? We never can tell until it happens."

"That's very true," Alexandra replied.

The conversation continued late into the evening and all too soon it was time for everyone to say good night. Each went into their own bedroom and Lucian found himself sitting by the window contemplating the day's events. His mother was right; they'd never had a problem with sharks in that part before. There was a different part of the shoreline that often had sharks, which was why the family rarely went there to swim. They preferred the safer waters closer to the castle. So then why had there been a shark? He supposed his father was probably right. The shark had probably run out of food within his own territory and decided to wander inland in hopes of finding a better food supply. Shaking his head, he crawled into bed. He was too tired from a long and very exciting day to worry about it too much.

During the next few days, Kaelen spent much of his time with Allegra on the beach healing from the bite to his leg. Adrian and Lucian would also join him as often as they could, though nothing could keep Lucian long from the sea. One afternoon as he sat thinking, Kaelen wondered how Achilles would react to discovering that Kaelen had not only wrestled the shark, but managed to beat it. In his mind he could just see the jealousy. Surely Achilles had never taken on so dangerous a foe. Then he reminded himself that despite looking young, Achilles was centuries older than he was. With a slight amount of depression he realized that it was entirely possible that Achilles had fought much more dangerous enemies than a simple shark. Perhaps the news wouldn't be impressive to him at all. If anything he might think it such a simple victory that he would give Kaelen even harder work to do in order to get him better prepared for what might be out there. This thought was hardly as comforting as some of his others, so Kaelen quickly pushed it aside and returned his attention to watching the others out splashing in the crystalline ocean shallows.

Soon he heard Lucian calling to him. He and Moira were both coming up to sit down in the warm sand. "How's the leg feeling?"

"Itchy," Kaelen replied. The fur was beginning to grow back and being bound in the cloth bandages was less than comfortable. "I would kill to have the fur all grown back the same length and get rid of these confounded bandages.

Lucian laughed. "I'm afraid those bandages aren't going to be going anywhere for a while. If anything my dad is extremely cautious. He's not going to risk you getting an infection because he doesn't cover up the wound. Until those stitches come out and he thinks you're fully healed, you can expect more itchy bandages and poultice applications."

Kaelen growled, "Better happen soon. This is driving me nuts."

"I'm sure you'll be better in no time at all," Moira said kindly. "Where's Allegra?"

"She went to the castle for a moment," Kaelen replied with a shrug. "Said she needed to take care of something but wouldn't give me any other information."

"Oh," Moira said as though she understood exactly why Allegra would need to go off on her own. "Well, I'm sure she'll be back down soon."

"Why do you girls always seem to understand everything where we remain clueless?" Lucian asked teasingly.

"Because we're girls," Moira retorted with a grin.

"Actually," Kaelen replied with a teasing tone, "I think it's just to irritate us and make us feel even more in the dark than we already are.

"Well, that may be part of it too," Moira admitted slyly.

The friends laughed and continued to chat until Allegra returned and joined in their conversation. Adrian had decided to go fishing with Lysander for a while. In truth, he was still trying to avoid spending time around anyone he thought might get suspicious of the changes that were happening. He'd noticed that his mother kept looking at him oddly and Nana certainly knew something. He could see it in her eyes and the way she looked at him. As of yet, Moira seemed to still be unaware of any change, but even there he wasn't certain. Perhaps he was becoming paranoid, but he was beginning to see suspicion in everyone's eyes and he was sure that if he didn't get back to school soon, his family was going to figure out that something wasn't quite right with him. Even Lucian's family seemed to be getting the idea that there was something different.

"Are you feeling alright, Adrian?" Lysander asked as they were sitting on a large rock near the ocean's edge.

"Hmmm?" Oh yeah," Adrian replied, "I'm fine."

"You just seem preoccupied," Lysander said gently.

"I guess I was just thinking about school," Adrian fibbed, hoping that Lysander wouldn't catch him in the lie.

Lysander didn't look fooled for a moment, but simply said, "It's coming up quickly isn't it?"

"Yeah," Adrian agreed, though he didn't believe that for a moment. If anything, this summer was the absolute slowest summer of his entire life.

"Well, I'm sure whatever's bothering you will resolve itself in no time," Lysander said comfortingly.

Adrian nodded but didn't reply. What could he say? The only way his worries would resolve themselves was with his princess breaking the spell put on him and he already knew that Allegra had a deep hatred for amphibians, though he knew Lucian was trying to downplay it to make him feel better. What he didn't know was that she didn't just hate frogs, she was terrified of them. Lucian absolutely wouldn't tell his friend something that would take his chances of success from slim to absolute zero.

Just before Adrian's family returned to Lictthane, a package arrived at the castle. Inside were the promised gifts from Uncle Sebastian. Each person was given their package and Kaelen was surprised to see that there was even a small package for him. They all opened them at the same time. Each of the women gasped as they picked up jewelry inlaid with amber and bits of turquoise. Beautiful and intricately carved leather belts were given to each of the men, though each piece was different. Kaelen was the only one who had not received a belt. In his package he found a little note that read:

> *If you believe the stories of the ancients, there is a mystic quality to the turquoise stone. Coupled with amber makes it even more powerful and especially lucky. For my beastly friend, a token to carry with you for good fortune and in hopes that it may someday be given to your bride.*
>
> *Sebastian*

Inside a soft, leather pouch was a unique amulet of turquoise and amber embedded in an engraved silver circle and dangling from a silver chain. He wasn't sure how he could give it to his bride as the chain was very thick and masculine, but perhaps if put on a more delicate chain the amulet could take on a more feminine appearance. Kaelen also didn't know the stories of the ancients. Perhaps in one of his spell breaking classes he could speak to Calypso about the amulet and see what insight she could offer. School was after all, only about a week away.

Chapter 2

As school began, Lucian found himself wishing that he could go back to summer. His schedule was far busier than ever before with sometimes daunting classes. When he had finally taken a moment that summer to look at his schedule, he had been shocked by what he found.

Class Schedule

Day	Time	Class	Teacher
Monday, Wednesday	8:00-9:30	Fencing	Raphael Peregrine
	9:30-11:00	Fencing	Raphael Peregrine
	11:00-12:00	Healing	Morghana
	12:00-1:00	Lunch	
	1:00-2:00	Botany	Russett Snapdragon
	2:00-3:30	Dragon Fighting	Vulcan Firebrand
	3:30-5:00	Dragon Fighting	Vulcan Firebrand
Tuesday, Thursday	8:00-9:30	Botany	Russett Snapdragon
	9:30-11:00	Horsemanship	Phillipa Rosepetal
	11:00-12:00	Healing Animals	Althea
	12:00-1:00	Lunch	
	1:00-2:30	Seamanship	Achilles Stardust
	2:30-4:00	Foreign Language	Lorelei
	4:00-5:00	Language Arts	Airlia Willowlimb
Friday	8:00-9:30	Fencing	Raphael Peregrine
	9:30-11:00	Orientation	Honoria Peregrine
	11:00-12:00	Spell Breaking	Calypso
	12:00-1:00	Lunch	
	12:00-1:30	Hunting	Diana Foxglove
	1:30-3:00	Etiquette	Gelasia Stardust
	3:00-4:00	Gardening	Lucretia
	4:00-5:00	Foreign Language	Lorelei

Most of his classes hadn't really surprised him. He'd known that some of them were continuing from the last year. He hadn't, however, expected the new classes. Seamanship had seemed odd for a boy who grew up by the ocean, but he soon learned that the class was all about sailing and ships; something that Lucian had surprisingly little experience with. He wasn't thrilled about the double dragon fighting. That had seemed entirely unfair. It was made worse by the fact that the second session had only two students; George and himself. Having only two students to pick on seemed to delight the dragon. But perhaps the worst of his new classes was gardening. He'd almost been embarrassed to tell the other boys about it. Perhaps most of his bad feeling towards the class was because it seemed so odd put in with all of his other classes. The rest was likely due to his temperamental instructor. "I don't really think this class is going to help me at all with my quest," Lucian complained one evening after a particularly bad lesson with the young witch. "When she's not mad at me for messing something up, she seems to be flirting with me."

"Well, mess up less," George teased. "Then she'll flirt more."

"Somehow I think that would make Moira jealous," Lucian retorted. "The last thing I need is to go back to year one when she wouldn't talk to me at all."

"Just don't start messing up more," Jacobi warned. "That would probably end badly."

"Think of it this way; she's not the youngest anymore," Adrian said. "So she probably won't lash out as easily as she would have then."

Lucian laughed, "I doubt anyone would have had her teaching gardening while she was the youngest. She hated all of us so much she probably wouldn't have gotten through the first day without turning the student into a slug."

"At least Russett is more forgiving of mistakes," Kaelen said. He and Lucian shared one of the botany classes, studying flower arranging; particularly the creation of beautiful bouquets. Kaelen was the only one who knew about Lucian being in a flower arranging class. The truth was that Lucian was the only one who knew Kaelen had flower arranging. Both had agreed that the only reason either knew about the other was because they were in the class together. "Otherwise I wouldn't have told you about it," Kaelen had admitted.

"That's true," Lucian said, bringing Kaelen back into the present conversation. "Anyway, how were your classes today?"

The boys continued to chat until they agreed that they'd best get their homework done, much as they'd like to continue putting it off. Lucian said he was going to do his in his room. "I just have reading to do and if I'm in the common room, I'll just end up talking to everyone."

"Understandable," George replied. "See you in the morning."

"See you," Lucian returned before heading upstairs to his room. Rusty stood as he walked in and pressed his head into Lucian's hand. "Hello boy," Lucian said, rubbing his dog's head. "I wish I could actually spend some time with you, but I've got lots of homework. You can sit on the bed with me if you want."

Rusty woofed understandingly and hopped onto Lucian's bed before curling up in the middle. Lucian lay down with his book for his animal healing class. This had also come as a surprise to him on his schedule. Why didn't Morghana simply teach him about healing animals in the other class? He supposed that part of it was the fact that Althea's gift involved things with animals while Morghana's gift was healing. Perhaps he should have counted himself lucky that the two witches weren't teaching it together.

Shaking his head, Lucian tried to concentrate on the chapter he had been assigned. He wasn't sure why it seemed that the witches always gave the longest reading assignments. Even Airlia didn't assign as much reading in their language arts class. He read the chapter for as long as he could before finally giving up and pulling out a different assignment. Luckily he didn't have much left to do because he was starting to feel sleepy. Rusty snoring on the bed wasn't helping him any. Lucian shook his head again as he started reading the other assignment. It was just as difficult to concentrate on as the first one had been. Before he knew it, the words on the page slipped away as his eyes drooped closed.

Lifting his head from where he was, Rusty looked over to see Lucian sleeping with the book open next to him. He woofed softly, which caused Lucian to jolt awake. "Sorry about that boy," Lucian yawned. "I guess I fell asleep. We should probably both head to bed."

Rusty jumped down off the bed and curled into his bed while Lucian blew out the candles. He crawled under his covers before promptly going back to sleep.

The next morning dawned so lovely that Lucian just couldn't stay inside. After breakfast he and the other boys went outside with their hounds and their homework. As the dogs chased after whatever they tossed for them, the boys worked on their homework. It was a nice, summery day with a slight breeze rustling the leaves above them. The sunshine was warm, but not overly so; which may have been in part because it was being filtered through the maple's abundant, large leaves. Kaelen, who had less bookwork than the others, soon began playing with Knight once he finished. They wrestled together under the shade of the tree until both were exhausted. Knight lay panting while Kaelen sat against the trunk of the tree, scratching behind Knight's ears. As the other boys finished, conversation soon turned to the summer and what all they had done.

"Just how much did you grow, Lucian? Four inches?" Jacobi asked.

Flushing, Lucian replied, "No, only two and a half."

"Two and a half in just over a month? What were they feeding you?" George teased.

Lucian didn't respond. Kaelen stepped in by saying, "It can't have been the food. I was eating the same stuff and I didn't grow at all."

"That's still crazy," George said. "I've never grown that fast in my life."

"Trust me, it's not all it's cracked up to be," Lucian groaned. "Between growing pains and never being able to find clothes that fit, I'm not sure it's worth the trouble."

"It can't be that bad," Jacobi replied.

"Try it sometime," Lucian retorted. "I just hope that I'm done. When the tailor took my measurements so they could do my new uniforms, I was nearly six five. I don't think I want to be any taller."

"You're probably done," Adrian said comfortingly. "And if not, we'll just take Uncle Sebastian's advice and cut your feet off at the ankle so you're closer to the rest of us."

"I'm not sure I like that plan either," Lucian said, laughing along with the rest of them. The boys continued to laugh and work as the afternoon progressed into evening, going inside only once so they could have their lunch. The day continued to be beautiful and filled with laughter. After finishing his own work Lucian asked, "Does anyone else want to go for a ride?"

"I'd love to, but I doubt any of the horses would let me," Kaelen admitted gruffly. "But if you guys want to go for a ride, go ahead. I'll stay out here with the dogs. Then you won't have to worry about taking them with you or taking them to your rooms."

"I'd like to go too, but I can't reach the stirrups anymore and there's just something wrong with getting a boost up at our age," Adrian admitted with a sheepish grin.

"What are you going to do for the fall meeting with the princesses?" Jacobi asked. "It's only a couple weeks away."

"Hope for rain," Adrian replied with a smile. "I'll stay back with Kaelen for today."

"Are you sure?" Lucian asked. "None of us would mind giving you a boost. Even at seventeen," he added teasingly.

"Yeah, I'm sure. You guys go on ahead," Adrian insisted. "I'm sure Kaelen and I will find plenty to occupy ourselves."

"Alright," George said. "You guys have fun." The three boys then left Adrian and Kaelen as they walked towards the barn.

"So, did you ask Calypso about the amulet my uncle gave you?" Adrian asked as the others disappeared.

"Yeah, she gave me a book to read," Kaelen replied with a moan. "Why can't anyone ever just give us straight answers? Instead they give us clues and books."

"I guess we're supposed to try to figure things out on our own," Adrian suggested. "I'd like it if they gave us clear answers, but it doesn't seem to happen often around here."

"Must be a fairy and witch thing," Kaelen added.

Adrian chuckled," Must be. So, is it at least a short book?"

Kaelen laughed harshly, "Not even close. It's got to be the longest book I've ever seen. I think the title is *Gems of Sanalbereth: Their History and Their Uses* or something really lame like that. It's got to be like a thousand pages. All I wanted to know was the story behind turquoise and amber. I didn't want the world's anthology of gemstones."

"Well, maybe you'll learn something interesting," Adrian replied. "And, you might be able to just look up the stones you want."

"I doubt it, but truth be told I haven't even opened the stupid thing yet," Kaelen admitted. "I was so disgusted when I saw it that I stuck it in my bag and left it there."

"I can understand that. Unfortunately, you won't be able to find any answers unless you crack the book. Figuratively speaking," Adrian added teasingly.

Kaelen growled, "I'd rather crack it literally, but Calypso blessed it so that I can't shred it like I did the last book she gave me."

"Smart," Adrian said. "Well, you'd best get started."

With a grimace, Kaelen opened the book and began trying to read. His thoughts wandered to the day Calypso gave him the volume. "I've blessed this so that your claws won't shred it," Calypso had said. "It'll be as though the pages were made of steel, but it'll still maintain a light weight."

"Light?" Kaelen had asked incredulously.

Calypso had given him a look that clearly said she wasn't amused. "In any case it's blessed so you can't destroy it. The Sisters and I have had quite a time repairing the last book we allowed you to borrow."

Before she could finish her complaint, Kaelen had interrupted, "Lucian has been blessed hasn't he?"

"I don't see why you're asking," Calypso had replied, avoiding the question.

"Because I've seen that glow around him, like a blessing. Adrian is green and Lucian occasionally has a white glow. It's faint, but it's there. He's been blessed. What with?" Kaelen had asked. "Is it with plants? It is, isn't it?"

"Whether or not he has been blessed is between the Sisters and Lucian," Calypso had said with a warning tone to her voice. "It is dangerous to know everything, Kaelen. Do not ask about him again."

"Kaelen," Adrian said, pulling him back to the present, "daydreaming won't get that book read either."

"Yeah, I know," Kaelen replied. He turned his attention back to the pages in front of him. The book had to be the oldest he'd ever encountered. It was hand-written with fancy lettering that Stefanos called illumination.

> *The gems of Sanalbereth have been a source of mystery and wonder for centuries. The use of gems began in the time before records as fairies tried to discover their purpose...*

"Oh boy," Kaelen grumbled. "This is going to be worse than I thought." He forced himself to continue reading, though the writing didn't get any better. If anything it became even more dry and boring. He flipped through to the back of the book, hoping to find an index. But there was none to be found. There weren't even chapter headings for him to look through. Kaelen realized with a sigh that he would have to read the whole book, page by page, in order to find what he was looking for. "I hate her," he mumbled as he turned to page two.

The weeks passed and it was soon the day before the fall meeting. It had been stormy all week, much to Adrian's pleasure. However, new problems had presented themselves within the last few days. His tongue, which had been shooting at insects for a while, had gotten longer and turned an awkward pinkish-purple. He could barely speak without it rolling out of his mouth. His fingers and toes had also started to web together.

"The toes aren't too big of a deal," Adrian told Tallia as he sat in the infirmary. "I mean, she won't see those because I wear shoes. But how am I supposed to hide webbed fingers?"

Tallia contemplated his hands with her turquoise eyes. "Well, um, I'm not entirely sure how we'll hide that, Adrian. Let me talk to the witches and then come back after dinner. By then I'm sure I'll have some kind of solution."

Adrian picked at his plate all through dinner. "I hate being an amphibian. Worse, I hate being half an amphibian. I mean, look at me. I'm a pasty-green color, my fingers and toes are webbing together, my tongue is purple and my eyes are starting to bug out. I'm the most hideous-looking thing in the world."

"No, Nathan still has you beat," Lucian replied. "In fact, he probably looks even worse now than when he was expelled."

"I guess so," Adrian agreed half-heartedly. "But still, how are they ever going to convince Allegra that I'm still the regular me looking like this? Those shoes Gelasia has been making are getting ridiculous. They're eight inches tall now. There's no way Allegra won't notice."

"Cheer up," Jacobi said brightly. "It's been raining the whole time, so we won't be horse-riding tomorrow."

"Great," Adrian said without enthusiasm. "We'll be inside where there's lots of opportunity for close examination."

"Don't be so negative," George chided gently. "I'm sure they'll think of something to mask all these changes. You've just got to be confident in them."

"Sure," Adrian sighed. He continued to pick at his meal until finally saying, "I can't eat. I'm going to Tallia's and then to my room. I'll see you in the morning."

"You sure?" Kaelen asked. "You need to eat up."

"I'm not hungry," Adrian replied. He slumped out of the dining hall and down the hallway to the infirmary. When he walked in, Tallia was sitting at her desk. She motioned for him to have a seat as she finished writing on a piece of paper before sending it flying out the door.

"Alright, I think I may have a temporary solution for you," Tallia said cheerfully.

"Really? What?" Adrian asked.

"Well, I've got a fresh batch of that make-up from Gelasia to hide the green" Tallia began.

"I wish you wouldn't call it that," Adrian groaned. "Girls wear make-up."

"What do you want me to call it?" Tallia asked. "Face paint?"

"That would be better," Adrian said.

Tallia rolled her eyes. "Moving along, these glasses will hide the bulging. Just tell your princess that you need them for reading."

"You want me to lie to Allegra?" Adrian asked.

"No," Tallia said slowly, "I want you to misinform. It's very different; at least that's Achilles' excuse for telling me something that's not quite accurate. Anyway, there's the glasses and here's a numbing solution to put on your tongue. It'll prevent it from being quite so unruly and because of the interaction it has with human saliva, it will make it look a normal color too. And last but not least, we're bandaging your hands. You had a rough time in dragon fighting."

"I'm not in dragon fighting," Adrian argued, still trying to take in all that she'd said.

"Oh, well then, you had a rough time in fencing," Tallia amended.

"I'm not in fencing either," Adrian said.

"Well, pick a class that's dangerous," Tallia snapped. "That will be the one you injured your hands in and so they have to be bandaged. And now, Allegra won't notice any difference."

Adrian tried to be grateful as Tallia wrapped thick white bandages around his hands, but he was starting to feel mutinous. Now instead of figuring out that he was cursed, Allegra would simply think him clumsy. "When should I use the solution?"

"Solution?" Tallia asked.

"For my tongue," Adrian clarified.

"Oh, of course; sorry, it's been a long day," Tallia apologized. "Use it first thing in the morning when you wake up. Just rub a little bit on the end and spread it backwards. When you've finished, say 'Tongue be numb' and it'll be complete."

"Really?" Adrian asked

"I know it sounds lame, but that's the way the potion works," Tallia explained. "You don't have much choice unless you want to be spitting and fly-catching throughout your meeting tomorrow."

Adrian sighed, "Alright. I guess things could be worse."

"That's the spirit," Tallia said with a smile. "Now run along. I'm sure you've got homework or something that you could be working on."

"There's always something," Adrian admitted before turning to walk away. "Thanks Tallia," he threw over his shoulder.

"My pleasure," Tallia replied.

The next morning, Adrian carefully dressed for the day. It was difficult to do with his hands bandaged up. Only the very tips of his fingers were outside the bandaging and they were nearly impossible to move. After a half-hour of fumbling with buttons, he was finally dressed and had his make-up on. The last thing he needed to do was add the numbing solution to his tongue. Carefully following Tallia's instructions, he spread it toward the back of his mouth. There was a slight tingling sensation as he worked and when he'd finished he looked in the mirror and feeling rather sheepish said, "Tongue be numb." Instantly, he felt as though his mouth were on fire. His tongue turned a vibrant shade of red-orange and started to swell. "Aaaaargh!" Adrian yelled as he jumped up and down. He grabbed a piece of paper and started fanning his tongue, but it did no use. Finally, he pulled open his door and went barreling down the stairs to the infirmary. "Ta-ya, Ta-ya! Ma ton, ma ton!" he shouted as he barged into the room.

"Adrian, what on… good heavens!" Tallia exclaimed as she saw Adrian's face. "What happened?"

"Ah dun o," Adrian replied crying. The pain was worsening and his tongue was still swelling.

Tallia was digging through a medicine cabinet, "Oh I know there's some in here. Ah, here we are!" She grabbed a vial of vivid violet liquid and poured it down his throat. Some splattered onto his shirt, but the swelling immediately began to go down. "Are you feeling better?" Tallia asked.

Adrian nodded. "Wath it thuppothet to boo that?" he lisped around his numb and still slightly swollen tongue.

"I've never seen anyone react like that before," Tallia said shaking her head.

"Are you sure you did exactly as I told you?"

"Yeah," Adrian said.

"Well, that's the worst allergic reaction I've ever seen," Tallia admitted. "I'm so sorry, Adrian. I never would have given that to you if I had known."

"It'th okay," Adrian replied. "How bad do I look?"

Tallia hesitated, "Oh, not too bad."

Adrian looked in a mirror. "Tallia, my fathe ith pink and my tongue ith orange!"

"I'm really very, very sorry," Tallia said apologetically. "There's nothing I can do about that."

"Perfec'," Adrian mumbled. "Ath if I didn' already look terrible."

Tallia patted his arm reassuringly. "It'll be fine. I'm sure your princess will be more than understanding."

"Tallia, I was wondering… oh my," Calista said upon entering the room. "Adrian what happened?"

"It's my fault Calista, I gave him a potion to make his tongue a little more normal and I fear he's had an allergic reaction," Tallia explained.

"Can I thtay in my room?" Adrian begged.

"Certainly not," Calista said. "I see no reason why you can't simply tell Allegra that you had an allergic reaction to some medication. It would be telling her the truth. You'll meet with your princess just like everyone else."

Adrian sighed and then walked towards the entryway where the others were waiting for him.

"Wow, Adrian, what happened to you?" Jacobi asked.

"I don' want to talk about it," Adrian said bitterly. The princesses started filtering in and Adrian grabbed Lucian by the arms. "You're tall; hide me," Adrian begged, pulling Lucian in front of him.

"Nice try," Lucian said, rolling his eyes and trying to move away.

"Come on, you're the talletht boy in our clath," Adrian said pulling him back. "Pleathe hide me."

"It wouldn't matter how tall I was," Lucian said, pulling away. "Allegra would still be able to find you."

"Thome friend you are," Adrian mumbled just before watching Allegra give Lucian a hug.

"I hope you start writing again soon, Lucian. I've very much missed your letters," Allegra chided.

"I've been busy," Lucian laughed. "But I'll try to write more often."

"Moira hasn't missed any letters," Allegra teased. She then turned to Adrian. "Oh, Adrian! What happened? You aren't in trouble are you?"

"Not exthactly," Adrian said. "I had an allergic reacthion to a medicathion."

"Oh you poor thing!" Allegra exclaimed. She patted his arm. "I'm so sorry. Is there anything I can do to make you feel better?"

"Pretend you can't thee me?" Adrian suggested with a mild grin.

Allegra laughed, "Oh Adrian, even vivid pink and orange won't scare me away. I still think you're the handsomest guy here. Except maybe for Lucian; he is my brother after all."

If he wasn't pink before, Adrian was then. He blushed to the roots of his hair. "Well, thankth Allegra. Thall we go to breakfatht?"

"I'd be delighted," Allegra replied, taking his arm. "Did the reaction affect your hands too?" she asked.

"Thort of," Adrian said. "It'th a lon' thtory."

Moira caught sight of Adrian as she walked to Lucian. "What's wrong with Adrian?" she asked him.

"Allergic reaction," Lucian replied. "I'm sure he'll be himself soon."

"Are you sure that's all?" Moira persisted. "He seems different."

"I'm sure it's just the reaction," Lucian said.

"You're not keeping secrets from me are you?" Moira asked seriously.

Afraid she would catch him in not telling her the whole truth, he asked as teasingly as he could, "Me? Would I keep secrets from you, Moira?"

"You would if you thought that was the best thing for me," Moira retorted with a wry grin. "Seriously, Lucian; is Adrian alright?"

"Moira, I would never lie to you about Adrian," Lucian said. "He'll be just fine. It's just a reaction. Tallia's doing what she can to make it go away."

Moira eyed him for a moment. "Alright, I trust you, you know."

"And I appreciate that. Shall we go to breakfast?" Lucian asked, offering her his arm.

"I see the topic is closed," Moira laughed. "But yes, I will join you for breakfast." She walked with him into the dining hall and they soon joined a table with their friends. As the meal progressed, she found herself watching Adrian closely, as though to find something more than just a reaction at work. She was sure that both Adrian and Lucian were keeping something from her, but she couldn't figure out what it was. It was really frustrating her and she wanted them to both be truthful with her. Why wouldn't they trust her with whatever it was?

She was pulled out of her thoughts by Clarissa saying, "My Lucian, you've certainly grown again. How tall are you now?"

"I'd really rather not say," Lucian said with a blush.

"I'll tell you," George piped up. "He's six foot seven."

"How did you find out?" Lucian asked.

"I was going to see Gelasia about some hemming I needed done while she was measuring you. I overheard the conversation. Sorry," George said sheepishly.

"What are you, half-fairy?" Eleanor asked teasingly.

"No, as far as I know I'm just tall because, well, I'm tall," Lucian stated. "There's no fairy blood in my family."

They were interrupted by Melantha announcing that they would be having games in the gym followed by lunch in the dining hall. "I'm afraid the weather won't permit our usual festivities," she explained with a smile. "However, I'm sure you'll enjoy the games and activities just as well."

After everyone had finished eating, the group of friends went to the gym. When they arrived in the gym, they found that an elaborate obstacle course had been set up. "Well, this looks interesting," Kaelen said as they entered. There were ropes hanging from the ceiling, large wooden platforms raised high above the ground, narrow balancing beams, and strange pits that none of the boys could remember having ever been in the gym before. "How do they plan on fixing all this?"

"Fairy magic?" Clarissa suggested.

Achilles walked in front of everyone and began instructing them on what they would be doing. "The first activity today is an obstacle course. Normally I would set this up outside, but obviously with it raining we don't want to get the ladies sick."

"Never mind the rest of us," Jacobi whispered with a grin.

"Instead it will be an indoor obstacle course," Achilles continued. "At each platform there is a fairy there to ask either the prince or the princess a question. If you answer correctly, you will be allowed to proceed to the next platform. If you answer incorrectly, you will have to return to the beginning and your way back will be even more challenging. Any questions?"

"I'd ask do we have to, but I don't think I'd like the response," Kaelen told the others. He had been paired with Leticia again. It made sense since they were the only two without their own partner, but it was frustrating since he didn't really know anything about her.

"We'll muddle through somehow," Leticia replied with a warm smile.

Before anyone else could speak, the light in the room dimmed dramatically and there was a sudden sound of growth and movement. Soon the only bright places were the entrances to the course. Above each entrance was a number. "I can only assume that the number is what year we are," Lucian observed. "May as well get started." He offered Moira his arm and together they walked under the entrance. Shadows danced about the course from flickering torches. The once lifeless gym seemed to be crawling with vines, plants and the sounds of scampering animals.

"I have to say," Moira whispered, holding more tightly to Lucian's arm, "they certainly make you feel like you've been transported elsewhere. This is creepy."

"Don't worry, I'll keep you safe," Lucian promised.

"You better," Moira said teasingly. "I think allowing your princess to get into danger is considered a failure."

Lucian laughed and led her by the hand over a vine-encrusted beam. "Careful that you don't slip."

They reached a break in the enchanted woods and found themselves facing Vulcan. "Lucian and Moira, you're the first to reach me. My question is for Lucian. Are you ready?"

Lucian nodded, but didn't speak. He was beginning to feel nervous.

"Where is your princess from?" Vulcan asked.

Shocked by the simplicity of the question Lucian stated, "Lictthane."

Vulcan stood aside and they realized he had been standing before a narrow passageway leading deeper into the jungle-like maze. "Proceed."

"Is that it?" Lucian asked, still confused.

"We don't start you on the hard questions, Lucian," Vulcan explained. "But if you wish something more challenging, I'm sure I could think of something."

"No, that's alright," Lucian replied quickly. He walked slightly ahead of Moira, keeping hold of her hand in his as they went under a canopy of vines. The air became damp and close as they continued on through the course. The torches seemed to be placed farther and farther apart, leaving large areas of darkness.

"I always wanted to go with Uncle Sebastian on one of his adventures," Moira said in a voice that was almost a whimper. "It used to make me so angry that he'd never let me go. Because I was a lady, he'd say. Now I'm glad he never took me."

Lucian turned to look at his princess. Moira's face was pale and her eyes shone with unshed tears as they darted around her. "Here, we'll stop a moment. It'll be okay," he said gently. He led her to a large stone that she could sit on. "I'm sure you'll feel better if you just rest a moment."

"I feel fine," Moira said stubbornly. "I'm just…"

"Scared?" Lucian finished for her. She didn't answer but he could tell he was right. "There's nothing wrong with being afraid of something. Everyone has fears."

A wild scream caused Moira to leap out of her spot and into Lucian's arms. "What was that?" she asked, quivering as she clung to him.

"I don't know, but it's probably just an effect of some kind," Lucian replied. "The fairies would never put you into any real danger."

"Are you sure?" Moira whispered.

"I'm positive," Lucian said. "Come on, I think I see another platform that way. We'll answer our next question and be that much closer to leaving."

"Okay," Moira whimpered. She stayed close to Lucian, clinging to his arm as they walked. Lucian stopped suddenly and she asked, "What is it?"

Lucian pointed. Ahead of them was what appeared to be a stream; only it wasn't clean and clear like ones Lucian was used to. This one was covered in slime and he couldn't tell looking how deep it was. He let go of Moira's hand. "Stay here a moment." She nodded and he looked around for a moment to see if he could find some way of crossing without getting into the water. There didn't appear to be any sort of bridge. There also weren't any vines hanging across. He took a tentative step into the murky water. It wasn't so deep after all. He took another step and found that it was the same as the step before. If he carried Moira, than he'd be the only one to get dirty. He was sure it wouldn't be quite that easy, but he returned to where Moira was.

"Maybe we missed a turn," Moira suggested.

"I don't think so. I think we have to cross, but I'm going to have to carry you," Lucian said.

"You most certainly will not," Moira retorted. "I am perfectly capable of walking on my own thank you very much."

"It's filthy in there. Do you really want to ruin that dress?" Lucian asked.

"No, but I don't want you carrying me either," Moira said.

"Well, we only have three choices: I carry you, you stay here, or you ruin the dress. If you stay here, we never get out. If you ruin your dress, than you'll be mad at me and the fairies would have a field day over it. I don't even want to imagine what they'd let the witches do to me," Lucian pointed out. "But if I carry you over, we get out of here, you don't get dirty and the fairies don't have me turned into a bug. It's not that far of a distance. I'll be able to carry you over easily and it'll be so quick you'll barely notice."

Moira looked thoughtful for a moment as though desperately trying to think of another way out of it. She sighed, "Fine, if you must; but you better be quick about it."

"We'll be at the other side in no time at all," Lucian promised. He scooped Moira up into his arms. It wasn't quite as easy as he had imagined it to be. Trying to get into a good position was awkward and she wasn't as light as perhaps he had thought she was. It didn't help that he needed to put her down a couple of times to make sure he had her skirt about her in such a way that it wouldn't drag along in the muck.

"Just how soon will we be across this?" Moira asked as Lucian took a step in.

"Before you know it," Lucian replied with as much of a grin as he could manage. He could feel the swampy ooze filtering into his shoes as he walked farther into the mess. To his chagrin, the platform seemed to be getting farther away rather than getting closer. It was several minutes before they were even halfway across the slime. He was surprised that they hadn't seen other people about.

"I thought you said this would take no time at all," Moira groaned after another few minutes had gone by.

Lucian grit his teeth. "It's not as quick as I thought." He was trying not to panic. The water had slowly risen from his ankles to halfway to his knees. Trying not to let Moira see him nervous he asked, "About how much further do you think we have?"

Moira looked ahead. She could see the platform and a pale aqua fairy standing on it. "Maybe a couple hundred feet?" she guessed.

"Good," Lucian said. "I'm starting to get tired."

"I could walk on my own," Moira offered.

"No," Lucian insisted as the water sloshed about his knees. He was fairly sure something had slithered past him too, but he wasn't about to say that to his already nervous princess. "I'm fine and I really don't want you to ruin that dress. It's very pretty on you. And it's my favorite color."

"If you insist," Moira replied with a small grin. As they got closer and closer to the platform, they could see the fairy watching for them. "What would you bet that she's going to tell us that there was a bridge or something?" Moira asked in a whisper as they got to the platform.

"I wouldn't take that bet," Lucian retorted. "Knowing my luck I just missed seeing it."

"Actually, Prince Lucian, you didn't miss anything," the fairy said with a smile. "You were meant to wallow through. However, I must congratulate you on not dirtying Moira's gown. You would have lost points had she gotten dirty."

"Wait, we're getting points for this?" Moira asked.

"Yes, didn't they tell you?" the fairy replied. When neither responded she continued, "Well, they must have forgotten. Anyhow, this question is for Moira. What is your prince's favorite color."

Moira blanched. "I, um, I..." She looked over at Lucian who was trying to point at her skirt without being too obvious. She looked down at herself. "Yellow?"

"Very good," the fairy said with a smile. "You may proceed. But before you go, I'll clean up those trousers for you." She waved her wand and instantly Lucian's pants were as clean as they had been before entering the maze.

"Thanks, I don't know how long they'll stay this way," Lucian replied honestly. He then led Moira on to the next part of the maze.

"Yellow? Your favorite color is seriously yellow?" Moira asked.

"Yes," Lucian replied, "it's like being in sunshine."

"Well, it's a good thing you were giving me a hint because I would have guessed blue or something like that."

Lucian laughed. "As much as I like blue, it's not my favorite."

They continued through the dense jungle-like maze, deeper and deeper as they stopped at platforms answering question after question until they reached a platform with both Calista and Melantha standing. "You've made it through. Now the final test to see if you leave the course or if you return to the beginning."

Moira and Lucian glanced at each other nervously. "Alright," Moira said.

"Lucian, if you could describe your princess with only one sentence and without commenting on her beauty, how would you describe Moira?" Calista asked.

"Can I have a moment?" Lucian asked.

"Take as long as you need," Calista replied.

Lucian thought for a while. There were many ways he could describe Moira, but which would he choose if he had only one sentence to do it in? "Moira is," Lucian began and then paused. He glanced at Moira. An encouraging smile brightened on her face. "Moira is my princess and gives me encouragement, light-heartedness and love."

"Well spoken," Calista stated with a smile.

Melantha nodded and said, "Moira, given one sentence, how would you describe Lucian?"

"Lucian is the very embodiment of Prince Charming in manner, action and word," Moira replied, barely pausing to think it over.

"You have both done well. You may now exit the course and retire to the dining hall where luncheon is waiting for you. Here is your final score," Melantha said, handing Moira a small slip of dark blue paper.

The two walked out of the maze and headed hand-in-hand towards the dining hall. Moira looked at the slip in her hand. "According to this, there were ten platforms and each platform was worth ten points. Then going through the course also had another ten points for each part, so all totaled there were two hundred points available. Of those we got one hundred eighty-seven. I wonder where we lost points."

"How soon did we get it finished?" Lucian asked.

"It says we completed the course in three hours and fifteen minutes," Moira replied.

"Not bad," Lucian said as they entered the dining hall. They saw several of the younger students and a few of their own age group. Allegra and Adrian were sitting together at a table by themselves. "I guess we should go join them."

"Before we do, Lucian," Moira began, "I need to ask you to do me a favor."

"Sure, what do you need?" Lucian asked.

"I want you to promise me that if there's anything you can tell me about Adrian, that you will," Moira said seriously. "I know there's more to this than a simple allergic reaction. Something that neither of you is willing to tell me. Now, I don't need to know everything, but I do need to know if there is anything you can tell me. He's my brother, Lucian; my twin. I've never known life without him. I need to know that he's okay."

Lucian took Moira aside and held her hand gently. "Moira, as I said before, I would never lie to you. Adrian will be fine. I promise."

Moira nodded. "I wish you would say more, but I suppose I'll have to just accept what I can get. Come on; let's join them before they think we got lost in there."

They walked to the table where Allegra and Adrian were sitting. Allegra was surprisingly quiet and Adrian was scowling over something. "Is everything alright?" Lucian asked.

"Everything is just fine," Allegra snapped.

Moira and Lucian looked at each other a moment. Lucian shrugged and they each decided to leave the matter be. "Well, has anyone else emerged?"

"You two are the only ones we know of," Allegra said. Her voice was still edgy and she refused to look at Adrian, but at least she wasn't snapping.

"I guess we'll just have to wait for everyone else to show up," Moira said gently. She was looking at Adrian as though by staring she might get him to talk to her. Instead he turned further away from them.

There was an uncomfortable silence until Leticia and Kaelen showed up, followed soon after by Jacobi and Clarissa. "I think I saw George nearing the exit, but I'm not sure," Jacobi said as they sat down.

"You did," Eleanor replied as she and George had a seat. "That was quite the challenge; especially that last question. They certainly made you think didn't they?"

Adrian scowled even deeper as Allegra retorted, "Well it made some of us think."

"Oh dear, I seem to have hit a nerve," Eleanor said apologetically. "I'm sorry. Well, how did everyone like the effects of the jungle? That was so real-looking. I very much believed we had somehow wandered out of the school and to an entirely different realm. The snake pit was terrifying."

"Snake pit?" Leticia asked. "I don't remember there being a snake pit. There were some very realistic alligators; though I'm sure they were fake."

"Oh they were real alright," Kaelen replied ruefully. "If I ever figure out who the wise-guy was who thought of that I'll strangle him."

Jacobi laughed. "Somehow I don't think that would look very good on your report card if you strangle the head of the school. But honestly, I don't remember having snakes or alligators. Do you, Clarissa?"

Clarissa shook her head, "No, I'm sure I would have noticed something like that."

George looked thoughtful for a moment. He then looked at Lucian. "Did you have snakes or alligators?"

"No," Lucian replied. "None that I saw anyway."

"Maybe you're just going blind," Kaelen teased as George continued to look as though he were puzzling over something.

There was laughter around the table. Even Allegra cracked a smile. Adrian continued to ignore everyone which made the conversation awkward and halting. They were all relieved when Calista stood to announce the day's winners. "We've chosen a winning couple for each age group. The points were based on correctly answering the questions and how well you made it through the maze. If you had to stop or got lost, you lost points. If you hear your names, come see Melantha and myself after luncheon and you'll receive your prize basket. Our first year winners were..."

As she continued to talk Jacobi asked in a whisper, "Alright, how did the rest of you do? We got one sixty-seven."

"Not surprisingly, Leticia and I only managed one hundred forty-three," Kaelen replied. "I know we lost points on some of the questions and had to start over."

"Well, we were at a slight disadvantage," Leticia said understandingly.

"We got one eighty-seven," Moira said. "Eleanor, how did you and George do?"

Eleanor was spared answering as everyone's attention returned to Calista who announced, "Our fifth year winners are George and Eleanor with a perfect score of two hundred points. They were the only couple to gain all the points available in any age group."

"You guys got a perfect score?" Clarissa asked. "Wow, that's really impressive."

It was difficult to say who had flushed more. "We just worked well together, I suppose," Eleanor said modestly.

The conversation continued between most of the friends. Adrian was still ignoring the group which was frustrating the others. When Calista announced that it was time for the princesses to go, Allegra hugged Lucian and without a word to Adrian followed the rest of the girls out to the carriages. Lucian said goodbye to Moira and the others before returning to the dining hall where Adrian was still sulking. For the first time in a long while, Lucian was glad to see the princesses go. It gave him an opportunity to talk to Adrian alone. "Alright, what is eating you?"

"I don't want to talk about it," Adrian mumbled.

"Well, like it or not you're going to have to say something," Lucian retorted. "You've been antisocial since the end of the course. Now come on, what's going on? Did you and Allegra get into an argument?"

"How are you supposed to describe your princess without talking about how beautiful she is, huh?" Adrian asked. Before Lucian could reply the rant continued, "I mean, really? Yeah, Allegra is talented and she's fun to be around and she's got a great personality, but she is truly beautiful inside and out. And so when I had to think about it and I tried saying that she was beautiful in mind, Calista said that I couldn't use the word beautiful. I couldn't think of anything else, so we had to go back to the part before and work our way back. And there were creepy crawly things all over the place. Allegra was whimpering that she was scared and I was trying to be encouraging and then that stupid potion wore off. At least, it wore off to the point that I started shooting at flies again and there were flies everywhere. Allegra asks what's wrong with me and then gets mad when I tell her that it's just the reaction because she doesn't believe me. So I told her she just didn't know what she was talking about and to mind her own business."

"What?" Lucian asked angrily.

"I know, I know, it was stupid, but what was I supposed to tell her?" Adrian demanded. "'I'm sorry Allegra; I'm turning into a frog. Yes I know you hate them but you'll have to kiss me anyway.' Really? Really? Who's bright idea was this anyway. I hate being a Prince Charming. I'd rather go back home and live out my days as a hermit frog thing."

"Would you really?" Lucian asked seriously.

Adrian sighed, "No. I'm just so tired of lying to her. I'm tired of lying to Moira. I'm tired of lying to my mother and to Nana and Uncle Sebastian. I'm tired of lying to your family. I'm just so tired of lying in general. Why can't I just tell them all the truth? Wouldn't that make it easier? I mean, Allegra could prepare herself, right?"

Lucian frowned, "I don't understand why it has to be this way either. But we have to believe that the fairies know what they're talking about, right? I'm sure everything will be just fine. You're not the only one lying about this you know. Moira won't believe me either. Hopefully she understands that it's not that I don't want to tell her. I can't tell her. Do you think this is easy on me? Do you think it's easy on the other guys? We all have to lie for you. We have to lie to the women we love because we're not allowed to let them know what's going on with you. All of us are feeling the stress because it's not easy to hide anymore."

"Yeah, well, I really flubbed it this time. I don't know that Allegra will talk to me again for a while. By the time she does, it might be too late," Adrian admitted.

"I'm sure she'll forgive you soon enough. She loves you," Lucian said.

"Whatever," Adrian replied. He walked away towards his room before Lucian could say anything else. No one really understood what he was going through. No one.

Chapter 3

It was several days before Adrian would talk to any of them. When he did, the conversation briefly started on the meeting they'd just had. "Did anyone else notice that none of the courses were the same for any of us?" George asked at lunch one afternoon.

"I did while we were talking about it," Lucian replied. "Everyone had different challenges they had to face."

"I guess I hadn't noticed," Jacobi admitted. "I just know I never want to do something like that again. There were eyes everywhere. I don't know if Clarissa saw them, because I didn't say anything to her about them. I figured having me scared was bad enough."

"There weren't any eyes in mine," Lucian said. "Just a never-ending pond that was slowly getting deeper." It was quiet for a moment and then he asked, "Do you think the reason each of our courses was different is because each of our quests will be different? I mean, Kaelen is a beast and will probably face a lot of danger on his quest which could explain the alligators."

"I'm turning into a frog which would mean it makes sense for there to have been all those flies in there," Adrian added.

"Exactly." Lucian explained, "I think that obstacle course was more than just a fun activity to do with our princesses."

"Fun?" Jacobi questioned teasingly.

George thought for a moment. "I think you're right. Did anyone else have a dragon? I mean, I didn't have to fight it or anything, but I thought poor Eleanor was going to faint when it stepped into our path."

"I didn't see it, but I heard it a few times," Lucian said.

The others shook their heads. "No dragons for me," Kaelen replied. "But there were a lot of dangerous plants in there and of course, the alligators."

"I saw dangerous plants, but the weird thing was as we'd get closer, they'd start, well, blooming. Maybe Moira scares the plants," Lucian teased.

There was some laughter followed by Adrian saying, "Flies, gnats, and other disgusting bugs in mine. And swamps, lots of swampy areas."

"Well, if that's a taste of what our quests are going to be like," George stated plainly, "than we have a lot of work to do."

Outside the world was doing a rapid progression from fall to winter. A mere two weeks after seeing the princesses, a snowstorm hit. Boys would scramble to the classes that were held in some of the outer buildings. As Lucian and Kaelen sat in their botany class arranging flowers, Lucian teased, "I'm jealous of you, all that fur."

"Be careful what you wish for. I'm sure we could arrange for you to have a nice thick coat too," Kaelen retorted teasingly.

Lucian laughed, "That's alright; I think I'll pass. I like myself just the way I am."

"Yeah, I did too," Kaelen said. There was a tinge of regret in his voice. "Do you think she'll come back to me?"

"Who?" Lucian asked.

"Esmé," Kaelen replied.

Lucian was quiet for a moment. No one had been allowed to tell Kaelen the real fate that had befallen Esmé. "Whether she does, or a better princess, I know that somehow or other you'll have a happy ending."

"That didn't really answer my question, Lucian," Kaelen said seriously.

"I know it didn't, but that's all I know. There's a beautiful young woman out there for you. Maybe Leticia," Lucian suggested.

Kaelen shook his head. "No, Leticia's wonderful and all, but I don't think she's my princess. I'll just have to believe that Esmé will see the light and come save me."

Lucian didn't say anything but continued to work on his arrangement. "Ugh, this is terrible," he said miserably.

"It's not nearly as bad as the first one I did," Kaelen assured him comfortingly. "It's not even as bad as the first one you did. Maybe try adding a little more greenery there. Yeah, right there. See? Looks better already."

"You have a great eye for this," Lucian replied. "I do okay, but you really do have a gift with these things."

Kaelen shrugged, "I don't know. I just like doing arrangements and stuff. It helps me think, like an escape. At any rate it's better than portraiture."

Lucian laughed, "How's that class going for you?"

"Terribly. Can you believe Stefanos is making me do a portrait while wearing a blindfold?" Kaelen asked bitterly. "I mean really? Even he couldn't create great art without looking at it."

"Why is he having you blindfolded?" Lucian asked.

"Some fiddle-faddle about painting from the heart the face of my true love," Kaelen replied. "How am I supposed to paint anything if I can't look at it?"

"Wow, that seems really hard," Lucian admitted. "Do you get to look at it after class ends?"

"No, and that's the other weird part. As soon as it's time to clean up for the day, Stefanos covers up the painting before he allows me to take off the blindfold," Kaelen explained. "And I can't even sneak a peek while I'm working because he's got this blindfold magically fused to my face or something. I can't move it at all. I don't even know what colors I'm using. For all I know I could be painting a green-skinned, purple-haired, demon-eyed monster."

Lucian couldn't help but snicker a little. "I doubt Stefanos would allow you to paint anything that bad."

"Hey, you didn't see my portraits last year," Kaelen retorted with a rueful grin.

"But I seem to remember Leticia thought you were pretty good," Lucian pointed out.

"Leticia is way too nice for her own good," Kaelen replied. "Even if I'd done horribly, she would never say so. She's too much the lady."

They were interrupted by Russett coming to check on them. "How's it coming boys? Lucian, you've got a bit much on that side, why don't you take off a bloom? It'll make it a little more balanced. That's it. Very nicely done, Kaelen. I think this may be one of your best arrangements. Well, I think it's time for you to dash to the castle before you get much colder."

"I don't know, Russett," Lucian said with a smile, "I'd rather stay here than go to dragon fighting."

"Just smack him upside the head a few times," Russett teased. "Maybe then he'll learn."

The boys laughed and Lucian retorted, "I doubt it."

"I do too," Russett admitted. "Well, go on now. No sense being late."

"Bye Russett," the boys said as they left the greenhouse and sprinted through the snow to the castle.

As Lucian went to the arena for his first session of dragon fighting, Kaelen wandered down the hallway to the witches' classroom for spell breaking with Adrian. As it turned out he was a little bit early. Calypso was sitting at her desk writing when he walked in. Adrian had not yet arrived. "Prince Kaelen, you're a tad early. Did Russett let you out sooner than normal?"

"I don't think so. It's just really cold so I ran all the way," Kaelen replied.

"I see. Well, how is your reading coming along? Have you found any answers about the gems you asked about?" Calypso asked.

Kaelen grimaced slightly. "I'm only about a third of the way through the book. I've found a little bit about amber, but it didn't mention turquoise there at all. So I'm still reading."

"Well, perhaps since you are early," Calypso began, "we can discuss what you've learned so far and perhaps I can help you gain some new insight."

"Okay. Um, I read that amber promotes warmth and is thought to give strength to the wearer like the strength of trees," Kaelen explained. "But I didn't quite get that."

Calypso smiled. "It's really very simple, Kaelen. Amber is from ancient tree sap; the blood of the tree if you will. It is blood that gives life, strength and warmth. There are those who believe amber to be a gift from nature, the sacrifice of one living entity to strengthen another."

"I don't remember reading about that," Kaelen admitted.

As Adrian walked into the room, Calypso said, "I believe that comes later in the book." Turning her attention to Adrian she chided, "You're late."

"I'm sorry," Adrian replied, "I was held after swimming for a while because my eyes went all blurry. Achilles wanted Tallia to look me over before I went to any other classes."

"Ah, and are you feeling better?" Calypso asked.

"Yes ma'am," Adrian said.

"Then let's begin." Calypso turned to the chalkboard and began writing notes on it while beginning her lecture. The two boys got out paper and pens before feverishly taking notes.

In dragon fighting, George and Lucian were listening to a hopelessly boring lecture about dragon behavior. "I do hope you are paying attention, princelings," Draconus sneered at one point, "because you will soon be put to the test."

Lucian rolled his eyes as he finished jotting down the notes on Draconus' magic chalkboard. He glanced over at George who shared his look of disgust. By this point each of them had been successful in defeating the dragon at various points throughout the semester. Lucian knew it wasn't because Draconus was backing off any. If anything, each victory against him spurred the dragon to become swifter and more cunning.

Draconus continued the lecture as George and Lucian silently took notes. It was a great relief when the two dragon fighting classes were over. They walked to the dining hall where their friends were already waiting for them. "You know, I'd rather deal with a test than listen to that dragon for that long." George said as they sat down with their tray.

"Me too," Lucian agreed. "I was going nuts listening to him."

"Long day in dragon fighting?" Kaelen asked.

"The longest," George moaned. "We had to listen to three hours of dragon behavior. It wasn't as bad during the first part because at least there were a few other guys in there. But the second part when it's just Lucian and I was torture."

"Well, maybe he'll give us that test next time and we can have a whole class period where he doesn't talk," Lucian said hopefully.

"I wouldn't count on it," Kaelen said.

"Yeah," Lucian agreed miserably. "Well, how was your day, Adrian?"

Adrian shrugged but didn't speak.

"That bad?" Jacobi asked.

"He's not talking to anyone," Kaelen answered for him. "His tongue grew again during spell breaking and he hasn't been able to say anything without spitting, ribbeting or catching what few bugs are left in the school."

"Shut up," Adrian muttered.

"Hey, it's not my fault," Kaelen retorted scowling at Adrian. "Nobody here caused you to turn into an amphibian. Ignoring everyone isn't going to make you feel any better."

"Adrian," George said, "we're your friends. We're not going to make fun of you."

When he turned to them, he sighed, "I'm sorry, ribbet, guys. It's just, ribbet, so frustrating. What, ribbet, are they going to do in, ribbet, December when the princesses, ribbet, come? They can't, ribbet, hide this any, ribbet, more."

Lucian tried to smile, "Why worry about that now? It's still over a month away. I'm sure the fairies will think of something."

"Yeah, I'll be banished, ribbet, to my room like Kaelen is," Adrian moaned.

"Hey, I could use the company," Kaelen teased gently. "And being stuck with me for a day wouldn't be so bad, would it?"

Shrugging, Adrian said, "I guess not. Ribbet, but look at my hair. It's starting, ribbet, to fall out."

"Doesn't look any thinner to me," Jacobi said. "You know, maybe if you stop worrying so much about it, then you won't notice as much."

The other boys joined Adrian in glaring at Jacobi. "Really?" Adrian asked sarcastically.

"It was just a thought," Jacobi replied quietly.

"Well, I don't see how it needs to be the only topic of conversation today," George stated. "Why don't we change the subject? I for one am planning on going to town this coming weekend for some new shirts. Does anyone else want to come along?"

To everyone's surprise, Adrian said, "Yeah, I'll, ribbet, come along. But it might be easier, ribbet, if we waited a week or so."

"Great," George replied honestly. "I think I can wait that long. Anyone else interested in joining us?"

Soon they were talking about the upcoming trip to town. Lucian had already decided that he wanted to get something for Moira that he could give her at their next meeting. He had a feeling that she would need something to cheer her up. Adrian's change had become so obvious that he was sure Calista would have to meet with his family and with Allegra to gently break the news to them. Although, how one could break such news gently was somewhat of a mystery to Lucian. But he was also sure that the fairies had dealt with similar situations before.

On the Saturday they were going to town, Adrian had so much make-up on that he felt sure people would notice. He was wearing mittens to cover his hands and to keep him warm against the cold outside. The colder it got the sleepier he began to feel. He had trouble focusing in some of his classes as chilly drafts entered the rooms. As they rode in the carriage towards town, he felt himself drifting to sleep. The others would poke him and at one point Kaelen stomped rather viciously on his foot. "Ouch!" Adrian yelped, jumping from the seat and causing the carriage to rock precariously.

"Stay awake, Adrian," Kaelen warned. "We don't want to try to get you out of hibernation mode if you fall fully asleep."

"Sorry guys," Adrian yawned. "I'm just so tired."

Lucian took off his coat and wrapped it around Adrian's legs. "There, that will help keep your body temperature up some."

They finally arrived and the boys split up to do their own shopping. Adrian soon realized that Lucian was heading the same direction he was. "Let me guess, Moira's accessories are too limited," Adrian said teasingly, trying to stifle another wide-mouthed yawn.

Lucian shrugged, "I just figured since I'm in town anyway I'd get a little something for her."

Adrian nodded, "That was my thought. Well, actually, for your sister, not Moira. The hard part though is I have no idea what to get her."

Laughing, Lucian said, "Well, if you help me out I'll return the favor."

"Deal," Adrian yawned. "Please tell me we're almost there. That dirt looks so inviting and I'm so very tired."

"Just hang in there," Lucian said encouragingly. "We've got just two more buildings to go. Why do you want to go to the dirt anyway?"

"Oh, I don't know," Adrian replied sleepily. "I might dig a little bed out of it to sleep in. Or maybe I'll just lie down on it. I'm too tired to dig right now."

They walked inside a shop with large windows and a sign hanging outside that read *Fernando's Fine Jewelry* in fancy script. "Good morning young sirs," a frail-looking old man said in a heavy accent they weren't able to identify, "and what can I do for you?" The man was small, with silver hair and a well-groomed goatee.

"We're just looking for winter gifts for our princesses," Lucian replied.

"Well, you've come to the right place," Fernando said with a smile. "What did you have in mind?"

"That's part of the problem," Lucian admitted.

Fernando laughed. "I see, well come this way my young friends and I'll show you what I have. Now, describe your princess to me. We'll start with the short one."

Flushing, Adrian said as he concentrated on not ribbiting, "Well, Allegra is a beautiful girl, in every way. She's got wavy auburn hair and warm, brown eyes. She's always smiling and there's a light in her smile that makes every problem seem easy to overcome. She's the world to me," Adrian finished softly.

Fernando said something in a language neither understood before continuing, "Well, I'm sure I've got just the thing for her. Step this way." He took them over to a case of stunning necklaces. "For a little ray of sunshine, I give gold to add sparkle and glow to her light. And then for love and fire, ruby. Finally, diamond to make it last forever. This necklace here was designed by fairy craftsmen years and years ago. It is perhaps a mortal's poor reproduction, but no doubt you see how beautiful it is. Imagine this around the neck of your beloved."

Adrian looked over the necklace that was being held before him. A heart-shaped pendant of gold with inlaid ruby and diamond chips amidst delicate scrollwork hung from a delicate gold chain. He noticed small hinges to the side. "Is this a locket?"

"Very perceptive of you," Fernando said. "It is indeed a locket. Inside, your princess can stow a portrait of you, to always be carried above her heart."

"What do you think, Lucian?" Adrian asked.

"I think it's lovely, just then sort of thing Allegra would love," Lucian replied.

Nodding, Adrian said, "That's what I was thinking. I'll take it."

"An excellent choice sir," Fernando said, placing the necklace inside a box. "And now for your very tall friend; what of your princess?"

Describing Moira in detail, Lucian painted a portrait in words of his princess.

When he finished, Fernando led them to a different case. "I believe that your princess would do best with rose gold, giving the necklace fire and a brilliant glow. For beauty and serenity, sapphires. And always there are diamonds. They represent the everlasting nature of love," Fernando explained as he pulled a necklace out of the case. "This is also fairy design. Look at how delicate the workmanship is. Can you see your true love wearing this when you rescue her?"

It was exactly what Lucian would have imagined and more. Tiny chips of diamond and sapphire swirled around a pendant of rose gold. The pendant was not a locket, but Lucian didn't necessarily think Moira needed one. This pendant, a star with swirls of blue and white was exactly what he wanted. "It's perfect," Lucian said. "Don't you think so, Adrian?"

"She'll love it," Adrian agreed.

"Then we will wrap these and take care of payment over here," Fernando said with a smile. He led them over to a desk where he carefully wrapped each boxed necklace in paper and tied a small ribbon around them. The boys paid for their purchases and then walked back out into the cold. They met the other boys at the clothing shop they'd gone to many times before.

"Where did you guys go?" Kaelen asked.

"Jewelry shop," Lucian replied.

"It's a little early to be purchasing rings, don't you think?" George teased as he paid for his shirts.

"It is," Lucian admitted. "That's why we didn't buy rings."

The boys laughed and soon headed back to the carriage. For much of the ride they were poking and prodding at Adrian to keep him awake. The temperature was swiftly falling and by the time they reached the castle, everyone had given Adrian their coats and he was still drifting in and out of sleep. They half-carried him into the castle. Calista was in the hallway when they arrived and saw them. "What happened?" she asked as they helped him sit on a chair.

"Nothing happened, it's just really cold outside," Jacobi said.

Calista sighed. "Of course, he's becoming more like an amphibian. He can't maintain his own body temperature and so he's going to sleep. Bring him to the infirmary. I'm sure Tallia can help us get him warmed up sufficiently."

Carrying Adrian between the two of them, Lucian and Kaelen made their way slowly to the infirmary. George and Jacobi followed along behind. When they walked in, Calista was leaving. Tallia had a tub steaming in the middle of the floor. "Take the extra layers off of him and then set him in the tub. Lucian, can you bring a fresh set of clothing for Adrian to wear please?"

"Sure," Lucian said as he walked back out. He quickly went up to Adrian's room and went through his dresser looking for clothes. When he'd collected everything, he went downstairs to the infirmary where everyone else was sitting around the tub.

Adrian opened his eyes sleepily. "It feels nice in here. What happened?"

"You started hibernating," Kaelen replied. "Nothing we did could keep you warm enough."

"I'll just stay in here then," Adrian sighed. "It's warm right here."

Tallia laughed, "You can't stay in there forever, Adrian. You'll get all pruny. But I think we'll give you another ten to twenty minutes until you're feeling a little more alert."

"Alright," Adrian said calmly. "Hey, Lucian, where's, ribbet, the box?"

"I already took it to your room," Lucian replied.

"Oh come on," George said, "you're not going to let us see what you got for them?"

"Nope," Lucian retorted. "It's going to be a surprise."

"Yeah, for her not for us," Jacobi pointed out.

Lucian shook his head. "I don't want to unwrap it. I'd never be able to get it looking as nice, no matter how hard I tried."

"I'll wrap it for you," George offered. "I'm pretty good at it."

"Go on, ribbet," Adrian said. "You should, ribbet ribbet, show them."

"Oh alright," Lucian relented. He unwrapped the long, flat box and opened it to show the others. "I'm not sure why you're so interested anyway," he continued as the boys crowded around him. "It's not like you'll be wearing it."

"No, but if we like what we see, we may go back and get things for our princesses too," George explained.

Laughing, Lucian said, "I guess I hadn't thought of that."

"You don't have much time left if you're going to do that," Kaelen replied. "There's just under a month until our winter visit."

The weeks seemed to fly until finals. Adrian's change had become more noticeable than ever. He had several bald patches where greenish-hued skin showed though. His eyes were constantly bugged out and more yellow than green. Perhaps the worst of it was that he could barely speak at all. He had to put all of his concentration onto speaking without croaking. Sometimes he concentrated so much on that, that he was unable to remember what it was he was trying to say. The day before the meeting he had his spell breaking final. He mustered up his courage and said, "Calypso, I need to, ribbet ribbet, ask a question."

"Of course, Adrian, what is it?" Calypso asked.

Adrian paused to gather his thoughts and focus on sounding human. "Calypso, is there any way, ribbet, for me to be normal tomorrow?"

Calypso eyed him for a moment. She then turned to where Kaelen had just taken his seat. "Stay after class, Adrian. We'll discuss your options in private."

The final seemed to last eternity as Adrian tried to answer the questions. He had difficulty using his pen properly. It would become stuck to his hands at awkward angles and he'd have to try to dislodge it before continuing. Worse, Kaelen was going very slowly about his final. Adrian knew he wasn't really doing it on purpose, but silently wished his friend would speed things up. When Kaelen finally left the room, Calypso beckoned to Adrian to sit at a seat right next to her desk.

"In answer to your question, Adrian, yes, there is a way," Calypso began. "But mind you, it comes at a price."

"Whatever it is, I'll do it," Adrian said fervently. "I just want to be normal for one day."

"Don't rush into this decision, Adrian," Calypso warned. "All magic comes at a price, whether from you or from someone or something else. In this particular case, the scenario is that yes, you would be completely human for a single twenty-four hour period. However, at the stroke of midnight of that day's end, your transformation would be complete. You would never be human again until the spell is broken by your princess. Due to the nature of this, I would ask you to speak with Calista before you make your final decision."

"I don't need to talk to her," Adrian replied. "I'm willing to do it."

"All the same," Calypso said kindly, "something of this magnitude needs the headmistress' knowledge and approval. I'll send a message to her to meet at the hovel at seven-thirty tonight. You should also arrive at that time. A spell this powerful cannot be done by a single witch, not even the Head of the Sisters. Also, do not tell your friends about our conversation. There is no need to give them a false sense of hope for you if Calista should turn down your request."

Adrian nodded. "I understand."

"Then I'll see you tonight," Calypso replied.

All through the remainder of the day, Adrian was quiet and thoughtful. He wanted desperately to at least be able to speak to Lucian about this. But having given Calypso his word, he dared not break it. The others tried to engage him in their conversation, but he couldn't remain focused. His thoughts were entirely devoted to the conversation he would be having that evening with Calista and the Sisters. He hoped that Calista would agree with him.

"Are you even on the same planet as us?" George asked teasingly, pulling Adrian away from his thoughts.

"I guess so," Adrian replied.

"Anything you want to talk about?" Lucian asked.

Adrian tried to smile. "I'd love to talk about it, but I'm not allowed to."

"Does it have to do with tomorrow?" Kaelen guessed.

"Guys, I really can't talk about it, as much as I'd like to," Adrian said. "I promised that I wouldn't."

"Well, we don't want you to break your promise," Jacobi said. "We'll leave it alone."

The rest of the meal seemed to pass by in hours rather than minutes. When it was finally time to head outside, he said goodbye to his friends and headed out to the hovel. It was so cold outside and the ground looked so tempting, but he concentrated on getting to the hovel. When he finally arrived, he knocked on the door. "Can I, ribbet ribbet, come in?" he asked sleepily as Maeve answered it.

"Oh, yes, of course, Adrian," Maeve replied. She opened the door and helped him inside. "Sit by the fire, you'll be warmer there."

"Thanks," Adrian said. He looked around and saw all of the witches sitting near a merrily crackling fire. Calista was also in the room already, speaking with Calypso. It didn't look like whatever the conversation was about was going at all well. He had a sinking feeling that she was about to crush his hopes of being able to see Allegra normal.

"It's good to see you, Adrian," Calypso said warmly. "We were just discussing your request."

"Adrian, I simply cannot allow for you to go through with this," Calista interrupted. "How will you finish your schooling if you are turned into a frog before the end of even this school year?"

"Calista, as I've tried to tell you," Maeve interjected sweetly, "he's going to be a frog by the end of this year one way or the other. Allow him this opportunity to be with his princess in a way that both are comfortable and happy with."

"Allow Adrian to speak for himself, Sister," Morghana rasped. "Adrian, why do you want to do this?" When he began to hesitate she continued, "Don't worry about your speech; within these walls, your voice will be heard."

"There are many reasons," Adrian began. "First, I can't hide this any longer, Calista. My skin isn't even human when I put the make-up on. My hands and feet are almost completely webbed. I'm losing my hair, my eyes are weird-looking and my mouth is totally out of proportion with the rest of my face. No matter what you or Tallia did, Allegra would notice. Second, I don't think there's much else you or anyone can teach me to prepare for my quest. I've realized that I don't have a quest. I have to wait for Allegra to be ready to save me. You can't teach me how to sit and wait patiently; I can already do that myself. Well, sit anyway. I'm not so good at the patient part. And third, I deserve one night to truly be myself with Allegra. I've never once gotten in trouble, not officially. I've done everything that has been asked of me and I think I deserve this one night to tell Allegra how much she means to me without having to worry about sticking my tongue out at her."

"Adrian, I know this is difficult, but please consider," Calista began.

"Quite frankly, Calista," Adrian interrupted, "I don't care what you or any other fairy here has to say about this. I've made up my mind. I accept Calypso's offer."

There was a strange pulse through the room. Calista looked slightly crestfallen. "It's too late now, Calista," Calypso said gently. "He's made up his mind and he is old enough to make this kind of decision himself. His words cannot be taken back."

"I know," Calista whispered. "Adrian, I wish I could tell you to reconsider, but I see there is no turning back. What I will say is that because of your transformation, we will do things differently than we normally would. At the stroke of midnight when this spell is reversed, you will be automatically transferred to the place you will await your princess. There will be no time to say goodbye to your friends, to your family, or to Allegra. It will be instant and irreversible. This is how it must be."

"You never planned on meeting with Allegra and I," Adrian said.

Calista shook her head, "I couldn't. Part of being on a quest is having unknowns. To tell Allegra the nature of your transformation would take away from her ability to complete this quest. It would make one part easy, but that would by nature make other parts even more difficult. It is better for her not to know."

Adrian nodded, "I see. However, I would request that I be allowed five minutes during my end of semester interview to talk to my family. I understand not having time with Allegra, but my mother needs to know that I'm alright. And so does my sister."

"I'll grant that request," Calista agreed. "Calypso, I'll return now if you don't need me any longer."

"I believe my sisters and I can take things from here," Calypso replied.

"Very well," Calista said as she stood from her seat. "I'll see you in the morning, Adrian. Good night."

"Good night, Calista," Adrian returned as she left the room.

Once she was out of the room, the Sisters stood and circled around Adrian. "As I've said, Adrian, there is now no turning back. By your own choice and your own words, this spell has begun."

"I understand," Adrian said. "I want to do this."

"Then we will proceed," Calypso said as the lights in the room flickered and the air crackled with energy and magic.

Chapter 4

The next morning, Adrian awoke and sat up blearily. The night before had seemed so long. He had spent an untold number of hours at the witches' hovel having them do their spells. If he had known it would take so long, he would have asked them to do it a bit earlier so he could get more sleep. After getting out of bed, he walked over to the mirror. He couldn't help but stare at his reflection for a while; he was normal. Smiling, he got dressed and then frowned. "Why are my pants too short?" he asked aloud. He put on a shirt and the sleeves pulled far past his wrists. He sighed, "I guess I've been growing. What am I going to do? Maybe Lucian can help me." He walked down the hallway to Lucian's room and knocked on the door.

"Adrian!" Lucian said in surprise when he opened the door. "You look, normal."

"It's what I couldn't tell you about. I made a deal with the witches yesterday," Adrian replied. "But I have a problem. None of my clothes fit."

"Well, makes sense," Lucian said as he pulled the door forward so Adrian could come in. "The fairies have been keeping your height at what it was two years ago. Obviously you did some growing in that time. You're a good four inches taller than you were. I think I still have a set of old uniforms that might fit you." He looked through his dresser drawers. "Here, try these on for size."

Adrian changed into the uniforms and looked in the mirror. "Other than I'm a bit broader than you are, they're pretty good."

"Well, try this set then," Lucian suggested, pulling one out of his closet. "It was made by someone a little less experienced in tailoring than I normally go to. All the pieces were just a tad too wide for me. It may just fit you the right way though."

Changing into the new uniform, Adrian stretched his arms around. "That feels better. In fact, it's almost a perfect fit. Thanks, Lucian. I couldn't think of anyone else tall enough to have clothes that might fit me."

"No problem," Lucian grinned. Then getting serious he asked, "So, how long do you have like this?"

"Twenty-four hours," Adrian replied.

"Well, let's not waste a moment," Lucian said as he buttoned his jacket. "The princesses will be here any time now. Do you have everything from your pockets?" he asked as he buttoned his own jacket.

Checking his pockets for the little wrapped box from the jewelers, Adrian stated, "Yeah, I've got everything."

"Then let's go," Lucian said. They walked out of the room and down the stairs. "Oh wait, we should go say hi to Kaelen first though. Kaelen is having breakfast in his room with Gelasia so that there will be no chance of anyone seeing him."

"That's a bummer," Adrian said as they returned back upstairs and went to Kaelen's room. They knocked and Kaelen welcomed them in. After saying hello to Gelasia, the boys sat down for a minute to chat.

"Adrian, you look like a normal human being. I'm jealous," Kaelen admitted.

"It almost didn't work out," Adrian told him. "But I get one day to be normal for Allegra. After that we'll just have to see what happens." He hated lying to them, but he had been forbidden to say anything to his friends. It would hurt to leave and not have them know where he was going. Although truth be told, he didn't even know where he was going. He just knew that this was his last day with any of them. "So are you going to be at the ball tonight like you were last year?"

"Maybe, Calista told me that she had received a letter stating that my mother had heard rumors that I was here and would be most displeased to learn that they were true. As long as Mom and Dad leave before the ball begins, Calista might let me come down for a bit. Or, she might not simply so that more rumors don't get spread," Kaelen explained. "We don't want my mother taking Anna out of school just because I'm still considered worthy of being a Prince Charming."

"That's awful," Lucian exclaimed. "I wish there was something we could do."

Kaelen shook his head, "I know, but there's not so no use worrying over it. Here, give this to Anna if you could. I know it's risky sending her a message as she leaves for break, but I need for her to read it." He handed Lucian a carefully folded sheet of paper.

"I'll make sure she gets it," Lucian promised.

"Thanks," Kaelen said with a sad smile. "Now, you two best get downstairs. You'll be late meeting your princesses. Tell them all hi for me."

"Will do," Adrian replied. "And in case I don't see you before I go, have a good break. You're a great friend and I'll miss you."

"Miss me?" Kaelen laughed, "It's only going to be a month."

"It'll seem longer," Adrian said sadly.

Kaelen and Lucian both looked at Adrian for a moment. "Is there something we should know?" Kaelen asked.

"No, I just want you to know that you're a good friend. I hope you have a great break and that you have the best of luck with everything. I'm going to go downstairs now," Adrian finished, stammering a little. He walked quickly out of the room before either could say a word.

Lucian raised an eyebrow. "That was weird."

Shrugging, Kaelen said, "Maybe it's all that human emotion getting to him. I'm sure everything's just fine."

"You're probably right," Lucian replied, though he didn't believe it for a moment.

"Well, if you don't get downstairs, you're going to be late," Kaelen warned teasingly. "I'll be fine up here. I've got a beautiful lady here to keep me company."

Gelasia laughed and Lucian said, "Alright, I'll see you tomorrow morning, if not sooner." Waving behind him, Lucian walked down the stairs. When he got down there, the princesses were already beginning to mill about. Allegra spied him coming down and ran to give him a hug. "I've missed you too," he teased when she finally released him.

"Doesn't Adrian look wonderful?" Allegra asked. "And he's grown a lot since the last time I was here."

"I take it you're not mad at him anymore then," Lucian guessed.

"No, it's clear that there's nothing wrong with him," Allegra said. She smiled over at him as he talked to some of their other friends. "It must have been just as he said."

"You should trust your prince," Lucian agreed.

Allegra didn't respond as Moira came over. "I suppose I owe you an apology," she said.

"For what?" Lucian asked.

"Not believing you. I was sure that you and Adrian were hiding something from me," Moira explained. "But he looks just as happy as can be. It must have just been my imagination."

Lucian swallowed. "Apology accepted. Let's go to breakfast." He offered his arm which she took graciously and together they walked into the dining hall. "Oh, by the way, I need you to give this to Anna, Kaelen's sister."

Moira frowned. "Don't you think that's a little risky with her parents coming and all? We all know what could happen if they found out."

"I know," Lucian replied, "and I agree with you. But I made a promise."

Sighing, Moira took the piece of paper from Lucian. "I just don't know how much longer we can get away with this. They're both getting a little reckless with these."

Lucian admitted quietly, "I know, but we've got to do something for them. We would all do the same thing put in a similar situation."

Moira nodded, but didn't reply. She placed the letter in a small pocket on her gown. "I'll do it during the activities today."

"Thanks," Lucian said with a smile. "That's a beautiful color on you. It really brings out your eyes."

"Well someone told me that I should wear blue today," Moira replied teasingly, looking down at the dark blue gown she was wearing. "Do I get to find out why you made that request?"

"All in good time," Lucian said mysteriously.

They continued talking with their friends until the fairies dismissed them to the gym for games and activities. Agreeing that they'd like some time just to be together, the group found a magical fireplace surrounded by comfy armchairs and sat down. There was laughter and chatter amidst the group as they watched younger students and older students filter around them. Anna walked meaningfully towards the group and asked in a whisper, "How's my brother?"

"He's doing fine," Lucian replied quietly.

"Here," Moira whispered, handing Anna the letter from her pocket. "He wanted us to give this to you. Just be careful with it," she warned.

Anna nodded and walked away to rejoin her prince who had been beckoning to her from a table with a game set up on it.

"It's tragic that things must be that way for them," Eleanor said sadly as they watched her leave.

"It is," Moira agreed, "but I do wish they would exercise more caution. We can't keep up this charade forever. At some point, they're going to be caught."

"Well, let's not discuss it further," George said kindly. "We'll just do all we can for each of them and stand by them when the time comes to do so. Ladies, how did your finals go?"

Eleanor laughed merrily, "Oh, George, of all the topics you could have picked why on earth would you choose that one?"

"I'm curious," George replied genuinely.

Leticia smiled, "I suppose our finals went as they always do. Lots of tests, lots of writing and balancing and such."

"Balancing?" Jacobi asked.

"A lady always has proper posture, no matter what she is doing," Clarissa explained. "So part of each final is balancing something on our heads so that we have to maintain the appropriate posture. If it drops, you have to begin again with something bigger."

"That's just mean!" Adrian exclaimed. "I'd have a two-story building on my head by the time I was done."

Allegra laughed, "I doubt that. You tend to have good posture anyway. But I'll admit that it is very challenging; especially when you're in a horsemanship final. It's not easy to balance a book on your head when you're working through a dressage course. And having Sunset Rose become skittish at the last moment didn't help."

"Oh, I'm sorry," Leticia said. "Is that what happened? I couldn't tell."

"Yes, something must have spooked her," Allegra replied.

"Do you get any kind of special recognition?" Lucian asked. "I mean, we get medals in classes we've shown great improvement in and that sort of thing. Do you have anything like that?"

"It depends on the class," Eleanor said. "I think Moira must have enough certificates and handkerchiefs from sewing to paper her walls."

Moira blushed, "I don't have that many."

Laughing Leticia said, "You're just being modest. And Eleanor is perhaps exaggerating a touch. Some classes give a certificate, some give a small token like a handkerchief; it all depends on the teacher and the class."

The morning progressed rapidly and Adrian wished that time would slow down. He knew this was the last time he could be with his friends. All too soon, it was time for lunch and parents began filtering into the castle. He was greeted warmly by his mother and Nana and to his surprise, Uncle Sebastian. "We didn't expect to see you!" he said as Sebastian wrapped him in a hug.

"Well, I could always leave," Sebastian teased with a grin. There was a twinkle in his eye that lit the room.

"No, I'm really glad you're here," Adrian said sincerely.

"I thought you might be," Sebastian replied knowingly. "Now let's go eat. I'm sure the food is quite as excellent now as it was when I was in school."

"I'm sure it's improved," Nana countered with a grin.

They headed into the dining hall along with Lucian's family. The others were still waiting for their parents to come. "We'll join you in a bit," George said. "You go on ahead."

Everyone else began their lunch and they were soon joined by their other friends. "What are you doing over winter break?" Lucian asked everyone.

"Well, ours will be a bit chaotic," Leticia began.

"I have an art competition starting the same time as the winter dressage finals in Rendorlin," Eleanor explained. "Leticia obviously will be going straight to Rendorlin to begin the preliminary competitions and then we'll be going after my art competition is over just in time to see her win the grand prize," she finished confidently.

"I wouldn't count on," Leticia said blushing. "As I understand, Allegra will be entering the same competition and she's very good. Am I right, Allegra?"

"That is my plan, we should travel together," Allegra suggested.

King Julian said, "I would certainly feel better if she did. I don't like the idea of her traveling alone."

"Oh Daddy," Leticia teased, "I'm not a little girl anymore."

"You'll always be his little girl," Lysander said with a smile. "Our children never grow up. At least, not in our eyes."

"Too true," Julian agreed.

The conversation continued to ebb and flow as they talked about all the things that would be going on over the winter and into the next semester. Soon they were going to the hallways to await their meetings. Calista came out and surprised everyone by calling Jacobi first. "That's odd," Lavinia said suspiciously. "She normally begins your year with you, Adrian."

"I'm not sure why she didn't," Adrian fibbed. "Maybe she just wanted to change things up."

"Well, I certainly hope she doesn't expect us to do your meeting during Moira's. I will not be torn between the two of you," Lavinia stated.

"I'm sure she'll keep that in mind, Mother," Adrian replied gently. Nana was looking at him though she knew something everyone else didn't. Even Uncle Sebastian seemed to know something as his gaze drifted from Adrian to his mother and back again.

"What made you choose to come now, Uncle Sebastian?" Adrian asked, hoping to get him to turn the intensity of his stare down a little.

"Oh now you know I never reveal my intentions," Sebastian teased. "That would spoil all the joy of seeing you. Suffice it to say I felt missed and decided to grace you with my presence."

Moira laughed, "Well, I'll have to start missing you more so that you come more often."

Laughing as well, Sebastian retorted, "Ah my dear, it doesn't work that way. I'm afraid my visit will be very short. I'm taking Nana away with me for a trip to Rendorlin. I know how she loves to watch the dressage finals and I'm not taking no for an answer, Bethany," he added as she looked ready to argue. "I've already taken the liberty of having your maid pack your things. Like it or not, we're going on a road trip."

Resigned to the idea, Nana said, "Well, that certainly explains why Maryanne was rummaging through my things before we left and why she insisted that I bring that trunk. I tried to tell her it was far too big to be an overnight bag. And when, may I ask, do you intend on returning me?"

"Oh, I haven't decided yet," Sebastian replied with a mischievous wink. "I may decide to keep you forever."

"Now that would never do," Lavinia said. "I couldn't possibly be without you both for that long."

The family laughed and soon it was time for Moira's meeting. "Adrian, send Nana to knock on the door should Calista start your interview while I'm with Moira."

Adrian nodded. He already knew he wouldn't have to. He watched as the others went in for their interviews and came out. Soon Moira had returned and they were waiting Adrian's turn. He was the last boy of his age left to be interviewed. Calista came out and said, "Adrian, if you and your family would please join me inside."

"All of us?" Lavinia asked.

"Yes, I have something very important that I need to discuss with you all," Calista replied.

Moira looked suspiciously at Lucian whom she had been talking to as they waited. Lucian tried not to look guilty as Moira and the others followed Calista into her office. "I apologize Sebastian, I had not known you would be coming. I'm afraid I'm one seat short," Calista said as she closed the door.

"I'm afraid I do have a bad habit of showing up unannounced," Sebastian replied. "I'll be fine standing."

"Thank you," Calista said warmly. "Now, to begin with I want you to know that Adrian is not in trouble. He has done a fine job this semester and has overcome many, many obstacles. His improvement in all of his classes has been commented on again and again by his teachers. They are all most pleased with him."

"Even Achilles?" Adrian interrupted.

Calista laughed, "Yes, even Achilles. Now, I'm afraid I have some bad news; news which must not leave this room. Part of it will make itself known as is, but much of what I tell you cannot be repeated to anyone, not even your closest friends."

Everyone was quiet and Adrian was looking at the floor. He suddenly couldn't bear to look at them anymore. He could see fear and disappointment on the faces of his family. "We'll keep this knowledge to ourselves, as you've requested," Lavinia said softly, not turning her gaze away from her son. "What has happened?"

"It is a long and complicated story, one too long to go into right now," Calista began. "I'll make it as brief as possible. Despite not being ordered to, a witch punished Adrian for a slight offense. For the past three years he has been slowly transforming into, well, I really shouldn't say."

"If you don't, I will," Adrian warned. "I'm not lying to them anymore."

"Very well," Calista sighed. "Adrian is turning into a frog. We did try to have this reversed," she continued as Lavinia and Moira both looked furious and Nana was looking thoughtful. "However, I was informed by Maeve that this is part of his quest. His princess, Allegra, will have to find him and break the enchantment. I realize that this may seem to be opposite of what things normally are, but it has happened in the past that the princess was the rescuer. These stories also had happy endings. However, it is imperative that you not tell anyone outside this room, particularly Allegra. It would make things more difficult rather than helping. It's all a part of how the quests work as I'm sure each of you will remember from your own quests. Moira, it is very important that you not say a word to Allegra, I need your promise."

Moira was fighting tears. "How long have you known?" she asked Adrian angrily.

"I'm sorry, Moira, I couldn't tell you," Adrian said.

"How long?" she shouted.

Adrian looked at the floor again. "About a year."

"And you never told me?" Moira asked accusingly, hurt coloring the tones of her voice. "Not once did you mention to me. I'm your sister, your twin!"

"He wasn't allowed to Moira," Calista said gently. "I forbid him from saying anything to any of you for fear that one of you would say something to Allegra. Please understand that she can't know. It is better this way."

"Why? Why is lying the answer?" Moira asked bitterly. "How will that help?"

"Moira," Nana interjected as Calista had started to speak, "it is better because if we make that part easy, another part will be made twice is hard. That is the nature of a quest. If we tell Allegra the nature of Adrian's transformation, she may have an even harder time finding him. Or the spell may become more challenging to break. You must trust us."

"How can I?" Moira demanded. "You've all lied to me."

"Moira Elizabeth, no one has lied to you," Lavinia chided. "Adrian did what he was told, as a gentleman would. I had begun to wonder about him. His eyes were always so like Martin's and then they were different. But he didn't lie. He never said he wasn't changing. None of us asked him if he was. And Calista has not lied either. She didn't tell us because she knew it was what was best at the time. Frankly, I don't think it was her choice to tell us this much," Lavinia added, looking again at Calista. When she nodded, Lavinia continued, "If no one else trust me. Trust Nana and Uncle Sebastian. None of us knew of this."

Putting her face in her hands, Moira sobbed, "I won't tell anyone. I promise."

"Thank you, Moira," Calista said. "I know how hard this must be."

"Do you?" Moira asked. "Do you really?"

Raising an eyebrow, Calista replied, "Do remember that I am many centuries older than anyone in this room. I have seen this before and yes, I know how hard it is. Now, I'm going to leave you alone for a few minutes and then it will be time for our feast. Adrian looks like himself because he has made a deal with the witches. He gets this one last day to spend with you and with Allegra before the transformation is complete. At midnight tonight he will disappear as you've seen princesses do at graduation. He will instantly be transported to the location at which he will await Allegra. You will not see him again until that time. This is also per Adrian's request. You have five minutes. Say your goodbyes and then get yourselves ready to be merry. Enjoy this night, it is the last you will have together for quite some time." Calista then rose from her seat and left the room.

Adrian finally looked up at everyone, tears glistening in his eyes. "I'm so sorry, I wanted to tell you, I really did," he began.

"Hush, dear," Lavinia said, taking him in her arms in a tight hug. "I understand. You couldn't tell us. Calista was right in doing what she did. I'm just sorry you had to bear this alone. I wish we had more time, but know how proud I am of you. I love you, very much."

"I love you too, Mother," Adrian replied, his voice muffled. When his mother let him go, he looked at Moira. She was looking away from him. "Moira, I'm sorry. Please, believe me."

Moira turned to him. "You could have trusted me. You should have trusted me."

"I know, I'm sorry," Adrian said.

Throwing her arms around his neck, Moira asked quietly, "What am I going to do without you?"

"Hey, it won't be forever," Adrian replied as cheerfully as he could. "I'm going to miss you though."

"I'll miss you too," Moira said through tears. She finally let him go so that Nana and Uncle Sebastian could take their turns.

"Well, my boy, the adventure of a lifetime awaits you," Sebastian said, shaking Adrian's hand. "Make it count." He then hugged Adrian and moved so that Nana could talk to him.

"You knew all along, didn't you?" Adrian asked.

"I suspected," Nana admitted. "My dear, dear boy," she said as he fell into her arms. "Be strong. You are both capable of this. The fairies would never give you a quest nor your princess a quest that you weren't capable of turning into a happily ever after. We'll be waiting for you."

"Thank you," Adrian said.

They were quiet together for a few moments before Lavinia sniffled and said, "Well, I suppose we should try to regain our composure and join the others downstairs for supper and the ball. Adrian, you are so like your father. Continue to be like him."

Adrian nodded and they all walked out of the office and downstairs. They found Lucian's family and Allegra waving to them to join the group at the table.

"Are you alright?" Allegra asked.

"I'm fine," Adrian replied with a smile.

"Okay," Allegra said. "You'll never believe what just happened."

As she jumped into a story about what had been going on while they were upstairs, Adrian only half-listened to what she was saying. He focused on every aspect about her that he loved and cherished. The way her voice lilted when she was excited, the sparkle in her eyes, the soft wave of her hair. He wished more than anything that he could make this one night last forever.

"You're not even listening to me, are you?" Allegra asked teasingly, bringing him out of his thoughts.

Adrian smiled sheepishly. "I'm sorry, Allegra, I'm a bit tired."

"No matter," Allegra laughed. "I wasn't really saying anything of importance anyway."

The meal continued with light-hearted chatter. Lucian noticed how quiet Moira was and that she looked more than just sad, she looked angry. He had no doubt that as soon as they had a moment alone, he was going to be in for a talking to. And he didn't have long to wait. As the fairies cleared the hall to make room for a dance floor, Moira grabbed Lucian's hand and dragged him out of earshot of anyone else. "You knew didn't you?" she accused.

"Moira, I'm sorry," Lucian began. "I wanted very much to tell you."

"So instead you lied to me?" Moira asked bitterly. "Lucian, Adrian doesn't stand a chance. We both know that Allegra is terrified of frogs. She doesn't just dislike them; she loathes and fears them. How can she save him if she can't stand to be in the same room as a frog?"

"I hope you didn't tell him that," Lucian said.

"Of course not," Moira snapped. "But tell me how this is going to work out."

"Allegra will simply have to overcome her fear, that's all," Lucian said.

Moira glared at him. "You told me that he would be fine. You lied, Lucian."

"No I didn't," Lucian argued. "Yes, Allegra is afraid of frogs, but look at them." He paused and pointed to where Adrian and Allegra were standing. "She loves him and will do whatever she has to in order to save him. If that means she has to kiss a frog you better believe she'll close her eyes and pucker. It may scar her for life, but she'll do it because she loves him. Love is more powerful than fear."

"Then why did your mother's real prince abandon her?" Moira spat. She wished instantly she could take back the words.

"My mother's real prince is my dad," Lucian said calmly, though barely masked anger was in his voice. "Her original prince didn't truly love her."

He started to walk away but Moira grabbed his arm. "Lucian, I'm sorry, I shouldn't have said that. I'm just, I'm worried about him. I don't want to see him trapped for eternity as a frog."

"You won't," Lucian relied gently. "I promise."

"I'll hold you to that," Moira warned.

"I know; that's why I said it," Lucian said with a smile. "Now come on, we're missing the dance and you're losing valuable time with your brother." He offered her his arm and she accepted as they walked back towards the rest of the group. Soft strains of music were beginning and couples were out on the dance floor. Moira watched as Adrian led Allegra out to dance. She could see that they were deeply in love with each other. She only hoped that the love Allegra felt would be enough to see past the frog her prince would become.

"Well, you two look like you've been having quite the discussion," Leticia said with a grin. "Anything I should know about?"

"No," Moira replied, "just getting a few things straight."

Leticia smiled and said, "Alright. They all look so happy out there don't they?"

"They do," Lucian admitted. He then cleared his throat. "Moira, my timing may be terrible, but there's something I'd like you to do for me."

"Oh really?" Moira asked. "And what's that?"

"Close your eyes," Lucian commanded mysteriously. Raising an eyebrow curiously, Moira did as she was told. Lucian pulled the box from him pocket and took Moira's hand. "Now open them," he said as he placed the box in her hand.

"You're right; your timing is terrible," Moira replied, trying not to smile. "I'm still mad at you."

"Oh, well, maybe this will help," Lucian countered as Moira took off the wrapping. Moira gasped as she opened the box and saw what was inside. For a moment no one spoke at all and Lucian asked nervously, "Do you like it?"

Leticia looked over and said, "Lucian, that's stunning. Moira, don't you think so?"

Moira couldn't speak to anyone. Her eyes had filled with tears and she was just staring down at the box. "Where did you get this?" she finally choked.

"The jeweler's in town," Lucian replied, not sure this was the reaction he was looking for. "If you don't like it, I'm sure we could exchange it."

Shaking her head, Moira tried to regain her composure. "My mom," she began and then faltered. Clearing her throat she finally managed to say, "My mom has a necklace just like this. My dad gave it to her."

"Oh," Lucian said dumbly. He wasn't sure exactly what to say. For a long moment there was an awkward silence as Moira pulled herself together. "Do you like it?" Lucian repeated after a while.

Moira threw her arms around Lucian's neck. "I love it," she whispered. "I'm sorry, it's just, Mom hasn't worn that necklace in so long, but every now and again, I see her take it out of its box and admire it. It's beautiful, I really do like it."

"May I then?" Lucian asked, taking the necklace from the box.

Nodding, Moira turned and Lucian put the necklace around her neck and carefully closed the clasp. "For my beautiful, sapphire-eyed princess," he said gently. "Hopefully this gets me at least outside the doghouse, even if I'm still stuck in front of it."

Laughing, Moira said, "I think you've very effectively gotten me to forgive you."

Lavinia rejoined them from having enjoyed a waltz with Uncle Sebastian. "Why Moira, where on earth…?"

"Lucian gave it to me, Mother; isn't it lovely? Just like yours," Moira said.

Fighting tears, Lavinia replied, "It is exactly like mine. I'm assuming you went to Fernando."

"Yeah, how did you know?" Lucian asked.

"Martin always went to Fernando for jewelry," Lavinia explained. "He said there was no one with a finer eye for the exact piece to take your love's breath away. And he was right, as usual."

A soft waltz began and Adrian took his mother out for a dance. Lucian offered Moira his arm. "May I?"

"You know you don't have to ask," Moira replied with a smile.

"Just because I know the answer, doesn't mean I shouldn't ask," Lucian said, returning her smile. For much of the song, they were silent, enjoying the beautiful music and the enchanting room they were in. "I'm not sure how the fairies manage to make this more beautiful every year," Lucian said softly as the music crescendoed.

"Perhaps we simply appreciate it more now," Moira suggested.

"I suppose that could be true," Lucian agreed. "Or perhaps they just strive for perfection each year and it comes out just a little better than before."

They were quiet for a while and after a moment, Moira teased, "You know, you weren't supposed to get so tall that I couldn't reach your shoulder."

"I'm sorry, should I shrink some for you?" Lucian retorted with a grin.

"No," Moira replied. "I like you just the way you are, even if you are too tall."

"And too freckled, too red-headed, too blind," Lucian said teasingly. "If we're going to list my flaws, we'll be here all night."

"I don't think I'd mind being here all night," Moira admitted with a smile. "But all good things must come to an end," she continued as the music began to fade.

"Not all," Lucian corrected, "just most."

For a moment, Moira simply looked deeply into Lucian's eyes. "I suppose you're right. Not all things end."

The music finished and Lucian led Moira back to the group. For the next song Adrian took his sister to the dance floor. "I am sorry, about what we talked about earlier, Moira," he said as they danced.

"I'm sorry too, Adrian," Moira replied. "I shouldn't have gotten so mad at you.

You know I love you, right? Even when we fight and disagree and when I'm being an emotional basket case. You know I love you?"

"I know, Moira," Adrian said, spinning her gently. "I love you too. Besides, I'm sure I'll be back to normal before you know it and then we'll have a great laugh about how I spent some time as an amphibian."

"Only you would get yourself put under a spell without actually getting in trouble," Moira laughed.

Adrian chuckled, "Yeah, I guess that's true."

They enjoyed the rest of the dance and at the end, Adrian kissed Moira's cheek. "Take care of Allegra for me, baby sister."

Moira choked back tears and simply nodded. "You haven't called me that in a long time, Adrian," she said when she found her voice again.

"I know," Adrian admitted. "It's been a long time since I felt I needed to. You're hardly a baby anymore."

"Neither are you," Moira teased.

When they arrived back at the group, Adrian pulled Nana out to dance with him. He saw Lucian dancing with Allegra, spinning her gently with the music and laughing as they discussed whatever it was they were talking about. "Don't you worry about a thing, Adrian," Nana said as they danced. "Everything will work out just fine."

"I hope so," Adrian admitted.

"Well, you trust your old grandmother," Nana said with a wink. "You'll see."

All too swiftly the last dance of the evening came. Before taking Allegra out to the floor, Adrian said, "I need you to turn around and close your eyes."

"Whatever for?" Allegra asked suspiciously.

"I can't tell you, you'll just have to trust me," Adrian replied.

Allegra turned around and dutifully closed her eyes, a smile playing about her lips. Adrian took the necklace from its box and moved Allegra's hair to the side as he clasped the chain about her neck. "Am I allowed to look now?" she asked teasingly.

"Yes," Adrian replied.

Opening her eyes, Allegra looked down at the pendant about her neck. She lifted it so she could see it more clearly. "Adrian," she gasped. "It's perfect. Thank you."

"A little something to have with you when I can't be," Adrian said gently, stroking Allegra's cheek. "And now, we're going to go enjoy this last dance."

Smiling brightly, Allegra accepted Adrian's arm and walked out to the dance floor with him. For much of the dance they were quiet. Midnight was only a few short minutes away. Concentrating on these last few moments being perfect, Adrian took her around the floor, spinning and twirling with the music as it floated through the room. As the clock got closer to midnight he held Allegra close and whispered, "Allegra?"

"Yes?" she asked looking up at him.

"I need you to know something," Adrian began.

"What is it, Adrian?" Allegra asked, her brow furrowing with concern. "You look upset."

"Allegra," Adrian said softly, just as the minute hand of the grandfather clock moved to midnight, "I love you."

The clock chimed and in an instant there was a flash of white. When the light cleared, Adrian was gone.

Chapter 5

Suddenly the room was a place of mass chaos. Calista tried to keep things in order, but there were students screaming, Allegra was having a panic attack followed by a shouting match with her brother, parents were demanding to know what was going on, and Adrian's entire family was being bombarded with questions. Lavinia was speechless, Moira sullen and Nana refused to answer. Sebastian didn't help by simply asking mysteriously, "What do you think happened to him?"

Just as Calista was about to give up hope of getting things calmed down Vulcan roared, "Silence!"

In an instant the room became dead quiet. "Thank you, Vulcan," Calista said quietly. He merely nodded. "Will Prince Lucian, Princess Allegra, King Lysander and Queen Alexandra please join me in my office?" she continued in a somewhat louder tone. "The rest of you will kindly go to your quarters and get some rest. Many of you have long journeys in the morning and I don't wish to be up all night answering questions. This matter is between myself, the fairies and the two families involved. No one else has any part in this and therefore is not entitled to any explanations whatsoever. Good night." She turned and Lucian's family quietly followed her out of the room.

Queen Alexandra was gently steering Allegra from the room. They could hear the steady buzz of whispering growing as people guessed what had happened. She hoped that Allegra wouldn't listen; despite the party they were in, there were a few people thinking the worst possible scenario. She was grateful when she heard Gelasia's sweet voice, "Now, now, my dears, this isn't the first time a prince has disappeared. You're all making a mountain out of a molehill."

As soon as they had reached the safety of her office, Calista closed the door and said, "Now, we can discuss what has happened and what this will mean for Allegra."

"Where is Adrian?" Allegra demanded angrily. "What have you done with him?"

Calista began slowly. "Where Adrian is, I cannot say. I can tell you that he is perfectly safe and in no danger at present."

"What does that mean?" Allegra asked.

"Try to be patient, Allegra," Calista said gently, though there was a seriousness to her tone which no one missed. "I will explain to you all that I can, but then you must accept the answers that I can give you. Adrian is, as I said, perfectly safe. His exact location is known only to the witches as they are the ones who transported him."

"He's been expelled?" Allegra asked, horrified.

"No, not expelled," Calista assured her. "Adrian was a very good student and there was no need to expel him. However, he has been put under a spell, the nature of which I cannot tell you. You see, Allegra, Adrian was never the one with a quest. You are."

Allegra's eyes widened in shock. "I have a quest? No, no that's not right. That can't be right. I'm the princess. I'm supposed to disappear and he's supposed to save me. That's the way it works."

"Allegra," Alexandra said gently. "It's not always the prince who goes on a quest. There was a young lady in my age group who had to rescue her prince."

"But, Mother, I'm not prepared to go on a quest," Allegra argued. "This isn't the way it was supposed to happen. I was supposed to disappear and he would save me. That's how it's supposed to be."

"There is no cookie cutter recipe for a quest, Allegra," Calista explained kindly. "Each quest is uniquely designed for the prince and princess it involves. Even if Adrian were the one with a quest, you would find yourself challenged in some way. Your mother did not sit idly in a tower. She had to entertain the dragon holding her prisoner to ensure her safety and survival. She spent time sewing and filling her hope chest for the time when she would be rescued. She also had to execute great patience, which between us was never one of your mother's strengths before the quest." Alexandra allowed for a tiny smile before Calista continued, "My point is, Allegra, that this is a unique and wonderful opportunity for you."

"Wonderful?" Allegra spat. "Wonderful? No, you bring Adrian back and you do it now. I want my Adrian."

"That is not going to happen, Allegra, as I'm sure you are aware," Calista replied sternly. "In the mean time, you will continue your schooling for the next two years."

"No," Allegra countered. "If I must rescue Adrian, than I'm doing it right now."

"Without finishing school you will be unable to complete this quest and neither of you will have a happy ending to this story," Calista warned. "It is imperative that you finish your last two years at Fair Damsels. During that time you will be given all the knowledge and tools you need to find Adrian, break the enchantment and live out your days happily."

Lucian had been sitting very quietly during the whole meeting, staring at his lap. Allegra suddenly turned on him. "You knew," she accused.

"Yes, I knew," Lucian admitted. "But I wasn't allowed to say anything to you or anyone about this."

"How long have you been lying to me, Lucian?" Allegra yelled. "How long have you been covering up what was going on?"

"I don't remember exactly," Lucian lied. "But I wanted to be able to tell you. I really did. I wasn't allowed to. It would have made things worse for you."

Allegra's eyes, filled with tears and anger, narrowed to slits. "I don't care," she said in a voice filled with bitterness and so quiet that it was almost a whisper. "I hate you, Lucian. And I will never, ever forgive you. Never!" She then turned on her heel and ran out of the room.

Lucian stood to follow, but Lysander put a hand on his shoulder. "Let her be, son," he suggested gently. "I know you want to make amends, but for now, let her be. She needs to come to terms with this and it's a lot to digest." He then turned to Calista. "I understand that there are reasons for this secrecy and also that you cannot tell us everything. But if I'm to help my daughter cope, I need to know everything I can. You've hurt her greatly and caused Lucian to be a part of that pain."

"I know I have," Calista admitted sadly, "and I wish it could have been done without Lucian's involvement. He is however extremely bright and excessively observant. I doubt we could have kept the secret from him, despite our best efforts. As I understand it, he was aware of the spell before even Adrian was. However, that is neither here nor there. What I can tell you is that Adrian is safe. I promise on my honor that he is in a place of safety. Allegra's schooling, while she will continue to learn the finer arts of being a lady, will also incorporate classes to teach her the skills of questing. She is more than capable of turning this experience into a wonderful story with a happy ending. But a word of caution: she must overcome her anger. She will need to rely on all of you and on Adrian's family in order to complete this successfully. Particularly, she will need to rely on her brother. Lucian is very knowledgeable about many things and his knowledge and guidance will be invaluable to her. When Allegra graduates, she will be given her quest. I believe she will find it less intimidating than it seems right now. That is all that I can tell you. For now, it is very, very late and I'm sure you want to get some rest before your travels tomorrow."

"I doubt there will be any sleeping tonight," Alexandra said sadly. "But we will not bother you any longer. Good night." She accepted Lysander's arm and left the room.

For a moment, Lucian stayed behind, angrily looking at his lap. "Is there something you wish to say, Lucian?" Calista asked.

"Why did you make me lie to her?" Lucian asked in voice that showed hurt and anger. "Don't you see what has happened because of it?"

"You never lied, Lucian," Calista said gently.

"Well, I now get to spend winter break with her ignoring me and she's going to hate me forever because of you," Lucian spat.

"I'm sorry you think so," Calista replied, seemingly unfazed by the accusation. "Good night."

Without returning the farewell, Lucian left the room and went to his own. It was going to be a long, hard break.

Early the next morning, weary from a restless night, Lucian's family, Leticia and Kaelen packed their belongings into their large carriage and began the trip to Rendorlin. Before leaving, Lucian took a moment with Calista to apologize. "I'm sorry about last night. I was tired and frustrated, and caught off guard. I wish I had known when he'd be leaving. I know how Allegra thinks and I could have made that even slightly easier."

"No, it wouldn't have been easier," Calista said gently. "I know you think it would have been, but it really wouldn't. Give your sister time, she'll forgive you."

"I hope you're right," Lucian had replied. Now as they began the drive away from Charming Academy, Lucian was glad that the dressage final would last all of break, because then maybe Allegra would get so busy she'd forget to be mad at him. The ride was awkward and quiet. Kaelen and Leticia both tried to start conversations, but they all ended in awkward silence as Allegra glared sullenly out the window. Lucian didn't try to join any of the conversations either. Anytime he would speak, Allegra would glare at him before returning her gaze outside. Finally Leticia said, "Allegra, I know you're upset, but you really have to try to focus on something else. If Calista said that Adrian's safe than I'm sure he is."

"It doesn't matter," Allegra replied.

"Yes it does," Leticia continued. "You're not going to do well at the final if all your concentration is on Adrian and what's happened. Let go of your anger so you can do well."

"I don't care anymore," Allegra said.

Leticia scoffed, "I don't believe that for a moment. You've been working all semester on your program. Augusta said she'd never seen a more dedicated horsewoman. You shouldn't let her down. Let it go."

"How would you feel?" Allegra spat.

"Don't forget, Allegra," Leticia replied angrily, "I don't have a prince anymore. There's no one waiting for me to rescue them. No one is out there preparing for me. I'm going to school for a happily ever after that will never be."

The sadness in Leticia's tone drew Allegra out of her melancholy and she began a long rebuttal of Leticia's chances at a fairy tale wedding. Soon Kaelen and Lucian's parents were drawn into the conversation as well. Lucian remained outside, listening rather than contributing. At one point, Leticia caught his eye and he mouthed a silent thank you. She smiled and then continued talking to everyone, making the once painfully awkward trip lively and fun.

It didn't seem like too long before they arrived in Rendorlin. They stopped at The Dancing Fairies as they had the last time they were in the area. Prepared with the news that they would be arriving, the proprietress welcomed them each inside "It is so good to see you again. I have missed your company. And thank you so much for everything you did. It was quite unexpected and very much appreciated."

"We had such a lovely time here that we couldn't go without leaving some token of our gratitude," Alexandra said with a smile.

"Yes," the proprietress said, "well, again I thank you. You'll be staying in the upstairs rooms. As you can see, I've had some improvements made while you were away. There is more space and more rooms available. If you'll follow me, I'll show you where you will be staying." She led the way upstairs and to the familiar rooms. They could see where additions had been made.

"How many rooms did you add?" Lucian asked curiously.

"Only three, but I have plans on making one more addition," she replied. "I've had the most gracious gentleman staying with me and he has kindly helped me sort things out and begin the process of refurbishing. So very thoughtful," she added with a sigh.

Lucian and Kaelen exchanged grins. It was quite obvious that the older woman was in love with Adrian's uncle. He was the only one they knew of who would be staying here. "Will he be here during our stay?" Kaelen asked.

"Why yes, as a matter of fact he will," she answered. "How did you know?"

"Just a guess," Kaelen shrugged.

"Ma'am," Alexandra said as they went into their room, "I don't recall your name. I'm so sorry; I am just terrible with names, what was it?"

The older woman looked startled and then smiled, "My name is, well, my name is of no importance. Most people just call me Mother."

"Oh, very well then," Alexandra replied. She stifled a yawn.

"You must be very tired. I'll prepare lunch for you all and while I do that, you must get some rest. I insist," she added when the others looked about to argue. "Get some good sleep and I'll have everything ready for you." She then left before anyone else could even attempt to argue. Although truth be told, they were all so tired that they quickly found themselves heeding her council.

Lucian woke to the smell of vegetable stew wafting up the staircase. He had been so tired he hadn't even bothered to close the door to his room. Stretching, he got out of bed and headed downstairs. "We were wondering when you would join us," Alexandra said with a smile, handing him a plate with rolls on it. "Here, I'm sure Mother will bring out an extra bowl for you shortly."

"It'll only be a moment," Mother assured them.

"Thanks," Lucian replied as she handed him a bowl. He served himself some stew before eating. He could see that Allegra was still avoiding looking at him.

"Lucian, how did your semester go?" Leticia asked pointedly.

He could tell she was forcing him to join the conversation, so Lucian said, "It went well. All of my classes had high marks and Raphael was really impressed with how George and I are doing in our class."

"What have you been working on?" Alexandra asked.

"Double-handed fencing," Lucian replied between bites. "Raphael says I'm a bit ahead of where George is, but between us I don't think that's true. George is a very good swordsman."

"That's probably why the two of you share that class," Lysander said.

"Probably," Lucian admitted. "Although, it would sure be nice if we weren't in two classes of dragon fighting. Dronecus is such a tyrant."

Lysander laughed, "I seem to remember my good friend talking about the dragon that way. I suppose he hasn't changed since then."

"I would guess not," Lucian said.

Their conversation was interrupted by Sebastian entering the room. "I hope you'll forgive an old man being late, Laura," he said as he placed his bags on the floor. "Last night was very long indeed."

"No matter," Mother replied with a bright smile. "And that's not my name. But where is your sister? I expected her to join you."

"Due to a family emergency, she has chosen to stay at home with her daughter and granddaughter," Sebastian explained. "She hopes you'll forgive her."

"Oh I do hope that everything turns out alright," Mother said warmly. "No need to ask forgiveness. Life happens. Will this cut your visit short?"

"I'm afraid it will," Sebastian admitted. "But rest assured that I'll come again soon. After all, I have a room to finish."

Mother laughed. "Well, come have some luncheon. You must be starved."

"I am feeling a mite peckish," Sebastian agreed. He joined everyone at the table.

"I'll bring you a bowl," Mother said and walked from the room as everyone greeted Sebastian enthusiastically.

"So, have any of you been able to discover her name?" Sebastian asked after greeting everyone.

"No, she simply said she goes by Mother," Alexandra said.

"Bah," Sebastian scoffed. "I can't call her Mother. She can't possibly be a day older than me. In fact, I'd wager she's not even the same age as me."

Laughing as she came in, Mother said," It won't work, Sebastian. They don't know either. You'll just have to get used to it."

"No, I shall make up a name for you every day until I finally pick the right one," Sebastian retorted. "Today your name shall be Felicity."

"Wrong again," Mother said, shaking her head. "But I'll accept the epithet for a day. But eventually you'll run out of names."

"Ah, there aren't that many names in the world," Sebastian declared. "At some point I'm bound to pick the right one and then perhaps you'll stop being so mysterious."

"But if I lost my mystery, you might lose your interest," Mother half-teased.

"I never lose interest in a lovely pursuit," Sebastian retorted with a wink.

Flushing, Mother excused herself to begin the dishes.

"Most frustrating," Sebastian complained as she left. "Of all the familiar faces in the world, I would forget the name to place with it."

"Do you know her?" Kaelen asked.

Sebastian frowned, "I'm quite positive that at one point I did know her. But I can't seem to remember her name. I suppose she might just look like someone I once knew because I've never forgotten a name before."

"Never?" Allegra asked in disbelief.

"Never," Sebastian repeated. "And we won't talk about how many years I've had that record going."

"Well, maybe she just looks like someone you knew, like you said," Leticia suggested.

"It's possible, I suppose, but I don't think so," Sebastian replied. "There's more to some people than meets the eye. That's what makes meeting new people so very interesting."

They continued their meal chatting and then left the inn to take care of signing the girls in for their competition. The necessary veterinary checks were done and the girls were each given a schedule of when they would be performing with their horses. After getting everything in order, the group wandered the town visiting various shops and stops along the way. Allegra spoke to everyone, except Lucian. He decided that perhaps it would be best to remain in the background and try to give her some space. But even as he thought what a good idea that was, he couldn't help feeling that Allegra was being vastly unfair. It wasn't his fault that Adrian had been transformed. It wasn't his fault that Adrian had disappeared. While part of him understood that she was just scared and angry, he didn't think it at all fair that all her anger was directed at him. *Couldn't she at least be a little angry at Adrian?* he thought as they stopped at a small café for some mulled cider. *Just a tad?*

When they arrived back at the inn, they had a very short supper and then everyone immediately went to bed. The day had been very long and the travelers were tired. Soon, unable to sleep, Allegra had wandered downstairs to the parlor. She sat before the fire watching the slowly flickering flames. As she watched the flames dance in the hearth, she tried to let go of her hurt and frustration. But the more she thought about the situation she found herself in, the more difficult it became. The odds went from challenging to insurmountable in a matter of minutes as she stared into the fire. Everything she'd ever believed about being a princess was suddenly wrong. She wasn't going to be rescued from a dragon or giant or even an evil queen. Instead, she was supposed to go on a quest. But, she didn't know how. How could they make her go through this? "It isn't supposed to work this way," Allegra muttered, angrily dashing tears from her face.

"You're a bit young to be talking to yourself, don't you think?" Sebastian asked. Allegra, startled, whirled around to look at him. His tone was light and teasing, but his expression serious.

Allegra shrugged. "I just can't make it work out in my head."

Laughing Sebastian replied, "My dear girl, it never works out in our heads. That's what makes having a heart so important. When our head gets lost in the details, our heart finds a way to make even the most impossible task possible."

"But this is different, Uncle Sebastian," Allegra argued tearfully. "I can't rescue Adrian. I'm a princess for heaven's sake. I'm just a princess."

Sebastian sat next to her on the sofa and took her hand. "You are anything but 'just' a princess. You have courage, spunk, and vivacity for life that makes you a joy to be around. You're a clever girl. No matter what lies before you, you'll find a way."

"But I'm not supposed to," Allegra cried. "I'm supposed to be rescued, not Adrian. I'm not a Prince Charming."

Sebastian smiled teasingly, "Well, no I suppose you're not a Prince Charming. All the wrong type of person for that role. But let me tell you a story. There was once a young woman named Charlotte. She was much like you, a beautiful, bright girl with the world before her. Now, being a student at Fair Damsels, she too believed that she would be swept off her feet by her prince. And figuratively speaking she was. Her prince was bold and handsome, daring and charming; everything that Prince Charming should be. The day of graduation, Charlotte waited impatiently for her turn to walk across the stage and disappear into oblivion like so many girls before her. As Melantha called her name, she seemed to float across the stage and took her diploma. But to her embarrassment and dismay, she didn't disappear. Instead, she was still standing there. 'When you have a moment, you should read your diploma,' Melantha said. 'It will detail your quest.'

"Confused, Charlotte said, 'There must be some mistake.'

"'No mistake,' Melantha replied. 'But you are blocking the next graduate.'

"Blushing furiously, Charlotte returned to her seat, refusing to even look inside the diploma she'd worked so hard to earn. She watched as the rest of her class graduated and then the princes began to graduate. There was her handsome beau, regal and tall, walking across the stage for a copy of his quest. To her surprise and to the surprise of all around her, he vanished. Such a thing had never happened before. There was chaos in the room as people wondered aloud what could possibly have happened to the young man in question.

"Calista got things settled down and Melantha took Charlotte to an empty classroom and said, 'Charlotte, you are getting the chance of a lifetime. It is your quest to find your prince and bring him safely back to Biberseth.' In those days you had to bring your princess back, the fairies didn't simply appear when your quest was finished. Anyway, continuing on, Melantha added, 'Use the knowledge you have gained from your family, friends and schoolwork to discover Samuel and bring him home.'

"It goes without saying that Charlotte was terribly confused. She begged for them to bring him back, yelled at each of them for not caring, and finally left, feeling doomed to life as an old maid. She was, after all, a princess. She was not meant for adventure or rescuing. Heartbroken, Charlotte went home and stayed there for over a year, trying to ignore the unopened diploma she had thrown on her desk. She couldn't throw it out, even as suitors came to call on her.

"Then, one spring night, she had a strange dream. She dreamed that her prince was with her again, but he was stuck. He begged for her to help him, to save him. She asked him what could be done and he directed her to read the diploma.

"Charlotte wasted no time on waking. She opened the diploma and read the quest aloud. 'Through briar and bramble you must seek your love in the place of no return.' Terrified, Charlotte collapsed on her bed and cried all the more. She was a princess! She couldn't possibly travel that far. And she didn't have the slightest clue how to get there. At length she fell asleep and was visited again in her dreams. Her prince told her to look at her father's map of the world and there she would find the answer to her questions.

"Again Charlotte did as she was told. She snuck into her father's library and looked at the map on the wall. She found on the map a small spot marked 'Thremidrial' which in old fairy meant 'place of no return'. Still frightened, but determined not to fail her prince, Charlotte resolved to travel to the small spot deep within the mountains. She packed only the things she thought necessary and took her journey.

"It was very long indeed, almost three years in going, for her horse was old and wearied easily. She camped at night in what places she could find; sometimes an inn, others a cottage. Occasionally she found herself taking shelter in a barn for the night. Finally, she reached the mountains and began her way through, searching in earnest for Thremidrial. For days upon days she walked through the woods. Trees and brambles blocked her path, ripping at her clothes and tearing her skin. Her hair became wild and tangled. Nighttime was frightening as the animals would come out of their hiding places and lurk about her. Here there were no cottages, no inns, not even a drafty barn to keep her safe. She stayed close to her fire, a large stick in hand to fight off the enemies of the night.

"When the five years were coming to their close, Charlotte finally found a large pool of strange water. She could see through it clearly, as though it were merely glass. At the bottom was her prince. Terrified that he had drowned, she leapt into the pool, taking no thought of her clothes or supplies. The waters were enchanted and would not release their hold on her. She could not reach the surface for air. Her lungs in pain, she knew the only way out would be rescuing her prince. She swam, deeper and deeper, trying desperately to make the shallow breath she'd taken last. At long last she reached him. It seemed that he was sleeping, but she knew that it must be part of the spell. She took him in her arms and kissed him, the water suddenly vanishing away in a blazing column of light. She shielded her eyes against the glare, all the while keeping hold of her prince's hand. When she opened her eyes, she saw that they were before the castle in Biberseth.

With not a moment to spare, she pulled him along into the castle; the victory was hers! She had defeated the challenges and rescued her prince.

"I don't think I need to say that they lived happily ever after," Sebastian finished. "But that's true all the same."

Allegra looked at him thoughtfully, "Is that a true story?"

"As true as I'm sitting here," Sebastian replied. "In fact, I wouldn't be sitting here if it wasn't. Charlotte and her prince, young Samuel of Rendorlin, were my eighth great-grandparents. Their story was the first in which a princess was the one who completed the quest. I hope that it gives you courage. The odds may seem impossible to overcome right at this moment, but I assure you, there is a way. Love always finds a way."

Allegra considered this with a barely suppressed yawn.

"Ah, I saw that," Sebastian teased. "Off to bed with you, now. You need your rest. Tomorrow is a big day for you and I'll be cheering for you in Adrian's place."

Smiling sadly Allegra said, "Alright. Good night, Uncle Sebastian."

"Good night, dear Allegra," Sebastian said, hugging her gently. He watched her climb up the stairs toward her bedroom. "Pleasant dreams."

True to his word, Sebastian joined Allegra's family in the stands, watching and cheering her as she performed. In fact, he stayed for nearly the first half of the competition. Towards the end of the second week, he told everyone at supper, "I must be going to Lictthane now. I have overstayed my visit far longer than I ought to have."

"Must you go now?" Allegra asked pleadingly. "We enjoy your company so much."

"I do," Sebastian replied. "Bethany will be needing me to help with Lavinia and Moira. I can't very well leave them on their own. But have no fears, I will visit again. I always do."

"When?" Mother asked.

"That I will never tell," Sebastian said impishly. "But, I am packed and ready, I must simply take my leave and be out the door."

"Have a safe trip," Alexandra said as he stood from the table.

"Yes, and tell Moira hello for us," Leticia added.

Sebastian nodded to everyone and soon was walking for the door. His bags were on the floor next to it.

"Sebastian," Mother said from behind him.

He turned to face her. "Yes?"

"Please do be careful," Mother requested. "There is rumor amongst the innkeepers of a band of highwaymen who are attacking carriages along the roads you will likely travel. They are merciless, killing everyone within them and leaving nothing of value behind."

"I'll be careful, Melody," Sebastian guessed.

Smiling and shaking her head, Mother replied, "No, not Melody."

"You can't keep your name a secret forever," Sebastian said teasingly. "I'm close to figuring it out."

"Well, I wish you'd do it sooner rather than later," Mother teased back. "You've picked out so many new names for me I do believe my head is spinning. I doubt I'd remember my own name if I heard it."

"You'd remember," Sebastian said seriously. "I can tell."

Mother smiled. "Perhaps I would. Now, if you're going to go tonight, go quickly before it gets dark. And please do be careful. Send word when you reach Lictthane, just so I don't worry too much about you."

"I'll be sure to do that," Sebastian replied. He raised her hand gently to his lips. "Farewell my lady."

"Until we meet again," Mother returned. She waved to the carriage as it rolled away from her inn, smiling at no one in particular.

Sebastian didn't travel far that night, keeping to his promise to stay safe. When he put in for the night, he talked to the innkeeper privately about the rumor Mother had confided to him. "It's true enough, all right," the innkeeper said. "We've been losing customers as no one wants to travel now. It's a bad business I tell you; a bad business."

"Indeed," Sebastian replied thoughtfully. In the years he'd been traveling, he'd heard of highwaymen, he'd even run into them from time to time, but never had he heard of there being a gang of them together. Highwaymen tended to travel alone, in pairs at the most. It was more difficult to catch them that way. These men must have been very sure of themselves to be traveling as a pack. In any case, Sebastian decided it would be best for him not to travel at night until he had safely reached Lictthane. It would still be a few days' journey and he planned on stopping briefly in Traifloran before continuing on to Lictthane.

The next morning, Sebastian awoke early and made plans to begin his travels again. He paid the innkeeper generously before packing his light curricle and leaving the inn. A light flurry of snow was dusting the wintry world around him. He wrapped his winter cloak about him a little tighter. The horses continued at a lively gait and he stopped once for luncheon in a small town along the roadside. Soon he was on the road again; he should arrive just outside Traifloran by nightfall if he kept up his pace. He enjoyed the scenery and the soft glow of the winter snows as he rode swiftly past. He slowed the horses as the snow began to fall a little thicker. Soon dusk was falling over the mountains. It was nearing time to stop, but he had not yet reached his destination. A few more hours surely would be alright. He was still as swift with his sword as he'd ever been. If the highwaymen were foolish enough to stop him, they'd get a whipping they'd not soon forget.

Dark had just crept over the land as the glow of a fire showed over a hill in front of him. He slowed the horses to a silent walk. "I wonder what that could be?" Sebastian wondered aloud. Stopping the curricle all together, he tied the horses to a nearby tree and walked carefully towards the blaze, keeping out of sight in the trees. Upon reaching the crest of the hill, his heart sank and a sick feeling entered the pit of his stomach. A large carriage was ablaze. The horses were nowhere in sight and he couldn't see any people either, but somehow he knew the victims were still there. Throwing caution to the wind, Sebastian swiftly descended to the site. He could see crimson drops of blood in the snow. A broken sword lay in pieces next to the cold hand of the man who had fought so bravely to protect himself. Nearby was the body of a woman, more than likely his wife judging by age and the sorrowful expression captured on her face. Tears filled Sebastian's eyes. He was too late. A slight whimper made him turn. A young woman was lying in the snow, her lips blue with cold and blood staining the front of her gown.

"Please, don't leave me," she begged in a voice barely a whisper.

"Oh my dear," Sebastian said earnestly, "don't worry. I'll help you."

"Mother, Daddy," the girl whispered as he removed his cloak and began to wrap her in it.

"I'm very sorry, dear, they're gone," Sebastian replied as he lifted her gently in his arms. He had to get her indoors and fast.

"Can't leave them," she mumbled against his chest. "Promised."

"I promise I'll see to them as soon as I get you to safety," Sebastian assured her.

Once in the curricle, he held the young lady close to him so that she could gain some warmth from his presence. He then cracked the reins over the horses' rumps. "Fly my friends, make haste!"

Taking his command, the horses cantered quickly to the nearest town. He stopped the curricle and took the young lady out with him and shoved his way inside the nearest inn. "I need a room with a fire quickly, and bandages."

"Of course," the proprietress said. She sent a serving boy to fetch the things needed and led Sebastian to the parlor fire. She shooed away several other guests. "Another victim?" she asked sorrowfully.

"Yes, but she's still alive, if only just," Sebastian replied.

"Surely she wasn't alone," the proprietress exclaimed.

Sebastian shook his head. "Her parents are dead. I didn't have time to give them proper burial. When I realized she was alive, I knew I had to come quickly. As is, I don't know that she'll make it." The serving boy had returned with a bowl of warm water and several rags. "Thank you," Sebastian said as he took them.

"Let me know if I can at all help you," the proprietress replied sadly. She went to the doorway and chided the guests who had gathered about. "This is not a show for entertaining. Let that poor creature alone. To your rooms all of you, or I'll turn you out, so help me."

This was met with some grumbling, but the guests did in fact leave. Sebastian stayed at the young lady's side, cleaning the multiple wounds and gently rubbing in ointment against infection. She had clearly lost a lot of blood and he could see that she was becoming feverish from her long exposure in the elements. Who knew how long she had lain in the bitter cold, waiting for someone to help her? Gently wrapping bandages about her, Sebastian softly hummed a tune, the name of which he'd long forgotten. Night lengthened and turned to dawn. The young woman's condition did not improve; if anything it steadily got worse. Exhausted, yet determined to see her well, Sebastian spoon-fed her cups of broth and took the time to bathe her wounds and redress them. It was mid-afternoon when the young woman awoke from a feverish sleep. "Sir," she said weakly.

"Yes, child," Sebastian replied, "I'm here."

"I need you," she began, her voice weary and strained. "I need you to tell George…tell George that I love him."

"But, my dear, I don't know your name," Sebastian said, trying to control his emotions.

The girl smiled as her eyes closed. "Tell George, Eleanor loves him." With that, Eleanor took her last breath and lay still in Sebastian's arms, the slight smile still playing on her lips.

Chapter 6

Winter break was almost finished when Calista and Melantha unexpectedly arrived in Rendorlin. They found Leticia at the dressage final in the middle of her final performance. "Should we ask for her now?" Melantha asked Calista quietly.

"No, allow Leticia this moment," Calista replied.

They watched in silence for a few moments, before leaving a message with one of the judges and then leaving to await them at the castle in Rendorlin. On arriving at the castle, King Markus and Queen Tabitha welcomed them cordially. "We hope you will like the rooms we've had made available for you. They have the finest view of the land."

"I thank you, Your Majesty," Melantha said kindly. "I'm sure they will be adequate."

"Is George at home or at the dressage finals?" Calista asked.

"He's at the finals. He's watching his princess' sister finish her routines. It's a very close tie, as I understand, between Leticia and Princess Allegra of Maltisten," Tabitha replied.

"You're not here about the dressage finals," Markus interjected, looking between the two fairies.

"No, I'm afraid we're not," Calista said. "But we shall wait until George and Leticia arrive before I share my news. It concerns both of them."

"I'll have the parlor arranged for tea," Tabitha replied. "Please, go sit down and warm yourselves."

No sooner had she said this than Samantha and Kieffer walked into the castle. "My dear daughter," Markus said, enveloping Samantha in a hug, "why are you here?"

"I was summoned by Calista," Samantha replied. "She said George needed me, so we left immediately."

"In your condition?" Markus asked in shock as he looked more closely at her. "You're with child! You shouldn't be traveling."

"Daddy, I'm fine," Samantha said with a smile, placing a gentle hand on her bulging stomach. "When I read the note I just knew I had to come immediately."

"Well, go join Calista and Melantha in the parlor and warm yourselves," Markus commanded while hugging Kieffer. "And you young lady, you will certainly have some explaining to do for your mother. You never told us."

Samantha smiled, "I wanted it to be a surprise."

It was many hours before George and Leticia arrived. When they did, Leticia looked as though she already knew what was going to be said. Her cheeks were tear-stained. As she took the seat offered to her, she looked straight at Melantha and said tearfully, "My sister is gone, isn't she?"

"Yes, my child, I'm afraid she is," Melantha replied sadly.

Leticia's fragile composure was shattered and she buried her face in her hands, her sobbing the only sound in the room.

"You mean, Eleanor is dead?" George asked. He felt numb all over, as though doused suddenly with a bucket of ice water.

Calista nodded. "Leticia's family was found by the emeritus king Sebastian while he was traveling to Licthane to be with his niece and her family. King Julian and Queen Rebekah were dead when he arrived. Eleanor survived only a day under Sebastian's care. I can assure you that he did everything that he could for her. My children, I'm so sorry."

"How did they die?" Leticia asked.

Melantha hesitated before saying, "Highwaymen. There has been a rash of attacks along the road. Your father fought bravely, but was overcome. They killed your parents, took everything of value and left Eleanor to die. I suppose they may have thought she was already dead."

George stared at his hands, trying not to allow his emotions to get the best of him. "What is to be done now? Eleanor," his voice broke and he stopped. Clearing his throat, he continued, "Eleanor was my princess. Leticia now has no family, her grandparents passed away last summer."

"Leticia still has Benjamin," Melantha corrected. "Although at present his location is unknown. He is still on his quest seeking Grace. As soon as he returns, he will be crowned King of Traifloran. In the meantime, the kingdom of Traifloran will be ruled by the emeritus king and queen living there. Leticia, you will be staying with Princess Moira and her family. There you will be safe and be given time to heal from this tragedy. Upon Benjamin's return, if you are still in school, you will be allowed to stay with him or you may choose to stay with Moira. We will leave that decision to you and Benjamin."

"George," Calista began when Melantha had finished, "you will continue going to school. We have spoken with Maeve and she feels it would be best for you to remain in your current coursework. During the remainder of this school year, you will also meet with Gelasia once a week, or more often if you need, for counseling and time to heal."

"Leticia, you will meet with Myrtle," Melantha added.

"Upon your graduation of Charming Academy," Calista continued, "we will discuss the options for your future."

"What future?" George asked, sorrow tinting his tone. "Eleanor was my princess, my love, my world. And now she's gone."

Samantha came and put her arms around her brother, holding him close as he sobbed against her. "My dear brother," she said gently. "Don't allow the future to appear so bleak. There will be light again." She lifted his chin so he was looking up at her. "I promise."

George merely nodded. Consumed by grief, he excused himself from the room. Samantha made to follow him, but Kieffer gently took her arm. "It'd be best to allow him some time to regain his composure, my love. Men don't like being seen so vulnerable."

Nodding, Samantha took a seat as Leticia also excused herself. "I'll be missed at the hotel."

"Of course, we'll have our best carriage take you back," Tabitha offered.

"I thank you, but I already have King Lysander's curricle waiting for me," Leticia replied graciously. "I assure you I'll be perfectly safe."

"Very well," Tabitha replied. "Please accept our condolences."

Leticia nodded, but didn't speak. Curtsying to everyone she said in a voice strained with emotion, "Thank you for your hospitality." Unable to bear another moment, she turned and left.

There was a long pause of silence, followed by Samantha saying, "I'm not sure why you summoned me, Calista. Your message was for George."

"I summoned you," Calista explained, "because I knew you had a strong relationship. I knew that you could be a shoulder for him to cry on as it were. The bond you have will give him strength. I do apologize however for making you travel under your circumstances."

"No matter," Samantha replied with a smile.

"I hate to force an unpleasant topic," Markus interrupted, "but I would like to know what is to be done for George."

Calista took a deep breath. "It is a little complicated," she began after a moment. "The witches were counseled, particularly Maeve who reads the stars. She is certain that there is still a quest for George. I realize that at present it may seem impossible, however with your permission I would request that he continue to come to Charming Academy so that he can prepare for that quest, whatever it may be."

"I see," Markus said. "Do you have any words of comfort we might give him? He loved Eleanor very much."

"We all did," Tabitha agreed.

"I'm afraid I have no magic cure for heartbreak," Calista admitted sadly. "Like all wounds, this must run its course and heal on its own."

By the time school had started again, everyone at the two schools was aware of what had happened to Eleanor and her family. Allegra still refused to talk to Lucian, but redoubled the time she spent with Leticia, offering support and friendship. Lucian did the same for George, knowing that it would be more difficult at the quarterly meetings when Eleanor wasn't there. About a week after school had begun again, he received a letter from Moira.

> *Dear Lucian,*
>
> *I understand that Allegra is still not speaking to you. On the first day back, we had a large school assembly commemorating Eleanor's life and bidding her farewell. It has been incredibly difficult for everyone, but especially Leticia. I'm doing all I can to help cheer her up, as is Allegra. I am hoping that by losing herself in helping Leticia, Allegra will overcome her anger with you. At present, she refuses to speak about the quest or anything related to Adrian. I hope you're right about her and everything else.*
>
> *Anyway, I know this is brief but I must get some sleep tonight. Do well and keep in touch. Keep writing to Allegra too, perhaps it will help.*
>
> *Love,*
> *Moira*

Lucian wasn't surprised to hear that there had been a special meeting honoring Eleanor's life. She had been well-liked by everyone. Her death was a true loss not only to the schools, but to the students as well. Her sweet nature and gentle heart made her friends with everyone and she would be sorely missed.

At supper that evening, the boys did everything they could to keep George's spirits up. They talked about their classes and about the weather, anything to pull him from his melancholy. Every now and again he would spark at something and be like himself again, but between losing Eleanor and not having Adrian there with his quick humor, the boys were struggling to keep George happy. As the meal ended, George stood and said, "I know it's probably frustrating, what you're doing, but thanks. I'm glad I have such good friends."

"We're here for you," Kaelen said sincerely.

George nodded and went upstairs to Gelasia's office. He knocked on the door before entering.

"Well, good evening, George," Gelasia said brightly. "Is it that time again?"

"Yeah, it is," George replied.

"Have a seat," Gelasia said, waving to one of the chairs. After George had taken his seat, she waited for him to speak. When he remained silent she asked, "How was your day?"

George shrugged. "It was alright, I guess. Long."

"Describe it to me, dear," Gelasia requested.

"I doubt it would be very interesting," George admitted. He went through his day, describing each class. "Dragon fighting was terrible. I guess I just don't understand what the point is of me staying here. Eleanor is gone and no quest will bring her back."

"You're right," Gelasia said simply.

"I beg your pardon?" George replied. He hadn't expected Gelasia to agree with him. He'd been expecting a rebuttal.

Gelasia smiled. "There is no quest that can bring Eleanor back, in that aspect you are correct. However," she continued, "that does not mean that your education here is wasted or unimportant. When it happens that a prince or princess loses their companion before the quest is completed, there is always another way provided."

"But, Gelasia, I loved Eleanor, with all my heart," George countered seriously. "How can I offer the shattered remains to someone else? It wouldn't be fair to them or to me."

Patting his hand tenderly, Gelasia said, "My dear boy, heartache too can heal. Even the deepest and most painful wound can heal. You must simply be open to healing. If you close off your heart, than you will always be a broken man. But, if you can find the strength within yourself to heal than you can find love again. It will be a different love than that which you shared with Eleanor. And there will perhaps, always be a touch of sorrow there, a sadness of lost love. But love will spring anew in your heart if you let it."

"I suppose so," George agreed reluctantly. "It just hurts so badly."

"I'm afraid there is nothing I can do to amend that, George," Gelasia replied. "But, I can tell you that the pain won't last forever."

They spent another hour in the room talking before George left to return to his own room so he could finish his homework and get ready for bed. When he arrived, he sat on the bed for a while and just thought. The more he thought, the more he hurt. Finally angry and upset, he threw his pillow across the room. Soon he was tearing the bed apart, throwing bedding, pillows, papers, books, anything that reached his hands went flying away until he crumpled on the bed in tears. Queenie came over to him from her box in the corner. A blanket had fallen on her head, waking her from sleep. She nuzzled his hand and began licking it. George looked down and stroked her long ears. "Oh, Queenie, I wish it would just stop."

Queenie whined softly, continuing to lick his free hand. She placed a paw on his chest. She wasn't sure why George was so sad and angry, but she wanted to help him feel better. She was surprised when George put his arms around her and cried. She licked his ears and sat quietly, waiting for him to be ready to let her go. He was her puppy and she would take care of him always.

Winter continued as it had begun and soon glimpses of spring were visible in the grounds of Charming Academy. The boys were busily preparing for their princesses to come, while trying to downplay it so as not to hurt George's feelings. They knew the constant reminders were painful to him, and so they talked about other things. "I wonder where Adrian is right now," Jacobi said one afternoon as they sat under their favorite tree.

"Your guess is as good as anyone's," Kaelen replied. "I doubt that any of us would know."

George shook his head. They were all quiet and then suddenly George muttered, "Being a prince stinks."

Everyone looked at him in surprise. "Why?" Jacobi asked.

"Look at Kaelen, he's a beast," George began. "And Adrian's heaven knows where as a frog. I've got no princess and Lucian's princess hates him."

"Hey now," Lucian argued with a slightly teasing note in his voice, "Moira doesn't hate me anymore."

"Great, you two don't have any problems," George retorted. "What's so great about being Prince Charming anyway?"

"George, I know you're upset and all," Kaelen began.

"Do you?" George interrupted. "Do any of you know what this is like? Day after day knowing that I'll never get the happily ever after that I was working so hard for because Eleanor is dead." He ignored the catch in his voice and continued his rant. "You at least have princesses, well most of you. Kaelen, you're the only one without a princess, but yours isn't dead she just thinks you're scum."

"Hang on now," Lucian said warningly as Kaelen glowered menacingly, "there's no call for that George. We know you're hurting, but there's no sense in hurting the rest of us too."

"Who cares?" George asked bitterly. "None of you get it."

"Well, Mr. Know-it-all," Kaelen sneered, "why don't you try telling us?"

"You're too dumb to understand anyway," George spat.

This was the final straw for Kaelen and he jumped on George, hitting him dead in the face. Jacobi and Lucian jumped in to pull the two away from each other. "Enough!" Lucian shouted when they finally managed to pry them apart. George was wiping blood from his face and Kaelen was snarling angrily. "We're princes, not animals. Both of you knock it off." He glared from one to the other. "Is this really going to make either of you feel better? Really? Hurting one another isn't going to help anyone. Don't you see that we're all we've got? If we start picking at each other than none of us will succeed. We need each other. George, I'm sorry that Eleanor died, I am, but you've got to get over your anger. The three of us here are the only support you've got, George. If you alienate us, you'll be alone. Really alone and you've never once in your life been that way. Kaelen, he's hurt and angry. He's going to say stupid things that he doesn't really mean. It doesn't make him right, but breaking him in half isn't going to solve the problem either. Right now, who knows what's going to happen for any of us? Life is unexpected and changes in the blink of an eye. Otherwise none of us would be here. So both of you relax and start leaning on each other rather than fighting each other."

Calista was watching from her window with Calypso. "Do you need me to intervene?" Calypso asked as the boys sat once again under the tree. They could see Jacobi handing George a handkerchief to wipe the blood off with. Kaelen was sitting against the tree, his arms folded over his chest, but speaking quietly to the others.

"No, I don't believe I do," Calista replied. "They seem to have taken care of the situation on their own. Lucian is quite the leader."

"And Jacobi a calming influence," Calypso added as they watched Jacobi keep the conversation flowing. "I suppose any other group we would have been down there taking care of matters ourselves."

"Younger groups, yes," Calista agreed. "But as they age, I try to allow them to settle their own differences so they'll learn. If they don't learn how to problem solve in an appropriate manner, than I've done them more disservice than allowing a few bloodied noses and black eyes."

"I agree," Calypso said. "Well, I believe that concludes our meeting anyway. Might I recommend that you send George to Maeve within the fortnight? He can be with her to consult the stars and perhaps that will help ease his mind."

Calista thought for a moment. "I might, but I don't want him knowing too much too soon."

"It will be as you wish," Calypso replied. "It was merely a suggestion. You may do with it as you will."

"Thank you," Calista said, "I will consider your advice. Perhaps if he is able to overcome this on his own in that time, I'll forego having him meet with her. If not, a meeting might indeed do him well."

"Indeed," Calypso agreed. "Well, I must go. I'm late for a class as it is. Good day, Calista."

"Good day," Calista returned. She returned to her desk and wrote a brief note for Gelasia asking her to get some information from George about his day, particularly the fight.

That evening when George met with Gelasia, he was pretty sure he was in for a talking to. His face was swollen so much that he could barely open his left eye. "Good evening, George," Gelasia said sweetly. "Might I ask what happened?"

"I'd rather not say," George returned, blushing.

"Well, I'm afraid that like it or not, I'm not letting you leave until I know what has happened to you," Gelasia replied.

"Would you believe me if I said I walked into a door?" George asked.

"I most certainly would not," Gelasia retorted. "I cannot abide lying. Out with it, George, what happened?"

George sighed and proceeded to tell her all that had happened, knowing that even if he tried to leave out details, she would somehow know. When he'd finished telling her everything he said, "I know I shouldn't have done it. I was just so angry."

Gelasia sat quietly for a moment. "I suppose I don't have to say how disappointed I am in your conduct. You know better. However, I also know that sometimes heartache leads to being angry. Did you feel at all better when you snapped at Kaelen?"

"No," George admitted. "If anything I felt worse."

"Then I'd say you learned the lesson," Gelasia replied. "Forcing our own pain on others does not make things better. It only makes you feel more isolated and more pain."

George nodded and the conversation continued, talking about other things. It was a longer meeting than they normally had. He supposed that it was in part because the spring meeting was that Saturday and she wanted to be sure that he was prepared emotionally for the fact that Eleanor would not be there. As they had prepared to wrap things up he asked, "What will I do, Saturday I mean?"

"Well, I suppose you'll be placed either with Leticia or Allegra," Gelasia guessed. "I don't know for certain, but as their princes are not available, I'm sure you will be with one of them."

"Leticia doesn't have a prince," George said.

"Doesn't she?" Gelasia asked mysteriously. "I will tell you now, George, that we don't keep students at these schools if they are missing half of the partnership. The very fact that Leticia is still in school states quite clearly that she does indeed have a prince, even if we do not know his identity."

"So that means Kaelen has a princess?" George said slowly. "Even though Esmé was expelled?"

"Yes, and so do you; though it is understandably too close to Eleanor's death for you to be considering who she might be," Gelasia added. "A little secret about life; when one door is closed, another is opened. Anytime there has been such a tragedy at either school, the stars have been consulted. If it is found that the prince or princess in question no longer has a quest, than they are placed in a different school setting so as to still gain the proper education as befitting their rank, but to ensure that they do not befuddle someone else's quest."

"What do you mean?" George asked.

"It has happened that people have fallen in love with the wrong person," Gelasia explained. "While they certainly enjoyed happiness, it has left others with only heartache and sorrow. There are many quests which were never finished because one party fell in love with someone else."

"What happens to the other one?" George asked cautiously.

Gelasia smiled sadly. "It depends on the nature of the quest. There are some who are instantly returned to the school and they are then taken to their homelands to court or be courted by someone else worthy of them. Others, however, are stuck as they were and where they were until the quest is completed by another. There are cases, though few and far between, where quests have never been completed."

"How awful!" George exclaimed. "Shouldn't the fairies do something for them?"

"I'm afraid, my dear, that's not how it works," Gelasia replied. "We do our best to promote for you the match that will make you happiest. It is why we ask your parents so many questions about you and your interests before you even come to our school. However, there is no magic spell we can place to ensure your love and devotion to the one you've been paired with."

"But if you know that there are princesses out there who have never been saved, can't you do anything for them?" George demanded.

"My dear boy," Gelasia said kindly. "You have so much love for everyone. The fairies only have limited power on these quests. In many cases, we do not even know where they are. We only know that the quest has not been completed because we are not summoned by the spell's breaking. We do not have the power to save them. That is in the hands of the parties responsible for that quest."

George suddenly got a stubborn look on his face. "Gelasia, when I graduate, I'm going to rescue all the princesses who are still out there waiting."

Slightly amused, Gelasia asked, "What? And marry them all too?"

"I'm serious, Gelasia. I can't marry all of the others because I already have a princess," George replied. "Since she is taken from me, I will spend the rest of my life saving the lost and forgotten. No one deserves to be alone forever."

"You wish to do this, even though it could mean that you are alone forever," Gelasia said, hoping that he would understand what he was offering. "You would travel to every corner of Sanalbereth, searching for the lost princesses."

"Yes," George said, "I would. It's not fair to be just forgotten about. Eleanor wasn't forgotten, she died. But I won't let other princesses live out their days in towers or swamps or dragon's lairs or whatever if I can do something to save them. I've been paying attention in spell breaking; there are multiple ways to break a spell. It's not always as simple as kissing the girl and she's suddenly yours."

Gelasia looked thoughtful for a moment. "And the princesses whose spells depend upon love's first kiss? What will you do for them?"

"I'll find another way," George replied.

"Hmm," Gelasia said noncommittally. "Well, it's very late and you should be in bed. Good night, George."

"You don't think I can do this, do you?" George asked as he rose.

"George, dear, if anyone in the world could do it, it would be you," Gelasia assured him gently.

Saturday came quickly and soon there were princesses milling about the castle looking for their princes. Lucian soon spied Allegra and went to say hello. She nodded, but didn't speak to him. She walked away to talk to Clarissa and Jacobi as Moira came up to him. "I'm sorry, Lucian. It doesn't seem to matter what any of the rest of us say, she simply won't forgive you. She's forgiven the fairies, Adrian, even the witches! I'm not sure why she's holding out against you."

"Because it's easier to blame me than anyone else, I guess," Lucian replied. "How's Leticia doing?"

"She's holding on," Moira said. "She and Allegra spend a lot of time together. I try to be there as often as I can too and so does Clarissa. It's just so hard to fill that void. Eleanor always knew just what to say to make anyone feel better. I've tried talking to her because I'm at least a twin; I understand some of what that feels like having lost Adrian the way I did. But even that's not the same; Adrian isn't dead. Eventually, he'll come back. Eleanor is gone and there is no bringing her back. How's George handling it?"

Lucian described in brief detail the fight George had gotten himself into. "He seems to be doing better since he talked to Gelasia, but you can tell he's still hurting."

"I don't doubt it," Moira said sadly. "I can't imagine what either of them must be feeling right now. I suppose the best we can offer is to be there as much as possible when they need us."

Lucian nodded as they walked into the dining hall for breakfast. George had been paired with Leticia for the day while Allegra was with Kaelen. It was the most awkward conversation the friends had ever shared. Between Allegra refusing to speak to Lucian and Kaelen not speaking to George, it was strange trying to keep the conversation flowing. More than ever they missed Eleanor's ability to smooth ruffled feathers.

"I don't think I've ever been so happy to see a meal end," Lucian admitted quietly to Moira as they began the annual scavenger hunt.

"Me neither," Moira agreed. "I couldn't believe how quiet it was." They continued their search and their time together seemed to fly. Soon they were having an outdoor luncheon with everyone. "Do you mind if we kind of sit off to ourselves?" Moira asked quietly as they were about to take their seats.

"I don't," Lucian replied, "But I don't know that our friends will appreciate it much."

"Lucian, half of them aren't speaking to anyone anyways," Moira pointed out. "Please, I really want it to just be us."

"Well, you can tell them," Lucian said. "I'm not getting myself in any more trouble than I'm already in."

"Wimp," Moira teased. She handed Lucian her plate and walked to the group and told them about their plan.

"I hope we didn't do anything to upset you," Leticia said gently.

"No, no," Moira replied. "I just have a few things I wanted to talk to Lucian about that I didn't really want everyone knowing about." Allegra muttered something under her breath and Moira continued, a warning note to her voice, "I'm going to pretend I didn't hear that. But I will warn you that if you say something like that about your brother again, so help me I'll ensure that you can't speak for a week."

"How do you plan on doing that?" Allegra asked angrily.

"Now, now, girls," Clarissa began.

"I don't know," Moira interrupted, "but I'll find a way. Your brother is going out of his way to be nice to you and to make up for not telling you and you're treating him like garbage. Well I've had it. You want to be mad at someone, be mad at the witch who cursed him. Don't take it out on Lucian."

"You can't even begin to understand what this is like," Allegra hissed.

"Try me," Moira snapped. "Do you think I don't miss him? Do you think Lucian doesn't miss him? They were best friends for crying out loud. Why don't you quit moping and acting like a baby and start trying to figure out how you're going to save him? Or do you plan on just leaving him out there?"

Allegra started to rise from her chair, but was prevented from speaking as a terrifying blast of thunder roared overhead. The once sunny sky had been so quickly overshadowed by storm clouds that no one had noticed them until it was too late. Giant drops of rain began pelting the ground and small hailstones rained upon the party. Girls were screaming and boys shouting as they ran towards the building to get out of the thunderstorm. The fairies were desperately trying to keep order while getting everyone indoors as quickly as possible. Lightning danced about and thunder crashed as the massive group scurried inside. Not a person was dry as the doors finally closed. There was sniffling and crying as people rubbed painful welts from hailstones and girls tried desperately to wring out their hair. Several fairies began bringing warm towels and those that were with the group tried to dry everyone by magic, only to find it wouldn't work.

When Calista finally got things quiet she said, "I believe our storm was a punishment on the whole group. There must have been bad feelings between many people. Only when there are multiple people in the wrong do the witches perform a mass punishment like this. You know who you are if you are among the guilty. I would suggest that you settle your differences and let go of your anger so that the ladies can have a pleasant trip home, rather than be hit with more rain and hail. There is just as much danger in holding a grudge as there is in picnicking in a storm."

There was some shuffling about as various people throughout the room made quiet amends with people they had hurt or been angry with. As more people forgave and were forgiven, the storm outside lessened to a gentle rainfall. Allegra looked sullenly at Lucian. "You should have told me," she said. "I could have prepared myself for it."

"I couldn't Allegra, I'm sorry," Lucian replied. "But I promise you that I will do everything I can to help you be successful. That's all I can give."

Sniffing, Allegra nodded. "I'm sorry," she said at length, falling into Lucian's arms. "I just miss him so much."

"I know," Lucian said gently, stroking his sister's hair. "I miss him too."

Within moments, the sun was shining and birds chirping. Melantha gathered her girls together and prepared them to leave. They would have to forego the luncheon as all the food had been soaked in the storm. Moira smiled at Lucian as she got ready to leave. "While I didn't appreciate getting rained on, it seems to have done the trick."

"Well, they do have several centuries experience getting us to see the light," Lucian said teasingly.

"Yes, they do," Moira replied. "Well, goodbye, Lucian. I'll see you at the end of the year."

"Goodbye, Moira," Lucian returned. He waved as the girls left the castle and headed out to the carriages. Looking outside, Lucian could hardly believe that there had been a storm, though he had several welts and soaked clothing to prove that there had been.

Calista ordered all the boys to their rooms to change into dry clothing. "I'll have the cook staff make a light luncheon of soup and bread to prevent anyone getting sick."

The weeks seemed to go by as days toward the end of the school year. The boys spent most of their time outside working on homework together under the maple tree. Queenie was sitting near George, playing with a stick, but not letting him too far from her side. If he got up and moved, she would stand and move with him. "Doesn't she know you're safe?" Kaelen teased after Queenie had done this the third time in a row.

"It doesn't matter," George laughed. "She thinks I'm her puppy."

"What?" Jacobi asked.

"It's a common occurrence in dogs," Lucian explained. "Especially females. They tend to adopt their master as though they were a puppy. My dad sees it a lot in his hounds. They are profoundly loyal and ferociously protective. My dad's first dog took on a bear once while he was hunting. He managed to shoot the bear before too long, but not before Mitzy gave her life defending him. Because Queenie sees George as her puppy, she will be there in whatever way he needs her. And if he's in danger, she'll protect him."

George laughed, "What he said. Anyway, she's been like this since the end of winter break."

"She senses that you need more attention," Lucian said.

"Yeah, well, I'll just be glad to go home for a bit; have time to think and all that," George replied.

"Don't wish too hard," Kaelen warned. "Summer is coming far more rapidly than I'm prepared for."

"Not me," George admitted. "I am more than ready to go home. I just need some space and time to really think and put together what I plan on doing."

Jacobi thought and then asked, "Won't you be lonely?"

"Are you kidding?" George asked. "Samantha's going to be visiting home with her new baby. Mom and Dad are thrilled because one of my sisters finally had a boy. It's all been granddaughters up till now."

"Cool, what did they name him?" Lucian asked.

George blushed. "You don't really want to know."

"Yeah we do," Jacobi insisted.

"We're going to start making up names otherwise," Kaelen added.

"Go for it," George retorted, "You'll never guess."

"Alright, boy names, hmm, Markus?" Lucian suggested.

"No, that's my dad's name," George replied.

"Well, sometimes people name their kids after their fathers," Lucian said. "Maybe it's because they want to get even with their parents for all the lectures and yelling. I don't know."

"Not Markus, Robert?" Jacobi guessed.

"Nope," George said.

"Thomas?" Kaelen tried.

"Wrong again," George laughed. "I'm serious, you'll never be able to guess."

"Well, since the question made you blush the name is either really terrible or," Lucian began suddenly smiling as he got it, "they named the baby George after you."

Blushing again George said, "Bummer, I was really hoping you wouldn't catch on. Yeah, they named him George."

The others started laughing. "Really?" Kaelen asked.

"Yeah, I told them George was a boring name and they should give him a better name," George replied. "I won't even begin to tell you the response I got. I'm sure Gelasia would faint if she heard the kind of language Samantha used. As it is, that's probably the only letter I've ever gotten that I actually tore up and threw away. I figure Samantha would rather I not keep it."

The boys continued to laugh and chat as the sun slowly sank over the horizon. Lucian had to admit, if only to himself, that he was looking forward to summer break as well. He desperately needed some time by the sea and time to be with Allegra and do whatever he could to help her prepare for the quest ahead of her. After all, he only had one year left before graduation. Then all of them would part ways as they journeyed on their own to complete their quests. He was pulled out of his thoughts by George asking, "Lucian, what has you so engrossed that you can't answer a question?"

"Sorry, I was just thinking about how close we are to graduating," Lucian said. "Soon we'll be leaving for our quests."

"Okay, you could have gone all day without saying that," Kaelen teased.

"No seriously," Lucian continued, "haven't any of you ever thought about that? Soon we're going to be the ones out there fighting dragons, climbing towers, searching the land over for our princesses. I mean, don't you think about it sometimes?"

"I try not to," Jacobi admitted.

"It is pretty crazy," George added. "I don't know, I guess I think about it sometimes. But really it seems so unreal, so far away."

"It's not far away at all," Lucian said. "I feel totally unprepared."

"Well, I guess you've got one year to figure things out," Kaelen said with a laugh. "Seriously though, don't sweat it. We're all doing pretty good in our classes. Finding our princesses and breaking the spells should be a piece of cake!"

"I doubt I'd call it a piece of cake," George countered, "but I think Kaelen's right. No need to worry about it now. That's still a whole year away. We've got plenty of time to get ready."

"Besides, before our quests, we still have to survive finals," Jacobi added miserably.

Finals week soon came and Lucian's last final of the year was in gardening. Lucretia hovered over his shoulder, breathing down his neck as he wrote the answers on his test. He was tempted to ask her to move, but didn't want to offend the witch. The last thing he wanted was to spend summer vacation lime green. Over the past few weeks, boys unlucky enough to be punished by her spent several days the awkward color. It was slightly better than the purple of his first year and infinitely better than the baby pink of his third year. He considered himself lucky that he'd never run afoul of Lucretia and planned on keeping it that way. When he finished the written part of the exam, Lucretia pulled it from his hand so fast that Lucian got a paper cut. "Ouch!" he exclaimed.

"Sorry," Lucretia threw over her shoulder, not sounding sorry in the least. She scanned the test and said, "Well, I suppose that will do, although I know you could have given me more detail here, Lucian. I'm disappointed." She pouted slightly and then continued, "The last part of your final will be identifying four plants out in my garden. You will also show me how to properly removed weeds and pests from the garden. Lastly, you will tell me the proper amount of fertilizer to water for three plants of your choice and demonstrate how they should be applied."

Gritting his teeth, Lucian got to work. He pointed out moonflax, silverweed, eastern dogwood, and greater snapdragon before getting on his hands and knees and pulling the weeds out of the garden. Lucretia watched him work, smiling to herself as the sun beat down from overhead. He then watered the garden, being sure to verbally explain what he was doing. "There," he said, standing again.

"Hmm," Lucretia replied.

She was silent for a moment and Lucian asked, "Well, did I pass? Am I done?"

"You're done," Lucretia said. "Good day."

"Did I pass?" Lucian repeated.

"You'll see," Lucretia replied in a falsely sweet tone.

Lucian rolled his eyes as soon as the witch couldn't see him and headed back to the castle. Of all the classes to end on, that was the most disappointing. Even dragon fighting had gone better than that. Although, Lucian was grateful to be out of that class for the year. He and George had been forced to battle two dragons at once and neither took to it easily; even with the second dragon being an ancient, decrepit excuse of a dragon. They could usually take her out easily if Draconus wasn't paying close enough attention. But if he was really on top of things, and he usually was, he defended her as though defending himself. Part of that may have been the fact that Draconus claimed that this dragon was his mother, but the boys thought it more likely that he just liked proving how weak humans were. It was worse on the rare days when she seemed to actually have some interest in making things challenging. Then it was impossible to defeat either one.

"All done?" Kaelen asked as Lucian plopped into a seat at their normal table.

"Finally," Lucian replied. "Ugh, I hope I don't have that class next year. I don't think I can stand one more simpering, sugary smile as she says, 'I am disappointed in you.' It's maddening."

"Could be worse, I suppose," Jacobi said.

"I'm not sure," Lucian admitted. "I've got classes with every one of them except Maeve and every now and again I'm sure that's because of an oversight."

"Don't say that too loudly," Kaelen teased. "You might just get a class with her next year."

The boys laughed and continued chatting as they ate their supper. They talked about summer plans and the things they hoped to get done before school started again. The next day would be graduation for the oldest boys and the final meeting with their princesses for the year. Then they would enjoy their last summer before heading out on their quests. Calista made some announcements at the end of the meal and the boys decided, all weary from the long week of tests, to call it an early night.

In the morning, George, Jacobi and Lucian all stopped by Kaelen's room to talk for a bit. They stayed until Gelasia arrived before going downstairs to meet their princesses. There were also parents starting to arrive. Lucian soon saw Moira and her mother talking to Alexandra and Allegra. He joined them and was told excitedly by Allegra, "We're going to Lictthane this summer!"

Lucian couldn't help but feel a little disappointed. "We're not going to the seaside this year?" he asked his mother.

"No," Alexandra replied. "Lavinia and her family have seen how beautiful our land is at this time of year. I thought it'd be nice to get an idea of what Lictthane is like in the summer."

"But, I was looking forward to going to our little castle," Lucian said.

"Don't worry," Moira said with a smile. "There's a great little pond near our home that you can swim in. I realize that it's not quite the ocean, but I am sure there must be some kind of shells in there for you to look for."

Lucian smiled, "I'm sure I'll find something to do to entertain myself."

Moira returned his smile and soon they were separating for their meetings. Calista welcomed Lysander and Lucian into her office. "Well, another year has passed, Lucian. You are doing incredibly well."

"Thanks," Lucian blushed. "Can I ask how I did in gardening?"

Calista laughed, "I take it Lucretia refused to say?"

"Yeah," Lucian replied.

"Well, I'll let you look into that when you look at your grades. They will be with your schedule for next year and your supply list," Calista said. "For now, it's time to seriously consider your quest. We have but one year left to get you completely prepared. Here is a list of things your teachers have compiled for you to do over the summer. I hope you'll make time to work in each area. This will be the shortest summer break you'll have. Come the beginning of August, you will once more be in our classrooms doing your last classes and then you'll be out making your story come to life. This is an exciting time for you. Make the most of this final year and do enjoy your summer."

"Is there anything else we should do to help him?" Lysander asked.

"Not for Lucian," Calista began, "but for Allegra. Both of you have had a very hard year. You've each lost best friends; both temporarily and permanently. Take this summer to really spend time together as siblings. You won't get another opportunity. Help Allegra learn and see what you can learn from her. It's amazing the things that our siblings know that help us succeed in the end."

"Okay," Lucian said. "Will we see Adrian again before we finish school?"

Calista shook her head. "I'm sure you realize that once a princess or prince is transported we are unable to bring them back, even for a moment. You'll see Adrian again when your quest and Allegra's quest have been completed. Until then, Adrian is in a safe location waiting for her."

"I thought you'd say that," Lucian replied. "I just wish I'd had an opportunity to talk to him before he disappeared."

"You'll have many chances to talk when you're both successfully in your places as kings in Sanalbereth," Calista said warmly. She rose. "And now, if there are no further questions, I will give you your final grades and we'll meet again in August."

"Will we be taking Kaelen this summer?" Lysander asked. "He is, of course, still welcome in our home."

"He may," Calista replied. "I'm really not sure, he has not revealed his summer plans to myself or anyone else that I am aware of. He seems to be reaching a difficult point in his own transformation and may wish to be alone for the summer. However, I will make you aware of his decision after I have met with him."

"Very well," Lysander said. "Thank you."

Calista nodded and the two headed back downstairs to wait for Alexandra and Allegra. While they were downstairs, Lucian found George and Jacobi. "How'd you guys do?"

"I've got a mix," Jacobi admitted. "Some classes were definitely better than others. But for the most part I did pretty good."

"A's and E's" George replied. "I thought getting an A in dragon fighting to be rather generous. I hate that class so much."

"I hear you on that," Lucian replied as he opened his grade card. His jaw dropped and George started laughing. "Well, perfection strikes again. E's across the board I take it?"

"Almost," Lucian admitted blushing. "I got an A in dragon fighting too. But everything else is an E."

"Not surprising," Jacobi said with a smile. "Lucian, you're really smart."

"Yeah, but Lucretia gave me an E," Lucian retorted. "Lucretia who's constantly disappointed in me. How does that translate to an E?"

"Maybe she gives you bonus points for being cute," George teased.

They were interrupted when the sound of shrieking from upstairs drew everyone's attention. "You've lied to us!" a shrill woman's voice screamed. "I knew I should have taken Anna from that school. Liars!"

"Wait, don't take Anna from school," Kaelen's voice was heard as he came barreling down the stairs after Queen Angelique who was dragging a terrified and sobbing Anna behind her.

"Don't speak to me, you animal!" Angelique shrieked.

"I'll go," Kaelen replied, ignoring the hatred in his mother's voice. "Don't punish

Anna, it's not her fault. I lied, I made the mistake." His voice fell as hurt filled his face and expression. "I was wrong in thinking you could ever learn to love me again. Please, don't hurt Anna by taking her away from school and the people she cares most about. I'll leave, I give you my word."

"The word of a beast," Angelique spat.

"The word of a gentleman," Kaelen replied, holding his head high. "I'll gather my things and leave this very night. Please, Anna needs to finish school."

"Angelique," King Roland began timidly.

"Quiet," Angelique hissed.

A flash of anger passed over the king's face and, for the first time in many years, he stood his ground. "No, Angelique. You listen, for once in your life. Anna will finish school. Kaelen has given us his word and I believe him."

"You would," Angelique sneered. "I'll not have my daughter attending a school that makes excuses and lies."

"You will," Roland retorted strongly.

Angelique stared at him. "I beg your pardon?"

"I'm still Anna's father and I am still the one responsible for her education," Roland continued, his voice becoming stronger with every word. "Anna will finish her schooling at Fair Damsel's Academy if I have to write her off as a ward of the school."

"You wouldn't dare," Angelique began.

"Oh wouldn't I?" Roland asked. "I've had enough of your bitterness and hatred. I'll not take one more moment of it, do you hear me? Not one more word of it. Anna will go to Fair Damsel's and Kaelen will be true to his word. I taught him better than to give his word of honor as a falsehood. I will stand by my son and trust him to make the right choice. You will learn your place and accept what is."

Angelique's face turned white and then furious red in a matter of moments. She suddenly seemed aware of the crowd that had gathered and quickly pulled herself together. "Very well, it shall be as you wish," she hissed. She then grabbed Anna's hand once again and started pulling her towards the door. "Come, we're leaving." She turned to see Roland still standing where he had been. "Come!" she commanded.

Roland turned to Kaelen. He took Kaelen's large paw in one of his hands. "Kaelen, I'm sorry that it's had to be this way. When you complete your quest, please come home. I know we've been awful. But, please, please come home."

Tears filled Kaelen's eyes. He couldn't speak, but merely nodded. He heard his mother shout for his father again and watched as Roland followed meekly out of the castle. But despite his continued obedience, there was a new strength in his stride. Kaelen knew his father would ensure that Anna returned to Fair Damsel's for the next school year. In fact, he doubted that life would ever be quite the same for his mother again. He began to turn away from everyone when he heard his name. "Kaelen, I need to speak with you," a strange man said. "We can speak in your room if you wish. I can help you pack."

Kaelen shrugged, "Alright." He led the way to his room while Calista got everyone else's attention and announced that luncheon would soon be ready and they needed to adjourn to the dining hall. Upon entering he said, "Who are you?"

The man laughed, "Donovan was right about you; you don't mince words. My name is Maximillion. I'm," he paused. "I'm your uncle."

"Uncle?" Kaelen questioned. "I don't have any uncles. Both of my parents were only children."

Maximillion shook his head, "No, your father has a brother; me. Your mother didn't think me worthy of being family."

"Why?" Kaelen asked.

"Failure isn't looked well upon by most people," Maximillion admitted sadly. "When I returned from my quest having not only failed it, but having it be completed by a random stranger with no training whatever, Angelique quickly saw to it that I was no longer welcome in my brother's house. I was forbidden to visit any of you and my children ignored."

"You were Queen Alexandra's prince," Kaelen said, remembering Lucian's parents' story.

Maximillion nodded. "Yes, I was once. However, I'm not here to discuss my past with you. I'm here about your future. As kind as Lysander is, I believe it is time for you to begin life on your own. I spoke with Calista about this when you were first disowned."

Realization dawned on Kaelen and he interrupted, "You were the family friend who offered me a home."

"Right again," Maximillion replied. "I have kept it in order for you to go to whenever you like. I think now may be the time to move there and begin your quest. Following Donovan's meeting, I spoke briefly with Calista about when you should move there, and we agreed that sooner would be best. We had no idea that Angelique would go snooping about looking for you. I suppose, however, that she would have found out sooner or later."

"Mother always could smell out a scandal," Kaelen replied with a mirthless laugh.

"Well, be that as it may," Maximillion replied, "let's visit with Calista and we'll make all the necessary arrangements."

After the graduation ceremony, Calista gave Kaelen and his friends time to say their goodbyes before the others headed home for the summer. She then oversaw Kaelen and Gelasia packing their belongings. "You've known you'd be leaving me for a while now, Gelasia, haven't you?" Calista asked.

"Yes, my dear," Gelasia replied, taking Calista's hand. "This is where I am most needed. Kaelen needs someone who can help him keep as much humanity about him as possible. Between my magic and my simply being there, I can help him adjust to his new home and help him make the final part of this transition as painless as possible. I've known this was my destiny since meeting with Maeve that night in Kaelen's fourth year."

Calista cleared her throat, trying to downplay the emotion she felt. "We won't see you again, will we?"

Gelasia laughed, a marvelous sound like bubbling water. "Ah, my dear Calista, you know that even when I'm gone, my essence will remain. But I'm afraid that yes, this is goodbye."

Forgetting her normal reserve, Calista threw her arms around the tiny, frail-looking fairy. "We shall miss you terribly. I'll miss you terribly."

Patting her back gently Gelasia said, "And I you. But know that a bit of me shall always remain, right here in your heart."

Calista sniffed and replied. "Well, safe journey my dear friend."

Gelasia hugged Calista again while saying, "Goodbye, my dear one. Take care of my students for me."

Laughing, Calista said, "I always do."

"This I know," Gelasia replied seriously.

Calypso had arrived as well to bid farewell. Kaelen walked over to her with the book he'd borrowed. "I found the answers I was looking for," he said. "I won't need this anymore."

"You found turquoise, I take it," Calypso replied with a smile, though she didn't take the book from Kaelen's hands.

Nodding, Kaelen explained, "Turquoise is like a gem made of water. It's supposed to carry healing properties and can cool an angry heart. Amber and turquoise are both considered element gems; amber being tree and turquoise being water. Together, their unique properties fuse and double in strength, almost like a tree gets strength from rainwater. But anyway, I really don't want you to lose your book, so here."

Calypso smiled, "Why don't you keep it Kaelen? Consider it a housewarming gift. I'm sure you'll find a way to use it." She then walked away without waiting for any response.

Kaelen shrugged and placed it in his bag before turning to Gelasia and Calista. "That was the last of the baggage. Are you sure you want to join me, Gelasia? I'll understand if you want to stay here."

"I'm quite sure, my dear," Gelasia replied. "You still have many things to learn before you get started on your quest."

Calista came over with a folded piece of parchment. "Kaelen, normally I wouldn't give this to you until graduation, however under the circumstances, I will give it to you now. Open it when you have time to really consider your quest. Then, do everything you can to fulfill that mission. Good luck, Kaelen."

"Thank you," Kaelen said. He offered Gelasia his arm. "Shall we begin our journey?"

"No time like the present," Gelasia replied with a smile. She followed Kaelen into the carriage and waved happily out the window after giving one last look at Charming Academy and Calista. Just before the carriage began to pull away she imparted a final farewell using an old fairy greeting, "Be joyful and merry for always."

Wiping a tear from her eye as she waved in return, Calista said, "And you, dear Gelasia."

Year 6

Chapter 1

Lucian's family did spend one week by the sea before traveling to Lictthane to visit Lavinia and her family. Lucian spent as much time as he could with his sister, while still taking time to enjoy the ocean surf. All too soon, they'd packed their bags and were heading to Lictthane. When they arrived Lavinia met them apologetically. "I know you've just arrived, but we received an urgent message from Uncle Sebastian to meet him in Rendorlin. I've no idea what he could want, as he didn't say anything, but I'd rather not wait too long."

"I do hope that everything is alright," Alexandra said. "We're already packed; we can leave as soon as you're ready."

"Thank you," Lavinia breathed. "It's so difficult with him liking mystery as much as he does. You never know if he's saying it's urgent simply because he thinks it's interesting or because there really is an emergency."

"We understand," Alexandra assured her. "Is there anything we can do to help you be ready?"

Lavinia smiled, "We've actually spent all morning packing. I believe everyone is packed and ready to go."

"Well then, I think the best course of action would be to have a brief luncheon so our horses can get some rest and then begin on our way again," Lysander suggested.

"I thought that might be wise," Lavinia replied. "I've had Cook making something light for us to eat. We can take an hour or so and then we really must begin our journey. It's a couple of days away and we absolutely are not to travel after dark."

Lysander nodded. "Wise words."

The group went into the dining hall for their luncheon. Nana spent much of the meal puzzling over what Sebastian could want them for. "It is so very frustrating that he never gives us any hint as to what he wants. Someday he must learn to be more specific."

"That will never happen, Nana, and you wouldn't want it to," Moira replied teasingly. "He wouldn't be Sebastian otherwise."

"Touché, my love," Nana retorted with a smile.

They finished their meal and then headed out to the carriages. Because of how much people had grown, Nana declared that it would be too crowded to travel together in one carriage. "And in some ways there is safety in numbers. Having two carriages looks like a larger party," she added knowingly. She, Leticia and Lavinia were going to go in one carriage. "Alexandra, we'd love to have you join us."

"I couldn't think of anything better," Alexandra replied. "Darling, will you ride with the other children as chaperone."

"Certainly. Although," Lysander teased with a grin, "I doubt we could call any of them children anymore."

"They are quite grown up," Lavinia admitted somewhat sadly.

"It's settled then, enjoy the ride loves. We'll stop just outside Rendorlin tonight at the halfway point," Nana explained. "Then tomorrow we'll go as far as The Dancing Fairies."

"We'll see you tonight then," Lysander replied.

Waving, the ladies entered their carriage and they waited for Lysander's carriage to be in the lead. He had insisted upon it when it was decided that they would need two carriages. As the carriage pulled away from the castle, Lucian asked, "So, what do you think Uncle Sebastian wants?"

Moira shrugged. "I'm guessing that there's some sort of festival that he thinks we should see and that's what he wants. I don't think there's actually any emergency. Although, between us, I think he has special feelings for the proprietress at The Dancing Fairies."

"Really? What makes you think so?" Lucian asked.

"Uncle Sebastian has never stayed in one place for so long," Moira said. "Mom has said that even when Aunt Isabelle was alive, the two were always out adventuring. Yes, they stayed at the castle as often as needed for meetings and general running of a kingdom, but every summer they would travel to some new exotic place. Sometimes they traveled in winter as well. When she died, it was like his wanderlust doubled. He stayed around the kingdom only at the very most important of times and as soon as the new king was crowned, he was off. Now, he spends more time in Rendorlin than anywhere else, including his own place. And he constantly mutters about figuring out her name."

"Why do you think she won't tell anyone?" Allegra wondered aloud. "I'm sure she must have a nice name."

"Perhaps she can't," Lysander suggested.

"What do you mean?" Allegra asked.

"Wait, George told me that when he met with Gelasia, she said that some quests are never completed," Lucian recalled. "I remember, because he said that when he graduates he's going to go save the lost princesses. He wants to do it for Eleanor because she wouldn't want for them to be alone. Do you think Mother, you know from the inn, do you think she could be a lost princess?"

Lysander shrugged, "It is possible, I suppose. We won't know unless something happens. If she is, she certainly can't tell us."

"Why not?" Moira asked.

"It's the way quests work," Lysander explained. "As I understand, when a princess disappears as part of her quest, she can't tell anyone that she is a princess. So, for example, Moira, if you were to be suddenly transported to a small village in Bordington, you wouldn't be able to tell any of the people that you were a princess. Granted, they may find out on their own by your manner and dress, but you cannot reveal your identity. It's part of the romance and mystery of questing."

"Well," Allegra stated, "I think it would be wonderful if Uncle Sebastian and the proprietress fell in love. Wouldn't that be the perfect end to the summer? A wedding!"

Soon Allegra and Moira were busily talking about the perfect, summer wedding. Lysander leaned over to Lucian and said quietly, "I think I'll take a nap. I want no part of planning someone else's wedding, particularly when there's no engagement."

"Can I take a nap too?" Lucian whispered teasingly.

Lysander chuckled and leaned back against the seat, tipping his traveling hat over his face. Lucian thought it vastly unfair that now he would be stuck listening to the plans without having at least someone to talk to. Instead, Lucian half-listened, but spent most of the trip looking out the window watching the landscape fly past. It didn't seem long at all before the sun was beginning to set and they pulled into a small town called Glendale for the evening. They ate a small supper before each heading to their rooms. The next day would be very long if they wanted to arrive in Rendorlin before nightfall.

In the morning, Lysander spoke with the innkeeper as to the swiftest route to their destination. "Mark me words," the older man said, "you'll be wanting to take caution in traveling these parts. Those ruffians ain't been caught and they're gettin' bolder. Been makin' attacks during the day too, right under the sun."

"Has no one been able to catch them?" Lysander asked.

"Not a one o' them," the innkeeper replied, shaking his head. "'Tis a bad business indeed. Were only three days ago we were sent to bring in the last victims. All dead, rest their souls."

"Has anyone been able to make a description?" Lucian asked.

"Son, you need survivors to tell what they looks like. Nay, there be no descriptions," the innkeeper said. "So, you travel careful. Don't let none of those ladies be without a man travelin' today. Mark me, they need protection."

Lysander paid the innkeeper for their stay and for the supplies they had bought for their journey. "Thank you, sir," he said.

"And you. Safe journey," the innkeeper called.

When they reached the carriages, Lysander explained in brief what the innkeeper had told him. "Lucian will go with Alexandra, Lavinia, and Nana. I'll stay in the other carriage with the three girls. We stay close together at all times. Lucian, if something should happen, you are in charge. Protect the women and they will listen to you. Girls, same to you about me. If we have a plan of attack, we're more likely to be successful in a battle. But if everyone goes off half-baked, there won't be any chance at all."

"I understand, Dad," Lucian said seriously.

"Here," Lysander added, holding out a sheathed rapier. "Just in case you need it. And take this horn. Use it only if in danger."

"I will," Lucian promised.

Lysander instructed the carriage drivers before getting in with Moira and Allegra. Lucian handed his mother, Lavinia and Nana into the carriage before getting in himself. He sincerely hoped that the freshly sharpened rapier would not be needed. As they began their journey, he found himself jumping at the slightest sound and listening more intently to the sounds outside.

"Lucian, dear," Alexandra said after about an hour, "you're going to wear yourself out, fretting so. Being cautious doesn't mean exhausting your energies looking for the fight."

"I'm not being taken off my guard," Lucian replied stubbornly. He did try to make a show of worrying less, but he was fairly sure that his mother hadn't been fooled.

No one was happier than Lucian when they finally arrived at The Dancing Fairies. Mother welcomed them in joyfully. "Come in, come in, all safe and sound I see. Bless you, child! You look asleep on your feet," she added as Lucian came inside.

"Someone was being very watchful," Nana explained.

"And right he is too," Mother said seriously. "It's a dangerous time to travel. I told Sebastian not to send for you."

"But they needed to be here, Agatha," Sebastian countered as he walked into the parlor.

"That's still not my name," Mother laughed as Sebastian hugged everyone.

"I'll get it one of these times," Sebastian retorted. "Come, come, everyone. We have supper all waiting for you. That will perk you up in no time flat. And during supper, you must tell me everything about your journey."

"Uncle Sebastian," Lucian replied, "I doubt you want to hear my report. Because while I can tell you how many bumps there were in the road and how many strange whistles through the trees, I can't tell you anything at all of what the scenery looked like."

"Seriously took your role as protector I see," Sebastian laughed heartily. "Well, then the ladies must describe the journey for me as I'm sure Lysander will probably have the same report as Lucian."

"I'm afraid so," Lysander admitted laughing.

They enjoyed their supper and soon the group decided to call it an evening. It was late into the night when Sebastian was writing busily in his travel diary. He wrote in it daily, whether or not he was actually traveling. It was a way of remembering his many adventures. He planned to leave it to his darling niece and nephew when the time came to do so. That way a record of all he had learned would remain forever. A knock on the door interrupted him. "Enter," he said simply.

"Someday, dear brother, you must learn to go to bed earlier," Nana teased.

"Ah, Bethany dear, you know I never will," Sebastian said.

"Indeed I do," Nana retorted. "So, what was so important that you brought us all the way out here under such dangerous circumstances?"

Sebastian waved a hand, "Bah, it wasn't dangerous. You had Lysander and Lucian with you. You were perfectly safe, otherwise I never would have sent for you."

"And you think Lucian ready to take on a band of highwaymen?" Nana chided. "He's a boy."

"Not anymore, Bethany, he's a man now," Sebastian corrected. "And yes, he's ready."

"Man or boy he is still in school," Nana insisted. "Grown men with years of experience and training have been defeated by this group. I hope that this was not a wasted trip. Lucian was terribly worried."

"No journey is ever wasted," Sebastian replied seriously. "I summoned you because I have decided to make the proprietress here my wife."

"As happy as I am for you," Nana said, "couldn't you have written it?"

"My dear sister, this isn't something you simply write. I wanted you all to be here," Sebastian explained. "This is something special."

"So, have you asked her?" Nana asked.

"I can't ask her if I don't know her name," Sebastian retorted. "And I most certainly will not propose to her as 'Mother'. There's just something wrong about that. No, I shall discover her name by summer's end and make her my wife."

"And I suppose you brought us out here to help you discover her name?" Nana guessed.

"I have indeed," Sebastian replied. "And because the summer festivals here are the best in Sanalbereth. Jousting, swordsmanship, food, laughter; it will be the perfect summer."

Nana laughed, "Very well, Sebastian, but next time, don't say it's urgent. Poor Lavinia was becoming sick thinking something had happened to you."

"She should know better," Sebastian chuckled. "But I will consider it. Perhaps next time I shall write, 'of great importance' instead of using urgent."

"That would probably be best," Nana agreed.

"Well, either way, you're here and that's what counts," Sebastian said. "We are on the verge of a grand adventure."

Throughout the week, the group went into the towns to participate in the festivities. Moira sat one evening with Sebastian and asked, "Have you considered making a list of names that you've already tried? I know you're still trying to learn Mother's name."

"I know her name," Sebastian replied with mock indignation. "I just can't seem to remember it."

"Whatever," Moira laughed. "Have you made a list?"

"Well, no, I suppose I haven't," Sebastian said. "Do you think I should?"

"I think it would be helpful," Moira replied with a grin. "Here, you tell me every name you've tried and I'll write them all down."

"You'll be there for a while," Sebastian warned.

"I can handle it," Moira said.

"You're going to get writer's cramp," Sebastian teased.

"Well, then I'd best have a warm compress when I'm done," Moira retorted. She had already picked up a quill and was waiting patiently. "The names?"

Sebastian smiled and went through the list of names he had tried. Moira obediently wrote down each and every one. "And yesterday I tried Susanna and Serena."

Moira looked through the list she had written. "Uncle Sebastian, did you realize that you haven't tried any names that start with 'r'?"

"That's not possible," Sebastian replied, looking over Moira's shoulder. "I've tried too many names to have missed an entire letter from the alphabet. Good heavens! You're right! I haven't at all. Let's see, names that begin with 'r'. Hmm, this is quite the challenge. Thank you, my dear, you are a jewel!"

Smiling Moira replied, "No problem. But, I think I smell something. Supper must be ready."

"Indeed," Sebastian agreed. "And I have a whole new letter to test out."

They laughed as they headed down the stairs to join everyone else. "We were beginning to wonder if you'd gotten lost," Lavinia teased.

"Just lost in thought, dear," Sebastian replied, kissing his niece on the cheek. "What have we for supper today?"

Mother came out of the kitchen, carrying a large platter, "Fresh caught fish from the market broiled with herbs and garlic, honeyed cinnamon bread and a salad of lettuce and vegetables from my garden outside. Allegra and Leticia were kind enough to help me gather my ingredients and make everything."

"And it all looks scrumptious, Rose," Sebastian tried.

Mother's eyes widened. "Well, not my name, but certainly better than some you've chosen," she said, regaining her former composure.

"Aha! I am getting close," Sebastian stated.

Mother quickly disappeared back into the kitchen while the rest of them continued their meal. Could she dare to hope? It had been so long since she had heard her own name. Was it even possible? She quickly shook her head and cleared her thoughts. It had been too long; she would not get her hopes up. Picking up a platter of bread, she pasted a fresh smile on her face and went out into the dining room. "Here we are everyone, fresh slices of bread. Moira, you must tell me about the design I saw on your bedside table. I apologize if that seems nosy, but I've done some sewing in my time and wondered what you're planning with it."

"Oh," Moira replied blushing slightly. "I was just toying with some ideas. It's, well, it's just a gown."

Smiling knowingly, Mother said, "I doubt it's just a gown, but I'll talk to you about it later. What was the detail work on the sleeve though?"

"I was thinking of embroidering on the sleeves, but I hadn't worked it all out yet," Moira explained.

"Well, it looks lovely," Mother said kindly.

They continued their meal and chatted late into the evening. The fire in the hearth was beginning to die when they finally decided that they should go to bed. Everyone went to their own rooms after Sebastian announced, "Tomorrow we shall all go to the fair."

In the morning, everyone got ready for a long day outdoors. Allegra, Leticia and Moira laughed with Mother as they packed a picnic lunch. Sebastian, Lucian and Lysander were busily preparing the carriage while Lavinia, Nana and Alexandra were packing enough parasols and hats to keep everyone protected from the sun's rays. Soon they were heading out the door and into town. They laughed and chatted the entire time they were traveling until they arrived at the fairgrounds. There was joyful clamor about them as they got out of their carriage and began walking. Soon they were surrounded by various people wandering about. Men in armor were riding horses, carrying large jousting sticks and shields. The smell of various venders' wares filled the air with spice and smoke. It was one of the liveliest places Lucian had ever been to. He offered Moira his arm as they walked through the fair. "Make sure you spend some time with Allegra too," she said teasingly as they walked past a jeweler's booth.

"I will," Lucian replied, "don't worry. For now, I'm going to enjoy some time with my princess. Besides, right now she's helping Leticia."

Moira laughed, "I'm not going anywhere."

"Doesn't matter," Lucian teased. "Right now, I'm completely at your service."

Blushing Moira said, "That's an awful lot of attention for one person."

"You deserve it," Lucian returned with a smile.

The group continued through the fairgrounds, enjoying the various diversions the fair had to offer. About an hour after arriving, the joust competition was beginning. They took their seats in the stands. Trumpets sounded the beginning of the match. "Do you learn jousting at Charming Academy?" Allegra asked as they watched the first battle.

"I did a semester," Lucian said. "Some guys have done more. I think it just depends on what the fairies have you focusing on."

"Hmm," Allegra replied, returning her attention to the jousting.

The day progressed and soon they were sitting together in a nearby field enjoying their picnic lunch. "I've made up my mind," Sebastian said suddenly, interrupting the conversation they had been having.

"Oh really?" Nana asked teasingly. "And what have you decided this time, brother?"

"I am not leaving this spot until I figure out your name," Sebastian said.

"Why? You haven't had any need to know before this point," Mother pointed out, looking almost nervous.

"I have needed to know, I've just been playing at finding out," Sebastian replied. "And now I will find you out. Rachel?"

"No," Mother said. She shook her head sadly, "Sebastian, you can't just spend the day guessing."

"Rosalind?" Sebastian persisted.

Mother didn't respond. A mix of emotions played on her face as Sebastian tried name after name. Finally she snapped, "Enough, Sebastian. Enough. Why, why must you do this? Couldn't you just pick a name and stick with one name?"

"I can't just stick with one name unless it's your name," Sebastian said gently. "I love you and want to be able to call you by your name."

Everyone else stared as the two looked at each other. Mother looked heartbroken and sad. "If you love me, Sebastian, then you'll find my name. You won't have to try." She then stood and walked away, hugging her arms about herself.

"I do believe you pushed too hard this time, Sebastian," Nana chided gently.

Sebastian did not reply, but rose as well and walked away; following the direction Mother had gone in. At length he had to jog to catch up with her. "You know, my dear, I'm not as young as I once was," he teased as he tried to catch his breath.

"Well, maybe you should have tried calling for me," Mother retorted with a slight smile. "I'm sorry I snapped at you."

"No, I should be sorry," Sebastian interrupted her. "I was being bull-headed and obstinate."

Mother laughed. "I'm fairly sure it won't be the last time you are."

Laughing as well, Sebastian replied, "Oh probably not. I'm known to be quite stubborn when I put my mind to something. But I did want to apologize to you. I was pushing and I ignored that you were hurting."

"Consider yourself forgiven," Mother said. As the rest of the family caught up to where they had stopped they watched Sebastian kneel down in front of Mother. "Sebastian, what are you doing?" she asked nervously.

"This is a proposal, my dear; surely you recognize that," Sebastian replied teasingly. "I want to marry you."

Mother blushed. "Sebastian…"

"Marry me," Sebastian said. "I would happily stay at your inn the rest of my life if you would promise to be mine."

Tears filled Mother's eyes. "Sebastian, you can't properly propose if you don't know my name."

"Well, I just did," Sebastian teased.

"Sebastian," Mother said gently, "it doesn't work that way and you know that."

Sebastian rose slowly. "Well then, my dear, there's only one thing I can do."

"What is that?" Mother asked suspiciously.

"I'll have to marry you without your consent, Rowena," Sebastian replied.

Mother caught her breath. "What did you call me?"

"Rowena," Sebastian said gently. "That's your name, I know it is."

Crying and laughing at once, Rowena said, "I haven't heard my name in so very, very long."

"Nor have we," a familiar voice said from behind them.

The whole group was surprised to see Calista, Raphael and Melantha standing nearby. "Rowena," Melantha said joyfully, "it has been too long."

"Yes, it has," Rowena replied, not keeping the pain from her voice. "I've been waiting nearly fifty years for someone to find me."

"And now you've been found," Calista stated. "I suppose it is your desire to accept Sebastian's proposal?"

"Well, Oliver hasn't shown himself in all this time, so I very much doubt he's been missing me," Rowena replied candidly. "Yes, I have every intention of accepting Sebastian's proposal."

"Then we will be in touch with the fairy king and queen and you can begin making your arrangements," Calista said. "In the meantime we will begin the process of writing your story."

"No," Rowena said.

"No?" Raphael repeated. "What do you mean no?"

"Sebastian has already completed his quest," Rowena began, "and I have been waiting for so very long, that the story doesn't really matter to me anymore. I have found someone who is in love with me and I am in love with him. That's all the story I need. And as far as our wedding is concerned, I am not waiting for the king and queen to be available. They are invited of course, should they wish to attend, but I would rather just have a quiet, simple wedding as soon as possible."

"Very well," Calista replied. "We will respect your wishes. The story will remain unwritten and you shall have the quiet wedding you desire, if that is also your wish Sebastian."

"Whatever Rowena wants is what we'll do," Sebastian said.

Rowena smiled brightly, "Say my name again."

Sebastian turned to her and held her face in his hands. "Rowena," he said gently before kissing her; the world forgotten as a princess finally won her happily ever after.

    True to his word, Sebastian helped Rowena plan a small wedding for the end of summer vacation. Rowena began preparing to sell her small inn so that she and Sebastian could continue his adventures once they were married. However when she'd mentioned the plan to Sebastian, he refused to hear of it. "Absolutely not," he said firmly. "We're keeping the inn. This is where I fell in love with you and this is where we shall stay when we're not off gallivanting."

    "But darling, we surely don't need so much space," Rowena argued gently. "Wouldn't it be more prudent to sell the inn and purchase a small cottage in the village?"

    "I refuse to budge on the matter, Rowena," Sebastian replied. "Besides, the extra rooms will be a blessing when family comes to call. I forbid you to sell it."

    Rowena raised an eyebrow. "You forbid me?"

    "Okay, perhaps forbid is too strong a word," Sebastian admitted with a sheepish grin. "But I would really rather we keep it. If anything, I'll sell my castle in Bordington and we can live out our happily ever after right here."

    Laughing merrily Rowena said, "Oh very well, darling. I won't sell the inn."

    Wedding plans continued and Moira began working feverishly on the gowns for everyone. Lavinia and Nana had insisted on going to town for theirs, but Rowena had asked that Moira design her gown and ones for Allegra, Leticia and Moira as they were to be her bridesmaids. Moira had taken on the challenge with delight, sheepishly admitting that the design Rowena had found in her room had actually been a wedding gown for her in the first place. "I suspected that something like this might happen," Moira had said once while she, the girls and Rowena had worked on sewing.

    The village was in a frenzy of delight over their very own secret princess. Many of the oldest members of the village claimed to have known all along that she must be a princess. Excitement built as invitations were sent and arrived. Rowena had lived in the village for so long that they had become her only family and she was anxious to allow them to partake in her joy. At the inn, checking off accepted invitations became a daily chore. Lucian was most often the one in charge of looking after the guest list. He was glad to see that George and his family had accepted the invitation to come to the wedding. After all, it was only proper to invite the king and queen of the province to the wedding.

    When not busy preparing for the wedding, Lucian, Allegra, Leticia and Moira would sit out under a shady maple tree near the inn and talk late into the evening about everything there was to talk about. Lucian sometimes felt out of place as the only boy and found himself missing Adrian more than ever. He also missed Kaelen and knew that his last year of school would also be his loneliest. Adrian had always been the one he could go to for anything. While George and Jacobi were every bit his friends, Lucian knew it wouldn't be the same without Adrian. Kaelen being gone just added to the pain. Despite their awful beginning, he and Kaelen had also developed a strong friendship that would last their whole lives through. However, he wasn't given much time to be melancholy as he checked off guest lists, talked with Allegra about everything he could say about spell-breaking and going on quests. "I feel like the last person in the world qualified to teach you about this," Lucian admitted one evening as they sat watching the sunset. "I haven't even started my quest yet."

    "No matter," Allegra replied sweetly. "Just tell me all you can."

    Lucian had launched into a discussion about the topic and soon they were once again sitting quietly under the maple tree, stars beginning to sparkle in the heavens.

    It was a long while before Allegra asked, "Can you imagine waiting for fifty years for someone to come rescue you?"

Shaking his head, Lucian said, "No, I can't. I guess it would get really lonely."

"Yeah," Allegra said softly. "Lucian?"

"Yes?" Lucian replied.

"Do you think I can do this?" Allegra asked. "I mean, honestly?"

"Allegra," Lucian said gently, "I know you can. The fairies would never have allowed it otherwise."

"But you know they have no power over the witches," Allegra pointed out. "I guess I'm just afraid that I won't be able to do this and Adrian will end up like Aunt Rowena, waiting fifty years for someone better to come and rescue him."

Lucian put a gentle arm around Allegra's shoulder as she tried to maintain her composure. "Allegra, I know it seems impossible now, but I promise you that you can do this. I know that you'll find a way to make this the most amazing fairy tale ever."

"You really think so?" Allegra asked, wiping the tears from her eyes.

"I know so," Lucian replied, hugging her tight.

The day before the wedding, Allegra, Leticia, Lucian and Moira went to the village to buy their school supplies and uniforms. Lucian had looked over his schedule five times to be sure he'd read it correctly. Nowhere did he see a gardening class. He was sure he must have missed it, but it really wasn't there. Instead it had been replaced by an art class. "Heraldry?" he mused aloud.

"Oh, you get to do heraldry?" Moira asked. "I'm jealous; I've always wanted to try my hand at it."

Lucian laughed, "Well, after the quest is done, maybe I'll teach you a bit."

Moira blushed and then quickly regained her composure, "I guess I can wait for a couple years."

They laughed and continued to do their shopping. Lucian went separate from the girls for a while since they didn't need armor, swords or any other weapons for that matter. He went by himself to a store Sebastian had recommended to him on a far corner of the town. As he walked in, a small, delicate looking man approached him. "Good day, young sir. What can I do for you?"

"I need some new swords and a couple daggers for school," Lucian replied, handing the man his list.

Taking out a pair of spectacles, the man looked over the list. "Hmm, I have several fine daggers available and we'll do some measurements to determine the grip for your swords. I've got several blades suitable that are prepared. Follow me."

Lucian followed the man to a back room where dozens of blades and sample grips were kept. The man suddenly grabbed Lucian's hand and started to examine it. "Small hands for one your height," he stated after a moment. "Delicate bones."

"Um, yeah, my hands have always been small," Lucian replied, feeling very nervous. He very much wished he'd gone to Bill in Maltisten for his school supplies.

"Do you fence right-handed or left?" the man asked, dropping Lucian's hand and walking towards a back wall.

"Both," Lucian said, not sure if he should follow or stay put. He decided to stay where he was. "I'll need a sword suitable for each hand."

"Of course, of course," the man mumbled. He looked through several grips and brought a few before ruling all of them out. "Come back in the morning and I'll have your order ready."

"Do you need me to write it down for you?" Lucian asked. "I need to take my list with me."

"Oh no, I'll remember," the man said softly. "And don't worry about the wedding. I'll make sure you've got them in plenty of time to be there."

Highly disturbed, Lucian left the shop as quickly as was politely possible. He soon rejoined the girls. "Next time, we stick together," he said.

"Lucian," Allegra reminded him, "there won't be a next time."

"I don't care," Lucian retorted. "I'm not going to that man's shop alone again. That was undoubtedly the creepiest place I've ever been in my whole life."

"Creepier than the dark part of the jungle with the weird hissing?" Moira asked teasingly.

"Much," Lucian replied seriously. "I can handle a dragon. But that man was so, I don't know how to describe him. Weird I guess, definitely intense."

The girls laughed. "Well, when you go to pick up your order, we'll go with you," Leticia promised.

"You won't be able to," Lucian said miserably. "Tomorrow's the wedding and I'm sure you'll be busy beautifying yourselves and Rowena. Then there are decorations to be put up, flowers to arrange and all the rest of those little details you girls like to fuss over. No, I'll have Sebastian go with me. He's the one who recommended that shop anyhow."

Continuing to laugh, the girls walked with Lucian back to The Dancing Fairies, their arms laden with purchases from various shops. When they arrived each went to their own room to put things away. Lucian began packing his trunk. The day after the wedding he would be returning to Charming Academy for his final year in school. The idea was rather terrifying as it meant there was less than a full year until he would be sent on his quest.

As dawn crept over the sleepy village, The Dancing Fairies was a beehive of activity. Sebastian and Lucian briefly went to town to pick up Lucian's order before returning to the inn to help with preparations. A part of the fairgrounds had been made available for the wedding and they spent much of the morning setting up seats, putting together a large wooden trellis and dangling plants about it. As Sebastian and the girls noticed how easily the plants moved for Lucian, they left him to finish the work. "That's quite a gift you have, son," Sebastian said before moving on to another area.

"Yeah, right," Lucian muttered. He continued to try to weave the vines of flowers through the small trellis openings. Though he had noticed that the vines would often seem to do it themselves, he wanted it to look perfect. As though reading his thoughts, parts of the vine that had been bare suddenly bloomed with flowers. "I don't know who is responsible for this," Lucian mumbled as he stood up, "but I'm glad the plants are cooperating for me."

"Oh Lucian," Moira breathed as she came over with ribbons and thin strips of tulle, "it's so lovely. How did you do it?"

"I wish I could say," Lucian replied. "Here, let me help you with those."

"Alright," Moira said, "but I'm not even sure where we would put these. There's not really a lot of room between the flowers. I don't remember it having been so full before. You must have a magic touch."

"I don't know what I have, but it's nice at times like this," Lucian admitted. "Here, I'll take some of them and we can just weave them in where they fit best."

The two worked side by side for a while and Moira suddenly said, "Lucian, can we have a garden?"

"What do you mean?" Lucian asked.

"I mean when you rescue me and we get married and have our own place," Moira replied, a slight nervousness in her voice. "I'd like to have a garden. You have such a way with plants that it would be a shame not to take advantage of that. Everything you touch becomes so beautiful. Please plant me a garden. Please?" she added, batting her eyelashes and smiling pleadingly

Lucian laughed, "Very well, Moira, we'll have a garden. You tell me what you want, and I'll make it your very own paradise."

Smiling, Moira said, "I'll take anything you give me."

For a while, Lucian just looked back at her. Her smile was so inviting and her eyes so mesmerizing. Not a moment too soon, Sebastian noticed them and interrupted them, "Well, now, you two have certainly been busy."

The moment broken, Moira blushed and said, "Yeah, um, I need to go get dressed."

"You do that," Sebastian replied. "I'm going to stay here and help Lucian finish." As soon as she was out of earshot, he turned to Lucian. "Be careful with the mooneyes," he warned gently. "That leads to kissing and we both know that's not allowed for you yet."

"Why not? Maybe she won't have a spell that depends on love's first kiss," Lucian argued half-heartedly.

"Are you willing to take that chance?" Sebastian asked seriously.

Lucian sighed, "No, I guess not. She's just so…"

"I know," Sebastian said with a chuckle. "Believe me, my boy; I've been in your shoes. My first wife, Isabelle, was a gloriously beautiful creature. Raven black hair soft as silk and vivid blue eyes that stared straight to your soul. And the most beautiful voice in the world. But, had I kissed her before finding her in my quest, and believe me there was many a tempting opportunity, she would have been stuck as a green-skinned, seaweed-headed mermaid for life. Somehow I don't think that's what you want for Moira. Keep that in mind when your heart runs away with your head." He winked and walked away to another area.

Even though he knew Sebastian was right, Lucian couldn't help feeling a bit disappointed. Moira was so beautiful in so many different ways. It seemed unfair not to be able show her how much he loved her with a simple kiss. But he quickly cleared his thoughts and continued working.

As the sun reached its pinnacle, the group busily readied for the ceremony. Moira, Leticia and Allegra had already changed and were helping Rowena get into her gown. Lucian and Lysander were standing with Sebastian, waiting for the ladies to arrive. A local minister was there to perform the ceremony. Soon music filled the air from a small band borrowed from the fair. Alexandra and Lavinia welcomed guests as they arrived and helped them to their seats. Lucian smiled and waved to George and his family as they sat down. Soon everyone was seated and Lucian took his place off to the side holding the rings. The doors of the tent Rowena had changed in slowly were drawn open and the three girls stepped out, slowly taking their walk down the aisle before standing to the opposite of where Lucian was. Rowena then appeared. She looked stunning in a pastel blue gown. Her brown eyes sparkled and her silver-white hair had been woven with flowers and ribbons. She was carrying a large bouquet of summer flowers and her face was radiant with joy. When she reached her place, Sebastian took her hand. "You are breathtaking, my love," he whispered.

She simply smiled and the ceremony began. Lucian's thoughts kept straying from the wedding he was currently in, to the one he would be the groom in. His eyes flitted to Moira at moments he thought she wasn't looking. She was everything to him, his world. As soon as he finished his quest, they could be married like this. He hoped that it would be summertime or maybe spring. Or maybe it would be better in the fall, when the world was a symphony of color and the harvest was in. No, summer; they could be married on the seashore surrounded by the calls of gulls and the sound of crashing waves. Yes, a summer wedding at the beach would be perfect.

His thoughts were interrupted by a cheer as Sebastian gently kissed his new bride. They both seemed younger almost, as though any cares they'd had were suddenly wiped away. The music began again and Sebastian led Rowena to the nearby field which had been cleared for dancing. They began their first dance together and were soon joined by many other couples. "Shall we?" Lucian asked Moira.

She smiled, "There's music. Why not?"

As he took her out to dance, Lucian said, "You know, I never thought I would be excited about the prospect of getting married."

Moira laughed, "Me neither. It's beautiful isn't it?"

"Not as beautiful as you," Lucian admitted, smiling down at her.

Smiling in return, Moira said, "Careful, dear, we don't want to get ahead of ourselves."

Lucian couldn't help but laugh, "That's what Sebastian told me."

"I had a feeling he was planning on having that little chat with you," Moira giggled. "He is very protective."

"And he has every right to be," Lucian replied.

Moira leaned against Lucian for a moment before looking up at him again. "Am I the only one terrified that this is our last year at school?"

"No," Lucian said honestly. "It's scary to think about."

"Yeah." Moira looked concerned for a moment. "Lucian, promise me you won't give up, no matter how hard the quest is. Don't make me wait fifty years."

"I won't make you wait that long," Lucian assured her. "I promise."

Moira smiled. "Good, because if you do; I won't be as forgiving as Rowena."

Laughing, Lucian said, "No, Moira, I don't expect you would be."

The celebration continued late into the evening and even after nightfall. Lucian enjoyed the time with his princess and with Allegra. He made sure to spend time with each of them because in the morning, he would be returning to school once again.

Chapter 2

As the school year began, the boys were surprised to find that they all shared one class together; heraldry. On the first day, Stefanos had everyone sit down and listen for the class period. "I know for those of you who have had me multiple times, it must seem very strange for me to do a lecture all day, but there are many things about heraldry that are very important for you to understand. First of all, you need to know that your coat of arms will be unique to you as you design it. We will use the school coat of arms as an example and then we will discuss the symbolism and terms used in heraldry. Before I begin, please take out paper and pen to take notes because you will definitely need them."

There was some shuffling about as students pulled out the supplies requested while Stefanos pulled out a chalkboard and pointed his wand at it. Immediately the image of a coat of arms appeared. "This, class, is the Charming Academy coat of arms. I shall describe it using the heraldic terms that you will need to be familiar with in this class. You would do well to write the description down as there will be a quiz later." There was some groaning and Stefanos began, "As you can see, we have two supporters, the azure unicorn rampart and the purpure dragon rampart. The shield is vert with the following charges: argent crossed swords and below that or palm leaves."

"Those are palm leaves?" Jacobi whispered. "They look like feathers."

Lucian nodded as Stefanos continued, "Each color and charge has meaning and symbolism. Even the supporters were not chosen idly. Azure or blue, as found in the unicorn, stands for loyalty while the unicorn itself is virtue and courage. Purpure, purple, stands for royalty; the dragon is a symbol of valor. The swords stand for justice; in argent, the word for silver, meaning sincerity. And the palm is victory, conquest and royal honor while the color or, gold, stands for reaching above oneself or in other words, generosity. The vert, green, of the shield stands for hope and the loyalty to your love. The decision to use these particular symbols and colors is simple; these are the traits we expect our students to have. In using this as our coat of arms, we are reminded of the tasks ahead of us and the traits that we desire."

"Why can't they just call the colors by their actual names?" Jacobi mumbled.

"Those are their actual names," George replied quietly. "We just don't use them anymore."

"That and I think they come from different languages," Lucian added.

"And now," Stefanos said, ignoring the boys' conversation, "we will continue to speak on the meaning of all these new words I have thrown at you."

"Good," George said quietly, "because I'm starting to get confused."

"That makes two of us," Lucian agreed.

The class continued with the boys taking notes on the different colors, animals, symbols and other parts of heraldry. When it was over, George said, "That class will be far more interesting when we're actually making a coat of arms rather than just talking about it. That was kind of boring."

"I don't know, I thought it was interesting," Jacobi admitted. "Although, some of those pictures all looked the same to me and I still think the palm leaves looked like feathers."

"Well, you try to draw it better," George teased.

"No thank you," Jacobi retorted. "I have every intention of creating my blazon and having a professional do the rest. I'm a terrible artist."

"Looking at some of those examples Stefanos showed, so are a lot of people," Lucian pointed out with a grin. "Besides, I don't think it's the beauty that matters; it's simply another way of identifying someone from a distance. Besides, you can always make yours something really simple. There's nothing that says you have to make it complicated."

"Yeah, well, I don't know what all he expects us to do anyway. I mean, none of us do much metallurgy, if any. How are we supposed to make a shield?" Jacobi asked.

"That's probably why we have to know the proper words for a blazon," George replied. "Then we can have a real herald make it out for us on shields, flags, and other stuff. I bet we won't have to do it at all."

"You know, if this class is reserved for your final year," Lucian said slowly, "how will Adrian and Kaelen take it?"

"They already have," Stefanos said behind them, startling them. "The witches suggested that they take heraldry last year. Turns out they were right as usual. Oh," he added as he prepared to walk away, "you will be making your own shields."

The boys groaned. "Me and my big mouth," George mumbled.

"Come on guys, we're late for our next class," Lucian said with a smile.

As the day progressed, Lucian didn't think much more about the heraldry class. He was too busy trying to figure out the knots Achilles was teaching him. "A fine sailor you'd make," Achilles grumbled as he untangled the rope Lucian had been working with. "When you tie a knot, it is important to tie the right one. Just making a mess out of the rope will get you or someone else killed."

"Sorry, Achilles," Lucian said, rolling his eyes. "I am trying."

"Well quit trying and start doing," Achilles snapped.

Lucian scowled. He didn't care what problems Achilles may have been facing, there was no call for snapping at him. When Achilles thrust the rope back at him, he started the knot again. *Like I'm ever really going to use this*, Lucian thought miserably. The more frustrated he felt, the worse the knot looked until he was stuck with the same tangled mess he'd had before. Angry, he threw it down on the ground. "This isn't working at all. Can't I work on something else? Signal flags? Rescue swimming?"

"You're not leaving this room until you get that knot done right," Achilles replied angrily.

"Achilles," a feminine voice chided from the doorway, "just because you're having a bad day doesn't mean you can take it out on everyone else."

"Hi Tallia," Lucian said as the fairy entered the room.

"Hello, Lucian," Tallia replied with a smile. "Let me help you with that." She waved her wand and the rope straightened itself out. "Here. As for you," she continued, turning on Achilles, "you're not going to make any more students miserable just because you are. I don't want one more boy coming to my office telling me that you've bitten their head off." Despite being short for a fairy, Tallia seemed to grow as Achilles glared at the floor. "Your mother chose to leave for a purpose we can't fully comprehend. It was her choice. No one forced her, no one coerced her. She chose to go with Kaelen because she felt that he needed her. Quit pouting and start doing your job."

"How would you feel?" Achilles spat.

Tallia's eyes narrowed and sparks flew from her wand. "You forget, Achilles, my parents have already turned to fairy dust. I've been on my own for quite some time."

Feeling incredibly awkward Lucian squeaked, "Is class over."

"No."

"Yes."

There was a glaring contest between Achilles and Tallia until sighing, Achilles said angrily, "Yes, Lucian, class is over. You'd best do better next time."

Not waiting for even a second longer, Lucian walked as quickly as he could from the room as Tallia and Achilles began another long argument. Because he wasn't watching where he was going, he ran headlong into George.

"Ouch!" George said. "Hey, Lucian, so nice to bump into you again," he teased.

"Sorry about that, I wanted to get away from the fireworks," Lucian replied.

"Tallia and Achilles again?" George asked.

"Yeah, and this time it's nasty," Lucian said. He briefly described what had gone on.

George whistled. "I guess I can understand where Achilles is coming from. I mean, if my mother just up and left I'd be pretty ticked off too. But I didn't know that Tallia's parents were both gone."

"I guess even fairies die eventually," Lucian said.

"It's not precisely dying, as I understand it," George explained. "They turn to magic fairy dust which acts almost like a fertilizer wherever it lands. Everything grows beautifully with flowers and bushes. Stories say that there's one specific flower that grows right at the heart of where the fairy dust was that is like the fairy's essence or something like that. That flower never fades and never dies, but blooms forever. So, they die, but they don't. It's kind of weird."

"Where did you learn that?" Lucian asked.

"I was doing a lot of research this summer and I came across it," George shrugged.

"About the lost princesses?" Lucian guessed.

"Yeah," George replied. "I'm trying to find out as much as I can before graduation. It's hard because all the details are sketchy. A lot of the quests have been forgotten too, so I don't have a lot to go on, but I'm working on it. I'll figure it out somehow."

The weeks continued and Lucian found himself on sunny afternoons sitting out under the tree with George, helping him piece together the quests he was trying to complete. Jacobi often joined them and would offer insight that neither had thought of. "You know, George," Jacobi teased one afternoon as they took a break, "you're going to get way more stories than the rest of us."

George shrugged, "I doubt these princesses want a story that ends 'And Prince Charming rode off into the sunset after the next princess on his list of lost princesses to save.' I mean, it's not necessarily a very happy ending for the princess. And some of these princesses may not even be there anymore. They may have given up and left somehow. I just don't know. There's so little to work with."

"What are you going to do if you actually fall in love with one of them?" Lucian asked.

"Then I'll marry her and we'll ride off into the sunset after the lost princesses," George retorted. "I've made up my mind. If it takes my whole life, I'm going to find all these lost princesses."

Lucian couldn't help but laugh. "I can see the end of your story now: 'Prince Charming and his lovely bride headed out under the moonlit skies in search of the forgotten, the lost and the lonely and traveled happily ever after."

George cracked a grin. "Okay, so maybe it's a stretch, but really I think it's terrible that they're just left out there."

The others agreed and they continued working until it was time for supper. Calista announced that the princesses would be coming for their fall visit that Saturday. "Can you believe it's already been two months?" Jacobi asked.

"Time sure has flown by," Lucian admitted. "It's kind of scary really."

In the morning he went to double fencing with George. This was Lucian's long day between double fencing, double dragon fighting and double botany. The only class that wasn't doubled was spell-breaking.

"Good morning, lads," Raphael said as they entered the classroom.

"Good morning, Raphael," they said together.

"We're going to have a bit of a challenge this morning," Raphael began. "You've both gotten very good at fighting a single person double handed. In fact, you've come along much faster than anyone I've ever taught before. So, today we will be fighting as a trio. You will have to be on constant guard, paying attention to every detail in both opponents. I assure you that this is no easy task. We will pace ourselves slowly today and as the semester progresses we shall liven it up until your fighting at full speed."

"Okay," Lucian said nervously.

George simply nodded and gulped. They had learned over the years that slow for Raphael was what most people would consider swift.

"Now, in fighting amongst three, it is especially important to be aware of your footwork. It's like dancing, you must count and watch and be ready to strike at any moment," Raphael explained. "When in such a match you cannot afford to miss opportunities. Missing an opportunity can be the difference between victory and defeat. And now, get your equipment and join me on the mat. You will need a vest, a mask, and two rapiers each."

"Why do I get the feeling we're in for a beating?" Lucian muttered quietly.

"Because we are," George retorted as they walked to the mat where Raphael was waiting.

When class was over, the two glumly walked down the hall to dragon fighting. "That was awful," George complained. "Couldn't they at least give us one successful class between these ones? This is killer!"

"I know," Lucian agreed. "But there's nothing we can do except make the best of it."

On walking into the new class, they saw Draconus and his mother talking about something in dragon. As soon as she saw the boys, the older dragon narrowed her eyes at them, smoke curling up from her nostrils.

"Oh, is it that time again?" Draconus asked languidly.

"Quit wasting time, Draconus," Vulcan barked. "We've got a schedule to keep."

"Oh, in that case, the short one will be a good victim to begin with," Draconus said hungrily.

George rolled his eyes as he put on his armor and grabbed his sword and shield. The battle lasted longer than most. The older dragon was tired and it showed as George got strike after strike with no rebuttal. Lucian watched anxiously, hoping that his friend could somehow pull off a double win. But all too soon, Draconus started working around the older dragon, snapping and breathing fire to block George's attacks. In a sudden blur of movement, George thrust his sword between Draconus body and arm. "You're out," George shouted.

Draconus glared and the older dragon roared in fury. Suddenly she no longer seemed tired and old. As though the defeat had brought on new strength and courage, she charged George, snapping at him as he jumped out of the way. Instead of the fight slowing down, it became even more rapid. Snaking her tail around the room, she swept George off the ground and began hissing in an old form of dragon that he had difficulty deciphering. But he could make the gist of it: if he didn't do something soon he was going to be lunch. As her tail loosened to drop him, he slid down it before jumping on her neck and shoving her sword in the fake kill zone. She screamed and snapped at him once more.

Draconus muttered something in dragon and she backed off, still hissing angrily. "Very well, done, George," Draconus sneered. "But you're lucky to be alive. The first rule in fighting against two dragons is to take out the female first. Often she is the mother and as you saw, will become twice as ferocious if her baby is killed."

"And yet, I managed to get her anyway," George retorted. "Maybe you both should quit looking at yourselves as invincible."

Glaring at George, Draconus hissed, "We're far less frail than you are."

"Maybe being frail isn't so bad," George snapped. "It reminds you that you have weaknesses and can be harmed."

"Alright," Vulcan cut in. "That's enough. Lucian, your turn."

George turned on his heel and went back to his seat. He took off his armor and sat quietly, watching Lucian take his hand at it. He felt almost badly for Lucian; the older dragon was now fighting with twice the energy, blocking his attacks nearly as soon as he started them. But no one was as surprised as Lucian was when she suddenly snapped down, taking him in her mouth.

"Andromeda, you drop him this instant," Vulcan shouted. "Draconus, tell her to drop him, she'll kill him."

"That is the general idea," Draconus said lazily.

"Now, Draconus!" Vulcan barked angrily. "Or I'll turn you into the largest leather coat the world has ever seen."

"Oh very well," Draconus began. "Mother, drop him." But Draconus came too late. With a scream, Andromeda opened her mouth, hissing and bleeding. Lucian had slashed through her mouth and was now falling towards the ground, covered in steaming saliva. Vulcan used his wand to slow Lucian's fall, thinking that the boy was unconscious, but Lucian took advantage of the levitating feeling to put his sword through the fake kill zone on Andromeda before turning on Draconus with the same strike. It all happened so fast that for a while Draconus didn't even react. "What?!" he roared. "You should be dead. You can't attack after you've been killed."

"Well I'm not dead, no thanks to you," Lucian snapped. "You know, George is right. The sooner you two imbeciles get it through your heads that you're not invincible and this is a classroom, not reality, the better. Vulcan, with your permission, I'm going to Tallia. I've got a pretty nasty bite on my leg."

"I'll go with him," George offered.

"Please do," Vulcan replied, his orange eyes aglow with anger. "I'll deal with the dragons. Lucian, I am very sorry."

"Not your fault," Lucian threw over his shoulder as he continued out of the classroom. When they arrived at the infirmary, they found Achilles and Tallia talking quietly at her desk, each smiling. "Sorry to intrude, but I've got a bite and I'm really not feeling so well," Lucian said weakly before slumping onto the ground.

"Oh not again," Tallia said, jumping up from her desk and using her wand to lift Lucian to an empty bed. "I've told Vulcan a thousand times, maybe even a million times to get rid of Andromeda. Draconus at least understands that this is a school. That old bat always tries to eat someone. George, how long was he in her mouth?"

"Maybe a minute, is he alright?" George demanded.

Tallia's eyebrows furrowed, "I don't know yet. Dragon saliva is highly venomous. Most grown men won't survive more than five minutes after exposure. Achilles, quickly, the antivenin on the third shelf, grey bottle.

"George, I need you to tell me everything that happened," Tallia continued. "It's a miracle the boy could walk at all. I suppose it was the adrenaline rush."

Taking a deep breath to keep from panicking, George described the fight as best he could. He tried to remember each detail as Tallia rubbed the antivenin over Lucian's body.

Vulcan walked in and Tallia snapped, "You get out of here before I put you in the bed next to him."

"I was going to tell you that Andromeda is dead," Vulcan said quietly.

"Good," Tallia retorted, "now get out."

Doing as he was told, Vulcan left the room. After several minutes, Lucian slowly started to come to. "What happened?" he asked quietly, his voice strained and his breathing shallow.

"You nearly died, that's what happened," Tallia said angrily. "How are you feeling? Can you feel your fingers? Your toes? How old are you?"

Lucian smiled weakly, "Which question would you like me to answer first?"

Tallia took a deep breath, "I'm sorry Lucian. Are you feeling alright?"

"I feel kind of numb and tingly all over, almost like my whole body fell asleep," Lucian replied slowly. "And just so you know, I'm eighteen."

Laughing in relief, Tallia said, "Yes, I know you're eighteen. Alright, that's the antivenin making the tingling sensation. I think you'll be alright, but I'm keeping you here for now so I can watch you. You came awfully close to death there, Lucian. You ought to consider yourself lucky. I'm going to go apologize to Vulcan; I shouldn't have bitten his head off like that. You stay here and rest, Achilles will send notes to all of your teachers explaining your absence. George, I've got it from here. You can go; thanks for your help."

"Sure," George replied. He waved to Lucian before leaving the room.

Tallia walked to the arena classroom where Vulcan was standing with Calista over the large, violet carcass of the dead dragon. "I believe the boys have had enough experience," Calista was saying as Tallia walked down. "Tallia, how is he?"

"He'll live," Tallia replied. "I came to apologize, Vulcan."

"No need to," Vulcan said gently. "You were right. I should have listened years ago. But Calista, George and Lucian surely won't be the only boys to go this far in dragon fighting. There will need to be another dragon found."

"Then I suggest we find a young one that can be trained. Andromeda was truly too old to understand her role here anyway," Calista pointed out. "And I highly doubt that Draconus really explained it to her well."

"How did she die?" Tallia asked, looking at the thick pool of blood about the dragon's mouth.

"Ironically enough, she was poisoned by her own venom," Vulcan replied. "Had Lucian cut her anywhere else, she would have healed from it fairly easily. But having venom leaking into her bloodstream at that rate, she didn't stand a chance. Draconus is down in his cave sulking so I can't get any help from him. It'll take the whole staff to lift her out of here."

"I'll speak to the Sisters and see if they'll take care of her for us," Calista suggested. "I'm sure there are parts that they can use in their magic."

"You do realize that by defeating her, Lucian has won her treasure trove," Vulcan added.

"But she was a school dragon," Calista replied, confusion on her face. "She didn't have a trove."

"Calista, all dragons have a trove," Vulcan said, as though this was something obvious. "Even Draconus has a trove down in his cave. He just keeps it hidden away out of sight. Andromeda was less secretive. Hers takes up the bulk of her part of the cavern under the school. It's now Lucian's."

"Well, we can discuss that later," Calista replied, rubbing her temples. "For now we should make sure that Lucian is okay and prepare for the meeting with the princesses. After all, the meeting is tomorrow."

The next morning as princesses filtered into the school, Moira and Allegra found Lucian standing next to George, his leg bandaged and holding crutches. "Lucian! What happened?" Allegra asked.

"I got on the wrong side of an overly protective mother dragon," Lucian replied with a smile. "But don't worry; I should be just fine in a few days."

"More like a week or so," George corrected.

"Well, how are you going to ride your horse today?" Moira asked.

"We're not going to be riding," Lucian replied. "Calista and Phillipa have arranged for us to take one of the school phaetons to enjoy the woods in today."

"Do you know how to drive?" Moira asked teasingly.

"As a matter of fact, I do," Lucian retorted with a smile.

The conversation was interrupted as Melantha began making announcements about the meeting. Once she was done, George escorted Leticia and Allegra out to their horses while Lucian led Moira to the phaeton. As Lucian clicked his tongue to get the horses going, Moira, her tone half-teasing and half-serious, said, "So, you didn't mention anything about a dragon in your last letter."

"That's because it just happened yesterday," Lucian replied. "There really wasn't time to write you a letter."

"Would you have, if you'd had the time?" Moira asked.

Lucian turned to her briefly, before turning back to watch the horses. "Yes, I would have. You said you wanted to know what was going on."

Moira nodded. "I did. So, how bad was it, really? Don't just say it's nothing because I won't believe you. You're red all over like you've got a bad sunburn."

"Not sunburn, scalds," Lucian corrected.

He hesitated and Moira added, "I'll just ask George if you don't tell me yourself."

Laughing Lucian replied, "Oh alright. It was bad. I wasn't just bitten; I was trapped in her mouth for about a minute. So, I slashed through her mouth, yelled at the other dragon and then went to the infirmary and blacked out. I guess dragon saliva is really toxic."

"You almost died, didn't you?" Moira asked.

"Not really," Lucian said haltingly. "I mean, Tallia reacted really quickly and so I was able to get better fairly quickly. Of course, the dragon didn't fare so well. She's dead and now I've got a huge treasure trove under the school."

"What are you going to do with it?" Moira asked.

"I have no idea," Lucian said honestly. "I mean, I wouldn't know the first thing to do with a trove. I haven't even seen it. I tried telling them to give it to Draconus, but apparently that will offend him, so I told them to keep it and they said they couldn't. Maybe I'll give everyone really big birthday presents this year."

Moira laughed. "Why not donate it to a museum or something? I'm sure there's got to be someplace that will take it."

"Yeah, maybe," Lucian replied. "I figure I'm just not going to worry about it right now. It's not all that important to me."

They rode together in silence for a while, enjoying the beauty of the fall foliage and the stillness of the woods. "So how did she bite your leg?" Moira asked after a while.

"I'm still not quite sure. I remember suddenly being in her mouth and my leg being caught between her teeth," Lucian replied. "Tallia said that was the most serious injury. All the venom was getting into my blood, but she gave me a potion to help that go away once the antivenin for the saliva on my body started working."

"So, what will happen for you now in dragon fighting? Will you fight three dragons?" Moira teased.

"I hope not!" Lucian retorted. "One is quite bad enough, two is a nightmare. I don't know that anyone could battle three dragons and win."

"I suppose not," Moira replied. She was quiet for a while and then said, "What do you think will happen when we graduate?"

"What do you mean?" Lucian asked.

"Well, do you think I'll disappear like so many others have? Or will you disappear? What will happen?" Moira wondered.

"I don't know," Lucian said. "I guess we'll find out soon enough."

"Too soon," Moira admitted. "I don't know that I'm ready to be a damsel in distress."

Lucian laughed, "Is anyone?"

"Point," Moira agreed.

"Don't worry about it so much," Lucian said after a while. "I can promise you that whatever happens, I will search the whole world over if I have to in order to find you. And I promise it won't take fifty years."

Moira laughed, "Good."

Soon they had reached the end of the woods and Lucian handed her out of the phaeton so they could join their friends at the picnic. Jacobi and Clarissa were sitting together while George sat next to Leticia and Allegra. "It's so nice being here together," Clarissa said. "I wish these days would go on forever."

"It would sure be nice," George admitted. "I enjoy the company."

Lucian added, "And it's so nice out today. I think this is the most pleasant fall meeting we've ever had."

"It is lovely," Moira agreed. "Leticia, my mom sent me a letter wanting to know if there was anything she could do to make your room at our castle more comfortable for winter break. She felt that summer was lacking I suppose."

Leticia laughed merrily, "Your mother is far too kind, Moira. I had everything I needed. Besides, we were only there about a week and a half. The only possible thing that I could say was missing is my horse collection. My mother bought me a new figurine for every birthday," she added with a sad smile. "If that could be brought from Traifloran, I would be most grateful. However, if it is inconvient, she needn't worry about it."

"I'll let her know," Moira replied.

The day continued in chatting and laughter as the group ate their meal and enjoyed the warm, fall day. There was the slightest chill in the air, but not so much that the sunshine couldn't warm it. The leaves were a beautiful blend of yellows, oranges and reds. Everything was crisp, clear and beautiful. Lucian couldn't help but feel slightly disappointed that this was the last fall meeting he would have with his princess. It was always one of his favorites; even when it didn't quite go as planned.

All too soon they were saying goodbye to their princesses. "Keep writing to me," Moira said as they prepared to leave. "I truly enjoy your letters. You really can write beautifully, even if you don't think so."

"Well, don't say that too loudly," Lucian teased. "Airlia will have me start writing sonnets again."

Moira laughed, "I don't know; that might be a good idea."

Lucian smiled and said, "I'm sure that it's not. Enjoy the rest of your semester."

"I'll see you in December," Moira returned as he gently kissed her hand. "Goodbye."

"Goodbye," Lucian repeated.

Chapter 3

Fall soon progressed into winter and the boys spent a lot of time indoors. Homework was almost always done in the common room with their hounds sitting nearby. Lucian was surprised to receive a letter from Gelasia one evening that he was to share with the group.

> *My Dear Young Friends,*
>
> *I wished to write to you to inform you that Kaelen is doing alright. Well, as much as to be expected. His transformation is nearing completion and I fear it has been very difficult on him. I would ask that you each make an effort to write him at least one letter. He needs something to help him remember to be human. I know that the time for your quests is coming very quickly, but he needs this. You are his greatest support group and to be cut off from you has deeply wounded him emotionally. Before semester's end, I would ask each of you to please write to him about your friendships. I feel that he will need these to rely on. I will use what magic I have to protect these letters from his claws, but as I age, I weaken; my magic will likely be only a temporary fix.*
>
> *I do hope that you are all well. You have come so very far since I first met you. Each of you is a true gentleman in word and in deed. I consider myself privileged to have known you and blessed to have taught you. Do not forget your friendships. It is our friendships that make us successful more than any other asset we are given. I am certain that Adrian is also safe and doing well.*
>
> *Again, please write to Kaelen. He will need strength from each of you to get through this troubling time. The transformation he is undergoing is difficult and at times painful. Give him hope and encouragement. He needs it.*
>
> *Thank you and may the sun always shine upon you.*
>
> *With Much Love,*
> *Gelasia Stardust*

"She sure knows how to make you feel guilty," George said when Lucian folded the letter again and placed it in his pocket. "I hadn't even thought of writing to Kaelen. I didn't think we were allowed to."

"I didn't either," Jacobi admitted.

"Well," Lucian said, grabbing paper and pens, "I suppose there's no time like the present."

Each sat down at a desk and began writing. Lucian looked into the warm fire dancing in the hearth as he wrote:

> Dear Kaelen,
>
> I know what you are going through must be challenging. We're all rooting for you here at Charming Academy. The winter snows are beginning to fall and the grounds are enchanting right now. The snow sparkles under the sunlight and at night glows blue under the full moon. It is beautiful and I wish you could be here to see it. Don't forget your quest. You can be successful, I have no doubts. If you ever have need of me, send for me and I will find you. You are one of my best friends and I will gladly do all I can to help you.
>
> I hope that you have a wonderful winter. Enjoy having Gelasia with you. She is certainly missed here at the school. I've heard that the new fairy teaching etiquette is not at all like Gelasia. I think her name is Treasa Rosemary. I've seen her at the staff table and she's the most awkward shade of purple I've ever seen in a fairy. But, she is very proper, so I suppose she would be a good teacher for etiquette.
>
> Anyway, I've got to be getting back to my homework. Write anytime you need something and I'll be sure to respond.
>
> Your Friend,
> Lucian

After writing the letter to Kaelen, Lucian opened up his book for spell-breaking. One of the other students in the class had made a smart remark to Calypso and as punishment they were all reading chapters three through six, a one hundred-fifty page section. Many of the others had wanted to strangle the other prince, but had said nothing about it. They all knew that Calypso would simply add to their assignment if anyone else got out of hand. Lucian decided that sometimes getting some kind of curse was probably better than getting yet another essay or reading assignment. George was the only one in the class who didn't seem too upset over the assignment, but Lucian figured that he was probably using the assignment to further his research about the lost princesses and how to break the spells to set them free.

George was in fact using it as research. The next day after class, he stayed after a moment to talk to Calypso about it. "Calypso," he began nervously, "what would it take to break an enchantment meant for a kiss without a kiss."

"That's an odd question, George," Calypso replied. "Why do you ask?"

"I want to help the lost princesses," George said honestly.

"I see," Calypso said. "Well, I'm afraid that such an enchantment doesn't usually leave a whole lot of room for substitution. However, I believe if you read chapter thirteen in this book," she continued, pulling a book from her shelf, "you may find an answer to your question. That's quite an undertaking for one person, George. There's a reason each prince is assigned his own quest."

"And when he fails a girl is left out there alone and miserable," George retorted, trying not to allow his anger through. "Just because everyone else has forgotten about them doesn't mean that I will."

"Hmm," Calypso replied simply, not missing the anger in his tone. "Well, I suppose then that will make your own quest that much more challenging. I do hope you won't allow your own princess to be forgotten as you save everyone else's."

She left the room before he could ask what she meant. He shrugged and later that evening he pulled out the book she'd let him borrow and began reading. The chapter was entitled "Spell Substitutions: Breaking a Spell through Alternate Means". He read on late into the night with Queenie asleep on the bed next to him. It gave some fascinating answers. There was usually more than one way to break an enchantment. He supposed that some of why they were never really taught about that was so that they wouldn't kiss their princesses early. Writing "and Prince Charming mixed a paste of rose petals and mint leaves which he smeared lovingly over her eyes" wasn't nearly as romantic as "Prince Charming kissed his princess and the spell was broken." But according to what he was reading, almost all enchantments had alternate ways of breaking the spell, particularly if you weren't meant to be the prince in the first place. Unfortunately, it did say that there were some spells, though rare, where only one means would break the spell and that was almost always a kiss. Stretching his arms over his head, George finally put the book up for the night and went to sleep. He'd read it again in the morning.

As the winter progressed, the boys prepared for their winter finals. Most of their free time was now spent studying rather than researching the lost princesses. Anytime they were brought up George would shake his head. "We'll go back to them when spring semester begins. I can't rescue anyone if I fail my classes," he said one evening when Jacobi asked if he'd learned anything new about any of them.

"Good point," Jacobi admitted. "Alright, back to our classes. So, for heraldry, does anyone know what to expect for that final?"

"Stefanos said it would be both written and practical," Lucian replied. "I'm pretty sure that means we'll have to remember all of those heraldic terms and then draw out a coat of arms based on a blazon he gives us."

"Oh goodie," George said without enthusiasm. Heraldry had shaped up to be one of his least favorite classes, though it was still behind dragon fighting. "I think our dragon fighting finals are both going to be written."

"Yeah, Draconus still hasn't forgiven us," Lucian agreed. "I think the lectures may just last to the end of the school year."

"That bad?" Jacobi asked.

"Well, I suppose we do deserve it. After all, you did fight him and then kill his mother," George pointed out.

"Hey, I wasn't trying to kill her," Lucian countered. "I just didn't want to get eaten! How was I supposed to know that she could be killed by her own venom?"

"I think it's just because you taste bad," George teased.

Lucian couldn't help but grin too. "I guess I'm bad for a dragon's health. Maybe I should put some kind of warning label on myself."

Laughing, Jacobi said, "Well, either way, I really don't have anything that I need to super study for, except maybe heraldry. Everything else is going to be practical exams for me, so there's really not much to study. I can either do it or I can't."

"My seamanship final will be that way, if Achilles doesn't kill me first," Lucian added with a grim smile.

"Is he doing better?" George asked.

"Yeah, I guess so," Lucian replied. "I mean, he hasn't totally bitten my head off and he and Tallia seem to have overcome their little disagreement too. So, yeah, I guess that one should go okay. But apparently he's never seen anyone tie worse knots than me. He said I was the worst the world has ever seen."

The others laughed and George said, "You can't be. He's never seen me try to tie knots."

After a long evening of studying, the boys finally called it a night and went to their rooms for bed. Lucian stayed up for a while, writing letters to his family and to Moira. Once that was finished, he finally blew out the candles and went to sleep.

In the morning, finals began. Everyone started with the heraldry final. As Lucian had suspected, they were expected to recall the heraldic terms and define them in the written portion. They were then given a piece of paper and brushes with bottles of colored ink with which to draw out the coat of arms based on the blazon given to them. "Each of you has a different blazon, so looking at your neighbor won't do you any good," Stefanos said as he passed out the papers.

"Like any of us would cheat anyway," George muttered. "I wouldn't trust anyone to know how to draw this stuff."

"Did you have a comment, George?" Stefanos interrupted.

"No, sir," George replied blushing.

"I didn't think so. Now," Stefanos continued, "you have precisely an hour and a half in which to complete both sections of the final. Use your time wisely, but do not rush. Good luck, gentlemen."

Lucian decided after looking at each part to do the blazon first. He read the blazon through before beginning.

> Arms: Gules an argent saltire cantoned with four bull's heads argent.
>
> Crest: Helm gules
>
> Supporters: Dexter seahorse sejant gaurdant gules sinister lion sejant guardant argent.

As Lucian painstakingly drew out the various parts and used the inks to color them in, he promised himself that when it came time to make his own blazon, he would make it something ultra easy to create. He wasn't surprised that on the written part of the exam, the first part was to write out your blazon in layman's terms. He wrote:

> Red shield divided with a silver "x". Four silver bull's heads, one in each red quadrant. Red helmet as crest. Supporters are red sitting seahorse facing viewers on left and silver sitting lion on right also facing viewers.

He then went through the rest of the final, defining terms and writing out meanings of symbols in heraldry. None of his other classes had required so much writing and it took him the entire hour and a half to complete the final.

"Boy am I glad that one is finished," Jacobi said as they walked out of the room.

"Me too," George agreed.

"Yeah, now on to advanced healing for me," Lucian replied. "Maybe Morghana will have pity on me and let me explain verbally rather than writing. I've got writer's cramp now."

"Don't count on it," George teased as Lucian waved to go out to the witches' hovel.

"I know," Lucian muttered as the door to the castle blew closed behind him. The winds had picked up and snow was rapidly falling around him. He walked quickly to the hovel and knocked on the door to the hovel classroom.

When Morghana let him in, she said, "Well, good morning, Lucian. I'm going to have you do a few practical tasks for me before we do our written exam."

"Oh, thank you," Lucian breathed.

Morghana looked confused and said, "Well, you're welcome dear. Why are you grateful?"

Lucian described the last final he'd done. "My hand is a bit sore from all the writing. It'll be nice to have a little break from writing."

"I see," Morghana replied with a smile. "Well, don't get too excited about it; you've a lot of work to do in here too. Shall we begin?"

"Yes, ma'am," Lucian said, taking his seat.

The rest of the week continued with the rest of their finals. Lucian was glad when the semester was finally over and nervous too. It suddenly occurred to him that the year was half-gone already and he still didn't feel like he was ready to go out and rescue his princess. As the princesses arrived for the meeting, however, he didn't allow his feelings to show. Instead, he proudly pinned his new medals to his jacket and walked downstairs with a smile on his face.

"Lucian," Allegra said with a smile as he came down the stairs, "we were beginning to think you'd gotten lost up there."

"No, I didn't get lost," Lucian replied. "Just thinking."

"I see your leg has healed," Moira added as she came over.

For a moment Lucian couldn't respond. Moira was stunning in a blue dress that was almost purple. She was wearing the necklace he'd given her and it sparkled bewitchingly in the soft light of the chandelier. Her hair was up in an elegant knot with tiny ringlets surrounding her face. She looked at him expectantly and he said lamely, "Uh, yeah, it healed."

Laughing Moira asked, "Do you like the new dress?"

Trying to regain some composure, Lucian cleared his throat. "It's really nice, Moira. I mean, you really look radiant. I can't think of a time you looked lovelier." And Lucian meant it. Six years ago she was a sullen, plain girl with little to like. Now, she was easily the most beautiful young woman Lucian knew.

Moira smiled, as though she'd been able to glimpse Lucian's thoughts. He blushed as she said, "Thank you. I hoped you would like it. Shall we join everyone else for breakfast?"

"Yeah, that would be good," Lucian replied. He shook his head while walking with Moira into the dining hall. He was acting like a love-sick puppy. *I am a love-sick puppy*, he thought to himself as he watched Moira sit down at the table and give him a brilliant smile. When he sat down he saw Allegra talking with Leticia about winter break. "I believe I'll be in Lictthane. There's been no word from Benjamin about completing his quest, so as of yet I still don't really have a home to go to."

"Mother told me she had all of your horses moved to your room at our castle," Moira said gently. "She hopes that will make it more homelike for you."

"I do appreciate it," Leticia replied graciously, "though she didn't have to do it."

"Actually, for my mom it's like having a second daughter," Moira said. "She's absolutely thrilled and wants to make sure everything is just so." She shrugged. "That's just the way she is."

Everyone laughed as they continued their meal together. Once finished, they headed to the gym which was once more an enchanting winter wonderland with snow encrusted pine trees and warm fires burning in magical hearths. The group of friends decided, like the last year, that they would stay at one of the hearths and just chat. It was hard to really break into pairs because they had an uneven number. At one point Moira leaned over to Lucian and asked, "Would you like to go play a game of chess with me?"

Lucian laughed, "You'll win!"

"Well, yeah, but it will be fun anyway," Moira retorted with a smile. "I promise to not win in five minutes like last time."

Still laughing, Lucian agreed, "Alright, I get the hint. We'll see you all a little later." He followed her to a table with a chess board set up on it. They sat down and started playing, silently at first. After a few minutes, Lucian said, "So, why did you want to be on our own? The last few times, you've been more interested in being with the group."

"Just wanted some time alone," Moira replied honestly. "I like being with everyone else, but we really only have two more days after this to be together at all. I want to enjoy some time with you."

"You could have gone all day without reminding me of that," Lucian teased.

"Sorry," Moira laughed. "Do you feel nervous about it?"

"Probably about the same as every other prince before me," Lucian admitted. "It's scary to think that I won't be in school for much longer. Soon I'll be graduating and you'll graduate and I'll have to complete my quest."

"I'm sure you'll do a great job," Moira said with a smile. "Checkmate."

"Hey, I thought you said you weren't going to win so fast this time," Lucian pointed out.

"I said I wouldn't win in five minutes," Moira replied impishly. "It's been at least ten."

"I don't know why I bother playing that one with you," Lucian said as Moira set the pieces up again. "I'm so terrible at it."

"Well, we can go play fairy stones now if you'd prefer," Moira suggested.

"That one I'll at least stand a fighting chance at winning," Lucian retorted.

They continued to go from game to game until it was time for luncheon. They walked with their friends to the dining hall and enjoyed laughter and chatting as they ate. Then they went up to prepare for their semester meetings with the headmistresses of the schools. Several parents had arrived and were waiting for their children in the foyer. Lucian soon saw his parents and he and Allegra went over to talk to them as they waited for their meetings. There wasn't much of a wait before Lucian and Lysander were called into Calista's office. "Well, Lucian, time has flown. It seems only yesterday you were a timid boy walking through those doors for the first time," Calista said with a smile. "But you're not a boy anymore. King Lysander, this is the last meeting you will be present for. His final meeting with me will be private so that we can go over some of the particulars of his quest."

"I understand," Lysander replied.

Calista smiled, "Well, Lucian, your grades this semester are superb. Morghana was very impressed with your final in healing. Considering we both know how picky she is, I hope you will take that as a compliment." Lucian nodded and she continued, "Vulcan says that Draconus is still mourning his mother's death, but that you have been doing very well with the lectures and written assignments. He hopes that you will continue to work hard on those, even though they are dry and boring."

"Do you have any idea when we'll actually be fighting in that class again?" Lucian asked.

"I don't," Calista replied honestly. "Dragons are very proud creatures, Draconus in particular. He is not going to forgive you easily, if ever. It doesn't matter that it was not your intention. Between us, I don't think he's actually mourning at all. I believe he's realized his vulnerability and is distancing himself from it. If needed, I will have a discussion with Draconus about the class and get him back in the proper frame of mind. As far as your other classes are concerned, nothing but positives from everyone Stefanos would like you to practice your drawing of the heraldic symbols and parts over winter break, but if you miss getting to it, I don't believe it will be the end of the world. Lysander, do you have any concerns or comments?"

"No, I don't believe I do," Lysander replied. "It sounds as though Lucian is doing very well."

"Indeed he is," Calista agreed. "I've rarely had the pleasure of having so many gifted and generous boys in one class. Lucian is certainly a light in our school and we'll miss him very much when the time comes for graduation."

Lucian blushed to the very roots of his hair at the praise. "Thanks," he mumbled.

"Do have a wonderful winter break and I'll see you here again in January," Calista replied.

They left her office and went downstairs to the dining hall to wait for everyone else. Soon they were joined by Moira and Lavinia. Nana was still in Lictthane awaiting their return. "She was feeling a bit under the weather and asked that I extend her apologies," Lavinia said as others filtered into the room.

"No apology necessary," Lysander replied. "Everyone gets sick occasionally. I certainly hope that she is well again soon."

Lavinia smiled, "I'll tell her."

Supper was soon ready and the friends sat together and enjoyed their meal. As they were eating, Allegra asked, "How are Uncle Sebastian and Aunt Rowena?"

"Just fine. They are currently up north near Greyshores," Lavinia replied. "Rowena grew up there and missed the province of her birth. Naturally Uncle Sebastian decided that meant they needed to go on a trip. The last letter I received, they were both doing very well and as happy as could be. I must say, Rowena has been a wonderful influence on him. I've received a letter at least once a month since their marriage."

"Well, hopefully Uncle Sebastian won't rub off too much on her," Moira said teasingly. "Otherwise we'll be back to random letters once a year or so."

They all laughed and Lucian admitted, "I don't think Aunt Rowena would allow for that. She can be quite stubborn in her own right."

"Very true," Moira giggled.

Laughter and light-hearted chatter filled the air about them as the meal progressed. Soon Calista and Melantha were dismissing the youngest students and the dining hall was being transformed into a ballroom. As lightly fluttering, magical snow fell silently about, seeming to dance around the music floating in the air, Lucian led Moira out to the dance floor. He spun her gently before holding her close in his arms. The music and atmosphere of the room was enchanting and his princess beautiful. It was the perfect moment and he wished it could go on. For a long time, neither spoke as they swayed with the music. Moira leaned against Lucian, listening to the deep, but gentle sound of him humming with the music.

"You have a nice voice," Moira said after a while.

"Not really," Lucian replied, grinning. "I just don't know how to stay quiet."

"Well, I think you sound nice," Moira retorted, returning his smile. They were quiet again for while until she said, "Oh Lucian, why can't nights like these last forever?"

Lucian sighed, "I don't know. I guess we need to experience the other times in our lives just as much. They help us learn and grow."

"I suppose so," Moira agreed reluctantly. "But everything is so perfect right now as it is."

"Yes, and who knows?" Lucian asked with a grin. "Tomorrow might be even better."

"Well, it might be if you were joining us," Moira teased.

"I'm afraid that's not possible this time," Lucian replied with a smile.

The music ended and Lucian led Moira back to her seat. He then took Allegra out while he watched Jacobi and Clarissa attempt a simple waltz. He chuckled, "I guess some things never change."

Allegra smiled, "No I suppose they don't." She frowned for a moment.

"What's the matter?" Lucian asked.

"He's been gone a full year now," Allegra replied, a mist of tears in her eyes. "I miss him so very much, Lucian. His last words to me were that he loved me, but I never told him. Do you think he knows? Could he possibly know how much I love and miss him?"

Lucian pulled Allegra into a hug. "I'm sure he knows," he replied gently. "How could he not? You showed it every day."

Allegra nodded, but didn't speak. Even though the song had not yet finished, Lucian gently led her back to where their parents were standing. She threw herself into Lysander's arms and just cried. Alexandra stroked her hair, softly soothing her cares with reassurances that all would be well as Lysander simply held her. When he had a moment, Lucian went to Moira and said, "I think we're going to go ahead and go. Allegra's..."

"She needs rest," Moira finished for him, an understanding smile on her face. "Don't worry. I was thinking of calling it an early night too. I'm sure Mother and Leticia wouldn't mind."

"I'll see you in the spring then," Lucian replied.

"Yes, in the spring," Moira repeated. "Have a good winter, Lucian."

"And you, Moira," Lucian returned. He then followed his family out of the ballroom, disappointed to leave early, but knowing that his sister needed him more than the dance floor did. Once they had left the room, they took their carriage to the Glass Slipper where they would be staying for the night. It was a long time before anyone went to sleep. Allegra was very upset and it took a long time to truly console her. When he finally was able to go to his room to sleep, Lucian felt not just physically tired, but also emotionally. It was hard to watch his sister feel so much pain and be so powerless to do anything for her. After a long while of lying silently on his bed, Lucian finally began to drift to sleep.

The day after arriving in Maltisten, the family spent together in the parlor, talking about the things that had happened and how the semester had gone for the two children. Allegra described her new classes in great detail. "Calypso comes and teaches me spell breaking. Lucian, you were so much more interesting. All she does is have me read out of boring, long books. The worst of it is that I'm in the class by myself, so there's not anyone else in the class to answer her questions. It's always me and if I don't give just the right answer I get huge essays and reading assignments."

"Trust me, it's not much better in a full class," Lucian replied. "She gives out those assignments if there's anyone not paying attention too. And that happens more often than not."

"Well, then there's the water life studies, which is really weird and I have no idea how that's supposed to help me," Allegra continued. "It's taught by this ancient fairy, Zinnia Toadstool, and she's obsessed with frogs." Shuddering she said, "It's really creepy. But the good thing is I'm still in dressage. Augusta is helping me come up with the program for the summer dressage finals. She expects me to do even better than at last winter's final. It's a shame you'll miss it, Lucian."

"Why would I miss it?" Lucian asked.

"You'll be on your quest then, dear," Alexandra pointed out.

"Oh and I'm also still in glassblowing," Allegra added before Lucian had time to really dwell on the fact his mother had presented. "Rhianna has me working on making spheres infusing metal in glass. It's really challenging, but I'm really enjoying it. So far I've only managed to do it twice. The others have had some pretty major flaws. I think I like the first one I did best though. It's a clear glass with tiny gold strips infused into it, so it looks like a shower of gold inside. It's really beautiful. She won't let me bring it home until the end of the school year though."

"Any particular reason?" Lysander asked.

"No, she's just picky like that," Allegra replied. "She never lets us bring anything home until the very end of the school year. I suppose she wants to be able to enjoy them the whole time. I don't know."

Allegra continued to describe school to them and then Lucian was given a turn to do so. He found that he really enjoyed these talks with his family. It was nice to just sit around the fire and talk about everything they had been doing. When Lucian described the fight with Draconus and Andromeda his mother said, "I almost feel badly for her."

"I do feel badly, sort of," Lucian said. "I really hadn't meant for her to die, I just didn't want to become her midday snack."

"Well, I'm amazed they had a dragon like her at all," Lysander replied. "That's a dangerous situation and they're lucky none of the princes died in that class."

"Dad, all of our quest classes can be dangerous," Lucian pointed out. "We have to learn somehow."

"Still," Lysander grumbled, "teaching you doesn't do anyone any good if you die."

"Well, I just won't die then," Lucian said with a grin.

The family continued to chat and laugh late into the evening, while the butler brought in trays of goodies for them to enjoy by the fireside. Lysander often stood to stoke the fire and add more pieces of wood. When Cook finally could not take it any longer, she walked into the parlor. "You can't survive on toast and cakes alone," she said with her hands on her hips. "Come to the dining room for a real supper."

Laughing, Alexandra said, "Alright, Cook, we're coming."

They walked together to the dining room and sat around the table, continuing their conversation. They enjoyed the peaceful time together, talking and laughing about anything that came to mind. Lucian hadn't really thought of it much before, but he really did have a wonderful family. He hoped that when he finished his quest and he and Moira started a family of their own that they would have nights like this; nights of talking late and laughing often. He couldn't think of a better way to spend life.

Throughout winter break, Lucian and his father continued practicing Lucian's swordsmanship and Lysander watched as Lucian practiced his symbols for heraldry.

"I've always wanted to create a coat of arms," Lysander said one afternoon while watching Lucian work.

"Well, here, Dad, grab a piece of paper and I'll teach you. It's fairly easy," Lucian replied.

Lysander laughed. "I doubt that it's easy, but you're welcome to teach me what you can." He picked up a sheet of paper and a pen and listened as Lucian described the parts and symbols involved in making a blazon.

They worked together long into the afternoon until Allegra came in a newly hemmed gown and said, "Supper is ready. If you're hungry you'd best come along."

As they followed her out of the room, Lucian said, "Hey, Dad?"

"Yes, son?" Lysander replied.

"Dad, I just wanted to say thanks," Lucian began. "You always believed in me, even when I didn't. I don't know, I guess I just really appreciate everything that you've done for me. You're really awesome, you know."

Lysander chuckled, "Son, you don't have to thank me. I know how you feel. It's been a joy watching you grow up. Doesn't seem long ago at all that you were terrified of the very idea of going to Charming Academy."

"I didn't want to go at all," Lucian admitted.

"I know you didn't. I knew at the time too, but I knew if I said anything, it would become all too easy to allow you to have your way and not go. And I knew that you needed to go to Charming Academy. You're more than just a regular old prince. You truly are a Prince Charming," Lysander explained with emotion. "Your story will be one of the ones people tell for generations to come."

"I hope so," Lucian said. "It's a scary prospect; being Prince Charming."

"I can't think of anyone better suited for it," Lysander said proudly.

"I don't know, Dad," Lucian teased. "George is a pretty much the poster boy for Prince Charming."

Laughing the two entered the dining hall. "Maybe, son, maybe," Lysander said as they sat down. They enjoyed a light luncheon before heading back to their activities. Alexandra came and watched for a while before leaving again. It was late evening by the time Lucian and Lysander were both satisfied with their work. "I'll have to take that into town and see what Angus can do with it. I'm sure he could make a wonderful shield with that on it for the hallway. Or perhaps a simple plaque would do."

"I think either would be really cool," Lucian said.

Just before Lucian and Allegra were to return to school, Lucian and Lysander made a trip to town to pick up the purchases that Lysander had made. Unable to decide which he wanted more, Lysander had decided to get both. "Whichever one doesn't go in the hall can go in my study," he had said. Lucian had also wanted to stop by Tom's to fix a seam in his trousers. They were still plenty long as Lucian had thankfully stopped growing, but a small hole had developed. So he and his father stopped by the shop before going to Angus to pick up the shield and plaque.

While they were in town, Allegra and Alexandra spent their time packing Allegra's trunks for school. Allegra tried not to think of the fact that this was Lucian's final year in school. When graduation came, there would be no one to lean on when she was sad or upset. At least, not while she was at home. She knew that while at school she would have lots of friends watching out for her, but it wasn't the same as having Lucian nearby. She would miss him terribly.

She was forced to push this thought away after double-checking that they had everything they would need and that everyone had packed their belongings. Once everyone had gotten everything, they climbed into their carriage and began the long journey to Biberseth for school to begin once again. They enjoyed the time together, laughing as they carriage seemed to fly past buildings and fields until at last they reached Charming Academy. Lucian got out of the carriage and gathered his trunks from the back of the carriage. His parents and Allegra followed him out. He hugged each of them in turn before entering the school, feeling nervous but prepared for this final semester.

Chapter 4

School began and all at once, Lucian fell back into the regular routine. Now that their winter finals were behind them, the boys went back to researching the lost princesses with George when they had finished their homework. It was a difficult process as there was so little information to go on. Lucian was scanning a fairly recent book discussing the lost princesses one evening when he said, "You know George, some of these princesses have been out for so long; how do we know they haven't simply left on their own and found someone else to love?"

"We don't," George replied honestly. "But I'm going to look for them anyway. Calista said that some of them return to the school, and I'm fairly sure that somewhere there must be a record of those princesses."

"But George, isn't it more likely that a list like that would be kept at Fair Damsels?" Jacobi asked.

George frowned. "Probably, but I don't know how to get to something from over there."

"Well, that's easy enough," Lucian replied simply. "We have friends going to school there. I'll write to Allegra and ask her what she can dig up. Maybe that will help us find some answers for you because right now we're hitting a brick wall."

"That could work," George admitted.

Lucian got out a piece of paper and his pen and began writing.

> Dear Allegra,
>
> I hope that the semester has started off well for you. I'm helping George with a little project here and wondered if you could help. You see, George wants to save all the lost princesses, but he doesn't really know where to start because there are many who returned to the school after their time was up. Not all, because many were left with whatever enchantments that may have befallen them. There is no such record here at Charming Academy. So, I was hoping that you would be able to get the information either from Melantha or someone else there at the school. I'm not really sure who you should talk to or where you should go, but if you could try, that would be great.
>
> School is still going well here. My classes are all long and, some, boring. Draconus still hasn't gotten out of his lecture mode. Calista said she's going to go talk to him after the spring visit if he's still pulling his "I'm in mourning bit." I have to admit, I almost like the break I'm getting, but I know that I need the practice so that if I meet a dragon on my quest I can defeat it.
>
> Anyway, I hope you're having a good day. Keep working hard in your classes. I'm sure you'll do great!

With Love,
Lucian

The boys continued to do their research until it was time for bed. For the next few days they didn't have much time to work on it as the fairies piled on more and more homework, as though to make up for the weeks without any. But the break was also long enough for Lucian to get a response from Allegra.

> Dear Lucian,
>
> Classes have been going fairly well. I stay busy, as I'm sure you do. I went to our library to look for things about the lost princesses and was able to find a journal-like book that has been kept for about the last three hundred years. It has a list of every princess who ever graduated from Fair Damsels in that time. Obviously that's an awfully long list and I don't want to copy the whole thing down for you, but I was thinking that if you give me a specific time frame, I can narrow things down that way. The journal is very interesting because not only does it list the princesses, but there are places to mark those that were found, sadly which ones died before their princes found them, which ones returned to the school single and which have never returned or been found. I even found Rowena, Queen Lavinia, and Mom in there. I'm still trying to find Nana and Grandma, but I'm sure they must be in there somewhere. After all, both of them attended the school too!
>
> Anyway, let me know what exactly you and George want and I'll get it to you as soon as I can. Maybe I'll just copy it out and bring it to you at the spring meeting. That's only about a month away anyway!
>
> Lots of Love,
> Allegra

Lucian shared the letter with George and Jacobi as soon as he received it. "So, tell me exactly what you want and I'll send it to her."

"I'd say the last fifty years," George said thoughtfully. "Anything past that it's more than likely that the princess moved on, whether to someone else or through death. But within the last fifty years is reasonable enough. Here, I'll write a little note that you can attach to your letter to her."

"Sounds like a plan," Lucian replied. They each wrote their notes and when they separated for the night, Lucian placed them in an envelope and sealed it. After addressing it, he placed it in his mailbox to go out the following day.

The weeks went by and slowly winter melted into a lush, glorious spring. Lucian was out in the greenhouse with Russett the day before meeting with the princesses. He was working on a large floral arrangement as the sun shone through the glass ceiling. "It's looking pretty good, Lucian," Russett said after a while.

"I hope so," Lucian replied. "I wish Kaelen were still here. He always knew exactly what to put where."

"I wish he were here too," Russett admitted sadly. "But, we can't always control things in life. Challenges make us grow stronger."

"Russett, why do plants become so easy for me to handle?" Lucian asked suddenly. "I know most people have to work at it more than I do. And I'm not totally ignorant of how tame my plants have been in my dangerous plants classes."

"I wish I could tell you, Lucian," Russett replied. "It's not something I can explain."

Lucian sighed, "I was afraid you'd say that. Oh well, I guess I should be grateful, it'll make some things easier."

"Hey, you'll always have a lovely garden," Russett pointed out with a smile.

"Yeah, Moira told me she wants me to give her a garden when my quest is finished," Lucian remembered.

"Are you going to?" Russett asked.

"I never thought I'd be one to garden," Lucian began, "but I actually like it. I know now why my dad spends so much time with his roses. I enjoy gardening, though maybe not if I'm being watched by a witch. That gets really disconcerting really fast."

Russett laughed. "I understand that feeling, believe me. Lucretia does have a bad habit of hovering somewhat."

"I bet she doesn't tell you that she's disappointed in you," Lucian said.

"No, I can't say that disappointed is ever a word she used on me," Russett admitted. "Bull-headed, stubborn, and often ignorant, but never disappointed."

"Ouch," Lucian chuckled. "I guess I'll take disappointed."

"I wouldn't worry about it too much, Lucian," Russett said. "Lucretia thinks that because she is incredibly gifted in gardening that she must know everything there is to know about the subject. And she really doesn't like to be told that she's wrong. But really, if you let her do her thing and at least listen to what she has to say, she's not too bad. And it's always easiest when she's on the older end of the Sisterhood. She mellows out somewhat."

"I'll have to take your word on that," Lucian teased. "I doubt I'll see her reach the older side of the Sisterhood."

"No, I don't suppose you will," Russett laughed. "Well, it's time for you to head to your next class. I suppose you'll want to give this arrangement to someone special tomorrow?"

"Actually, that one and the one I did earlier this week," Lucian admitted.

Russett nodded. "I'll have both of them ready for you tomorrow morning."

"Alright, goodbye Russett," Lucian said as he walked out into the sunshine. The air was still cool from winter's frost, but the sunshine felt good on his face. Little green shoots were poking through the soil and the trees were heavy with blossoms and buds. *Tomorrow is going to be a beautiful day*, he thought as he continued inside for his next class.

Early the next morning he went to the greenhouse to pick up his flower arrangements. He knew there was no way to hide them, so he simply put them on a table he was standing next to. When Moira and Allegra came to greet him, he handed the white roses and lavender to Allegra before handing the larkspur and daisies to Moira. "I love larkspur," Moira said with a smile. "How did you know?"

"Lucky guess," Lucian replied. "Shall we go to breakfast?"

"Yes, that sounds lovely," Allegra said while Moira nodded. Each accepted his arm and they went into the dining hall for their breakfast. They chatted easily with Jacobi, George, Clarissa and Leticia. There was a lot of discussion about the next meeting.

"Can you believe we're graduating this year?" Jacobi asked.

"Well, you might be," Clarissa replied, "but Allegra and I both still have a year left after this one."

"I'm sure it will fly by for you like this year has flown for us," Moira said.

George and Leticia were both quiet until Lucian asked, "Leticia, do you have any new ideas on what will happen at graduation?"

"I have no more idea about it than anyone else here," Leticia admitted. "Melantha has given me no hints or anything. It'll be as much a surprise for me as it will be for everyone else. I will admit to being very curious about what is going to happen, but I try not to dwell on it. There's still much for me to do in school and I want to do my best."

Their conversation was interrupted by Calista announcing that they would be enjoying their annual scavenger hunt. The boys soon found themselves holding a slip of paper with a list of items written on it. When Lucian looked at his slip, he saw that Allegra and Moira's names were written on it. "I think you're going with me today, Allegra."

"What makes you think so?" Allegra asked.

"Your name is on my slip," Lucian replied.

"I have Leticia on mine," George added.

"Funny," Jacobi said, "my slip doesn't have anyone's name on it."

"Well, I suppose that answers the question about who's going with whom," Leticia said with a smile. "Shall we begin?"

George smiled, "Yeah, let's go. We'll meet the rest of you out at the picnic." The two left quickly and the others were swift to follow suit.

Lucian was fairly sure that with three of them they would be more at a disadvantage than the others and it turned out he was right. It was more challenging to choose directions to go in because instead of there being only one person to convince there were two. It also slowed them down as they had to make sure everyone was together. As it turned out, they were the last ones to return for the outdoor picnic. "Oh well," Lucian said as they sat with their friends at a picnic table. "Do you guys know who got out here first?"

"We did," Leticia replied with a smile. "I must say, George, I didn't realize you were quite that competitive."

"I am sorry," George said apologetically.

"What, did the two of you sprint?" Moira teased.

"Just about," Leticia said grinning. "But it's the most fun I've had in a long time. I really enjoyed myself. We were racing I think three other couples to the table Melantha and Calista were sitting at."

"Only two," George corrected, blushing.

"Oh, just two," Leticia repeated with a smile. "It was wonderful just having fun again. I guess you never realize when you've gone a little melancholy until someone pulls you out of it. Thank you, George."

George blushed but didn't answer. In fact, he wouldn't look at anyone in the group. Lucian was worried that perhaps George was feeling guilty for having enjoyed himself despite Eleanor being gone. But he didn't have long to contemplate it before he was pulled into the conversation. Even George wasn't immune and soon the group was laughing and chatting as they did every time they were together. The afternoon went by far too quickly and no one was ready to say goodbye when the princesses were gathered to leave. As Lucian walked with Allegra and Moira to the carriages, he said, "I hope you both enjoyed yourselves, even if we did lose."

"Winning isn't the most important thing, Lucian," Moira replied.

"Just second most," Allegra said teasingly. The three laughed and she continued seriously, "I had a great time Lucian. Besides, George and Leticia could both use a basket of goodies more than any of us. They needed some cheering up and I think this was just the thing to do it."

"Well, have a safe journey and I'll see you both in June," Lucian said.

"One last time," Moira added.

"Yeah," Lucian admitted. He waved as the carriages left. He saw George standing by himself, the basket hanging loosely by his side. He walked over. "Hey, are you alright?"

"It's not right," George said quietly. "I shouldn't feel like this."

"Like what?" Lucian asked.

"Liking her," George replied. "It's not fair. Do I actually like her for who she is? Or is it simply that she reminds me of Eleanor and I'm still very much in love with her? Well, the memory of her. I shouldn't be giving Leticia any kind of hope that maybe I'm her prince. I lost my princess, I'm not the right guy for Leticia."

Trying to lighten the mood, Lucian teased, "You got all of that out of a simple scavenger hunt?"

"I'm serious, Lucian," George snapped.

"Okay, well, here's something for you to think about," Lucian retorted, trying not to lose his own temper. "Eleanor isn't coming back. Eventually, whether Leticia or someone else, you're going to fall in love again. If you don't, you'll simply be miserable. Leticia and Eleanor do share a lot of similarities. They should; they're twins. But, they're also very different. If you think the only reason you like Leticia is because she's like Eleanor than you are absolutely right. It's not fair. It's not fair to Leticia because you're not trying to look at who she really is. You're looking at her as a replacement."

Before George had a chance to reply, Lucian walked away. Lucian knew he'd been a little harsh, but he also knew somehow that George needed to hear it. He needed to pull himself out and really evaluate what his quest was going to be. Lucian didn't think it so far-fetched at all for Leticia to be George's princess. They actually would work really well together. It would be different than George and Eleanor, but it would still work and they could both be very happy.

At dinner that evening, George sat next to Lucian and said, "Hey."

"Hey," Lucian returned.

It was quiet and George continued, "Look, you were right earlier. I'm not being fair to Leticia. It's just so hard sometimes. I guess it's only natural to wonder about things. Who knows? She may have some other prince we don't know of."

"It's possible," Lucian agreed. "And I'm sorry I came down so hard."

"No, I deserved it," George interrupted. "I was being very selfish. By the way, did Allegra bring the list we asked her for?"

"Yeah, she did," Lucian replied. "It's in my room. I'll grab it after dinner and we can look through it."

"Lost princesses, here we come!" Jacobi said with a grin.

After dinner was over, the three went to Lucian's room and he got out the list. He handed it to George. "It's really long, sadly enough."

"I kind of expected it to be," George replied. "Just by the way Gelasia talked about them when I talked to her last year." He scanned the list. "Wow, that's just sad. There are princesses from as little as six years ago who are still waiting. We knew some of those guys."

"Yeah, it is sad," Jacobi agreed.

"These poor girls," George said sadly.

"Poor families," Lucian added. "Can you imagine the five years ending and still your daughter doesn't come home? I can't imagine how painful that must be for them."

"Especially if all your friends' daughters come back and get married," George stated. "Alright, well, this gives me a starting place. I think I'm going to call it a night; I'm beat!"

"I agree," Jacobi said.

"Me too," Lucian replied.

"Good night all," George said. He and Jacobi left Lucian's room. Once they were gone, Lucian changed into his pajamas before blowing out the candles and flopping into bed.

His dreams carried him to a distant castle. There were storm clouds thundering as lightning danced about the place. He could hear a dragon hissing somewhere, but couldn't see it. Rain pelted him, ringing against his armor and dripping through his hair. He had no helmet and his shield was dented badly. His sword flashed as lightning split the sky. The dragon was still speaking in its own language. "Do you really think you can defeat me?" it asked bitterly. "Really, tiny human? Come out of hiding and I'll end your suffering."

Lucian ignored the dragon and continued trying to find it while staying in the thick branches around him. Rather than thorns, the closer he got to a new branch, the more it would blossom and grow. He wished the plants would stop doing it since that was going to give away his position. Just because he couldn't see the dragon didn't mean the dragon couldn't see him.

As more flowers bloomed the dragon mocked, "Planting flowers for your funeral? There's no need, there will be nothing to bury." A scaly, orange snout burst through the branches, snapping at Lucian. He slashed at it with his sword. The dragon screamed and Lucian ran to a different spot to hide, but each time he did the thorns of the thicket disappeared and in their place grew beautiful blossoms. Over and over again, the dragon's snout darted in and out of the flower-laden branches. Lucian dodged and swerved but it finally was not enough. The dragon had snuck his tail around and now held Lucian dangling above the air. As he began speaking again, the dragon slowly changed from orange to green. It was Draconus! "You won't be saving your princess this time, young princeling," he sneered. And with an evil chuckle, the dragon dropped Lucian into his open mouth.

Lucian bolted upright out of bed. His heart was racing and his breathing heavy. He sat there for a few moments. Rusty lifted his head and whimpered softly. "It's okay, boy," Lucian said quietly after a moment. "It was just a nightmare." He leaned back against the pillows, tightening the blankets about himself. "Just a nightmare."

Time, it seemed, got faster each day and before they knew it, they were finishing their finals. Calista had announced during their heraldry final that she would be meeting each sixth-year boy individually in her office that afternoon after they finished with their classes. When all the boys were waiting patiently outside, she called Jacobi into her office. He followed her nervously. "Relax, Jacobi," Calista said gently. "There's nothing to be worried about. This is simply your end of year meeting, just as you've done every year prior to this. The only difference is we will now discuss your quest in brief and how you did this semester."

Breathing a sigh of relief, Jacobi said, "Oh."

Calista smiled and continued, "You've done well, Jacobi. All of your classes ended on high notes this year. Tell me a little bit about what you've learned here, particularly in your specialty classes."

"Well, I've learned to be more observant and to notice the little details," Jacobi began. "I can handle myself with a sword; I can fight a dragon if I have to, but not well. I don't know, I guess I learned a lot of stuff."

"Do you feel that you are prepared to take upon yourself the responsibilities of a Prince Charming?" Calista asked.

To his own surprise Jacobi said, "Yes, I do. I've done my best and will continue to do that as I search for Clarissa in any place I need to."

"Very good," Calista said. "Now, there are a few things you need to remember. First, quests are very individualized; they are based on your personal strengths and weaknesses. Magnify your strengths and overcome your weaknesses and you will be able to make this a happy fairytale. Second, make sure that you read the quest very, very carefully. A simple word slip can change the whole plan. And lastly, follow your heart and stay true to yourself. You will receive your diploma with a copy of your quest. We will also have a copy of that quest for our own records. Once you have successfully completed your quest, we will begin the arrangements to have the fairy king and queen come and preside over the wedding. Do you have any questions?"

"No, I don't think so," Jacobi replied.

"Well, then, I will let you go. We are very proud of you Jacobi, you have come a long way," Calista said with a smile. She led him to the door and then allowed George in his place. "Well, George, how are you doing?"

As he sat down, George said, "I'm doing fine."

"Good," Calista replied. "That is very good. So, what all have you learned here at Charming Academy, particularly in your specialty classes?"

"I've learned mostly about myself," George admitted. "I learned how to control myself, how to defend myself in all types of situations, and that it takes a lot of work to make things happen. They don't just come into existence. If you want specifics, I can fight and win a battle against a dragon, or even two! I can take care of and recognize dangerous plants and remove them."

"Well, I have heard only the greatest praise for you, George, from all of your teachers. They seem to think that you have been working extra hard," Calista added with a smile. "Do you think you are ready for the responsibilities of being a Prince Charming?"

"I'm not really sure," George replied. "But I am ready to give it my best."

Calista smiled. "And now a few points for you to remember. First, Eleanor is not the only love of your life. You will find your princess and you need to be able to recognize her wherever she is. Second, do not overextend yourself. You have a great capacity for love and kindness, but don't do it all at once or you will become weak. Take small steps one at a time and you'll go far. Third, rely on your friends and family. Your friends have been with you here for six years. And you have a charming family who will help you to be able to succeed."

"Thanks," George said.

Calista nodded and continued, "Now, tomorrow when you graduate, you will be given your diploma and a copy of your quest. You need to read it often so that you remember all parts of it. Don't despair or give up. While Eleanor is gone and nothing can bring her back, there is a princess for you who will be counting on you to save her. Only you can find out who that princess is. Once you have found her and completed your quest, the fairy king and queen will be contacted and plans for your wedding will begin. Is there anything you wish to ask?"

"No, I think I'm as ready as I'll ever be," George stated honestly.

"Well then, for tonight enjoy this time with your friends and I will see you again tomorrow evening at the graduation ceremony," Calista replied with a smile. "We are so very proud of you, George. You have overcome some very difficult challenges and we are looking forward to seeing what you do after graduation."

George blushed to the roots of his hair as Calista let him out of the office. Lucian waited for a few more boys to go through before it was his turn. "Lucian, it seems impossible to believe that we sit on the brink of graduation," she said as he sat down in her office. "You have grown so much. Tell me what you think you have learned, specifically in your specialty classes."

"I've learned my strengths, my weaknesses," Lucian began. "I've learned how to look beyond the obvious and how to make do when things aren't quite what I want them to be. I think most of all I've learned patience."

"Do you feel you are ready to accept the responsibilities of being a Prince Charming?" Calista asked.

Lucian thought for a moment. "I suppose whether I am or not, they're coming. I think I'm fairly prepared. I have a lot more to learn, but I'll have to do that as I go."

"A good answer," Calista said. "Now I'm going to give you three keys to help you in your quest. First, be aware of your surroundings. Really pay attention to what goes on around you and what you are capable of and not capable of. Second, trust in those around you both your friends and your animals. They know you best and can help you succeed. Third, at times when you are ready to give up hope, remember the real reason you are going on a quest. It's not just to earn a title or have a story; the real reason is to find your true love and create a happily ever after with her. Tomorrow is graduation and you will be given your diploma and a copy of your quest. Read your quest very carefully and be aware of the exact words that are used. They will tell you everything you need to know. You are about to begin a marvelous adventure. Think of it that way. Do you have any questions?"

"Actually, I do have one question," Lucian admitted. "Were you able to find someone to take that silly dragon trove? I hardly need it."

"We haven't yet," Calista replied. "However, we are looking into a couple of other places. If we haven't been able to get rid of it before too long, we'll find a way to contact you and get it sent to your home."

"Alright, I think that does it for me," Lucian said.

"Then I will say good night. Enjoy being with your friends," Calista said as she waved Lucian out of her office.

The boys did enjoy their last night together. They talked late into the night, long after the glowing fire in the common area was little more than embers. Finally, exhausted and knowing that they needed to rest for their big day, they went to their own rooms and crashed for the night.

The next morning, the school was full of parents, princesses and those getting ready to graduate. Lucian met Moira and Allegra for breakfast and enjoyed being with them, but also felt nervous at the same time. As their parents began walking towards them, Moira pulled Lucian away. "Here," she said, handing him an envelope. "Do not open it until after you begin your quest."

"Why?" Lucian asked.

"Because I said so," Moira retorted.

"That's a silly answer," Lucian replied. "What if I want to read it now?"

"Lucian, I'm being serious," Moira said. "I don't want you to open it until after you've started your quest. Promise me that you won't read it until then."

Laughing, Lucian said, "Oh, alright, I promise I won't read it until I start my quest."

"After," Moira corrected.

"After," Lucian repeated. "I won't read it until after I start my quest. I promise."

Moira smiled. "Okay then." She took his hand and they rejoined the group. Lucian savored every moment they were able to spend together, despite the fact that there were lots of people around and they really weren't able to say or do anything. Feeling her hand in his even for just a few moments at a time was enough. It spoke to him volumes more than either of them could have said.

All too soon the graduation ceremony was beginning. Melantha made her usual announcement about how some of the princesses would disappear. "This is perfectly normal and I assure you that they are each placed in a safe location."

She began calling names. Lucian watched as girls he knew and girls he didn't walked to get their diplomas. He saw Leticia go and to his surprise, she disappeared. It must have surprised some of the others because there was a collective gasp. However, it died away without any whispered theories. Everyone knew that she must have been the damsel in some quest and they left it be. Lucian then watched as Moira walked across. "I love you," he mouthed as she reached for her diploma. She smiled and then in an instant was gone. Despite knowing that it would probably happen, Lucian felt his heart sink. Where was his princess and how would he find her?

When the last of the princesses was announced, Calista rose and started with a small speech. "Every year it is my honor to announce the graduates who will begin their quests for true love and happily ever after. A fairy tale is what each gentleman strives to be worthy of. I receive these young men as boys and watch them grow and learn. Now, I will give them their quests and anxiously await their triumphant return." She then began calling names. Lucian watched George and Jacobi get their diplomas and waited for his turn. When she reached Lucian's name, he walked forward and took his diploma. "Good luck, Lucian," Calista said while shaking his hand.

"Thanks," Lucian replied. He took his seat near his family and began to open his quest, but his father's hand stopped him.

"Wait until we can all hear it," Lysander suggested. "You won't have an opportunity to tell us about it otherwise."

Lucian waited for the ceremony to be over and then followed his family outside. They were stopped by Lavinia who took Lucian's and Allegra's hands into her own. "Please, find my children," she said, her voice a mixture of pride and worry. Find them."

"We will," Lucian promised.

Lavinia smiled and then said, "Good luck to you."

Lucian nodded and then opened the copy of his quest and read aloud:

In unending night and lonely sleep, your princess silent vigil keeps
Your quest to seek her where she lies, at home underneath the starry skies
Awaiting true love's first embrace, a kiss to waken the sleeping face.

"Well, son," Lysander said with a choke of emotion. "This is the day we've all been waiting for. Go out and live your very own adventure. We'll be waiting for you." He then hugged Lucian tight before allowing Alexandra and Allegra their turns. They then entered their carriage and left for home. Lucian turned and read his quest again. He whistled for Zephyr and the horse came to him, Rusty loping at his side.

"Well, boys," Lucian said, "it's time to go rescue our princess."

Epilogue

"We're home," a feminine voice came from outside the room as the little boy asked, "That's it? You can't end the story there?"

"But your parents are home," the babysitter replied.

"No, Mom, you have to go back," the boy said as his parents entered the room.

"Whatever for?" the mother asked.

"She hasn't finished the story yet," the boy replied sullenly. "I have to know what happened to Adrian and Kaelen." He yawned. "And why is Leticia gone and where's Moira?"

"How about I tell you more of the story the next time I babysit?" the babysitter suggested with a smile.

"Okay, Dad, take Mom on a date tomorrow," the boy demanded.

His parents chuckled while his dad said, "Maybe not tomorrow, but I'll make sure it's soon, okay sport?"

The boy yawned wider. "I guess so."

As the babysitter and the boy's parents left the room, the mother said, "He never goes to sleep that easily. What did you do?"

"I simply told him the truth about fairy tales and where they began," the babysitter replied.

"Well, we'll certainly have you back next time," the father stated. "Are you busy next Wednesday?"

"Nope," the babysitter said, "I'll make sure I'm available to babysit."

"And bring that story with you," the mother added as they paid the babysitter and walked towards the door.

"Don't worry," the babysitter replied as she walked out the door, "I always do."

Made in the USA
Charleston, SC
09 August 2011